Where Eagles Never Flew

A Battle of Britain Novel

HELENA P. SCHRADER

Where Eagles Never Flew: A Battle of Britain Novel

Cross Seas Press
91 Pleasant Street
Blue Hill, Maine 04614
www.crossseaspress.com

ISBN: 978-1-7353139-4-8 (paperback)
ISBN: 978-1-7353139-5-5 (eBook)

Library of Congress Control Number: 2020921145

Foreword and Acknowledgements

I first became fascinated by the Battle of Britain while going to school in England as a teenager. While still in University, I made my first attempt at writing a novel set in the Battle, but the task eluded me. I went on to other themes, other stories. Yet the Battle of Britain never left me alone. I devoured every first-hand account of the Battle, read scholarly histories, and collected the usual commemorative picture-books.

While living in Berlin and writing a dissertation on the German Resistance to Hitler, I became interested in the German side of the Battle. Yet, it was the former RAF and WAAF that I met and corresponded with while researching *Sisters in Arms: The Women who Flew in WWII* and *The Blockade Breakers: The Berlin Airlift* who inspired and encouraged me to make a new attempt at a Battle of Britain novel.

While I owe thanks to all the pilots, WAAF and ground crew, whose memoirs, comments and correspondence contributed to the authenticity of this book, I am especially indebted to Edith Heap Kup. Edith, who served in Fighter Command during the Battle of Britain, provided me with her unpublished but insightful memoirs and corresponded with me for more than a year, answering my many questions. She also allowed me to use one of her photos on the cover.

Finally, in the summer of 2007, my novel was released under the title *Chasing the Wind*. Promptly, a review copy fell into the hands of Wing Commander Bob Doe, one of the few surviving RAF Battle of Britain aces. In a hand-written letter dated August 11, 2007, Wing Commander Doe wrote: "This is the best book on the life of us fighter pilots in the Battle of Britain that I have ever seen. ... I couldn't put it down." As a historian, no compliment could have been greater. My long years of listening to participants had paid off.

Later, Paul Davies, then President of the Battle of Britain Society, wrote that my book "would become a classic.... Never was so much owed by so many to so few. These men now have a book to tell it like it was." Aviation expert Simon Rodwell wrote: "... it is hard to imagine that a new novel could be written that would make the Battle of Britain seem fresh. Yet this is exactly what Helena Schrader has achieved."

In light of these endorsements, I felt I did not have the right to let this book languish in self-published purgatory. For the 80th anniversary of the Battle of Britain, I am releasing this new edition. Without altering the fundamental story which resonated with veterans of the Battle, I have attempted to improve the literary quality of the work.

Thanks to the heroic efforts of Stephen Tobin — to whom I am eternally thankful — the manuscript has also been meticulously scrubbed for "Americanisms" as well. This is not to say that none exist, but hopefully the American nationality of the author will be less obtrusive to the British reader.

Last but not least, I wish to thank Chris Goss for opening his splendid personal photo archive and allowing me to select some evocative images for inclusion in this novel.

Front Cover:

"B" Flight, 85 Squadron, RAF, Summer 1940. This photo shows, left to right: John Bickerdike, killed in a flying accident July 22, 1940; Patrick Woods-Scawen, killed when his parachute failed to open after bailing out during a dogfight on Sept. 1, 1940; James Lockhard, who survived the Battle of Britain but was killed in action in 1942; Flight Lieutenant Richard "Dicky" Lee, lost over the North Sea pursuing German aircraft on Aug. 18, 1940; Leonard Jowitt, killed in action, July 12, 1940; Flight Lieutenant Bieber, the squadron medical officer, and Ernst Webster, both of whom survived the war.

The photo was taken between May 19, when the squadron returned from France, and July 12, 1940, when Jowitt was killed. The setting was the "grass and tented" satellite airfield of Castle Camps. According to the photographer Edith Kup: "At the time the photo was taken, Dicky Lee... was not fully recovered from a wound in his leg and still limped fairly badly. However, he was soon airborne and inverted before one would think it possible and gave an exhibition of flying a Hurricane I have never seen surpassed." This photo was provided and is used with the permission of Ms. Kup.

Back Cover:

The pilots of JG53, France, 1940. Photo courtesy of Chris Goss. Interior photos were likewise all provided and used with the permission of Mr. Goss. A complete list of photo captions is provided after the Historical Note.

High Flight

Oh! I have slipped the surly bonds of Earth and danced the
skies on laughter-silvered wings;
Sunward I've climbed,
and joined the tumbling mirth of sun-split clouds,
— and done a hundred things you have not dreamed of
— wheeled and soared and swung High in the sunlit silence.
Hov'ring there, I've chased the shouting wind along, and flung
my eager craft through footless halls of air...
Up, up the long, delirious burning blue
I've topped the windswept heights with easy grace Where
never lark, or even eagle flew —
And, while with silent, lifting mind I've trod the high
untrespassed sanctity of space, Put out my hand,
and touched the face of God.

Pilot Officer John Gillespie Magee, Jr,
Royal AirForce, Spitfire Pilot
Killed flying in the UK at age 19 in December 1941

PART I

The Call
to Arms

Chapter 1

**RAF Duxford
18 May 1940**

Only fourteen of them would be making the sortie to France and Flying Officer Robert "Robin" Priestman was glad to be among them. Their orders were to proceed by air to Plievaulx (wherever that was), refuel, and from there to rendezvous with and escort some Blenheims which would be bombing the German bridgeheads on the River Aisne. The Blenheims, it had been explained, were part of a massive, all-out effort on the part of the British and French air forces to stop the Germans at the Aisne, ground troops having proved insufficient to the task. All fighter squadrons in France and several from the UK would be providing protection. After they had flown their mission, No. 579 Squadron would refuel and catch a meal on the Continent and then return to Duxford.

They had been rather disappointed to hear that bit about returning. Ever since the German offensive had started a week earlier, the entire squadron had waited with bated breath for the call to arms. Flying defensive patrols over the peaceful English countryside or circling around slow-moving convoys as they ploughed up and down the North Sea could not satisfy their appetite for action. Not when just across the Channel the Germans were apparently smashing through everything that tried to stand in their way. On May 14, Holland had surrendered. On the 17th, Brussels had fallen, and – even more shaking – on the same date the Germans had bypassed the Maginot Line and crossed into France.

Allied strategy had clearly been based upon the conviction that the Maginot Line was impregnable. After all, improvised trench networks had held for four whole years the last time around. How could massive fortifications built in peace fail entirely? It was worrying, and rather hard not to conclude that the Germans were bloody good. In fact, they were beginning to seem very nearly invincible. But that only made the pilots of 579 Squadron anxious to *do* something. As one of them had put it in the Mess the other night, they'd been *training* for this for the last three to five years.

The frustration of comparative inactivity had been aggravated by the claims of the squadrons already in France; they had reportedly downed

11

hundreds of enemy aircraft. No one seemed to know for sure just what the score was, but it seemed that the RAF was putting up a more spirited resistance than the men on the ground or the *Armee de l'Aire*. It didn't seem fair that these other squadrons should have all the fun and glory.

So the selected pilots had followed the lead of their CO and Flight Commanders and retired early after a rather subdued night in the Mess. Priestman, finding he couldn't sleep so early and after fewer beers than usual, took the precaution of writing to his mother. It wasn't that he expected to die the next day, but you never knew. Besides, his mother was a widow, he an only child. He'd been raised on his mother's laments about having no last "farewell" from his father because his father had had the inconsideration to go down with his ship, taking all his personal belongings with him. Priestman had never known him; he'd been born posthumously in the summer of 1916.

Having done his filial duty but still not feeling sleepy, Priestman had dashed off a rather more heartfelt letter to his Aunt Hattie, his mother's elder sister, who had helped raise him, and last but not least to his paternal grandfather (known in the family simply as "the Admiral"), to whom Priestman owed his education and any standing he had in the world. By then it was almost midnight, and wake-up calls were set for 4 am.

Priestman slept soundly for four and half hours; then his batman woke him with his tea. He washed, shaved and dressed rapidly. From the rooms on either side of him came the clumping and knocks of the others as they, too, prepared to meet the day and with it what promised to be their first encounter with the enemy. Priestman wasn't aware of any nervousness, but rather an alertness and keenness, as he had often enjoyed before an air show.

For most of the last year before the war, Priestman had been a member of the RAF's aerobatic team, performing around the country and internationally, in both formation and individual aerobatics. It had been a very heady time, full of excitement and celebrations, but he had requested the transfer back to an active squadron even before the team was disbanded. It had been a risk. Rather than belonging to No. 1 (Fighter) Squadron like most of the aerobatics team, before he joined the Team he had been with a torpedo-bomber squadron based in Singapore, flying hopelessly out dated bi-planes. He might have been sent back to Bomber Command or to the Far East. He had been pleased, therefore, with the posting to a fighter squadron, even if it was a newly formed one with no great traditions or reputation. Of course, on arrival, both his new CO and flight commander had made it clear to him that he was still on probation.

"Being an aerobatics pilot doesn't make you a fighter pilot," the CO had said sternly. "We'll give you a fair chance and if you work out, good enough. If not, off you go!" Priestman had said, "Yes, sir" dutifully and saluted. But the CO stopped him. "And there'll be no repeat of the sort of thing that happened in Singapore, or it won't be a posting but a bowler hat! Understood?"

From that remark Priestman knew the Singapore incident was still held very much against him, and the threat of the chop was still hanging over his head. But they *had* included him in the sortie today, *and* he'd been given command of a section in apparent belated – or was it grudging? – acknowledgement of his seniority. Most of his class at Cranwell, if they were still in the RAF, had made Flight Lieutenant by now. Then again, they hadn't incurred the displeasure of their superiors in such a flagrant manner, either...

There was no breakfast at this time in the morning, so just half an hour after wake-up, the pilots taking part in the sortie to France climbed aboard the waiting transport and were driven out to their aircraft. They were still too sleepy for chatter – or maybe they were preoccupied with their own thoughts. In the darkness it was hard to see faces, anyway.

The ground crews were clambering over the 14 Hurricanes which were slated to fly, working mostly by feel and habit in the near darkness. They removed dew-covers, checked tyres, oil, petrol, oxygen, and R/Ts and gave the canopies a final polish.

Priestman jumped down from the tailgate of the lorry as it paused alongside his assigned aircraft, "Q." He had his para- chute over his shoulder and was kitted up in helmet, flying jacket, and 'Mae West' – as the inflatable flying jacket was affectionately called.

LAC Douglas emerged from under the wing, grinning. "Morning, sir."

"Morning, Douglas. Everything OK?"

"Can't ye hear her champing at the bit, sir?"

Priestman smiled and nodded. He pulled on his parachute, tightening the straps. They had done one practice jump in the last 7 months, and he hadn't had the straps tight enough. *Not to be repeated!* Then he put his foot in the stirrup and reached forward for the handhold. No sooner had he settled into the worn seat in the narrow cockpit, than Douglas leaned over him to help with his straps. Inside the cockpit Priestman pulled his helmet tight but left the goggles up until he was finished with the cockpit check. To his right he felt more than heard the spinner of the next Hurricane start to tick over.

LAC Sellers, his rigger, stood beside his engine with the starter cable connected, anxiously awaiting a signal. Priestman leaned out of the cockpit and gave a thumb's up. He pressed the starter button. The propeller started to spin slowly, and then with a cough it came to life. Priestman smelt the petrol smoke as it belched back at him and saw the exhaust flames spitting into the darkness. He glanced to the east, where the sky was starting to lighten. The trees beyond the perimeter fence were gradually becoming silhouetted against the night.

One after another the Hurricanes rumbled to life, and when they were all purring contentedly, Squadron Leader Sharp nosed out of his blast pen and started towards the head of the runway. The flare path had been lit for them and winked faintly in the pre-dawn twilight. They had practiced squadron take-offs hundreds of times these last six months, and every man knew his place. They took off in sections of three: led by the CO with his two wingmen of Red Section, he was followed by Yellow Section, led by the senior Flight Lieutenant, Yardly, then came Blue Section with Flight Lieutenant MacAllister leading, followed by Green Section led by Priestman with Pilot Officer "Shakespeare" Stillwell and Sergeant Pilot "Driver" Bennett on either side of him. The two, reserve aircraft took off last.

They were formed up in "Aircraft Close Vics, Sections Close Echelon Starboard," with the two reserves tucked in behind Red Section but parallel to Blue so they wouldn't get in anyone's way. The entire formation swung onto a course for France. The eastern horizon was starting to take on a luminous, sapphire-blue tinge, and the aircraft to Priestman's left were black against it. The little fighters looked wonderful and purposeful to him as they gracefully rode the winds against the increasingly orange sky to the east.

Overhead, some scattered cloud caught the rays of the rising sun and the soft, ruffled bellies were suddenly clothed in dazzling purples and pinks. Below, the English countryside slept beneath wisps of milky mist that stretched in an uneven sheet across the valleys. Here and there the stone steeple of a village church rose up triumphantly above the fog, and the first birds were rising from the fields in great flocks.

The Thames Estuary glistened in the morning light like molten copper. Beyond lay the Straits of Dover and France. The haze seemed to be worse up ahead and Priestman hoped that Sharp, who was the only one with a map, didn't get lost. They were all simply formatting on him without doing any navigating of their own. When Priestman had served on a Torpedo- Bomber Squadron at RAF Changi in Singapore, he had become rather fanatical about navigation because of the high risk of being lost over the sea. He didn't really like just tagging along behind his leader but reminded himself to be grateful that he was here, flying one of the best monoplane fighters in the world, and not still flying biplane Vildebeests in Singapore.

Soon the clearly identifiable coast at Calais came into view, although partially obscured by haze. Not ideal bombing weather, Priestman thought, but no doubt the haze would burn off as the sun got higher and hotter. Sharp shifted course once or twice, acting a little lost, Priestman thought, but then he settled onto a course and barked once: "Close up! Close up! Black Section" (that was the two reserves) "gain 1000 feet and keep a sharp lookout!"

Everyone was very keyed up by now as the unfamiliar French countryside slid past below them. Priestman strained his eyes, squinting hard against the bright sun, looking for hostile aircraft. He presumed they would come from the east, out of the sun, and so kept a particularly sharp lookout in that direction. But the sky remained empty.

Sharp started to lead them down towards the haze. It was very murky down here, and Robin didn't like this feeling of not having the foggiest idea where he was. But Sharp was good, and they soon spotted an airfield with several rows of bombers lined up neatly along the periphery. "Aircraft Close Vics, Sections Close Astern! Sections Close Astern! Go!" Sharp ordered, and the Sections slipped in behind one another. In the new formation they wheeled around and lined up into the wind.

Suddenly an alarmed cry went up. "Look out! There are bomb-craters all over the place."

"Abort!" Sharp ordered, throttling forward and zooming upwards again. They followed him upwards and now circled the airfield eyeing it suspiciously. It was indeed badly pockmarked by bomb craters. In fact, one aircraft, which Robin could not readily identify, lay on its back. Its burnt-out belly was exposed obscenely – rather like a gutted fish.

Sharp ordered them to spread out and land individually, one after another.

By the time Priestman was down, a lot of Frenchmen had poured out of the airfield buildings to greet them. It seemed they were not at the right airfield after all, and the French language skills of the English commanders left something to be desired. Sharp eventually remembered that F/O Ibbotsholm had spent much of his youth in Swiss boarding schools and called him over. Ibbotsholm soon sorted things out enough to make it plain that Sharp needed to get in touch with the British Advanced Air Striking Force. Things appeared to be happening very fast, and there was some change to their orders. Mean- while, the other pilots were taken into the French Mess for breakfast – something Robin heartily welcomed, as by this time he was starving.

After the meal, however, the pilots became increasingly restless. The time for their rendezvous with the bombers came and went. It was now nearly 8 am and the sun was bright and quite high. It was getting quite warm as well. They had removed their helmets long ago, and now unzipped their flight jackets or took them off entirely.

"Listen!" Pilot Officer George "Spotty" Millman called out, sitting bolt upright.

They all lifted their heads. In the distance they could distinctly hear some low, dull booms. They looked at one another. It sounded harmless enough, but because they were in a country at war, the distant thuds took on an ominous note. Further- more, the thumping didn't stop. "Bombs?" Roger Ibbotsholm speculated.

"Ack-ack?" S/P "Granddad" (so-called because he was already 29 and came from the Volunteer Reserve) Pierce countered.

"Artillery?" P/O "Shakespeare" (English teacher before the war, also VR) Stillwell suggested.

"Look!" "Driver" (former bus-driver, VR) Bennett leapt to his feet and pointed.

"Crikey!" There seemed to be swarms of gnats in the air off to the east.

"Maybe they're our bombers – this big raid we're supposed to be protecting?"

They stood and stared. "No. They're flying west."

Their instinct was to rush to their Hurricanes, to take off, to engage – anything but just sit here. But they had no orders to do anything of the sort. They looked about sheepishly. The French countryside in the immediate vicinity of the field seemed even sleepier than the English countryside they had left. Just beyond the fence a peasant was ploughing the field with a team of stocky horses. He would not have looked out of place in a Bruegel painting, and he ignored both the distant thuds and the "gnats."

"I'll go and find the CO," F/Lt. MacAllister announced. "The rest of you prepare to take off at short notice."

They ran to their Hurricanes. Without their ground crews, they had to do all the checks themselves, and the French apparently had only one starter battery that was compatible with the Hurricane. Priestman, glancing frequently over his shoulder at the steadily growing armada of "gnats," managed to convince the French airmen to start up the waiting Hurricanes by using vigorous sign language. Christ! If he'd known he was going to end up in a situation like this, he'd have paid more attention to French at school!

They were all in their cockpits with idling engines by the time Sharp and MacAllistair appeared at a trot. Sharp paused to consider the large formation of approaching aircraft, shielding his eyes against the bright sunlight with a hand, then scrambled up into his Hurricane and got it started. Over the earphones came his commentary. "The bloody Frogs

16

are running about like chickens with their heads off. Nobody seems to know what the hell's going on, and I can't get through to AHQ. Let's go get the buggers!"

Sharp led them off the field and then away from their targets to enable them to get some height. Priestman was aware of a growing tension, but nothing worse than the first moments before an aerial display or competition. Sharp called for Echelon Starboard, and the aircraft spread out in a long, receding line. Priestman thought it looked rather too long to his right and registered that the two "reserve" pilots had exploited the situation to take off with them. He sympathised; he would have done the same in their shoes.

Besides, it was just as well. Even with these extra bodies, they were just fourteen aircraft and facing a tight formation of something between forty and sixty enemy bombers. The enemy formation was impeccable, Priestman noted. A vic of three in the lead, followed by five vics of five aircraft each. The vics were stacked up slightly so the whole formation was like a moving stairway.

It registered that such tight boxes of bombers would be able to put up quite a murderous amount of fire, but Priestman noted that with absolute calm. He was more concerned with switching on his gun sight, taking the safety off the gun button, and then doing a last-minute check of his instrument dials, looking for abnormalities. The Hurricane was purring like a great cat.

"FAA 1!" Sharp ordered. Fighting Area Attack 1. "FAA 1! Go!" They had practised it scores of times. Now they would see if they were as good as they thought they were.

The bombers had seen them long ago, of course. As the RAF fighters started their attack, Priestman saw glowing beads start to slowly drift through the air in his direction. It took him several seconds to register that these must be tracer bullets. They looked rather lovely and slow – utterly harmless – until suddenly they were whizzing past like lightning. Abruptly, there was a hammering sound so close that it made his heart leap clear out of his chest. The Hurricane bucked. Priestman looked sharply right and saw a huge hole explode out of his wing. Smoke and fire were flashing over the wing surface – from behind him!

He wrenched around in his seat, causing the Hurricane to lurch and tip upwards slightly as he moved the stick unintentionally, and then his heart seized up as he realised there was an Me110 right on his tail. The monster wasn't more than 200 yards away, spewing cannon and machine-gun fire at him. He could see the explosions and hear the rattle of the bullets going home, and for a split second he looked Death in the face. "Behind us!" he screamed into the RT, as he kicked the rudder and flipped on his back before smashing the throttle through the wire with only one thought: escape!

The Me110 was right behind him. Suddenly Priestman remembered all the things he'd heard about this prize German fighter. With its two engines, it was faster than either the Hurricane or the Spitfire, and it was better armed as well, firing both cannon and machine guns. Hadn't someone said they would make single-engine fighters obsolete? Priestman was now truly terrified. He fish-tailed and swooped up and down – anything to muck up his pursuer's aim. He quarter-rolled and turned, but nothing seemed to shake the bastard off. They were racing down the sky. Tracer smudged the air first on the left and then the right, and every now and again – as a little reminder – bullets rattled against the Hurricane.

A detached part of Priestman's brain wondered how the Hurricane could take so much punishment and keep flying. Another part of his brain said that it surely couldn't take much more. He was down on the deck now, dodging farm buildings, hopping over stone walls, ducking under high tension wires. This was sheer madness! The Messerschmitt was still right behind him. The tracer kept reaching for him. Wouldn't the bastard ever run out of ammunition?

A church with a tower loomed up in front of him. Robin aimed for it and bent the Hurricane around the tower in the tightest turn he dared. The manoeuvre caught the Messerschmitt by surprise. It missed the turn, slued out as it tried to follow, and lost ground. Priestman flogged the Hurricane, but it was already going flat out. The engine started to smoke from overheating. He really couldn't keep this up much longer. In desperation, Priestman flung the Hurricane over into another tight turn in the other direction, hoping to catch the Messerschmitt off guard again. It worked. It started to register on his still stunned and frightened brain that his turning radius was significantly smaller than the enemy's. Thank God! He started a shallow spiral away from the earth, luring the Messerschmitt after him while waiting for the opportunity to get it into his sights. In a split second he had turned from hunted into hunter.

As he tightened the turn, his vision "greyed" out on him as his blood was forced from his brain. His consciousness became constricted to a single point: the gun sight. Those slow, glowing beads were coming at him again from the rear-gunner of the Me110 now. They sped up to flash past the cockpit, but Priest- man ignored them. Only with frustrating slowness and extreme concentration could he get the sight to nibble at the trailing edge of the larger aircraft. He held the gun button down, lifting the nose of his Hurricane. At last a piece of tail fin broke off the Messerschmitt and flew back at him. He ducked instinctively; the Messerschmitt slid out of his sight. Cursing, he strained to get it back in his sights.

Now it was the Messerschmitt that was jinking and dodging. It also was drawing away. Damn it! Frustrated, Priestman jammed his thumb on the gun button again, but all that came was the hiss of compressed air. He was out of ammunition.

When he realised that, the tension eased instantly. He throttled back and lifted the aircraft several hundred feet higher into the air. The German was belting down some railway tracks, gushing black smoke from both engines. That was from straining them, not from any damage Priestman had done. He knew that. The duel was over. A draw.

Not really a very good showing, Priestman reflected, when one considered how much time and money the British tax-payer had invested in him. Very nearly six years of education, flight training and experience flying a variety of aircraft, and what had he achieved? He'dmanaged to knock a tiny bit off the tail of the German, who was obviously still flying very well indeed, thank you. He was going to have to do a lot better than that if he wanted to be of service to his country. Which he did.

Priestman gradually became aware that his heartbeat was slowing down from what must have been an excessive rate. He was also drenched in sweat. The oxygen mask was particularly uncomfortable, and he unclipped it and wiped the sweat away from his chin with the back of his leather sleeve. He was still climbing gently, trying to get high enough to look around, because he was now completely lost. As far as he could see, there was not another crate in the sky, and below him was nothing but farmland, dotted by occasional barns and houses and this railway line, all half lost in a milky murk. The haze was still remarkably thick for so late in the day. What was he talking about? A glance at his watch showed it was only 9.20 am.

Priestman tried to raise the squadron over the R/T, but, as expected, all he got was static. The range of the R/T wasn't exactly brilliant. Meanwhile, his fuel was more than half gone, and he couldn't just circle around up here indefinitely. Hehad to find an airfield. Priestman decided to follow the railway tracks in the opposite direction from the German. They must lead to a town, and airfields were likely to be nearby.

Just when he was beginning to get seriously worried, he spotted an airfield and gratefully set his Hurricanedown. Hewas even more grateful to see a couple of Blenheims on the edge of the field. Priestman shoved the hood back, gulping in the fresh air, while he looked over the side to see around the long nose. He used his brakes alternately to swing the aircraft's snout from side to side as he carefully drove the Hurricane around the bomb craters littering the field. A couple of erks waved to him, and he followed their signals to a spot on the edge of the field. At their signal, he cut the engine and climbed out of the cockpit. He was stiff all over.

A grey-haired and weathered Flight Sergeant emerged. "Where did you come from, sir?" He was eyeing the squadron letters on the Hurricane with evident bafflement.

"I left Duxford this morning just after 5 am. We were supposed to fly escort to a bombing raid, but something went wrong. We ran into an incoming raid and attacked."

"Well done, sir. Did you get anything?"

"No. I saw a bit break off the tail, but that was all, I'm afraid. Look, do you think you could tank her up and let me make a telephone call? I haven't the foggiest idea where I am, much less where the rest of my squadron is."

"You're at Plievaulx, sir. 139 Squadron."

"Oh, how extraordinary! That's where we were supposed to land this morning. 579 Squadron."

"I'll take you over to the CO, sir. Let me just get some petrol organised. You'll want those holes patched up, too, I should think."

Priestman glanced over to where the Flight Sergeant was pointing and felt a short moment of dizziness as he saw the huge gaping holes in the fuselage of the Hurricane. He hadn't realised she'd been *that* badly hit.

He nodded. "Yes. Better check the controls, etc. while you're at it."

"Of course, sir. One moment."

The Flight Sergeant went over to the two airmen who had just put chocks around the Hurricane's wheels. They nodded and set to work right away. You certainly couldn't complain about the service, Priestman thought to himself, except that the erks weren't as cheerful as his own crew.

"I gather 139 is flying an operation?" Robin remarked to the Flight Sergeant as they started across the field together towards a large, camouflaged tent.

The Flight Sergeant glanced over at him and shook his head. "No, sir."

"But where are the rest of your aircraft?" "There aren't any more, sir."

"What?"

"Just what I said, sir. We only have three Blenheims left, and more than half the crews are dead or wounded."

Priestman was speechless. No wonder the ground crews were looking sombre.

A Wing Commander was coming towards him. Robin saluted. "Priestman, 579 Squadron."

"You're *alone*? You're all that's *left*?" The Wing Commander asked in horror.

"No, sir. I got separated during a dogfight and then lost. It was pure luck that I landed here."

"But where is the rest of your squadron?"

"I don't know, sir," Priestman admitted, feeling foolish.

The Wing Commander gazed at him numbly. His eyes were bloodshot and he had a three-day beard. "Well, let's try to find them," he suggested at last and, taking charge of Priestman from the Flight Sergeant, led him into a tent which apparently served as an Ops Room. There were maps of Northern France hanging on the walls, a telephone manned by a corporal, filing cabinets and two camp beds. The clerks raised AHQ, and learned that 579 Squadron was refuelling at Pontavert and preparing to return to England. Priestman had been presumed killed, along with two other missing pilots. They didn't have the names of who was missing, but Priestman wasn't worried, thinking no doubt they'd turn up just as he had. AHQ asked if Priestman could get himself to Pontavert?

The Wing Commander agreed to give him a map and some instructions. "Keep clear of Reims," he warned. "The Ack-Ack there is trigger-happy." Priestman thanked him. They shook hands, and Priestman started back towards his Hurricane. He could see the ground crew refuelling it from four-gallon drums. The sound of aircraft engines made him look up automatically. Two bombers were coming in quite low. Priestman followed them with his eyes as they swung around and lined up to land. They didn't look like Blenheims; maybe a French bomber type?

A voice from across the field was screaming, "Get down! Get down!" The voice was far away, and so rather faint and half carried away by the wind. Priestman looked over, baffled. He noticed that the erks who had been refuelling his Hurricane were running for the edge of the field, the petrol drums abandoned beside his Hurricane. "Get down!" someone shouted again, and at last he located the Flight Sergeant standing near one of the Blenheims and apparently waving at him.

The bombers must be hostile. Priestman looked back at them, anxious to make a correct identification. He saw the bomb-bays open and bombs start to drop. It was like a film. And then he was face down in the dirt and the earth was leaping and shaking under him. Dust got in his eyes and debris rained down on him. The explosions came one after another. One was higher pitched than the others and followed by a wave of suffocating heat, drenched in the smell of aviation fuel. Priestman glanced up in time to see his Hurricane collapse inwards in a ball of flame. They must have landed a direct hit, he registered in amazement. And then the bombers were directly overhead, and instinctively he crossed his arms over his head and lay flat on his stomach with his eyes pressed closed.

As suddenly as it had started, it was over. The humming of the unsynchronised engines gradually grew fainter, leaving the humming of the bees in their place. Slowly, Priestman uncrossed his arms, and lifted his head. The air was full of stagnant dust, just hanging above the ground. His Hurricane was a wreck, slowly burning itself out. He pushed himself to his feet and walked over to it. The erks and the Flight Sergeant also converged on the wreck and stood staring at it. "Sorry to waste your petrol," Priestman remarked at length.

"Not to worry. The Blenheims are already fuelled up." Priestman glanced around at the three Blenheims. They were untouched. In fact, his Hurricane appeared to be the only casualty of the raid – and, of course, the field, which was now even more torn up.

Priestman returned to the Ops tent and reported what had just happened. It was decided that 579 Squadron shouldn't wait for him any longer. They would return to England and he was to take ground transport to Seclin aerodrome, where 85 Squadron was based. 579 Squadron would meet up with him there in two days' time, as it had been decided to rotate 85 out and bring 579 in to replace them.

The Wing Commander was as obliging about ground transport as he had been about the map and the fuel. One of his dead pilots had left behind a battered old Renault; if Priestman could drive it, he could have it. The Wing Commander then carefully showed him the best route to follow to get to Seclin by road. "The French army is moving up reinforcements along these main arteries, and with the increasing number of refugees coming the other way, you'll never get through. You're much better off taking the side roads, skirting major cities as much as possible."

Priestman was provided with three extra canisters of petrol, bread, cans of bully beef, tea-bags and 200 francs in cash. As a last thought, the Wing Commander also gave him a pistol. "I hope you know how to use it. There have been repeated warnings about parachutists landing behind our lines. They use any number of disguises, so trust no one."

Priestman nodded, but the gun felt very heavy and awkward. He was a reasonably good shot, but he'd never pointed a handgun at anything except a target before – not even a clay pigeon. There was something much more brutal – criminal almost – about pointing a pistol at someone than pointing one aircraft at another.

It was early afternoon by the time Priestman set off, and it was very hot. He put his flight-jacket, parachute, Mae West and helmet into the boot of the car with the food and the extra petrol. He turned onto the road leading past the airfield and found himself at once in the midst of a slow-moving trek of civilian traffic. There were cars, lorries, tractors, horse-carts, bicycles, and people on foot. Everyone was caked in dust, and a cloud of dust hung over the road. Priestman found that the people moved out of his way if he honked, so at first he made quite good progress. After an hour or so, however, he started to fall asleep at the wheel. He would wake up just as he started to swerve one way or the other. He decided he would have to stop and sleep. Just half an hour, he told himself. To avoid jamming the road, he turned off into a field and parked the car under a line of large chestnut trees beside an irrigation ditch. He locked the car from the inside and fell instantly asleep.

Priestman woke with a sense of both terror and confusion. Something was roaring overhead, people were screaming. A horse galloped past dragging a man tangled in the reins of the harness. Branches rained down onto the top of the car. Jesus Christ, the Germans were strafing the road!

Priestman flung open the door and rolled out of the car into the ditch. There was about a foot of water in it, and his right foot was instantly soaked, but he didn't notice it at the time. Looking up, he could see two Me109s wheeling around and coming back for a second run. The bloody bastards! There wasn't a legitimate target for miles.

The roar of engines low overhead, the chatter of machine guns, the screams of refugees and horses, the branches cracking and falling, repeated themselves. Twice. Then apparently the Messerschmitts ran out of ammo or lost interest, because they flew away.

Shaken and shaking, Priestman pulled himself up out of the ditch. His uniform, which his batman had gone to so much trouble to clean and press just last night, was now filthy. Priest- man tried to brush off the worst dirt, but then gave up. He went to the Renault and looked it over. Except for a dent or two from the falling branches, it appeared undamaged.

Then he turned with dread to look at the road beyond it. Along the length of it, the refugees were picking themselves up, dusting themselves off, and checking their own vehicles. But here and there were crumpled bundles that did not move, or only barely moved. The hysterical screaming of a woman drew his attention to the right, and he saw a woman on her knees before a lifeless bundle. An older woman was trying to calm her. Priestman approached, planning to offer transport to the next hospital, but the child's head had been blown open and half torn away by the impact. He retreated. A little farther away, however, a man was rocking back and forth clutching his shattered shin, his face screwed up with pain. Robin went to him and tapped his shoulder. *"Monsieur. J'ai une Auto."*

In the end, Priestman loaded no less than six of the injured into the little Renault and set off. Later he could not explain how they communicated. His French was spotty at best, and the refugees spoke a dialect that was far removed from school French.

Somehow, they got to a town, and a gendarme on a bicycle led Priestman to a hospital. But the hospital was completely over-run with patients already. Dazed and bleeding civilians sat or lay like a carpet across the reception area.

Priestman left the injured in that sea of misery and returned to his Renault. The heat had finally gone out of the day. The sun was sinking down the western horizon and turning golden yellow. He realised that he was starving. He'd had nothing since breakfast. Deciding to keep his rations for later, he went into the nearest café.

Filled if not refreshed, he returned to the car and started off again. As darkness fell he discovered new hazards. The roads were not lighted and the headlights of the car he was driving had also been "blacked out" – that is, covered except for a small slit. Thus, he could hardly see the road or what was ahead of him on it. Carts or slow-moving vehicles seemed to loom up suddenly out of the night.

Once he crossed a major road, on which lorries of the French Army were rolling up towards the front. It took Priest- man considerable honking and gesturing to get a lorry to stop long enough for him to cross the road. The weary soldiers could be seen swaying back and forth under the canvas covering, their lighted cigarettes glowing briefly in the dark. Beyond them the night sky was lit by flashes of light. With a shudder, Priestman realised it was artillery.

After that, traffic got lighter and Priestman tried to drive faster. But this only ended in a near-accident when he abruptly ran into a herd of cattle trotting towards him. He just managed to screech to a halt in front of a massive bull that glared contemptuously at the little Renault. Priestman held his breath until the bull decided to saunter majestically past. He dropped his head on the steering wheel, and as soon as the adrenaline pumping through his veins had eased away, he fell asleep from exhaustion.

When Priestman woke, it was already getting light in the sky behind him. It was, he guessed, roughly 24 hours since he had taken off from Duxford. He was now somewhere in Northern France, driving a dead pilot's automobile to a destination he'd never heard of before. In the last 24 hours he had been in his first dogfight, been on the receiving end of both bombing and strafing, watched his Hurricane blown up before his eyes and seen his first casualties. He was stiff, tired, sticky with dirt, unshaven, and uncombed, and he had an unpleasant taste in his mouth reminding him he hadn't brushed his teeth, either. He could not remember ever feeling this foul at any time in his short life. And the grumble of artillery sounded nearer than ever. Today looked like it was going to be a re-run of yesterday. Was it really just yesterday that he had been eager and anxious to come over here to do his part?

Merville, France
20 May 1940

Priestman had never been so glad to see his comrades – or his ground crew. 85 Squadron had taken off (in their few remaining Hurricanes and a couple of Ansons) almost an hour before the neat vics of 579 Squadron appeared in the morning sky. In the meantime, he had been feeling very lonely and endangered. The artillery was beginning to get on his nerves, incessant as it was, and Priestman honestly didn't see how he would get out of this mess if 579 didn't show up.

But then they were there. Thirteen Hurricanes (so they'd brought their last reserve aircraft with them), two Ansons and a Lysander. Priestman was standing by the wing when Sharp stepped down. The squadron commander did a double-take before he recognised Priestman. "I say! What's happened to you?"

"What *hasn't* happened, sir? – bombed, dive-bombed, strafed, played ambulance to civilian casualties and slept in the open – and I didn't have a change of clothes or a razor with me." "Right. Well, your batman packed some of your kit for you." Sharp was looking around, watching the rest of the squadron land, making dispositions in his mind. "Not much here, is there?"

"No, sir. Who's missing?"

"Sergeant Putnam is dead; Ned is still missing. He may be a POW, but we don't know. At least no one's found his body yet." This said, Sharp strode away towards the Lysander, from which the Flight Sergeant was emerging.

Within a very short space of time, Priestman felt his confidence returning. They had tents up, the aircraft dispersed, and telephone connections to HQ Advanced Air Striking Force and to a mobile control room. Sharp had chalked an Order of Battle on a blackboard, which put Priestman as Green Leader again, flying the reserve aircraft, "B."

Priestman went over to put his parachute and helmet into the new kite; Douglas and Sellers met him. Douglas was smiling, while Sellers looked openly worried. "Good to see ye, sir," Douglas opened. Robin thought the two erks were eyeing his three-day beard with a degree of wonderment, but they made no comment. "We were a wee bit worried when ye didn't come back the other day."

"So was I!"

They laughed. Then, back to business, Douglas nodded towards the waiting Hurricane and assured him, "B's a dandy, sir. She's been fitted with armour plating behind the seat, see?" He proudly drew the Flying Officer's attention to this new feature.

The idea of providing Hurricane pilots with armour plating behind their seats had been proposed by No. 1 Squadron earlier in the year, but the Air Ministry had resisted the idea. They claimed that such armour plating would alter the aircraft's centre of gravity and so impair its flying ability. Fortunately for the pilots of Fighter Command, the CO of No. 1 Squadron was not about to take "no" for an answer – not after seeing how vulnerable his pilots were and noting that the Luftwaffe provided this protection to *their* fighter pilots. He found some scrap armour, had it fitted in one of his operational Hurricanes, tested it himself – and then sent one of his pilots to perform aerobatics with the modified Hurricane directly over the heads of the gentlemen at the Royal Aircraft Establishment. Since then, all new Hurricanes issued to operational squadrons had this seat armour. "B," furthermore, looked brand-new and still had a factory smell about her.

"And we've brought your kit, sir," Sellers announced, going over to a pile of kit-bags and boxes in a heap near the tail of the Hurricane. He pulled out a package neatly wrapped in paper and tied with string. Priestman opened to find a clean shirt, two sets of underwear, three pairs of socks, his toothbrush and shaving kit. The latter he thought he'd use right away, but he didn't get very far.

After the last 72 hours, Priestman's ears were highly sensitised, and he heard the engines before his ground crew. He looked up at once, located the beehive of approaching bombers and glanced back at his Hurricane, trying to calculate if they could get airborne in time to attack this lot. "Get her started!" he ordered and ran over to the ops tent, into which he had seen Sharp disappear.

He burst in a bit breathlessly, "German bombers, sir. Shouldn't we take off?"

"No! That's not our job. We're here to provide support for our own bombers. You have no idea what a bollocking I got for taking off last time."

"But, sir, if we don't, they're very likely to get us on the ground."

"The last two days seem to have got your wind up a bit, Priestman. I don't doubt that you've had a bad moment or two, but get up off your knees and —"

He was cut off by an explosion that went off not more than 100 yards away. It flung them down and blew half the tent off. Tables and filing cabinets crashed over, and already the rest of the bombload was raining down. For the first time in two days Robin was almost gratified by it, but he had no chance to really enjoy it.

Holding his hands over his head, Priestman listened with every muscle of his body. He felt the detonations receding, the sound of the engines moving away, and when he judged it was safe, he scrambled up and ran back out into the open. Just as he'd suspected. A pair of bombers had apparently detached themselves from the larger formation to come over and investigate the airfield. Liking what they saw – all those new Hurricanes on the ground – they had dropped their own loads, but they were now circling. They were probably calling up their chums and suggesting that this was a delectable target.

The CO was beside him, staring at the bombers too, and he apparently came to the same conclusion. He gave Priestman a look as if reassessing him. He nodded once. "Right. Get them up – now!" As they started for their Hurricanes, Sharp gestured and shouted to the other pilots picking themselves up off the ground.

Priestman had his foot in the stirrup when Douglas emerged beside him. The Scotsman was shaking, but he helped his pilot with his straps nevertheless. Sellers rolled the starter trolley alongside as the sound of bomber engines returned. They all glanced up. Five German bombers were lining up for a run at the field from about 10,000 feet overhead.

Priestman returned his attention to his instrument panel, and his crew went through the drill with trained precision. You had to hand it to them, Priestman thought; he already felt like a veteran, but his crew was under fire for the first time. As Priestman leaned out of the cockpit to wave the chocks away, the first bombs were already going off behind him. As soon as Sellers jumped clear, Priestman threw the Hurricane into a racing start, ignoring the wind direction, and praying he'd be able to get off the ground before encountering a bomb crater. The bombs were falling fast now, but they were a bit too far to the right, and so falling harmlessly into a field. Must have mis-judged the wind, Priestman registered professionally, as he felt the Hurricane come unstuck from the earth.

Behind him, at least six other Hurricanes were also either in the air or rushing to takeoff. However, they were much too low to catch this lot of bombers, so the question became whether more Germans were on the way or not? Sharp apparently decided they were not, because he gave the order to land again.

On the ground, Priestman was amazed to discover that a field kitchen had been set up by four airmen cooks in a tent – despite the bombing. The corned beef and beans they offered lukewarm might not qualify as gourmet cooking, but Robin had never been so grateful for a cup of tea in his life. The ugly airman who was serving grinned at him, "Looks like you could use a cuppa, sir."

"I would have killed for one, if you hadn't come along." They laughed together.

14.15, Priestman was back in the cockpit. The squadron had been ordered to rendezvous with some bombers again. Douglas and Sellers strapped him in. "Try not to get lost this time, sir," Douglas suggested with a wink.

"No chance. I have a map now!" Priestman tapped the map given him by the WingCo at 139 Squadron, which he had stuffed into his right boot.

Douglas gave him the thumbs up and jumped down off the wing. They took off on time and in formation. Sharp led them up in a climbing spiral, while Priestman tried to memorise the countryside around the field. During his drive here, he had spent a great deal of time studying his map, and he recognised much of what they were soon flying over. Seclin Airfield, where they had originally been scheduled to take over from 85 squadron, came into view quickly.

Funny that there seemed to be aircraft on it. Priestman had presumed when 85 Squadron pulled back to Merville that no other squadron would be moved in, but apparently, he had been wrong. Then the first crack of flak shook his Hurricane as it exploded just a hundred yards ahead of him. He flew right into the stinking blossom of cloud, and the next cracks were exploding around them. The aircraft on the ground were Messerschmitts.

Sharp ordered them to climb out of range, but someone was shouting, "I've been hit! Half the wing's gone!"

Priestman glanced left towards the bulk of the formation and saw a Hurricane falling out of it in a spin. Even as he watched, other pieces of fuselage appeared to break off. He tried to see the ID, but the aircraft was going down too fast.

"Get out, Blue Two!" Sharp ordered.

Robin tried to see if someone got out of the cockpit, but he couldn't see over his shoulder well enough to be sure what happened.

"They're coming for us!" a new voice reported in obvious excitement.

"Who is that? Make a proper report!" Sharp insisted. "Kapock Leader, Kapock Yellow Three here. Those Messerschmitts are taking off."

"Don't worry about them; they'll never catch us."

Priestman wasn't so sure. If he remembered the gen they'd been given, the Me109 had a rate of climb something like 600 feet per minute faster than a Hurricane. Sharp was ordering "Aircraft Close Vic, Sections Close Astern, Flights Close Echelon Port."

Priestman cursed inwardly. That was a bloody tight formation – the kind of thing bombers did. Flying it called for a lot of concentration just to avoid collision – and Priestman didn't want to concentrate on formation flying. He was much more concerned about those Messerschmitts. He eased his section back to avoid the risk of colliding with Blue Section and kept looking over his shoulder.

"Green One!" Sharp barked. "Close up!"

"Yes, sir." Priestman made a half-hearted effort to do so, but then sank back unintentionally as he searched the sky behind them again. Maybe he was losing his wool, but he couldn't avoid the thought that those aircraft on the ground might well have comrades already in the air.

He sensed it more than anything. Then the sun blinked. "BREAK!"

They were all over the place. At least 20 of them. They fell out of the sun. One minute they were nothing but a winking of the light, and the next they were blotting it out entirely while their wings lit up with flashes. The smoke of tracer smudged the sky, and then Yellow Three started spewing black smoke. Wasn't that Roger? Whoever it was, he flipped over on his back and started downwards. More Robin didn't have a chance to see, because he yanked his own Hurricane instinctively into a tight turn and was temporarily blinded as the blood drained from his head.

Priestman unhooked his oxygen mask and shoved the hood back before he landed, gulping in the fresh air. When he set down on three points, he thought he had never in his life been so glad to have ground under him. He was aware of a pulsing headache and his eyes felt swollen in their sockets. He taxied absently to the side of the field, too tired to notice if someone was signaling him somewhere else. He cut the engine and pulled off his helmet and ran his hand through his hair – it was wet and sticky.

He heard someone pant up beside him. "Robin?"

He glanced over; it was Roger Ibbotsholm. So he hadn't been in Yellow Three after all.

"Aye, aye." Robin was having trouble unclipping his straps for some reason. Roger was on the wing and bent over to help him.

"Are we glad to see you! We thought you'd bought it."

"They did rather catch us out again. Is everyone else back?"

"The CO's gone for six. Flamed out and went straight in from 10,000. Guy had to hit the silk over Seclin. Driver swears he saw a parachute land just beside the field and so he's almost certainly a POW. Shakespeare says Spotty didn't make it either – crate flamed before he could get out."

Douglas and Sellers reached Priestman. They too were panting, having run over from the far side of the field. "Are you all right, sir?"

"I've got a terrible headache, actually," Robin admitted rubbing his forehead.

"There's a ruddy great hole in the back of your seat, sir!"

"Oh, that. Yes. Good thing about the armour plating."

"You can say that again, sir! Look!"

A crowd was gathering. This Hurricane didn't look nearly as tattered as his old one, but the one neat puncture it *did* have indicated a cannon shell that had lodged deep in the armour plating behind his seat.

The others scrambled up the off wing and peered into his Hurricane. There were a lot of admiring whistles and excited comments. Priestman left the others to it and slid to the ground, leaning back against the trailing edge of the wing. Only once before had he been so conscious of divine protection – after capsizing a small boat in a Force Five gale in the Solent. Then he had been a foolish 15- year-old boy who over-estimated his abilities, and for whom God had no doubt felt pity. Today, with so many others dead, it was hard to understand why he should have been one of the lucky ones.

Priestman noticed Yardly approaching but didn't think anything of it – until the Flight Lieutenant opened his mouth and said: "I'm acting CO now, if you're wondering." Robin hadn't got that far, actually, but he didn't like the sound of this. Priestman had never really warmed to Sharp, but he was a first-rate pilot and a conscientious commander. Priestman had trusted him. Yardly was something else again. From the day he joined the squadron, Yardly had seemed to resent him. In short, this was not a good development.

Yardly, meanwhile, was remarking, "I see you were lucky a second time, Priestman."

"It would seem so." It obviously did not occur to Yardly that maybe Robin was particularly skilled or a talented dogfighter.

"And the Blenheims got slaughtered again." Yardly made it sound as if it was Priestman's fault alone. Priestman kept his mouth shut. He might do stupid things when he got backed into a tight enough corner, but he wasn't inherently insubordinate or stupid.

Yardly was compelled to continue his lecture without new fuel. "Our job is to protect our bombers, not go rushing off on our own. Don't forget it! I'm not going to put up with your nonsense the way Sharp did."

What nonsense? Priestman asked himself. He'd been behaving himself like a bloody goody-two-shoes ever since he'd joined the Squadron!

At six pm they were sent up again – this time to patrol a certain piece of sky. Unlike Sharp, who had been careful to share any intelligence he had with his pilots, Yardly either didn't know or didn't tell them why they were supposed to fly back and forth between two harmless-looking towns, and after 1 hour and 50 minutes of stooging around, they returned to Merville.

The sun was setting at last. They sat around in the cooling May evening waiting for release. The Adjutant had organised billeting in the village of Merville via their French liaison officer. "Is there a café in Merville?" Driver asked generally but looking in Robin's direction because he had driven through the town on his way here.

"Not that I saw," Robin answered. "But it was dark."

"There *has* to be a café. No self-respecting French village is without a café." Roger intoned knowingly.

"Who said this village is self-respecting?"

At 9.30 pm they were stood down. A French Army lorry picked them up and took them the three miles into the village. Priestman really only wanted a bath and bed, but the others insisted on going to the café – and of course, Roger was right and there was one. They crowded into the little, dingy building and overwhelmed the bar.

"*Vous êtes les Aviateurs Anglais!*" exclaimed the buxom proprietress with curly blond hair and a double chin. She then proceeded to give them each a loud, wet kiss on the lips.

"Could you ask if she has a daughter, Milord?" Driver suggested to Roger (who was the best French speaker among them).

"Granddaughter would be more like it," Shakespeare muttered, wiping his mouth with his handkerchief as discreetly as possible.

Roger ordered six bottles of red wine instead.

Priestman caught Shakespeare's eye; they had been billeted in the same house. "I'm going to turn in."

"Right oh. Good night."

Priestman left the stuffy café, with its pervasive smell of stale wine and cigarette smoke, gratefully behind. His headache had been almost unbearable inside, but in the fresh air it eased somewhat. He found the address he'd been given. It was a narrow house with a rough plaster façade and wooden shutters closed over the tall windows – typically French. He knocked, already practising his French in his head. The door cracked open and a timid, little voice asked, "*C'est qui?*"

"*Je suis Rober' Priestman, Madame. Je suis Aviateur Anglais. Il Capitain—*"

"*Oui, oui, Monsieur!*" The door was flung open and Priestman was gestured inside with vigorous, sharp motions. He found himself towering over two little old ladies. Both were dressed in black, from their high-necked dresses to their black hose stuffed into wooden clogs. They both had grey hair, combed to the back of their heads in neat little buns. And both wore gold crosses that glimmered in the dull light coming from the kitchen.

Priestman was just a hair under 6'0" and towered more than a foot above his hostesses, but they went on tip-toe to deliver kisses on both cheeks. He could understand little of their words, but their gestures of welcome were so effusive that they hardly needed language at all. He was hustled into a kitchen lit by oil lamps. The door to the kitchen garden was open to let in a little fresh air – and the cackle of fowl in the yard.

Priestman was pushed into a chair and before he knew what was happening, a meal of braised liver in onions with mashed potatoes and carrots in parsley was set before him, along with a bottle of wine. It would have been impossibly rude to refuse, and after one mouthful he realised how hungry he was – and how good this tasted.

Priestman tried to apologise for his uniform and general state of disorder, but the sisters (at least that was what he presumed them to be) appeared to misunderstand him. They showed him the washbasin and iron and made gestures to indicate they would clean everything for him. Robin tried to explain he wanted to clean *himself*, not for them to clean his things. *"Oui, oui, Monsieur! On a compris! C'est bien!"*

One of the two old ladies pulled out the washbasin and started to pour water from the kettle into it. Her sister started pumping cold water from the sink. Ten minutes later, he found himself being urged to undress right here in the kitchen, and embarrassing as it was, he felt he had no choice. Feeling incredibly foolish and de-sexed, he stripped down to his underpants, but then he insisted on being left alone so vigorously that, giggling at his modesty, the two old ladies withdrew.

Feeling half-way human again after the bath and shave, Robin wrapped himself in the ancient dressing gown they had left for him beside the towels, and tip-toed out of the kitchen. He was intercepted and led upstairs to a crowded little room filled with furniture, a sewing machine and stacks of mending (maybe they took in mending work to earn extra?). Amidst it all was a narrow bed with a frilly bedspread, and here Robin was supposed to sleep. Although it was uncomfortably soft, he did – instantly.

21 May 1940

Shakespeare woke him in the dark. "Time to get up, Robin."

"What time is it?"

"Time to get up."

"What time is *that*?"

"If you insist on the ugly details: 3.25 am. The lorry will be in the square in 5 minutes."

"Dawn Patrol."

"Isn't that the name of a flick?"

"With David Niven, I think."

"I don't think it had a very good ending."

"Not for everyone."

They patrolled various positions in the sky five times that day and did not encounter the enemy once. There was something terribly ominous about the situation. Like the calm before a terrible storm. The horizon to the northeast was dirty – as if the haze were mixed with increasing smoke. Artillery rumbled constantly. As dusk gathered from the east, the sky pulsed with flashes of light punctuated by flares. God knew from whom, or what they meant.

The villagers of Merville were getting very nervous, too. When the pilots of 579 squadron reached "their" café, they found that many of the houses had carts and cars parked in the street in front of them. They were being loaded up in preparation for departure. The situation was even worse in Robin's billet when he and Shakespeare arrived. The two sisters pulled them inside, wringing their hands and gesturing to their possessions. They begged Robin and Shakespeare for advice on what to do. They had heard that Amiens had fallen! Amiens! How was it possible? Where was the Grand Army of France? The brave British? Would the Germans continue westwards or turn south towards Paris? What should they do? They looked to two strange young Englishmen for the advice and guidance they should have had from their own sons. But their sons were buried somewhere north of here, victims of the last German onslaught.

"Stay put!" Shakespeare told them — with vigorous supportive nodding from Robin.

"The roads will soon be clogged to a stand-still, and the Germans attack the people on the roads," Robin tried to explain via Shakespeare. "They shoot at everything. You are safer here in your house."

"But what if the Germans come? What if the town is occupied?" the two sisters asked nervously, their eyes wide with fear and their wrinkled faces creased with worry.

Despite Robin's less than pleasant encounters with the Germans, he honestly did not believe they would do any harm to two little old ladies. He said as much to Shakespeare in English. "The problem is, old boy, the Boche has been their bogeyman ever since they were children," the former teacher explained patiently. "As little children they were raised to blame the Boche for all the hardships imposed by the Peace of Paris. Then they had to fight them again in the Great War, and now he is on their doorstep again."

"They're still safer here than on the roads! What on earth are the Germans going to do to two old ladies? On the roads they'll just get exhausted, hungry and footsore – if not worse. You've got to make that clear to them."

The English teacher-turned-pilot did his best, including some nice talk about the German thrust being too thin and how it was going to be cut off by a pincer movement by the British Expeditionary Force (BEF) and the French army. After a while, the two old ladies seemed to feel less distressed.

The airmen went up to bed, and Robin asked Shakespeare in a low voice, "Do you really believe that pincer stuff?"

"Christ, Robin! That's what *has* to happen! If we can't crush the Germans between the BEF and the main French Army, then the Germans will continue on to the Channel, because they can't afford to turn south towards Paris with the BEF at their backs." Priestman could follow that logic, but the Germans were in Belgium, too. That meant that the BEF was being pushed westwards towards Calais. If they turned south to strike at the Germans in Amiens, weren't they exposing their *own* back to the Germans pressing them from Belgium? He didn't think of himself as any kind of strategist, but it rather looked to him as if the BEF was itself *caught* in a very daring pincer movement.

Robin didn't sleep very well that night.

22 May 1940

At 3 .30 the next morning they were on the lorry again, heading back for the airfield. Only this morning, the darkness was incomplete. The fires from Amiens lit up the sky in a murky red colour. As the sun came up, turning the red glow of the fires to dirty brown, 579 Squadron was sent on patrol again, which seemed rather ridiculous. Surely there was something more useful they could do? But Yardly insisted that they just fly back and forth along the pre-determined flight line.

Whatever it was they were supposed to be protecting, the Germans didn't appear to have any interest in it. Just under two hours later they were back on the ground, having accomplished nothing but the consumption of many gallons of precious aviation fuel. Unhappy and unsettled, they waited in the shade of the poplars beside their airfield.

"I can't believe we wouldn't be more effective strafing the bloody Germans than just stooging around at 15,000 feet!" Priestman complained. (Yardly, as usual, was in the operations tent and so not within hearing of this complaint.)

"I suppose our 30mm guns aren't very effective against panzers," Driver suggested with a little helpless shrug.

"The Germans aren't *all* in panzers, for God's sake! They've got infantry and supply convoys, too. We could be raising hell in their rear, not just wasting aviation fuel." Priestman had seen what a couple of Me109s did to the French lines of communication; he couldn't believe they couldn't be making *some* contribution to the fight.

"Robin's right," Shakespeare agreed, sitting up and clasping his arms round his knees. "If the Germans are fighting in Amiens, we have the range to hit their lines of supply and communication."

"Yes," Roger agreed, pulling himself upright. "But," he glanced over towards the Ops tent to be sure Yardly wasn't within hearing and then remarked, "it would appear that our noble *acting* CO is not very keen on actually encountering the Hun, is he?"

The awful words out, they hung in the still, hot air like an unpleasant smell. Granddad shifted uncomfortably, kicking the dry dirt with his boot. That was just it. Yardly kept telling them what their orders were, and somehow their orders were always to be somewhere where the Hun was not. Maybe Air Advanced Striking Force (AASF) was so confused that they got it wrong all the time, but even when the Hun did show up, Yardly ordered them *not* to attack. The only fights they'd had since Sharp had been killed had been forced on them by the enemy.

Not very long afterwards, an excited Frenchman drove onto the airfield and started spreading panic. He was a Colonel, and he gestured very wildly and seemed to be demanding support for his unit. Yardly, even with the help of Ibbotsholm's impeccable French, had some difficulty explaining to him that they were a fighter squadron and could not provide the kind of close support he seemed to expect. Angry and bitter (Priestman thought he heard some rather impolite phrases mixed with references to "perfidious Albion"), the French Colonel withdrew, promising that they would soon have Germans rather than French to deal with!

Not an hour later, French tanks rattled past on the road in apparent flight. The steady and growing stream of refugees on the road was forced into the ditches to make way for the French armour – going the wrong way.

Next, orders came down from AASF to withdraw 14 miles to the west. There was no time to collect the things left at their billets. The pilots were told to fly out their own Hurricanes, while the ground crews, supplies and equipment were loaded onto the remaining French lorries to follow by road.

Their new quarters proved so inhospitable that Yardly set off by car to try to find something better, leaving MacAllistair in charge. He at once took the squadron up on an aggressive patrol that led them towards the enemy. One hour later, the squadron had finally done what it had come for: successfully attacked an enemy bomber formation and broken it up.

Priestman could not resist a victory roll as he came in to land. He came low over the field counting 10 aircraft on the ground, and did a slow roll at 1000 feet, then banked sharply to the right and set down on the grass.

Even the dour Sellers was smiling as the two erks caught the tips of his wings to swing the Hurricane around and back it onto the edge of the little field. Priestman shoved the hood back and shouted out to them, "A Heinkel! The crew jumped and I saw it go in!"

"Good show, sir! That makes 4 altogether. Flight Lieutenant MacAllistair, Flying Officer Ibbotsholm and Sergeant Pilot Bennett made claims as well."

Douglas was on the wing already, helping him with his straps.

"Is everyone back safe?"

"Yes, sir. Sergeant Pilot Turner took a bit of lead in the tail, and Pilot OfficerSmith couldn't get his undercarriage to come down, so he had to belly-land it. Bit nasty, that, as we haven't got the spares or equipment to repair it over here. But he's all right."

By the time Priestman's feet hit the grass, Ibbotsholm and Shakespeare were there to greet him. "Congratulations and all that," Shakespeare offered, while Ibbotsholm threw an arm over his shoulder and remarked, "Well done, my boy." (He was two years older than Robin and affected this fatherly manner when it suited him.)

"We have some good news and some bad news. Which would you like first?"

"Let's start with the good."

"Can you imagine? In the midst of all this chaos where no one knows what's going on or where the enemy is, a telegram has arrived promoting you to Flight Lieutenant."

Priestman was taken aback by the timing. He'd hoped for the promotion all through the winter. He'd even spoken to Sharp about it, who had told him to "just give it time." So maybe they had forgiven him after all? Then he remembered the bad news. "What's the bad news?"

"Bit of a graveyard promotion, you might say, and Yardly's all in a dither. You see, it seems the Germans have taken Abbeville. The BEF is cut off."

Robin stared at them. Maybe it was time to start praying – seriously.

After that, things only got worse. The days started to blur into one another. They were flying frantically – usually led by MacAllistair rather than Yardly, who had to "keep things together" on the ground, and Robin found himself acting "B" Flight Commander.

They were soon out of spare parts and had to cannibalise Smith's Hurricane. Bizarrely, 11 Group sent them four replacement Hurricanes and pilots in the midst of this chaos, but the new pilots were so wet behind the ears that Yardly told them to just keep out of everyone's way. Which left the remaining pilots of 579 flying 4-5 times a day. When they weren't flying, they generally stretched out in the shade of their Hurricanes and tried to sleep.

Priestman had done just that when an airman crawled under the wing beside him. He opened one eye, and honestly didn't recognise the ugly little man who was shaking his arm. "You've got to eat something, sir," the AC1 urged.

Priestman sat up, forcing himself to focus. It was a cook from the Mess. He was in his forties, with crooked yellow teeth, and he was thrusting a sandwich at Robin. "You 'aven't eaten all day, sir. You can't keep going on an empty stomach."

"How did you know I haven't eaten?" Robin asked, taking the thick sandwich from the airman.

"Do you think I can't keep track of my pilots?" The AC1 asked indignantly. "You 'aven't been eating proper for two days, sir. It ain't good." The little airman was genuinely upset.

Priestman registered guiltily that he hadn't given a thought to the ground crews of late. They were getting bombed sporadically, and the possibility of the airfield being over-run by enemy was a constant threat. Furthermore, now that the Lysander and one of the Ansons had been damaged and cannibalised to keep the Hurricanes flying, they might have to rely on the Royal Navy to get home – which hardly seemed very likely. The Royal Navy couldn't take the *whole* of the BEF off, after all, so what were the chances that the ground crews of an RAF squadron would get special treatment? Very slight, and they must know that. They must know that in all probability they were going to be prisoners of war within the next few weeks, even days. And this airman was worrying about whether he'd eaten properly?

"What's your name, Airman?"

"Thatcher, sir."

"Thank you, Thatcher," Robin managed between mouthfuls of rather dry bread and beef. It didn't taste like anything, actually, but the airman was right: he needed it.

Priestman shot down an Me110 the next day, but before he could congratulate himself on it, he was bounced by a 109. His engine seized up. Oil was spewing back at his windscreen, covering it with filth so he couldn't see out. The 109 was hammering him still, and Priestman decided it was time to take a walk. He scrambled out of the cockpit and dropped into space, pulling the ripcord after the recommended count to ten. He landed in an abandoned village, in which an overturned ambulance still lay at the crossroad — replete with fly-covered corpses being picked at by the crows.

Priestman walked backwards out of the junction, then turned and started searching the abandoned houses until he found a bicycle. He climbed on it and pedalled back to the airfield.

"Am I glad to see you!" MacAllistair greeted him. The more senior Flight Lieutenant was looking a little the worse for wear, Priestman registered. He had the same 5-day beard they all had. His uniform was covered with a mixture of dust, sweat, oil, petrol (they often helped the ground crews with the bowsers) and spilt tea. But that was just normal dress these days. What struck Priestman was that he had his arm in a sling. "I've knocked my shoulder out, Robin. You'll have to lead the squadron. Take my Hurricane if you like."

Priestman was about to ask how he'd done his shoulder in if his Hurricane was all right, when a shout went up. "Here they come again!" Priestman just had time to fling himself into a slit trench before the strafing Messerschmitts were over-head again. Not hard to hurt yourself in such a situation, he realised, and refrained from even asking MacAllistair for details.

Teatime. Priestman joined the other pilots sitting in the shade of the Mess tent. They were drinking tea. No sooner had Priestman sat down than the airman/cook shoved a mug of the hot, sweet stuff into his hand. Priestman smiled up at him, "You are a marvel, Thatcher."

"Just doing my job, sir."

"Doing a damned good job, if I may say so, Thatcher."

"Thank you, sir." The airman actually looked embarrassed, as if he didn't know what to do with appreciation – and that made Priestman feel guilty: obviously he and his colleagues were a little too sparing with praise and thanks.

The telephone was ringing in the ops tent. They turned their heads and stared at the tent, waiting.

"Maybe it is just someone ringing up to see how the weather is over here."

"Or someone calling to ask if there is anything we lack?"

"Maybe someone has just signed a surrender."

No, it didn't look like that. Yardly was standing in the entry, waving furiously at them.

"Once more unto the breach, dear friends, once more," Shakespeare intoned as he set his mug aside.

"Shut up!" Roger told him irritably – much too irritably. You could tell his nerves were a bit frayed. He'd had an ugly belly landing the other day and hadn't been the same since, really.

"What's the matter?" Driver asked innocently. Yardly was shouting at them to "get cracking," but they ignored him. After all, *he* wasn't flying, and they didn't presume it would make much difference to the war if they were a minute or two later. It was all a cock-up, anyway.

"It's the next line," Priestman explained to Driver, putting his own mug aside carefully.

"What's that?"

"'Or close the wall up with our English dead.'"

Most of them slept on the field that night. They felt happier together, near their Hurricanes, than scattered out among the houses where they were allegedly billeted. The erks felt the same. They were gathered in the maintenance tent, and you could hear occasional volleys of laughter from that direction. What there was to laugh about, Robin couldn't imagine, but it was a tribute to the ground crews that they still had it in them. The pilots, except for Yardly who was billeted with the local mayor along with the adjutant and intelligence officer, preferred the open air. It would have been different if the weather hadn't been so warm and clear, or if any of them had had a change of clothes. As it was, they were warm enough under the stars, and far too filthy to worry about any more dirt.

They collected on a little rise that gave them a view across the field in one direction and towards the coast in the other. Not that they could actually see the coast, but the glow of distant fires and the faint crack of Navy guns told them roughly where Boulogne and Calais lay.

"Do you suppose they're putting troops ashore or taking them off?" Driver asked with a nod in the direction of the burning cities.

"Didn't all our armour come out with the BEF?"

None of them knew, so they fell silent. Secretly, they rather hoped that troops were being taken off. Then again, how could the Navy ever embark 300,000 men or more?

"They can see those fires in England, too," Granddad reflected. "Must make people nervous."

"They certainly make *me* nervous!" Driver readily admitted, speaking for all of them. "The bloody Germans are rolling up the coast. If they take Calais, what's left?"

"Dunkirk, I think, and Ostend."

"Haven't the Belgians surrendered?"

Nobody knew. They weren't being told much of anything. "Calais was English once," Shakespeare reflected in the silence that followed.

"And the country has been going down-hill ever since we lost it!" Roger answered and they laughed, but then fell silent again.

"Today was Sunday," one of the new pilots, whose name Robin had forgotten, remarked with his chin on his knees.

"Was it?"

"My father's a vicar," he continued, "so I've got this internal calendar."

"Useful, I suppose."

"They'll have prayed for us all across England."

"A lot of bloody good that's likely to do!" Roger snapped bitterly.

"Who knows? We're still here, aren't we?" Robin countered.

Priestman couldn't sleep. He was exhausted beyond all measure, but everything seemed to keep him awake – the dampness of the earth, the roughness of his parachute pack under his head, the snoring or uneasy stirring of his companions, the distant bark of navy guns. It should have been reassuring that the Navy was there, he supposed, but the rest of that quote from Henry V kept going through his head, too: "Dishonour not your mothers; now attest that those whom you called fathers did beget you."

Wasn't it odd that Shakespeare, 400 years ago, could write something that fitted so perfectly? Nearly all the pilots had fathers who had been here in France last time around, and they had fought it out four years. It was barely two weeks since the German offensive had begun – and it was very nearly over. If Calais fell, they were all trapped.

The thought of being a German prisoner made Robin shudder. Such a grim, humourless people! And the arrogance of them! That was really the worst of it: the way they would gloat and lord it over you.

The sky was lightening to the east already. God! It couldn't be. He needed his sleep! Please let me sleep! God ignored him, as he so often did. The birds were waking. From the airfield came the sound of someone whistling.

Robin wanted to scream or cry. He was exhausted. He couldn't take any more. Not without a good night's sleep. A Hurricane engine coughed into life as the fitters started to warm them up. Around him the others started to sit up. Most looked as if they had slept as little as he had. They straggled back down towards the field, found their way into the Mess tent, and fell heavily upon the benches lining the somewhat precarious trestle tables.

Two hours later they were scrambled to intercept bombers attacking the British in Calais. Priestman could sense he was in trouble from the start. At take-off, his Hurricane hit a small hole and bounced. He over-reacted, pulling back on the stick much too soon. He didn't have enough speed. The Hurricane fell back to earth and he was running out of grass. When he did get airborne, he barely cleared the trees.

The adrenaline pumping from the near miss, he had to throttle forward to catch up with the others as they swung west towards Calais, the sun behind them bright and blinding. It was obvious that they were going to get bounced. But ahead, a gaggle of ugly Stukas was peeling off and going down to drop their loads on the ruins of Calais – because that was all that was left of the city. The buildings the Stukas were hammering had long since turned into heaps of rubble. Still, guns were being fired out of that rubble, and with a twinge of pride Robin realised that there were British troops down there in that wasteland, and they were flinging defiance back at the overwhelming might of Germany.

They were so small, so weak, their arms so inadequate for the task facing them, and their situation was patently hopeless. In fact, the town had apparently already fallen to the Germans. The ugly swastika flag fluttered over the major buildings, but the Union Jack cracked defiantly from the ancient medieval fortress.

Robin hated Stukas more than any other aircraft. They were ugly, vicious planes without any kind of natural grace. They had bent wings and massive, fixed undercarriages like the extended claws of an attacking eagle. They had been designed to intimidate without majesty, and were even equipped with sirens whose sole purpose was to increase the noise, and so the terror, they created as they dived. They symbolised in his mind all that was most objectionable about the Nazis – the brutality, the brashness, the bragging. Robin was determined to get one – and confident, too.

Bringing one down was not the problem. The Hurricane could fly circles around a Stuka, and Priestman, Ibbotsholm, Stillwell and Bennett all brought one down on their first pass. Robin's mistake was that he wanted more. As soon as he'd finished off one Stuka, Priestman spiralled up the sky to get enough altitude for a new attack. He kept watching the Stukas, afraid they would get away before he could attack again. He was not watching his tail or the sun.

The canon hits from behind took him completely by surprise. He reacted as he had taught himself over the last ten days, with a flick quarter-roll and a tight turn. It worked, the Me109 overshot him, and Robin straightened out and turned inland. He'd made a second mistake: he'd forgotten the wingman.

The minute he straightened out, machine guns and cannon raked along the side of the Hurricane. He felt as if it had been wrenched violently out of his hands as it spun out of control. Still shaken by the suddenness of the dual attack and the terrifying sensation of losing control of the Hurricane, Priestman was close to panic as he tried to pull out of the spin.

Nothing happened.

The pedals and stick were dead.

His brain registered what had happened. His tail and/or the control cables had been shot away. He had no control of the aircraft and the Hurricane plunged down, spinning so fast the earth was only a whirling blur.

He struggled to get clear of the aircraft, tearing off his helmet to free himself of oxygen and R/T, but the centrifugal force pinned him in the seat. The hood jammed. He battered his hands bloody trying to free it. At the very last minute it broke free, and with the super-human strength of panic he flung himself over the side of the cockpit. But he was far too close to the ground. His 'chute didn't have time to open properly.

He crashed into a steep sloping railway siding and tumbled down to the bottom lifelessly.

Chapter 2

Labour Service Camp, East Prussia
Early June 1940

Klaudia paused to wipe the sweat from her forehead with the back of her arm. In the distance a ragged line of men moved forward methodically, mercilessly swinging their scythes. Behind them, the girls of the *Reichsarbeitsdienst* (RAD) in their blue shirtwaist dresses, white bibbed aprons, and red headscarves, raked the hay into stacks.

It was a familiar scene, something Klaudia knew from home, even though the landscape here was very different. East Prussia was both flatter and wilder than her native Silesia, but after almost six months here, she was beginning to see the beauty in it.

Klaudia had been with the RAD almost a full year and was now accustomed to the work just as she had adapted to the drill and the group living. As her time drew to a close, she realized she would miss being with the other girls and part of the collective effort to make Germany greater than ever.

Klaudia was shaken from her thoughts by someone calling her name. She straightened, and with a sigh again wiped at the sweat that dripped off her forehead with the back of her arm. Her back seemed to ache even more when she stopped raking than when she worked. "Ja, Frau Krüger?" she called out from where she stood.

"Come here!" Frau Krüger ordered as she waved frantically from the edge of the field. "The Camp Commandant sent a messenger all the way here! You must report to her at once!"

Klaudia was instantly alarmed. She wasn't conscious of having done anything wrong, but a year in the RAD had taught her to assume the worst whenever one was ordered to "report at once." The leaders at the camp had absolute authority over the young women serving under them. They could order any number of unpleasant punishments such as extra duties, exhausting exercise or even house arrest. Klaudia, who had only two more weeks before her scheduled release from the RAD, did not want any trouble at this stage.

All the way back to the camp, Klaudia tried to think what this could be about. She had always tried very hard to obey the rules and to fit in with the others. That had been difficult at first because she knew so little about National Socialism.

In her village, Berlin had seemed very far away. Ever since Kaiser Wilhelm had been forced to abdicate, the governments in Berlin had appeared to come and go more often than some people changed their socks. After the "Seizure of Power," things settled down a bit, of course. There were no more elections to worry about. A so-called *"Ortsgruppenleiter"* appeared now and again in a big, chauffeured car and a brown shirt, but the pastor, the policeman, the schoolmaster and, of course, Klaudia's father the *Landrat*, "ran" the village between them as they always had. People still said "Good morning" rather than "*Heil* Hitler," and everyone went to church on Sunday.

In a village that abhorred the "Reds," no one had been arrested in 1933 or afterwards. When compulsory military service was reintroduced in 1935, it was celebrated in the village tavern by the entire male population. So was the reoccupation of the Rhineland, the liberation of the Sudetenland, and the bloodless victory over Czechoslovakia.

Admittedly, the mood during the invasion of Poland this past autumn had been tense. Many of the older men had worried that the French would attack Germany along the Rhine, while the Wehrmacht was tied down in Poland. But things had turned out all right in the end, and so everyone had celebrated another victory and then life had continued as before. Everyone still said "good morning" rather than "*Heil* Hitler" – although they now revered the "*Führer*" almost as much as the *Kaiser*.

Klaudia thus arrived in the RAD without even a rudimentary knowledge of National Socialism. She hadn't known about "Living Space" or "Racial Politics" or the "Leadership Principle." Nor had she been familiar with all the seemingly endless numbers of organizations and uniforms from SA and SS, Hitler Youth and League of German Girls, to the Labour Service itself. Yet Klaudia had been anxious to fit in and be accepted. As soon as her fellow "Labour Girls" and her "Leaders" recognised her willingness to learn, they did their best to help her. She had never been called upon to "report at once," much less dragged away from her work in the middle of the day.

The camp came into view, and Klaudia spotted another Labour girl, Rosa Welkerling, arriving at nearly the same time. Rosa served in a different unit and so Klaudia did not know much about her – except that she had a working-class Berlin accent and had been active in the League of German Girls (BDM). She was widely thought to be "leadership material," and it was hard to imagine her being in any kind of trouble.

Then Klaudia noticed the large, but rather battered, old car parked out in front of the Commandant's office. It had the distinctive number plates reserved for the Wehrmacht. A driver in the uniform of a Luftwaffe airman was lounging against the front fender, reading a magazine. He glanced up and grinned at the sight of the two girls pushing their bicycles.

"Have you been summoned, too?" Rosa asked Klaudia, astonished.

Klaudia nodded, and asked in a nervous whisper, "Do you know what this is all about?"

"No," Rosa admitted.

In the Commandant's outer office, the Deputy Leader told Rosa and Klaudia to change into their best uniforms and clean themselves up. "A Luftwaffe Major wants to meet you."

Rosa and Klaudia looked at one another in utter amazement. "But why?" Klaudia wanted to know.

"Don't ask questions. Do as you're told!" came the sharp retort.

Together the girls hurried down the wooden stairs and sprinted across the dusty parade ground towards the barrack huts. "Do *you* know a Luftwaffe major?" Rosa asked Klaudia suspiciously. After all, Klaudia was not only a Junker, she was related to the Red Baron from the last war.

Klaudia shook her head. Although she supposed there might be a Luftwaffe major among her many relatives or neighbours, there was certainly no one with that distinction whom she knew well.

The two Labour Girls washed side by side in the wash-hut, changed and then reported again. They were dressed now in the navyblue uniform skirt, white blouse and black tie with a swastika brooch. This time they were admitted to the "inner sanctum," and came to attention with outstretched arms and a simultaneous *Heil Hitler!*"

The Camp Commandant was a woman in her late 20s who had risen rapidly in the RAD. She sat behind her desk, while her visitor sat back comfortably in the leather armchair reserved for visitors. The girls were both disappointed. Unconsciously conditioned by the Propaganda Ministry, they had assumed that all Luftwaffe majors were tall, blond, and dashingly handsome. This man was middle-aged, over-weight, balding and not in the least handsome. He looked rather like an ordinary shopkeeper dressed up in uniform.

The Commandant considered her two charges critically. Neither would qualify as beauty queens or movie stars. Rosa was round and dark, a short, stocky product of the slums, but she was alert, quick, and ambitious. From the day she arrived, she had demonstrated the kind of dogged determination to get ahead that could be quite sickening if it were paired with fawning or arrogance. But Rosa wasn't that kind. She seemed to be genuinely enthusiastic about the work here. The Commandant felt she should be given a chance to make more of herself.

Klaudia was prettier than Rosa, but not glamorous. She had blond hair, pale blue eyes, and freckles. Her face was pleasant but not strikingly so. Her figure was slender but lacked enticing curves. She was willing and obedient. She never made trouble of any kind and was obviously anxious to fit in with the other girls and to please her superiors, while the farmers had never complained about her shirking, either. To be fair, however, all this could have been said about dozens of other girls at the camp. The only reason that Klaudia was standing here and not one of the others was because of her name. When the Luftwaffe major had asked her to recommend two suitable girls, the Camp Commandant had automatically thought of the Labour Girl v. Richthofen.

The Commandant introduced the girls standing at attention before her to the Luftwaffe major. Then she explained to them that the major had come over from Air District HQ on a special mission. She nodded to the major to continue.

The major got to his feet and with his hands behind his back began to lecture to the girls. "Not a shopkeeper," Rosa thought in annoyance; "a schoolteacher!"

She was right. In civilian life Major Bayer was a high-school teacher, but in his capacity as Reserve Major he was responsible for recruitment in the East Prussian Air District. A few days earlier, a report had crossed his desk detailing the sudden and dramatic increase in the Luftwaffe's requirements for communications specialists. The report went on to say that despite the preferred position of the Luftwaffe in the allocation of annual conscripts among the armed forces, the short-term demand for manpower had exploded beyond what they could reasonably expect to call up. The report concluded that the Luftwaffe must increase reliance on female auxiliaries, as these could be recruited from the vast pool of untouched "manpower" not already being funnelled into the armed forces. A general request to increase recruitment efforts had been attached to this report.

Major d. R. Bayer – anxious to make a good impression upon his superiors – had seen this as an unequalled opportunity. Aside from contacting the local Employment Office, he had decided on this personal recruitment tour to all the RAD camps in the East Prussian Air District.

Bayer explained at some length about the new demands placed on the Luftwaffe. Aside from the need to monitor and control the airspace from Norway to the Italian border, they were now in the final stages of subduing France. Since the English had managed to escape at Dunkirk, however, there was no longer any doubt that they would have to invade England. For this last task – something not achieved since 1066 – the Luftwaffe would have to station bomber and fighter Groups in France and the Low Countries. It was going to have to concentrate these for a massive assault on the British Isles.

Up to now, Bayer reminded his attentive audience, the Luftwaffe had fought in *support* of German ground forces. It had acted like long-range artillery, softening up enemy positions in advance of a ground attack, and responding to requests for air support from the troops on the ground. But against England, the Luftwaffe would be spearheading the assault, and doing so virtually alone.

"Never in the history of the world," Major Bayer told the Labour Girls in front of him, "has an air force been asked to perform a comparable task. We have been asked – *by the Führer personally* – to destroy the British will to resist. Our beloved *Feldmarschall* has staked his personal reputation on fulfilling the Führer's wish. And the Luftwaffe will not fail him – I can assure you of that! The Luftwaffe burns to show the Führer what it can do. But," the teacher-turned-major stopped dramatically, "*but* the Luftwaffe needs help. It needs *your* help."

The astonished looks of the two Labour Girls were highly satisfying to the lecturer. "Yes, we need your help because our young men want to be at the forefront of the battle – flying, arming and repairing aircraft – but they can only do *their* jobs if there are enough communications specialists to direct them to their targets and bring them safely home. That is a job that even women can do. The Luftwaffe already employs thousands of young women who do exactly that – and we need many more. Women like you – women who are hard-working, conscientious, loyal and discreet.

"I say discreet, because your work will be highly classified. It is not work that can be entrusted to flighty girls. The jobs we demand of you are difficult and vital to national security. You will be members of the Luftwaffe Support. You will wear Luftwaffe uniform, eat at Luftwaffe messes, and be subject to Luftwaffe discipline. With luck, you could even be stationed at one of our new bases in France or the Low Countries. You could then take part very directly and personally in this historic struggle. You will be able to tell your children and grandchildren that you – no less than your brothers and boyfriends in our bomber crews – helped to subdue the stubborn British lion.

"Your Camp Leader has selected you two girls as the most suitable of all the girls currently in her charge for this awesome and inspiring task. Now I put the question to you: are you willing to help your Fatherland, your nation and your *Führer* by becoming *Luftwaffehelferinnen*?"

Bayer had not yet met two teenage girls who could resist his harangue.

Cherbourg, France Mid-June 1940

Leutnant Ernst Geuke stepped uncertainly off the train and looked about himself nervously. He set his over-loaded, badly stained and scuffed leather suitcase on the platform, and took his handkerchief out to wipe the sweat off his face and neck. Around him swirled the usual chaos of disembarking passengers and excited friends and relatives meeting the train. Young men fell into passionate embraces with thinly clad females. Children jumped up and down and waved frantically at respectable-looking middle-aged men. Businessmen hurried away purposefully, and soldiers – lots and lots of soldiers – shouldered their kit and moved in hordes towards the head of the platform. Over the loudspeakers, announcements squawked – first in French and then in German.

Geuke's orders had been to join JG 23 stationed "near Cherbourg" by 24:00 today. His orders authorised his travel from Berlin to Cherbourg. Nothing had been said about how he was to get from Cherbourg to the improvised base itself, and Geuke felt very uncertain in the alien surroundings. Born and raised in Cottbus, he had never travelled farther than Berlin on his own. After joining the Luftwaffe, he had been transported here and there during his training, but always in groups with officers in charge of everything. He had never been outside of the Reich before.

Today, however, he had seen Paris. He had even risked getting off the train and spending six hours in the famous city. He had seen with his own eyes the Eiffel Tower and walked up and down the Champs Elysées. He'd had a cup of coffee – real coffee! – in a café, and he still didn't quite believe it. Of course, he hadn't risked eating anything until he was back on the train. The menu had been in French, and that was as intimidating as the looks of undisguised contempt from the waiters.

Here, too, he could sense the hostility of the population, and it made him uncomfortable. Geuke was self-conscious because the uniform, which attracted the looks of hatred, was new to him. He had completed training and been promoted from cadet to *Leutnant* just five days ago. He'd barely had time to get the uniform fitted during his three days home leave, before he had to leave Cottbus to join his unit.

Geuke was extremely proud to wear the uniform of a Luftwaffe *Leutnant*. No one in his family had ever held a commission before. His parents were so busting with pride that he had been paraded about during these last days as if he were already an ace. But if it had been tedious and embarrassing at times, it had more or less matched his own mood. How often in the last two years had he doubted he would ever really make it? Geuke had wanted to learn to fly as long as he could remember. He had spent all his spare pennies on model aeroplane kits and gone to every film about flying or with a flying sequence in it. Once he'd even managed to beg more than buy his way into an air show at which Ernst Udet did some stunts. He was proud to have the same first name as the famous pilot. And it was the thought of Udet that reconciled him to the assignment to fighters six months ago. Bombers were much more prestigious, of course. The best pilots at basic flying school had been selected to train on Stukas, but for him just not "washing out" was achievement enough.

The training on Messerschmitts had been the most harrowing weeks of Gueke's short life. He'd managed to damage one in a groundloop, and he'd been put on notice. One more mistake, and he'd be grounded. There was plenty of work in communications, intelligence, and administration, he'd been reminded. Most Luftwaffe personnel didn't actually *fly*, after all. But Geuke hadn't joined the Luftwaffe to sit on the ground. If he couldn't fly, he might as well be in the army.

Somehow, he'd managed not to bang up another kite. Last week he'd passed his final flight test and here he was. In France.

He looked about himself again. The platform was almost empty now. Only a couple of porters were wheeling over-loaded carts down the platform from the luggage van, and an old couple with a silly, little, shaggy dog ambled slowly towards the exit.

Geuke stuffed his handkerchief back into his trouser pocket and readjusted his peaked cap. Then he bent and picked up his battered suitcase and started towards the head of the platform. Maybe there would be some sort of Luftwaffe office with information about how to get to his *Geschwader*.

Geuke had guessed correctly. In the terminal there was an office manned by all three services, and here he was told that the Luftwaffe provided regular transport from the station to the various bases in the vicinity after each train from Paris. Unfortunately, he had just missed the lorry, and would have to wait for the next – and last – shuttle of the day.

Although the NCO who gave him this information was careful to address him as "*Herr Leutnant*," Geuke was acutely aware that the *Oberfeldwebel* looked on him with the contempt of most veteran NCOs for newly baked commissioned officers. Geuke's uniform was too new, the rank insignia too bright, his boots too stiff for anyone to mistake him for an experienced pilot. Besides, he didn't look the part.

Geuke was too short and too fat to match anyone's conception of a pilot – much less a fighter pilot. When he'd first joined the Luftwaffe, the NCOs had promised to "toughen him up" and "melt all that lard" – but they had failed, just as his Hitler Youth leaders and his sports teachers and the Leader at the RAD Camp had failed. Geuke wasn't unfit, and he didn't eat excessively. As a Luftwaffe doctor had explained it best, he simply had an "efficient fuel-burning system"; with the same food and exercise that made others lean and tough, he remained round and superficially soft.

Afraid to miss the shuttle, Geuke hung about Cherbourg station, admiring the things in the closed shops. He was amazed by how much more of everything there seemed to be here. Even here in a provincial city which was – as far as he could tell – no more important than Cottbus, the shops offered things unseen in the Reich: perfumes in exotically shaped bottles, creams of indecipherable purpose, toiletry kits in fancy leather cases, fancy hair-clips and glasses cases, and, of course, make-up.

Geuke had been raised to think that only whores "painted" themselves, and certainly that was the way it seemed in Cottbus. But he noticed that here even very elegant elderly ladies – *real* ladies – did not disdain the aid of artificial colours. Wistfully watching the passing women, he wondered if he would ever have a girl friend of his own. Not something glamorous, of course – he knew better than to expect that. But maybe a girl like the one over there? With the short brown hair and trim little bolero jacket?

As soon as the Luftwaffe lorry pulled up at the designated spot, Geuke climbed aboard. Shortly afterwards the last train of the day from Paris arrived, and he was joined by roughly a dozen other young men in Luftwaffe uniform. Geuke, however, was the only commissioned officer among them, and the others acknowledged his presence with half-hearted salutes and then kept to themselves.

Geuke was told to get off the lorry at the first stop, Cherbourg West, where the Staff of JG 23 was based. Here he was directed to the Kommodore's office, where he was received not by the Kommodore but the *Geschwader* Adjutant. The latter grunted more than greeted, "Oh, yes, Geuke. We've got you down for II *Gruppe*, 5 *Staffel*. II *Gruppe* is based at our satellite airfield at Crépon. I'll have a staff car take you over. Report there to *Staffelkapitän* Bartels."

Half an hour later, Geuke climbed out of the open staff car and found the office of *Staffelkapitän* Bartels, but again he only encountered the Duty Officer. This man was more friendly, and after checking with the NCO in charge of accommodation, offered to take Geuke over to the Officer's Mess. This was located in a country inn. He was shown his functional room with a washbasin, cupboard and narrow bed, and a window overlooking the airfield. He was told to leave his suitcase there. "You'd better come with me if you want to get anything to eat." It was nearly 8 pm and Geuke was starving.

The dining room of the Mess was far less sterile than the bedrooms had been. It had gracious dimensions and was decorated in

Art Nouveau, including electric chandeliers. The tables were set with white linen, silver and crystal — as was standard for the Luftwaffe.There were fresh flowers on every table and the mess stewards, Geuke noted, wore white jackets rather than field grey, as if it were peacetime or they were in the Reich. Geuke was taken to the head table, at which the *Gruppenkommandeur* and his three *Staffelkapitäne*, including *Hauptmann* Bartels, sat.

Bartels was tall, blond, tanned and fit — a German officer straight out of an UFAfilm. He wore the Iron Cross First and Second Class on his tailored uniform and smoked long cigarettes. He considered Geuke with a mixture of disbelief and annoyance. Geuke could hear him thinking, "Have we really sunk so low that we have to take officers like *this*?"

Geuke wriggled uncomfortably in his brand-new uniform. The collar seemed much too tight. He wished he could have loosened his tie a bit, but instead he had to stand at attention, trying to cut a military figure.

Bartels seemed to overcome his disappointment and with a sigh, he announced, "Find yourself a free place to sit and have a meal. We're flying tomorrow at 09:00 — weather permitting. What do you think, Hartmann," he turned to one of the other officers, "can we trust Feldburg with a *Rotte*?" Then answering his own question, he remarked with obvious disgust, "I don't suppose we have much choice. At least he's seen some combat."

Then turning back to Geuke he said, "You'll be flying wingman to Christian Freiherr von Feldburg. I'll send him over to you after dinner."

The only table with vacant places was one occupied by non-flying officers: the intelligence officer, signals officer, paymaster, quartermaster, doctor and chaplain of the *Gruppe*. These men made Geuke welcome at their table perfunctorily, and then continued their discussion about the relative merits of the British and German early warning systems. Geuke tried to listen, but he knew far too little about either system to make any kind of intelligent contribution to the debate. He was relieved when the *Gruppenkommandeur* retired to the bar.

But Geuke's sense of relief was short-lived. In the bar, the officers clustered together in familiar groups, and Geuke was more of an outsider than in the dining room. Here men could shoulder him aside or turn their backs without being rude. Geuke hesitantly went to the bar and after everyone else had been served, he timidly asked the Luftwaffe bartender for a beer.

"Account number, *Herr Leutnant*?" the bartender demanded without even looking at him.

"Put it on my account," a voice said from behind him, and Geuke jumped and turned around.

The officer behind him smiled and held out his hand. "Feldburg. The CO just told me the good news that you will be flying wingman to me tomorrow. I think that calls for more than a beer, don't you? May I make that beer a glass of *Sekt*?"

Geuke was so taken aback he hardly knew what to say. This officer was another one of the propaganda-poster-types, and the hand he extended had the distinctive heavy gold ring with the inset coat of arms. Geuke heard the *Staffelkapitän's* words ringing in his ears, "You'll be flying wingman to *Freiherr* von Feldburg." The plumber's son did not believe he had ever shaken hands with a baron before.

"Ah, Herr – Freiherr—"

"Christian," interrupted the other pilot. "And let's go straight to " *Du*." As a *Rotte* we have to work together like brothers, after all. No room for formality. What's your first name?"

"Ernst," Geuke croaked out, still in a bit of a daze.

They shook hands again, and Christian insisted, "Champagne?"

"Of course. Thank you—" Geuke had a hard time not adding, "Herr Baron."

"Buying Champagne, Christian?" another officer joined them.

"Not for you, parasite," Christian countered good- humouredly, and the other pilot laughed without the slightest indication of being offended. Christian was proudly continuing, "Let me introduce my *wingman*." He clapped a hand on Geuke's shoulder. "Ernst Geuke."

This second officer also offered Ernst his hand with apparent warmth, and introduced himself, "Dieter Möller. Don't let Christian push you around. If he gets too obnoxious, just come to me. I've known him all his life – well, since he was three – and I know how to handle him."

"And vice-versa," Christian retorted.

Other officers drifted over. Like a magnet, Christian drew a crowd. He introduced Ernst to each of them: Busso Appelt, Max Mühlbauer, Otto Neufeldt and Hans Becker. Ernst and Christian's champagne arrived, and they toasted one another. Ernst sipped very carefully and remembered to raise his glass to Christian afterwards. He was glad that he'd been taught that in training; he wouldn't have known from home.... Better not think about home now.

The champagne warmed him almost instantly, and the tension he'd felt since stepping off the train started to ease. In the middle of the little group of pilots, the sound of their relaxed voices and the light music playing on a gramophone in the background seemed to blend together into a warm cocoon. He didn't feel so lonely any more. It started to sink in that he had really made it. He was an officer, a pilot and these were his comrades. He was one of them, and he started to have a sense of belonging.

Chapter 3

RAF Tangmere Late June 1940

The Mess was full of strangers. Flight Lieutenant Christopher Bainbridge, known to his friends as "Bridges," and more unkindly as "the Cyclops" on account of his one eye, stood rather dismayed in the doorway to the lounge and surveyed the scene. Bridges had seen and heard officers of No. 43 Squadron in the billiards room having a very rowdy time of it on his way past, while most of No. 17 Squadron was up at *The Green Man* on the road to Chichester at this time of night. This left No. 145 Squadron in a lively crowd by the fireplace and the new boys, No. 606 Squadron, clustered around the bar. The sight of them made him feel a stranger in his own Mess. They had flown in this afternoon with Hurricanes, replacing the Blenheims that had at last been withdrawn from this front-line station – none too soon, as far as Bridges was concerned.

Bridges hadn't expected to feel this out of place at Tangmere. He hadn't had much time to expect anything, really. After the accident, the first months had been filled with just coming to terms with the pain and the loss of an eye and getting back on his feet again. His parents had been wonderful about it, especially his mother, who must have been devastated, but she hadn't let him notice. She'd treated him as if nothing serious had happened – he might as well have had a cold or the mumps or whatever. So the ten days at home, even riding a little, had done him a world of good.

The summons to training had come unexpectedly, cutting short his convalescent leave, but he had welcomed them. It gave him a new purpose, focus, and a future. The Controller's course itself had been brutally intense. Air Chief Marshal Dowding had lectured them on the importance of the job they would be doing. He had looked out at his audience, most of whom were sporting wings, and said bluntly, "I know most of you would rather be flying, but for one reason or another, you are not currently fit to fly." It was true; the room was filled with men on crutches, with empty sleeves, burned faces. "Some of you will fly again, but in the meantime you have a job to do that is as important as flying." He had gone on to explain to them the current system for controlling fighter aircraft assigned to the Defence of the British Isles.

As the Air Chief Marshal and subsequent instruction and exercises made clear, Fighter Command was too weak (especially after the appalling losses in France and over Dunkirk) and spread too thin to maintain patrols over targets or on the borders. The only chance England had of defeating the Luftwaffe – and so just possibly of discouraging an invasion – was for the fighter squadrons to be deployed economically and effectively. This meant they had to take off only when targets were in range, go straight for them, and – hopefully – shoot them down. After which they must straight-away return to base to refuel and rearm in order to be ready for the next sortie.

The task was not just one of seeing the enemy well in advance, it was also one of correctly guessing the enemy's intentions, pulling together resources, and guiding the squadrons to their prey. That was the job of the Controllers.

The essence of Dowding's system was that the forward Radio Direction Finding (RDF) stations and the Observer Corps passed information about enemy aircraft (or unidentified aircraft) to Fighter Command HQ. Fighter Command informed the various Sector Stations, these being the Stations tasked with defending a certain "Sector" of British airspace. Each Sector had a number of fighter airfields at which were stationed several (from one to four) Fighter Squadrons.

The Duty Sector Controller was supposed to know at all times the strength in aircraft of each of "his" squadrons, and the state of readiness of each of these squadrons. On orders from Fighter Command, the Duty Controller sent squadrons into the air to intercept invaders. The Sector Controller's job was then to guide "his" squadrons to the intercept, ordering the squadrons to fly in a specific direction at a specified height, and to pass the information from RDF and Observer Corps about the enemy – their numbers, type, height, course, and so on – to his airborne squadrons. The controller also had to keep track of the location of each of his aircraft, plotting their course as well as that of the enemy. His job was also to keep HQ informed of the status of his squadrons – when they took off, sighted the enemy, engaged, returned for refuelling, and so on.

The more the trainee controllers learnt about their future job, the more difficult it appeared, and the training exercises only reinforced the point. Time and again they got things hopelessly wrong, sending bevies of squadrons after decoys, leaving targets exposed, failing to get their squadrons high enough to avoid being "bounced" by German fighters, etc., etc. The course was over much too soon, as far as Bridges was concerned, and he found himself posted to Tangmere – the most forward of Fighter Command's Sector Stations. There were just two airfields in the Sector: Tangmere itself and Westhampnett, a "satellite" with very rough accommodation and few facilities for support.

In the stress of learning his new job against the backdrop of the defeat and collapse of their Allies on the Continent, Bridges hadn't had much time to feel sorry for himself – until now. Now he stood in his own Mess feeling like an ancient outsider. The men who had taken over the bar were his own age and had only been here a couple of hours, but they owned the place already. They were fighter pilots, as Bridges had once been but was no longer, and he might as well have been part of the furniture for all they cared.

Bridges did not even try to join them. He found himself a corner table and settled down. A WAAF orderly appeared promptly. "Can I get you anything, sir?" she asked cheerfully.

Bridges ordered brandy. The WAAF orderly withdrew, only to be replaced by the WAAF OC on the Station, Section Officer Newton. Newton was a woman in her mid-forties, a sour woman with a face fixed in a permanent scowl. She wore her hair pulled back in a severe bun, confined by a hairnet, and the use of make-up was alien to her. Bridges had already had more than one unpleasant encounter with her because the station plotters, with whom he worked daily, were all WAAF.

Bridges, no less than the other controllers on his course, had been surprised to learn that WAAF were being entrusted with such vital and responsible jobs as RDF operators, filterers and plotters, but Dowding had been insistent. "They're intelligent, they're precise, and they're reliable. You will have no complaints about your WAAF plotters," he predicted, and he'd been right – so far.

Yet, while the plotters were operationally under Bridges' command, they were administratively under Newton's discipline. Within the past two weeks, Bridges had provoked the ire of Section Officer Newton because he had a) given a girl leave to take off one day (which he had no right to do), b) sent another girl who was obviously ill back to her billet (again not his prerogative), and c) given a girl a lift in his car in the pouring rain. Bridges would have given *anyone* from the Station – whether ground crew, WAAF, or Officer – a lift in that kind of weather, but Newton implied he was "undermining discipline" and – what was worse – taking "liberties" and "endangering the reputation" of her charges.

"You can't seriously mean I should have let her get drenched to the bone?" Bridges had protested after the rain incident, and Newton had answered (with every evidence of sincerity): "You most certainly should! A little rain never hurt anyone! These girls certainly aren't made of sugar!"

Having cornered Bridges in the Mess, Newton now addressed him pointedly, her lips pinched together, and her eyes narrowed. "Flight Lieutenant Bainbridge, have you noticed that ACW Roberts has a drinking problem?"

"A drinking problem?!" Bridges would have had a hard time believing this of any of the girls, but especially of Roberts. She was definitely a "nice" girl, dark and quiet and very well mannered. "I must say I find that very hard to believe," he managed to stammer out to the indignant WAAF officer.

"Whether you find it hard to believe or not, is not the issue, young man." Now she sounded very much like one of his aunts, Bridges reflected with an inward sigh. "I wish you to be alert for the problem, and report to me whenever you smell alcohol on her breath."

"Yes, of course," Bridges agreed willingly, not intending for one minute to do anything of the kind – even if he did smell something, which he certainly did not expect. However, his obedient compliance had the desired effect of convincing Section Officer Newton to withdraw. She moved away determinedly, apparently armed with an admonishment for her next victim – the padre, Colin Duport.

Bridges had been surprised the first time he met the padre to discover that he was a young man, no more than 28 or 29, and barely out of seminary. Duport had pointed out with a modest smile that all priests *started out* young. "We aren't born old and wise." No, of course not, Bridges thought, but it was a bit awkward turning for advice, guidance or comfort to a man hardly older than yourself. Bridges certainly did not envy Duport his job here with gaggles of irreverent young pilots, who generally took little note of priests even if they *were* grey and gnarled with experience. For the moment, however, it was the WAAF who were causing the padre problems, as he was getting a painful earful from Section Officer Newton. Bridges sympathised.

"Do you mind if we join you?"

Bridges had been so busy watching the exchange between the WAAF officer and the padre that he had not noticed the men who had come over to his table. He looked up, and then got to his feet respectfully at the sight of a gaunt Squadron Leader with wings but a wooden leg. He was accompanied by a round, soft-looking Flight Lieutenant with glasses and no wings. "You must be from 606," Bridges stammered out.

"Allars, Douglas Allars, the spy" (i.e., intelligence officer), the Squadron Leader introduced himself.

"Michaels – or Mickey, squadron adjutant," the Flight Lieutenant followed suit.

"Bainbridge, one of the Station Controllers," Bridges answered, adding a little awkwardly, "You'll probably hear me referred to as 'the Cyclops' on account of this." He pointed to his eye-patch, still not fully comfortable with the situation.

"France?" the Squadron Leader asked, settling himself opposite.

"Nothing as noble as that, I'm afraid. Motorcar accident last January. The road bent around to the left and I'm sure I put the helm over, but somehow I just kept going straight into the telephone pole and woke up in hospital."

"Dreadful ice all over the country last January." 606's adjutant commented sympathetically, and the "spy" agreed with a nod.

"Where have you come in from?" Bridges asked.

"Dyce. Operated from Debden during Dunkirk, however. Lost five pilots, three killed. We were quite surprised to be posted back into the thick of things so soon." This came pouring out of the adjutant, who was clearly more than a little shaken by the turn of events. "Things hotting up around here, I gather?"

"Not really," Bridges admitted. "More like the lull before the storm. Hitler appears to be giving his troops a breather and marshalling his forces before really letting loose."

"There are those who think he doesn't really want to attack us at all," the adjutant ventured with a slightly nervous glance around him. "I mean, why should we fight on now that the Continent is lost? If Hitler is willing to let us retain our Empire and command of the seas—"

"He's a bully, and the only way to keep bullies from oppressing you is to fight back!" Allars interrupted hotly, with a heavy frown. "Don't talk that peace rot to me, Mickey. Keep it for the CO."

"Your CO favours a negotiated peace with Hitler?" Bridges asked incredulously, before he could stop himself.

"Squadron Leader Jones' father is quite high up in the Foreign Office," Mickey was quick to explain, "and he says that if you read carefully what Hitler has written and said, it is very clear that he admires the British and never really wanted to go to war with us in the first place. Apparently, he sees Germany's destiny in the East and, according to Mr. Jones senior, has said that Britain and Germany are natural allies. He has said that with Britain as the dominant Sea Power and Germany—"

"Hitler also said he had no more territorial ambitions after the Sudetenland – and look what's happened since!" Allars interrupted again.

"Of course, of course, I know. I was just telling you what the CO's father reported...." Mickey fell silent.

Bridges felt sorry for the adjutant. He seemed very much to want to please, and it was not easy being a man without wings among pilots. Bridges might never be allowed in a cockpit again, but at least the wings on his chest proclaimed to this world of fliers that he had once been one of them. For the adjutant's sake he changed the subject. "606 is an Auxiliary Squadron, I take it. Where was it formed?"

"Somerset. Flight Lieutenant 'Tommy' Thompson's father – he's an MP with a coal fortune – basically founded it. He was a very keen hobby flier as a young man. He's been a keen supporter of the RAF ever since – and a bitter enemy of Lord Beaverbrook." The adjutant provided the information.

"Pure jealousy," Allars added. "Wanted the job at the MAP for himself."

Bridges glanced a little uneasily from one newcomer to the other.

"They used to require candidates for the Squadron to have a personal income of £1,000 a year just to apply," the adjutant reported, evidently impressed by the idea.

"Those days are over," Allars countered firmly. "Just an ordinary RAF squadron now."

Bridges glanced over to the men gathered around the bar, and something told him that *they* didn't think there was anything "ordinary" about them.

**RAF Tangmere
Late June 1940**

"Ripley, Appleby!" Flight Sergeant Rowe shouted into the hangar. The two Leading Aircraftmen, who had just sat down on one of the work benches for a well-earned cup of tea, looked at one another as if for an explanation. But neither of them had an answer, and Chiefy was already calling again, "Get cracking!"

With an audible sigh, Ripley clambered over the bench resignedly, while Appleby took a last deep gulp of tea and then scrambled nimbly after him. Ripley was a solid, good-looking young man with sandy hair. Appleby was a child of the East End slums, slight of figure, with a pointed weasel-like face under a shock of dark hair. Ripley had just turned 20, and Appleby was still 17.

They drew up in front of the Flight Sergeant. "See that Hurricane over there?" The Chief pointed to a Hurricane that was waddling towards them from the airfield. "The ATA just delivered it as a replacement for the CO's old kite. He wants his crest and name on it right away. It will be designated 'J' for Jones, and you are the crew. Make bloody sure you give the CO no cause for complaint, or you'll answer to me for it!" And that was it. No explanation as to why they had been chosen. Why the CO's old crew hadn't been given it. Presumably he'd had some cause for complaint....

Ripley and Appleby eyed one another warily. Ripley was an aircraft engine mechanic, a fitter; Appleby was an aircraft frame mechanic, or rigger. Although they had both been with the squadron for several months, they had not worked together before. There was no time for discussion, however, as the Hurricane was coming straight at them, and Appleby signalled it onto the hangar apron and gestured for the pilot to cut the engine.

The hood was shoved backwards, and the pilot pushed off his leather helmet to reveal long, grey hair that blew about in the wind. Appleby at once nipped under the wing and watched as a stiff, old gentleman in a dark blue uniform clambered out of the cockpit of the fighter. Inwardly Appleby shook his head. What was the country coming to?

Until the start of May, the RAF had collected new fighters from the Maintenance Units themselves, but now this civilian organization, the Air Transport Auxiliary (ATA), had been tasked with all "ferrying" work. The ATA collected new aircraft from the factories, ferried them to the Maintenance Units for radio and armament fittings, then ferried them on to the squadrons. By definition, all pilots in the ATA were, for age or disability reasons, not subject to military service, and the bulk of them were gentleman hobby fliers. This old boy looked old enough to be Appleby's grandfather.

Out of habit and upbringing, Appleby offered cheerily, "Can I give you hand, governor?"

"Thank you. I'll manage." The old man replied rather tartly, as he slowly and carefully stepped off the wing of the Hurricane backwards – in sharp contrast to the way the young pilots liked to jump down. Then he turned and faced the young rigger and announced solemnly, "The starboard wing seems a shade heavy on this kite. You might want to check that."

"Yes, sir. We'll look into it right away. This kite has been designated for the CO already, so we wouldn't want to let a thing like that interfere with his flying. Everything else all right, sir?"

"The engine hiccupped several times – almost as if the fuel mixture was off. You'll want to look into that as well."

"Yes, sir," Appleby agreed with a glance at Ripley, who nodded. "Do you want us to take her off your hands? Sign for her, I mean, sir?"

"Oh, can you do that?" He sounded sceptical.

"Of course, sir. Got the chit?"

The old man thrust a hand down the inside of his Sidcot suit and pulled out a flimsy with the particulars of the aircraft on it. Appleby took it from the old man, looked it over and then handed it to Ripley, who checked the aircraft and the engine numbers on the receipt before handing it back with a nod. Appleby signed for the aircraft with the stub of a pencil he had tucked behind his ear and added to the old gentleman, "I expect you'll want to get some tea over at the Mess, sir. Do you want to walk or shall I ring for transport for you, sir?"

The old man looked up at the bright blue sky and the fluffy clouds and decided to "hoof it." He set off, carrying his flying helmet in his hand, and Appleby watched him for a moment, making sure he was out of hearing before remarking to Ripley in his thick cockney accent, "Bloody dangerous letting an old bloke like that fly around in an 'urricane! It's a wonder he don't kill himself."

Ripley frowned. "You don't know that. For all you know he has hundreds of flying hours. Maybe even flew in the last war."

"What the hell good is flying experience if you can 'ardly walk! His reflexes must be slow as strawberry jam!"

"His job is to deliver aircraft safely to us, not throw them around in the sky."

"And what if Jerry happens along? Or something goes wrong with the kite?"

"Let's get to work and stop standing around nattering!" Ripley replied with a frown.

Appleby willingly complied, but he was one of those people who could work and talk at the same time. To Ripley's annoyance, he did. He explained at greater length than Ripley wanted to hear how the RAF recruiter had promised him that once he was in the service he could change trades. He could apply for transfer to Flying Branch. The recruiter said that deserving airmen were selected every year for flying training. "You don't have to be a gentleman to fly an aeroplane," he insisted.

"Maybe not, but it don't hurt. And what's more, I'd think twice about it if I was you! Look what happened over Dunkirk."

"We're all going to die some time."

"Well, burning to a crisp like Flying Officer Overington isn't my idea of how I want to go!" Ripley was definitive, and Appleby was quiet for a moment – but not for long.

"What I don't understand is that they keep saying they're short of pilots, so why not give us a chance?"

"We're short of trained riggers and fitters, too!" Ripley reminded him.

RAF Tangmere
Late June 1940

The two young men stood in front of the adjutant's desk with orders to report to No. 606, but (typical RAF) no one had told the squadron adjutant to expect them. Mickey looked frantically through the stacks of paper in his various "in" and "out" and "to do" boxes, but nothing yielded the slightest information.

Obviously, they *needed* more pilots. They had lost five over Dunkirk and so far only one replacement had arrived, but still these two young men didn't seem at all suitable, and Mickey was certain the CO wasn't going to like them. For a start, one was Canadian, of all things, with a hideous accent, and the other spoke with a broad West Country accent that suggested he had never been to a proper school in his life. Furthermore, both were Sergeants, and 606 had never had Sergeant Pilots until two days ago, when the RAF had sent them a certain Sergeant MacLeod.

The CO had had a fit about that, and Mickey agreed with him. He didn't think much of the idea of Sergeant Pilots generally. How could a squadron develop strong bonds between pilots if they lived in different messes? But at least MacLeod was regular RAF, with almost ten years' service. These boys were Voluntary Reserve (VR), and the Squadron had been spared these "weekend fliers" up to now.

"I really can't find anything at all," he said helplessly to the two young men opposite him. "You're sure your orders were for 606? Not 607? Or 602?"

"No, it says right here, 606." The Canadian handed over his own copy of the orders.

"Oh, dear," Mickey ran his hand through his thinning hair. "Well, let me call the Sergeant's Mess and see about some accommodation for you." He reached for the phone.

"Where's the CO?" the Canadian asked.

"He happens to be on a patrol, guarding a channel convoy," Mickey told the impudent young man in what he hoped was a sufficiently severe tone. He really disliked these colonials, he thought to himself, and this young man was too tall, broad and tanned by half. The other pilot was more to his taste; he looked and acted like a respectful young man, with reddish hair and a freckled face. "Why don't you go get settled in at the Sergeant's Mess and report back to me in an hour? Maybe the CO will be back by then." Mickey dismissed them.

The Sergeant Pilots heaved their kitbags over their shoulders and went back out into the bright sunshine. "Not exactly an enthusiastic welcome," the Canadian grumbled, clearly disappointed.

"No," the other Sergeant replied simply. He wasn't one for unnecessary words. He'd grown up in an isolated cottage on the moors.

The Canadian held out his hand. "Name's Harvey Green. From Kingstown, Ontario. My Dad owns a gas station there. How about you?"

"George – but everyone calls me Ginger – Bowles. From Devon. M'Dad's a carpenter." That was putting it nicely. Mostly he just did odd jobs and repairs for people. But he was good with carpentry if anyone gave him a chance. He could thatch too, and tile. He'd do just about anything to try to make ends meet.

Ginger was feeling very homesick at the moment. He would much rather have been heading home to his Dad's cottage than joining yet another unit. It seemed that since he'd been called up, he'd been thrown in with one bunch of young men after another. Ginger was tired of it all. He wished he could go home for a few days with his Dad, just the two of them, his Dad smoking his pipe and, Bessie, their dog, at his feet.

Ginger couldn't remember his mother. She'd died when he was three or four. A couple of faded photos of her adorned the mantelpiece, and his Dad kept her wedding dress in a cardboard box in the cupboard still. And that was all. It had always been just his Dad and him, and now he'd gone and left his Dad alone.

It wasn't fair, really, but his Dad had urged him to go. "Take the chance while you've got it," his Dad had said. The posters and adverts had been so inviting: "Join the RAFVR! Learn to Fly!" It sounded so wonderful. Flying was wonderful. But not the rest of it. Now they'd given him no leave between training and posting him to a squadron.

The Canadian was talking again in his loud, grating voice. "Devon, huh? I heard that's real pretty. Hope I have time go there sometime. We get some leave, don't we?"

"Theoretically," Ginger answered. He hadn't seen any in what seemed like an eternity. They started walking towards the Sergeants' Mess. Tangmere was an old station with the buildings built of dark brick and covered with ivy. The tall windows had white frames and everything had the comfortable feeling of a university – or at least what Ginger supposed a University was like, never having been to one himself.

It certainly sat in a peaceful location, surrounded by broad, flat fields of hay out of which a stone church tower rose. Somewhere just beyond the fields, invisible and yet intangibly present, was the sea. That was the only thing Ginger didn't like about Tangmere so far, that it was so near to the sea. He hated the sea, and his worst nightmare was to be out upon it – in a small boat or, worse still, crashing into it with an aircraft. The thought alone sent a shiver down his spine.

The sound of aircraft engines drew both pilots' attention towards the sky. At first they couldn't find the aircraft, but then they did, two. The pair was coming in low with the sun behind them. The Sergeant Pilots paused to watch them come into the circuit and land. Green shielded his eyes with his hand to see better.

There wasn't much to see. From head on, the body of a Hurricane was narrow and the wings razor thin. Furthermore, these two were approaching at a terrific pace. Of course, Hurricanes were fast, but.... "Aren't they going too fast to land?" Green asked.

Bowles had been thinking that, too. The next thing they knew, the lead Messerschmitt was spewing cannon and machine-gun fire at a Hurricane on the far side of the airfield.

"Hit the deck!" someone screamed from behind them, and Green dived for the ground. Ginger was a fraction slower. He saw the Hurricane leap into the air and fall back to the ground in three pieces, the back completely broken. The Messerschmitts thundered overhead, their cannon finding a second Hurricane. Then, as suddenly as they had come, they were gone. Not one of the AA-guns had fired.

Green got to his feet first, dusting off his trousers and tunic and gazing after the Messerschmitts that were climbing gently as they rapidly grew smaller.

Ginger was slower, shaken to the marrow of his bones. First, he'd failed to recognise the enemy when it was flying straight at him, and second, with just a three-second burst, they had utterly destroyed a Hurricane. True, it had been a sitting duck, but the sheer, awesome power of the cannon left him a little dazed. The next time they fired, it might be at him.

"Jeeze! Do they do that a lot?" Green wanted to know, beating his cap against the side of his leg to get the dust off it. Ginger had no idea, but he was very, very frightened.

The pub was crowded, of course. Pubs always were in the evening. The newcomers were late because as soon as the CO had seen their logbooks, they had been sent up on a "familiarisation flight." What the CO had said when looking at the logbooks still rang in Ginger's ears: "My God! What do the chaps in Personnel think they're up to? We haven't got time to train green pilots down here! I'm going to ring up in the morning and see about having you posted back to some Squadron in 13 or 10 Group – safely out of harm's way."

Ginger would very much have preferred to be in another squadron. He didn't think he was going to fit in here at all.

And now all this forced "conviviality." Why did the RAF expect squadron members to do everything together all the time? Ginger would have much preferred to spend the evening alone in his room writing to his Dad. He owed his Dad a letter to explain where he was and why he wasn't going to be able to make it home to see him any time soon. But, no, even though they got back from their flight after the rest of the Squadron had left for the *Fox and Hounds*, they found the padre waiting to take them over in his car. Obviously you couldn't say no to that – not if the CO ordered it and the very nice padre was waiting there with his battered old Bentley.

The *Fox and Hounds* was already very loud and smoky when they arrived, and there was an inordinate amount of Air Force blue about. Some sort of competition was on at darts – apparently between the ground crews of two different squadrons. The cheers and shouts of encouragement/ discouragement were deafening as they came in. The padre politely squeezed around the large crowd, and down a couple of steps into the lounge.

Here apparently the entire squadron was collected – at least Bowles recognised their CO. He was very debonair and reminded Ginger of Clark Gable on account of his dark moustache. He was currently surrounded by a bevy of other commissioned officers, including two Flight Lieutenants and a large number of Flying and Pilot Officers.

"Oh, there you are!" Squadron Leader Jones greeted them. "Come over and meet the rest of the chaps."

There were far too many names to remember, and all the accents sounded very posh to Ginger. He started to feel more out of place than ever, while Green grinned rather inanely at everyone. Almost at once one of the Flight Lieutenants, "Tommy" for Thompson if Ginger remembered correctly, turned to the two newcomers and announced (rather aggressively, Ginger thought), "It's the squadron tradition for newcomers to buy a round, lads, so—"

"I'll get this one," the young padre obliged, heading off to the bar while the others took their seats.

Ginger took the end seat and hoped he would be ignored. He was, for the most part. The others were talking about people that Ginger didn't know or care about, so he fell to thinking about his Dad again, alone in the cottage. He wouldn't know yet that Ginger wasn't coming home. He didn't have a phone, and Ginger's letter wouldn't reach him for a day or two. Maybe he should have sent a telegram? But his Dad said that in the last war a telegram meant another young man had died for King and

Country. If he sent a telegram, his Dad would think he'd been killed and have a heart attack before he even read it.

"Is something the matter, Sergeant Bowles?" It was the padre who asked the question very softly, soft enough so none of the others heard.

"No, of course not, sir."

"Please don't call me "sir.' We all use first or nick names here. I'm Colin. Andyou?"

"M' Dad calls me 'Ginger' – I mean, everyone does. It's just, I was thinking of him right now. He doesn't know I won't be coming home on leave – that I got posted straight here. He'll be expecting me, waiting up half the night, no doubt. Then thinking he got the dates wrong, he'll wait again tomorrow. He's got no phone, see."

"But that's terrible. There must be a neighbour we could ring? Or a telegram—" The padre seemed genuinely distressed.

Ginger shook his head and explained about telegrams and that his father lived in an isolated cottage. "Our next neighbour is two and half miles away and they've no phone, either. The nearest people with a phone haven't got a car, and it wouldn't do to ask them to cycle six miles just to tell m'Dad."

"Surely the rector has a car? Orthe doctor? There must be someone we can ring!" Colin insisted. Before long, he'd coaxed out of Ginger the name of the vicar of the village church. Ginger didn't know the telephone number, of course, but Colin got that from the operator.

They had just asked for last orders when the bartender called out in a loud voice. "Got a Sergeant Pilot Bowles anywhere in here? Telephone." The bartender jerked his thumb in the direction of the narrow passage leading to the toilets, where there was a telephone box.

Ginger almost tripped as he extricated himself from his seat and had to squeeze his way past the other customers. He took the receiver hesitantly and identified himself. His Dad was on the other end.

"The Vicar picked me up and brought me home with him."

Twelve miles there and back and there and back again, Ginger thought, embarrassed. "I didn't mean to cause so much trouble, Dad. I just didn't want you waiting up for me."

"Nowdon't you worry about me. Everything's fine. Are you all right? With your squadron now, are you?"

"Yeah, that's right."

"Are they a fair lot?"

"They seem to be, Dad, but it's hard to tell after so little time. I just got here this afternoon. I did a little flying, though. They sent me and another new bloke straight up. He's all right, I suppose – Canadian, though. The others, I don't know yet. I'm sorry I couldn't get home."

65

"Don't worry. You've got more important things to do right now. I'm proud of you, Ginger. Get a couple of Jerries. Make 'em think twice about invading."

"I'll do my best, Dad."

"I know you will, Ginger. Take care of yourself, too."

"Of course, Dad." He was seeing the way that Hurricane had disintegrated under a three-second burst of cannonfire.

"Got to hang up now, Ginger. Don't want to run up the Vicar's bill."

"Thank him for me, Dad."

"I will. Take care of yourself."

"I will." They hung up. Ginger wasn't sure if he was feeling better or worse, but he knew it had been the right thing to do. Who knew when he'd get another chance to talk to his Dad?

Chapter 4

Portsmouth, Hampshire
Late June 1940

Emily Pryce hoped to slip out of the house without waking her parents, but just as she started down the stairs, her mother called out. "Emily? Is that you?"

Mrs. Pryce stood in the doorway to her bedroom in her nightdress and barefoot. She was very thin, almost skeletal, with a long braid of grey hair hanging down her back. "Where are you off to this early?" She asked in an accusatory voice.

"I've promised to help at the Seaman's Mission, Mum," Emily answered, knowing her mother would disapprove. Her parents disapproved for two reasons. First, because the Seaman's Mission was run by the Salvation Army (a religious organization, and so part of the apparatus of the ruling class designed to keep the proletariat in darkness), and second, because work at the Mission was increasingly close to "war work," and her parents vehemently opposed the war.

"This really is getting out of hand!" her mother responded with a fierce frown. "I can't see what you hope to accomplish there!"

"We provide meals and a place to relax for lonely sailors who don't want to go to the pubs, Mum." Because her parents were passionate nondrinkers on account of the disastrous impact alcohol had on the standard of living and social behaviour of the working class, Emily hoped this reminder would soften her mother's opposition. She added, "In fact, today's the first day we're going to try offering a hot meal, which is why they need a little extra help."

"I don't know why you got a university degree if all you intend to do is work in a canteen!" her mother countered unfairly. Emily knew that if the canteen had been run by the Trade Unions, or better still, the Party, her parents would have had no objection to her working there. They had made it clear to her from the start that the only point of *any* education was to use it to enlighten the working class – as they had both done by becoming teachers at a council school here in the poorest part of Portsmouth.

Her parents came from humble homes, and each had been the first in their respective family to get higher education. They had met through the Communist Party, in which they were both active, and taken jobs together more or less because the Party had sent them here. Sometimes, Emily wondered if even their marriage had been directed by the Party. At best, it represented an alliance dictated by ideological and practical considerations. Certainly, they showed no particular affection for one another, and they had maintained separate bedrooms for as long as she could remember. But they remained true to the Party even now – despite the Molotov-Ribbentrop Pact and all that had followed.

Emily had become disillusioned with Marxism-Leninism long ago – or rather, when her friends from University went off to Spain to fight for the Republican government and came back, if they came back at all, with horror stories about the Republicans as well as the Fascists. Nor had she been able to stomach Stalin's treachery in making a pact with Hitler – and then dividing up Poland with him. Emily was through with Marxism and her parents' rigid devotion to the Party line, but she didn't want to argue about it with them. She knew she would never make them see things differently. Since her mother had not asked a direct question, she responded with a non- committal gesture of her head and continued down the stairs.

Rather than make herself breakfast (and risk her mother coming down and lecturing her), Emily decided to snatch something at the Mission. Taking her handbag, she went straight out into the street. Her parents lived in the end house of a row of grimy terraced cottages without front gardens. Coal dust darkened the mud-coloured brick facades, and the sidewalks were as likely to be littered with drunks and used French letters as dog shit.

This was not a "nice" neighbourhood. Emily hated returning home after work because there were always drunks loitering around in front of the corner pub, "The Queen's Head." Although she had been brought up here, she had never really liked it, and her three glorious years at University had turned a latent dislike into outright aversion.

She had gone up to Cambridge on a scholarship, and for the first time in her life she had found herself surrounded by beautiful things – magnificent historic buildings, green countryside, and healthy, articulate people. She had loved every minute of it – most of all, the freedom from her parents' dogmatic ideology and lifestyle. She had sampled a variety of political clubs, but after dabbling in everything from Atheism to Fascism, she had found a home in the Peace Society.

If only she had been allowed to take the Fellowship offered for a Master's Degree! If only she'd been able to find a job at a school or college! But England in the late 1930s had not been flush with jobs, and what academic positions were available went, naturally, to young men. One of the deans with whom Emily had interviewed had finally been honest enough to tell her that: that she didn't stand a chance despite getting a First Class Degree. So, she'd had no choice but to return to Portsmouth, to her parental home, and to take a job with an insurance company.

Because she was running late, Emily decided to take a bus, but the busses weren't running to schedule, and she ended up wasting rather than saving time. It was almost 9.30 before she reached the Mission. She was astonished to find that the place was very much alive already.

Emily could still remember the way it had looked the day of her first visit – glum and neglected. The grated windows suggested a prison, while the inhabitants consisted of mostly aging sailors sleeping off hangovers or trying to keep out of debt before going on the next binge. Since the start of the war, and especially since Dunkirk, however, the Mission had turned into a beehive of activity.

As Emily went through the main door, she glanced into the library. Once a yawning, echoing cavern, it was now filled with sailors, most of whom appeared to be writing letters. The mission provided free paper and envelopes for sailors often caught in Portsmouth on very short turnarounds. (Some sailors didn't like writing in the narrow confines of their ships where privacy was non-existent, the Mission's director, Major Fitzsimmons, had explained to Emily.) On the other side of the hall, an auction to benefit the orphans of Dunkirk was in progress. Meanwhile, the queue from the downstairs canteen wound up the stairs.

Emily hastened into the cellar, lit by a mixture of neon ceiling lights and ground-level windows covered with filthy glass. The room itself was functional in the extreme, without either plants or paintings, but on tables which had been pushed together, large vats of boiling water kept food in an upper tray warm. The cook, a man almost as broad as he was tall, with arms blue with tattoos, was carrying in fresh trays of scrambled (powdered) eggs. The Director herself, in her neat uniform, stood at the cash register, ringing up the bills with a stream of cheerful chatter, while Marjory, one of the women who had taken refuge here and never really left, was trying to serve both food and drinks.

The Director, Major "Hattie" Fitzsimmons, was the reason Emily was here. Emily had met Major Fitzsimmons on a train coming down from London the day of that fateful interview when she had been told she was never going to get a University position. She had been feeling depressed and sorry for herself, and somehow Miss Fitzsimmons had cheered her up without being the least bit patronising.

Miss Fitzsimmons was a trim but solid woman, with a face too strong to be considered lovely. People called her "handsome" rather than "pretty," and her appeal was in her good-humoured practicality. She had the capacity to be helpful and do good without pathos or an overbearing ideology.

At the sight of Emily she smiled and, rather than complaining that Emily was late, remarked sincerely, "How lovely that you could make it, Miss Pryce. You can see how much we need you! I've never seen so many sailors at one time in my whole life!"

Emily hung up her handbag on a hook on the wall and fetched an apron from the kitchen. "Where have they all come from?" she asked, as she tied an apron behind her back and took over serving the food from Marjory.

"Apparently both the *Prince of Wales* and the *Hood* anchored off Spithead last night," Miss Fitzsimmons answered.

"An' you'd think the Navy didn't feed 'em!" Marjory added in her Portsmouth accent.

As Emily set to work, she was struck by how terribly young the sailors looked. Of course, she'd always known the Navy took volunteers at 15, but she'd never realised just how *young* that was until she saw them here in front of her – their uniforms too large for them and their faces still spotted with teenage acne. Or was she getting old? With a sense of life slipping by her, she realised she was now 24, practically an "old maid," and no suitor or boyfriend anywhere in sight....

At about 11.30, the cook stopped bringing eggs, beans and sausage and brought peas, mash and gammon steak instead. By this point, Emily was feeling wilted, hot and sweaty, but suddenly Miss Fitzsimmons was called away. Some sort of "co-ordinating" committee with the various volunteer services from the WVS to the Red Cross. She asked Emily to take over the cash register. Shortly afterwards, the cook called for Marjory to "come quick" – there was some sort of problem with a delivery to the back. So, Emily found herself alone trying to serve food, then drinks, and finally collect payment from each customer in a queue that just wouldn't end.

She glanced towards the stairs, wondering just how long the queue was *outside*, and saw a young man coming down the stairs on crutches. Although he was young and in civilian clothes, out of respect for his injury the sailors squeezed to one side to let him through. His white shirt was open at the neck and the sleeves were turned up part-way to the elbows, revealing darkly tanned arms to match his face and neck. He had rather longish, dark hair – the way students wore it, not what would be acceptable in the services. Emily thought he was the best-looking young man she had ever seen.

When he reached the foot of the stairs, he paused to look around. He caught sight of Emily and smiled right at her; then he hobbled over. "Are you all alone here?"

"Not really. Marjory is supposed to be helping, but she got called away. I don't know why exactly, something about deliveries." Emily glanced over her shoulder at the door through which Marjory had disappeared a few minutes earlier.

"I better see if I can help, then," he offered at once, coming around the end of the table. Then propping himself up with both crutches under his left arm he started serving the food with his free hand.

The apparition was so extraordinary that Emily found herself quite incapable of protesting – as she knew she ought to do on account of his leg. Instead, she only nodded thankfully, while feverishly searching her brain for an explanation of where this young man could have come from and what he might be doing here. She remembered Major Fitzsimmons saying something about Conscientious Objectors being assigned to the various support services. Emily presumed they would be allocated to places like the Fire Department and St. Johns Ambulance Corps first, but it wasn't completely unreasonable to send one along to help here.

Although most of her friends from the Peace Society had answered the call to the Colours when the time actually came, she still had one friend who remained true to their common ideals, Michael Woolsey. Michael came from a Quaker family, and, like his father before him, he was a "conshy" who refused military service. Emily had had a terrible crush on Michael when they were at University. Even after a girl friend had gently explained the "facts of life" about Michael's sexual preferences, Emily hadn't stopped loving him.

"I was looking for Major Fitzsimmons," the young man beside her announced, drawing her attention back to the present. Although this young man was darker and taller than Michael, something about him reminded her of him. He certainly had a warm smile and an unselfconscious helpfulness and maybe, just maybe, he wasn't "one of them"?

To the young man she answered easily, "Oh, I'm terribly sorry. She's off at some co-ordinating committee, and I have no idea when she might be back. They want to get all the various support services working more closely together, but I think they spend more time bickering over turf and titles. So, it could take rather a long time – seeing the way committees are and especially committees of do-good ladies." Emily risked a quick smile at the stranger.

He laughed appreciatively, giving her a new, more discerning look that sent a little shock through her. The smile he shot her was clearly approving without being predatory.

"I hope you don't mind me asking, but what is a nice girl like you doing in a place like this?" He put his look into words.

"What makes you think I'm a nice girl?" Emily quipped back. Without even thinking, she fell into the kind of repartee that was so much a part of her University days.

He laughed but retorted without missing a beat: "Innocent until proven guilty – or some such thing." Then he gave her another quick but observant glance.

Emily was starting to feel *very* self-conscious. She wasn't exactly dressed to meet the man of her dreams – not in an old, threadbare apron over an ancient cotton blouse and skirt, flat shoes, naked legs, and her hair pinned up at the back of her head out of the way. And on top of that, she was sweating, and her hair was coming down in random strands.

"So, what *are* you doing here?" he pressed her.

"Oh, well, in case you missed it, there is a war on, and I wanted to do something useful."

"Most girls seem to be flocking to the Women's Services – WRNS and WAAFs and all that. A bit more glamorous than the *Salvation* Army, surely?"

Ah ha, Emily thought, he was trying to test her commitment to the war before admitting to being a conscientious objector. It must be horribly difficult to be a "conshy" at a time like this, when the country was truly threatened with invasion for the first time since the defeat of Napoleon.

"Well," Emily drew a deep breath to answer his question with the sufficient forcefulness to assure him that she was *not* the kind who had eyes only for a uniform. "Glamour is not the issue. I simply don't want to be a member of a military organization. I admit, Hitler has to be stopped and only military force is going to stop him now, but that does not mean I have to *personally* join an organization whose *raison d'etre* is war."

"Well, it's not as though the women's services are being asked to carry guns or drop bombs. Most of what they do is just clerical, answering phones and all that," the young man pointed out reasonably.

"That may be, but I'd still be part of an organization that quite frankly has been involved in a great deal of oppression – particularly in our Colonies. And furthermore, our military leadership is probably rather grateful to Herr Hitler for giving them an excuse to buy all the toys they wanted to have anyway." Emily was surprised to discover that she still felt quite strongly about this. It was one thing to admit Hitler and the Wehrmacht had to be stopped, and another to forget that the British military had brutally suppressed people all over the world for the last hundred years. Emily was a vehement opponent of Empire.

The young man laughed. "Fair enough. We'd never have got the budget for monoplane fighters without the Luftwaffe frightening Parliament to death. I take it you belonged to one of the university peace societies that voted 'under no circumstances to die for King and Country'?"

"That was the Oxford Union, actually, but yes, I did belong to the Peace Society. And you?"

"Oh, no! Too dim for University." He waved the thought aside, almost losing his balance in the process, and for a moment they both concentrated on serving again.

Emily didn't believe him. His accent was upper class without being "over the top," and his self-confidence suggested a man used to authority, even privilege. And then there was the long hair and the civilian clothes. He had to be a "conshy" and still afraid to admit it. Emily felt she had to say something to put him more at ease. "Actually," she tried, "I think we're almost as much to blame for this war as Hitler is."

"What?" That surprised him so utterly that he stopped serving to stare at her.

The sailor in line at once complained in a heavy Australian accent. "Give us a break, Mate. You can flirt with your Sheila later; I've been waiting in this line half an hour!"

"Right!" The young man turned back to the sailor, serving him an extra-large portion. They exchanged a grin that was almost conspiratorial.

Emily felt compelled to explain herself, feeling more self-conscious than ever. "What I mean is that we more or less drove the German people into the arms of Hitler. If we hadn't imposed the Treaty of Versailles on them in the first place, they would not have had the economic crisis which drove them to despair. Have you ever read John Maynard Keynes' *The Economic Consequences of the Peace?*"

He shook his head.

"Well, Keynes was with the British Delegation at Versailles, and in 1919 he predicted almost exactly what would happen. He couldn't foresee Hitler, of course, but the—"

The door from the kitchen swung open, and Marjory burst in with loud apologies and explanations. She stopped dead in her tracks when she saw the young man beside Emily. "Where did you come from, dear boy?"

"Oh, I just dropped by to see Aunt Hattie, and seeing a damsel in distress, I offered to give her a hand."

"That was very kind of you, I'm sure, but you shouldn't be standing about on that leg. Go and give Cook a hand in the kitchen. He's starting the sandwiches, and you can sit down to do that. I'll take over here." She shooed him out of the way and into the kitchen before Emily and he had a chance to exchange another word.

Emily noted, however, that he had referred to Major Fitzsimmons as "Aunt," and Marjory clearly knew him. So maybe he wasn't a conscientious objector after all? In that case, he must have a reserved occupation – a scientist perhaps? Or cipher work for the Navy? Or translating? He seemed slightly foreign in an indefinable way, and he might speak a foreign language well without having gone to University. Perhaps he had gone to Swiss boarding schools as some of the wealthy boys did....

She was still pondering it when the hot food gave out, and Marjory sent her into the kitchen to help with the sandwiches. She found the young man behind a massive table with loaves of bread, slabs of butter and packages of cheese and ham. Emily joined him at the table. Before she could even get a word out, he smiled over at her and put down his knife to offer his hand. "I'm afraid I've been terribly rude. I should have introduced myself. I'm Miss Fitzsimmon's nephew, Robin Priestman. And you?"

"Emily Pryce." They shook hands.

Before Emily could get out another word, he urged with a decidedly wicked smile, "You were about to tell me how we started the war?"

"Well, not *started* it," Emily corrected, feeling a little silly. She got the feeling that this young man was highly amused by her, but not in a malicious way. On the contrary, he seemed to be intrigued by her in exactly the way she had always *wished* Michael had been: as an *intelligent woman.*

Before she went up to Cambridge, she had had her brief encounters with men, mostly sailors, who were interested in her as "a skirt" only. She had hated it intensely. Nothing had made her more uncomfortable or angry than wolf-whistles and compliments referring to parts of her body. In a way, that was what had first attracted her to Michael and his crowd. They had always treated her as a person, a mind, a fellow human being first and a woman second. And then she found out why....

But this young man seemed to be interested in both – in what she was saying as well as in what she was sexually. She wanted to retain that interest and to convince him that she had a brain and something to say. "I just wanted to explain how our *revanchist* policies resulted in the economic collapse and the humiliation of Germany, which in turn gave rise to political extremism, including National Socialism. After all, the main reason Hitler was so popular was because he promised to 'tear up Versailles' and restore German sovereignty on the Rhine and give it back an army suitable to a nation of its size. Territorially, until the invasion of Czechoslovakia, all he was asking for was the same 'self-determination of peoples' that Wilson had promised in his Fourteen Points and which all other peoples – except the Germans – had been granted."

Too late, Emily realised maybe she had been talking too much politics. Her best girl friend at College had warned her that she tended to do that. Emily had never been a debutante, after all, and her intellectual parents had never taught her the "social graces" expected of a young "lady." She wasn't *supposed* to be a "lady," but the vanguard of the proletariat. Her roommate at college had tried to give her some tips, the most important of which had been: "Men love talking about themselves. The best way to make them think you're brilliant is to ask them questions and then tell them *they're* brilliant. Oh – and you can never go wrong by asking a young man about himself."

"You must have a very important job," Emily ventured, "to be exempt from military service."

That clearly startled him. He cocked his head and asked, "What makes you think I am?"

"Oh, well, *everyone* wears a uniform now-a-days – if they have one." Emily pointed out with a laugh. It was so true.

"Ah."

Suddenly Emily got the feeling she had made a terrible mistake. He *was* in the services, and she'd been babbling on about the military being almost criminal and how she would never want to be part of it, and all because she'd wanted to please and impress this young man. She was an absolute fool! She had done everything wrong – just as her roommate said.

But meanwhile the attraction was so strong that she found herself asking timidly, almost pleading, "But you aren't one of these gung-ho types who wants to go out and kill the Hun, surely?"

"No, I'm worse than that," he told her cheerfully, clearly enjoying himself.

"What do you mean?" she asked, baffled. What could be worse than that?

"Well, you said you were in one of these peace societies that see war as fundamentally wrong, and I'm a professional. Did Cranwell and all that."

"Cranwell?"

"RAF training college."

"Yes," Emily whispered. It wasn't that she didn't *know* what Cranwell was, it was that she was beginning to grasp the magnitude of her error. "Your leg?" she asked almost inaudibly.

"Broke it jumping out of my Hurricane. Seemed a shame to rip up a uniform to accommodate the cast, so I've been wearing civvies while on convalescent leave."

Emily couldn't take it any more. This wonderful young man had walked into her life, offered to help her in an awkward situation, looked at her with the interest she so longed for, and he was a professional soldier. Not only that, but she had made an absolute fool of herself by jumping to wild conclusions without proper evidence. The embarrassment and confusion was so intense she felt she had to leave. She got up and started to back out of the kitchen. "I'm so sorry."

"About what?" Robin asked, baffled.

"About – oh, dear." She turned and fled.

Before Robin could even find his crutches and get to his feet to follow, Hattie Fitzsimmons swept into the kitchen. "Good heavens, where was

Miss Pryce off to in such a hurry? Robin! What are you doing here?" She looked from him to the door where Emily had disappeared and frowned slightly.

"I'm completely innocent!" Robin protested, reading her thoughts.

Hattie Fitzsimmons didn't look convinced, but with a glance towards the Cook she said firmly, "We'll talk about it later. Where's Marjory?"

Robin took a taxi home to his mother's house on Clifton Terrace in Southsea. The Victorian terraced cottages looked across Southsea Common to the Solent and the main sitting room, located on the first floor, had a lovely bow window with a window seat which invited residents and guests to enjoy the view. On a good day the Isle of Wight seemed just a stone's throw away, but in haze or rain it was just a blue-grey shadow beyond the green-grey sea.

Robin had grown up in this house, when he wasn't away at school or visiting his paternal grandparents in Yarmouth, Isle of Wight. He had spent hours on this window seat watching the Royal Navy ploughing its way purposefully in and out regardless of the weather. He sat down on the window seat, his crutch propped up beside him, and his attention was, as usual, drawn to the sea.

A destroyer was battling a choppy sea as she made her way southeast – probably going to join a convoy, Robin reflected. She looked splendid with the white ensign fluttering stiffly behind her, crisp and clean against the greyish background of sea and sky. From this distance you couldn't see the dents, tears, and bullet holes, he reflected. Robin would never forget the tattered and bloody state of the destroyer that had taken him off the beaches.

He turned away from the window to survey the room behind him. It had not changed in 24 years – except that everything was a little older, more faded, more threadbare, more yellowed and old-fashioned. He sighed.

On the mantel over the fireplace was the "mausoleum." Throughout his childhood this had consisted of his parents' wedding photo, his father in the dress uniform of a RN Lieutenant with cocked hat and sword, flanked by a portrait-photo of his father in service uniform and a photo of his mother at his christening, already wearing black.

To this collection had been added three new items. One was a framed newspaper clipping showing him with a lovely girl in a floppy brimmed hat on his arm and shaking hands with the Duke of Windsor. Then there was a photo of him standing beside a Hawker Fury in flying kit and grinning like an idiot. His hair was rather too long and hanging in his forehead in the photo. It reminded him he'd needed a haircut ever since he got back from France. Better see to it tomorrow.

The other new item on the mantel he had never seen before. He had to get up and hobble over to the mantel to see what it was: a telegram flimsy with the ten words which – according to his mother – had nearly killed her: "F/Lt R Priestman missing in action over France. Regrets."

In the chaos of Dunkirk, it had been almost a week before his mother learnt that he had, in fact, been found by the French, taken to the retreating BEF, and given a lift in the back of a supply lorry as far as Dunkirk. There he had waited, under constant attack for almost two days, before finally being taken off in a long-boat and delivered to an RN destroyer. However, he had broken his ankle badly on landing, snapping every ligament and tendon, and since it had been days before he got to hospital and the ankle could be operated on, the recovery was not as smooth as one would have liked.

Robin hated being immobilised, a fact made harder by the fact that he had no friends in Portsmouth and found his mother's company tedious. His friends from school and Cranwell were now widely scattered, having joined various services or been posted to different squadrons. Even the remnants of 579 were now up in Scotland. Roger had been taken prisoner. Driver had been badly burned. Shakespeare was still MIA. But Robin had been glad to hear the ground crews had been flown out at the very last minute.

As for his mother's company, the problem was that they had nothing in common. His mother had married at 17, been widowed at 18, and spent the rest of her life playing the role of "grieving widow" – when she wasn't setting her cap for one new beau or another. Uneducated as she was, with no job (she lived on her husband's pension in the house he'd left her), her only interest in life seemed to be the society pages of the newspapers.

Indeed, she had never been happier than when her son, as a member of the RAF's aerobatics team, had occasionally found his way into those pages. Travelling about England and the Continent, taking part in air displays and competitions, had brought Robin briefly in contact with socialites and even the court. His mother had then spent the better part of her waking hours (as far as Robin could tell) fantasizing about what life would be like for her if he married one of the heiresses with whom he had occasionally been photographed.

As usual, she was talking even before she entered the parlour with the tea tray, "… and she left a number where you can ring her back."

"Who?"

"Robin! Haven't you heard a thing I've said to you? *Virginia Cox-Gordon!*"

There had been a time when he would have been excited to hear that Virginia Cox-Gordon had rung. He had, for a short time, been fascinated by her. She was pretty, witty, rich, and he liked being seen with her. But Robin couldn't afford her. His paternal grandfather, Admiral Priestman, had put him through public school but had flatly refused to pay for anything as "nonsensical" as flying. He had only made it through Cranwell on money Aunt Hattie raised by mortgaging her house. As for his Flight Lieutenant's pay, you could book that under "petty cash" as far as the Cox-Gordons of the world were concerned. Robin hadn't inherited a fortune and he wasn't going to make one either – and Virginia wasn't going to give sustained attention to anyone without.

Besides, Robin reflected on his reaction to his mother's news, Virginia had lost her allure. Before the war, Virginia had been good for his image, and he'd been flattered that she would go out with him at all. But he hadn't given her a thought since the war had started in earnest.

His mother set the tea-tray down on the coffee table, and Robin took his crutch and hobbled over to sit on the sofa. "I dropped by the Mission to see Aunt Hattie today," he remarked.

"In your condition?!" his mother answered, horrified. She had never approved of him "hanging about" the Seaman's Mission, because he came in contact with "bad company" there. Robin, on the other hand, had been starved for masculine role models as a boy, and so he had been fascinated by the tattooed and weathered men who washed up at the Mission. He'd always spent time down there when he could, often helping Cook because the retired seaman had a wealth of fascinating – and by no means completely sanitised – stories. "There was a new girl working there. Emily Pryce."

"Good heavens! What do you want with the girls Hattie drags in? For all you know she was a you-know-what! She might well be diseased."

"With a Cambridge education and quoting John Maynard Keynes?"

His mother had no answer to that but didn't need one. The telephone started ringing out in the hall, and she rushed to answer it.

"Yes, yes!" Robin heard her say breathlessly into the phone, and then, "He just got in. I'll go fetch him." She rushed back into the sitting room and stage-whispered at Robin. "It's Miss Cox-Gordon!"

"I don't want—" He thought better of it, took a crutch and limped into the hallway. He took up the receiver. "Hello?"

"Robin, darling! I was *so* worried! Are you *really* all right?"

"Brilliant. Wizard. Nothing but a bashed ankle. Cast comes off in a couple of weeks or so. Then I'm back on ops."

"So soon? Then we *must* get together at the *first* opportunity. What are you doing tomorrow? I'm having a few friends down to the country." She meant her father's country estate in Kent. "Why don't you join us?"

"Sorry. Can't drive yet. Not until the cast comes off. Nice of you to think of me, though. Just have to wait until I'm fit. I'll give you a ring."

"Look, if you can't drive, how about if I come down to Portsmouth one evening and pick you up?"

"Wouldn't want to impose. Besides, Portsmouth's pretty grim at the moment. Navy all over the place."

Virginia tittered. "Honestly, Robin, there's nothing *new* about the *Navy* in Portsmouth. Besides, it must be quite exciting, really. London is *dreadfully* boring these days. Black-outs and air raid wardens and everybody in some silly uniform – and, oh yes, you should *see* the Americans. There seem to be American press people *everywhere* these days." She interrupted herself to ask him, "You know I've got a job with the *Times,* don't you?"

"Congratulations. Society Page?"

"No! Who cares about that now-a-days? I'm covering London. You wouldn't believe all the silly questions these Americans insist on asking everyone! 'Will Britain bear up?' 'Can the RAF stop the Luftwaffe?'"

"Can we?"

Virginia tittered again. "You're a card, Robin. You should know."

"Haven't the foggiest. Look, Virginia, my aunt just got in, and I must entertain her." He was looking at Aunt Hattie, who having let herself in was coming up the stairs. "I'll ring you later in the week. Thanks for calling."

"But –"

"Bye."

"Bye."

He'd already hung up.

"Just who was that?" Hattie asked giving him a piercing look.

"Virginia Cox-Gordon."

Hattie's eyebrows went up. She didn't read the gossip pages, but many of her staff – and of course her sister Lydia – did. She knew exactly who Virginia Cox-Gordon was: daughter of a millionaire, debutante, the "catch of the season" just last year, before the war started.

"You know your *other* girl friends call *my* flat," she told him in a low, reproachful voice.

"I'm sorry—"

"Just *how many* girls did you give my number to?"

"Only two." He thought about it. "Three."

Hattie sighed and gazed at him sadly.

"I *am* sorry they bothered you," Robin insisted, looking sincere. "I told them not to call unless it was an absolute emergency, and—"

"Yes, well, I'm sure things look very different from your superior male vantage point, but to us poor females here on the ground, the fact that you were last seen duelling with two Messerschmitts over the ruins of

Calais in the midst of the worst rout in English history seemed very much like an 'emer-gency.' I can't say I blame *them*, but I do wonder about you sometimes...."

Robin concluded it might not be the best moment to ask her for Emily Pryce's telephone number.

Chapter 5

Stukageschwader 22, III Gruppe
Late June 1940, Northern France

Klaudia hardly knew how to react. At training it had been drilled into them that they were "soldiers" and that they could not expect to be treated like "ladies" any more – at least not when in uniform. Quite the contrary, it was for them to get to their feet for superiors (i.e., any NCO or officer). Furthermore, they were to speak only when spoken to and to obey without question. They had been drilled hard during training – mostly by professional soldiers old enough to be their fathers. These men took "no nonsense" from the girls entrusted to them. The girls who had tried to flirt had quickly learnt different manners, and those that tried tears and hysteria were washed out entirely. The survivors of the rigorous, compact course felt very proficient at the various tasks they were expected to perform – whether manning the telephone switchboard, the telegraph machines or the wireless. They felt ready to perform their duties like good "soldiers."

Now, suddenly, they were being treated like ladies again. Well, maybe not ladies, but certainly like young women rather than soldiers. The airmen were all but falling over themselves to carry their luggage, and the whistles and invitations to dinner were like an artillery barrage. Klaudia found herself grinning out of sheer embarrassment and – well, yes – excitement, too.

Never in her life had she found herself surrounded by so many men. Not just men, either, but young, healthy, high-spirited men. It was absolutely intoxicating – especially when added to the thrill that she felt just to be here. She, along with just a handful of other "privileged" *Helferinnen,* had been sent to France. Better yet, they had been sent to a *Stukageschwader*, the absolute crème-de-la-crème of the Luftwaffe.

Klaudia still couldn't believe her luck. She wanted to think it was because she had passed her training with flying colours, but of course there was no denying that her name was worth more in the Luftwaffe than it had ever been in the RAD. A distant cousin, Wolfram, commanded the *Fliegerkorps* VIII, the Stuka corps stationed in France, and of course her father's second cousin had been the famous "Red Baron" of the last war.

So here she was along with Rosa and four other girls at *III Gruppe, StG*

2, stationed just south of Falaise in Normandy. On leaving training, they had been warned that they were going to a war zone. Their lecturers, veterans of the last war, had been careful to point out that the *Luftwaffehelferinnen* stationed in France would be confined to base most of the time. They had been reminded that they would be expected to work "front-line" hours – which could mean around the clock in a crisis. They would be subject not only to military discipline but to military justice as well – and that meant they could be sentenced to death for infringements of the military code.

A stern *Stabsfeldwebel* had warned them, too, that they would very probably be subject to enemy air attack. The "bestial British" had already bombed unprotected cities, aiming at "innocent civilians." It was only to be expected that they would soon target the bases of the planes that would – in due course – be launched against them. By the time they boarded the train in Berlin, Klaudia and Rosa had almost had second thoughts. After all, the *Helferinnen* stationed inside the Reich lived at home and worked "normal" shifts with regular days off – and they were safe.

But as Klaudia and Rosa passed through Paris and rolled through the rich, green countryside of Normandy, all doubts vanished. Even if they only had half a day off each week, what an opportunity! Surely, they could get down to Paris now and again. Klaudia, after seeing a map, thought too of Rouen Cathedral and Mont St. Michel, which she knew from pictures in one of her father's books. In Falaise itself, of course, was the oldest castle in Normandy, seat of the Dukes of Normandy. It was the castle from which William the Conqueror had set out to conquer England. Surely there could be no better omen for the impending German invasion of the impudent island? Klaudia and the other girls were absolutely convinced of it.

And now this. They were picked up at Falaise station by grinning Luftwaffe airmen, who gallantly carried their things and escorted them to a bus, which took them straight to their new quarters. This was nothing like the barracks of the *Reich-sarbeitsdienst*! The 1st *Staffel*, III *Gruppe* of StG 2 was stationed at an improvised airfield just south of Falaise itself, directly on the banks of the river Orne – and they were to be housed in the wonderful old Chateau in which the officers were also billeted. Admittedly, they were put up in three cramped servant's rooms under the eaves, and they had to share a single bath and toilette between them, but what a place!

Klaudia and Rosa, who were sharing one of the rooms, looked about themselves and couldn't believe their luck. There were two narrow beds under the eaves with a dormer window in between. Everything about the room – the low beams, creaking floorboards and flowered wallpaper was romantic. They even had a view out of their window across a somewhat overgrown but still discernible formal garden to the meandering river that glistened in the late afternoon sun. Beyond the river, cattle grazed peacefully in the long, green grass bathed in golden afternoon sunlight. It was like a painting. "Isn't it beautiful!" Klaudia exclaimed.

"You must be used to it," Rosa remarked with a sidelong look. She still couldn't quite make head or tail of Klaudia. She ought to have been arrogant, self-important, spoilt and lazy, but she was none of those things. She had even helped Rosa with the theoretical subjects that had almost brought her to ruin. Without Klaudia's help, Rosa would have washed out. In turn, Rosa helped Klaudia with the Nazi stuff. They had worked so well as a team that Klaudia had graduated top of her class and Rosa in the respectable middle field. On account of Rosa's experience as a leader in the BDM, however, she had been promoted directly to *Oberhelferin* and entrusted with disciplinary responsibility for the six girls assigned to this base.

Rosa had been astonished by how thrilled Klaudia had been for her. Not once had Klaudia suggested that her birth entitled her to privilege and power. That surprised Rosa, who as the daughter of a Communist activist, had been raised to think of aristocrats as "the class enemy." But Rosa supposed much of what her father had spouted off all those years was nonsense. He was certainly wrong about the Führer and the Nazis, the silly old fart!

"Oh, our house is nothing like this," Klaudia assured her new friend sincerely. "It's much smaller and nothing grand at all. This is the most beautiful place I've ever seen!"

Just then, with a suddenness that made both girls jump, three aircraft roared right over their heads – so low that they instinctively ducked. The airfield, it turned out, was just on the other side of the house, and a "*Kette*" of three Stukas had just taken off. Before their eyes the lead aircraft of the tight vic seemed to stand on its wingtip and start banking sharply away to the right. The two wingmen clung to the leader's wingtips in perfect, precision flying. The engines roared and the windowpanes in the old chateau rattled. Gone was the idyllic peace of the French countryside, and back was the thrill of being part of Germany's magnificent air force.

The *Luftwaffehilferinnen* did not eat in the Officers' Mess, of course. They had been carefully instructed to use the servants' stairs of the chateau and cross the airfield to the large "other ranks" Mess, which was housed in a gigantic converted medieval tithe barn. Their arrival here was greeted with cheers, clapping, and whistles – enough to make even Rosa blush. But the girls ignored everything, and soon a grizzled Sergeant Major had quelled the friendly rebellion. They were shown to a separate table for exactly six, and here they sat a little apart, acutely aware that their every move was watched. It was very awkward, at first, and they only dared whisper among them- selves, but Klaudia supposed they would get used to it eventually.

Just as they were about to leave, another sergeant came up to their table. "We've organised a dance in your honour, ladies. May I escort you?" He held his arm out to Brigitte, by far the prettiest of them, and she – with a little uncertain glance at the others – took it. Instantly, there were other NCOs in attendance on all the remaining five girls. Klaudia found herself being led away by a cheerful young sergeant who introduced himself as Hans Detweiler. He chattered away, giving Klaudia no chance to get a word in.

In another out-building of the Chateau, a large room had been turned into an NCOs' club. It was decorated with flags and photos of Stukas, and here a gramophone was being wound up. There was also a long, improvised bar at one end, and with only six girls to nearly forty NCOs, most of the men clustered around the bar for a beer.

Klaudia had been taught to dance, of course. All the other landowners in the neighbourhood held balls on various occasions. At Christmas and the New Year there were usually a half-dozen or so. Klaudia and her parents were always invited and usually attended. At those dances her dinner-partner dutifully danced the first dance with her, and the other gentlemen at the table each asked her for a dance in turn. After that, however, Klaudia usually sat out the rest of the ball with her parents. Once, just once, someone's cousin had been visiting from Austria, and he had danced almost every dance with her. But then he went home, and she never saw or heard from him again.

This was totally different. She couldn't finish one dance before someone else cut in. It was impossible to keep names straight any more, and she found that "Klaudia" sufficed as far as these men were concerned. She was infinitely grateful to be in sturdy, tie-up Luftwaffe shoes rather than high heels, and – strange as it seemed – she felt prettier in her tailored uniform than in any ball gown she had ever worn.

Suddenly there was a great commotion at the door. A voice bellowed, "Achtung!"

The young corporal she was dancing with frowned and glanced over his shoulder, as if expecting it to be a joke. But in the next instant he dropped hold of her and went into a parade-ground salute. Coming through the door in a little crowd was a bevy of commissioned officers. Not just officers, Klaudia rapidly realised, as she remembered the charts on rank and speciality insignia from training. Leading the little horde was a Major/ *Gruppenkommandeur* with a Knights Cross at his throat, and around him were apparently all the pilots of the Staff and First *Staffel*.

Beside her the Corporal started swearing under his breath, something about "bleeding pilots poaching our game." And there was little doubt about that.

The pilots made straight for the six girls, and the NCOs could only retreat, even if they looked sullen rather than polite about it. Klaudia could hardly take in what was happening when the *Gruppenkommandeur* came straight for her. His eyes were levelled at her from the start – strong, hunter's eyes in an angular face. No, he wasn't handsome, but there was an unmistakable attraction about him, a charisma so strong that Klaudia thought she'd faint as he took her in his arms.

"Jako Paschinger," he introduced himself simply. "As Senior Officer at this base, I feel it is my duty to welcome you here personally and make sure that everything is to your satisfaction."

"Thank you," Klaudia stammered.

"I didn't catch your name?"

"Klaudia." And this time she played her trump. "Klaudia v. Richthofen."

Jako guffawed. When he had himself back under control, he grinned at the perplexed Klaudia and declared. "Don't you see? Brilliant instincts. I picked you straight out as the only one for me." Then he seemed to have second thoughts. "Not Wolfram's sister or anything like that, I hope?"

"No. His grandfather and mine were second cousins once removed," Klaudia explained.

"Ah," Jako digested that, and then grinned. "Excellent! Excellent! Now can I buy you a drink? I'm much better at drinking than dancing."

By the time Klaudia tripped back upstairs to her attic room, she was more intoxicated than she had ever been in her life. In fact, she was so light-headed that Rosa warned in her brusque Berliner dialect, "Get your feet back on the ground before you crash into the ceiling."

"Oh, Rosa! I can't believe it! I just can't believe it! He spent almost the *whole* evening with me."

Rosa, uncomfortable with the officers and their funny manners (clicking heels and bowing over her hand and all that), had escaped them at the first opportunity. She'd spent most of the evening with the ground crews, particularly a certain *Stabsfeldwebel* Axel Voigt, who was also from Berlin. Voigt was the Chief Mechanic of the *Stabsstaffel*, and the man responsible for the *Gruppenkommandeur's* own aircraft. She'd heard enough from him not to have a very high opinion of Major Paschinger. In fact, he sounded like what her father called an "Officer-Pig."

To Klaudia, who was obviously head-over-heels for the arse already, Rosa said simply. "He still puts his trousers on one leg at a time. Come on, Klaudia, we have to report for duty tomorrow, and don't count on the Herr

Gruppenkommandeur protecting you if you get the codes wrong."

"Oh, I wouldn't dream of taking advantage!" Klaudia assured her friend, genuinely shocked by the thought. Duty was duty. But as she drifted to sleep that night, Klaudia did not think she had ever been happier in all her life.

Crépon, France
Late June 1940

Ernst's mechanic was tightening his straps for him, but across the airfield the CO was already swinging into position for take-off. Ernst was late. He'd felt such an urgent need to relieve himself before take-off that he was the last one into his cockpit. The others were bouncing and swaying across the field from their respective dispersal points, all converging on the head of the runway.

"Everything's fine, fine!" Ernst waved the mechanic aside irritably, cutting the checks short. He could identify Christian's aircraft trundling over the uneven ground to get into position, while the CO was already rolling down the runway with his wingman just a couple lengths behind. Ernst hauled the hinged canopy down and clipped it shut. He waved the chocks away and bounced off to get into position for take-off.

The CO and his wingman were already in the air, and they tucked up their wheels as they started to climb. The second pair of planes raced along the grass as the next pair swung into position.

Ernst tried to hurry up, but the Me109 was a bitch on the ground. He had to swing the nose back and forth to see around it, and the narrow undercarriage felt particularly unstable as this grass field was quite uneven. Adding to his discomfort was the low sun that slanted right into his eyes. He squinted into it as yet another pair of fighters took to the air.

At last Ernst was in position. He looked anxiously to Christian on his right. Christian's Messerschmitt danced about like a high-strung horse anxious to gallop away. Ernst saw Christian turn his head in his direction expectantly, and Ernst gave him a thumbs up to indicate he was ready.

At once Christian's Messerschmitt was away, racing straight across the field, the slipstream from the propeller bending back the grass in its wake. Ernst eased off his own brakes and his aircraft rolled forward. His vision blurred as the Messerschmitt gained speed rapidly and shook itself more and more, until at last it was airborne. The rattling and shaking faded into a heady sense of lightness.

They formed up and the CO called their course: 140. Ernst checked his compass briefly, but mostly he just followed Christian as he swung onto the new heading. They were ordered up to 10,000 metres, taking part in a "reconnaissance in force" sweep of the Channel. The *Gruppe* climbed steeply.

As Ernst followed along, he was thinking about a heated discussion they'd had in the Mess the night before. The *Führer* had made a generous peace offer to the British. He had suggested that two great nations, one the pre-eminent sea power and the other the pre-eminent land power, should share the world between them. The *Führer* suggested that if Britain gave Germany a free hand on the Continent, Britain could retain all her colonies.

The *Führer* clearly wanted peace with Britain, and Ernst had been rather excited about the idea. He wasn't really all that confident about going into battle and would be just as happy flying in a peacetime Luftwaffe. That seemed the best of all worlds, being paid to fly wonderful aircraft without being shot at by anyone.

But most of the other pilots had been angry, saying the peace offer would rob them of the chance to eradicate the RAF. Particularly the younger pilots complained that a "premature" peace would rob them of the chance to become aces.

There were lots of clouds about, Ernst noted from habit – towering pillars of cumulus. It was getting cold in the cockpit. The CO called out a course change and the whole *Staffel* swept about in a graceful curve, still straining for altitude. Ernst concentrated on keeping in formation, his eyes darting from his instrument panel to Christian on his starboard bow. Why was he feeling nervous? This was just another routine sweep, his fourth since joining the squadron. It ought to be child's play by now. But his head was killing him, and he couldn't seem to focus or concentrate. No matter what he started to do, he got distracted.

When his eyes fell closed and he had to shake himself awake, something clicked in his memory and he wondered if he was suffering from oxygen deprivation. He glanced at the altimeter. They had passed through 6,000 metres. Ernst pressed the mask more closely to his mouth and drew deep breaths, but it was no good. The mask must be defective.

Ernst started to panic. He had to dive. He had to get back down where he could breathe. He couldn't just dive. He had to tell someone. The CO. In his mounting panic, he just barely managed to find the radio switch and croak out, "Herr *Hauptmann*! Geuke, here! My oxygen isn't working!"

"All right, Geuke. Return to 1,000 metres and see if you can sort it out. If not, return to base."

Without thinking Ernst shoved the nose down and turned away at the same time. He didn't register that by doing that he was flying away from the rest of the *Gruppe*.

Only slowly did he come to his senses. He remembered that he was supposed to see if he could repair the oxygen supply in flight. He dutifully checked the tube leading from the oxygen tank. It was hanging loose. It wasn't plugged in at all! Broken? No, just not plugged in. He'd been in such of a hurry to take off, he'd waved his fitter aside before he was finished with the drill.

Ernst was overwhelmed by shame. It was bad enough to have forgotten something, but he'd not only shouted about his problem over the R/T, he'd also absented himself from the flight. And now, at last, he realised what he'd done when he'd peeled away while diving. This was terrible! Rather than simply flying along with the Staffel at a lower level, he was now miles away from them. It would be almost impossible to find them again. But if he returned to base, they would accuse him of just running away. Ernst swung his Messerschmitt about again and tried to remember the last course they had been on. He thought it was 110, and he climbed back to 8000 metres.

Rather than finding the *Gruppe*, he found only increasing cloud. The sky was thick with the stuff, and it blocked his vision almost everywhere he looked. Ernst changed his course several times, but he found nothing but more cloud. Now a sheet of low cloud was creeping inland below him.

Afraid of getting lost entirely, Ernst abandoned all hope of finding the *Gruppe* and dived below the cloud cover. He found the coastline and followed it eastward, expecting to find a landmark he recognised. After flying almost ten minutes, he decided that he must have turned the wrong way. He reversed and flew along the coast in the opposite direction for fifteen minutes. He could find nothing he recognised.

The cloud continued to increase and sink. Ernst descended to 500 metres to keep below it, but mist started forming on his windscreen as he flew just beneath the dense, dark clouds. The wind had picked up as well. The little, delicate Messerschmitt was buffeted about harshly, and the engine strained against the headwinds. Abruptly, rain started pelting him. It smashed so hard against his canopy, that it overwhelmed the feeble efforts of the windscreen wiper. He could only see out of the side windows, but these too were streaming rain and steaming up.

Ernst tried to beat back his mounting panic. He started flying very carefully in an increasing square looking for a landmark, but as his fuel gauge steadily recorded his diminishing fuel reserves his hopes faded. He resigned himself to the coming crash, yet he knew that the crash investigation would reveal that he'd made one mistake after another. He'd be washed out. They'd never let him fly again. And they were right. He didn't deserve to fly. He was worthless.

When the engine finally cut out, it was almost a relief. The agony of trying was over. He had only one task left: putting the Messerschmitt down with as much skill as he had. Or should he just smash it and himself into the earth at a speed that would put them both out of their misery? Ernst thought about it, but his survival instinct was still stronger than his despair.

The countryside was open and there were plenty of pastures. There were hedges and stone walls, too. You don't want to go into a stone wall at 100 km an hour! Or trees, either. No, over there. He banked a little, gliding towards a field cut in two by a little stream. Ernst spiralled down towards the outer edge of his chosen field so he could see around the long snout of the Emil. He was so low the cattle were galloping away in terror. He eased the throttle back, straightened, pulled the nose up and applied more flap. Whop! With a horrible crash she was on the ground, slithering along on her belly, and Ernst was flung against the instrument panel so violently that he was knocked out.

When he came to again, he was being hauled out of the cockpit by solicitous Luftwaffe medics. They asked him if he was injured, and groggily he denied it. Ernst couldn't understand where the Luftwaffe medics had come from until, ten minutes later, he discovered he had crash-landed less than 10 km from the base of a *Zerstörer Gruppe*. He was taken directly to the *Gruppe* medical officer, who determined he had a concussion. Ernst was feeling a bit dizzy and queasy, and they made him lie down. Everyone just assumed he'd been trying to make the base after a sweep over the channel when his fuel had run out. The Medical Officer gave him a shot, and he fell asleep still in a state of bewilderment.

Then Christian was there. He'd driven over from JG 23 to pick Ernst up. Still feeling very confused, Ernst thanked the medical officer, pulled on his flying boots and carried his helmet, life vest and parachute out to the waiting staff car. It was pouring rain and dark as dusk – or maybe it was dusk?

"What time is it, Christian?"

"19:10. Hungry?"

Ernst thought about it. He'd eaten nothing since breakfast. "Yes, I am," he decided.

"Good, I saw a very nice little café on the way down. We can stop there." Christian sounded cheerful.

Ernst didn't understand why. He must be annoyed to have to drive all the way over here in the pouring rain. Timidly, Ernst remarked, "It's very nice of you to pick me up, Christian."

Christian waved it aside. "I was delighted to have an excuse to get away

89

from base. Bartels got it into his head he ought to put on a programme. Pure Party shit!"

Ernst was so shocked he laughed nervously. Then he looked sidelong at Christian. This wasn't the first time Christian had been irreverent towards either the CO or the NSDAP. Ernst didn't quite know what to make of it.

Christian tossed an apologetic smile at Ernst and admitted, "By the way, I had to promise the CO I'd take a look at your Emil and see what state it was in – whether it's worth sending a salvage crew over or not."

"I don't know where it is exactly," Ernst admitted miserably.

"I got the directions from the ambulance crew that picked you up. Here." Christian pulled a slip of paper from his breast pocket and handed it to Ernst, without taking his eyes off the road. "We have to turn right after a big barn. That could be it up there."

The road they turned onto was rutted and full of puddles; the engine groaned as they wallowed in mud. Ernst could already picture them getting stuck. But Christian proved as adept a driver as a flier, and after a few hundred metres the road improved. They turned left and right again, and then Ernst recognised his field even before they saw the wreck.

His Messerschmitt looked miserable. It was splattered all over with mud, and it lay with its snout shoved into the guck. The propeller was bent back, and the tail wheel dangled in the air above the level of the canopy. The canopy hung open untidily.

"Not bad," Christian remarked. "You didn't break anything. They should be able to unbend it. Better close the canopy, though."

Ernst looked over to see if Christian was being sarcastic or what.

Christian grinned at him. "Come on. Let's close the canopy and then get in out of the rain and have a nice meal with some good wine. You look like you could use it."

They dashed out to the Emil through the wet grass and puddles, hauled the canopy closed, and then dashed back for the staff car. Somehow Christian managed to turn the car around without getting stuck. Soon they were back on the main road, and Christian located the café he had selected on the way over.

It was an old stone house at a crossroads. They had to push through a bar full of hostile locals in smelly dungarees, mucky boots and sweaty berets, but the back room was empty. Here, there were a mere handful of neatly set tables under low ceiling beams. It was lit by a smoky fire and felt cosy after the rain outside. Christian chose a table near the fire. The scents from the kitchen were mouth-watering, and soon they had wine as well. Ernst tasted it sceptically, but it was very good. He drank faster than usual.

"You all right, Ernst?" Christian asked with apparent concern as he poured wine for himself. "The MO said you had a concussion and no other injuries, but..." Christian looked at him intently. "What's bothering you?"

Ernst couldn't take the scrutiny. The tension was just too much. Ernst wasn't someone who could pretend anyway. He burst out, "Christian, I'm a wash-out, aren't I?"

"Whatever for? You did a great job putting your Emil down without breaking anything."

"But – I mean – that I had to crash at all. I mean...." Too late, Ernst realised that Christian didn't know about the oxygen and that he'd been lost. But they would find out as soon as they investigated. Ernst's head was killing him. He dropped it into his hands and just held it.

"Come on. What's eating you?" Christian urged in a friendly tone.

"My oxygen."

"What about it?" Christian asked confused.

"There wasn't anything *wrong* with it – I'd just forgotten to plug it in." Ernst was so ashamed he didn't dare meet Christian's eyes as he admitted this.

Christian just laughed. Ernst stared at him. "And? Who *hasn't* done that once or twice?"

"But I – I *panicked!* I peeled away when I dived instead of staying below the *Staffel*. And I didn't realise what was wrong until I was back on the deck and, and..."

Christian leaned his elbows on the table and looked Ernst straight in the eye. "If you aren't getting enough oxygen, you can't think properly. That's all there is to it. It's normal. Don't let it get to you. What's important is that you plugged in and tried to catch up with us."

"Yes – but I couldn't find you."

"Of course not. The weather closed in too fast that the sweep was scratched."

Ernst stared at Christian, hardly daring to believe what he was being told. Christian acted as if he wasn't to blame for what happened. He tried to explain, "I got lost, Christian. I didn't know where I was. I followed the coast in both directions, but I couldn't find anything familiar – not even Le Havre. It – it was just luck that I landed so near the ZG base."

"How long have you been with us, Ernst? Ten days?" Ernst nodded.

"And how many of those days have we flown? – not even half." Christian answered his own question. "So, you've flown in France all of four times, right? – and rarely the same route. And in better weather. Any of us might have lost our way in this muck."

Ernst stared at him, afraid to believe him. Yet Christian really seemed to mean it. "Cheer up, Ernst!" Christian urged with a smile. "If I have to spend the evening with you rather than Gabrielle, then at least try to make it a pleasant evening, all right?"

"Gabrielle? Is that your French girlfriend?" Ernst ventured timidly. "Didn't the CO order you to stop seeing her?"

"We've signed a truce with France, for God's sake! Half the Gestapo has French girlfriends nowadays! What do they expect us to do? Live like monks? That's not healthy!" Christian declared with conviction.

Ernst snickered in embarrassment. He had never had a girlfriend, and he was far too inhibited to go to whores. The very thought of them made him feel dirty. He didn't want it like that. He wanted a nice girl, who was there just for him. She didn't have to be beautiful, just kind and sympathetic, and nice. He found himself gazing at his wine, wishing, while Christian continued his commentary.

Christian was telling him about meeting Gabrielle, and somehow he made it so amusing that Ernst soon found himself laughing. He forgot about his headache and getting lost and crashing, and when he remembered again, it didn't seem so bad.

Christian guided him through the menu. He spoke French, of course, and he ordered and chatted with the waiter. The meal was wonderful, and when they left, Christian picked up the bill. He wouldn't hear of Ernst paying his share. "It's your turn when I've got a concussion from a crash, OK?"

Outside the rain had stopped and the clouds were tearing apart, revealing the occasional star. "Glorious!" Christian exclaimed, gazing up at the night sky with his hands on his hips. "I wish I were up there!"

They climbed back into the car, and Christian put it in gear. He twisted around to look out the rear window as he backed out into the street, speaking to Ernst without looking at him. "You're a good pilot, Ernst. A hell of a lot better than I was just three weeks out of flight school! All you need is to gain a little more confidence."

Ernst didn't really believe him, but from that moment on he didn't just admire Christian, he *liked* him.

Chapter 6

RAF Tangmere Late June 1940

606 Squadron was slated to do a patrol this morning and for the first time since joining the squadron, Ginger's name was on the Order of Battle. He stared at the blackboard. He was chalked in as Blue Three, and his stomach started to feel queasy at once. Flight Lieutenant Hayworth and two other senior pilots were on leave, so that all three newcomers – Green, Bowles and Pilot Officer Debsen, who had joined them a couple days after Green and Bowles – were down to fly. Jones himself was leading.

"Just a routine patrol," Jones assured the three sprogs from where he lounged in a deck chair, one leg thrown over the arm, and a newspaper opened at the racing results. "The last three times we were up we just stooged around. Jerry hasn't bothered us at all. Doesn't seem at all keen to mix it, if you ask me. Must have taught him a lesson at Dunkirk, after all."

"I don't mind if Jerry puts in an appearance," Debsen assured his CO, sounding rather boastful, Ginger thought.

Ginger didn't like Debsen. He was as inexperienced as Green or himself, but simply because he held the King's commission, he preferred to associate with the veterans rather than the other newcomers. He'd gone to a good public school, too (as he made sure everyone knew), and his father was apparently someone "important" at the Ministry of Food.

Ginger could have accepted all that without acrimony, but Debsen had also dubbed Green "Rabbit." Obviously thinking himself very clever, he had announced on hearing Green's name: "Harvey was a Rabbit, wasn't he?" The others had laughed at his joke (which Ginger didn't get at all), and since then they all called Green that.

In addition to dubbing him "Rabbit," the others tormented Green about his Canadian accent. They pretended they didn't understand him sometimes or repeated some of his more unique phrases accompanied by great guffaws of laughter. Other times they exaggerated his manner of speech, making it sound ridiculous. Ginger cringed at each attack, but Green just grinned and shrugged it off. Ginger envied Green his thick skin. He knew he'd be a lot happier if he could develop the same self-assurance that left him impervious to the ridicule of others. But how did you do that?

Ginger sat down in a sagging armchair and swallowed, trying to settle his stomach with an act of will. The problem was well known to him. As a boy he'd always been the butt of ridicule at school – his uniform was second-hand, his socks darned, his shoes often had holes in them. Nor was it just a matter of being poor; a lot of the boys in the county school had been that. It was something about his Dad that made him an object of universal contempt. His Dad was called not only "thick" and "lame-brained," but also "half-breed" or even "gypsy." When Ginger proved to be brighter than average, the other boys all joked that his mother must have given his Dad "horns." It had been a long time before Ginger realised what that meant, and he had never learned how to fight back. Instead he would flee into the surrounding moors or – if it he couldn't do that – rush to the toilets and be sick.

He was feeling the same way now: as if he needed to be alone with God and nature or he was going to be sick. Just when he was about to stand up and go out into the fresh air, Jones folded up his newspaper with a loud rustle, stood, stretched, and announced: "Time to mount up, lads."

They separated to go to their respective Hurricanes. Ginger had been assigned to fly "Q." He found the Hurricane already ticking over; the efficient ground crew had started it up and done the checks already.

Ginger was rather intimidated by the ground crews. The senior NCOs had served in the last war and were awe-inspiring veterans, while even the younger men had mostly joined up as apprentices at 14 and 15. They had in consequence received years of very high quality technical training – far more than Ginger had ever had. He was acutely aware of his own inferiority whenever he confronted them and found it awkward that they called him "sir" and deferred to him as to an officer.

As Ginger arrived, the fitter climbed out of the cockpit, and reached out a hand to help him onto the wing. Ginger hoped the erk wouldn't notice that his hand was icy cold and wet with sweat. Would the fitter be able to read the fear in his face as he bent over to help him with the straps? Ginger intentionally looked down, avoiding the fitter's eyes.

"There you are, sir," the young man said cheerfully. (Ginger thought his name was Sanders.) "Don't forget your helmet." He handed it to Ginger. How had it been left on the wing?

"Thanks," Ginger muttered, embarrassed, and still avoiding the fitter's eyes. He was sure the man could sense how terrified he was.

The squadron taxied out and began forming up along the far perimeter of the field. When they were all there, Jones signalled takeoff and led them into the air by section, each section of three following the one ahead.

At first the need to concentrate on flying distracted Ginger from his unease. They circled around the field once, forming up, and then set off in a shallow climb to the west to intercept the in-bound convoy they were supposed to protect. A convoy meant ships, and ships, obviously, were at sea, so this patrol would take them over the water – something Ginger dreaded more than anything. At least during training, they had only flown over land.

To make things worse, the weather was very hazy, Ginger noted, and the contours of the land below them were murky and difficult to decipher. In fact, he wondered how they were ever going to find the convoy that they were supposed to be protecting.

Jones ordered them into Close Vics, Sections Close Echelon Port, and Ginger had to concentrate on flying again. As Blue Three, he had to keep tightly tucked in behind Blue One's port wing and farther behind Yellow Two's starboard wing. Blue One was Flight Lieutenant "Tommy" Thompson, and Ginger didn't like him very much either.

Everyone had made a point of telling the newcomers how Thompson's dad had sponsored the squadron and withouthim they wouldn't have been formed at all. Apparently, he had a big "pile" somewhere, to which the squadron had been invited now and again. It was so big and so magnificent, with its own tennis courts and swimming pool.

Ginger found that all rather intimidating, and he didn't like opening his mouth around Thompson because the latter found Ginger's West Country accent almost as offensive to the ear as Green's.

Ginger was brought back to the uncomfortable present by the bored-irritated voice of the Flight Lieutenant over the R/T: "Come on, Blue Three, get your finger out!" Ginger pressed in closer to his leader, sweating from the effort of not colliding at such close quarters. With his wingtip just a couple of feet away from his leader's, any clear-air turbulence or a sudden gust of wind could result in contact – and at 260 mph that was not recommended, Ginger thought.

"Cotton Ball Leader, Beetle here. Can you read me?"

"Cotton Ball Leader here. Reading you loud and clear, Beetle."

"We've got a lone bandit approaching the coast at Portsmouth. Can you detach a Section to look after it?"

"Will do."

"Intercepting section should steer 080. The bandit is at Angels 26, so you'll want a few thousand feet more, so make that Vector 080, Angels 30."

"Roger, Beetle. Tommy, take your Section, will you, old boy?"

Ginger's stomach flipped over as he registered that meant *him*, too. Before he knew it, his leader had shoved his nose down and started banking to starboard to lead them safely out of formation. Ginger was almost left behind and had to throttle forward. He heard Jones calling for

Green Section to close up with Yellow Section, and Thompson was urging him to catch up in his annoyed-despairing tone of voice. Ginger got the feeling that Thompson considered him "hopeless" – and he was beginning to wonder himself whether he'd ever make a fighter pilot. Maybe it had all been a mistake. Maybe his instructors had been too optimistic about him....

After that, they got a lot of directions from Beetle (that was the Controller), and they turned this way and that. Ginger was so busy staying in position that he lost track entirely of where they were – except that they were over the dreaded Channel. It gleamed menacingly, a metallic grey beneath him. It looked rather like molten lead, in fact, and Ginger was sure that if you went into it you would never re-emerge.

After ten or fifteen minutes of this, however, and with still no sight of the "bandit," Thompson's voice came forcefully over the earphones. "What the bloody hell is going on here, Beetle? We're just going around in circles! I'll bet you 50 quid some bloody WAAF can't read the tube right and we're chasing our own bloody echoes out here!"

After that there was a rather long silence from Control. Then they were ordered to "pancake" – i.e., return to base.

On the ground, Thompson was still fuming about the "silly girls" that had been brought in to read the radar, and insisted he wanted to have a word with the Controller. He stormed off, but Ginger was just glad to be back on the ground without encountering the enemy.

Unfortunately, F/Lt. Thompson was right, and they had been chasing their own echo, but Bridges had spent time in training staring into the RDF tubes and he knew just how difficult it could be to interpret the odd shapes that appeared. He thought it was marvellous that anyone could learn to make sense of the shadowy, oscillating blobs, and found nothing surprising about a WAAF getting confused. Of course, it was a waste of fuel, as F/Lt Thompson claimed – but a lot less of one than if they'd had no RDF and needed to patrol along fixed lines.

To the irate Flight Lieutenant, Bridges responded firmly, "I can understand your irritation, Tommy, but I'd appreciate it if you wouldn't barge in here and disrupt things. You look after your flight, and I'll look after the Operations Room."

"Well, one does wonder if you can *see* all that's going on here – under the circumstances!" Thompson retorted with a slight curl of his lip.

Bridges flinched, and felt the way his assistant, Warrant Officer Robinson, stiffened sharply. The girls below were stock still; none of them dared look up towards the gallery where he and Thompson stood, but he could tell by their unnatural poses that they had frozen, listening.

"If you have any doubts about my competence, then I would ask you to see the Station Commander, not come barging in here," Bridges answered evenly.

"You can be *very sure* that I will take this up with the Station Commander," Tommy answered in his precise, schooled voice, which had a way of reminding you that his father was an MP with all sorts of friends in the right places. Bridges felt as if he could see his entire career going down the drain before his eyes. Not fit to fly, incompetent controller....

Thompson turned with casual slowness and went down the steps of the platform and out the door. The heavy, reinforced door clanged shut behind him very loudly – almost as if he had given it an extra push. The girls glanced up towards the gallery. Robinson leaned over the rail and ordered, "Look sharp, girls. We've still got the rest of the squadron airborne!"

They came off watch at 4 pm and Bridges turned over the Operations Room to the other Controller, Gage. He made a brief reference to the incident, trying to play it down, but mentioning that F/Lt. Thompson had been upset.

"Silly sod," his fellow controller remarked. "A little flying around in circles never did anyone any harm." He was a reserve officer from the RFC who'd re-mustered; in the meantime, he'd been a very successful stockbroker with no shortage of self-confidence.

Bridges thanked him and left feeling a little better. The damned thing about "Tommy," he reflected, was that he made you *feel* inferior and insecure even when there was no reason for it! Damn him. If only one could be *sure* his influence wasn't as omnipotent as he made it seem....

Leading Aircraftman Appleby had been looking for an opportunity to talk to Sergeant Pilot Macleod ever since Ripley mentioned that he'd come up through the ranks. But that was easier said than done. Appleby wasn't assigned to MacLeod's aircraft and MacLeod was a dour Scotsman, who made no effort to be friendly. Rumour had it that he'd been transferred to the squadron after being thrown out of his old squadron for drunken brawling. Appleby could believe it. The Scotsman carried a flask of Scotch in his inside breast pocket – according to his fitter – and he was a stocky man with the build of a boxer.

Fortunately for Appleby, the Scotsman seemed to have taken a fancy to a certain WAAF working as a supply clerk. As a Sergeant Pilot, MacLeod didn't have any business hanging about the supplies office, but Appleby did. Appleby carefully saved up a couple of items he needed to draw from supply until he noticed MacLeod was loitering near the supplies office again, and then he went over, whistling casually.

At his entry, the WAAF drew back, blushing, and MacLeod gave him a look from narrowed eyes. But Appleby had his alibi and cheerfully stepped up to the counter to place his order, looking at a dirty and crumpled little list. He rattled off the items (with RAF inventory numbers) that he needed, and then with his back to MacLeod he winked at the WAAF. She looked more flustered than ever. Silly thing! She wasn't his type at all, too frail and windy.

When she hurried off to find all the things he had asked for, Appleby turned around, leaning on the counter, and remarked conversationally to MacLeod – as if he were just passing the time while waiting, "Excuse me, sir, but is it true that you started your career in the RAF as an apprentice?"

MacLeod started slightly, and then growled back, "That's right, laddie. I joined at age 14, trained three years at Halton and worked two years as a signaller before I was allowed to start flying training."

"Would you mind telling me, sir, how I might best go about following in your footsteps, so to speak?"

"You can't, laddie. Your feet are too small," MacLeod told him, with a rather contemptuous jerk of his head in the direction of the little rigger's feet. MacLeod was wearing flying boots, which made his feet all the bigger at the moment.

Appleby wasn't put off for a moment. You don't grow up in the East End of London if you are thin-skinned, and Appleby's Dad had abandoned his Mum when Appleby was 7. He was used to remarks of this kind, and grinned as he shot back, "You've got it backwards, sir. I can tread in your prints, but not you in mine."

MacLeod liked cheek. He laughed, but he insisted, "You don't have a chance, laddie. There are too many bleeding erks who dream of being fly-boys."

"But if I'm really outstanding, sir. I mean I am the best rigger on the squadron—"

MacLeod was shaking his head. "Then they can't let you re-muster, can they? Made yourself too valuable to them, see?"

"But how did you do it, sir?" Appleby persisted.

"Boxing. I was RAF boxing champion in '37. Beat the Army champion in a match, too. That made 'em like me."

Appleby didn't like that answer. He wasn't a bit athletic. There hadn't been time for sports in his childhood. Appleby would have dropped out of school if his Mum had let him, but she was a demon about making all three of her children attend and even do their homework. She'd wanted them to make something of themselves. But she needed the extra money they could earn doing jobs, too. Appleby had worked for a baker, doing deliveries between 5 and 7.30 before going to school. That meant getting up at 4.30, and he often fell asleep in class.

"But there must be some way—"

The WAAF was back, with the first of the items Appleby had ordered. She started putting them on the counter, counting and checking off items, making him sign forms. By the time he was finished, MacLeod was gone.

PART II

Warm-Up

Chapter 7

RAF Hawarden
Early July 1940

Priestman had never heard of RAF Hawarden and he didn't know what the hell an Operational Training Unit was either, but he didn't like the sound of either. From the moment his orders arrived and he'd discovered he was not going back to his squadron, he became increasingly unsettled, but he had no one to confide in. His mother was still annoyed with him for refusing to see Virginia Cox-Gordon, while Aunt Hattie was browned-off with him because those silly girls had rung. He'd only just managed to wheedle Emily Pryce's number out of Marjory – together with a lecture on what a "nice" girl she was and how he ought to "behave himself" with her. He hadn't dare ring her after that. Besides, what was there to confide?

After the promotion to Flight Lieutenant and with four credited kills in France, he had assumed (naïvely, it appeared) that he was "off probation" – that he had been forgiven his injudicious escapade in Singapore. But apparently not. Apparently, they had decided he wasn't suited to fighters after all and were going to re-train him. Train him for what, he wondered. What did they do with ex-torpedo-bomber, ex- aerobatics, ex-fighter pilots whom they didn't trust? Assign them to Transport Command or towing targets for the ack-ack boys perhaps? The thought made him hot under the collar with shame. And all because he hadn't been able to take the taunting of the Japanese in their new fighters any more.

Robin's squadron had been sent to locate a foundered freighter full of refugees whose distress signals had been intercepted by the navy. Flying in a cloth-and-wood Vildebeeste, an ancient bi-plane held together by string and glue, he had witnessed how a squadron of Japanese in monoplane Claudes had swept in and strafed the survivors. Then they had come and flown mocking circles and done aerobatic manoeuvres around the helpless RAF. Even now, even knowing what it had done to his career, he couldn't repress the feeling that he'd *had* to do it! He'd had to challenge them.

Priestman was so lost in his memories that he wasn't watching where he was driving. Abruptly he was stopped by a policeman and a barrier. Beyond, he caught a glimpse of what appeared to be a huge airfield behind a very large complex of buildings that looked for all the world like a factory. It was hard to be sure, but the aircraft lined up in front of it – rather too neatly for someone who had been to France and seen what the Luftwaffe did to aircraft lined up in rows – appeared to be brand new. At any rate, they had no camouflage paint and no squadron markings. But they *looked like* Wellingtons.

The policeman was at his window, asking him where he was going.

"RAF Hawarden."

"Oh, you've made a wrong turn, sir. This is the Vickers-Armstrong factory. The RAF station is on the other side of the airfield."

Robin dutifully followed the policeman's instructions, splashing through deep ruts and puddles brimming with rain. In fact, it was still spitting a bit, although the heavy cloud appeared to be tearing apart and lifting. The whole thing looked more than a little dubious to him. The only building on the far side of the field was a Victorian house with dormers and lacecurtains. As he pulled up in front of it, however, a Wing Commander leaned out one of the downstairs windows and waved to him, a pipe in his hand. What was the world coming to?

There was a hand-painted sign beside the front door identifying this as the O.T.U. headquarters, but Robin felt rather like an intruder just walking in – a feeling reinforced by lavender wall-paper and family photos still on the wall.

The Wing Commander with the pipe, however, put his head out of a room on the right and waved him in. As Robin walked through the door, he noted a sign that said: W/C Kennel, Station Commander. He entered what must have been a downstairs parlour, now somewhat awkwardly accommodating a large desk, and saluted smartly. "Flight Lieutenant Priestman, reporting as ordered, sir, although I honestly don't know what I'm doing here."

"Oh?" The Wing Commander, who had looked quite benevolent up to this point, raised his eyebrows and answered with a very cool, "And you think the Air Ministry owes you an explanation for every posting in your career?"

"No, sir, but unless I'm greatly mistaken, the German Wehrmacht is about to launch an invasion of this country, and His Majesty needs every fighter pilot he has in the air."

"That is one – if rather melodramatic – way of putting it," the Wing Commander agreed, now managing to look slightly amused.

"So, what am I doing in training, sir? Why aren't I back with my squadron? Even if they're now with 13 Group, sir, they're still on ops. What am I doing here?

"You're here for the reasons you just stated, Flight Lieutenant. We need every trained fighter pilot we have – and more. It takes only hours to assemble a fighter plane, but it takes years to make a fighter pilot. Fighter production is coping with the losses; pilot production is not. If you go back to your squadron, you are one pilot; your job here is to produce dozens. It's as simple as that." The Wing Commander rested his arms on the desk in front of him and fixed his gaze firmly on the baffled Flight Lieutenant in front of him.

Priestman couldn't grasp it. "Sir? Are you telling me, I'm here as an instructor?"

"Of course; what did you think?"

"I hadn't the foggiest, sir, but...." Priestman cut himself off. He still couldn't grasp it. He was 24 years old. When he'd been in flying school, all the instructors had been men with greying sideboards and receding hairlines, men who had fought in the last war, men with a lifetime of experience coddling and harassing aspiring young pilots. He couldn't picture himself as an instructor.

"But what?"

"Aren't I a bit young for an instructor, sir?"

Kennel smiled faintly, leaned back in his chair, and picked up his pipe. He carefully pressed the tobacco down into it and then lit up. Only after he'd taken a few puffs did he direct his attention to Priestman again.

"Have a seat." He indicated the worn leather chair in front of his desk with his pipe.

Priestman sat down and looked at the Wing Commander expectantly.

"What good is an instructor whose experience is from a different war, on different aeroplanes, against different – in terms of aircraft anyway – opponents? Our operational squadrons are too hard pressed at the moment to provide operational training, so this unit and others like it have been established to provide pilots with the final stage of training before going on ops. The young men who come here are on their last leg of training before being thrown at the Luftwaffe. Who better to get them ready for that, than someone who has faced all the Luftwaffe has to offer?"

Priestman thought of the four sprogs that had been sent to 579 Squadron in France and hadn't been of any use to them. He decided it made sense and concluded, "This is Hurricane training?"

"Spitfire."

"But I've never flown a Spitfire!" Priestman protested.

Kennel glanced out the window; the wind was tearing the clouds apart, and sunlight was stabbing down through the gloom in places. "Then I suggest you get a couple of hours in before your trainees arrive."

Priestman was twirling his cap in his hands. His hair was falling on his forehead. He gazed at Kennel, and then he got to his feet. "Right-O. Will do. Where do I find the CFI?"

"You're talking to him. We've only just been established. I'm Station Commander *and* Chief Flying Instructor all rolled into one at the moment. You'll meet the two other instructors, Flight Lieutenants Bradford and Dockery, at 14.00, when I want you to report back. We will go through everything together from the assignment of the trainees into flights, the schedule, lecture content, disciplinary procedures and all that. The idea is to give the trainees 30 hours or more on Spitfires over the next couple of weeks. But the fog and rain is definitely lifting, so go up for a quick spin first."

"Yes, sir."

Just as he was about to go out the door, Kennel stopped him. "Priestman."

"Sir?"

"Your record says you were an aerobatics pilot before the war."

"I did a show or two."

"Hendon, Zürich, Paris, Rome, and I can't remember what more...." Kennel corrected him. "I'll be interested in your assessment of the Spitfire." Kennel had expected a smile for that. All he got was a solemn nod and another "yes, sir." Robin was still in shock at the prospect of being an instructor – on an aircraft he'd never flown.

Out on the airfield, the crews were crawling out of the damp hangars to soak in a bit of sun. A couple of Spitfires had been rolled out and were being worked on. Robin changed into flying kit and then wandered over to the nearest Spitfire, trying not to limp.

"Hello."

The fitter and rigger stopped what they were doing and offered a cautious, "Hello, sir."

"Priestman. Just arrived. Some bloody fool in the Air Ministry sent me here as an instructor. Must be some kind of cock-up, because I've never flown a Spitfire in my life."

"No problem, sir. Climb in." At once he was given a hand. His bad ankle wasn't as flexible as it should be yet, and it was tender. But it felt good to be scrambling up a wing and into a cockpit again. The fitter helped him with his straps and started to go over the control panel with him. "Flown Hurricanes, I presume, sir?" Robin nodded. The mechanic concentrated on the differences, rattling off take-off, stalling and landing speeds and other vital information – like how fast the Spit overheated during take-off. Then as he finished, he flashed Priestman a grin and concluded with: "You'll like her, sir."

The starter battery was rolled up and plugged in, and the engine sprang almost instantly into life at the touch of the button. It roared, belched smoke and flame at him and then, as he throttled back, it fell into a steady purr. The whole cockpit vibrated with energy.

Priestman felt the familiar thrill, and his heart lifted. In fact, he felt like an 18-year old again, sitting alone in the cockpit of an aircraft for the first time. He smiled over at the fitter, whose name he didn't know yet, and gave him the thumbs up. He waved for the rigger to pull the chocks away. As he released the brakes, the Spitfire sprang away like a race-horse at the gate. Together they bounced their way across the grass, while he swung the nose left and right to see where he was going. He had the canopy open all the way and had not bothered with a helmet as he did not need R/T or Oxygen for a short familiarization flight. The wind ruffled his hair, but the sun poured down hot, making him sweat in his sheepskin flight jacket and boots. It was burning away the last traces of mist and drying the grass.

Priestman raced the engine a moment or two against the brakes, and the Spitfire shuddered and grumbled in protest at the restraint. The tail danced a little behind him and without someone to hold it down, he didn't dare really open up standing still. He eased off the brakes and throttled forward. The Spitfire galloped across the grass and almost at once the tail came up. Then the whole wonderful frame lifted itself into the air almost before Priestman could believe it.

There was no sensation on earth like this moment of take-off. Suddenly he was free of gravity and all the drudgery of earthbound life. Everything was left behind but the sheer joy of flying. Overhead was an expansive pale blue sky, below the rich, rain-soaked green of the Welsh Marches – and in between was unfettered freedom. Robin's soul extended to the tips of the curving wings and he did not have to think about flying – any more than did a bird.

Of course, the ground crews paused to watch "the sprog" take off. "M"'s crew, Fletcher and Smitty, watched particularly closely. They weren't surprised by how easily the Spitfire took to the air – she did that on her own, even for bad pilots. But they were surprised she didn't waggle as the pilot had to change hands to get the undercarriage up. Still, the big question was how this pilot would handle the landing. They expected him to do a couple of circuits and bumps, practicing landing and take-off. Instead Priestman started larking about.

At first, they were annoyed. "Show-off," muttered Fletcher irritably, as overhead the Spitfire swept into a series of climbing rolls, stall-turned, sped down in a dive, and levelled off, inverted, righted again. The next thing they knew, the Spitfire came chasing across the airfield so low that several men flung themselves on the ground, thinking it was crashing.

Soon the other ground crews came out of their hangars to watch. "Who the hell is that?" someone asked.

"New bloke. Priestman."

"The CO's going have his arse for that."

But then they noticed that Kennel was standing on the edge of the airfield watching closely – and without the slightest indication of indignation.

Priestman was climbing again, looping. The engine overhead sang a melody. After half-rolling off the top, he reefed the Spitfire into a turn, tighter, tighter, tighter – "like a cat chasing her tail," Smitty whispered, and his eyes shone with pride. Overhead the engine stalled, and there was a moment of shock among those on the ground until they saw how gracefully the Spitfire was being slipped sideways on the wind, the way it glided on the air, manoeuvring with majesty in slow motion now. They watched appreciatively as this pilot spiralled leisurely on the wind and touched down gently at the far end of the field – only to restart the engine and take off again without a pause.

"Bloody hell," Fletcher said, and they stood transfixed as they watched the Spitfire pirouette about the sky once more. Across the field at the Vickers factory, the workers too paused to watch the show. The cooks came out of the canteen and the lorry drivers left the motor pool. The clerks and secretaries left their desks. All around the field people stood about, squinting into the bright sun and shading their eyes as they followed the plane dance in the sky.

It climbed higher and higher and higher until it was almost invisible and then it started spiralling down at them, tighter and tighter. Spinning, it came closer and closer, looking for all the world as if it were out of control. At seemingly the very last minute, the Spitfire screamed overhead, lifting gently, swinging around with a raised wing. She did a slow "victory" roll before she was set neatly and gently onto the grass again. She bounced and hopped a bit on her way back to her crew. She trundled a bit awkwardly to face out again. The engine was cut and the propeller slowed. The hood was shoved back, and a transformed young man grinned out at the world.

Fletcher and Smitty were up opposite wings to help Priest- man out of the cockpit. "You were right," Robin declared, twisting to look from one to the other. "I like her."

Chapter 8

Stuka Gruppe 22, Northern France, Mid-July 1940

After only a month "on the job," Klaudia had a feel for the routine in the Communications Centre. As expected, the atmosphere was very professional. Not that there was no camaraderie or joking, but it was between colleagues rather than flirting, and even that was kept very much in bounds by the eagle eye of the Duty Officers. These were either Major d. R. Lendle or, on Klaudia's watch, a Civil Servant loaned from the Post Office with the temporary rank of *Hauptmann*, Herr Schneider. Schneider was a thin, slightly nervous man in his mid-forties who was very concerned about everything being "exactly correct."

Work was done in shifts (or watches, as they were called) of six hours at a stretch, twice a day. Klaudia's job was Radio Surveillance, listening for and jotting down in shorthand any messages other than those on their internal frequency, and passing these on to a de-coder. Rosa worked at the telegraph machine and Brigitte was a telephone operator. All the others working in the CC during Klaudia's watch were male NCOs.

Already most watches were routine. The night watches were usually so boring that it was hard to keep awake. The NCOs played cards much of the time, and Rosa sometimes joined them; Klaudia preferred to read novels and Brigitte knitted. But when the *Gruppe* was flying, the atmosphere was charged with suppressed excitement. Even if they could not see the aircraft, they were connected to them by radio, and hence were instantly aware of developments. It was, Klaudia felt, almost like being in the cockpit with the pilots.

Klaudia had witnessed two raids already. Each time, Klaudia found it hard to concentrate on her own work, particularly when she heard the controller call out the various stages of the battle. First came, "rendezvous with escort complete," then "target in sight," "attack commenced," "attack complete," "heading home."

But today Klaudia sensed that things were not going well. The *Gruppe* had taken off just half an hour earlier to bomb a British convoy. The fighters failed to show up at the rendezvous, and the bombers had continued without escort. Then instead of "target in sight," the controller called out: "English fighters over target!"

Everyone in the CC looked over at him. It was perfectly normal for the escort to encounter English fighters, but rarely more than six. For an escort of up to 40 Messerschmitts this hardly called for comment, but without an escort the situation was very different. The decision to press ahead without now seemed foolish.

When the controller called out "attack commenced" shortly afterwards, Klaudia sat biting her lip and hoping no radio contact would interrupt her in the next tense minutes. Rather than "attack complete," however, the controller exclaimed – more loudly than required – "More Indians!" And almost before they could all turn to stare, he shouted, "Helfritz is hit – down! Air-Sea Rescue!" The latter was directed at the Radio Operator responsible for liaison to the Luftwaffe's excellent Rescue Service. The next thing he said was: "Pfeiffer's on fire!"

A murmur swept the CC; one or two of the NCOs jumped up and started to move towards the controller, but Schneider ordered them to return to their places. Klaudia guiltily turned her attention back to her own duties, absently turning the dial in search of other frequencies that might be alive. But all her nerves strained to hear what the controller would report next.

"Attack suspended!"

That again brought a wave of astonished exclamations from the men in the CC. Klaudia gathered from their comments that no one could remember this ever happening before.

At last came the report, "Attack resumed," followed by "attack complete" and "heading home" in short succession. But the atmosphere in the CC remained charged – so charged, in fact, that at the first sound of returning aircraft, the men jumped up and rushed to the windows – and nothing Schneider could shout at them could stop them. Schneider gave up trying and went over to the window himself. Klaudia followed him.

They saw the powerful planes curving around to land into the wind, and with a collective in-take of breath registered that the *Stabskette*, Paschinger's own leading vic of three aircraft, was missing a plane as it swept in to land. In #1 *Staffel* another plane was missing, and another was belching black smoke as it came in very clumsily. At once, sirens started to wail as the fire engines and ambulances rushed out to meet the wounded aircraft.

"Back to your posts!" Schneider commanded angrily, but his voice broke from excitement. He was also a fraction too late. Already Klaudia and the others had seen an ambulance rush up beside Paschinger's Stuka. Klaudia caught a glimpse of a limp body being handed down. Then Schneider chased them all back to their posts.

But the losses hung over them like a gloomy cloud all day. The three girls of the relieving watch told Rosa, Klaudia and Brigitte in agitated tones how they had seen the wounded gunners taken out of the planes. Although rapidly whisked away in ambulances, one of the men had been whimpering and moaning from pain. They had seen the ground crews using hoses to clean away the blood in the cockpits. The girls were badly shaken.

Klaudia, Rosa and Brigitte started towards the NCOs' Mess for their dinner in a sober mood. Lost in their own thoughts, none of them spoke. Axel Voigt emerged out of the darkness by the hangars and fell in beside Rosa, offering her a cigarette that she gratefully accepted.

"Kites are a bloody shambles," he announced without preamble. "Two complete write-offs, and three should take days to repair. Crews will be working all night because you- know-who wants every damned kite fully operational first thing in the morning. We'll never make it. You wouldn't be an angel and bring me and the boys something from the Mess, would you?"

"Not likely," Rosa answered with her usual cheek, before adding with a smile, "But miracles do happen now and again. Coffee and cake for four?"

"Four?"

"I'm not going to drag it over and—"

"Look out! Arschinger!"

Klaudia had not heard this rude corruption of the CO's name before and didn't realise what Voigt meant until she saw Jako emerge from the nearest hangar. He stopped, and then, having trouble making out features in the fast-falling dusk, asked, *Fräulein* von Richthofen?"

"*Jawohl*, Herr Major."

"Glad I ran into you." He had her by the arm. "Come back to the Mess with me."

"I'm just coming off duty, Herr Major—"

"So what? I'll buy you something at the Officers' Mess." His grip on her arm was uncompromising, and Klaudia was not inclined to resist anyway. Even if he'd taken no notice of her since that enchanted evening of her arrival, she still found him irresistibly attractive.

Jako took long, rapid strides, and Klaudia had to run to keep up. She was a little out of breath when they reached the chateau. Jako didn't notice. He led her straight to the salon with massive sixteeth-century tapestries, and directed her to a large, winged chair whose seat was so worn she fell into it more than sat on it. The *Gruppenkommandeur's* appearance instantly conjured forth an orderly. Jako rattled off orders for a meal and wine.

The orderly withdrew, and Jako lit a cigarette and stared into the empty fireplace as if Klaudia wasn't even there. She was beginning to feel very awkward. Then he started talking.

"I sank three British ships, including a destroyer, during the evacuation of Dunkirk.Three! That's why they gave me this!" He flicked at his Knights Cross. "And not once did I lose a pilot! Not one! Two planes were shot down, but the crews bailed out safely. We lost one plane and crew at Sedan to ground fire. And one plane crashed from technical difficulties in Poland." He turned and looked straight at Klaudia, telling her proudly, "I made sure *that* ground crew will never go near an aircraft again – unless it crashes on top of them, that is. All were transferred to the infantry!"

The Mess orderly arrived with a tray, which he set before Klaudia. He removed the cover over the plate to reveal a steaming dinner, re-warmed from the officers' evening meal. There was steak in an onion and mushroom sauce, peas and new potatoes with parsley. It looked delicious, and Klaudia realised how very hungry she was.

"*Guten Appetite,*" Jako wished her absently, and then checked the wine offered him, before nodding and telling the orderly to pour for two.

When the orderly was gone again, he stood with his left elbow resting on the stone mantel while holding the wineglass in his other hand and told Klaudia as she ate, "Helfritz and I have been flying together for two and a half years. We've been in Poland, Holland, and France together. *Meine Güte*, we were both in Spain – though not in the same *Staffel* then. Gone. He didn't have a chance. They pounced just as we came out of the dive. Weiss – that's my gunner – shouted and at the same moment I felt the Stuka shudder. I glanced back and saw Hel- fritz's kite disintegrate as it cart-wheeled into the ocean. There was a heavy swell running. One wing went in and broke off at once, and then the tail broke off. I didn't have a chance to see any more. There was a Spitfire on my tail blazing at me from all eight guns. Weiss was firing back furiously, but then they got him. My only hope was turning – a Stuka can out-turn anything – but that was what killed Helfritz – trying to turn too low. He must have stalled. I don't know." He shook his head, as if he still couldn't grasp what had happened. It was as if he had believed he was indestructible. At last he resumed. "I saw Pfeiffer smash into the water already ablaze, and you could see him and his gunner still in their seats – burning. You could *see* them."

Klaudia could only stare at him. Her appetite was gone. "I'm so sorry," she whispered at last.

Jako's glass was empty. He poured for himself and said fiercely, "And not a God-damned Messerschmitt anywhere in the whole God-damned sky! They'd all slept late and missed the rendezvous! If Rosskamp thinks his boys can get away with leaving us in the lurch like that, he'll soon be taught a lesson! Fatty gave me this," again he touched his Knights Cross, "personally. He said I could call him any time I liked. He said I could come straight to him with any request. So I did." He looked hard at Klaudia. "I asked him to come out here."

"You talked to the Herr *Feldmarshall*?" Klaudia was awed. Jako shook his head and frowned irritably. "He was in a meeting with his *Luftflotten* Commanders, but I left a message with his *Ordonnanzoffizier*. He promised to get back to me. I told him the crews wanted to see Fatty personally. Let him think we're just a bunch of hero-worshipping schoolboys. Once he's here, he's going to hear what happened." Klaudia was impressed. She was excited by the idea of actually seeing Feldmarschall Goering – even if only from a distance. Goering was not only the C-in-C of the entire Luftwaffe, he was an intimate of Hitler. It was even more exciting to think that the man opposite her was on such familiar terms with him, that he could ask the C-in-C to come and "visit" him. He was only a major, after all.

Jako was gazing at her from the other side of the room, and for the first time this evening he seemed to see her. A smile twitched across his face. "When was the last time anyone mentioned to you, *gnädiges Fräulein*, that you are a very attractive young woman?"

Klaudia felt as if her breath had been knocked clear out of her. She couldn't remember anyone ever saying that to her. "I – I – can't remember."

Jako smiled again and cocked his head. "You are, you know? 'though you don't make nearly as much of yourself as you should."

As if Jako had just noticed that Klaudia's glass was empty, he took the bottle from the mantel and came towards her. He bent over as if to pour and then turned and pressed his lips to hers.

She hadn't been expecting it. She'd never been kissed by anyone before. And for almost four weeks Jako himself had ignored her almost entirely – nothing more than the occasional stiff nod. But now he had the tray out of the way and onto a side table. He pressed her against the back of the chair and set his own wineglass aside. Then he slipped his hands into her hair, pulling it down from its neat pins. At last he pulled back and considered her. "You have such beautiful blonde hair. You are much prettier with it down," he told her smiling.

Klaudia was completely confused. She had never been looked at by a man like this before – certainly not by a man like this. She honestly didn't know what to do.

Jako read her confusion easily and he laughed. Smiling, he poured for both of them and put Klaudia's glass right into her hand. His face was close to hers, so close she could smell the wine on his breath, and he spoke very low and caressingly. "You seem surprised, *gnädiges Fräulein*; didn't any of your noble friends ever pay court to you?"

She shook her head and tried to explain. "We, my family, have terrible debts, you see, the whole estate is mortgaged and—"

Jako cut her off with a quick little kiss, then drew back smiling deeply at her, his eyes just inches away. "What do I care about your father's debts, *liebes Fräulein*? You are what interests me. Do you know how often I have thought about you these past weeks? I wanted to see you, but I let duty get in the way. But after what happened today – I need you. Need a sympathetic ear, and the comfort that can only come from a woman's smile – a woman's touch." He reached out and stroked the side of her face.

It was wonderful. Klaudia felt herself in a fairy tale. Here she was in a romantic French Chateau with Gobelins and wine – and the most thrilling man she had ever met in her life was telling her he *needed* her. She lifted her chin just a fraction, and Jako accepted the invitation willingly, kissing her again, more passionately this time. Without even realising what she was doing, Klaudia lifted her arms and slipped them around Jako's neck. Part of her felt that she was alive for the very first time in her whole life.

By the time she crept back up to her room under the eaves, Klaudia was already having her first doubts. It had all happened so fast. She had wanted to kiss and be kissed. She had even welcomed the invitation to go up to his room, so they could be somewhere where no one could just walk in on them. She had wanted to lie with him in the moonlight and listen to his compliments and feel his caresses forever. But at some point she realised that he wanted *more*, and then it was hard to say "no." How could she explain that she didn't want *that* just yet? She had tried, but he had silenced her with kisses, and his hands had done things to her body that she really didn't understand. It had hurt a bit too, but then again, his very ardour was a compliment – wasn't it?

She was reminded of novels she'd read in which the hero needed his sweetheart so desperately that he *couldn't* wait. In the novels, couples made love in all sorts of unlikely places. But what could be more romantic than under the canopy of an eighteenth-century bed? Or more exciting than being desired – desperately – by a man with a Knight's Cross? It had been intoxicating – and, of course, they had drunk at least two bottles of wine between them by then. Or rather, she had drunk most of it....

Oh, dear. She was slightly dizzy and queasy, and really didn't feel all that well. She accidentally knocked something off the dresser as she tried to wriggle out of her tunic.

Rosa growled something from her bed.

"I'm sorry!" Klaudia whispered, adding apologetically "The *Herr Gruppenkommandeur* asked me to have dinner with him and—"

Rosa sat up and turned the light on. She took one look at Klaudia and knew exactly what had happened. She wasn't really surprised – except that Klaudia had made such a point about still being a virgin and being unable to imagine doing "it" before she married and all that. But Rosa was fairly cynical by now, and so she just remarked, "So that's what's been keeping you up until the middle of the night! I should have known." She flopped back down on her bed and turned on her side, the bed making loud squeaking noises as she squirmed once or twice to make herself more comfortable.

"It's not what you think—" Klaudia protested. "We had a glass of wine and—"

Rosa sat up again. "So, where's your tie? And what happened to your stockings? Look, I don't care if you sleep with Arschinger or not, but don't try to make a fool out of *me*! I wasn't born yesterday!" And with that she flopped down again, turned on her side and pulled the covers up over her head.

Klaudia hastened to undress, worrying now about how to get her tie back so she wouldn't be out of uniform tomorrow. Somehow Rosa's reaction made it all seem so *common* – as if it hadn't been wildly romantic and exciting after all.

JG23, Crépon Mid-July 1940

The aircrews were already in flying gear, their heavy boots and jackets unbuckled because of the heat here on the ground. Most of them carried their life jackets and parachutes, but Ernst had pulled his Mae West on already. That made it uncomfortable to lean back on the little wooden chair in the briefing room, and he wriggled uncomfortably, making the chair creak. The Intelligence Officer was pointing at a large wall map showing the Channel and the coast on both sides. RAF and Luftwaffe bases were marked with little aircraft symbols and ports with anchors. With a wooden pointer, the Intelligence Officer indicated the last known position of an English convoy. "StG 22 has been ordered to intercept it here," again he pointed, this time to the tip of the Isle of Wight. The Luftwaffe liked to intercept the ships while they were in relatively confined waters, with little room for manoeuvre and evasive action.

"II *Gruppe* of JG 23 will provide escort in echelon. 4 *Staffel* high, 5 *Staffel* mid, 6 *Staffel* low – directly above the Stukas."

This was to be their third mission giving fighter cover to bombers attacking targets in the Channel, and Ernst thought he wouldn't have been so nervous if the *Geschwaderkommandeur*, *Oberst* Rosskamp, hadn't flown down specially with his Staff-*Schwarm* to lead this mission. He now stepped into the centre of the stage. He had been standing to one side with his arms crossed, listening, up to now.

He faced his pilots. "I know it wasn't our fault about the missed rendezvous, but the Stukas took a battering last time. Paschinger gave me a piece of his mind and went whining to Fatty, too. Furthermore, I *know* just how hard it is to protect the Stukas when they're flying at stalling speed. I also know the English try to avoid us and go straight for the bombers, but we *have* to protect the Stukas. That's what we're paid for. When we reach the target and the Stukas start their bombing dive, I want the lowest Staffel to circle around the target at 1,000 metres. The mid-Staffel circles in the opposite direction at 2,000 metres. I'll be up with the high Staffel, ready to pounce on any English fighters. Clear?" He paused, but no one said anything -although from the expressions of the men staring back at him, none of them were particularly enthusiastic about the task they had just been assigned.

Next the *Gruppenkommandeur*, Major Frischmuth, stepped up beside his CO and took a deep breath. His tone was brusquer. He ordered rather than informed: "We stick with the bombers regardless of what happens. I don't want to see – or hear about – any one of you chasing off after English fighters! If you do, you'll be grounded! You are to stick to the bombers, and you are to see that they get in *and out* safely! Any questions?"

Feldburg raised his hand instantly. Frischmuth grimaced and nodded to him warily. Questions from Feldburg were almost always ticklish.

"Herr Major, how can we win air superiority over England by attacking merchant ships?"

Ernst caught his breath at the impudence, and someone else groaned. Neufeldt even muttered sharply something like "You ought to have more respect for the leadership (*Führung*)" – or had he said "for the *Führer*?" Ernst twisted in his chair to try to see Neufeld, but that made the chair creak, and Major Frischmuth scowled at him before addressing Feldburg with a sour expression. "You have a brother in the General Staff, don't you?"

"*Jawohl*, Herr Major."

"Well, ask him!" Frischmuth snapped and then turned away with a sharp, "To your aircraft and prepare take-off." Further questions were clearly not wanted.

With a scraping of chairs and boots and a murmur of voices, the pilots got to their feet and crowded out of the room. Ernst automatically fell in beside Christian, who was complaining to Dieter Möller. "That's just the point! Philipp says that the only way to prepare for an invasion is to destroy – or at least badly maul – both the Royal Air Force and the Royal

Navy in advance. He says we ought to be focusing on those two targets and nothing else. He says we're wasting time, aircrews and aircraft on irrelevant targets like merchant shipping and docks."

Dieter shrugged, "Philipp usually knows what he's talking about, but orders are orders."

"Idiotic!" Christian countered.

They were out into the brilliant sunlight of the field, and from seemingly all points of the compass aircraft engines coughed and grumbled. Dieter waved good-bye and headed for his own aircraft, while Christian and Ernst continued together to their "Emils," which were parked side-by-side. Ernst worried that Christian made himself sound disrespectful and even disloyal by his remarks. He wished Christian wouldn't be so critical – at least not in public – but he didn't know how to tell him.

They reached Christian's Messerschmitt first. The ground crew had already started it, and it vibrated and purred as it waited for its pilot. Ernst wished Christian luck.

Christian clapped him on the shoulder. "Keep my tail clear, and maybe I'll get something this time."

Despite having flown throughout the French campaign and encountered the English twice in the last week, Christian still had no confirmed kills, and it bothered him. He was very keen to get one now that the RAF had started to come up to fight. Ernst, frankly, was happy if he kept station and didn't get shot down. If something hostile happened to cross his bows, he hoped he'd remember to squirt his guns at it, but that was the extent of his ambition for the moment. Christian, in contrast, was a hunter.

Ernst scrambled up into the waiting cockpit of his own aircraft and let the fitter strap him in. He carefully connected his oxygen and R/T. He rechecked his controls, ignoring the sound of other aircraft already taking to the air. He'd learned the hard way not to let anything rush him at this critical moment, and he mentally blocked out all distractions until the preflight check was complete. At last he was ready and looked over to give Christian the thumbs up. He took a last deep breath of clean air, and then closed his canopy as Christian's Emil started to trundle away. Yes, he was nervous, he admitted, but he also told himself he was getting more confident with each sortie. The routine was starting to tell.

The minute the bouncing and vibration of the take-off ceased, Ernst allowed himself a moment just to enjoy flying. He looked ahead to the nearly 40 other aircraft flying in loose and staggered formation ahead of him, and he thought they looked very impressive. He didn't understand where the English found the courage to attack them. The English were always out-numbered, and Ernst wouldn't have wanted to be in their shoes. He supposed if he were, he would attack just as they did, because he'd be ashamed not to. But he admired them, all the same.

Because of the slow speed of the Stukas (their maximum speed of 230 mph was just 2/3s of the Me109's cruising speed), it was almost impossible to fly with them; the idea was, therefore, to meet up with them almost over the target. The problem with that, of course, was timing. Last time, they had been over the target too soon, and had run out of fuel before the Stukas (or the RAF) showed up. This time, although they had no direct communication with the Stukas, it had been agreed that both formations would call in their position to their respective controllers, who then passed it on to their counterparts, who then relayed it to their respective units.

Ernst heard Rosskamp calling control several times, and then they were ordered to change course a bit and increase speed. A few minutes later they were told to slow down again. Then speed up. Ernst took deep gulps of oxygen and told himself to stay calm.

They left the French coast behind, and in the distance was the white line marking the English coast. A cackle on the R/T drew attention to the Stukas off to their right, and the *Gruppe* curved around onto a new course.

"*Scheisse!*" Someone called out imprecisely but with feeling.

Ernst sympathised as the next report came in. "Indians north-by-northeast at 2,000 metres, coming up!!"

"6 Staffel! Intercept! Go!"

The lowest Staffel visibly accelerated away below Ernst. The Stukas, meanwhile, were lining up for their attack, and Ernst hadn't even found the convoy yet. He searched the sparkling water of the channel.

"5 Staffel circle the Stukas clockwise!"

"*Scheisse!*"

Ernst sympathised with the comment again – whoever had made it. The order to circle the Stukas meant going down nearly to 1000 metres and probably getting bounced by the English. At that altitude even the Hurricane was a match for the 109. But the Staffel dutifully dipped their wings and peeled off in pairs. Ernst watched Christian closely and slid down after him.

At last he found the convoy – and saw the great columns of water bursting into the air like fountains as the lead Stuka straddled but failed to strike any of the ships. The ships started zig-zaging about irregularly to evade the attackers. Their escorts were sending little puffs of smoke into the air. It looked quite harmless from up here, but Ernst knew from unpleasant experience that the closer one got to it, the more terrifying it would become. That was the other disadvantage to "circling the Stukas" – you put yourself in range of the anti-aircraft fire, and the Emil wasn't built for it.

Obediently they started to fly around in a great, sweeping circle while the Stukas continued to dive at the convoy.

"Spitfires"

"*Scheisse!*"

Ernst looked up sharply, twisting his neck around, but he never saw it. The sound of machine guns was so close it was as if they were inside the cockpit. His Emil shuddered and the right-hand side of the canopy turned white from shattered glass. Then a shadow blocked off the sun, and Ernst screamed: "Christian!!! Behind you!"

Only a second later did he remember to press his trigger. No good, the safety was still on. What an idiot! Ernst pulled the throttle back to full power and chased after the English fighter, while Christian broke right, yanked up into a sharp climb and then fell on his back. The Englishman shot past him, tracer going into blue nothingness. Ernst kicked at his rudder and tore at the stick to try to stay with Christian, cursing himself the whole time.

"Hans! Get out! Now!"

Ernst twisted around, trying to see what was happening, but the whole right-hand side of his canopy was opaque from shattered glass. He felt blind and vulnerable. It made him nervous to see all those bullet marks just inches from his face.

An explosion rocked his Emil, and he whipped his head around in time to see a huge black cloud of smoke spitting pieces of aircraft. The nationality and make of the plane were no longer identifiable, but the certainty of the death made Ernst's stomach heave once. He tasted vomit in his mouth and swallowed it down. Where the hell was Christian? He twisted about in the cockpit and dropped his left wing to see through the ceiling of the canopy to his right.

"Stay with the Stukas! Circle the Stukas!" The order came from Rosskamp who, presumably, was flying well above the fight and looking down on it.

Ernst swallowed again and tried to locate the Stukas. He couldn't, but he rapidly located the convoy by the smoke that was billowing up from it. The Stukas had made a least one hit. What he didn't understand was what the convoy was doing way over to the left. But then he found Christian, who was already heading back towards the fight, and a moment later nearly collided with a Stuka that came lumbering towards them, belching smoke and dragging a broken wing. They skipped up over it and proceeded towards the convoy. No other aircraft around. Where had they all gone?

Christian gained altitude, while over the R/T came loud static interrupted by snatches of communication: "stch-stch-stch-down—stch-

stch-out!—stch-stch-stch—steer 210—stch- stch-sch-HEEELP!!"

Ernst's hair stood on end. The scream was full of terror and pain. And it went on and on. He tried to search the sky again, but he saw nothing but Christian. Christian's head twisted about as he searched overhead, and then he dipped first one wing and then the other. Far away, a vertical black streak lengthened and lengthened like a black crayon on a pale-blue board until it ended in the drink. The scream was silenced. The smudge left behind in the air started to smear.

"Let's go home," Christian suggested curtly, and banked about for a course towards France.

Ernst followed him silently.

When they put down, the bulk of the *Gruppe* was already there. Most of the aircraft were being serviced around the periphery of the field.

As soon as the Emil trundled to a stop, Ernst unclipped and thrust up to open the canopy and gulp real air. He made no effort to climb down. The aircraft's mechanic scrambled up on the wing root. "Are you all right, Herr *Leutnant*?"

Ernst nodded and started to release his straps automatically. He was afraid to open his mouth.

"What happened?" His mechanic asked him.

Ernst shook his head.

"Becker is over-due."

Ernst nodded, remembering the shout to Hans to jump. But there could be any number of pilots named Hans in the other *Staffels*, too.

At last he pushed himself up out of the cockpit and slid down the wing. His legs almost collapsed as he hit the ground. Christian came around the aircraft. "Are you all right?"

Ernst nodded again.

"Your Emil looks a trifle the worse for wear." Christian had come from the right and had had a good view of the damage done.

Ernst nodded, and very gradually his heart started slowing down.

Chapter 9

RAF Tangmere
Mid-July

For the third time in as many flights, Ginger's aircraft developed trouble. To make things worse, they were responding to a scramble, not just on a patrol. "Bandits" were approaching the coast, and all the duty pilots had rushed out to their aircraft. It had happened so fast that Ginger almost didn't have time to get nervous. Then his engine started to pack up. He tried everything he'd been taught, but it just kept spluttering, almost dying. It roared back to life if he gave it more oil, then faded again. When they made a sharp turn in response to a new vector, it went out on him altogether.

Ginger managed to get it re-started, but only after hectic seconds of trying. By then he'd been left rather far behind, drifting away from the rest of them, and the CO was furiously calling for him to catch up. When Ginger throttled forward, the engine gave off a bang and started making a horrible racket. Really frightened now, Ginger had no choice but to report that he had engine trouble and he was ordered back to base.

As he nursed the Hurricane back to Tangmere, he noticed that if he kept the revs down below a certain point, the noise was less threatening, but at that level he had barely enough power to keep the Hurricane in the air. As he went into the circuit for landing, there seemed to be an inordinate number of people standing about watching him. It was worse than being on a check flight. He did his best to make a good landing for such an audience, but at the critical moment the engine cut out on him again. He fell out of the air and bounced badly. Ginger cringed with embarrassment.

He rolled to a stop and tried to re-start the engine, but now nothing seemed to work at all. Suddenly Flight Sergeant Rowe, the Chiefy, was on his wing telling him off in an exasperated tone that he was "never going to get it re-started that way" and "asking" him to get out of the cockpit so someone else could move it off the landing strip.

Humiliated, Ginger climbed down from the Hurricane, and Rowe himself slipped into the cockpit. An instant later the Hurricane roared back into life, puffing smoke to be sure and making a horrible racket again, but running well enough to trundle off towards a hangar. Ginger was left standing in the middle of the field, holding his helmet and his parachute and feeling foolish.

After a moment, he decided he ought to follow his aircraft on foot and find out what was wrong with it – or at least report what had happened during the flight. By the time he reached it, it stood on a hangar apron with Rowe still at the controls, revving the engine while the ground crew removed the cowling and took a look at it. Ginger waited off to one side until Rowe had switched off and climbed down. The aircraft's fitter and rigger were already starting to take things apart.

Rowe caught sight of Ginger and came over to him looking very sour. "Well, sir? What happened?"

Ginger tried to describe the problem, but Rowe seemed very displeased with what he had to say. What speed and altitude had he been at when the problem developed? Hadn't he noticed the oil pressure? What had the oil temperature been? Why hadn't he tried this, that or the other? Had they been climbing when the engine cut out entirely? After a few minutes of cross-examination, Ginger had the impression that there had never been anything wrong with the engine at all – only with the pilot.

Ginger was relieved when a telephone call drew Rowe away. While the "Chiefy" went to his office in the small shed that ran along the length of the hangar to take the call, Ginger stood gazing at his Hurricane in despair. He just wasn't cutting it. He was never going to be a fighter pilot – and he hadn't faced the enemy yet!

"Tea, sir?" It was the aircraft's regular fitter. Ginger had been so lost in thought, he hadn't noticed the LAC coming up beside him. The young man was offering him a mug brimming with steaming tea. "It's got two sugars in it, if that's all right with you, sir?"

"Thank you," Ginger took the tea gratefully.

"You mustn't let the Chiefy get to you, sir." Sanders was roughly Ginger's own age, but he had been a Halton apprentice and so had six years in the Service behind him already. "He won't admit that there's anything wrong with any of his chicks." He nodded towards the aircraft generally. "But, just between you and me, sir, 'Q' hasn't been the same since P/O Davis ground-looped it up in Scotland last month."

Ginger clung to his tea mug and gazed at Sanders with more gratitude than he could put into words.

"Just leave it to us, sir. We'll either find the problem or write it down for a factory refit."

"Thank you," Ginger managed at last. Sanders smiled. "Just doing our job, sir."

Ginger would have liked to say more but at that moment Rowe emerged from his office calling out. "Look sharp! The Station

Commander's on his way over with visitors!"

Sanders dashed back towards the aircraft, and Ginger decided to make himself scarce.

RAF Tangmere

606 squadron had encountered German fighters for the first time since Dunkirk, and there'd been quite a fight from the sound of things. Both Jones and Thompson were claiming "probables," while Ringwood insisted he'd actually seen his German go into the drink. They'd had quite a bash to celebrate it, too – the commissioned officers at least. For the ground crews, however, it meant overtime.

There wasn't one crate that didn't need work of some kind. If there weren't holes and tears from enemy bullets, there were jammed guns, overheating engines, faulty oxygen feeds and bum R/T sets. Everyone seemed to have one complaint or another, particularly P/O Debsen, who had furiously rattled off a whole list of ills – enough to keep his crew working all night, although the kite looked untouched.

Jones' own aircraft had the greatest damage, however. There were some cannon holes in the canvas of the fuselage, and a piece missing from the rudder. But the biggest problem was that the canopy runner had been damaged by something blown back at the squadron leader when he shot pieces off an enemy aircraft. The ground crew had only been able to open the canopy by using a crowbar – and that, of course, had done more damage to the runner and canopy frame. Clearly the aircraft was unserviceable until the entire runner and canopy had been replaced, but Jones insisted he did not want to take another aircraft. He wanted *his* aircraft serviceable by 5 am the next morning.

Appleby took one look at the job and knew it couldn't be done. Not alone. He reported to Flight Sergeant Rowe, and Rowe came to take a look for himself. He made a face, but he kept his opinion to himself and shouted for Tufnel.

Tufnel worked with Sanders on "Q," one of the reserve aircraft usually assigned to the sprogs. It was still u/s after the engine packed in yesterday, and so had not been flown and was not in need of repair. Together Appleby and Tufnel set to work removing "J's" entire canopy and the fittings for it, and then installing a new one.

They took a break for tea but returned to finish the job by artificial light in the blacked-out hangar. The sound of their tools echoed in the otherwise empty hangar, and Appleby was beginning to get muscle cramps from trying to hold himself in place on a ladder and still get enough force behind his tools as he worked. Tufnel was looking tired, and when he dropped a spanner for the second time and had to climb down, Appleby said in sympathy, "Ain't no bleeding reason why the CO couldn't take up one of the new kites!" He nodded towards two new aircraft that had been delivered by the ATA during the afternoon.

Tufnel glanced over at Appleby and shook his head. "That may be, but it ain't our job to question it. If the CO wants to fly 'J' then we got to stay up all night, if that's what it takes."

"Why?" Appleby wanted to know.

"Because he's got a right to fly the aircraft he prefers. He's the one facing the bloody Hun!"

It had started to rain, and the sound on the broad roof of the hangar made conversation difficult, so they fell silent for a bit. With the rain came a noticeable drop in temperature, too. Now, in addition to the discomfort of working in awkward positions on ladders by poor lighting, came the added unpleasantness of damp cold.

A door opened somewhere, sending a gust of wind through the hangar, that rattled anything loose and made both riggers look over sharply. It was Sanders – and he was carrying a thermos and several mugs. Tufnel started backwards down his ladder at once, and Appleby followed a little hesitantly. Sanders put the things down on one of the work-tables on the side of the hangar, and smiled over at Appleby. "Thought you could do with something warm."

Although Appleby knew that Sanders was doing this for Tufnel more than himself, he still appreciated it, and said so. The three men sat together on the work benches and sipped the hot, sweet cocoa.

Tufnel asked his fitter, "Did you get a chance to see the Adj?" At once Sanders' face fell. He nodded. "Same answer. The CO's been too busy to look at it."

"But he's had the request for a week!" Tufnel protested.

Sanders, noticing Appleby's blank look, explained. "I was planning to get spliced to m'popsie on July 1, but then we got our orders here and I had to call it off. I've been trying to get three days leave ever since. It took me a month to talk Chiefy into forwarding it and now the CO won't act on it!"

"Jones won't give you three bleeding days leave to get hitched?" Appleby asked incredulous.

Sanders shrugged. "He hasn't said 'no.' It's just he's too busy to sign off on it. According to the Adj, even some of the officers haven't got the leave that's coming to them."

Appleby frowned sceptically. Jones had time to go to the pub this evening, after all. It didn't seem fair. Tufnel was frowning too, but Sanders just looked sad. And then Flight Sergeant Rowe found them, gave them a bollocking, chasing the riggers back to work and ordering Sanders not to "distract them."

Stuka Gruppe 22

Goering came and went in a whirlwind. He flew in with what seemed like a huge entourage. He waddled (that was really the only word for it) over to Jako, who stood in front of his pilots saluting. He patted him on the shoulder, apparently cracked a joke, and everyone within hearing laughed with him. Klaudia, Rosa and Brigitte weren't close enough to hear, but they watched it all from the CC along with the NCOs on duty.

Was it less than a fortnight since Klaudia had been excited by the thought of seeing Goering personally? Was it less than a fortnight since she had been thrilled to think she knew a man who could ask favours of a man so powerful and favoured that the Reichstag had created a new rank just for him, "*Reichsmarschall*"? It seemed a lifetime ago. The intervening fortnight had been such a roller-coaster of alternating ecstasy and despair. The expected roses and proposal had not come, but then Jako was the *Gruppenkommandeur* of a crack Luftwaffe unit in the midst of war. Klaudia kept telling herself she should not expect too much. He *had* sent for her a couple of times after duty, and his ardour and compliments reassured her again of her place in his heart. And yet...

Now, as she watched Jako grinning and nodding beside the *Reichsmarschall*, she felt intense – almost unbearable – pride. That was *her* man that the *Reichsmarschall* was jesting with like an old friend! Nor had Jako ever looked more splendid than now in his tailored uniform, grey gloves and the leather riding boots that gleamed in the sun.

"He's coming this way!" someone called out.

Instantly the personnel of the CC bolted back to their respective places. By the time the *Reichsmarshall* reached the door, they were all intent upon their respective tasks. A loud "*Achtung!*" preceded the C-in-C into the room. Everyone sprang to attention.

Staff officers poured in, and then came Goering himself with

Paschinger still beside him. He greeted the staff of the CC by touching his glittering marshal's baton to the peak of his cap. He was smiling and nodding, and then he caught sight of the *Helferinnen*. "Ah, so you have some of our charming, brave *Helferinnen* here! How are they working out?"

"*Jawohl, Herr Reichsmarschall*. Very well, so far. May I introduce the *Herr Reichsmarschall*?" Jako led Goering directly to Klaudia.

There she stood, rigidly at attention, hardly daring to breathe. What could be a better sign of Jako's good intentions than the fact that he brought the *Reichsmarshall himself* over to introduce him to her? She sucked in her stomach and kept her chin up; she wanted to do Jako proud. "This here is Klaudia *von Richthofen*."

"Ah ha!" Goering was delighted. "I didn't realise Wolfram had a niece! How do you like it here, *Fräulein*? Are my young eagles treating you properly?"

Klaudia couldn't help smiling. "*Jawohl, Herr Reichsmarschall*."

"Good, good. Glad to hear it." Already Goering was moving on. Turning away from Klaudia and addressing Jako, he remarked, "Seeing these lovely girls reminds me of your own charming wife, Jako. How is she doing these days?"

"In her seventh month now, *Herr Reichsmarshall*," Jako answered happily, his back to Klaudia as if she didn't exist.

"Ha!" Goering laughed approvingly. "A Christmas leave baby."

"*Jawohl, Herr Reichsmarshall*," Jako agreed, "and I hope we will have tamed the English lion in time for me to be with her at the birth."

"Certainly, certainly," Goering agreed as they moved away. Klaudia wanted to scream – or just fade away into nothingness. He was married. He had been married the whole time. Not once, not even for a moment, had his intentions been honourable. He had used her. That was all. Used her like a common whore! Rosa had been right about him the whole time. She couldn't cope with the implications. She was ruined! Absolutely ruined. She could never go home and face her parents.

A sharp order from Schneider brought her back to the present. Jako and Goering were gone. She had work to do. Work. That was all that was left to her now, her identity as a *Luftwaffehelferin*. She was ruined socially. No man would ever marry her. A message was going in over her earphones. She had to concentrate, but her insides were tied in knots.

As always when they came off duty at 9 pm, Rosa, Brigitte and Klaudia went across to the Other Ranks Mess to get their dinner. Klaudia was still in a daze of disbelief about what Jako had done to her and wasn't really listening to the others as they chattered, but as they entered the Mess, they could sense that the atmosphere was charged. Men were standing around talking excitedly – agitatedly – and no sooner were they sighted than someone called out to Rosa. "Did you hear what happened? Voigt was demoted and sent to a *fighter* squadron." Only the infantry would have been a worse disgrace.

"What?!" Rosa came to a dead halt. Then: "Why?"

The explanations burst out from all directions as a crowd formed around the three young women. Everyone was talking at once, and it was hard to sort through it all at first. But gradually the picture formed. During his tour of the base, Goering had remarked casually to Paschinger that the ground crews and hangars "looked a bit sloppy."

"Christ! We'd been up all night for the third time this week."

"No one told *us* the Herr *Reichsmarshall* was coming!"

"Where are we supposed to get a haircut here, anyway? We have to go to Falaise even for our laundry!"

"If we spent our time polishing our boots, half the kites would be u/s."

"Arschinger thinks we're nothing but machines! He resents having to feed us or let us sleep!"

"The only thing wrong with the hangars were the tools lying around from the overhaul! What are we supposed to do? Sign them out in triplicate every day?!"

"What happened to Axel?" Rosa demanded, cutting through the resentful chatter.

"Arschinger called the crews together and said we'd disgraced him in front of Fatty!—"

"Fatty didn't really take offence. It was just an off-hand remark—"

"What difference does that make?! Arschinger acted as if Fatty'd torn his head – or at least his Knights Cross – off! He said he'd teach us a lesson in smartness."

"He charged up and down finding fault with everyone."

"My hair was too long. Klein had an oil-stain on his uniform trousers. Rezka's sleeves were frayed."

"Arschinger screamed: 'When I'm through with you, you're going to be able to lick your dinner off the floor of the hangars.'"

"He said he'd inspect the hangars tomorrow in white gloves, and if the tips of his fingers were dirty when he was finished, he'd cancel all leave for the crews for the next month."

"And that's when Voigt couldn't take any more. He stepped forward and saluted and then asked: "Then the Herr *Gruppenkommandeur* does not want the aircraft operational until the day after tomorrow?"

"Arschinger turned the colour of a boiled crab. He was so furious he was shaking."

"He grabbed Voigt's epaulettes and tore them off—"

"I thought he was going to choke Voigt with his bare hands—"

"He was spewing insults which I don't intend to repeat in the presence of ladies."

"Where's Axel?" Rosa wanted to know. "He's on his way to JG 23—"

"If Arschinger had had his way, he'd have been transferred to the infantry, but *Fliegerkorps* refused. They said mechanics were too highly trained and couldn't be wasted."

"He was demoted *two* grades! To Feldwebel—"

"And sent to JG 23, the bastards that left us in the lurch." The contempt and outrage was blistering.

"He's already gone?" Rosa asked, disbelieving.

"Hours ago. Paschinger said if he ever laid eyes on Voigt again, he'd shoot him."

Rosa turned on her heel and left the Mess.

The feeling of queasiness as he approached his Hurricane was familiar to Ginger now. It was his fourth patrol this week. So far, all had been uneventful, but after the fight yesterday, he was certain they were in for it now.

Ginger reached his Hurricane, and Sanders swung himself out of the cockpit and offered Ginger a hand as usual. Ginger took it gratefully with a nod and a smile of thanks. Sanders had kept his word, and "Q" had been sent back to a Maintenance Unit for a complete re-fit. Sanders was now assigned to Ginger's new aircraft, "H," along with the rigger, Tufnel. Ginger no longer felt shy with either of them; they were both first-rate blokes. They seemed to really like their work and were proud to keep their aircraft in the best possible condition.

Sanders smiled as he helped Ginger pull the straps tight. "I hear Jerry's getting cheeky. The blokes from 43 Squadron were telling us their pilots bagged a couple of Stukas that were going for a convoy right off the Needles."

"I guess it had to come sometime. France surrendered a month ago," Ginger answered stoically. Somehow when he'd joined the RAF, all he'd thought about was flying – not killing and dying.

"Good luck then, sir!" Sanders flashed him a last smile and jumped down off the wing.

"Thanks!" Ginger called after him, and then turned and waved to Tufnel to pull the chocks away. Tufnel was looking tired. He'd been up half the night helping the CO's rigger repair the CO's kite.

Today they were flying in three sections of four aircraft rather than vics, and once they were in the air, Jones ordered them into Sections Line Astern. This put Ginger, Green and Debsen respectively into the "tail-end Charlie" position of their respective sections.

Ginger didn't like this formation *at all*. While the three aircraft ahead of him flew one behind the other in a neat row, he had to weave back and forth behind Blue Section and, theoretically, keep an eye out for any Huns that might try to "bounce" them from behind. But how could he watch the sun and the sky around him when – if he didn't watch where he was going – he might lose the squadron or crash into Debsen? After just ten minutes of flying like this, the back of Ginger's neck was completely rubbed raw, and unconsciously he stopped turning his head because it hurt too much. Instead of turning his head, he twisted his upper body, and that was when he came within a hair's breath of colliding with Debsen.

Twisting around, he'd unconsciously applied too much right rudder, and all of a sudden there was Debsen flying straight at him. They both yanked the stick over and veered off in opposite directions just in the nick of time.

His heart was still thudding from the near miss, when Ginger got a blistering in his ears from Jones. "Stop mucking about back there! You are supposed to be keeping a look-out, not playing games!"

Ginger, his nerves still very shaky, resumed his position behind Blue Section, but now he hardly dared turn in his seat at all. He concentrated on just weaving back and forth as if he were keeping a look out, even though he didn't dare take his eyes off where he was going to look behind him.

The next thing he knew, his Hurricane bucked for no reason at all. Then a great hole appeared in his wing, and for a whole second Ginger thought his Hurricane was disintegrating around him for no reason. Then the sound of gunfire penetrated to his brain, and he realised he was under attack. He wrenched around in the cockpit and to his horror discovered a huge, twin-engine, twin-tailed German fighter was not more than 300 yards away and firing at him.

"Look out behind!" he screamed into the R/T (forgetting all the proper jargon). But it was too late. The Messerschmitts were all over them. Tracer was piercing the air every which way. The squadron seemed to explode as every aircraft abandoned the formation for the safety of diving, rolling, turning, and jinking.

Ginger, too, was doing all he could to get away from the Messerschmitt on his tail. He had been weaving when he had been hit, and without even thinking he up-ended onto one wingtip and pulled the stick back into his stomach. The blood drained from his head so fast, that his eyes could not focus and all he saw was a sheet of grey. He realised he was on the brink of blacking out entirely, and then he must really have blacked out, because he came to floating in his Hurricane in a thick haze.

He heard only silence, and for a moment Ginger thought he was dead. He did not know if he was right way up or upside down, whether he was diving or climbing.

Then he realised that his engine was still rumbling in his ears, and so he decided he might not be dead after all. He looked out the window and with a jolt saw the leaden sea, heaving, dark and ominous, no more than a thousand feet below him. The sight filled him with sheer terror. Instinctively he pulled back on the stick to rush upwards towards the heavens − away from the murky darkness waiting to swallow him and his aircraft whole.

After the initial, panicked response, however, Ginger concentrated on his instruments. He straightened out, righted his slight left bank, and climbed steadily through the haze into clear sunshine. Here he looked in all directions, straining to find the others. But there was not another aircraft in sight. After looking about for several minutes, trying to decide where he was, he gave up.

Timidly he switched on his R/T. "Beetle, Cottonball Blue Four here. Do you read me?"

To his amazement, the response came instantly, from a very nice, clipped voice. He recognised it as the man with the eye-patch, the man the others called "the Cyclops" − another cruel nickname for a man who had a suffered such an awful injury. Ginger couldn't remember his real name, but he was relieved to hear his voice: "Reading you loud and clear, Cottonball Blue Four, over."

"I − seem to have blacked out for a minute."

"Are you hurt?"

"No, no. I just turned too tightly, I expect," Ginger felt an absolute fool. "But I can't seem to see where I am."

"Not to worry, Blue Four. Circle while we get a fix on you." A short time later a course was given to him, which Ginger gratefully followed back to Tangmere.

To Ginger's horror, however, only a little more than half the squadron was on the ground when he returned. Surely the others hadn't *all* been shot down? As tail-end Charlie, he should have seen those Messerschmitts before they attacked; he had failed entirely. He stood miserably on the edge of the field, searching the sky. At least there was one Hurricane coming in to land. Ginger watched it come down easily, undamaged, but with guns fired. He wandered over to see who it was. (He hadn't memorised which pilots flew which aircraft yet.)

The hood was shoved back, and Ginger saw that it was the Scottish Sergeant Pilot Malcolm MacLeod. He had a very strong Glaswegian accent – particularly when he was upset – and a reputation as a brawler and a drinker that made him very much an outsider in this genteel squadron. Ginger had heard rumours that the CO was doing everything he could to get him posted away again.

When the Scotsman's fitter clambered up onto the wing to give him a hand, asking the usual: "Any joy, sir?" MacLeod responded with a bitter volley. "How the bloody hell should I get anything when I have to spend my time playing nursemaid to the squadron's sprogs?"

Ginger winced at that, ashamed that he needed a nursemaid. The Scotsman was continuing, "All three arse-end Charlies got clobbered again. Why the hell do we keep flying the bloody formation?!"

This obviously being a rhetorical question, the Scotsman's fitter wisely said nothing. MacLeod dropped down from his cockpit, and completely ignoring Ginger, took out a packet of cigarettes and lit up immediately – something that was strictly forbidden in such close proximity to an aircraft due to the risk of fire. Behind them, another pair of aircraft landed.

MacLeod was still raging, his accent more pronounced than ever. "Jerry joomps us everrry Goddammed time! Eats the bloody Cherrrlies alive, larrrks hooome unscathed. Y' want to know what I call it? coverrring the officers' arses w' the youngest and weakest."

Just at that moment the CO himself had come around the tail of MacLeod's aircraft with the spy, S/LAllars. Both senior officers had heard MacLeod's last insulting remark. Allars raised his eyebrows, but Jones – looking more than ever like Clark Gable with an open collar and silk scarf at his throat – scowled darkly.

"You're out of order, Sergeant – and put that cigarette out!" the CO ordered sharply.

Although MacLeod was taken by surprise, he was a professional. He dropped and stamped out the cigarette instantly and came to attention with a "Sir!"

Jones' gaze shifted to Ginger and the ground crew, his intention clearly one of sending them away before he gave MacLeod a piece of his mind. But when he recognised Ginger his eyes narrowed. Frowning furiously, he pointed an angry finger at Ginger. "What the hell were you doing out there, Sergeant? Napping?! You very nearly got us all killed! If anyone's bought it, it's your fault!"

Five minutes later the last aircraft returned. There had been no casualties after all, but Ginger still felt guilty.

Chapter 10

Portsmouth
23 July 1940

Emily was doing the washing-up after dinner with the radio playing softly in the kitchen. The walls of the terraced cottage were so thin that the music could be heard throughout the house. Fortunately, she was listening to classical music, which did not disturb her parents as they sat together in the parlour. Mr. Pryce was reading *Pravda*, his Russian dictionary beside him for reference, and his wife was correcting exams, as it was end of term.

The telephone rang.

Mrs. Pryce scowled and remarked indignantly, "Just *who* can be ringing at *this* time of night?" as she went into the hall to answer it. She was even more annoyed when a strange male voice asked for Emily and with pub noises in the background. She stepped into the kitchen doorway and announced sharply, "Emily! Some man is calling you *from a pub*. You certainly will *not* meet him there."

"No, of course not, Mum. Who is it?" Emily was not "seeing" anyone. Or could it be Michael? Maybe he was in the area for some reason? A little breathless with hope and apprehension she said, "Hello?"

"Miss Pryce?"

"Yes." She didn't recognise the voice.

"Robin Priestman. We met about three weeks ago at the Salvation Army Mission." He sounded as if he wasn't sure she'd remember, but Emily remembered all too vividly. In fact, she'd agonised over the encounter countless hours since then, trying both to understand her feelings and dissect her behaviour so there would be no repeat of her incredible faux pas.

The voice in the receiver was continuing, "Look, I'm flying an old Spit down to the Supermarine works near Southampton for factory re-fit tomorrow, and don't have to get back here until late. I thought maybe we could do something together. Dinner perhaps?"

"Dinner?" Emily was blind-sided. She had never expected to see this young man again. She had certainly never expected him to ask her out. And having dinner with a young man she hardly knew was something she had never done before. She had always assumed that anyone she actually went *out* with would be someone she knew from University or work ....

"Yes, why not?" The young man was replying lightly. "Although, actually, I'll have to catch the 8 o'clock train, so it would be better if we could meet earlier." The pub noises in the background were loud – evidently young men in very high spirits. Robin raised his voice to be heard over it all. "More high tea, really. Is that all right?"

"Yes, of course," Emily stammered.

"Four o'clock, then? Where can I collect you?"

Emily registered that she would be at work at that time, and she would have to take time off if she wanted to go early, but she would worry about that tomorrow. She just managed to give Robin her work address before his coins ran out, and the loud buzzing of the telephone cut them off.

Dazed, Emily drifted into the parlour where her parents looked at her expectantly, her father over his reading glasses and her mother very rigidly from her desk chair. "And just who was that and what did he want?" Mrs. Pryce demanded.

Emily perched on the edge of the nearest chair, the dishcloth still in her hands, and said in a dazed voice. "It was a man I met at the Seaman's Mission."

"A sailor?!" Her parents said in horrified unison.

"No, he's Major Fitzsimmons' nephew. He's a pilot in the RAF."

"Not much better!" Mrs Pryce concluded. "One hears they drink like fish."

"Well, I expect that's a little exaggerated," Mr. Pryce conceded. "I don't see how they could be fighting off the Luftwaffe, if they all drank too much all the time."

"And what did he want with *you*?" Mrs Pryce ignored her husband.

"He's asked me out to tea tomorrow."

"And you *accepted*?" Her mother sounded shocked.

Emily looked up and straight at her mother. Suddenly she was no longer uncertain and confused. She was 24 years old and earning her own living. She was tired of being treated as though she was still a schoolgirl. "Yes, Mum. I accepted, and I'm going to go to tea with him whether you like it or not."

Emily stood and went back into the kitchen to finish the drying up, leaving her startled parents gazing at one another baffled.

One thing was clear: she was attracted to this young man as she had been only once before, to Michael. But after finding out he was in the military, she was intimidated by him, too. The military was an alien and rather frightening world. She wasn't at all sure she could handle it, but she was determined at least to get to know Robin Priestman better. Surely nothing that came out of the friendship could be worse than spending the rest of her life here in this horrible house with her fanatical parents, doing nothing of any significance.

RAF Hawarden
24 July 1940

The weather was pretty miserable. Low, drizzling cloud hung over the airfield and the windsocks were limp. Priestman was annoyed. The Met officer was reporting cloud, in layers, up to 15,000 feet. Flying above that would be cold even with a flying jacket over his tunic, so normally he would have bundled up in a turtleneck or two. Today, however, he was dressed in his best blues for tea with Miss Pryce. He hoped the Met was right about the cloud cover clearing as he flew southeast.

Fletcher gave him a leg up into the cockpit and strapped him in. "Don't forget this prop isn't variable, sir."

Priestman nodded.

"And the brakes are a bit sticky too, I'm afraid." Priestman nodded again.

"We've armed her, though, sir. Just in case you run across something tempting." He grinned.

Priestman thanked him automatically and went through the pre-flight check, gave the thumbs up and taxied out on the wet grass. The brakes were a real nuisance, grabbing very unevenly. Landing would be a bitch on a short field. Worry about that on landing, he told himself. He revved up and set off. At the instant of lift, he felt the weight of the world start to dissolve.

He was not at all happy in his job as an instructor. The young men entrusted to him seemed so hopelessly incompetent. He knew it was not *that* long since he had been in their shoes, five to six years only, and he reminded himself over and over again that it did take *time* to learn to fly. In fact, it took *hundreds* of hours, and most of these young men had less than 200. W/C Kennel had reminded him that he'd loged more than three times that number of hours before he started flying powerful, monoplane fighters.

As Kennel had put it, "It's as though they've just learnt to ride their Dad's aging draught horse, and someone has plopped them on the back of a nervous, young thoroughbred and said 'right, off you go.' There they are, hanging onto the saddle for dear life."

Although not much of a rider himself, Robin had found the simile apt. When he watched his trainees take off in a Spitfire, it did seem very much as if the Spitfire was in control rather than the pilot, while their landings made him wince more times than not. It was a wonder the Spitfires – not to mention the long-suffering ground crews – could put up with it. The trainees broke things all the time.

Nor could Priestman get over the fact that they made so many *stupid* mistakes. One idiot had gone up on a night circuit and forgot that the Spitfire's nose would block his forward vision when landing just as much as when taxiing. Or there had been the brilliant trainee who forgot to release his compass gyro before take-off.... It seemed a miracle to Priestman that none of them had been killed yet – but they'd managed to prang more aircraft in a couple of weeks than he'd done in his entire career.

Priestman had meanwhile climbed steadily through cloud and broke clear at just over 6,000 feet. Above him was another layer of cloud, blocking off the bright sun, so he was in a world of grey, cloud both above and below him, but he had good forward visibility. He decided to level off here. He didn't need to go on oxygen that way, and so could leave the uncomfortable mask hanging open rather than clipped over his mouth. He turned on his course for Southampton, automatically checking over the dials to be sure everything was reading normally. The Spitfire purred contentedly, and he could fly her with the lightest touch of his fingers or toes. His thoughts were still at Hawarden.

He found it extremely difficult to know how to handle the trainees entrusted to him. Some were obviously very frightened of where they found themselves – as if they had been moved along far too fast from their innocuous civilian lives as draughtsmen, salesclerks and solicitors just a year ago. They did not see themselves as RAF officers and pilots yet – nor did they act like it. They tended to be timid, unsure of themselves, excessively deferential, and at the same time casual and imprecise. They often over-reacted to criticism, with despair or desperation. Or there were the over-confident types, youths full of themselves, who tended to think they were above all the "nonsensical rules" and "juvenile regulations." They were often offended by criticism, even resentful of it, because they seemed unable to accept that it was justified.

It was obvious to Priestman that he couldn't treat them all the same, but to do otherwise was to risk being seen as unfair or having favourites. In retrospect, he found himself admiring his instructors with new appreciation of their professionalism. How had they managed to correct and encourage so skillfully?

As he'd hoped, the cloud petered out just east of Bath, and after that Priestman had a splendid view all the way to the Channel. Magnificent. He could pick out one landmark after another, flying entirely by the living map below him rather than by compass or chart. He left Salisbury behind, the elegant Cathedral spire compressed optically into insignificance, and set his sights on Southampton Waters shimmering in the distance. He could see the barrage balloons floating above the city like great silver elephants and was surprised when puffs of cloud started to form just above them. Anti-Aircraft.

Only then did Priestman stop sightseeing and realise that there was what looked like half a hundred aircraft flying towards Southampton from the south. Looking more closely, he identified roughly 20 bombers and above them twice as many smaller dots – not the tiny Me109s, but the more powerful but less manoeuvrable twin-engine Me110s.

Up to now, the Jerries had concentrated on Channel shipping, but this air fleet was clearly heading for Southampton itself. He counted again: definitely more than 50 aircraft. No one could expect him to attack such a gaggle of aircraft alone. No one expected him to attack at all. He was posted to Training Command. He was flying a machine over-due for an overhaul back to the factory. He had the day off.

But that was *Southampton* they were attacking! Just beyond it was Portsmouth – home. Besides, he could now see seven Hurricanes hanging on their propellers as they strained valiantly for height. Must have been scrambled from Tangmere a bit late. Priestman clipped his oxygen mask over his face, pulled down his goggles, and started spiralling up another 10,000 feet so he could dive shallowly at the bombers.

At least if he had to jump this time, he'd land practically in his back garden, he told himself. No risk of being taken prisoner, either – at least not bloody yet! He switched on the gun sight, set it for Heinkel 111, and turned the guns to "fire." Then he went straight in at them head-on.

For a moment Robin was caught up in the thrill of closing at nearly 600 miles an hour. What an amazing thing that someone was actually paying him to do this, he thought irreverently. Of course, head-on attacks didn't leave a lot of time for shooting, and the tactic was better designed to just break up a bomber formation, upset their nerves and aim a bit. Then again, if their targets were in the middle of a city like Southampton, making them miss their military targets only meant dropping the bombs on innocent civilians. Not exactly what he was being paid to do, Robin realised a little late.

By then he was through the formation, however, and swinging about in an S-curve to come back on the bombers from behind. Around him planes were shooting past like meteors. The 110s had bounced the Hurricanes, and they were all darting about in the familiar chaos of a dogfight. Priestman sensed more than saw a 110 start lumbering around to discourage his attack on a bomber as it turned for home. The 110 was well out of range, however, and after his experiences in France, Priestman wasn't concerned. Instead he concentrated on the bomber in his sights.

He pushed the throttle through the safety-wire and opened fire, holding down the trigger-button with urgency, wanting to score hits before the 110 had a chance to drive him off. Frustratingly, only bits of the bomber's port wing broke away, and it continued to fly apparently undisturbed. Priestman pressed in closer and aimed more directly at the port engine. It started to smoke and then burst into flame. Abruptly, damaged portions of the wing fell away, and the pilot lost control of the aircraft. It went into a flat spin going down fast – and then tracer was flashing past Priestman's own wing.

He felt the Spitfire shudder slightly, and the sound of cannon punching holes in the fuselage was unpleasantly familiar. He kicked the rudder and stood on the wing-tip, greying out as he slid down and away from his assailant – consciously delighted by the manoeuvrability of the Spit. He felt even better in it than he had in his Hurricane. The Me110 didn't have a hope of following him – and so it ignored him and started for home.

Below, two parachutes blossomed and swayed, incongruously peaceful amidst the dirty bursts of anti-aircraft fire. To Robin's amazement, the parachutes were falling not on Southampton, but over what was very nearly Gosport. Robin could make out Southsea Castle and Palmerston's Follies beyond. If he flew just a minute or two more, he'd be right over his mother's house. Or he could beat up Aunt Hattie at the Mission – if it weren't for those barrage balloons.

A very odd feeling, to be in the midst of combat and at home at the same time. No time for philosophising with 110s still around, he reminded himself. Furthermore, his fuel gauge was reading nearly empty. Time to find the Supermarine factory – and hope it hadn't been hit by the raid.

He climbed and swung hard left to return to Southampton Water, beside which the Supermarine factory lay. On the way, he located the wreck of his Heinkel; the port wing was completely charred, and the rest lay at an awkward angle on the mudflats before Portchester. Low tide, the sailor in him registered.

The factory, of course, had been a target in the raid. Fortunately, the German bombers hadn't been terribly accurate, but the near misses marked the factory out with columns of smoke rising into the air all around it. Priestman circled a couple of times before the balloons were lowered to make a landing lane for him. They were rather miserly about it, Robin thought, and the lane created by the lowered balloons was not only very narrow, it was not properly into the wind. The crosswind blew smoke from the near misses right across his path, further com- plicating his landing. At least the runway, built for testing new machines, was quite long.

He touched down rather nicely under the circumstances, and relaxed at once, feeling quite pleased with himself about the Heinkel. In his satisfaction with his kill and his nice landing, he forgot about the sticky brakes. He applied the brakes too hard. The starboard brake caught much firmer, and before he could correct, the wing-tip touched the turf and whompf, he was hanging from his straps upside down in the cockpit as the aircraft ploughed a rut in the runway. Priestman's first thought was: thank God my trainees can't see me now.

Fire engine, ambulance, assembly-line workers, technicians and even secretaries (or so it seemed to Robin in his embarrassment) were soon swarming around to help him out. Helping hands, reassuring voices, all promising immediate help, urged him not to worry. "Important thing in this situation," someone declared in a stentorian tone, "is not to release the straps."

"Thank you," Priestman retorted in a precise, annoyed voice. "I may have botched the landing, but I'm not a complete idiot."

The workers of the Supermarine factory could see that his guns had fired. They saw, too, the cannon holes left by the 110. They naturally assumed that the crash had been caused by battle damage or pilot injury rather than incompetent flying. They had feared that the pilot might be seriously hurt. His tart reply, therefore, caught them by surprise, and his rescuers laughed with relief. Then, well cushioned by multiple pairs of arms, he was told to release the straps, and they dragged him out of the cockpit carefully.

As Robin got his feet under him, his knees were shaking. He was both shaken by the crash-landing and feeling foolish for having it witnessed by such a crowd. But the crowd saw a young man who had evidently just clashed with the enemy – risking his life for theirs – and who had nearly died landing. Most could not see that he was shaking, but his annoyed remark about having "botched the landing" was already being passed back to the edges of the crowd and beyond. It would soon become legendary among the factory workers.

A man in a suit with a white technician's coat over it pushed his way through the crowd. "Where did you come from?" he demanded.

"RAF Hawarden, actually. The brakes – as you may have noticed – are a bit sticky, and she's not fitted with variable pitch yet, either. Didn't Wing Commander Kennel warn you?"

"Flight Lieutenant Priestman?"

"That's right."

"That's good news, then. You were over-due, and we were rather worried that you might have been mixed up in the raid we just had."

"I was, actually. Got a Heinkel."

"Good show!" Now they all started congratulating him and clapping him on the back. The next thing he knew, he was being taken to the factory canteen – which was quite all right, as he felt he could very definitely use a stiff drink even if it was only mid-morning.

A growing gaggle of factory dignitaries, men with greying hair and balding heads, escorted Robin. They all seemed extraordinarily keen to meet him. Men in suits and ties under white coats were being introduced to him, and they all seemed to want to shake his hand. In a group they entered a huge factory canteen in which men in grimy overalls stood in line for food or sat at long, battered tables. The smell of boiled cabbage, cooked potatoes and hot fat filled the room. The clatter of trays and cutlery counter-pointed the drone of voices.

Priestman knew the Supermarine factory was working around the clock in three shifts, seven days a week. The newspapers had reported cases of men falling asleep standing up on the assembly line, of men having heart-attacks while working, men collapsing from exhaustion. The men here certainly *looked* exhausted, Robin thought. The average age must have been near 40. These were men too old for the services, men with families to feed.

Evidently, word of his kill had reached them because someone started clapping and others took it up. It never occurred to Robin that they were clapping just because he flew and fought – whether he shot down anything or not. The sound spread across the vast hall as the men seated at the tables got to their feet, clapping louder and louder.

Priestman stopped dead in his tracks, overcome with emotion. This was completely different from winning a prize at an air show. There were no photographers and no socialites, no fluttering flags, silk scarves and silk dresses. No flowing champagne. Just tired men in oil-smeared overalls in an echoing hall that smelt of over-cooked food.

The managers around him stopped with him. They waited uncertainly, not knowing what he wanted.

Priestman tried to put it into words. "I couldn't have done it without the Spitfire." He told the men around him. But that wasn't enough. He wasn't sure they'd pass the message on. He reached out to the nearest man in dungarees, standing in front of a long table and clapping vigorously like the others. He was a short man with a fringe of grey hair around his shining head. His hands were black with ingrained oil. He continued clapping even as Robin leaned closer to his ear to be heard above the roar of clapping. "The Spitfire! It's a magnificent machine! We couldn't do a damn thing without her." (Unfair to the Hurricane, but at the moment it didn't matter.)

The man nodded vigorously, grinning, and clapped more wildly still. Then Robin was led away to the management dining room behind its solid oak door, and the sound of the clapping faded away.

Portsmouth

Emily rushed into work late. Just what she didn't need when she wanted to get away early, but she had changed three times after getting up this morning. How can you possibly dress for an ordinary workday *and* the most important date of your life?

She told herself that any young man as handsome as Robin must have dozens of girlfriends. The very fact that he hadn't called her until the night before suggested he'd tried other girls first, or maybe his original date had cancelled at short notice. Emily firmly told herself that she mustn't get her hopes up about any long-term prospects.

But whether they had a future together or not, she was determined to start living her own life. That had been almost the last thing Michael had said to her when they parted the last time: "Don't let your parents harness you to their outdated dreams. You have a right to your own life." Even if she couldn't imagine what it would mean to have a friend in the RAF (a fighter pilot, of all things!), she was determined to break out of the rut she was in. She was going to enjoy this one date as much as possible. It was her first – and for all she knew it might be her last – chance for a better future.

She had decided to wear a smart, tailored suit with velveteen collar and cuffs that she had bought for graduation from Cambridge. It was two years old and had served at every "official" function since, from funerals to weddings. She had a white blouse with a lace collar to go with it, and patent-leather shoes with straps – not working dress at all. She also wore pearl earrings and a pearl ring – the only jewellery she owned, left to her by her grandmother. Most significantly, she wore her hair down.

Obviously, all the other girls in the office noticed that she was "tarted up" (as one of them ungraciously put it), and the word spread like wildfire (from the boss's secretary to the others) that she had asked to leave early. "What's she up to, then?"

"A big date, it seems," the secretary said in a stage whisper.

"Emily?"

"Wonder what *she's* dragged in?"

"Oh, I heard her say she'd met him at the Salvation Army," the secretary confided.

The others roared with laughter. "Do you think he was a customer or the old man who beats the drum?" There were more delighted giggles.

"I just wonder why it has to be so *early*, don't you? I mean: you don't suppose he's *married* or something like that?"

"*Emily*? With a married man?"

"Well, she might not *know*. She's *so* naïve!" They all laughed again.

The whole delicious incident gave the office something to gossip about all day, particularly after Emily went out on her lunch break and bought lipstick.

The receptionist was quite as distracted as the others, and then suddenly the most gorgeous young man that she'd ever laid eyes on was standing in front of her. She could hardly take it all in: the dark wavy hair falling over his forehead, his large dark eyes, his left hand casually stuck in his trouser pocket, *two* rings on his sleeves, and the silver pilot's wings on his tunic. "Excuse me," he interrupted in an upper-class accent.

"Any time, love," she gazed up at him, feasting on the mere sight of him. "Any time."

"I'm looking for Miss Pryce. Miss Emily Pryce."

For the second time in one day, Priestman was conscious of everyone in a large room staring at him – only this time he hadn't the foggiest idea why.

Farther up the room, Emily got to her feet and waved to him. He smiled and waited while she packed up her things. She locked the desk, dropped the key into her handbag, and started towards him. She looked smashing. With her hair down she looked gentler and more feminine. The suit revealed a very delectable figure. Her legs were definitely a piece of nice. In short, streamlined with graceful curves, just like a Spitfire. He smiled and held the door for her.

Outside he returned his cap to his head and opened, "I thought we could go to the Queens."

"Yes, thank you," Emily managed. She was feeling as if she had swallowed a whole flock of butterflies. Seeing him in uniform for the first time drove home the fact that they were worlds apart, and part of her felt the whole thing was hopeless. What could an ex-pacifist and an air force officer ever find in common? Furthermore, his uniform was attracting more attention in this port city than an Admiral would have done – and that meant that everyone was assessing *her* as well. She had never been so aware of *jealous* looks from other women before. Last but not least, the Queens was a nice hotel right on Southsea Common. Despite growing up in Portsmouth, Emily had never been there because her parents considered it too "bourgeois."

As the Queens was within walking distance on such a pleasant day, Robin need only gesture, and Emily started along the sidewalk with him. She was obviously nervous, and Robin asked, "Is something wrong? I mean, why did everyone in your office stare at me?" He was beginning to think he had oil stains in unseemly places or some such thing, and unconsciously (and rather too late) remembered to button up the top button of his tunic.

"You just surprised them." Emily admitted, glad for anything to talk about.

"How?" Robin wanted to know.

"Well, I said I'd met you at the Salvation Army. I suppose they expected an ageing alcoholic on the dole."

Robin threw back his head and laughed, ending it with a piercing, sidelong glance and the remark, "And you did nothing to disabuse them of their expectations?" Emily intrigued him. He had never met a girl like her before. He supposed it might be because he'd never dated a University graduate before. At all events, she was challengingly unpredictable. As was her answer now.

"It was better the way it was," she observed simply.

Robin considered that answer, and then the girl beside him, more seriously. That was a wise answer, but it also suggested that her relationship with her co-workers was less than friendly. "Don't they like you?"

Emily looked up sharply, then shrugged. "It's just that we are so different. I'm the only one with a University education. Their chatter doesn't interest me, and they think I'm a snob to prefer reading books and listening to 'posh' music to going dancing with sailors."

"Why are you doing the same job as them – since you're so much better qualified?"

"Well, I'm *supposed* to be a 'management apprentice,' actually, and supposedly I *will* move on to better jobs, but no one seems willing to tell me *when*. Meanwhile, I just do clerical work while the young male graduates go right into Sales or Claims." There was a trace of bitterness in her voice.

"Sounds a rum deal to me. Surely with all the blokes getting called up, there are some really good jobs opening up? If not in that office, then somewhere else." When she didn't answer right away, he asked, "What did you read at University?"

"History. Medieval history. Not very practical, you see. My parents warned me this would happen – and never tire of telling me they told me so," Emily added, sighing unconsciously. That was another of their perpetual fights, like her leaving the Party and working at the Salvation Army Mission.

Robin looked at the slender, dark-haired girl beside him and felt an unexpected tenderness towards her. His usual dates, the ones who slept with him, were witty, self-confident working-class girls, happy to flaunt an officer boyfriend even if everyone knew what it meant, and his "nice" girl friends were the spoilt daughters of privilege, who expected to be courted or entertained. He hadn't been out on a so-called "serious" date since Singapore – and back then he'd made damn sure none of them had any reason to think he was "serious." They would have ruined his career.

They had reached the Queens, and Emily led the way up the stairs and into the lobby with its stained-glass ceiling. Being such a nice day, however, Robin suggested they sit on the terrace. This was quite crowded, but the waiter found a small table for them towards the back where they had almost no view. Still, it was sunny and the breeze was lovely. Emily was relieved she had put on her best. The other ladies were all in wide-brimmed hats, many wore gloves, and Robin had to salute more than once before they got settled. They ordered cream tea with scones and jam.

Robin tried to pick up the thread of their conversation. "Do you regret studying history?"

"Not for a minute!" Emily's face lit up with a smile, and suddenly she was so lovely it astonished him. When still, her mouth was rather too large and her nose too long, but when her face came to life it made all the pretty girls of his past look like pale, little dolls.

"I loved every minute of my studies," she was saying with real enthusiasm, "but increasingly Cambridge seems like a fairy tale. Once upon a time.... Real life, as my parents would say, is about tedious and unappreciated work – just like the rest of the working masses."

"Ah, your parents are Socialist." Robin concluded from this.

"Communist." Emily corrected. "They both teach at the Council school." Emily did not want to talk about them, however, and she did not want to make the mistake of talking too much as she had last time. She was determined to do as her roommate had advised long ago: ask about *him*, get him to talk. "And your parents? What do they do?"

"My father's dead, killed in the last war before I was even born, and my mother doesn't do anything that I can see," Robin replied candidly. "Aunt Hattie's the dynamic member of the family, and you know about her already."

Clearly, he did not want to talk about his family, either. She decided on an even more direct approach. "And you? What made you go into the air force?" Behind her question was the unspoken wish that he had been that civilian cipher wizard or translator that she had thought he might be when they met. If he'd been an intellectual in a reserved profession, things would have been so much easier!

It was Robin's turn to smile unconsciously. "I was mad about flying! I still am. I think it's marvellous that the British tax-payer is paying me to do what I love best."

"But what about the fighting part?" the pacifist asked. She couldn't help herself.

"I didn't give it a thought when I applied. Of course, the Selection Board asked at the interview, but it didn't seem all that real to me, and I told them what they wanted to hear: that I would be proud to die for

King and Country. Dim, I suppose. I told you I wasn't bright enough for University."

"But you went to public school, didn't you?" Emily pressed him. He had that finish about him, that understated self-assurance and impeccable good manners that she had only seen in her University friends.

"Not exactly Eton or Harrow. An obscure school up in Northumberland, actually. I suppose it's time to confess that my grandfather, although himself an Admiral, actually came from a Quaker family."

"What?" She was flabbergasted. How could a Quaker family produce an Admiral – not to mention an RAF fighter pilot?

"Well, I might point out that since the Society of Friends has no dogma, there is actually nothing inherently contradictory about a Quaker being a member of the Armed Services. Pacifism is a powerful tradition among Friends, but it is not theologically compelling." Emily noted that he could argue very eloquently indeed, and his tone suggested schooling in debate – not at all the popular image of fighter pilots!

"But to be fair," he continued in a more conversational tone, "according to family legend my paternal grandfather was so besotted by the woman who became my grandmother that he not only left the Society of Friends, but also took up a career in the Navy and rose to the rank of Admiral to win and retain her respect and affection. He insisted, however, that his sons and grandsons go to the school he'd gone to – which was emphatically non-denominational and the preferred school of the North Country Quakers – along with half the Jews north of the Trent, or so it seemed. There were only about 15% of us who were C of E. I have countless Quaker cousins."

"And what are they doing these days?"

"Oh, most of them are in the Merchant Navy. Ruddy dangerous place to be these days! One drives ambulances and another works in a large mental hospital in the Midlands."

"That's why you didn't mind what I said the other day." Emily realised.

"Of course not. You're entitled to your opinion. But I do hope you respect mine as well. My grandfather – to justify himself, of course – liked to quote the 'Tombstone of a Pacifist.' You know it?"

Emily shook her head.

Robin quoted: *"Pale Ebenezer thought it wrong to fight, – But Roaring Bill, who killed him, thought it right."* After a pause he added conversationally, "I decided against pacifism at a very early age. I think I was in the fourth form, to be exact. Anyway, I had made an enemy of an older boy and he felt he was entitled to teach me a lesson. He cornered me at dusk one autumn evening out beyond the playing fields, and although I tried to run he brought me down and, being a boxer, did a fair job of beating me up. In fact, I was in the infirmary for a week. All of which would have been bad enough, but as it happened my cousin Peter, who was the same age and no less fit than the bloke who beat me up, had been with me at the time. Because it was against his principles to raise a hand in anger, rather than help me he just stood there pleading with this other bloke to stop.

"The way I see it, pacifism landed me in hospital back then, and Hitler's not much different from that bloke now. I'd much rather fight the Luftwaffe than beg it to please stop bombing innocent people."

Emily nodded solemnly. "Very few people are so purist that they do not acknowledge the right to self-defence," she pointed out. "And the defence of the weak and defenceless is part of "self-defence." I *do* think this war is necessary and right. I didn't mean to criticise you."

She seemed genuinely distressed, and Robin thought maybe he'd said rather too much. "Sorry, I shouldn't have rambled on like that. Peter, by the way, has remained true to his ideals. He's the one at the mental hospital. Hard, gruelling, depressing work. I respect him for it – and I wouldn't change places with him for the world." With a grin, to lighten things up a bit, he added, "No Spitfires."

"I can't tell one aeroplane from another," Emily admitted, "but it must be wonderful to fly. I wanted to – I mean, take a joy ride," she added hastily, afraid he would be offended if she compared her humble desires with his own passion. "There was a flying circus that came to Haylings Island, near my school, and they were offering joy rides for a crown. I begged my parents to let me go. I promised to do the dishes for a week and – I don't remember what else – all the things a child can offer. My parents were unyielding. My father said it was dangerous, and my mother that it was an outrageous waste of money. Didn't I realise that children were starving all over Wales and the North? If I had five bob extra, then I should donate it to the miners – who were on strike at the time."

"Jolly nice of them," Robin observed sarcastically, taking an instant dislike to her parents. "Would you still be interested?"

"In a joy ride?"

"Yes."

"Oh, yes!" she said without thinking. "I tried again when I was at University, actually. A friend and I heard there were two women aviators giving joy rides from some airfield we'd never heard of. My friend had a car, and we set out to find this airfield but got rather lost. By the time we found it, it had started to rain and they closed the field to flying."

"What are you doing next weekend?"

"Sorry?" She wasn't following him.

"Next weekend, if you aren't busy, you could come up to Hawarden and

I'll take you up in the Maggie – the Miles Magister. It's a training aircraft. Two-seater."

Emily couldn't believe what he was saying. "Are you serious? Oh, I'd love to!" Then reality hit her. "But is that allowed?"

Robin laughed. "Certainly not – but we do it all the time. Besides, as they say, some rules are made to be broken – like giving rides to girlfriends and beating up places – that's flying very low. I've done much worse. Don't worry about it. Would you be interested?" He pressed her. None of his other girl friends had taken the slightest interest in actually flying. Not even Virginia.

"I'd be thrilled!" Emily told him forcefully. For some reason she felt as if she had never wanted anything so much in her whole life. Then reality came back to bite her again. "But where did you say you were?"

"Hawarden. It's very near Cheshire."

"Oh, so you're not involved in the air battles they talk about in the news all the time?" Emily was calculating that if he was stationed as far away as *that*, he couldn't be fighting over the Channel.

"No," Robin admitted, wondering what she meant. Were only "real" fighter pilots with "front line" squadrons status symbols at the moment? Virginia had been fascinated with his kills; she'd have no interest in him now that he was with Training Command. But he had assumed Emily was different. He didn't want to just be trophy, so he made sure she knew the whole of it. "I've been posted to Training Command and given a flight of fledgling pilots to train on Spitfires. Most terrifying job I've ever had!"

She smiled radiantly. "Oh, I'm so relieved. There was a terrible air battle just this noon over Southampton. The BBC said there were almost a hundred Germans and just 8 RAF aircraft. They claimed five bombers were shot down, but so was one of our aircraft. I was so afraid you might be up there."

Robin couldn't decide what to say, so he just gazed at her.

"Have I said something I shouldn't?" she asked, confused by his look of consternation.

"Of course not." He smiled. "It's flattering that you should worry. You mustn't, you know. It won't do any good. What do you say we have dinner?" It was getting on to six and he had to catch the train back to Southampton in a couple of hours.

"I'd be delighted," Emily agreed. She did not want this afternoon to end, and she didn't dare believe in the flying offer.

Just as she was dismissing it, he said, "There's a dance planned for end of the course. Nothing special, really. But we are sending the lot out to the slaughter, unready as they are, and something along the lines of a last celebration seemed the form. I gather some of the chaps are shipping in girlfriends, even sisters and parents. The CO thinks the instructors ought to give a little flying demo in the morning. So, you wouldn't be entirely bored."

"And we could fly? I mean, you could take me flying?" she asked hopefully.

That did it: she was more interested in the flying than the dance or the air show. Robin decided he liked this girl better than any other he had ever met. "That's the general idea," he answered with a smile.

Chapter 11

JG 23
24 July 1940

It took Rosa eight days to get the transfer to JG 23. More *Helferinnen* had arrived in the meantime, so there was no shortage of communications specialists, and the Luftwaffe was still somewhat unused to women and inclined to indulge them. When Rosa said she wanted the transfer for "personal" reasons, no one wanted to dig deeper. Klaudia found it easy to tag along, saying she wanted to stick with Rosa.

Admittedly, there was less red-carpet treatment for their transfer than there had been for their arrival. They had to find their own transport from one base to the other and ended up hitchhiking to a central spare parts depot with a lorry from StGr 2 in the expectation of being able to hitch a lift with a lorry from JG 23 from the depot onwards. The logic was sound, and they found themselves at the improvised airfield of their new *Gruppe* just after noon. Here, too, they were greeted considerably less jubilantly than had been the case a month earlier at StG2, but by no means unkindly. For a start, they were expected, and two airmen, who could now go on leave, were particularly hearty in their welcome. Rosa and Klaudia were told to settle in, and report for duty the next morning.

There were already six *Helferinnen* at this field, and they were housed in the Officers' Mess, just as had been the case with StG 2. The Officers' Mess was not in a chateau, however, and although initially disappointed, Rosa and Klaudia were quick to discover the advantages. Previously a country inn, this Mess had more modern conveniences. There were no romantic eaves and no grand marble fireplaces or Gobelins, but the eight girls shared two large bathrooms, had sinks in their own rooms, and furthermore had their own little Mess on the ground floor. Klaudia started to feel better almost at once. She was determined to make a new start here. She was not going to be taken in by any pilot. Instead she was going to concentrate on her career only. She fantasized about a commission and even doing something heroic. She would be in the papers and on the radio and Jako would feel like the cad he was....

The *Helferinnen* had been given a free hand to decorate their mess, and that made it homelier than anything at StG 2. Aside from feminine touches like lace curtains, fresh flowers, and pictures *other than* the Führer and Goering (the Alps and a flat farmland with cattle), one of the girls had found a sewing machine, and there was an ironing board. They also had a gramophone, a growing collection of records, and a small library of books – novels, not flight manuals. Their Mess was right next to the games room with the ping-pong and billiards tables. They were served their meals in their own Mess at a family-sized table, and they all took turns doing "Mess duty." That way no man ever set foot in their little preserve, the others explained, and Klaudia liked that thought immensely.

After Rosa and Klaudia had unpacked their things in their spacious if utilitarian bedroom, it was mid-afternoon. Rosa declared her intention of finding Axel. Klaudia considered staying cocooned in her new, safe world, but curiosity got the better of her. Axel would be able to tell them about the routine and the people here.

It was a bright, sunny day, and the airfield was alive with activity. The *Gruppe* had been airborne when they arrived, but had now returned. Everywhere the tiny Me109s could be seen trundling across the grass to their various dispersal points. The ground crews crawled up on them, helping the pilots out of their straps and down. It was a bad time to be asking questions or getting in the way, Klaudia pointed out, but Rosa ignored her.

Rosa scanned each crew for Axel, but she didn't find him. At last she spotted a cluster of crewmen waiting off to one side. She frowned slightly and pressed forward. These men were searching the sky anxiously as they waited, and they looked tense. At last she spotted Axel among them.

Axel caught sight of Rosa and his face lit up at once. "There you are! I was beginning to think you hadn't made it after all!" He flung an arm around her shoulders and drew her into the little group. To the others, he said, "This is Rosa Welkerling. She's another Berlinerin. And that's Klaudia." Klaudia was thankful he left her family name off. She found herself shaking hands with various young men who introduced themselves nicely. Axel still had his arm around Rosa possessively, which increased the interest in Klaudia somewhat – but not inordinately. The men were clearly preoccupied, and even while the introductions were going on they kept glancing at the sky.

Axel explained, "Möller – that's Meierhof's pilot," he indicated one of the other mechanics, "had to ditch on the way home. Feldburg, Geuke and Appelt – our pilots" – he indicated with a sweeping gesture the rest of them – "all stayed circling the spot where he went in, to keep an eye on his dinghy and help air-sea rescue or the navy to find him."

"Then it's certain the pilot is safe?" Rosa registered.

"Well, he got into his dinghy, apparently, but the kite went down in flames. Hard to know if he got out without being burnt. Besides, he was pretty far out when he had to jump. It will be hard to get air-sea rescue to him without them attracting attention from the English. That's the main reason the other three stayed out there."

"Trouble is the fuel." They all looked at their watches, and then at the sky again. Automatically Rosa and Klaudia followed their gaze.

Axel asked Rosa how she'd managed to get the transfer, and when she'd got in. She started to explain, but before she was finished they heard engines. Instantly the men's attention returned to the sky, and Rosa fell silent.

One of the NCOs saw them at last and pointed. "There!"

"There's only two of them."

"*Scheisse!*"

Tensely they watched the two 109s sweep around to the right in a wide circle to line up to land into the wind. They eased down gently, one leading the other by 100 metres.

"Guns have been fired," someone remarked. The others grunted or nodded acknowledgement.

"*Scheisse!*" Axel Voigt said, stamping his foot. Rosa glanced at him.

"That's Appelt and Geuke."

The crews of these two pilots were already on their way across the grass to intercept the two Messerschmitts that had landed.

"Better see what Geuke has to say," Stückardt suggested, and Axel nodded. He removed his arm from Rosa's shoulder, and together with Stückardt he trotted out towards one of the two 109s, as the engine cut off and the canopy pushed up and open.

Rosa followed behind at a discreet distance, while Klaudia, feeling very awkward and out of place, tagged along. The two girls kept back, anxious not to be in the way, as the men clustered around the returned aircraft. The pilot had already slid down the wing to the ground. He was a fat, round-faced officer – nothing like the propaganda posters. Furthermore, his hair was soaked with sweat from his flying helmet and his face was red with exertion and excitement. He looked very clumsy in his life jacket and big flying boots, and he was gesturing rather agitatedly.

Rosa crept nearer as unobtrusively as possible to try to hear what he was saying, "... so the bombers broke apart and Frischmuth ordered the escort to divide, but all the Hurricanes must have picked on us. Or maybe a second squadron engaged because there were at least nine or ten of them. It was impossible to see what was happening. The CO got one, I think, but Dieter was in trouble fast. Engine streaming black smoke. He dived for the deck and started for home, but a couple of the bastards were after him, and so Christian took us down to bounce them.

"We got them to break off, and would have followed, but Dieter called on the R/T that he had to ditch and got out. His machine burst into flames almost before he got away from it. Tank must have gone. We saw Dieter splash short of where the bird had gone in. He got out of the 'chute and into the dinghy and waved to us. There was only a gentle swell and good visibility.

"Christian started circling, calling out the position as best he could. Busso joined us there. I don't know where he'd been. The bombers had turned back by then, and a good part of the *Gruppe* appeared to be still with them. Christian wouldn't think of leaving Dieter alone out there anyway. So, we kept it up until my fuel gauge light blinked on. Busso reported that his light was on as well, so Christian ordered me to follow Busso home."

"And stayed out there?" Axel asked angrily.

The fat pilot looked quite worried. He wiped sweat off his face with his crumpled handkerchief. "I asked him about his fuel, but he told me that was his problem."

"*Scheisse!*" Axel and Stückardt searched the sky again, but it was silent.

"*Scheisse!*" Axel repeated and kicked at the nearest wheel of the 109 Geuke had just landed. "What good does he think he can do ditching next to Möller?!"

"Look! Over there!"

They spun around. Coming straight out of the north and quite low already was the silhouette of an aircraft. It was silent.

"He's gliding it in."

"Like hell he is!" Axel snapped back, but they all stared at the approaching 109 in fascination. It was sinking down very slowly, drifting down in an elegant, superior fashion; then just over the perimeter fence, the pilot seemed to get a touch nervous and put on the flaps rather heavily. The aircraft dropped, bounced up, bounced down again landing on one wheel, but the other joined it and the little machine hopped and tripped across the airfield straight towards the waiting crews.

Axel and Stückardt darted forward, caught the wingtips and brought it to a halt. The canopy was pushed up, and the pilot grinned out of the cockpit. He had crinkled, dark-blond hair over an open, well-proportioned face that was lit up happily at the moment. "Air-Sea Rescue made it! I saw them coming in low and met them with a wing-waggle. I'm sure they got him."

"What the hell did *Herr Leutnant* plan to do if they didn't show up in time?" Axel demanded. Klaudia caught her breath at the impudence of the remark – despite the correct use of the third person.

The pilot took no offence. "Oh, I knew I could put her down in a pasture, if I had to. There are plenty about. But – as you see – I made it here." The pilot was clearly pleased with himself.

"Pig's luck, *Herr Leutnant*! A little more headwind, and *Herr Leutnant* would have been belly deep in cow-shit somewhere!"

The pilot continued to smile unperturbed as he hoisted himself out of the cockpit and slid down to the ground. "I appreciate your concern, Voigt. Everyone else backsafe?"

"Yeah, except Möller, of course."

"He'll make it. Got a cigarette?" The pilot had already patted his own pockets without success.

Axel shook out a cigarette, and Christian took it thankfully. Axel gave him a light. As he straightened from bending over the match, the pilot's eyes fell on the two girls, still hovering just within earshot. He smiled at them at once, and Klaudia's alarm signals went off. She took a step backwards, but it was too late. "Has the Luftwaffe come up with the *delightful* idea of training *Helferinnen* to service Emils?"

Axel turned back from the waist, saw what Christian had seen, and with a somewhat annoyed frown signalled the girls forward as he explained. "No. They're both in Communications, but Rosa and I met at StG 2. After I'd told her how nice it was here, she got it into her head to follow me over."

Axel had his hand around Rosa's elbow as he introduced her. "Rosa Welkerling." Christian clicked his heels and bowed his head, smiling, but his eyes had already shifted to Klaudia. "Klaudia von Richthofen," Axel duly introduced her, adding for the benefit of the girls, "Christian Freiherr von Feldburg."

Again, Christian clicked his heels and bowed to Klaudia. Klaudia was so distressed to find herself attracted to him when she had barely recovered from what Jako had done to her, that she was immensely relieved when the fat pilot emerged beside them. He distracted the handsome baron, who turned on him to declare triumphantly, "I told you not to worry about me."

"You barely made it," Ernst pointed out.

"Perfect planning, as the CO would say," Christian assured him, flinging an arm over his wingman's shoulders.

"The CO won't say anything of the kind," Ernst retorted with a sour expression.

"He would, if *he'd* done it," Christian reasoned, and they all laughed a bit more loudly than the joke justified. Christian and Ernst started to turn away, but Christian remembered to nod politely to the girls. Then the pilots were gone, and Axel turned to the *Helferinnen* rather sharply. "We've got work to do. See you later."

"As you wish," Rosa answered, miffed, as she started to turn away.

Then she stopped and called out, "Axel?"

"Now what?"

"You never looked that nervous when Paschinger was late."

"Arschinger was an arsehole."

"And this baron's not?"

"Feldburg? No, he's all right."

Dinner was exceptionally good. It was still hot, and the meat was not overcooked, the vegetables were still crisp, the potatoes not soggy. Klaudia didn't think she had ever had a better meal in her whole life. "They kept the French staff of the hotel on, including the chef and his assistants," one of the other girls, Ursula, explained.

There was even a bottle of wine for the four of them not on duty, and there were candles. Klaudia told herself that she wasn't going to let any of the pilots – or ground crew either, for that matter – near her. She was going to keep to this little Mess and her duties, and she'd prove to them all that she was good. Jako already seemed hundreds of miles away, and she *wasn't* going to fall for Baron von Feldburg!

They chatted happily with Ursula and Gertrud until the sound of a motor stopping just outside their window disturbed them. Doors crashed shut. Someone shouted something. They heard other excited voices and went quickly to the window to see what was happening. A large Luftwaffe lorry had stopped at the steps up to the entrance of the inn, and a young man in Wellingtons and a roll-neck sweater climbed out.

Officers spilled out of the Mess and down the steps. Klaudia detected both Feldburg and Geuke among them. They were clapping the newcomer heartily on the back, flanking him in a little group as they returned up the stairs. Evidently it was the pilot who had ditched, returning to his *Staffel* unharmed.

The girls left the window and Ursula put a record on the gramophone. Gertrud set up the ironing board, and they continued to chat while she ironed. Ursula explained that the *Hauptfeldwebel* who commanded their watch in the Communications Centre was "a big Teddy bear." He had four daughters and he was very protective of the *Helferinnen*. "If any of the other blokes gets fresh, just call on Pappa Kahrs. He'll sort them out fast enough."

Klaudia liked the sound of that, too.

By about 10 pm, Klaudia was falling asleep upright. It had been an eventful day, and she was no longer used to wine with dinner. She stood, hiding a yawn behind her hand, and announced she was turning in.

"I'll come, too," Rosa agreed.

They said good night to the other girls and left their little Mess, crossing the darkened games room and making for the main stairs. But as they reached the stairs sweeping up beside the reception area, they could hear music and singing coming up from the Officer's Bar off to the left.

"Listen!" Rosa said with delight. "That's *Veronica, der Lenz ist da!*" When Klaudia looked blankly at her, she added, "You know, by the Comedian Harmonists! Surely you know the Comedian Harmonists?" Rosa might be a good National Socialist, but nothing could ruin her delight in the songs of the Berlin quintet. She tiptoed towards the stairs that led into the rustic bar with its flagstone floors and beamed ceiling half a floor below.

Someone was playing a piano very well, and several men were indeed singing in harmony. They could hear men clapping and stamping their feet in time to the music. Rosa tiptoed down four or five steps until, by bending, she could see into the bar itself. In a line with their arms around each other's shoulders, four of the pilots were dancing to the music as they sang. They had their tunics completely unbuttoned, their ties loosened, and the pilots on the ends – the fat pilot Ernst Geuke and a man she didn't recognise – were having some trouble keeping up with the steps. In the centre, very much the motor of the little act, was – who else? – Christian Freiherr v. Feldburg. Beside him – almost as good as he – was the rescued pilot, still in his borrowed roll-neck sweater and Wellingtons. The officers lounging at the bar or at the tables were clapping or keeping time with their feet.

Klaudia hissed nervously from behind her. "Rosa! Come on! We don't want to get caught here!"

"Why not? Who says we can't watch?"

Klaudia nervously crept down and crouched beside her more daring friend. The sight of so much uninhibited good spirits was attractive. She tried to picture Jako doing a sort of can-can with his tunic open and his tie loose. It was unthinkable.

Too soon the song came to an end. The pianist made a great flourishing finale, and the pilots went down on one knee – or three of them did. The fat pilot got left standing, to the evident amusement of the clapping audience. Everyone was clapping. Someone was even calling "Encore! Encore!" Feldburg made a gesture of "enough," however, and the pilots headed towards the bar.

Rosa reluctantly got to her feet, sorry that the show was already over. "Axel was right," she concluded as the two girls went up to their room together. "It is a lot nicer here."

Chapter 12

RAF Tangmere
25 July 1940

Bridges stood tensely at the balcony of the gallery, looking down on the map table below. The WAAFs were diligently trying to plot the position of the hostile aircraft based on RDF and Observer Corps reports. They were very smart and neat, their hair rolled above their collars, buttons and shoes polished, and their stockings straight. Not a word was uttered. They listened and responded with calm efficiency although the RT transmissions from the pilots had disintegrated from disciplined reports into shouts of warning, cries of alarm and screamed curses.

Bridges, seeing the young women before him and hearing the language crackling in over the airwaves, stiffened with embarrassment. He knew his girls, and he knew they weren't used to hearing such things. But they didn't even glance up, much less giggle in embarrassment. They concentrated on their job. They already understood what that blistering language implied – mortal danger.

While the pilots were clearly fighting for their lives, focused only on what they had in their sights or on their tails, Bridges had the misfortune of seeing the whole picture. The squadron had been sent to assist the escort squadron of a westbound convoy, CW8, which had just passed through the Straits of Dover. The Germans had hit it so hard with E-Boats and from the air that several ships were reported sinking. In consequence, the Royal Navy had sent two destroyers, *Boreas* and *Brilliant*, sallying forth from Dover to the rescue of the convoy. Just minutes later, the RN liaison officer reported that both destroyers had been so heavily damaged that they were being withdrawn. The Navy could not afford to lose any more destroyers. The Atlantic lifeline was practically undefended as it was. The remnants of this convoy were being sacrificed to what appeared to be the entire Stuka force of the German Luftwaffe, while still trapped in the narrowest part of the Channel.

Bridges felt not only helpless but chilled. They had put up the best defence they could – and it had proved inadequate. Furthermore, reconnaissance showed that the Germans were now installing heavy long-range guns at Calais that would be able to reach Dover itself. Guns like that would close the Straits altogether and make it unsafe even for the Navy. If the Royal Navy was no longer safe in the Channel, how could one consider it an *English* waterway? And if the Germans controlled the Straits of Dover, then they became a highway for invasion.

Napoleon, Bridges reflected, had been stopped in his tracks by the Royal Navy alone, but now the combined might of the German dictator's Navy *and Air Force* had tipped the scales in favour of the enemy. The Navy and RAF Fighter Command just weren't strong enough to stop the Wehrmacht. Bridges' morose thoughts were interrupted by the sound of returning aircraft, and he forced himself to focus again on the immediate job.

Doug Allars also heard the sound of returning aircraft leaned forward to try to get a glimpse of them from his office window. He was too slow, however, so he stood, took his cane and limped outside to the field. One Hurricane was down and trundling towards its sandbag bay, while a second, "T" for "Tommy," was beating up the airfield and doing a victory roll. Allars watched it with his cold pipe clenched between his teeth. He disapproved of this kind of antic. Any aircraft returning from combat might have damage to it that could cause a crash. A crash at low altitude directly over the airfield endangered not only the pilot, but ground crews and station personnel as well. Allars had mentioned the fact to Jones more than once, but the Squadron Leader had brushed off his warnings. "Can't stop the lads from having a spot of fun! Don't really want to. Keeps up morale – and the ground crews like it, too."

"Until it kills some of them." Allars had replied, but Jones was clearly not receptive.

Hayworth was apparently back, too, Allars noted as he stopped to watch the next vic of Hurricanes put down. So far, all aircraft had fired their guns, and none of them appeared seriously damage. They had sent up a full complement of 12 aircraft and seven were back, including Jones and both flight commanders. In short, the "experts," as the Germans called their more senior and successful pilots, were all safe, but all the sprogs and two of the older but less successful members of the squadron were missing, and their fuel must be running out.

Allars didn't like the look of this. He started limping over towards Jones to get his report. The Squadron Leader was still flushed with excitement, and his dark eyes flashed with anger. "It was a bloody slaughter! There were only two merchant ships left steaming when we had to turn back. The rest were either sunk or sinking – not to mention the destroyers that got it! How much longer is the Government going to allow this kind of thing to go on?"

"Did you get anything, sir?" Allars pointedly distracted his commander from the topic of whether the Government should make peace or not. He heartily disapproved of Jones' advocacy of making a deal with Hitler. Furthermore, his frequent hinting that Halifax had secret channels open to "the other side" ready to "put an end to this nonsense" if only "that madman Churchill" could be put aside was dangerously bad for morale in a fighting unit.

"One Stuka for certain – Tommy can confirm it – and then the 109s hit us. I got some good shots in, but nothing definitive. Tommy got a 109, though, didn't you, old boy?"

Tommy had joined them, and the two confirmed each other's claims. They were joined by Fl/Lt. Hayworth and F/Os Ware and Dunsire. Meanwhile, the rest of the squadron was straggling in. The Canadian landed with his engine belching black smoke and running very rough, but he climbed down without apparent injury. Allars went over to talk to him.

The Canadian was, as always, very talkative, and gushed at some length about the confused combat. They had gone straight for the Stukas attacking the ships. "Bunches of ships were laying there dead in the water; one had already rolled over on its side, and you could see all these little round things in the water that were the survivors trying to swim to the lifeboats. At least one of the lifeboats had capsized and was rising and falling on the waves like a dead fish. And one of the other ships was down by the bows, the whole front end awash with water, while the stern stuck out of the water so you could see the big propellers and the red paint."

"Surprised you had time to notice so much," Allars remarked.

"Damn right! I shouldn't have let myself get distracted! I got hit from behind while I was looking down. Never even saw what hit me. The engine started making a horrible racket! Soon it was shaking the frame so bad, I thought the whole thing was going to go to pieces. I dove down for the deck. No idea why the Jerry didn't follow me. I guess he thought I was done for and wanted to hunt something else. I nursed my Hurri back here, sweating the whole way. I wasn't sure I was going to make it until I felt the grass brush my wheels."

"No claims, then?"

"Nope." He shook his head. "Just lucky to be alive, sir." He grinned as he admitted it, and Allars nodded. The Canadian was going to be all right. They'd all been a bit sceptical at first, but he was a solid, honest lad, who could assess his mistakes without tying himself in knots.

Allars was more concerned about the pilot he approached next: Sergeant Bowles. Although his guns had not been fired, Bowles' aircraft had some very minor damage to one wing and a few holes in the fuselage far behind the cockpit. Allars professionally judged that an Me109 had tried a deflection shot at too great a range. Probably the German had also been a relatively inexperienced pilot.

Bowles, however, was looking more than a little shaken as he climbed down from his aircraft. Allars caught a whiff of vomit and noticed that one knee of Bowles' uniform was soiled. Bowles swallowed and looked ashamed. "Sorry, sir."

"Were you sick?"

"Yes, sir. But I'll clean it up—"

"No need to do that. The ground crews will see to it – although it is customary to tip them two-and-six for it."

"Yes, sir," the pilot answered, but he unconsciously shook his head as if he meant the opposite.

"What happened?"

Bowles swallowed again, still looking rather green.

"Don't worry. Go clean out your mouth and we'll talk later," Allars suggested.

Another aircraft was down; it was Debsen, and Allars limped over to meet him. Debsen's aircraft had not a scratch on it, but its guns had fired. That was odd. The other two "tail-end Charlies" — Green and Bowles — had taken hits for none of their own. How did Debsen escape the bounce, yet find an opportunity to engage?

Even before Allars had a chance to ask him, Debsen started explaining that he'd got a Jerry. He claimed to have chased it half-way back to France — which was why, he said, he was late landing. "Got it in the end, 'though. I saw it crash into the sea."

"Jolly good," Allars praised automatically. "What was it?"

"One of the big fighters, a 110."

"And you took no hits from the rear gunner?" Allars tried not to sound sceptical.

"He was already dead," came the quick answer. Too quick. It was as if Debsen didn't even have to think about it. Most pilots straight out of combat had confused images that only got sorted out as their pulse slowed and they could review what had happened in slow motion.

Allars nodded. "Can you tell me more about the whole engagement? From start to finish."

"When we arrived over the convoy, the other squadrons were already mixing it with the escort, so we went for the Stukas — but there was a second escort, or maybe the Germans reinforced the escort from the Pas de Calais. Anyway, the 110s came for us, but I saw them coming and turned into them. Then I managed to get on the tail of one of them and followed him until I got him."

Too glib, Allars noted professionally. Getting on the tail of an Me110 after confronting it head-on was not all that easy to achieve; a pilot who had really managed such a manoeuvre would normally have been eager to describe each move in detail — using both hands to do so. But Allars only asked calmly, "What happened to the rest of the squadron?"

"I don't know. I suppose they didn't hear my warning and got hit from behind." Debsen glanced around the field a little nervously. "Is anyone missing?"

"Two aircraft are still missing," Allars informed him, watching his reaction carefully. It wasn't anything you could put your finger on, but Allars thought Debsen looked just a little ashamed. In any case, there were a number of things Allars didn't like about his story, quite aside from the pilot's delivery of it. For a start, no one else had mentioned 110s being involved. Secondly, since the engagement had taken place just west of the Pas de Calais, there wasn't much channel for a German plane to ditch in. Any German pilot with a wounded gunner would make for France and the many nearby airfields there. Worst case, they could ditch in a field. Debsen's story might have made sense if they'd been fighting in their usual airspace, where the channel was much wider, but not today. It was as if the story had been concocted in advance.

Back in his office, Allars was told that P/O Hughes had broken several ribs crash-landing his Hurricane and had been taken to hospital. It would be weeks before he would be fit to fly and rejoin the squadron. But there was no news of P/O Davis until the next day; it seemed P/O Davis had been forced to abandon his aircraft and bail-out in the Channel. His body was washed ashore near Eastbourne; cause of death: drowning. His life jacket had a puncture and failed to inflate.

Allars, meanwhile, had had time to compare the combat reports filed by the surviving pilots. There was the usual confusion and fragmentation, but they all shared the same outline – except Debsen's. The others agreed they had been bounced by 109s, not 110s, and no one had heard any sort of warning from Debsen. Allars sought out Bridges in the Controller's office.

"You were on duty during 606's sortie yesterday, weren't you?"

"Yes." Bridges admitted, already unsettled by the expression of the intelligence officer. Allars' face was deeply carved by the "phantom" pain he often had in his missing limb. Nor was he a man of frequent smiles, but even so, he looked more grim than usual somehow.

"Mind if I have a seat?" Allars asked. "Sorry. Please."

Allars took out his pipe and lit up. He shook out the match and dropped it in the ashtray on Bridges' desk, already filled with matches and cigarette stubs. "Can you remember the bounce?"

"What do you mean?" Bridges asked.

"Well, according to most of the reports, 606 saw the convoy and the attacking Stukas, and saw some dogfighting above and behind it to the east. Jones said they went straight in, but the tail-end Charlies were bounced from behind. Did you hear that on the RT?"

Bridges thought back. "Jones gave the tally-ho, and Hayworth drew attention to the dogfighting to the east. Several pilots reported on the damage to the convoy. Jones cut them off and ordered an attack — saying very clearly: 'Go for the Stukas – now.' And then, seemingly, all hell broke loose. MacLeod started cursing in very rude language, I remember. I was rather embarrassed for the WAAFs, you know. He was the one who shouted a warning to Bowles, too – twice. And Green reported – rather loudly – that he'd been hit. Hughes was quite agitated, too." Bridges fell silent.

"Did you hear anything from Debsen? A warning of any kind?"

Bridges tried to reconstruct the frenzied transmission of the day before in his memory, and then shook his head. "Not that I can recall. Is it important?"

Allars shrugged, pretending to be pre-occupied with his pipe. "Just trying to re-construct what happened. You know what it's like. The boys can't remember half of what happened after a bad fright."

Bridges hesitated, but then admitted, "I've got a WAAF on the watch, ACW Roberts, who's absolutely wizard with short- hand. She used to be a court secretary, doing transcripts and that sort of thing. If it would be useful to you, I could ask her to keep a log of R/T transmission – at least during combat."

"Good idea – if it wouldn't disrupt your routine too much?"

"We'll manage," Bridges assured him.

Allars next sought out Sergeant Pilot Bowles. Since 606 was stood down for the day, most of the pilots were not on the station at all, but Bowles was in the Sergeant's Mess. Allars asked the Sergeant to come to his office, and Bowles appeared at his door a few minutes later, slicked down and nervous. He also looked as though he hadn't slept very well. He had dark circles under his bloodshot eyes, although he was not a heavy drinker and had not been out with the rest of the squadron at the *Fox and Hounds* last night.

Allars asked him to come in and sit down and offered him a cigarette from a box on his desk. "Smoke?" Bowles shook his head. "Mind if I do?"

Ginger shook his head again. He was sure this had to do with being sick in the aircraft yesterday. It had been horrible. When he'd seen the ships down there, one lying on its side with people swimming around it while bombs were still going off all around them, he'd been unable to control his stomach. It had heaved, and he only just managed to rip his oxygen mask off before being sick on the floor of the cockpit. And then suddenly they were hammering him from behind as well. He didn't know how he'd survived. He remembered trying to turn, and his foot had slipped off the pedal in his own filth. He'd been sure he was just seconds away from death. He couldn't remember much more. Someone had shouted a warning to him. But he'd already been doing all he could....

Allars had finished stuffing tobacco into his pipe and pressing it down meticulously. He put a match to the tobacco, puffed into the pipe and when it was burning properly, he shook out the match. "You were tail-end Charlie for Yellow Section yesterday, weren't you?"

"Yes, sir."

"And Debsen was flying on your left, correct?"

"Yes, sir."

"And the German fighters bounced you from the east, correct?"

Ginger had to think about that. They had come out of the sun. "Yes, sir."

"So, they must have hit Green, the other tail-end Charlie, first, right?"

Ginger nodded.

"Did you hear a warning from anyone?"

"MacLeod shouted to me, sir."

"That was after the bounce. What about before?"

"No, sir."

"Not from Debsen?" Ginger shook his head.

"Did you see Debsen turn into the enemy?"

Ginger thought about it, and then shook his head. He had been too wrapped up in his own crisis – the vomit and his feet slipping and the machine-gun fire going into his Hurricane. No, he hadn't noticed anything that happened to anyone else.

Allars thanked him and let him go.

Ginger returned to the room he shared with Green. Green was out somewhere, and Ginger had the little room to himself. He sat down at the desk and stared at the unfinished letter to his Dad. He knew his Dad waited anxiously for his letters and that he would worry if one didn't come when expected. He knew, too, that his Dad didn't read very well and agonised over each word, reading it out loud, syllable by syllable. He had to keep his letters short and simple, and positive. But what could he possibly say that was not a lie?

He was far too ashamed of what had happened yesterday to tell his Dad about it. His Dad knew about his stomach, of course; he'd always had a weak stomach. But Ginger couldn't admit about yesterday. Almost the worst of it had been trying to pay Sanders and Tufnel to clean up the mess as the Spy had suggested. The two airmen had refused to take his money, saying they'd have it hosed out in no time and with no fuss. "Not like you did it intentional," Sanders had insisted. "You've got enough to worry about, sir. We'll see 'H' is cleaned out and refitted in no time." Ginger had left it at that, but he felt worse than ever.

And he was absolutely terrified of having to go back up again tomorrow. He was terrified of being sick again, and terrified of having the whole nightmare of helplessness overtake him again. Ginger was certain that he was going to die soon. He should have died yesterday, and it was a miracle that he had not. But it was a miracle he didn't understand. Why had God spared him yesterday? What had he done to deserve it? Nothing. Absolutely nothing. It must have been a mistake, and you can't expect God to make mistakes two times running. Next time they caught him, it would be the end.

Allars, meanwhile, had gone in search of S/L Jones, but found only Mickey. The Squadron Leader had gone off, leaving the Adjutant struggling with the paperwork that was piling up. "I can't even hold him down long enough to sign off on the things I've prepared for him. Poor LAC Sanders has been trying to get leave to get married, and—" Mickey realised he was complaining, and at once regretted it. It never looked good for an adjutant to complain about his CO. Distressed, Mickey was unconsciously wiping his balding head with his handkerchief.

By the look of things, Allars guessed that Mickey had moved all sorts of files into his own office from the adjoining Squadron Leader's office. Wooden boxes were lined up not only on his desk, but on two chairs which he had placed beside it. Everything was well ordered but overflowing.

"Just where *is* Squadron Leader Jones?" Allars asked. Mickey sighed. "I think he said he was going to his tailor in Chichester."

Allars considered that. "And Davis's funeral?"

"Oh, I've taken care of that." Mickey assured him. "I've got everything arranged with the vicar at Boxgrove Priory. The padre will say a few words, and a squad from the RAF regiment will fire the salute. Hayworth, Dunsire, Ware, Ringwood, Parker and Needham will serve as pallbearers."

"And Jones?"

"No; six is enough, surely?"

"I mean, will he be back in time for it?"

"Oh, well, I assume so. It would be very bad form if he weren't," Mickey pointed out.

But he wasn't.

It was quite late in the evening before Allars finally caught up with the CO in the Mess. By then, Allars was tired and annoyed and in pain. He had no patience for beating around the bush, and he got straight to the point. "I've looked into the combat reports from yesterday carefully, and I have to tell you that I don't believe a word P/O Debsen told me. I don't believe he gave any warning – at least, no one heard him. I don't believe he turned into the enemy – or he would have encountered a little opposition and taken some damage to his aircraft. And I don't believe he chased and shot down an Me110."

"What are you saying?" Jones asked, drawing his dark, bushy eyebrows together and narrowing his eyes.

"I'm saying that I think P/O Debsen not only falsified his combat report and made a false claim, but that he absented himself from the fight at the first sight of the enemy – and before the bounce."

"But he fired his guns."

"He could have fired them into the sea. According to his erks, he fired less than a hundred rounds – making it even more unlikely that he shot anything down."

Jones scowled, his thick dark eyebrows almost meeting over his nose. "I don't like what you're implying, Spy. Debsen's a gentleman, and I don't think it's fair to question a gentleman's word behind his back. Have you told him about your suspicions?"

"Not yet, but I will if you want me to."

"No, damn it!" Jones replied forcefully. "Leave the boy alone! He's young. We all make mistakes. I'm sure that if he did do something not quite above board, he regrets it now and won't do it again. He's a good lad, I tell you. Comes from a good stable."

"If that's the way you want to deal with it, sir," Allars replied tartly. His leg – the one that wasn't there – was killing him. He'd been moving around too much today, standing too long at the funeral. He nodded once and started to go. Then stopped, turned back. "We missed you at Davis' funeral."

Jones' face, which had cleared when Allars accepted his decision, darkened again. "Yes. Things took longer at my tailor's than I expected. Couldn't leave in the middle, you know. Had to finish the fitting."

Allars nodded and limped out of the lounge. Davis had joined them in Scotland. He wasn't one of the "old boys." Just like Bowles and Green and MacLeod. But Debsen, the real rotten egg, was all right, just because he had the right accent and had gone to the right school. Allars shook his head. He didn't like it, but there wasn't very much he could do about it. Or should he call Air Vice Marshal Park?

No one at Tangmere knew that AVM Park was a personal friend, but the 11 Group Commander and Allars had served together in 48 Squadron in World War I – until Allars lost his leg. Park was largely responsible for Allars taking a reserve commission.

But Allars hated to take advantage of an old friendship, and really, what was there to report? It wasn't as if Jones had done anything *wrong*. He hadn't broken any law or violated regulations. He was a good, aggressive combat pilot. No, there was really nothing Allars *could* report. He sighed. It was time to go home to bed. His wife would be worrying. And tomorrow they were on readiness again.

That same day, the Admiralty cancelled all daytime merchant traffic through the Straits of Dover and abandoned Dover naval base. The Germans had achieved their first clear victory in the Battle of Britain.

Chapter 13

RAF Hawarden
26 July 1940

The Germans were winning another battle as well: the Battle of the Atlantic. Of the roughly 200 destroyers in commission at the start of the war, the Royal Navy had only 74 operational by the end of July 1940. The rest were either sunk or under-going repairs from the damage suffered at Dunkirk or on convoy escort. These few remaining destroyers had to be held back in Home waters to meet the invasion the German Army was going to launch across the Channel any day. That left the merchant ships responsible for supplying Britain with vital raw materials, agricultural products, munitions, oil and arms virtually undefended. Most convoys had, at best, an Armed Merchant Cruiser or an old trawler for an escort, and these were all but helpless. The U-boats were having a picnic.

The more the enemy knew about when convoys left port and what course they set, the better, while knowing when in-bound convoys were approaching the confined waters between England and Ireland was extremely useful to U-Boat Command. That was where the Luftwaffe came in. Luftwaffe recce aircraft kept a vigilant watch on the Western Approaches, passing on to the U-boats all they saw.

During the day, the fighter squadrons of 13, 12 and 10 Groups made the skies dangerous for them, but the RAF had no dedicated night-fighter squadrons and at this point in time no aircraft designed for night fighting. All the RAF had at its disposal in August 1940 were their standard daytime fighters – and far, far too few pilots with instrument ratings and experience at night flying. So, the instructors at the O.T.U. Hawarden, so close to the critical port of Liverpool, had been asked to lend a hand. Every night a Spitfire was kept fuelled and armoured, and one of the three instructors slept out on a cot in the dispersal hut, on "availability" in case an intruder was identified.

"Availability" meant that the duty pilot had to be in the air within 15 minutes of a scramble. That was enough time to pull on flying kit and run out to the waiting Spitfire. One ground crew was always on duty, and they slept in the hangar or – when the weather was warm and clear – under the wings of the fighter. At least, that was the theory. In reality, none of them really slept when "available." They napped perhaps, drifted in and out of dreams, and hovered between sleep and consciousness waiting for the telephone to ring.

They had been at it for two weeks now, and none of them had done any good. Both the other instructors had been scrambled once but found nothing in the darkness. Priestman had never even been scrambled, but the nights on availability exhausted him because he couldn't sleep properly.

He sighed and turned over again, the springs of the cot squeaking loudly. The dispersal seemed stuffy. Maybe he should open the door? What time was it anyway? He tried to read his watch in the dark, but he couldn't make out the hands. Annoyed, he kicked off the covers and went to the door of the hut. One-thirty am. Outside, the airfield was flooded by bright moonlight. One could easily read the ID letters on the waiting Spitfire, and the kite cast a sharp shadow on the silvery grass.

Priestman looked up. It was an exceptionally clear night. The stars stood out magnificently in the arch of the heavens – well, in that half of the heavens not lit by the rising moon. A light nor'wester had blown away the fumes of aircraft and factory smoke left from the day, and the air smelt wonderfully fresh. It was also a rare balmy temperature, more reminiscent of the tropics than England.

And then the telephone rang.

Priestman grabbed for the receiver and knocked it off. He heard the voice squawking at his feet. He recovered the receiver. "Hawarden dispersal. Duty pilot."

"We've got a lone bandit coming down the coast. Scramble and report in the air."

Priestman hung up and grabbed his trousers, pulling them on over his pyjamas. Then he drew a roll-neck sweater over his head and pulled on socks and flying boots. He glanced at the flight jacket, but the night was so warm, he decided against it. Instead, he took only his tunic and Mae West. The 'chute was awaiting him in the aircraft.

When he reached the Spitfire, Fletcher and Smitty were already fussing around her. The Spitfire coughed twice and then roared into life. Smitty throttled back and dismounted so Robin could climb up into the cockpit. The flames from the exhaust could be seen clearly in the dark, interfering with night vision, but Priestman was familiar with the problem. With the moonlight tonight, it was less irritating than on darker nights. He tested flaps, rudder and elevator and scanned the instruments – all glowing nicely – and then, somewhat reluctantly, pulled on his helmet and plugged himself in to the R/T and oxygen. On such a balmy night, it seemed a shame not to be able to fly bareheaded in an open cockpit.

He revved up once, eased back, gave the thumbs up, and Smitty stopped leaning his weight on the tail of the Spitfire. As the night was still and he was the only aircraft taking off, Priestman cut straight across to the head of the runway, swung into position and opened up. Suddenly he was wide awake. The tail wheel came up, and an instant later the Spitfire surrendered herself to the air. Priestman reached almost at once to pump up the undercarriage and banked away to the north. Still climbing and turning, he called Control and got a vector.

The sky was a luminous navy blue rather than black – lighter blue nearer the moon, darker farther away. The constellations were easily identifiable, and the Milky Way was a smear against the darkness. The land, in contrast, was a dark, ominous mass. The great industrial city of Liverpool was completely blacked out to hide itself from the predators in the skies.

The moon lit up the River Dee: a sheen of silver on which dots marked small craft floating at their moorings. The Wirall peninsula jutted out towards the Irish Sea and then a broad silver ribbon, the River Mersey, threaded its way between Birkenhead and Liverpool. Forming up in the Mersey and very visible against the bright sheen of the water was a convoy travelling in two columns line astern. The wake of each ship was clearly highlighted in a "V" of moonlight behind it.

Maybe Kevin was down there, Robin thought. His favourite cousin Kevin was Second Mate on a Merchant Navy tanker. Kevin and he had done a lot of sailing together in their grandfather's boats as boys. They had met up in Singapore, too, when Robin was stationed there and Kevin Fourth Mate on a passenger liner. They had also managed to get together once in London just before the balloon went up in France.

Just last week Kevin had rung him from Liverpool. Robin knew how bad things were from Kevin's few words. When a Merchant Navy sailor says the Royal Navy is "doing its best" – things are pretty bad. Worse: he had given Robin the name, address and telephone number of a girl. "Mum doesn't know anything about her," he admitted, "but she's got the right to know if something happens to me." Kevin was shy with girls because his face had been badly scarred by teenage acne. Robin had been glad to hear there *was* a girl. Kevin had added, "And if she needs anything, you know, please do what you can." That rather made Robin feel like Captain Hardy receiving Nelson's plea for Lady Hamilton.

Seeing those ships made Robin glad he had been dragged from his cot. What a waste to sleep on a night like this anyway, and if there was any way he could help protect those ships so much the better! But as he sped along the coast, he didn't have much hope of finding the enemy. It was damn-near impossible to find anything in the dark. Neither of the other instructors had caught a glimpse of the targets picked up by

RDF and so diligently followed and reported by the Observer Corps.

Priestman, therefore, scanned the sky but found himself dreaming a bit, too, when abruptly searchlights flared up ahead of him. At first they just waved about in the night sky, nervous and apparently without direction, but then one stopped dead. A Dornier was caught in the beam. A second beam coned in on it. Robin could even read its ID numbers and see the neat little black crosses.

The bomber pilot jinked, banked and dived sharply to shake off the beams. Unfortunately for him, he turned on a course that brought him right across Priestman's bows. Priestman barely had time to switch on the gun sight and release the safety on the guns before he was in range.

Things happened so fast that Priestman failed to slow down in time. Already he was upon his target, firing without really aiming, and the Dornier came to life, firing at him from its rear guns. Tracer lit up the night sky and then the searchlights found them both, just as Robin hopped over the back of the Dornier. He felt machine-gun bullets smashing into the underbelly of the Spitfire and flinched as the glass on one of his gauges shattered. But he was flying by instinct, pirouetting on the wingtip to wheel back around and get behind the bomber.

The bomber was still diving for the deck, leaning over hard, heading east for home. It had no doubt already radioed to U-Boat Command about the convoy, Priestman registered angrily, and he shoved his throttle to full power. The searchlights had lost them again, but that didn't matter in the moonlight. Priestman did not lose sight of the bomber, although it dived and dodged. The moonlight helped. It glinted on the panels of the glass dome over the cockpit and lit up the white markings around the crosses and along the fuselage.

As Priestman closed, he could see the four men inside squirming about, searching the sky to find him. The rear gunner found him and started firing again. Priestman ignored the tracer reaching out towards him and throttled back so as not to overshoot this time. He side-slipped irregularly, both to avoid the slip-stream and so the enemy gunner had to swing the gun back and forth. The tracer was always just a fraction behind the agile fighter. It was exhilarating to escape the gunfire, to be faster and nimbler than his opponent. The certainty that there were no German fighters to pounce on him from behind added to Robin's sense of invulnerability.

He pressed in closer. He saw the gunner clutch the machine gun and shuddering from the recoil. Priestman pressed his thumb on the trigger button. All eight Brownings hammered into the back of the Dornier. The gunner slumped down instantly, and the gun fell silent. Priestman eased off slightly to the right, and his guns ripped along the starboard wing. The starboard engine flared up like a lit match. Bright flames burst from it briefly, but then the flames eased back and only licked along the cowling of the engine. Even as he watched, they died out completely, but smoke continued to belch from the engine, and the bomber slid downwards.

The front gunner fired furiously as Priestman overshot the target a second time. Priestman turned across the bows of the bomber, drawing more fire from the forward gun, and curved around for a new approach.

Meanwhile, however, the bomber itself was jinking about the sky in an awkward dance. Robin couldn't decide if the pilot was trying to evade him or was just having trouble flying with only one engine. But the crate was still flying, so his job wasn't finished.

Priestman lined up for a new attack and pressed in from the port side, with the intention of going for the port engine. The forward gun spewed fire at him that harmlessly dropped off in a graceful curve into the night. Robin pressed in closer, slithering back and forth as before. Then when he was confident of hitting the mark, Robin lifted the wing up in a quarter roll and opened fire, flying with the wings at the vertical. The enemy gun went silent and the bomber's undercarriage dropped down – a gesture of surrender among aviators, the same as raising one's hands was to the infantry.

Priestman peeled away, looking over his shoulder to be sure this wasn't a trick. But the undercarriage was definitely down, and the bomber had stopped jinking about. The pilot looked over directly at him, and then commenced a shallow dive, apparently looking for a place to land.

At first, Robin tried to stay with it, flying at full flaps, but couldn't fly slowly enough. He had to peel off, climb up and start circling from above. The bomber was down to just a couple hundred feet, skimming over the surface of the water, casting a racing shadow. The undercarriage come up in preparation for a belly-landing and Robin guessed the German pilot was aiming for the soft south bank of the Mersey west of Runcorn.

At the last instant, the bomber saw the Manchester Ship Canal, hopped over it, and then pancaked hard into the marshes beyond. The bomber bounced up once, landed hard a second time, lost one wing as it slewed around, and ploughed along sideways for a couple hundred yards before coming to a complete halt. Robin made one last pass over it, but couldn't see if there were any survivors. He swept up into a private climbing roll before turning for home.

Hawarden was still asleep and bathed in moonlight when he landed. Priestman turned off the engine and shoved back the hood. Only the crickets greeted him. He pulled his helmet off and ran his hand through his sweat-sticky hair. Sweat was running down the side of his face. That surprised him since it hadn't seemed that hot.

At last Smitty appeared on the wing, and his eyes widened. "Are you all right, sir?"

"Fine, but the oil pressure gauge is shattered." Priestman indicated the instrument panel, where the machine-gun bullet had hit it.

"But your face, sir." Smitty said, still staring at him.

"What about it?"

"You're bleeding, sir."

Robin felt his face again. It was dripping wet, but he'd assumed it was sweat. Only when he looked at his fingers did he realise he was indeed bleeding. "Must be a splinter from the instrument panel," he concluded sensibly. "Nothing to worry about." He held out his hand and Smitty hauled him out.

Fletcher came up and started, "Sir, are you—"

"Just a scratch. Better check what other damage was done—"

The telephone rang, and Fletcher ran back towards the dispersal. Robin waited, leaning against the wing-root.

"Sir!" It was Fletcher's excited voice. "It's Control. The Home Guard at Frondsham say you got a Dornier!"

"I know," Robin answered.

"Congratulations, sir!" Smitty declared delightedly, and Fletcher came running back grinning. "Well done, sir!"

Robin took a deep breath and wondered why he didn't feel any particular elation about this victory. For one thing, he supposed, it had been too easy. With no fighter escort to protect it, no cloud cover to hide in and the full moon to expose it, the Dornier hardly stood a chance once he'd found it. Furthermore, because he'd been able to attack at his leisure without having to look over his shoulder every other second, he'd had time to see the gunner slump and the pilot look over at him. He hadn't shot down an aircraft, he'd shot down four men. "Any news of survivors?" he asked Fletcher.

"Four, sir. All captured by the Home Guard."

Robin nodded. "Good. I'll go and get some sleep then."

Crépon, France
26 July 1940

All Klaudia wanted was to do some sightseeing on her day off. She checked the train schedules carefully and calculated that she could get to Mont St. Michel and back in a single day. She no longer felt inhibited about hitching a ride with one of the Luftwaffe lorries going into Cherbourg, and the driver obligingly dropped her at the station. With the French phrasebook she purchased, she navigated buying a railway ticket, and then even ventured to have a croissant and coffee in the station café.

The morning was wet with intermittent showers. Bad flying weather, she thought automatically these days, but just as she reached Mont St. Michel, the sun burst out. It made the wet cobbles glisten and even steam a bit – very dramatic. Better still, she was lucky with the tide. It was going down, and she had only to wait a little before crossing on the causeway and starting the strenuous climb up past the thousands of souvenir shops to the Abbey perched at the top. The view from here was breathtaking. She bought a guidebook in German and was enthralled by what she was seeing and touching with her own hands. She had never been anywhere so historic before. At once, Klaudia dreamt of visiting Rheims, St. Malo, and Paris itself.

Trouble started at lunch. She found what she thought looked like a nice little crêperie, but the owner shook his head and made gestures to indicate he was closed. She pointed to the other customers, but he pointed to his watch and shook his head and shooed her out. She was very hungry and getting foot-sore too. Although the only other restaurant she could find had dirty tablecloths and a sullen waiter, she was too tired and hungry to search further. The menu was remarkably limited, and the food was bad. Worse still, three sailors came in while she was eating and made a lot of noise trying to attract her attention. When she tried to leave, they blocked her way and wanted to know if she was "some kind of snob" or what?

She denied it, and they insisted that she come and sit with them. She countered by saying she would miss her train if they didn't let her out. They clearly didn't believe her, and they got more insistent and insulting – while the waiter looked on with evident amusement. Klaudia was becoming quite desperate, when four Luftwaffe NCOs arrived. She appealed to them at once, and they gallantly took her side, telling the sailors to clear off. The sailors didn't appreciate the advice and tempers flared unpleasantly.

Klaudia managed to slip out during the commotion and ran most of the way to the station.

The train back to Cherbourg was very crowded, and Klaudia couldn't find a seat. Standing with several other passengers in the aisle, she became increasingly aware of the hostility of the French around her. The women, particularly, looked her up and down as if she were trash, and they wagged their tongues in tones that were sneering.

Still, she preferred that to the oily man wearing heavy perfume who tried to coax her into his compartment. There was a seat free next to him, he told her in heavily accented German. Why didn't she join him? He grinned. His breath smelt of garlic. Non, non, non, she answered, and looked out the window to avoid him. She felt his breath hot on the back of her neck. "German whore!" he hissed into her ear. It made her feel filthy, and she fled from him down the length of the aisle. He called things after her, making all the other passengers stare.

In Cherbourg things only got worse. It was now raining again – hard – and she couldn't find any transport back to the base. She had been so sure that there would be a lorry at the station picking up personnel returning from leave. But the only Luftwaffe transport she found was bound for Caen. After waiting for over an hour, hoping something would turn up, she became desperate enough to try to hire a taxi. Fortunately, she asked the price first, and, once she'd heard it, she beat a rapid retreat. She didn't earn that in a whole week! She certainly didn't have it on her.

But her leave expired at midnight, and since she went on duty at 4 am, she really wanted to be back in time to get at least a few hours of sleep. It was already 6 pm now. Could she walk it? She decided that if she started walking, maybe a Luftwaffe lorry would come by.

She purchased a scarf at the station and replaced her forage cap with this non-regulation headgear in the hope of keeping her head dry. After just 20 minutes her hair was drenched anyway. Indeed, water was dripping off the edge of the scarf in great drops, and her feet were wet, too. As her stockings got wet, they started to give her blisters. Soon she could barely hobble along, and she wasn't half way there.

A black Mercedes with a uniformed driver screeched to a halt beside her, and a man in SS uniform rolled down the window of the back seat. "Can I give you a lift, *Fräulein*?" The way he smiled at her made her skin crawl.

"I'm all right," she managed miserably, and the man laughed outright. He flung the door open and moved over for her.

Klaudia was frightened. All her instincts said that she shouldn't get in this car with this man, but she didn't know how to say no. He was so obviously important, and she was so obviously in distress. "Hurry up," he urged impatiently. "Don't keep me waiting all day!"

Klaudia shook her head and backed away.

"What silly game is this? Since when did you *Helferinnen* become so fussy? I'll take you to dinner afterwards." Klaudia couldn't speak for shock and indignation. No one had ever said anything like this to her before. It was worse even than Jako! She shook her head and took another step back.

"Get in before I catch cold!" It was an order, but the remark about *Helferinnen* had been too explicit. Klaudia turned and tried to make her way back along the side of the road in the other direction, slipping and sliding in the mud. The SS car kept pace with her, going backwards, and all the time the man in the back seat was heckling her.

There was a curve in the road, and suddenly a car came around it and had to screech to a halt to avoid colliding with the reversing Mercedes. Klaudia cried out in fear, and then in relief. The officer getting out of the driver's seat was familiar. It was the fat officer who flew wingman to Feldburg. She couldn't remember his name, but it didn't matter. She ran to the car and threw herself in the passenger side. "Thank you!" she gasped out. "Thank you!"

"*Fräulein* von Richthofen, what's happened? Who is that?"

"Please, just take me back to the base." Klaudia was trembling from fear, cold and relief all at once. Ahead of them on the road, the door of the Mercedes slammed shut as the car went into forward gear and started accelerating.

Ernst glanced nervously at Klaudia. She seemed to be crying, but it might just have been the rain. "Did that man do something to you?"

Klaudia shook her head. "I – I didn't get in the car, but – he said things. I'm sorry. I must seem very hysterical." Her teeth were chattering.

"You're soaked through," Ernst registered. He stopped the car, got out, and removed his own tunic. He handed it to her as he climbed back in. "Put that on."

Klaudia wanted to say no, but then again it was warm, and so much too big for her that she could cuddle up in it. That was comforting. Ernst looked a little ridiculous without it, of course. His round belly was more exposed than ever, as were his trouser braces. The Luftwaffe uniform was not designed to be flattering without the tunic.

"If he did anything to harm you, *gnädiges Fräulein*, it ought to be reported," Ernst told her earnestly, glancing sidelong at her as he drove. He meant it. He didn't care if the other man was a senior officer of whatever service. Ernst had been unable to see the uniform, much less the rank, of the man in the car, but he had seen the German number plate. The type of vehicle and the driver indicated that he was powerful.

But that only made things worse. Ernst had been raised to believe that officers ought to be exemplary gentlemen; they had no right to harass an honest German girl like Frl. v. Richthofen.

"I'm sorry. I'm making too much of it. Please don't tell anyone. It's just been a long day. I'm so grateful you came along!"

"I'm very glad I could be of service, Frl. v. Richthofen," Ernst answered earnestly. He wished desperately that he wasn't fat and round-faced and the son of a plumber from Cottbus.

27 July 27 1940

Flying had been cancelled due to weather, and Ernst had gone into town for a haircut and just to get off the Station for a bit. Christian and Dieter were doing something with their French girlfriends, because now Dieter had one, too, so Ernst was on his own.

Ever since the encounter the day before with Klaudia v. Richthofen, Ernst's interest in the French girls had declined. Klaudia was the kind of girl he wanted – pretty without being sexy, modest, well-mannered, loyal, German....

He'd wanted to approach her, but he knew what he looked like from his mirror. Besides, she was an aristocrat from a famous family. No, he couldn't expect her to take an interest in him, but his interest in her made it hard for him to look at other girls.

Listlessly he window-shopped in the provincial town. He had coffee and cake at a café, and then went to a film. It was in French and he didn't understand it. When he came out it was drizzling rain, and he had nothing better to do than return to the Mess, so he drove back to the Station.

The Mess was nearly empty. Most of the others appeared to have gone to a local night-club. Ernst knew there was one not all that far away, with live music and a very alluring French singer. He supposed Christian and Dieter and the others would be there – or out dancing with their girls. Ernst wished he could enjoy things like that, but for some reason he found smoke- filled rooms with a lot of drunk men making lewd remarks to the "hostesses" mildly disgusting. He supposed there was something wrong with him – especially after tagging along once or twice and seeing the number of senior officers who frequented these places. Still, he never enjoyed himself, so there seemed no point in wasting all that money.

He went up to his room and tried to read Clausewitz' *On War*. During training, he had been advised that he *must* read this, but it didn't really interest him. He put it aside and decided to write to his mother instead. Not that there was much to report since his last letter, but he could answer the news from home and assure her that he was fine – getting enough to eat and all that. (She always worried about that, though he couldn't understand why, given his figure.)

He had been writing for quite a while when he became aware that noises were coming from the next room. That was Dieter's room. So Dieter, and Christian, were probably back, although when he checked his watch and saw that it was only just after 9 pm. That was early for them, but they had been put on alert for tomorrow morning, so it was just as well. He thought of knocking and seeing if they wanted to have a beer together downstairs but decided to finish his letter first.

A moment later he heard what sounded like a radio being switched on, static, and then a slightly distorted voice calling *"Achtung! Achtung! Der Führer spricht direkt von der Reichskanzlei!"* Ernst lifted his head. The *Führer* was giving a speech? Why hadn't they been warned? Usually the entire base was informed that the Führer would be addressing the nation, and it was broadcast in the lounge and the bar. Frowning, he turned towards the wall through which the sound came. It certainly sounded like the *Führer*, although he couldn't quite catch the words.

He got up and switched on his own radio, but all he got was static and then music. How could that be? A *Führer* speech was carried on all the German channels. He snapped off the radio. Still the speech came from the other side of the wall. It seemed to be coming to a crescendo. He could clearly catch phrases like *"deutsches Blut und deutsches Boden."* Maybe it was a recording of an older speech? But Dieter didn't seem like the type to keep records of the *Führer's* old speeches – Hans, perhaps, but not Dieter.

Baffled, Ernst decided to find out for himself. He went out into the hall and paused before Dieter's room. The speech was easier to hear through the door than the wall; now he could hear Hitler saying: "Today and only today this *great* German nation, this nation filled with *millions* of Germans in whose veins German blood flows, Germans raised on German soil, German potatoes, German cabbage, and German coffee – also known as Ersatz—" and then there were guffaws of male laughter, and Ernst knew something very strange was going on. He knocked on the door.

Stunned silence answered, and then Dieter called out, "Yes?"

"It's me, Ernst."

A pause, then "Come in."

Christian was sitting on the floor with his back against the wall, and Dieter and Busso were lounging on the bed, with their ties loosened and passing a bottle of schnapps between them. A shot glass was on the floor beside Christian, too. They were all looking at little dazed from too much alcohol, but both Busso and Dieter looked alarmed, too. Not Christian, of course. Christian staggered to his feet and drew Ernst into the room. "My dear wingman! We have been missing you. Come and join us for a little schnapps."

"I thought I heard the *Führer* giving a speech," Ernst found himself saying, feeling very foolish, since it was obvious that they had been making fun of the *Führer* and he didn't approve of that.

"Ah, did it really sound that way?" Christian asked as if flattered. "I must be getting better," he bowed to the others. They still looked wary. "Dieter, you must have another glass for my beloved wingman," Christian ordered.

Dieter produced the glass, handing it to Ernst with a probing look.

"Do you want to hear more?" Christian asked, hiccupping.

"Of what?" Ernst asked.

"My speech!"

"No!" Dieter cut it off. "We've had enough. Sorry we disturbed you, Ernst. We just had rather a bad night. First M. St. Pierre grounded both Gabrielle and Yvonne for some silly thing or other, and then the café we wanted to go to had a leaking roof and was closed for repairs, and worst of all, Christian's car stalled on us and we had to push it home the last two or three kilometres in the rain. So, we warmed ourselves up with rather too much schnapps and got silly. That's all. I'm sorry."

Ernst was torn. He didn't think they should have been making fun of the *Führer* – but then again, these were his closest friends, and if they were going to have a little fun together, he wanted to be included. He supposed there really wasn't any harm in making a parody of a *Führer* speech. They could be quite tedious sometimes – at least on the radio. Once he'd had the privilege of seeing the *Führer* speak in person. He'd been mesmerized and caught up in all the enthusiasm. He'd joined in screaming "*Heil!*" like mad, and it had been intoxicating and exhilarating. But on the radio, sometimes, the *Führer* seemed to talk on and on without ever coming to the point. So, Ernst shrugged and clicked his glass against Dieter's. "Why didn't you come and get me when you got back?" he asked a little plaintively.

"We assumed you were out enjoying the evening, my dear wingman," Christian assured him, an arm over his shoulders. "Having a good time." He waved the air vaguely, "But since you are *here*, have some more schnapps to make up for starting late. You can clear any hangover with a whiff of oxygen!" And Christian refilled Ernst's glass.

Chapter 14

RAF Hawarden
27 July 1940

From the way the trainees reacted, you would have thought *they'd* got the Dornier. It didn't help that a rain front had come in the next day and there had been intermittent showers ever since, inhibiting flying. This gave the trainees and ground crews the opportunity to cluster around his Spitfire, inspecting the bullet holes in the belly and starboard wing and – more fascinating – the bullets still inside the cockpit. Altogether they'd found seven in the cockpit itself, while another half-dozen bullets had been stopped by the armour plating behind his seat. Robin found it a fraction unsettling and thought it almost uncannily odd that he'd come away with only a scratch to his forehead, from which a fragment of glass had been promptly extracted. In short, All he had to show for his brush with death was a sticking plaster.

And then the reporters arrived. First came the local press, of course, which Kennel was used to handling; Priestman got off with a handshake and a photo next to the damaged Spitfire. But the day after, two American reporters and a photographer turned up.

The Americans had been in Liverpool covering "the convoy story" (as they called it): the courage of sailors facing an invisible enemy practically unprotected. That was the angle that fascinated the Americans, of course, because the United States had some fifty-odd de-commissioned destroyers, which the US government refused to lend, lease, sell or give to Great Britain. They argued it would be a violation of "neutrality." It didn't make Priestman feel particularly friendly towards Americans.

He was down at the dispersal hut, trying to catch up on some paperwork, when he heard loud American voices and Wing Commander Kennel saying, "Flight Lieutenant Priestman is just in here, and I'm sure he'll be happy to answer a few questions."

Priestman looked for cover. There wasn't any.

Kennel stood in the door of the hut and asked, "Robin, would you come out and meet some gentlemen from the American press?"

"No. I will not," Robin answered bluntly.

Kennel was taken aback – but only for a second. He was, after all, used to dealing with fighter pilots. "Yes, you will, Priestman, and that's an order." Kennel spoke softly to avoid being heard by the Americans, who were talking in loud voices behind him.

The Americans were asking someone if *that* was the Spitfire which had shot down the enemy bomber, and one of the trainees answered readily: "Indeed it is, sir. May I show you the bullet holes in the cockpit?" By the time Priestman emerged from dispersal, the Americans were already halfway to the aircraft.

Kennel remarked as they approached, "I'm quite surprised you don't want to talk to the press, given the way you've been behaving."

"What is that supposed to mean, sir?"

"Seems rather like you're trying to attract attention, doesn't it? First the Heinkel over Southampton and now this night intruder."

"It wasn't my idea to go on night ops – or fly to Southampton, for that matter." Priestman reminded him. "Besides, it was pure luck that I got anything. If the search-lights hadn't found it, I wouldn't even have seen the damn thing. Once they had it in the beams, even one of *that* lot" – he nodded towards the trainees – "could have bagged it. Piece of cake." Robin dismissed the episode.

He had something else on his mind. "Would you mind if I nipped over to Chester County Hospital this afternoon? I'll be meeting the train from Bristol anyway, and if I went over early I could drop by the hospital."

Kennel stopped his pipe halfway to his mouth and froze in his tracks, staring at the junior officer. Robin didn't meet his eye; he pretended to watch the American journalists inspecting his Spitfire instead. He felt Kennel's searching gaze and self-consciously tossed his hair out of his eyes. He had both fists stuffed in his trouser pockets.

"Now why would you want to go and do that?" The Senior Officer asked very seriously.

Robin shrugged. He didn't know why he wanted to, exactly, but it had something to do with being honest with himself. With being able to look himself in the mirror. With being able to face Emily again.

Funny how often his thoughts came back to Emily. He knew he'd been a bit of a cad in the past. Too keen on having fun to take any girl seriously, and – except for the predators like Virginia – most girls wanted to be taken seriously. He'd tried not to let things go too far with anyone nice. He'd done nothing he really had to be ashamed of, but he'd caused a lot of tears. It was hard to have fun with a girl and then leave her without her getting upset about it. That had always been his dilemma in the past.

And now? Now he often found himself wondering what Emily would think or do or say. Emily wasn't a trophy like Virginia. She would not enhance his reputation, but somehow that didn't matter to him any more.

What he cared about was whether Emily would like flying, and if she'd get on at the Mess, and if he'd have as much fun with her this time as he had before. "Don't do it, Robin," Kennel brought him back to the present.

"Are you forbidding it, sir?"

"No. Facing the men you shot down is between you and them – and God. No commanding officer has the right to interfere. But my *advice* is: don't do it. Now, we'd better go and talk to these American chaps before they're too filled with rubbish to see straight."

As they approached the Spitfire, one of the Americans caught sight of the approaching officers and rushed over. "Flight Lieutenant Priestman? Howard Briggs, *Detroit Times*. Pleasure to meet you. We've been hearing some great things about you."

"All lies, then, I can assure you."

The American started and then laughed heartily. "Love your English sense of humour! Wonderful!" He jotted something down, and Kennel raised his eyebrows at Robin. "Tell me about this kill of yours, Mr. Priestman."

"What kill?"

"Didn't you shoot down a Do17 the other night?"

"Yes, I shot down a Dornier 17, a twin-engine, monoplane aircraft of German manufacture. Maximum speed 250 mph – or thereabouts – range roughly 1,500 miles. All four crewmen aboard survived."

"Uh-huh. Would you tell us about it?"

"What?"

"About the dogfight," Briggs pressed him, a touch of exasperation creeping into his voice at Priestman's evident reticence.

"There was no dogfight. The Dornier is not a fighter and had no fighter escort. I intercepted an enemy intruder and, in accordance with standing orders, I did my best to shoot it down. This time I was lucky."

"How?"

"The Spitfire is equipped with eight Browning machine guns. They are quite effective. I suggest you inspect the wreckage of the Dornier for evidence of their impact."

"Love to, but your police or Home Guard or whatever it is won't let us near it. Top Secret. You make it sound very easy, Mr. Priestman – what's that expression you boys use, 'piece of cake,' eh?" How silly it sounded in that American accent, and Robin resented the reporter even more. Meanwhile, the reporter was continuing belligerently, "The way we hear it, Nazi planes are flying over here night after night – heard bunches of them myself – and most of them go home unmolested."

"Have you ever flown at night?"

"Once or twice."

"Did you find it easy to see other aircraft in the darkness?"

"Uh. I don't think I tried. But, look, don't you Brits have some sort of top-secret tracking device for locating aircraft?"

"I've heard rumours, but I wouldn't know."

"You mean you *don't* have any means of tracking the enemy aircraft?" The second reporter, who had not introduced himself, asked with open hostility. The reporters struck Robin as vultures. Both seemed to be hunching over their pads with their pencils poised, ready to tear him apart.

"We have the Observer Corps – extremely efficient and dedicated volunteers, mostly ex-service men and women from the last war. I highly recommend visiting one or more of our observer stations – particularly on a dark night."

It took them a moment to digest that answer and then Briggs asked, "What chances do you give the RAF of defeating the Luftwaffe?"

"None."

There was a collective gasp – and not just from the reporters. Kennel at once tried to intervene, "Now just a minute, Priestman—"

"In case you haven't noticed, *we* are not attacking Germany. We don't *have* to defeat the Luftwaffe. All we have to do is convince the German government that it is not worth *their* while trying to conquer England."

"And you think you can do that?" the second reporter insisted sceptically.

Priestman looked at the reporter and considered his answer carefully. Then he smiled. "Let me put it this way, gentlemen. I would not want to trade places with a Luftwaffe pilot for anything in the world."

"Why not? Don't you think their planes are as good as yours?"

"The Me109 is a very good aircraft. I was shot down twice by 109s."

"Then why wouldn't you want to trade places with a Luftwaffe pilot?"

Priestman shrugged and jammed his fists deeper in his pockets. The photographer lifted his heavy camera to his face and with a flash, a photo immortalised the moment. Robin stood in front of his Spitfire staring into the camera, with a plaster over his left eye and his hair falling over the right. "Never fancied getting my arse shot off for a dictator."

Robin was deadly serious, but for some reason the others all found the answer terribly funny.

*****

It was raining buckets by the time the train finally pulled into the station at Chester, and Emily felt like a limp hanky. She had foolishly worn her best suit so she'd look nice for Robin, but after almost six hours in trains – much of it standing – her blouse and skirt were crushed and rumpled, and her lipstick was gone, too. (How did other women always manage to look so neat and fresh?)

The station was only dimly lit on account of the blackout, of course, and, never having been here before, she felt forlorn as she followed the crowds through the unfamiliar tunnel towards the exit. What if no one was here to collect her? And what if he was?

Her parents had filled her with apprehension. In fact, they had thrown a fit when she announced she was going to spend the weekend with an RAF officer whom she hardly knew. Her mother had wanted to know where she was to stay, and when she admitted she didn't know, there had been a terrible row. Her mother accused her of being a hussy. Although her father defended her, saying she was just naïve, he had warned her against going. "You are being used, Emily. Can't you see that? An honest man wouldn't even *suggest* that you spend a weekend with him when he knows you so little! Why can't he come to Portsmouth if he wants to see you?"

"Because he's training pilots all day," Emily told him, afraid to mention the fact that she also intended to fly with him.

"Then he won't have time to see you whether you're in Wales or not!" her mother retorted pointedly, adding, "I can't believe my own daughter is so *desperate* for some man's attention that she is willing to traipse halfway across the country at her own expense and make an absolute fool of herself – if not worse." The remark hit home. Emily so wanted to see Robin again, that she would have travelled much farther than Wales.

So, her parents had raged and advised in vain. Emily closed her ears as much as possible, and stubbornly went and spent half her savings on a new cocktail dress, a new blouse and new shoes. She dug out a pair of riding breeches and boots (bought second-hand while at Cambridge for a week on a friend's estate and never used since), and she went and had her hair cut – not short, just styled more.

Now she stood in front of Chester station on a rainy night, feeling like an absolute fool. Everyone else was rushing purposefully, and he wasn't here. She'd been stood up. She should have expected it! A man like Robin must have all sorts of prettier girls—

"Sorry I'm late. I stopped by the hospital and it took longer than I expected." He loomed out of the darkness, reaching for her suitcase. "I'm parked just over here – in a no-parking zone, I'm afraid." He gestured with his head.

Emily took the hint and hurried, but she couldn't help asking, "The hospital? Has someone been hurt?"

"I shot down a German bomber two nights ago and the crew was taken to hospital. One gunner was in pretty bad shape, getting blood and fluids intravenously. The other gunner had a thigh wound but seemed cheerful enough. The pilot had a shattered shoulder and elbow. Really quite astonishing what a round of .303s can do to human flesh and bones! Only the bomb aimer was unscathed. He actually landed the aircraft. The pilot couldn't handle the bomber once his shoulder was shot up, and so the bomb aimer had to take over the controls with the pilot telling him what to do." Robin was still very much preoccupied by the experience at the hospital and not entirely attentive to Emily. He threw her suitcase in the back seat and held the front door for her.

Emily slipped inside and waited while Robin went around to the driver's side to get in. She was a little stunned. He hadn't said anything about flying "ops" last time, and if one was to believe the papers shooting down an aircraft, particularly at night, was quite an accomplishment. Yet the most incredible thing about the incident was this idea of going and visiting the captured enemy crew. She found herself asking in disbelief as he climbed in behind the wheel, "You visited the German crew of an aircraft you shot down?"

"It seemed the decent thing to do, don't you think?" Robin asked without looking at her. He was twisting around to see out the back window as he backed up. He sounded utterly casual, but in fact he was quite tense, wondering what she *would* think.

"I think that was very courageous of you," Emily told him in a low voice that she hoped conveyed her sincere admiration. She felt it took at least as much courage to meet the men you have shot and hurt face to face as it did to brave their guns in the first place. She could not think of one of her University friends who would have done that – except perhaps Michael....

"It was odd, you know. I used to compete in air shows and I ran into the Luftwaffe fairly regularly. They always seemed so arrogant and self-assured. I don't mean they were pompous and rude the way the newspapers portray them. It was subtler than that. It was more that they were so friendly and jovial that it was patronising." He glanced over at her to see if she was listening.

Emily was watching him with fascination. She nodded, not wanting to interrupt or distract him with words.

"Towards the end, the rivalry was getting a bit barbed – at least on our part. I mean, after Czechoslovakia we could see a war was coming, and it really galled me the way they assumed we'd just roll over and play dead. They'd tut-tut at us over a beer: 'Come, come, you don't *really* think you can take on our Stukas with your bi-planes, do you? Why, our *bombers* can fly faster than the bulk of your front-line fighters! Why can't we just be friends?'"

Now Emily was holding her breath. It was beginning to sound as if Robin had visited the men in hospital *not* out of concern but in order to gloat – to remind them of their former arrogance and rub their nose in their personal defeat. She didn't want to think of him being like that.

"I was curious how they would behave in the face of defeat. I have to admit they were really very nice – especially the bomb aimer. He seemed shy and modest, insisting that the landing was nothing special. I expect he'd had some flight training. Still, with one engine out and in the dark, it was no mean feat. The gunner who was not so badly hurt was full of curiosity and acted down-right excited to meet me. I suppose they were just ordinary airmen, while the officers I met at air shows were probably specially selected not just for their flying skills, but for their political loyalty as well. These men were different. The bomb aimer spoke excellent English, and he was solemn and soft-spoken. I can only hope I will behave as well if I ever find myself in his situation."

Robin paused, trying to sort out his own emotions. He knew that Kennel had not wanted him to go because he feared that seeing the enemy as human would make it harder to shoot at them. Seeing what machine-gun fire could do was certainly sobering....

"I had friends from University who went to fight in Spain," Emily ventured a little uncertainly in the silence.

Robin looked over expectantly; her response so far pleased him. Virginia had been morbidly fascinated by his "kills" and that was a major reason he didn't want to have anything more to do with her. Given Emily's pacifism, on the other hand, he'd known she wouldn't applaud his victory, but he had feared she might be appalled or disgusted that he'd shed blood. He'd worried, too, that she might consider him proud and gloating to visit the prisoners in hospital.

"One of my friends from Cambridge returned from Spain very bitter and cynical. He said both sides were guilty of unspeakable atrocities and that it was not possible to fight a war without becoming bestial. That confirmed my own pacifism at the time," Emily admitted.

Robin looked at her hard, sensing she wanted to say more.

"I hope this doesn't sound foolish or naïve," she continued, "but I don't *want* to think that any more. I want to believe that we all have a choice. I think that respecting the enemy and remembering that he is human is an important part of that. I think," she hesitated but then forged ahead, "if you recognise your enemy as human and *still* feel you have to fight him – and if necessary kill him – then you know you are fighting for a good cause.

If you have to turn the enemy into something sub-human or super-human or alien in order to motivate yourself, then you are deceiving yourself."

It took Robin a moment to digest that thought, but then he nodded. What she said made sense, and his opinion of Emily rose further. No girl he'd ever dated before would have said anything so profound. "Thank you."

Then, feeling embarrassed, he smiled and changed the subject. "I hope you don't mind. I've put you up at a B & B. I thought you'd be more comfortable there than in a hotel, and it's a little closer to the airfield."

"It sounds lovely," Emily responded, relieved. He'd said "you," not "us."

Shortly afterwards, they stopped at a neat little cottage with a thatched roof, a rose garden and a purring tomcat. The door opened before they reached the front steps, and an elderly lady with a white lace collar peeking over her cardigan welcomed them inside. The parlour was all stuffed furniture and silver-framed photographs of happy children on Welsh ponies.

"My dear Miss Pryce, what a delight to have you with me," the landlady, Mrs. Lloyd, exclaimed in a lilting Welsh accent. "Let me take your case and show you to your room. You must be terribly tired after such a long journey. We'll only be a minute, Flight Lieutenant Priestman. Have a seat by the fire and help yourself to tea. I made it for you just minutes ago."

Mrs. Lloyd led Emily up the narrow, wallpapered staircase, chatting as she went. "Now the lavatory is just here, and the bath is the next door. And up this way...." They went up a second flight of stairs into a spacious room under the eaves, with a frilly bedspread on a four-poster bed. Everything was neat and clean and polished. Just what one wanted in a bed-and-breakfast – especially Mrs. Lloyd, who was exclaiming in a loud whisper, "You must feel very lucky to have a friend like Flight Lieutenant Priestman. Such a nice young man! *Some* of them are quite wild, you know. They drink too much and then drive about causing accidents. But Flight Lieutenant Priestman is a perfect gentleman. Now, I'm sure you want to freshen up before dinner with Mr. Priestman, so don't let me stop you. What time would you like breakfast?"

"Oh, I haven't had a chance to ask Robin about tomorrow."

"Don't you worry, my dear. Go and freshen up and I'll ask him myself." She was already on her way back downstairs, and Emily took her little make-up kit down to the bathroom, feeling more comfortable already. At least her parents had been wrong about Robin's dishonourable intentions. This was not the place you brought a girl you thought was a tart.

Emily was woken by Mrs. Lloyd with a tea tray. "Flight Lieutenant

Priestman just rang. He's on his way over to pick you up in a half hour."

"Already?" Emily sat bolt upright and looked about, bewildered.

"I let you sleep in, dear. It's almost 9 o'clock."

Emily rushed down to bathe and change. Robin had promised to take her flying if the weather permitted. Emily peered out of the bathroom window, trying to decide if this was flying weather or not. What did she know about flying weather? At least it wasn't raining. She opted therefore for her breeches, boots and the smart "safari" blouse that she had purchased especially for the occasion. She also had a large square silk scarf to protect her hair – or would she be expected to wear one of those leather flying helmets?

She heard the bell ring and brushed her hair hastily as she heard voices waft up from the hall below. When she came down the stairs, Robin was waiting in the entry. He looked up, and the look he gave her made her warm all over. It was unmistakably approving. As she joined him she said self-consciously, "I don't own any other trousers, I'm afraid, and in the pictures women always wear trousers for flying."

"Awkward clambering in and out of a cockpit in skirts. Boots and breeches are excellent." Then with a wry smile he added, "Just what the Luftwaffe wears." Then he broke into a real smile and admitted, "Besides, you look smashing," before adding practically, "you'll be cold in just a blouse, however. Didn't you bring a jacket or jumper?"

Emily hadn't thought of it. "Only my rain-coat." She indicated the coat she had worn in the train.

"Not to worry. I'll find you something. Shall we go?" Emily nodded.

They climbed into Robin's battered old Austin, and a few minutes later they turned in towards the airfield. With a horrible blast that seemed to rock the little Austin and made Emily gasp, three Spitfires shot out of nowhere and flew just feet above their heads. They had just taken off and were still folding in their undercarriage, bobbing up and down a little as they did so. Emily was a bit shaken, but Robin didn't appear to have noticed them at all.

He parked by the Mess, and led Emily out to the waiting two-seater, which had been rolled out and tanked up for him. The ground crew greeted them cheerfully. There he left her to go and fetch a couple of fleece-lined flying jackets. When he returned, he was at first bewildered that neither Emily nor the crew were anywhere near the Maggie. Then he noticed, 20 yards away, that the ground crew was introducing Emily to a Spitfire. Fletcher was going on at great length and in great detail about the merits of the Merlin engine, and Emily was listening and nodding with so much attention that one would have thought she was genuinely interested.

Robin held back to watch for a moment. "Is it the engine that makes the Spitfire such a superior aircraft?" Emily asked.

"Of course not!" scoffed Smitty. "It's the design! Look at the curve of these wings," and he ran his hand lovingly over the leading edge of the distinctive wings.

"It's the combination," Robin joined the conversation. "The engine and the design. Shall I give you a leg up?"

"May I?" Emily asked, a little frightened.

"Why not? You can't do her any harm."

Robin showed her the handles and stirrups so she could scramble up the wing, and she sank into the narrow cockpit. It looked far more spacious with her in it than it felt when he was sitting there.

Emily felt her heart in her throat for a moment as her bottom sank onto the worn seat, and she was enclosed by the smell of metal and oil and aviation fuel. Directly in front of her was the confusing instrument panel and, beyond, the snout of the mechanical beast loomed up, cutting off her view. Before she knew what she was doing, her feet settled on the pedals, and with an audible clank the rudder shifted. She jumped slightly and yanked her feet back guiltily.

"Not to worry," Robin assured her from where he stood on the wing root. He pointed out the various instruments and the "joy stick." Emily's thumb slid over the trigger. How easy it must be to push, she thought. The thought frightened her. She pushed herself back up and gave her hand to Robin. "Take me up in the other plane, please."

Robin helped her out of the Spitfire cockpit and handed her a jacket as they walked back to the Maggie. "I borrowed it from the smallest of the trainees, but I'm afraid it's still too big."

It was too big but flattering, nevertheless. The thick fleece collar framed her face, and the brown leather went well with her breeches and boots. Her hands looked wonderfully slender and elegant, emerging from the turned-back sleeves that came halfway down her hand.

Robin gave her a leather flying helmet as well, and Smitty strapped her securely into the front seat. "Wouldn't it be better for me to sit behind you?" she asked, concerned, but Robin insisted she'd have a better view in front.

They bounced across the field to the head of the runway, turned into the wind and waited for a heartbeat. Abruptly the purring of the engine turned into a roar and the little plane rolled forward, faster and faster. Emily clung to the doors, almost frightened. But all excitement has to do with being just a little bit frightened. She almost missed the moment when the aircraft left the ground. She thought it had and then she wasn't sure and then she realised, oh yes, they were flying! It was amazing.

Absolutely amazing!

Robin banked and turned. She could see back and down to the Spitfires dispersed about the airfield and the new Wellingtons lined up beside the factory. The factory complex dwarfed the little brick house that served the RAF as a Mess. Everything was so clear and yet already so small. And the wind was rushing and cold and exhilarating.

They kept climbing, and the countryside was laid out beneath her like nothing she had ever seen before. She'd seen magazine photos taken from the air, but they were black-and-white and abstract compared to this. This was far more tangible and exciting. She could see the shapes of the fields, defined by hedgerows and stone walls. With wonder, she realised the little white dots must be sheep. Yes, they moved about in shifting patterns, and two horses bolted when the shadow of the plane caught up and passed over them.

Then the aircraft was nipping in and out of great, fluffy clouds. They plunged into the cloud and it was like being in a blinding fog one minute, and then they burst back out into the dazzling sunshine. Below, something shone like shimmering gold, and Emily leaned over to see more clearly around the propeller and the wing-struts: the sea! And there were ships upon it – dark and tiny with glistening wakes. Robin banked around tighter to take her closer and for a moment she was frightened, feeling as if she were about to fall out. But the fright passed quickly, and she gained confidence rapidly. By the time he did it again, she was leaning into it. Again, again! she begged him silently.

Instead, he swooped down and frolicked along the coastline, following the bays and inlets, their shadow dancing beneath them, sometimes on the water, sometimes springing over the land like a hunter effortlessly clearing fences. They leapt over cliffs and skimmed across bays and mud-flats. Then Robin dipped the wingtip again, and Emily clung to the sides of the cockpit and caught her breath as he banked sharply and raced inland. They left the sea behind, following a road with traffic. Their shadow overtook the cars and lorries. Emily saw the white faces of men in the back of an army lorry look up at her. She waved to them, and they waved back. Robin found a river — a ribbon of silver in the dark-green and golden countryside — and followed it until a great castle loomed up on their left: Ludlow.

Emily recognised it instantly. She'd done a paper on the Battle of Ludford Bridge and made a trip to Ludlow especially to get a feel for the topography. Now the town of Ludlow was below her, so she could see the plan of the streets and the market cross at which the Duchess of York had once courageously awaited the Lancanstrian Army to beg mercy for the town.

Emily was sorry when a quarter of an hour later she saw the airfield below them, and realised that Robin was preparing to land. She supposed she would never fly again – well, not like this on a private tour of the Welsh Marches. On the other hand, her feet and hands were frozen and she was very stiff. They circled once, letting a Wellington get off on its way to a Maintenance Unit to be fitted with radio and other gadgets, and then Robin put the Maggie down so gently and they hardly bounced. They returned to the RAF side of the field, and the ground crew emerged out of nowhere. The engine was switched off and there was an abrupt, unaccustomed silence. Emily twisted around in her seat and beamed at Robin. "That was wonderful! I wish it could have lasted for hours!"

"Flight Lieutenant Priestman didn't do any of his tricks, then?" Smitty remarked, with a grin and a wink to Robin as he helped Emily out of her straps.

"What tricks?" she asked, looking from Smitty to Robin as he slipped down to the ground.

"Flying upside down or under telephone wires, barrel rolls – all that kind of thing that he did with me!"

"Smitty!"

Emily stared at Robin, and he took her elbow. "Don't listen to him. Did you really like it?"

"I loved it! I'm beginning to understand how one could spend every penny and every waking minute just to learn how to do that!"

"Better when you get paid for it," Robin countered, his hand still on her elbow as he led her back towards the Mess. "We can do it again sometime, if you like."

"When?"

"Tomorrow, after the flying demo. Where do you want to go for lunch?"

"Can we go to Ludlow? I know a wonderful pub there."

"You know Ludlow?"

"I read Medieval History at Cambridge, remember? Ludlow is the seat of the Earls of March."

"Never heard of them."

"Roger Mortimer, the lover of Queen Isabella? And Edmund Mortimer, the friend of the Black Prince, and, of course, Edward IV himself—" She stopped, unsure of herself. There were lots of people who weren't interested in history.

Robin smiled and prompted, "Tell me."

She did more than that; she showed him Ludlow Castle from the ground. She led him through the ruins, up the narrow winding stairs and along the windy wall-walk. Under her outstretched arm, the armies of Lancaster and York re-mustered. She painted the great hall with the colours of the tapestries and carpets, the surcoats of the knights, and the gowns and veils of the ladies. She conjured up the ghosts of frightened children, terrified women and helpless clergymen facing the vengeance of a foreign Queen during the sack of Ludlow, and also brought to life again a 19-year-old knight, grieving the loss of a father and a brother, turning defeat into victory by his dogged courage. As she spoke, Emily was reminded that most of the pilots in training here were just about that age.

For the dance, the staff at the Station had gone to considerable effort to decorate the lounge, pushing furniture aside or removing it altogether to make a small dance floor. They had strung coloured lights and some wooden aircraft models from the ceiling. There was an amateur three-piece band drawn from the ground crews and the chief cook. The refreshments were catered from the local, and the bar was open.

Emily had never attended such an event and had been rather unsure what to expect. There were quite a few local girls in high heels and rather short skirts. And there were sisters in modest cocktail dresses. Mrs. Kennel and some of the mothers looked decidedly dowdy, however. Emily was relieved that no one was in evening attire and reassured by the way Robin looked at her. What surprised her most was that she became the centre of attention among the young pilots.

It started because one of them asked her how she liked her flight with Robin, and she had answered with honest enthusiasm and followed her remarks with questions about flying. The young trainees suddenly had an audience who knew even less than they did. That was intoxicating, and the next thing Emily knew there was a little crowd around her. Robin had to elbow his way in to deliver a drink. "Are they boring you?" he asked. "They really can't talk about anything except Spitfires, I'm afraid."

"I don't mind," Emily answered sincerely, but Robin looked sceptical and continued, "Sir Christopher, the Managing Director of the factory, and his wife have asked to meet you." He had her by the elbow and manoeuvred her back towards the sedate crowd around the Station Commander.

The usual introductions and pleasantries were exchanged, and then Mrs. Kennel turned to Robin rather pointedly (for the knighted audience, Emily suspected). "What's this I hear about you visiting wounded Luftwaffe pilots in hospital?" she wanted to know. Adding before Robin had a chance to answer, "I hope you made them feel their feathers had been well and truly plucked!"

Emily stiffened, and Robin squeezed her elbow in an intimate gesture of reassurance before remarking very calmly, "Not at all. They told me they had decided to land so the wounded gunner, who otherwise probably wouldn't have made it home alive, could get medical attention quickly. They were clearly not too concerned about spending a lot of time in prison, since they are certain the Wehrmacht will be here to free them within weeks."

Emily was never sure if it was the truth – or only Robin's way of putting the Station Commander's wife in her place. Her expression had certainly been worth seeing, and then, fortunately, the dance music started, and Robin excused himself to take Emily onto the dance floor.

Chapter 15

RAF Tangmere
1 August 1940

It came just as he knew it would. After almost a week of uneventful patrolling, the next time they encountered the enemy, Ginger didn't get away. His pursuer hammered him from behind at such close range and with such perfect aim that his engine burst into flames. Ginger flipped the crate over and dropped out before he even had time to consciously be afraid. He found himself tumbling head over heels and his brain screamed at him: Ripcord, ripcord! There had to be a ripcord somewhere. His hand groped. He started feeling sick – whether from the tumbling or the fear, he didn't know. With a terrible jerk, his parachute opened. He was no longer falling through the sky but gliding gently downwards.

Slowly, his breathing settled somewhat. Ginger had a moment to realise he was alive after all – and then he looked down and saw he was out over the water. Instantly, he was seized with new terror. It was his worst nightmare. Worse even then being burned to death in his aircraft. God was getting his revenge for letting him live a week longer than he should have. He was going to kill him slowly. He thought of Davis, washed up a day later, and he knew he was going to die down there all alone in the cold-blooded sea.

Ginger couldn't swim. If his life vest didn't inflate, he would drown at once. But even if it did, his chances of rescue were almost nil. He'd had no time to make an R/T transmission. The others wouldn't realise what had happened until he failed to land. No one would know where to look for him.

Despite his terror, Ginger couldn't entirely abandon hope. Maybe there was a ship somewhere that could see him? Ginger looked frantically at the sea beneath him. It was empty. Ginger searched the sky again, hoping for some friendly aircraft that could report his position. Instead, he saw one of the German bombers, billowing black smoke as it limped across the sky. He could hear the rough, irregular throb of its engines through the still air. One was running very roughly. Even as Ginger watched, it went dead. Maybe the pilot had turned it off to stop it from over-heating or to save fuel. Whatever, it was sinking faster now. Apparently, there was not enough power in the other engine to keep it aloft. Ginger watched as little black specks drop away from the bomber and realised it must be the crew bailing out. Seconds later, parachutes blossomed over them. He counted.

Four men were floating gently on the same breeze he was. Then the bomber sliced into the water and disappeared.

For a moment the death of the bomber was comforting. After all, it was more likely that someone from the shore would see those four parachutes than his lone one. Surely a boat would be launched for them?

Then he plunged into the water, and it was sheer terror again. The Channel was bitterly cold. Ginger went right under and struggled wildly to get back to the surface. The sheepskin of his flying jacket and boots absorbed the water and started weighing him down, dragging him under. Worse still, the parachute was spread out over him, so that even when he surfaced he could see nothing. The silk clung to the surface. Panicking, Ginger tore at it trying to get out from under it, completely forgetting the release button. Struggling against it and the waves and the weight of his boots was too much. He started drowning.

Swallowing huge mouthfuls of numbing, salty brine, however, triggered a survival instinct so powerful that it overcame his despair. He somehow managed to kick off his boots and release the parachute harness. Clawing at the silk, he found a way out from under it. He was back under the sky. His panic subsided enough for him to find the nozzle of his Mae West and start blowing it up.

That was not easy – not when you're dog-paddling about in cold water. His arms and legs were getting tired already. He knew that if he didn't get it inflated, he would definitely drown. He blew again and again. God, give me strength, he kept praying unconsciously. Give me air. Slowly, very slowly, the life-jacket puffed up and started to buoy him in the water. When Ginger realised it was actually holding him up, he closed his eyes and thanked God.

This sense of peace and gratitude did not last long. As soon as he recovered a little from the exhaustion of getting out of his boots, out from under the parachute and blowing up the life-jacket, he became aware of his surroundings.

There was absolutely nothing to see but the grey sky overhead and the grey sea around him. The gentle swells, invisible from the air and insignificant even from the deck of a ship, nevertheless blocked out all vision when he sank between them. Even when he rose up on them, the view was the same – endless sea and sky. He couldn't see the coast at all. He didn't understand that at first – until he worked out that there must be a very thin low-level haze over the water. Or maybe it was just "patchy fog." Whatever it was called, the visibility was much reduced in this spot of water. That made the sense of isolation – and his chances of rescue – worse than ever.

Ginger had always liked being alone. Walking alone on the moors was his favourite pastime. Though he wasn't alone on the moors. Usually, he had Bessie with him. And there were always rabbits and hares, birds of all kinds, mice and foxes.... Ginger had never felt alone on the moors or in the sky

Flying had always been like communion with God. But the sea had nothing divine about it. The sea was cold, contemptuous, and dark. It wanted to swallow him, to drag him down to the dark depths where only sea-monsters lurked.

For Ginger it was very simple. God was in Heaven – and that was the sky above him, which, just a few minutes ago he had been able to touch with the wings of his Hurricane. The sea, on the other hand, was worse than the earth: it was the Devil's territory. The thought chilled him even more than the cold water. The fog cut Ginger off from God as well as from observation.

Ginger tried not to think about where he was, but what else was there to think about? What would they tell his Dad? Missing in action. How long would his Dad hope for good news? How long before his Dad realised there was no hope? And what would he do then? Ginger could picture his Dad crumpled up in his old chair with Bessie whimpering in sympathy and distress at his knees. He could picture Bessie pawing helplessly at his Dad's knee with her soft white paw. He could picture his Dad clutching the old dog to him and crying until he'd soaked her silky head with his tears. His Dad didn't have anyone else in the whole world. It wasn't fair for him to be left alone....

Ginger lost all sense of time. He supposed that time seemed to crawl because there was nothing to do or see. His hands and feet started to feel numb. He forced himself to kick his legs and wave his arms. He knew it would keep his circulation going, stop him from dying of exposure. Funny that he could still hope for rescue. But hope dies last of all, perhaps.

The fog seemed to be thinning. The sun burned through it from overhead. That encouraged Ginger for a bit, but then he realised that, though better, it still wasn't good enough for him to see the coast.

Then he heard aircraft engines. Not distant aircraft engines far overhead, but the throbbing engines of an aircraft flying low. At first, he thought it must be another bomber trying to ditch. He searched the sky in the direction of the sound and could hardly believe his eyes. It was a flying boat! A rescue plane! It had large red crosses on its wings. It was flying lower and lower.

Ginger started waving and shouting. Although he knew they could not hear him over the sound of their own engines, he shouted for sheer joy. He shouted and waved, and the aircraft continued right past him at its stately pace. Ginger's shouting became more desperate, hysterical almost. "Over here! Over here! Can't you see me! Are you blind! God, help them to see me!"

The flying boat banked slightly and started flying in a large curve. A chill slithered down Ginger's back as he saw the German crosses on the body of the plane. It was a *Luftwaffe* Air-Sea-Rescue plane, apparently looking for the downed bomber crew. Following the flying boat with his eyes, Ginger saw a flare shoot up, and realised that the bomber crew was not very far from him. The flying boat waggled its wings in greeting and flew with a new purposefulness towards the downed Germans.

Ginger started "swimming" after it. It was too far away, of course, and he couldn't swim, but he could kick and paddle with his hands and somehow make his way nearer to it. Maybe he could get near enough to make himself heard. Maybe they would see him when they went to take off again. He'd be a prisoner, but prisoners weren't dead. He'd be able to write to his Dad. The war would eventually end; it might even be over very soon. At the moment, Ginger found it easy to believe the Germans would win the war rather fast.

What happened next was the most horrible part of the whole, horrible day. Out of the vast sky overhead, a vic of three Spitfires swooped down on the flying boat just as it was trying to land, and they shot it up.

Ginger was screaming again. Screaming at them to stop. Waving at them to stop. Leave it alone! It was on a rescue mission! It was his only hope of survival! It was the only way he'd ever see his Dad again. Stop it! Stop it!

But three undisturbed Spitfires are very effective weapons; the clumsy, slow, unarmed flying boat was an easy target. They tore its high wings from their struts, set its petrol tanks alight, and punctured its pontoons so it could not stay afloat. In just minutes Ginger's rescue became nothing but a stinking, spreading oil slick on the surface of the water between him and the bright yellow life raft with the four German airmen in it.

Ginger sobbed himself into a state of unconsciousness. Not only had he lost all hope of rescue, the injustice of what had happened overwhelmed him. It was against everything he'd been brought up to believe in. If only the enemy had done it. If only it hadn't been British planes that had shot it down. What was he fighting for? What was he going to die for? A country that shot down unarmed rescue planes? It was no better than shooting at Red Cross ambulances or medics. It was barbaric. It was what Ginger thought he was fighting *against*.

When he came to again, Ginger didn't know where he was at first.

He was still at sea. He could feel the sickening motion of the treacherous waves under him. He was also cold and wet, but he wasn't in the water any more. He was floating on it with the endless but now utterly inaccessible sky stretched over his head. He heard voices, but he couldn't understand them. He saw a face framed by a leather flying helmet. He was being offered a canteen. He accepted it almost without thinking. It contained water. He drank gratefully, only now registering how thirsty he was.

Gradually, he also registered that there were seven of them crowded in the little raft, and that one of the others was seriously wounded and another had his arm and hand bandaged. The seriously injured man had his head bandaged and lay under a blanket. It seemed that the Germans thought of everything – a life raft, flares, bandages, blankets, water, air-sea rescue planes....

"Thanks," Ginger managed. Straining his brain, he even remembered the German that they used in the films, "Danka."

"*Bitte schön.*" The man holding him didn't sound very friendly, but then who could blame him? First an English fighter had shot him down, and then three more had shot down the unarmed rescue plane that had been on the brink of saving them all from dying out here in the Channel.

"I'm sorry about the plane. I'm so sorry."

"Bastards! That's what you are! Bastards!" one of the other men shouted at him furiously in perfectly understandable English, but he was instantly hushed by two of the others. There was a short, heated discussion in German, and then silence. The man who had shouted at him looked away, out to sea. Ginger could see the fear and exhaustion in the faces of the others. They were grey, drawn, and anything but confident of survival.

We'll probably all die together, Ginger registered, and suddenly that seemed very appropriate. He didn't deserve to live any more than they did. His comrades had shot down an unarmed rescue plane. He had never been so ashamed of England in his life.

A long time later, the deep, grumble of a straining engine penetrated his consciousness. Or rather, the stirring of the other men in the life raft drew his attention to it. Someone said something. A short answer. Silence. Another short comment. Then a shout, and one of the Luftwaffe airmen pointed. Ginger followed the outstretched arm. It was as if the Archangel Gabriel himself was walking across the water: it was the Shoreham Lifeboat.

"Ship ahoy!" Ginger scrambled up on the slippery, unsteady bottom of the rubber boat and shouted with all his might. "Ship ahoy! Over here!"

The prow of the lifeboat swung noticeably towards them. Slowly, professionally, the lifeboat drew alongside the raft, and cut its engines. With grapples they were held alongside. The wounded were handed carefully up over the gunwales, and then the other men scrambled after them.

When he arrived at the dispersal hut to report back, Jones snapped at him. "Get yourself some dry kit and boots. Youcan't fly like that."

"But—"

"The Squadron hasn't been stood down. Get in proper uniform and report back here before we're scrambled again!"

They were finally stood down just after 9 pm. Ginger kept to himself. He hadn't been able to talk to anyone about what had happened to him. In fact, no one had bothered to ask – not beyond a cursory, "How did you end up in a *German* life raft?" Ginger replied that he didn't know. He'd lost consciousness in the cold water, and when he woke up he was in the raft. No one pressed for more details.

The commissioned officers were too tired for the pub and opted to stay in their own Mess, excluding the three Sergeant Pilots from their society. MacLeod climbed into the battered old MG that he had fixed up from a wreck and drove away into the night without a word. Ginger wished he could be with his Dad – and Bessie. The dog would have done him good. They could have gone for a long walk together. "Think I'll go for a walk," he told Green.

"In the dark?!" the Canadian asked incredulous. "So what?" Ginger countered, and slipped outside into the cool, clear night. He walked away from the Mess and housing, past the motor pool and the hangars. He walked out to the Hurricane he'd been assigned this afternoon. It was "H" and snugged down for the night in a sandbag bay, the canopy closed against the dew.

Ginger looked up at the stars, bright and vivid in the night sky, and it felt as though they were strangers to him. The whole world was alien. It couldn't really be that he'd watched three RAF Spitfires destroy a Red Cross flying boat. It had to be a nightmare – except that he could never have thought up something so horrible. He realised he must have been very naïve, and now he had lost his innocence.

"Oh, I'm sorry!" The upper-class accent made Ginger almost jump out of his skin. He turned and found himself face to face with the padre.

"I didn't mean to intrude," the young clergyman apologised, and started to retreat guiltily.

Ginger felt he had to say something. "It's all right. I was just looking at the stars."

"Beautiful, aren't they?" the padre agreed at once, stopping to look upwards. "Are you all right, by the way?" he asked, still looking upwards.

"I heard you'd been shot down and were in the Channel for hours. Have you seen the MO?"

"No. I'm fine. Physically."

"And otherwise?"

The question was put so softly, but so intently, that Ginger wondered if the padre had really just chanced upon him after all – or had he followed him out here intentionally? Suddenly it didn't matter. Ginger burst out angrily, "I saw three Spitfires shoot down a flying boat which was landing to rescue aircrew. It had red crosses all over it, and it was landing right beside the raft with the airmen in it! There couldn't be any question about what it was or what it was doing. And *we* shot it down – not Jerry, not the Nazis, not the Hun! Spitfires of the His Majesty's Royal Air Force with their roundels bright as day! Why?" Ginger turned to face the padre as he flung the last question at him. He saw the clergyman's eyes widen behind his thick lenses.

Colin was shocked. He licked his lips nervously. "I don't know," he answered honestly. "I suppose there must be a reason. I'll try to find out."

"Don't bother. It's too late." Ginger told him harshly, forgetting entirely that Colin was an officer and an Earl's grandson. "Two of the crew survived, wounded, and were in the raft with me. The others must have drowned – trying to help save their comrades. At least they try! We don't have anything like that, do we? We don't have air-sea rescue, and no one gives us rafts or flares or blankets. All we have is a silly Mae West that we have to blow up ourselves! If I'd had a lung wound, I'd have drowned before I could get the vest inflated!"

Colin was horrified to think that the Nazis showed more concern for their downed airmen than England did for hers. He felt indignant and was determined to say something to someone in the right place. His grandfather sat in the House of Lords, for a start. He could raise a question, even demand an enquiry. Colin firmly believed that that was the most important aspect of being a Peer of the Realm: having the means to make a difference. He took his responsibilities as a peer – or future peer – very seriously. However, he did not believe in boasting about that influence, so he said nothing to Ginger now. He just mentally noted that he must ring his grandfather in the morning and explain the situation to him. Hopefully the old man wouldn't go off about Nelson having done without air-sea rescue, or some such thing....

To Ginger, Colin said, "Sounds to me like you could do with a beer—"

"Alcohol isn't the answer to everything!" Ginger flung back at him bitterly.

Colin felt his own helplessness. "Tea, then. Would you like to join me?"

"No. I just want to be left alone."

That hurt, but Colin accepted it. "All right. Good night then."

No sooner had Colin retreated into the darkness than Ginger felt guilty about it. At least the padre had taken an interest – the only one in the whole squadron to do so. And he was right. Ginger could have used a beer – as long as it wasn't in a large noisy crowd. But it was too late; he'd chased away the only officer on the whole Station who had ever been nice to him.

Chapter 16

RAF Hawarden
9 August 1940

The weather, after clearing briefly at the start of the week, had closed in again, and for four days they'd been fogged in and grounded. The trainees were bored, fractious and unruly. They kicked about the Mess or walked across the sodden airfield, their flying boots slurping and squishing through the mud as they stared up into the shapeless murk. They drove 'round to the pubs at night and were much too loud and got far too drunk, causing problems with the locals. The ground crews were bored, damp and irritable. They generally kept to their hangars, playing card games among themselves. That led to a fist fight and three Airmen being put on charges. They too went down to the pubs at night, making life even more difficult for the local girls.

The staff was just getting nervous. They'd put on extra lectures – the Merlin engine, Spitfire design, tactics, enemy tactics, even an improvised "history of the Luftwaffe." And they'd drilled the pilots in R/T procedures and tested them in navigation theory. But quite aside from gradually running out of relevant topics, theory simply could not replace practice. With each day on the ground, the trainee pilots entrusted to them lost a couple hours of flying time.

Inevitably, when the cloud lifted to 3,000 feet late in the afternoon, Kennel opened the station to flying. The airfield came abruptly to life. The ground crews shoved the aircraft out and started up their engines, while the pilots eagerly changed into flying kit and collected down in the dispersal huts. Priestman, too, put on his sheepskin jacket and boots.

"The weather is very unstable," he announced to the six trainee-pilots gathered in front of him. "We can't risk going too far from the field, as the cloud cover could easily drop down on us at any minute. What I'm going to do with you is lead you up above the cloud cover – reportedly at 4,000 feet – and then have each of you in turn navigate us to recognizable landmarks. We'll see how well you do by dropping back below the cloud to see if you've got it right. For take-off and landing, remember the field is boggy muck. Keep the snout up at landing – or you'll be standing on your propeller. Hammond, Ward, and Powys, you're in the first section. The rest of you will go up as soon as we return."

The first exercise went fairly well, particularly when one considered that most of these pilots had done very little cross-country navigation on instruments. Some of them hadn't done it at all, or not solo. After all, some them had less than 50 hours solo altogether.

Priestman waited in the cockpit for the crew to refuel, and the remaining three trainees took over the returned aircraft. They took off again in line abreast. Same drill as before.

The wind had come up, however, and was quite stiff. Failing to calculate for it sufficiently, they missed their first target. Flying low under the cloud cover, now down to 2000 feet, they found it. They climbed above the cloud cover again, but by now they were being buffeted about badly.

Priestman called Hawarden for the latest Met. "Winds increasing to gale force. Veering north-northeast."

"Thanks for telling us," Priestman snapped sarcastically, and decided to break off the training at once. He gave McKeegan a chance to calculate the course back to Hawarden and let him lead, but Taylor wouldn't get his chance today by the look of things.

McKeegan announced that he thought they were over Hawarden, and Priestman took over the lead. The cloud had become ragged and rough. Priestman descended gently, watching the altimeter and the windscreen. He was sweating badly. They were down to 2000 feet and still not out of the cloud, but the windscreen was steaming up. He could feel the earth beneath him getting closer; the air around him was darker and darker. The Clwydian Range was too bloody close for comfort. It rose up sharply to 600 feet. At last, he came out of the muck with a good bit less than 1,000 feet to the ground.

They were too far west, just as he'd feared, carried on tailwinds past their destination. Priestman swung gently to the right, looking for a landmark. He knew the countryside well, and didn't expect to have a problem. Then he heard a dull boom behind him.

He flinched, then wrenched about in the straps trying to see behind him. Red Two and Three were both there, jinking about in the turbulent air nervously. Red Four was nowhere in sight.

"Come in, Red Four!" Silence.

"Red Four, where are you?" Silence.

"Red Three, when did you last see Red Four?"

"When we entered the cloud, Red Leader."

"Did you see him in your rear-view mirror as we emerged?"

"Ah. No, sir. I was trying not to lose sight of Red Two, sir." Of course, he was. Very sensible of him.

They were flying at just over 1,000 feet over hilly countryside in an increasing gale. They were being buffeted about, and there was only one place to be with two inexperienced pilots: on the ground. Priestman found a landmark and led the two remaining pilots back to Hawarden. He didn't let himself think about Taylor. Not yet. Not until he had the others safely on the ground. He circled the field carefully to bring them into the wind for landing.

"Remember the muck. Keep your kites properly trimmed."

Actually, there was little chance that they'd hash their landing: they hung on his wingtips and let him judge speed and altitude for them. They watched him more than the ground. He could see that. They imitated his every action until they touched down in a vic and rolled across the field. Robin's crew caught the wingtips and turned the Spitfire around neatly. He cut the engine, unplugged the R/T and oxygen, pulled off his helmet, and just sat there for a moment. Fletcher was already on the wing, shoving back the canopy. "What happened, sir?"

"I don't know." That was the worst of it. He didn't know. They shouldn't have been up there in these conditions. He should have brought them back sooner. He should have calculated the last course himself, but he might have misjudged the tailwinds, too. They shouldn't have been up there.

He shoved himself up and out of the cockpit. Kennel was waiting for him as he slipped to the ground. "The police have already found him."

Priestman just looked at Kennel, not daring to form the question.

"Flew straight in at an estimated 300 miles an hour."

"I wasn't flying 300 miles an hour."

"Maybe not but Acting Pilot Officer Taylor apparently was. Come back up to my office with me."

As they started across the field, the other trainee pilots clustered around. They all looked shocked and shaken. Kennel sent them away. "Stand down. There'll be no more flying today – or lectures."

"Is there any hope, sir?" One of the youngsters asked.

"No. He's been found dead."

Kennel led Priestman into his office. The Adjutant handed him a glass of scotch. Priestman took it and sipped at the golden liquid unhappily. He didn't know what to say.

"There will be an enquiry, of course. The Met was wrong. I shouldn't have opened the airfield. You should have returned sooner. God knows what Acting Pilot Officer Taylor should have done – but it wasn't fly into a mountain at 300 mph." He paused, sighed. "I'll write to the next-of-kin. Can you give me all the details you have on Taylor?" This latter was addressed to the adjutant, who nodded. "Anything you can add?" Kennel asked Priestman.

"He was..." Priestman searched for words to describe a young man he had known barely a week. "… insecure. He kept trying to cover it up with bravado."

"Do you think he'd drunk too much last night?"

"Very likely. I wasn't with them, but they crashed in late enough."

"We'd better talk to one or two of the others about that."

"What does it matter now? You're not going to put *that* in the letter to his next-of-kin," Priestman added a little alarmed.

"No, but it might help with the enquiry."

Priestman had already forgotten about that, but he supposed this would be the death knell to his career. He'd barely survived the last enquiry. They were bound to throw him out now. God help him, he'd be drafted into the Army!

His expression of foreboding was so explicit that it moved Kennel to remark, "Look, Priestman, there's no need to look as though you expect to be hanged. We all bear a share of the blame, but things like this happen in training all the time. Flying is dangerous. Flying Spitfires is *very* dangerous. Give a bunch of teenage boys an extremely fast, powerful aircraft, and the instinct of half of them is to crash it one way or another. It doesn't help that the Hun is killing, on average, three to four of our pilots every day. Fighter Command needs trained replacements, and it needs them sooner rather than later. If we close down every time conditions aren't ideal, we'll either not deliver enough pilots soon enough or we'll deliver untrained pilots to the operational units – and the Huns will have even more of a field day shooting them out of the sky."

"That's over a hundred pilots a month," Priestman remarked slowly, as he registered what Kennel had just said.

"And half again that many hospitalised," Kennel added.

"You're telling me Fighter Command casualties last month were roughly 150 pilots?" Priestman wanted confirmation. "That's roughly six squadrons."

"Yes, it is."

"At that rate, it doesn't matter how many of *them* we shoot down. Fighter Command will cease to exist by the end of the year."

Kennel made a gesture of helplessness in acknowledgement.

They stood together in silence. They could hear rain pelting against the windows and the wind howling as a gale tore down from the Irish Sea. They were all thinking the same thing: the Germans hadn't even started their main assault yet.

PART III

Round One

Chapter 17

Crépon, France
12 August 1940

The *Oberstleutnant* briefing them this morning did not wear wings, but he came direct from the intelligence department of the Luftwaffe General Staff. "The English," he announced confidently, "use radio to control their fighters. Each squadron is tied to a base, which directs it in the air. The bases in turn rely on information they receive from these special radio stations located along the coast." With a pointer he indicated the appropriate places on the map. "In preparation for the main assault tomorrow, raids will be flown against these radio stations and key RAF bases." With the pointer he indicated Manston, Lympne and Hawkinge.

"Bombers of KG2 will cross the Channel at Dover and then split up for their respective targets – Manston, Dover, Hawkinge, Lympne, Rye and Pevensey – taking the latter two targets from the east rather than the south. Since these radio stations can only transmit in one direction, they are blind in the flanks and the rear." He sounded very pleased about this, although, as far as Ernst knew, their own Freya system was also only capable of transmitting and receiving in one direction.

"II *Gruppe*, JG 23, will be escorting Junkers 88 of KG 51 as they fly from Cherbourg to make landfall here at Brighton, turn west and divide into two raids at Spithead. Half the raid will proceed to bomb Portsmouth harbour, in which the British prestige liner-turned-troop-transport *Queen Elizabeth* is currently lurking, and the remainder will turn south and take the radio station at Ventnor on the Isle of Wight from the rear. Any questions?"

There were none. Ju 88s were the fastest of the Luftwaffe's bombers. If the fighters were forced to do escort duty, then the fighter pilots preferred escorting these fast, elegant bombers with both high-altitude and dive-bombing capabilities. The pilots were dismissed to go to their aircraft.

As always, Ernst fell in beside Christian. Dieter and Busso, the other two pilots of the *Schwarm*, were on Christian's other side – just as they would be in the air. "Satisfied?" Dieter asked Christian with an amused expression.

"Absolutely. We should have done this four weeks ago. Mother of God! We've lost 5 pilots in the Gruppe since the French surrendered— and all for the sake of beating up a handful of ancient coal-ships that had probably been written off by their insurers years ago."

"Come on, Christian. We've been giving at least as good as we get – if not better," Busso argued, tossing his long hair out of his lean face and lighting up a last cigarette before take-off.

"So what?" Christian insisted. "What with illnesses and injuries, we're down to 80% strength, and that must be true of all the front-line *Geschwader*. An utter waste for the sake of 'closing the channel to British shipping' – pure propaganda rot! If they can't use the Straits of Dover, then the English just put the coal on trains or send it around the tip of Scotland. Do you think giving Goebbels a propaganda victory was worth Hans or Uwe's lives?"

As usual, Ernst squirmed uncomfortably when Christian challenged authority, but Busso protested outright. "That's not what it was about," he declared, frowning. "The point was to defeat the RAF, and we *would* have beaten them, if only they hadn't shirked the fight most of the time."

"Who shirked what when?" Christian asked, stopping in his tracks to stare hard at Dieter's wingman. "The RAF isn't shirking anything. They just refuse to play the game by *our* rules. We want them to come up and fight with us, and they aren't that stupid. They go for the bombers and then get out. JG 53 tried some pure fighter sweeps the other day. They flew all over the island as if they were on a sightseeing tour, while the RAF thumbed their noses at them. They won't be able to ignore attacks on their own bases and infrastructure, however. We may get away with it today, because they won't be expecting it, but the next couple of days are going to be the toughest we've seen yet."

They had reached Dieter's aircraft, and Dieter ground out his cigarette in the moist, dew-covered grass. "Well then, break a leg."

Ernst made for his own aircraft, uncomfortably aware of his usual pre-flight urge to urinate, but he also knew it would pass soon enough. He scrambled up the wing, and then lowered himself carefully into the cockpit, which was almost too narrow for him. At meals the *Staffelkapitän* often called out to him to stop eating or he wouldn't be able to fit into it at all. That always brought gales of laughter from the CO's table, and newcomers often laughed along, too. The first time it happened, Ernst had been shocked and hurt by the public humiliation – until Christian had hissed under his breath, "Stupid, tactless arse!" After that Ernst didn't mind as much. Still, his shoulders did brush the sides. Narrower than a coffin, an instructor had joked. Ernst was relieved when his mechanic started the pre-flight drill, distracting him from his morbid thoughts.

They rendezvoused with the bombers over Cherbourg. KG 51 had apparently sent up every machine that could fly – very nearly a hundred of them. And they were escorted by at least that many Me110s as well. It was the largest formation of aircraft Ernst had ever seen. The huge gaggle, with the Me109s flying top cover at 10,000 metres, flew first to the northeast, straight for the holiday town of Brighton. They then curved around elegantly and swept west along the channel coast, passing Hayling Island on the right and the Isle of Wight on the left.

As they approached Spithead, a small group of Ju 88s banked left and started back across the Isle of Wight to take the radio station at Ventnor in the rear, but 5 *Staffel* of II *Gruppe* stayed with the larger flock of Junkers. The latter was easing down to bomb Portsmouth dockyards, careful to keep above the barrage balloons. The escorts also shaved a couple thousand metres from their own altitude, and Ernst could clearly see a long white pier sticking out into the Solent. Beyond it rose a line of smoke thrown up by flak as the Royal Navy opened up with everything they had.

RAF Tangmere

Allars cut straight across the sunlit field. Most of the pilots were lounging in deck chairs, reading magazines or novels. Debsen was lying flat on his back on the grass, snoozing. MacLeod sat astride a chair opposite a card table, playing Black Jack with Green. Squadron Leader Jones was discussing with Fl/Lt. Thompson the handicaps in steeple-chasing; Jones' father owned a stables.

"Something up, Spy?" Jones asked casually from his reclining position.

"I'm afraid there is, sir," Allars answered seriously. "It seems that our RDF stations at Rye and Pevensey have both been attacked. Pevensey is completely off the air; Rye is so badly damaged that we now have a hundred-mile gap in the RDF chain."

That had their attention. All the pilots – still sprawled across the lawnchairs and lying on the grass – were staring at Allars.

"We rather assume that they will now pour bombers through the gap – possibly going for London. Then again, there is a large raid approaching Brighton."

"So, what are we doing on the ground?" Jones asked in an annoyed tone, folding his newspaper together with a crack and getting to his feet.

"The enemy could turn any way yet or go straight for London."

But just then the telephone in the dispersal gave its throaty ring, and the airman-clerk on duty shouted out to the pilots. "Stand-by!"

MacLeod knocked the chair over as he stood up, and Green tripped over the straps of his Mae West and fell flat on his face. The others were already sprinting towards the waiting Hurricanes. Ginger was completely out of breath by the time he reached his kite, but it was less from running than from sheer terror. This was clearly it: the attack they had all been waiting for for almost two months. And Ginger knew he was going to die.

The squadron was forming up along the far perimeter of the field. The Hurricanes trundled across the grass comfortably and then swung around to form a ragged line, their noses pointing into the wind. Here they waited for the order to scramble with their engines idling, the aircraft trembling slightly to the rhythm of the engine. Most pilots had their canopies open so they could see around the snout better during take-off.

Across the field, the Hurricanes of 43 Squadron were scrambling already. Jones' irritated voice crackled through the R/T. "What's going on, Beetle? We're overheating here and you're scrambling 43."

"There's enough trade for both of you, Cottonball Leader."

"Then let us get at it. The Merchant Navy chaps have to run the U-Boat gauntlet to deliver this precious green stuff. Let's not waste it, old boy."

"Stand-by," the Controller answered patiently.

"Fucking bastard," MacLeod muttered to himself, forgetting he had the R/T on.

43 Squadron was in the air and curving around in a battle climb.

Portsmouth

The air-raid sirens started wailing and there was a moment of stunned silence before Mr. Wyndham, the senior partner, emerged from his office and ordered, "Proceed to the air-raid shelter immediately."

Everyone started talking at once. The younger girls grabbed their handbags, while the older women chastised them for "vanity" and the men speculated openly whether this was the start of the invasion. Mr. Cassidy and Mr. Harper, the other two partners, took up positions flanking the door, and urged their employees to remain calm and orderly. "No need for panic now. Just move along briskly. For all we know this is just a drill. There you go, Mrs. Beedle." The senior partner gave the elderly secretary a hand as she stumbled. "Hurry along now, Miss Cutlip. Is that everyone, now?"

"I'll just go and check."

Emily was at the tail of the group. She saw Mr. Cassidy return into the offices to make a final check, while Mr. Wyndham prepared to lock the door. From the other companies in the office building, the employees were likewise evacuating in an excited but orderly manner. No panic was evident, but there was a heightened nervousness, Emily thought.

For weeks now, the papers had been reporting on the vast number of barges collected on the far side of the Channel. Furthermore, after a spell of rain, fog and storms, this was the first good day for flying in almost a week. "Bomber weather," the radio commentators had called it unabashedly.

Outside in the brilliant August sunlight, the sirens wailed furiously. Some people hesitated, looking up at the sky; others barked, "Move along! Don't block the pavement!" A number of people started walking much faster, almost breaking into a run. The entrance to the shelter was around the corner in Albert Road. People converged on it from offices and shops in Victoria and Albert roads in a steady stream. Emily thought it would be much too small for so many people, and she hung back.

Above the sound of the sirens and the jabber of the people came the first gruff barks of ack-ack and the higher-pitched, more frantic yakking of the naval AA-guns from the ships behind them off Spithead. Like a pack of hounds including Great Danes and Terriers, Emily thought. And then – like a subconscious drone that only slowly forced its way into her consciousness came a heavy, throbbing rumble that got steadily louder and nearer.

With amazement Emily registered that it must be aircraft engines – scores of them.

Someone called out, "Look! There they are!"

She looked up and a chill went through her. You really could see them: masses and masses of bombers flying wing-tip to wing-tip in neat rows: a vic of three followed by sections of five by four aircraft, a break, another "box" of 23 and above them, staggered upwards in steps, were other similar formations. They were flying directly overhead, and they seemed to darken the entire sky.

The thought of the Greeks at Thermopylae flashed through Emily's head: the Persians gathered against them had been so numerous that it was said their javelins would darken the sun. But the Spartan defenders had laughed and answered: "all the better, then we shall fight in the shade." The thought heartened her for a moment – until she remembered the Spartans had lost the battle and died to a man at Thermopylae.

"They're diving!" Someone shouted.

While the bombers overhead continued to fly straight and level, the lead bomber group – which was now a good three miles further – started diving at a steep angle. Emily was surprised, because by now she had spent a lot of time staring at the aircraft identification charts at Hawarden and knew these were not Stukas. They must be Ju 88s, she decided, which could fly both high-altitude and dive-bomb attacks. Meanwhile, the ack-ack barked furiously. Smoke hung over the entire northern part of the city, thickening with each crack of the anti-aircraft guns. Finally, Emily heard the first dull thuds as the earth jumped under-foot, and new blossoms of grey smoke erupted upwards as the first bombs exploded.

JG 23

From his bird's-eye view, Ernst saw one Junkers shudder and start to smoke, a victim of British anti-aircraft fire, but the other Junkers were making their bomb runs with apparent indifference to the British defences. Their formation was superb, and soon their bombs sent up puffs of smoke like pebbles thrown into the sand.

Still no sign of English fighters, Ernst noted, remembering to look over his shoulder and up at the sun – although the English fighters rarely had a height advantage over the Messerschmitts.

Below, the first *Kette* of bombers started to climb again. They banked into a curve and turned for home.

"Indians! Attacking the Junkers."

"Hurricanes," someone improved the report.

"Just twelve of them. One squadron. Hold your position!" Bartel's voice was sharp. "Wait until the RAF has fully deployed!"

Christian had already tipped his wing to slide down to the attack. Now he righted the aircraft and flew straight and level, but Ernst could see him looking down as the fight developed below. The Me110s, Goering's beloved "Destroyers," made no attempt to stop the Hurricanes. All they did was go into a defensive circle, flying around like a moving circus, covering each other's tails. A lot of good that did the bombers! Ernst thought in disgust; and apparently unnecessary as well! The English contemptuously ignored the frightened "Destroyers" and went for the Junkers anyway.

Portsmouth

Only a few people remained on the street now. Some of these frantically ran for the shelter, but the rest stood transfixed where they were, staring up the length of Victoria Road towards the north – where the dockyards lay. Emily stood with the others, astonished that she felt no fear. Even as the earth jumped and trembled under her, she was conscious more of fascination than terror. Somehow it *still* seemed unreal to her, even as she watched bombs falling on the city she had grown up in.

She had never believed it would come to this. Certainly not when she and her fellow students had marched through the streets chanting peace slogans and carrying large banners demanding "Unilateral Disarmament Now!" Nor when she gave standing ovations to the debaters in their boaters as they argued eloquently that "on no account would they fight for King and Country." She could still hear the vigour of the young male voices shouting "Hell, no, we won't go" as they drowned out a Parliamentary Candidate calling for more military "preparedness."

She remembered, too, how tensely she and her parents had followed the news of the Munich crisis. She remembered how they embraced each other in relief and sang *"The Internationale"* when Chamberlain announced "Peace in our Time." She had believed it. She had believed that reason had triumphed over fanaticism. The only seed of doubt had been planted by a German Social Democrat, a man who had fled Nazi Germany and taught German at Cambridge. He had claimed that the Munich Agreement would make Hitler more powerful at home and feed his ambition abroad. She hadn't wanted to believe it.

But Hitler's bombers were flying directly over her head and dropping high explosives on the Portsmouth dockyards. Emily registered that most of her neighbours worked in those dockyards. For all she knew, she was *watching* men she had known all her life being killed. Furthermore, they only had to miss by half a mile, and they might be obliterating her house, her parents, or the Salvation Army Seaman's Mission and Major Fitzsimmons. And she was just standing here – watching. It was perverse. But the only other thing she could do was look the other way. Would that be any better?

"Hurricanes!" one of the men shouted. "There they are!"

"How many are they?"

"They've got a bomber! Look at that! They've got it! They've got it!"

JG 23

Ernst watched the Hurricanes tearing into the Junkers with a vengeance. While the undamaged Junkers opened up to full throttle and, relieved of their bomb load, jinked and frolicked with almost as much agility as the fighters, any bomber that had suffered flak damage was cold meat for the Hurricanes. Ernst watched in horror as first one and then a second Ju88 sheered off, streaming smoke. One spiralled down, apparently out of control, while the other dived hard for the Solent and small figures started to drop out of it. Smoke was billowing back from both engines of a third machine that was struggling hard to keep above the barrage balloons, and then a fourth blew up in mid-air.

"Whose side are you on, *Herr Staffelkapitän*?"

"Shut up, Feldburg!"

Ernst sensed it, anticipated it, and he was thankful for it, too. The tension of just watching the bombers get shot to pieces was too much. Christian didn't say another word; he just dipped his wing and shoved the Emil into a power dive. Dieter must have read his mind, too, because he and Busso were right beside him. Ernst blocked out the acrid shouts in his earphones and concentrated on staying with Christian.

606 Squadron

"Scramble Cottonball."

The Hurricanes sprang forward raggedly, some of the pilots overeager and others caught off guard by the order when it finally came. Twelve abreast, they galloped across the broad field in the mid-day sun like a cavalry charge. In a ragged line they lifted into the air. The Controller was vectoring them to the north. Angels 15.

"Sure that's enough, Beetle?" Jones wanted to know. It was half the Messerschmitt's favourite cruising altitude.

"Your bandits are bombing Portsmouth dockyards. No point in going in too high."

"Fucking bastards," MacLeod commented again, although it was unclear if he meant the Germans that were bombing Portsmouth or Control for holding them back so long. They were vectored back to the west. The familiar countryside, soaked in mid-day sunshine, spread out green and apparently peaceful below them.

Ahead, the sky was smudged with the smoke of anti-aircraft fire and bombs. Ginger saw the smoke first and then the black dots – more like beetles than aircraft – except that they were in neat rows. Then he saw the little dots that tumbled away from the "beetles" and realised he was watching the bombs fall.

His stomach heaved so violently that he tasted vomit in his mouth. He tried to swallow it down, but he couldn't. Christ, he thought, I'm going to be sick all over the cockpit *again*. If he was, it would get on his boots, and his feet would slip on the pedals just like last time. In desperation he let go of the stick, pulled off his right glove, and was sick into it. He felt better after that, and let the glove sink down beside the seat as he wiped the sweat from his face with his sleeve.

He concentrated on flying. They were ordered into sections line-astern. He fell in behind Thompson and heard the "Tally Ho" as if it were miles or even light-years away. How did the poem go? "Cannon to the right of them, cannon to the left of them, cannon in front of them volleyed and thundered. Into the valley of death...."

Portsmouth

Over the dockyards the last of the bombers were still making their runs, although the formation leader had turned and started for home. The returning bombers would clearly pass a little more to the east, but Hurricanes were amidst them like wolves amidst the sheep. They careened in and out, overtaking the bombers, peeling off and curving around to attack again.

From where she stood, Emily could hear the rat-a-tat of the Browning machine guns and the high-pitched chatter of the answering bomber guns. She could see tracer criss-crossing in the air, leaving ugly, dirty streaks on the sky. Emily saw smoke burst out of a bomber engine, and a minute later the whole machine slowly tilted over. She could see the insignia on both wings; the cockpit glass caught the sunlight. She heard the engines screaming at a totally different pitch. Then little dots started to fall out of it, and she realised it must be the crew abandoning the dying aircraft.

"They've got another! Look over there!"

Emily looked over just in time to see another bomber slip out of sight behind the barrage balloons. A few moments later, an explosion rocked the ground and smoke billowed up in a huge cloud. Another bomber was smoking from both engines.

"More Hurricanes!" someone cried out excitedly.

Indeed, there were now even more fighters swooping in and out like frolicking swallows, and it took the observers a moment to register that these fighters were not attacking the bombers, but the other fighters. A Hurricane peeled off from the fight and roared right over-head at no more than 1000 feet, recklessly risking a collision with the balloon cables.

By the time Emily registered that it was being pursued by an Me109, it was too late to take cover. The German flew straight at them, its guns blazing. She could see the muzzle flashes. From behind someone flung her forward onto the pavement, and instinctively she covered her head with her hands. With a deafening roar, the shadow passed overhead and was gone.

Dazed, Emily got back to her feet. Both her knees were bleeding. Her stockings were in shreds. The palms of her hands were bruised and bleeding. Her hair was falling down from her bun. Around her the others also got to their feet and brushed off their trousers. Someone offered her a handkerchief for her knees. Emily realised only now that she was trembling all over. And the battle moved on at 250 miles an hour.

JG 23

Christian didn't waste time getting lined up astern. He took them in on a broad reach, and Ernst nervously tried to calculate a deflection shot.

But they were going much too fast and were soon being jostled by the slipstream of the bombers, and the Hurricanes were scattering in all directions.

The Emil's engine screamed in protest. For the first time in his life, Ernst thought the gallant little bird might fail him, as he tried to stay with Christian, who had reefed hard to the right firing furiously at an escaping Hurricane – but from too far away. Ernst could see his tracer falling away in a gentle curve, a good half-hundred metres short of the target. The Hurricane flipped onto its back and started turning the other way. Christian and Ernst tried to follow, but they had been caught by surprise and lost ground.

Then Ernst felt his Emil shudder and, amazed, wrenched around in his seat to look behind him. Spitfires! He tried to scream a warning into the R/T, but it was jammed. Only then did he register that someone had been screaming into it for some time. There were Spitfires all over the place! There had to be at least two squadrons of them. Ernst looked left and right in terror as he realised he'd lost Christian. He was absolutely alone in a sky filled with enemy.

"Christ!" Ernst shoved the throttle to emergency speed and started twisting and turning wildly to shake off his pursuer. Some part of his brain was saying "dive"; the Emil had an advantage in a dive. But there were those damned barrage balloons! The cables could slice right through a wing. He turned over Southampton water and then dived for all the Emil was worth.

After an eternity, the Isle of Wight loomed up. Smoke billowed up from a cluster of buildings around the soaring masts of the radio station. The other group of Junkers must have hit their target, Ernst registered, as he levelled off just above the ground and flew right through the smoke. Beyond, he dropped off the far side of the cliff to skip across the wave tops.

He was utterly alone in a sunny seascape. The shadow of his Emil danced over the wave tops. Men in a fishing boat threw themselves onto the deck as he swept over. He pulled the stick back a little and looked over his shoulder. Left. Right. He weaved backed and forth a bit. No one – except for the remnants of the bomber force limping home ahead of him.

606 Squadron

Ginger never even fired his guns.

Shamefacedly, he shoved back the hood of his Hurricane. Sanders and Tufnel were on either side of him cheerfully asking if he'd had "any joy," but then they saw his face and Sanders asked instead, "Are you all right, sir?" The concern in his voice was genuine.

"I'm sorry," Ginger pleaded. "I seem to have had an accident again. I'm so sorry." He felt terrible. His glove had turned on its side during the crazy flight and spilt his vomit over the floor of the cockpit after all. "I'll help clean it up," he promised, ashamed both of what he'd done and the fact that Sanders and Tufnel would be expected to clean up after him.

"Don't you worry about a thing, sir," Sanders answered evenly, as he leaned forward to help Ginger with his straps. "We'll have it cleaned up in no time. Just like before. Nothing to worry about, sir."

Crepon, France

Ernst was feeling miserable by the time he joined the circuit at Crépon. He had failed again. He had not even managed to stay with his leader, much less fire his guns and hit anything.

It looked like about half the *Gruppe* was back already, and he could see other Emils, in pairs or solo, converging on the field from the various northern points of the compass. But he couldn't spot Christian's aircraft, and that really frightened him.

If anything had happened to Christian, it would be his fault for not staying with him. As soon as he had turned off the engine and thrust the hood over to the side, he asked: "Is Freiherr von Feldburg back yet?"

"Ja, about five minutes ago. His feet hadn't touched the ground before the CO dissected him for disobeying orders and blamed him for all casualties. He threatened him with a court martial."

Ernst stared at the mechanic in disbelief. "But the Hurricanes were massacring the Junkers!"

"Bartels says if you'd waited, you wouldn't have been bounced by the Spitfires. He says if you'd obeyed orders, you would have clobbered the Spits too—rather than just the Hurris."

"Ja, and by then all the Junkers would have been shot down!"

"I hope you can testify to that at the court martial."

"How high were our casualties?" Ernst thought to ask next.

"Well, Wilke's kite is a complete write-off, and Kühn isn't back yet."

"Yes, he is," someone corrected. "Just got in." The speaker pointed to an Emil that was taxiing at the far side of the field. It was billowing smoke from a damaged engine, but Kühn was evidently still fit to fly.

"Then no pilots were lost?"

"Not in the Staffel. I don't know about the rest of the *Gruppe*."

Relieved by that, Ernst concentrated on Christian again. He was really in trouble this time. "I better go and find Feldburg," he announced.

Chapter 18

Crépon, France
13 August 1940

"Christian!" Ernst shouted. He hadn't been able to find him the day before, and after waiting up half the night in the Mess, he'd learnt that Christian had left the base entirely. Nor had he appeared at breakfast – but then Christian often skipped breakfast when it was scheduled before 8 am. (He said it was not civilised to eat too early in the morning.) But here he was, pulling on his leather gloves and apparently preparing to fly. It was 5.30 am. Although there was heavy and increasing cloud that would make it almost impossible for the bombers to find their targets, they were scheduled to escort KG 54 on a raid against RAF airfields.

At the sound of his name, Christian turned and smiled. He came back towards Ernst. Before he could even say "good morning," however, Ernst demanded, "Where were you?"

"I went to see Major Schulz-Heyn."

"Who's that?"

"The acting *Geschwaderkommandeur* of KG 51 – after their previous CO, Dr. Fisser, bought it yesterday. Do you know how many kites they lost yesterday? Ten! Ten aircraft and crew because that arsehole Bartels wanted to run up his own damned score against the RAF. He can't bloody take it that Galland and Mölders have left him standing!"

Ernst was appalled by the losses, but he still didn't think Christian should be talking like this about their CO.

"The whole system stinks!" Christian told him before Ernst had decided what to answer. "They only give away medals and promotions for kills."

Ernst decided it was better not to enter this discussion. He rather suspected Christian might be less contemptuous about rewarding kills if only he had one or two of his own. Ernst changed the subject. "The ground crews are saying you're going to be put before a court martial."

"Only the ground crews?"

"They heard the CO threaten you after you landed yesterday and were pretty shaken up. Dieter and Busso, however, say they can't afford to ground you. We're too short of pilots. They said the CO was just blustering."

"See. Nothing to worry about." Christian grinned and shrugged – unconvincingly, Ernst thought.

"They don't have to ground you to court-martial you, Christian. They could let you fly ops until your trial."

Christian shrugged. "When I walked into the Mess at KG 51, you would have thought I was a Jew. They all stared at me. Not one man nodded in greeting, much less smiled. They just stared at me. It was the coldest reception I've ever had in my life. And they were right."

"No, they weren't! You did your best! It's not *your* fault that so many of them got slaughtered."

"I didn't hit a damn thing – again. Not one goddamnned English fighter!"

"You fire too soon, Christian." Ernst said it softly, wincing even as he spoke, afraid Christian would be mad at him for criticising.

"What was that?"

"You fire too soon, before you're in close enough to do any damage."

Christian considered Ernst for a long moment, his head cocked. "Just when did you notice this?"

Ernst shuffled his feet unhappily and shrugged. "We've been flying together for weeks."

"You could have said something earlier." Christian sounded annoyed, but not angry.

Ernst took a deep breath and risked looking at him squarely. He answered honestly, "What right have I got to criticise? Most sorties I don't even fire my guns – just like yesterday. I *certainly* haven't hit anything. At least you try. And you scared the Hurricanes away yesterday. They broke in all directions at the sight of your tracer."

Christian smiled sadly. "Thanks, Ernst."

"It's true."

"*Jein.* They broke in all directions and some of our bombers made it home – yesterday. But the Hurricanes will be just as numerous today because I didn't get any of them. Maybe they'll get a Junkers today – because I didn't get any of them yesterday. We can't beat the RAF by scaring them off. We've got to destroy their aircraft and pilots faster than they can be replaced. It's as simple as that."

"Then the system of rewarding kills is right after all?" Ernst said it with a little whimsical smile, expecting a heated denial.

But Christian sighed and agreed, "Yes, it's right after all – although you're the last man who should be defending it! Do you know how many *Rottenhunde* Galland has gone through? Seven! Seven wingmen have died while he ran up his score."

That shook Ernst a little, and he didn't know what to say, so he said nothing.

Christian clapped him on the shoulder. "Come on, we better mount up." He nodded towards the waiting Messerschmitts. Just as Ernst turned to walk over to his own machine, Christian called out after him, "Don't worry about me, Ernst. Nothing's going to happen to me for what I did yesterday. Let's see if I can't do a better job today." He managed a real smile at last.

RAF Hawarden

Priestman was just heading out to the field when Kennel intercepted him. "Priestman, could you come to my office for a minute, please."

Priestman glanced towards the uncertain morning sky. There was quite a bit of cloud about and he worried about the weather closing in, but he dutifully turned around and went back in. "Sir?"

"I have two new pilots for you."

"Sir? Now? We're in the middle of the course. They can't possibly catch up with the others."

"These can. Both are experienced pilots. Only need to convert to Spitfires and learn a bit about tactics, formation flying and air gunnery. Just what you will be starting with the others shortly." They had already reached Kennel's office, and the two new pilots got to their feet and saluted – or tried to.

The contrast between the two newcomers could hardly have been greater. One was small, slight and pale with delicate, almost feminine features and piercing blue eyes. The other was darkly tanned, hefty, tending almost to fat, and a good six inches taller than Robin – and Robin was six foot. Robin was reminded of a lumberjack and mentally questioned if the man could fit into a Spitfire cockpit. The little man saluted smartly; the giant didn't seem to know what he was doing and stopped trying with a grin.

"These gentlemen are both volunteers on short service com- missions," Kennel introduced them. "Pilot Officer Goldman is from Canada," he indicated the small, delicate pilot, and "Pilot Officer Murray is from New Zealand."

The New Zealander was already holding out his big paw-like hand. "Nice to meet you, sir."

Priestman shook hands automatically, still distracted and irritated by the idea of two new trainees in the middle of the course.

Kennel was continuing, "Murray was a bush pilot who has flown a variety of aircraft in difficult situations. Goldman has been working as a pilot for a private bank. He has flown single- and twin-engine monoplanes for several years. Murray has over 700 and Goldman more than 1,200 hours flying. Both pilots should be able to convert to Spitfires readily."

"That's all well and good, sir, but we haven't got enough aircraft—"

"Yes, we have. Beaverbrook is really outdoing himself these days. Four more aircraft will arrive before noon. So, take the others up for some formation stuff this morning. When you get back, these pilots will be kitted out, and the new machines should have arrived. You can give these pilots their introduction to Spitfires before the afternoon flying with the others."

Priestman went out to the dispersal where his remaining five trainees waited impatiently. He apologised for being late, explained why, and then took them into the air. Leading a formation of six aircraft was a demanding job, particularly when the other pilots were so inexperienced. Knowing how pointless tight formation flying was in combat, Priestman wanted to teach the others to fly in a loose formation – but it was very hard to keep track of them all if they spread out too much. Yesterday, he'd lost one of his pilots; fortunately the trainee had managed to find his own way home. Today he decided he might as well teach them about flying line astern. After all, they had to know what a future squadron leader might expect of them. They practised the formation in various combinations, until their fuel ran low. Then they returned to the airfield.

The trainees headed to the Mess for lunch, but Priestman went back to dispersal and found the two newcomers dutifully waiting for him, all dressed for flying in boots and flight jackets.

Priestman found some lukewarm tea in a large, battered urn and poured himself some. Only after he'd fortified himself did he turn to face the two new pilots. Although they were very different in stature and looks, they were both considerably older than the other trainees, he noted.

"Have you had lunch?" Priestman asked.

"Yes, sir," Goldman assured him.

"If that's what you call the slops they served, Skipper," the New Zealander retorted good-humouredly.

Skipper? Robin wondered, but his only reply was a calm, "Would you mind if I had a bite to eat before we set off?"

"Of course not, sir." Goldman answered politely.

"No problem, Skipper," Murray added generously. Priestman winced again at the New Zealander's over-friendly attitude. Priestman rang over to the Mess and asked if someone could bring him some hot tea and sandwiches. Then he settled on the arm of an ancient armchair that someone had dragged into the dispersal hut. "Tell me something about yourselves. Where are you from? Where did you learn to fly and all that?"

"Oh, my father's got a farm on the North Island," Murray started instantly. "Nothing but sheep. Thousands of them. Hard work keeping them all together and rounding up strays, keeping away predators and all that. My Father heard about some other farmer who used an old fighter plane to keep track of his sheep and got it into his head he wanted to do the same. Only he had a bum leg, so I got the job. It was the biggest mistake of his life. Once I started, I just couldn't stop. I left home and tried to join the New Zealand Air Force, but they only have twenty pilots. So, I went over to Australia and do some real flying. Fire-fighting, crop-dusting, mail-runs, ambulance service. Anything and everything."

"What aircraft have you flown?"

"Question's what *haven't* I flown, Skipper," the New Zealander countered with a grin.

"I know the answer to that," Priestman shot back. The New Zealander looked baffled. "Spitfires."

The New Zealander laughed heartily, a loud booming laugh that seemed to shake the flimsy dispersal hut, but then he grinned and pointed at Priestman. "Your score, Skipper. That's why I'm here. The way I hear it, there isn't a better kite in the world."

Priestman was grateful for the arrival of a Mess steward with his tea and sandwiches on a tray. It enabled him to go over to the door, thank the airman, and busy himself with finding a place for the tray where he could help himself without actually sitting down. By then it was too late for any tart remarks about the "fun" of flying Spitfires being markedly inhibited when there was a 109 on your tail. He turned to the Canadian instead.

"And where are you from?"

"I was born in Wilhelmshaven, sir. But my family emigrated to Canada when I was 15, shortly after Hitler came to power."

"And when did you start flying?"

"Also, when I was 15, sir. I was always fascinated by aircraft even as a little boy and was in a glider club as a youth. My friends and I built our own glider. As soon as we arrived in Canada, I started with real flying lessons."

"Expensive pastime," Priestman remarked dryly, who would also have *liked* to take flying lessons at 15.

"My father is a banker, sir," Goldman answered.

"At the bank you were working for...?"

"Yes, sir, but mostly I flew for one of the other partners, sir."

Priestman understood; Goldman's father wasn't a banker: he *owned* a bank. "Didn't your father want you to join the bank? Follow in his footsteps?"

"Of course, sir, but fortunately I have an older brother."

"Still, he must be quite upset about you leaving them to come adventuring over here."

"No, sir. That is, sir, he doesn't see this as adventuring. The newspapers have been full of the news – how Britain is now fighting completely alone with just the Royal Navy and the RAF to stop an invasion. There was an article in the paper about how powerful the Luftwaffe is and how few pilots the RAF has. It said the RAF was offering short service commissions to qualified pilots from anywhere in the world. I showed that article to my father without comment, and he just nodded and said he would talk to the senior partner. The bank paid my passage over, sir."

Robin understood. "And what aircraft have you flown?"

Goldman listed a large number of aircraft, and finished by noting he was qualified for night flying as well.

"Right then, let's get cracking."

Out on the field, Priestman had them climb up opposite wings of his own Spitfire and from the cockpit showed them the controls. "The most important thing to remember," he concluded, "is that at normal flying speeds and altitudes it takes no strength to control a Spit. She'll respond to the slightest pressure of your fingers and toes – sometimes it feels as if all you have to do is *think* what you want of her, and she'll give it to you. She's willing – even eager – sensitive and nimble. But like a sensitive woman, she's easily insulted. If you muck about with her, she'll get nervous and difficult. Treat her too roughly and she'll kill you. The worst thing to do in a Spit is panic, and she doesn't really like spinning." He shoved himself up and out of the cockpit and assigned the new pilots a Spitfire each.

Before they took off, Priestman climbed up beside each pilot and had them run through the cockpit drill with him and repeat the vital statistics on thrust, speed and the like. Finally, he sent them off with orders to take off, circuit the airfield, and then land. After they'd done that four times each, he told them to fly off on their own for half an hour and get comfortable with their aircraft. "You'll have no trouble finding the station, will you?"

They both shook their heads. With their experience, navigation wasn't the problem.

By then it was time to continue the training of the other five trainees. When he landed again it was time for tea, but Priestman found the two newcomers waiting as before, still in flying gear and clearly eager for another hour of flying. If they were to have only half the training of the others, it was only fair to use all the time they had. Besides, Priestman hoped, the sooner he got them up to the same standard as the others, the sooner he could integrate them into the regular training and spare himself this double load. He wasn't on readiness for 12 Group until tomorrow night. Better to work overtime today.

Priestman took off with the newcomers this time, and he gradually increased the difficulty of the manoeuvres. It quickly became clear that although Goldman was a precise pilot very capable of neat, close formation flying, he was not comfortable with anything that required him to fly upside down or otherwise throw the aircraft about a bit. Murray could do both with ease – the trickier it was, the more he seemed to enjoy it. After about 50 minutes, Priestman decided to call it a day and started back for the station.

His thoughts had wandered ahead as far as the day after tomorrow, when Emily would be coming, but gradually his sub-conscious registered that something was odd about Murray. He looked over his right shoulder and realised that Murray was flying upside down.

"What the hell are you doing, Red Two?"

"Who, me?" The Spitfire rolled back to the upright.

"Haven't you had enough for one day?"

"No, Skipper. Can we do some more?" Priestman heard the challenge and knew he should ignore it, but part of him was genuinely provoked by the New Zealander with his placid self-assurance. "Red Three, do you want to do some more flying?"

"No, sir. Not just now, sir."

Priestman knew he ought to use that as an excuse to refuse Murray, but instead he heard himself ordering Red Three back to Hawarden, while he banked away in a climbing turn.

"Red Two, stay with me."

"Right, Skipper."

Half an hour later, Robin had to admit that the New Zealander could do everything he could – and some of it better. He consoled himself with the thought that it had been a long time since he'd practised some of the manoeuvres. He was not up to the standards of his competition days. On the other hand, he'd been flying Spitfires for weeks. It galled not a little to have this greenhorn clinging to his flank with ease whether he was flying at 100 feet or 30,000. When the fuel gauge started to register red, however, Priestman gave up. He curved around for home and flipped on the R/T to admit grudgingly, "Well done, Murray."

They eased down towards the field as the sun was setting. As the exhilaration of the contest with the New Zealander faded with the sunlight, Robin realised he was tired. He touched down and rolled across the field, thinking that he could really use a beer. It took him a moment to register that something was wrong. Everyone seemed to be running in the opposite direction; a siren started wailing; the ambulance and fire truck were rushing onto the field. He turned the Spitfire around and looked back at the field.

The New Zealander's brand-new Spitfire was crumpled up in the middle, its propeller completely savaged and the aircraft flat on her belly.

Priestman hauled himself out of the cockpit and jumped down. He ran out to the aircraft. The ambulance crew was already on the wing, helping release the straps. The New Zealander was hunched forward in the cockpit, but he stirred as the medics released the straps and groaned as he sat up. He had a big gash on his forehead that was bleeding profusely, but otherwise he seemed unhurt. He was helped out of the cockpit and staggered a bit as if dizzy as he hit the ground.

"What the hell happened?" Priestman wanted to know.

The New Zealander was wiping blood off his forehead with his handkerchief. "I – I'm sorry, sir. I – I'm not used to aircraft with a retractable undercarriage. I – forgot."

"Forgot?! Don't you realise men are working themselves practically to death to see that we have enough Spitfires to fight the bloody Hun?! And you prang a new kite just because you *forgot* to let down your undercarriage!? I should dock your pay to cover the price of the repairs! You're *definitely* grounded until we get a replacement aircraft! The other pilots shouldn't suffer because you're too bloody stupid to lower your undercarriage!"

Priestman felt a hand on his shoulder, and looked back at Kennel, who had now arrived. From Kennel's face, he realised he was overreacting a bit. It occurred to him that he was angry in large part because Murray had proved his equal in the air – and because he very much resented the fact that the New Zealander saw the war as a kind of lark.

In fact, when he thought about *that*, he became so furious that he could not risk saying another word. He turned on his heel and steered straight for the Mess. A scotch was more what he needed now. A scotch and a hot meal, and then he'd ring through to Emily to be *sure* she was coming up for the weekend.

He unzipped his flight jacket as he went, aware only now of how hot he was. Damnit! They were fighting not just for their own lives and freedom, but for Democracy itself and the Empire. Where the hell did New Zealand think it would be if the British Empire collapsed? And it wasn't just the RAF and the Navy and the Merchant Navy that were giving all they had! Robin thought of the men in the Supermarine factory in their worn-out overalls, saw their pale, strained faces and their grimy hands. They didn't work until they dropped so that some bloody playboy from New Zealand could prang a perfectly good Spitfire because he *forgot* his ruddy undercarriage!

Priestman entered the cramped little Mess still steamed up, and was confronted by an unambiguous, chilling image. Goldman was standing forlornly at the bar, and the other pilots were clustered around in a happy group at the opposite side of the room. They were sitting on the arms of chairs and crowded together around a table with their backs to the newcomer. Robin's anger boiled over, turning icy cold.

He walked up to the bar, right beside Goldman, and ordered a scotch. Without looking directly at him, he asked the newcomer softly, "May I ask why you're drinking alone?"

"I was told that Jews don't belong in a first-class club."

"I thought I was *fighting* Nazi Germany, not *living* in it!"

Priestman burst out, his worst suspicions confirmed. Then he clamped his left hand on Goldman's elbow, his scotch still in his right, and drew the reluctant Canadian towards the circle of pilots.

"Get up! All of you! On your feet!"

The trainees were taken by surprise. They looked around and gaped at the instructor in confusion.

Priestman repeated, even more forcefully. "On your feet! Now!"

They got the message this time and started to fall off the sofa arms, or push back the chairs, the legs scraping loudly on the floor. In the faces of the more intelligent an expression of guilt, or at least worry, spread.

When they were all standing attentively and facing Priestman, he looked them in the eye one at a time as he declared in a low, ominous voice, "You may think that the RAF is nothing but a first-class flying club, and that the only thing you're here to do is fly Spitfires at government expense, but, by God, as long as you wear the King's uniform you'll respect the King's laws – and one of them is freedom of worship. Pilot Officer Goldman can fly better than *any* of you. This country can count itself *lucky* that Pilot Officer Goldman has more in his head than beer, girls and Spitfires – like you lot. If any one of you ever makes a derogatory remark about Pilot Officer Goldman or his religion again, I'll see that you spend the rest of the war flying cargo crates! Is that clear?!" He looked each of them in the eye, and then stalked back to the bar with Goldman in his wake.

Behind them came the booming drawl of the New Zealander, "And if *I* hear any of you sneering, I'll beat your bloody brains out. Is *that* clear, mates?"

Priestman and Goldman turned as one to stare at the giant New Zealander as he now joined them at the bar. He held out his hand to Goldman. "My mother's a Jew."

Goldman smiled faintly as he accepted the giant paw offered him. "And *my* mother is Catholic."

Priestman registered that maybe Murray didn't think this war was just a lark after all – and started to like him.

Chapter 19

RAF Tangmere
14 August 1940

Colin went out for his nightly walk around the perimeter of the Station after dinner. He needed the walk, he found, not just for the exercise and the fresh air, but to give himself some time alone to think. Things had been happening very fast these last three days. Clearly, the Germans had opened the long-expected air offensive preparatory to the invasion. Portsmouth had been pounded – a clear effort to disable the Royal Navy – and the Harbour Station had taken a direct hit. The Luftwaffe had also gone for the RAF. They had hit hard at the RDF stations and forward airfields on three successive days. Fortunately, the Germans did not appear to know the difference in importance between Fighter Command, Coastal Command and Training Command airfields, and had distributed their attacks across airfields from all three commands, which meant Fighter Command had suffered less than it might have. But the situation was anything but good. Fighter Command had lost 11 aircraft on the very first day of the offensive, five of those from Tangmere squadrons.

These squadrons had, furthermore, been kept at readiness from dawn to dusk – and at this time of year that meant from 5 am to 9 pm. They had been scrambled several times a day, and whether they encountered the enemy or not, the strain was beginning to take its toll. After all, it wasn't as if they had been under no pressure up to now.

The station MO reported a rash of requests for sleeping pills, too. Obviously, pilots were finding it hard to relax after the tension of the day, and their drinking binges had, Colin thought, a touch of desperation to them now. He was particularly concerned about Bowles, especially after their last encounter. Bowles was clearly terrified, but equally determined not to give in to his fears. P/O Debsen was another problem. He was no less terrified than Bowles, but he was not prepared to admit it – not even to himself. And MacLeod.... Colin sighed.

MacLeod was another problem altogether. MacLeod had seduced one of the young WAAF, a girl who worked as a clerk in supplies. She was a sweet, timid girl from a strict Presbyterian family, and she had been completely unprepared for the persistent Scotsman. It was bad enough that he had taken advantage of her naïveté and timidity, but now he was flatly refusing to marry her. The girl had come to Colin several times, and she was in a terrible state. No matter how often Colin assured her that *God* would forgive her, she knew her *father* would not. "He'll throw me out," she'd explained miserably to Colin, begging him, "Can't you talk to Malcolm?"

Colin had tried, but not successfully. The Scotsman came from a rough part of Glasgow, and MacLeod said he'd left home at 14 after his father beat him up once too often. He proudly told the padre he hadn't let anyone tell him how to run his life since. "Ain't seen the inside of a church since I was eight, either," he announced aggressively. "So, keep your sermons to yourself, padre. It weren't rape and if the silly girl claims it was, I'll go to court and describe exactly what happened – word for word."

That was a cruel threat, as there was nothing poor Lettice Fields wanted *less* than publicity. Nor had she ever claimed it was rape. Colin, however, thought that MacLeod's actions *amounted* to rape, because it was obvious that Lettice truly didn't know what she was letting herself in for. Her upbringing had been so protected that it was assumed she would never be in a situation where she would need to be forceful.

Colin had just come abreast of one of the hangars, and his attention was torn away from his thoughts by shouting from inside. An instant later, one of the small doors cut into the hangar entrance crashed open. A long sheet of light spilt onto the grass – a dangerous violation of the blackout. A man ran out. He didn't see Colin, just sprinted towards the cluster of brick buildings in the darkness beyond. Excited voices came from inside the hangar. Colin slipped inside, closing the door behind him to blacken the field again.

A crowd stood just under the nose of one of the Hurricanes and as Colin entered he heard someone shouting, "Don't touch him! Don't try to move him! Get back! Give him air!!" An airman lay flat on his back on the concrete floor. Blood oozed from nose and mouth, and he moaned and twitched horribly.

"What happened?" Colin asked one of the men standing about in a low voice.

"Sanders was working on the engine of that Hurricane, and he missed his footing somehow and fell off. Chiefy thinks he might have broken his back."

Colin let his eyes sweep across the faces of the men crowded around. There wasn't one that didn't look exhausted and shocked. After all, it wasn't just the pilots who were under horrible pressure now. A couple of the younger men were ghostly white. One, particularly, seemed to be shaking.

The Station Medical Officer pushed his way in through the crowd.

He knelt beside the injured man, talked to him too softly to be heard, and then ordered a stretcher. In five minutes, the injured airman had been lifted carefully in accordance with the MO's instructions and taken out of the hangar. But the men left behind were still stunned.

"What are you all standing about for?" Flight Sergeant Rowe demanded gruffly. "We've got work to do!"

Some of the men started to drift back to their work, but the young man who had attracted Colin's attention earlier remained where he was, as if paralysed.

"Tufnel! Get on with it. I'll finish for Sanders." Already the ageing Flight Sergeant was hauling himself up onto the wing of the Hurricane from which the accident had occurred, but the LAC he'd addressed didn't move. "Tufnel!" the Flight Sergeant called again sharply.

The young man seemed frozen to the concrete. Colin went over to him. "Are you all right?"

"I saw him fall. He fell off right before my eyes," the young rigger admitted, staring at the place on the floor where his comrade had lain moaning just minutes earlier.

"Tufnel! We have work to do! This crate has to be serviceable tomorrow!"

"I heard something snap as he hit the concrete," the airman said to Colin, ignoring the Chief, still staring. "Just a soft snap– but I could hear it perfectly. Just snap. Then he was moaning and couldn't move."

Colin put his hand on the man's upper arm gently, tentatively. The rigger didn't even seem to notice.

"If his back's broken, he'll never walk again," the airman was saying in an awed voice. "He—"

Flight Sergeant Rowe suddenly loomed up beside Colin, took hold of the LAC by the front of his overalls, and started shaking him violently. He shouted into his face. "I gave you an order! We've got work to do! Get on with it!"

"*What do you mean, 'get on with it?'*" the young man shouted back in hysterical rage at his superior. "*Pete was crippled right before my eyes and all you care about is a damned crate! Don't you give a damn about **us**?*"

The Sergeant hit the airman so fast that neither his victim nor Colin saw the blow coming. The rigger doubled over, clutching his belly, and Colin protested in a high-pitched, outraged voice. "You can't do that, Flight Sergeant! You have no right to—"

"Then report me, sir! Tell the CO! But let me get these crates patched up first – or this squadron won't be at strength tomorrow!"

Colin stood in the middle of the vast hangar, and you could have heard a pin drop. He might have the law on his side, but Colin was not sure at that moment if Squadron Leader Jones – or Station Commmander Boret – would back him up. The country was about to be invaded, and the only thing that might *possibly* prevent that were these "crates." Maybe the Flight Sergeant was right? Maybe he could get away with hitting his men.

Colin wasn't naïve. It wasn't that long ago that it had been standard practice to flog men for minor infractions of discipline in the Navy. The RAF had a much better reputation, but in times like these it was hard to know for sure what would be condoned. Colin felt he had no choice but to retreat.

He turned on his heel and walked slowly out of the hangar. Behind him Rowe was shouting orders, bullying them back to work again. At least he heard one cockney voice say, "I'll finish the work on the crate, sir. Let Tufnel go to the infirmary and see how bad Sanders is."

"Haven't you got any work of your own, Appleby?" Rowe demanded.

"I'll finish it later, sir. Tufnel isn't going to do a proper job in the state he's in."

Good lad, Colin thought, and went straight over to the infirmary to find out the state of the injured man himself.

One look at the MO's face was enough. "I've given him a sedative and called for an ambulance. I'm sending him up to a hospital in Southampton with a specialty unit for spinal injuries, but, frankly, I don't think he stands much of a chance."

"To live?"

"To walk again. If he's lucky, he'll regain use of his arms but not his legs."

Stunned, Colin retreated to the chapel. He knelt and dropped his head on his clasped hands, praying silently and fervently – for Sanders' recovery, and for guidance. The job was growing harder and harder by the minute, and he had an almost panicked feeling of not being able to cope.

He didn't know how long he prayed. Eventually he got up, stiff but feeling vaguely better. As he turned to leave, he noticed a man sitting in the last pew of the chapel, huddling in an oversized overcoat. He stood as he saw Colin coming towards him. It was the fitter who had been so distressed in the hangar, Tufnel.

"Can I have a word with you, sir?"

"Of course. Come along to my office and I'll put a kettle on." The "office" was really the vestry, but that seemed to work best. The hanging vestments and stacked hymnals, etc., reminded visitors that they were with a clergyman, even if he was in uniform. Colin indicated a chair and plugged in his electric teapot.

The airman sat hunched forward with his elbows on his knees, the

233

shock still stamped on his face. Colin wondered if he was here because of the brutality of the Flight Sergeant or because of the accident.

"Sanders," the rigger started, "was engaged to be married."

"Oh, dear," Colin muttered involuntarily. "Had they set a date?"

"Yes, sir. July 1st, sir – but then we got our orders south, see, and Chiefy said he had to put it off. Pete put in for leave every week, but Chiefy kept turning him down until finally about three weeks ago. But we still ain't heard nothing, and it was – well, sir, Pete was worried that his girl would change her mind if he kept putting her off. She's pretty, you know, and she had lots of boyfriends before she agreed to marry Pete. She works at a canteen in a shipyard, and there are lots of blokes there earning bags more than we do."

Colin knew the situation all too well, and it angered him; the unions had shamelessly exploited the fact that certain professions were vital to the war effort in order to obtain wages and other benefits far in excess of normal. But at the moment, only Sanders mattered. "Is there any way I can help?" Colin asked.

Tufnel shrugged. "I don't know, sir, but I worry that if – I mean when – Pete's girl finds out he's been crippled, that she'll ditch him."

Colin was not shocked. In fact, he could sympathise with a young woman who didn't want to be tied to a cripple. It was bad enough for a married woman to cope with a husband who was crippled later in life, but how could you expect loyalty of a young girl who had not even had any good times with her husband? "How well do you know the young lady?" He asked the airman in front of him.

Tufnel shrugged. "We went out together now and again – me and my popsy and Pete and Dotty."

"And Sanders? Have you known him very long?"

"Oh, yes, sir! We was Halton apprentices together. He qualified as a fitter and me as a rigger just so we could be a team, and we asked for a posting together – regardless of squadron – too. We've been with 606 ever since. We've been friends for almost 6 years."

"Then you know Sanders' family. How do you think they'll react?"

Tufnel looked uncomfortable. "His Dad's been dead for years now, and his Mum's got her hands full with the younger kids. There are five of them, six altogether counting Pete, but he was the eldest, and he's got four younger sisters and a baby brother."

"Do you think his mother or one of his sisters will come down to Southampton?"

"Oh, no, sir! They live in Newcastle!" It might as well have been India or China, from the way Tufnel said it.

"We'd better see about getting you some leave, then," Colin concluded.

"Sanders is going to need support in the days ahead." Colin hesitated and then asked cautiously, "Are you all right?"

"Oh, yeah," the rigger shrugged uncomfortably. "Where I grew up, a punch now and then were sort of part of the package. I'll be all right."

"Does Rowe do that kind of thing often?"

"Oh, no, sir! It ain't like he does it a lot. It's just, well, what with the balloon going up and all, I guess even he's got the wind up."

Colin nodded.

"You aren't really going to report him, are you?" Tufnel sounded worried.

"I don't know." Colin answered honestly. "What he did was wrong. It was a serious breach of regulations."

"But, sir, in the middle of all this... I mean, we can't afford for him to go on charges – not now. I mean, at least you know where you stand with him, and he knows more about aircraft and their engines than the rest of us put together."

Colin understood: the devil you know is better than the one you don't know. So, he nodded, slowly and ambiguously. Then, noticing that the water was boiling away merrily on his desk, he asked, "Did you want some tea?"

The airman looked over wistfully but shook his head. "I think I'd better turn in, sir. We've got to have the aircraft ready for the pilots at first light." Colin nodded and pulled the plug on the water. The ground crews were being woken at 3 am so they could get out to the aircraft and do the DI (Daily Inspection) and warm up the engines *before* the pilots arrived at dawn. It was now already past 10 pm. They both stood, and Colin promised, "I'll see about getting some leave for you, and please let me know if there is anything else I can do – write a letter or whatever."

"Thank you, sir." Tufnel nodded and slipped out.

Despite the hour of the night, Colin decided to see if 606's adjutant was about. Not entirely to his surprise, he found that Mickey was indeed still in his office.

Mickey looked up startled at the knock on his door, but he waved Colin in when he recognised him. "Isn't it frightful?" he asked before Colin even got a word out. "The MO says he doesn't stand much of a chance of ever walking again. Such an experienced man, too! He was one of Trenchard's brats, you know, and he's been with the squadron practically since it was formed. I can't get over it: a fitter who's been doing this work for years just steps backwards into thin air and falls straight onto the concrete." Mickey shook his head again to emphasize his disbelief.

"Have you notified his family?"

"I've been trying, but I can't seem to get through. Trunk lines appear to be completely over-loaded – that or Jerry got something during the day. All I get is the engaged tone before I even finish dialling!" The exasperation was understandable. The adjutant was tired, too – and all but drowning in the overflowing stacks of paperwork filling the office.

"Do you know about the fiancée?" Colin asked next.

"Yes, it's here in the file. A certain Dorothy Morley – but I thought I ought to talk to his mother first. Maybe even have the mother break the news to the girl friend, don't you think?" The question was not rhetorical. Mickey sincerely wanted advice. He felt terrible and dreaded talking to either woman.

"Yes, if they live close enough, that is." Colin paused, and then continued. "I also think it would be a good thing if LAC Tufnel was given compassionate leave to go up to Southampton and be with Sanders when they give him the news. They were pretty close, I understand, and his mother and fiancée aren't likely to get down fast enough."

Mickey was shaking his head. "Not a chance."

"Why ever not?" Colin at once sat straighter, and for an instant the future Earl was very evident; Colin was prepared to fight for this.

Mickey shook his head. "Don't misunderstand me. I'd give him leave in an instant, but Jones hasn't signed off on anyone's leave in weeks. Look, here's the file!" Mickey knew exactly where everything was despite the appearance of chaos presented to strangers. He had his hand on a manila folder in an instant. "These are all the leave requests submitted to Jones since we came south. The only ones he granted were for Hayworth, Dunsire and Ringwood at the end of June. Apparently, he'd promised it to them before leaving Scotland. But nothing since then. Believe me, I've tried to get him to sign off. I used to leave the file on top of his mail every day, but he ticked me off for that! Look! Here are, what," Mickey counted, "seven requests from various erks – all duly signed off by the Chief – and here – oh, and here's one from Davis. I suppose I can get rid of that." He crumpled up the leave request from the dead pilot and tossed it into the wastepaper basket before turning the entire folder over to Colin.

Colin flipped through it and found Sanders' request form, dated July 19. "But there haven't been any orders to stop all leave, have there?" Colin asked.

"From the Ministry or Group, you mean? No, not at all. After all, things were comparatively quiet in June and early July. And when you think about it, throughout the last war we continued to have regular leave and rotations. Wars go on for years, and men can't stay at peak performance continuously. They need rest."

"They certainly do, and Sanders is going to need at least one familiar and friendly face around him when they give him the news. Surely, in this extreme situation, Jones could make an exception. We're only talking about Tufnel going up to Southampton for a day or two."

Mickey was unconsciously wiping imaginary sweat from his brow with his handkerchief. "I couldn't agree with you more, but I'm not authorised to sign these things on my own. I've got to pin Jones down long enough to make him do it, and frankly...." He sighed, defeated.

"How long will it take to get a replacement in?" Colin asked next.

"Oh, that's already organised. I put in for a fitter immediately after I heard the news, and Personnel said they'll have someone here by tomorrow morning. In fact," Mickey again put his hand on what he was looking for, "I've got a telegram stating a certain AC Fowley will be reporting to us in the morning. Coming straight down from the School of Technical Training."

"Doesn't that mean he's straight out of training? No experience?" Colin asked, a little alarmed.

"Yes, but, well, they can't very well steal from other squadrons, can they?"

Colin supposed that was right, but he didn't like the sound of it. It would be very difficult for a young fitter to start his first job in the middle of the most intense air offensive in history.

"Mickey?"

"Yes?"

"Have you ever heard of Flight Sergeant Rowe punching or hitting the men?"

"Good heavens! That sort of thing isn't allowed!" Mickey responded shocked.

"I know," Colin conceded, but then continued, "yet I just witnessed it with my own eyes."

"Good God! That's horrible! We can't afford to put Rowe up on charges in the middle of all this! You aren't going to make a formal report, are you?"

Colin thought about that answer and considered the look on Mickey's appalled face, and with a sigh shook his head. "No, I suppose not. Not now. Not this time.... But I don't think it's right." He said good night to Mickey and retreated up to his own room, feeling very dissatisfied with himself. His last thought as he fell asleep was a simple prayer: God, help me.

Chapter 20

Crépon, France
15 August 1940

It was their third sortie of the day, and Ernst was exhausted. They all were, actually – 'though of course no one said anything about it. You could tell the others were tired because they didn't joke around as usual. Even Christian was silent, almost grim. Of course, some of that might have to do with Mühlbauer not returning from the mission yesterday. He was now officially posted "missing, presumed dead" – although he might still turn up somewhere or have been taken prisoner. Bartels, too, had failed to return (not that Feldburg was upset about that), and Hartmann had been named acting *Staffelkapitän*.

The day had started off well. First, they'd escorted Stukas in an attack on one of RAF's forward airfields. The Stukas were excellent, as usual. From what Ernst could see through the smoke of the burning buildings and the dust thrown up by the bombs, the field had been a shambles by the time the Stukas were finished with it.

Of course, the RAF showed up too, but late. The Stukas had been finished and could rush for home while the Me109s held off the Hurricanes. Möller and Hartmann had both put in claims. Although two 109s had been damaged, both made it across the channel. Because Busso had to crash-land near the coast, he'd missed out on the second sortie of the day, when they were supposed to rendezvous with Ju88s on another low-level raid against the coastal radio stations. Somehow the fighters and bombers lost each other in the patchy cloud. II *Gruppe* never found the bombers they were supposed to escort, although they swanned around looking for them for twenty minutes, consuming precious fuel. Frischmuth then tried to tempt the English into coming up to fight while the *Gruppe* wasn't tied to the bombers, but it didn't work out that way. The English got the bombers – almost all of them – and II Gruppe got clobbered with vicious accusations of incompetence and even cowardice from *Luftflotte* 3 Command. Frischmuth passed the compliments on to his three *Staffelkapitän*, who "graciously" shared it with their pilots – at least Hartmann did.

They were now being given a third "chance to redeem themselves," by escorting a relatively small contingent of Ju 88s on what was explicitly called a "nuisance" raid. The principal target was RAF Warmwell, but the

Geschwader Intelligence Officer had suggested this was not very important, as it was probably no more than a training field. He said if they couldn't find it easily, the bombers had orders to hit any "target of opportunity." The point of the raid was to wear down British air defences rather than cause destruction on the ground, and it was part of a day-long campaign with this principal objective. Since dawn, not only had *Luftflotte* 2 and 3 in the Pas-de-Calais been at work, but *Luftflotte* 5, flying all the way from Norway, had launched multiple sorties. In short, the Luftwaffe had been pounding the British Isles from Scotland to Cornwall.

The idea of wearing down the British defences might be fine for the bombers that each only flew one sortie a day, Ernst thought, as he wearily heaved himself up his wing and sank into the cockpit again. However, the shortage of 109s – and the ever more apparent ineffectiveness of the 110s – meant that the 109s were being asked to fly more and more frequently. Then again, he admitted to himself as he strapped himself in, he wouldn't really have wanted to change places with the bomber boys even so. He didn't like being on the receiving end of a Spitfire's attention, but at least if he was, he had a fighting chance of escaping in his faithful Emil.

Ernst glanced over at Christian mechanically. Christian's engine was already purring, the Emil trembling. Ernst signalled to his own mechanic, and almost before he knew it, they were in the air again. Routine. Pure routine. Ja, he was getting better at it, he decided with a touch of satisfaction.

They found the bombers this time. Just 16 Ju88s, and they flew northwest, away from the main battle, probing for weaknesses in the English defences. The Intelligence Officer had said that the steady attrition in RAF Fighter Command over the last month had reduced the number of operable fighters down to less than half their Order of Battle. The remaining 300 or so fighters were naturally concentrated in the southeast, to protect the approaches to London and the narrowest parts of the Channel.

Taking advantage of this fact, the Luftwaffe had designed today's raids to exploit British weakness across the rest of the island. This was the main reason raids had been launched from Norway – to show the English people how vulnerable they were north of the Trent. According to the Intelligence Officer, the British people had no idea that the Luftwaffe possessed bombers and fighters (this was where the Me110s were valuable) with the range to attack the British Isles from Norway. When Edinburgh, York and Durham went up in flames, he told his audience, they would learn. As for this particular late-afternoon raid, the Intelligence Officer had explained, it might not be such a surprise to the

British that Devon and Cornwall were *within range* of the Luftwaffe operating from Northern France, but it ought to frighten them to realise they had no defences any more.

Ernst very much hoped that Luftwaffe Intelligence was correct and there were no defences in this region. Then they would go in and out without opposition. Christian would be disappointed if that happened, of course, Ernst thought with a glance towards his leader. Christian was still itching to get a confirmed kill.

During the brief fight this morning, Christian had pressed in much closer to the one target he managed to get in his sights. Ernst had been able to report to him that he'd seen bits and pieces of the Hurricane's wing breaking off – but the old crates were remarkably resilient. Say what you would about the Hurricane (and Ernst certainly wouldn't want to have to fly one of the humpbacks himself), it was very hard to shoot down for some reason. Ernst could have sworn Christian's cannon had chewed at the Hurricane's wing for 5 or 6 seconds, but the crate just kept churning along – and then managed to nip about in a tight turn, flip on its back and dive away. They hadn't been able to catch it because another of the beasts had come at them, and they had to break away from it.

The ragged English coast lay ahead of them in the late afternoon sun. Ernst could clearly see a peninsula that hung like a hook into the Channel with a deep harbour behind it. He tried to remember the map they'd been shown, and decided it was Poole.

"Indians to the left."

"That's to the west. I thought they didn't have any fighters in the west any more?" Christian commented helpfully, and Ernst groaned inwardly. Why couldn't he just leave it be? They could all see that Intelligence had been wrong – again.

"Shut up, Feldburg. Follow me down."

Hartman knew that Bartels had had his ears blistered for delaying his attack three days ago. He clearly wasn't going to make the same mistake. Besides, if the RAF was decimated, one could hardly justify waiting for more targets.

Busso had returned in time to be along on this sortie, so the Schwarm was at full strength. Ernst registered that he was tense again – so much for routine. He felt the need to urinate the minute he realised that the English fighters sweeping towards them were Spitfires. Ernst *hated* Spitfires.

For what seemed like a lifetime, the two formations of fighters charged at one another in almost equal strength. They were closing at something close to 1,000 km/h, and with every second Ernst's instincts to duck away grew more and more compelling. Just when he thought he couldn't take it any more, Christian himself put his nose down and led him just metres beneath the bellies of the Spitfires. Ernst pulled his head in instinctively. Then they were out from under the enemy and both formations swung about, scrambling like a pack of hounds in the turn to get turned around and come to grips again.

Ernst lost sight of Dieter and Busso completely and started to grey out as he tried to keep up with Christian in the turn. As his vision gradually cleared, he could see the Spitfire Christian was going for. It seemed to hang in the air, confused. Of course, it was also flying at over 500 km/h, but even so, Christian was going all out and clearly gaining on it.

Christian pressed in closer and closer. Ernst could see the English pilot looking about in his cockpit – overhead, left and right, but never really turning around properly to where the danger came from. Poor bastard, Ernst thought, remembering that Warmwell was a training base and thinking this pilot might be very young and inexperienced. He certainly seemed to be daydreaming. Then Ernst remembered himself, and twisted about so hard in his straps that he all but pulled his shoulder muscles in an effort to check his own tail. But there was nothing behind them.

When Ernst looked forward again, Christian's cannon were eating along the side of the Spitfire from the tail to the engine. Ernst could see the holes being punched into the metal. Then white smoke gushed out of the cowling, and rapidly turned black.

"You got it!" Ernst called out jubilantly. "You got it!"

"Not until it goes down! Cover me!"

Ernst looked over his shoulder again, weaving the Emil back and forth a little to be absolutely sure he could see everything that might be threatening them. But there didn't appear to be another plane in the sky. Ernst assumed they had been reinforced by 4 or 6 Staffel, which would have given them a little more than 2-1 superiority and make it hard for any Spitfire to go on the offensive. A little to the left he could see some smoke, apparently sent up by the bombs. Whether it was the RAF airfield at Warmwell or something else, he couldn't tell from here.

"Now I've got him!" Christian called out, drawing Ernst's attention back to his leader. Not only was the Spitfire going into a sharp nose-dive, but the pilot was evidently struggling to get out of the cockpit. He had the canopy open and after an awkward minute of frantic if indefinable gesturing, he was lifted clear out of the cockpit. Ernst winced as he almost collided with his own tail and hoped fervently that he would never have to do this.

Christian at once started curving around, his eye following both the crashing plane and the falling pilot. The parachute blossomed white and Ernst breathed out in relief. The Spitfire was leaving a filthy smudge of smoke in the sky and then, with a dull boom, it went in. The smoke billowed up from a wheat field that seemed to catch fire near the wreck. Christian flew circles around the pilot as the latter gently floated down the sky. Much as Ernst sympathised, he was getting nervous about fuel.

"Christian, *I* know you don't intend to shoot him, but I think you're making *him* nervous."

"All right. Let's go home," Christian agreed cheerfully, at once breaking into a slow "victory" roll. As he levelled off again, Ernst fell in beside him. Christian looked over and waved. Then he went back to flying, but Ernst could see him moving his head about in his cockpit – not cautiously checking for enemy but singing. Christian had a good voice, and he sang when he was happy. He was, Ernst knew, very happy at this moment.

It was the best party the Staffel had put on since Ernst had joined it, and clearly it had been planned long in advance. Christian must have left standing orders with the Mess sergeant, "The day I get my first kill...." Furthermore, Christian had deep pockets. His family owned large, prosperous estates in southern Germany, and he and his brother shared the rental income of an elegant five-story apartment house directly on the Landwehr canal in Berlin. Dieter said there were various other sources of income as well, stocks and bonds or whatever. Although Ernst had long supposed Christian didn't live on his salary alone, the baron had never flaunted his wealth before.

For this dinner, however, Christian provided not only French champagne, but also mussels in garlic butter, followed by wild-boar paté with apples, then there was steak and sorbet all of which Christian had ordered via the Mess Sergeant from a French source in Cherbourg. There was fresh salad with walnuts and vinaigrette, mushrooms sautéed with parsley in sour cream, potatoes roasted with rosemary, and French baguette, too. There was entertainment too: a singer accompanied on the piano sang French chansons.

Christian provided for the other ranks as well – albeit not as lavishly. He paid for several kegs of beer to be opened in both the Sergeants' and the Other Ranks' Messes. As for the eight Luftwaffe *Helferinnen*, they were invited to the Officer's Mess and explicitly warned not to appear in uniform. In uniform they had no right to eat at the Officer's Mess, but as ladies they could be guests of the officers.

The entire *Gruppe* was, of course, included in the party, so there were nearly 50 officers (pilots and non-flying commissioned personnel) and only the eight girls. Christian's seating arrangement carefully distributed the *Helferinnen*, one per table. Klaudia was assigned to his own table.

From Rosa, Klaudia knew that Axel thought the world of Feldburg, and she knew too that he reputedly had a French girlfriend. A couple of the other *Helferinnen* were quite outraged by this fact – pointing out it was against regulations, not to mention unpatriotic – but Klaudia thought they were only jealous. Still, having so meticulously avoided contact with the pilots of this *Gruppe* – particularly pilots like Feldburg, who were good-looking and self-confident and so reminded her of Jako – she wasn't entirely happy about the arrangement. Nor did she have anything appropriate to wear. She had never dreamed she might find herself at such a dinner.

The tables were set with white linen, cut crystal and silver. There were roses in vases, candles, and individual salt dishes with tiny spoons. The Mess stewards wore dress whites, the officers dress uniform with shoes rather than boots. Feldburg met the *Helferinnen* at the door to the dining room like a gracious host. They were each escorted into dinner by their dinner-partner. Klaudia felt transported back to the world of her childhood, as if she were attending dinner at a neighbouring estate.

At table, Klaudia found herself seated between Baron v. Feldburg and his wingman, the fat pilot who had rescued her from the SS officer on the day she went to Mont St. Michel. Feldburg made a point of saying that the celebration was partially to Geuke's credit, as "Without him, I couldn't have shot down anything."

Klaudia smiled at the wingman, but he wouldn't meet her eyes. He seemed a bit sullen and nodded moodily, his gaze fixed on his plate.

In contrast, Baron v. Feldburg was a splendid dinner-partner. He didn't just talk about himself as Jako had done. He asked her about herself, her family, her home. With him she had no need to be embarrassed or shy about her background, and he deftly put her at ease by enthusing about his own summers spent on his mother's family's estate in Mecklenburg. Although geographically distant, the experiences resembled one another: helping with harvests in the long summer days, visiting the neighbours by carriage or horse, swimming in the cool, shallow lakes, excursions to the Baltic, sandy beaches and smoked herring.

Not that Baron von Feldburg by any means monopolised Klaudia. He easily included other pilots in the conversation, drawing Klaudia's attention to one after another with little anecdotes about them. When he heard she'd been in East Prussia for her RAD service, he delightedly indicated a pilot who was from Königsberg. Klaudia found herself chatting about her RAD experiences; everyone understood, as they had been through it themselves. They groaned and complained and laughed at the memories, putting her even more at ease.

Only Geuke refused to join in. More than once Baron v. Feldburg made an effort to get him to take part in the conversation, but the fat pilot stubbornly refused to be drawn. He kept his answers monosyllabic and his eyes fixed on the table. Klaudia almost felt insulted, but she couldn't really believe he had something against her – not after the way he'd helped that day in the rain. She decided to make one effort on her own, and when Baron v. Feldburg was having a friendly argument with one of the other pilots, she turned pointedly to his wingman. "I understand your aircraft was badly shot up the other day. Are you sure you're all right?"

"Quite," he answered curtly, refusing to look at her, much less smile.

Klaudia shrugged inwardly, feeling she had made an honest effort to be nice. If *Leutnant* Geuke didn't want to respond, that was his problem. Just then Baron v. Feldburg noticed them and smiling widely, he urged, "Ernst, tell *Fräulein* v. Richthofen about the little boys who waved to us this morning."

Geuke cast Feldburg a look that would have killed him, if looks could kill. It dawned on Klaudia that there was some reason Geuke was furious with his *Rotteführer* – though she could not imagine what it was. They otherwise seemed to get along very well.

Meanwhile, however, Ernst dutifully started telling the story Christian had demanded. "On the first raid this morning when we were escorting Stukas – of your old *Gruppe* to be exact, *gnädiges Fräulein* – we engaged some Hurricanes to prevent them from following the Stukas. Somehow in the course of this little tiff, we were drawn inland. When we got bounced by a second squadron of the beasts, Christian took us down on the deck to evade them. We shook them off and turned for home. By then, we were very low on fuel, and to save it, Christian chose not to climb. That was the reason you chose not to climb, wasn't it, Christian?" He was focusing on Feldburg rather than Klaudia.

Christian shrugged, and with a smile for Klaudia poured her some more wine. "Actually, I was sight-seeing. I don't know that part of England very well, and there seemed to be an interesting Gothic church down there. Perpendicular, to be precise."

"Don't believe a word he's saying," the pilot on Feldburg's other side leaned across him to say. "He wouldn't know the difference between Romanesque and *Baroque*, much less high Gothic and Perpendicular."

"*That* is not true," Christian protested in mock outrage. "I—"

"Let Ernst get on with the story," Dieter interrupted, settling back in his own chair satisfied.

"Anyway, we were down on the deck," Ernst continued dutifully, "flying at under 200 metres, very near a village. You could see people standing in front of the shops and looking up at the sound of our engines. And there were some boys in shorts playing football in the field beside the churchyard. They stopped playing, forgetting the ball entirely in their excitement. As we came nearer, they waved at us eagerly. It was really heartwarming they way they jumped up and down and waved. You would have thought we were flying over a German town."

"They must have been *mortified* when we passed overhead and they saw the crosses on our wings," Christian added.

Everyone burst out laughing.

Christian continued, "no doubt they are still blaming one another for being the first to wave. '*I* knew it was a Messerschmitt straight off, Fat Head! *You* were the one who said it was a Hurricane, you silly sod!'" Christian imitated a schoolboy's high-pitched whine and they all laughed again.

"Really?" Ernst asked, incredulous, his expression stunned. "I thought they were Fifth Columnists!" His innocent claim produced a new round of laughter.

For an instant Klaudia was offended for his sake. She didn't like mocking anyone. Then she saw Geuke's lips quirk, and she realised he was playing the fool quite intentionally – and the others knew it. That made her feel better, and she laughed more easily. She saw *Leutnant* Geuke sneak a glance at her, and look away sharply when he realised she was watching him, his ears going red.

Thunderstruck, Klaudia realised that he liked her. He was tongue-tied because he was shy! She looked more intently at him, but he was stubbornly staring at his plate again, although it was empty. The thought unsettled her. She had vowed she would not "get involved" with anyone here.

Admittedly, it would have been easy to fall for Baron v. Feldburg. Already her defences against him were quite disabled. If he were to focus his attention on her just a little more, if he were to flatter her just a touch less routinely, if he would only be really attentive, rather than just exquisitely polite— She didn't even want to think about it. She knew she would weaken. It would be so easy to talk herself into believing he was different from Jako, because he was a nobleman.

But fortunately, he wasn't interested in her. He was no more interested in her than all her other aristocratic dinner-partners at countless dinners in Silesia. Baron v. Feldburg was a charming dinner-partner, but *Leutnant* Geuke was the one who was interested in her. And that was why she was sitting here: because Baron v. Feldburg knew how his wingman felt about her. And that was why *Leutnant* Geuke was so furious with his *Rotteführer*....

But Klaudia didn't want *Leutnant* Geuke to take an interest in her. Not if it was going to end as it had with Jako. The thought of that horrible incident still shamed her. Even here and now, in the middle of this lovely dinner, she felt herself getting hot at the memory of it. What would a nice young man like *Leutnant* Geuke think of her, if he learnt she was already deflowered? "Damaged goods," as she'd heard the NCOs call it. He'd either lose interest in her altogether, or he'd think she was a slut and expect her to sleep with him, too. Klaudia could have cried from self-pity. Jako had ruined everything – even her chances with the likes of a *Leutnant* Geuke.

Chapter 21

RAF Tangmere
16 August 1940

Although the weather was splendid, the sky over Britain was curiously empty for most of the morning. At Tangmere, the pilots of Nos. 17, 43 and 606 squadrons dozed in the sun in their deck chairs, waiting, but the klaxon remained silent. No. 145 had been pulled out. They had lost 11 pilots dead and 2 wounded since July 10 and effectively ceased to exist as a fighting unit; only the ground crews and administration were still intact. Dowding ordered the remaining four pilots to fly north to Drem in Scotland and sent a Spitfire squadron, 602, down to take their place. The latter deployed to Tangmere's satellite airfield at Westhampnett, leaving Tangmere in the hands of Hurricanes alone.

MacLeod lay with his head in the shade of an empty deck chair, his eyes closed, trying not to move his head. It was killing him, the result of the worst hangover of his life. He'd had another horrible fight with Lettice last night and then drunk a bottle of gin to comfort himself. Lettice had turned out to be a hysterical girl. She was threatening suicide if he didn't marry her! Good riddance was all he had to say. Bloody females!

As he lay in the shade of the deck chair, MacLeod vowed to keep away from women until the war was over. He couldn't afford to feel like this. The mere thought of having to look into the bright sunlight made him want to scream. He knew his exhausted eyes would send stabbing pains to his brain the moment they had to deal with the light. MacLeod could only hope that Jerry wouldn't show up today at all. Surely, they were getting tired, too?

Ginger, in contrast, was waiting for something to happen. He couldn't sit still today any more than yesterday or the day before, but he didn't want to risk being shouted at by the CO for "making them all nervous" as he had yesterday. Cautiously he slipped away from dispersal, walking over to the perimeter fence. He could hear the klaxon from anywhere on the field, and he could sprint to his Hurricane from anywhere. No need to hang about the dispersal hut with the others and their stupid, senseless conversations. Who *cared* what horses were running races or what teams were playing stupid games?

Ginger looked for signs of mice or rabbits in the long grass beyond the fence. Then he looked up to search the heavens, squinting against the sun. He saw them, but for several seconds he couldn't believe what he saw. The whole sky was full of specks. And then the klaxon started screeching like an outraged beast.

Ginger started running, realised he was running for the wrong Hurricane, changed direction, and nearly collided with a pilot coming the other way. 17 and 43 were scrambling, too. Over the tannoy came the voice of the Station Commander in a tone that betrayed urgency despite its pronounced calm: "All squadrons scramble! All squadrons scramble! This raid is directed at Tangmere. Repeat: Tangmere is the target! Get your aircraft into the air immediately!"

The drone of the bombers could be heard clearly, making the whole summer day vibrate to an alien, hostile hum. Hurricanes started coughing into life all across the field, and then the ack-ack started, drowning out the shouting and other noises.

Only as he slipped into his cockpit did Ginger remember he'd forgotten his paper bag, the one he now carried to be sick into, but there wasn't time for it anyway.

The Controller was ordering over the R/T, more alarmed than the Station Commander: "Get them off the ground! Get them into the air! They're coming for us! *Get airborne!*"

MacLeod was trying to see where he was going while keeping his eyes squeezed almost shut. The Hurricane was bouncing and leaping over the field, and suddenly there was another Hurricane crossing his path just a few feet in front of him. MacLeod gasped and swerved. The tail of the other Hurricane whisked by, just inches in front of his propeller. MacLeod's eyes were wide open now. Hurricanes were rushing across the field from all directions in complete pandemonium. MacLeod thrust his throttle forward with just one thought: escape this madness. Get into the air!

Debsen, cursing his crew for being so slow, was one of the last pilots into the air. He was only halfway across the airfield when he heard the howling of a Stuka behind him. He looked into his rear-view mirror and saw one of the crooked-winged beasts going straight down. Then the earth shook and his Hurricane came free of it. He pushed the throttle forward, screaming at the inanimate machine, "Come on! Come on! Come on!" It was total chaos. Three squadrons were in the air, and none of them in formation or even together. No one was giving orders. Not from the air or the ground. On the other hand, there was no need for vectoring and interception. They could all see what they were up against: 50-odd Stukas were lining up to dive at Tangmere, and above them were swarms of 109s and 110s so dense that it was impossible even to guess at their numbers.

For once, it made no difference that the enemy fighters had a height advantage. Having been caught on the ground, the three Tangmere squadrons found themselves on the same level as the dive-bombers as they finished their bomb-run, while the Messerschmitts were thousands of feet above. The English fighters flung themselves at the bombers as soon as they were airborne. They attacked the Stukas as the latter pulled out of their dives – their most vulnerable moment. The Hurricanes dashed in and out amidst the enemy, completely ignoring their own anti-aircraft guns.

MacLeod felt as if he couldn't see straight. It wasn't the hangover any more. His Hurricane was being shaken violently from the bomb blasts just below it. Then he found himself flying through smoke and debris. He could hear the clatter of fragments colliding with his wings and fuselage, but he had his sights on one of the ugly bastards, and screwing up his eyes, he held the trigger down.

Green reefed his Hurricane around to try to get back over the airfield. He saw first one, and then a second, hangar collapse in a cloud of dust and debris. Before he had fully recovered from the shock of what he'd seen, a Stuka loomed up right in front of him, trying to get away. Green's whole body tightened in terror, but he clung to the stick and pressed the gun button, just holding it down as he tried not to lose the Stuka. He saw his bullets shatter the glass of the canopy, saw the glass turn red. And then he was past the Stuka, shooting overhead, and he started aiming straight at the next one.

Debsen skimmed over the perimeter fence and just kept flying flat out at the lowest possible altitude. He had to save his aircraft. That had been the last order. Get them airborne. Save them. Suddenly an unfamiliar fighter loomed up in front of him, flying straight at him but climbing hard. It had to be a Messerschmitt! Debsen tried desperately to fire his guns. The safety was still on! He flipped it off and fired more desperately still. Then the aircraft was gone, overhead, still climbing. Debsen saw the roundels on its wings and realised to his horror he had been firing at a Spitfire – probably from their own satellite airfield at Westhampnett. The first time he'd ever fired his guns at a real target it had been at one of their own kites!

Ginger didn't manage to get his undercarriage up before he was confronted with a Stuka. It seemed to cross his bows at a leisurely pace, and without thinking Ginger fired his guns at it. To his utter astonishment, the Stuka exploded right before his eyes. Ginger couldn't believe it. It had been there one minute, and now it was just a black smudge of smoke in the sky. Did I do that? he asked in amazement. Then it dawned on him that maybe it hadn't dropped its load yet. Maybe he'd hit the bomb. Whatever, it was gone, and Ginger was being knocked about by his own ack-ack and decided maybe he should try to get some altitude. For some reason the Hurricane seemed very slow to climb. Ginger began to worry that it was damaged in some way. It was flying very strangely, and making too much noise. Of course it was! He still had his wheels down! As he reached forward to pump them up, he realized the surviving Stukas and their escorts were already half-way to the channel. The only sensible thing to do was circle around and land.

When he looked down, however, he could hardly believe what he saw. Several buildings had collapsed, including two hangars. One Stuka and one Hurricane lay in smoking heaps on the grass airfield. Another wreck was burning just beyond the fence. Smoke and dust blew across the field in undulating billows. Sirens howled. Ambulances darted about, and people tried to rescue things from the shattered hangars and the damaged buildings. Ginger registered also that the field was pock-marked with craters and, for all he knew, unexploded bombs. Unable to land in this chaos, he started to circle the field uncertainly.

As the earth stopped its convulsive shudders and the sound of explosions faded, Bridges picked himself up off the floor and looked down over the balcony at the scene below. Plaster dust covered all of them to various degrees, and the markers on the table had been knocked over and shaken into meaningless heaps. One of the large lights had burst, shattering glass everywhere, and Corporal Winters was already applying first aid to a girl who had been badly cut in the hand. Although she was still wearing her steel helmet, so he couldn't see her face, Bridges thought it was ACW Hadley. Whoever it was, she hadn't let out so much as a shout when she'd been hit by the glass.

"Are there any other casualties down there, Winters?" Bridges called.

The WAAF Corporal glanced up at him, her face white with plaster dust, and shook her head. "No, sir."

Around her the other WAAF were crawling out from under the table, dusting off their knees and removing their steel helmets. As he watched, they started replacing the displaced markers, talking among themselves in low voices about where things had been and also pulling their headphones back on. Even Bridges, who had always expected they would do well under fire, was impressed. This wasn't just an absence of hysteria; it was professionalism of the highest order.

"Sir." His attention was drawn by ACW Roberts, on the balcony beside him. He had reassigned her as his clerk so she could keep the transcript of combat transmissions that Allars had asked for. She also manned the switchboard.

"Yes, Roberts?"

"The telephone lines to Uxbridge are out of order, sir."

"Right. See if you can reach Kenley or Middle Wallop and have them relay messages to and from Uxbridge."

"Yes, sir."

"Robinson," he addressed the Warrant Officer, "see if you can find out exactly what damage has been done so we can report it to Uxbridge as soon as possible."

"Yes, sir."

Bridges leaned over the gallery. "Winters?"

"Sir."

"Anything else coming in?"

"Ventor's down again, sir. We're blind unless they come in east or west of here and then turn."

"Understood." That explained how it had happened.

Behind him Robinson was reporting. "Two hangars collapsed in direct hits, sir, and the motor pool has been obliterated under the collapsed garage roof."

The sound of sirens wailed through the walls, and the deeper-throated hooting of the fire engines penetrated, too. The door was wrenched open, and a man in steel helmet and Flight Sergeant's stripes stuck his head in. "I need volunteers to come out and mark a runway for our aircraft to get down between the bomb-craters and the unexploded bombs!"

"Go on, any of you who want to go." Bridges released them all. If RDF and the lines to Uxbridge were down, there wasn't a lot they could do here.

Appleby and Ripley had helped start up the CO's aircraft and strapped him in, and then had run for the nearest slit trench. Other fitters and riggers jumped in more-or-less on top of them as they finished with their aircraft. None of them had their "panic bowlers" with them, and they simply crouched down with their arms over their heads when the detonations seemed too near. As the earth-jarring explosions stopped, they hesitantly raised themselves up and peered over the edge of the slit trench to see what had happened to their world.

"Bloody hell!"

Smoke and dust were blowing sideways across the field, and from near at hand a Stuka was standing on its nose and burning furiously. The pilot and gunner were clearly visible inside the cockpit, the pilot collapsed over the control panel and the gunner slumped to one side. It wasn't clear if they were already dead or merely unconscious, but the readiness of the English airmen to risk the fuel fire that engulfed them was limited

– particularly as they realised from shouts on their left that some of their own comrades had been caught inside one of the collapsed hangars.

"Christ help us! There are blokes in there!" a corporal exclaimed, and they scrambled out of the slit trench and started towards the hangar. A Hurricane had collapsed on the apron, with one undercarriage leg folded up and a wing broken off, apparently from the pressure waves of near-by explosions. The huge metal doors had also blown outwards, crushing a small lorry that had been parked in front. The roof of the hangar had collapsed inwards, shattering the two Hurricanes inside for their 100-hour checks. They lay on their bellies with their backs broken by the beams of the roof, one pointing its nose upwards and the other lying on its side like a dead beast.

The cries for help, however, were coming from the side of the hangar, behind the work-benches that had fallen over, spilling tools and spare parts all over the concrete floor. As they came nearer, it was clear that two airmen had taken refuge under the work tables. One of the beams, however, had smashed down so hard that the table had collapsed onto the man's leg, which had shattered.

Appleby set to work with the others to lift the beam up and pull the injured man free, but then Rowe came into the hangar and shouted that he needed volunteers to dig people out of a collapsed slit trench. Since Appleby was towards the back of the crowd helping with the beam, Ripley nodded at him to go. Appleby and two others reported to Rowe, and Rowe led them around the back of the Airmen's Mess.

The Mess had taken what appeared to be several direct hits. Between craters, the rubble, dirt and debris were thrown up into heaps. Bits and pieces of clothing, furniture, cutlery and masonry were scattered about as if a giant child had thrown them. Bizarrely, some things were whole while others were in pieces. A silver trophy recording someone's success at sports lay next to a toilet seat; a framed photograph had landed atop a heap of kitchenware. Water was gushing from a broken pipe and flooding the surrounding area. A lone shoe was bobbing on the water as it spread.

When they reached the slit trench, they found that it had collapsed in on itself. That wasn't supposed to happen, Appleby registered. Men with shovels were already at work, and the grey-clad legs of a WAAF were exposed – all twisted around unnaturally. There were no shovels left, so Appleby went to work with a metal bucket. The earth wasn't packed hard – just heavy with moisture, suffocating.

They dragged the first girl out, her hair trailing behind her, her face covered with dirt. Beneath it she was ghastly white and strangely peaceful. The next body was also a WAAF, a plump little thing, not particularly pretty, but Appleby remembered she'd worked in the kitchen and had a penetrating, high-pitched laugh that carried right out into the diningroom. Now silenced forever, he thought swallowing, as he helped straighten out her limbs and pull her skirt down decently. One of the others took off his tunic to lay it over her.

After that came almost a dozen airmen. Appleby knew them all. They worked as Assistant Cooks in the Airmen's Mess and served out the meals. They were ordinary blokes. Many of them came from the same kind of background he did – but without the benefit of mothers who'd made them go to school. Growing up in the slums of London, Liverpool or the mining towns of the North, they were stunted and all but illiterate. At mustering, they were given the lowest skilled trades: cooks, orderlies, waiters and batmen.

One of the last bodies they pulled out was Jones' batman. Appleby remembered him well because he, too, came from the East End. In fact, they had been quite chummy, since they both served Jones. Whipple had been all but blind and wore very thick specs, but he had been dead set on joining the RAF. Didn't want to die in the trenches, he'd said. Yet that was exactly what had happened, Appleby reflected, laying him out gently, and removing the shattered glasses that had cut his eyes dreadfully – hopefully after he was dead. He was the last.

Appleby straightened and looked at the long line of broken bodies, and then up at the sky. Although smoke was still billowing up from several fires that were burning around the airfield, beyond it was a pale blue. He vowed again that if he were going to die, it would be up there. He had to talk them into letting him transfer to the Flying Branch.

By the time the ops room staff returned, looking even dirtier than before, the extent of the damage done to the airfield was becoming clear. Although only three fighters had been shot down in action with the loss of just one pilot, 14 aircraft had been destroyed on the ground, mostly in or near the hangars in which they were being serviced. Not only were the main telephone lines cut, but a water main had ruptured, flooding cellars full of stores. This greatly hindered the work of the Royal Corps of Engineers sent to defuse the unexploded bombs and the postal exchange men come to mend the telephone lines. In addition to the two aircraft hangars, the motor garage had been flattened in the attack, and large parts of the Other Ranks' Mess, particularly Married Quarters, had been damaged. The Navy Army Air Force Institute NAAFI had been obliterated.

In the slit trench that had taken an almost direct hit and collapsed, there had been 33 casualties altogether, 17 dead. The dead and injured were predominantly from the staff of the Airmen's Mess, male and female, as well as four of the pilots' batmen.

Towards dusk, a lone Hurricane landed at Tangmere and went almost unnoticed in the lingering confusion. No ground crew signalled the Hurricane to a dispersal point, and no fitter mounted the wing to help the pilot unstrap and slide down. The tall, thin pilot stepped carefully out of his Hurricane and let himself to the ground decorously. Although his white overalls and white flying helmet should have attracted attention, the people wandering about the field were still in such a daze that no one seemed to take any notice.

The pilot took advantage of the situation and went himself to look into the hangars. The ground crews had formed a chain to pass boxes of spare parts and supplies out of the collapsed hangars into a tent. A little to one side, technical crews from the postal service worked up to their knees in mud to get the telephone lines repaired. A team of army sappers had cordoned off an unexploded bomb and were preparing to disarm it.

The pilot made his way to the sick bay, and nearly collided with a doctor coming out. The MO drew up to avoid the collision and glanced up to apologise, and then his eyes widened. "Air Vice Marshal Park?"

"Yes, how are things?"

"We just lost P/O Fiske, the American, I'm afraid. It's his Hurricane that is out there smouldering on the field."

"I'm sorry to hear that. No doubt the press will make much of it. I'll go in, if I may, and have a word with the injured."

Afterwards, Park made his way to the Station Commander's office. Here he was given a full account of the damage and the progress and prognosis for repair. The Station Commander pointed out that their one Spitfire squadron at Westhampnett was completely unscathed. Also, pilot — although not aircraft — losses had been minimal for 15 Stukas claimed, the carcasses of nine of which were littering the countryside, testimony to the legitimacy of the claims.

When Park had convinced himself that Tangmere did not yet need to be written off, he asked the Station Commander to summon the four Squadron Leaders and the controllers. Park asked for their accounts of what happened. Everyone had had a shock, but only S/L Jones really seemed shaken. In fact, Jones fulminated bitterly against the duty controller for not warning them in time, shocking Park both by the tone and the sentiment. With Ventnor RDF down, the Huns had come in through the blind spot in their RDF, Park reminded the squadron commander. "It was by no means your Controller's fault that you had no warning. You might just as well blame me." Jones fell silent, but a sour expression settled on his face, as if he did not believe Park.

To lighten things up, Park suggested they go to the Mess for a drink. Here he stayed only for one brandy, however, before excusing himself.

The others assumed he was heading back to Uxbridge, but instead he sought out Doug Allars. In Allars' office they discussed the situation for about half an hour more, then Park flew back to Uxbridge.

Several things were clear to Park. First, Tangmere was very close to being inoperable, and if it were hit again like this tomorrow or the next day, they would have to abandon it. Second, Tangmere was the only station whose operations room was in a bunker; if any other station were hit as Tangmere had been, it would be nothing short of a miracle if the unprotected, above-ground operations room survived. Third, if the control room of any station *were* put out of action, the station would have to close down – at least temporarily. If a sector airfield closed down, he could disperse the squadrons onto satellite fields, but it would be almost impossible to control them and so ensure interceptions. With the Ventor RDF station down, he was going to have a very hard time making interceptions anyway.

Almost as unsettling was the fact that the Germans had apparently learned that if they flew in low, they could sneak in under the RDF. Several of the raids today – like the one on Ventor and the one on Brize Norton – had been carried out by small numbers of low-flying aircraft. These had all gone in and out without being detected or intercepted, and the damage at both had been devastating. The technicians at Ventor were saying it would take at least a week to get it fully operational again, and at Brize Norton they had hit hangars containing fuelled-up aircraft. The resulting conflagration consumed 46 aircraft, fortunately mostly trainers. If the Germans changed their tactics completely and concentrated on this kind of low-level, surgical strike on vital targets, the entire RDF chain could be knocked out in a matter of days – and Fighter Command would not have a fighting chance.

Park knew that he had committed every squadron of 11 Group in the course of this afternoon's fight. That was calling things very close, even if Fighter Command still possessed considerable reserves in the other Groups and aircraft production exceeded losses. Furthermore, the pilot situation was becoming critical. But Park refused to admit that he could not win. He refused to consider the possibility that the Nazis with their brutality, bigotry and banditry might win. The consequences – if they did – were unthinkable.

Somehow, Fighter Command had to beat the Luftwaffe back, and the key to that was good Squadron Leaders. Young pilots were always prepared to give their very best, but if they were poorly led, then they were little more than calves led to the slaughter. That had been the key lesson of the last war. Of the four men he had just spoken to, he had confidence in three – but not in Jones.

From what he had seen and heard, No. 606 Squadron had no esprit de corps and no vitality. He had seen for himself that the little clique of old Auxiliary pilots kept to themselves, leaving the younger pilots wandering about confused and bewildered like fish out of water. On top of that, Allars reported that the only professional Sergeant Pilot, MacLeod, was a loner and an aggressive drinker. Clearly, Jones had failed to mould his squadron into a team, and equally failed to set his pilots a good example. His attacks on the Duty Controller had been unprofessional and misplaced.

Then again, Park had no grounds for replacing Jones. He was quite effective as a hunter – at least he claimed five destroyed and three probables. Whatever his deficiencies, he was also a known quantity. Park had no reserve of combat-experienced squadron leaders to draw on. So, while S/L Jones was not good, Park had no way of knowing who would be better. It was always dangerous to change horses in mid-stream. Reluctantly he admitted to himself that he would have to leave Jones where he was, but Park flew back to London with a bad feeling about No. 606 Squadron. He couldn't shake off the feeling that it was going to get ravaged – probably soon.

Chapter 22

**RAF Hawarden
17 August 1940**

Robin went to the bar to get them another drink, and as he waited, he turned back and watched Emily. With each weekend she spent here, she seemed to gain confidence and grow in sophistication. She was chatting to Kennel at the moment and she had him laughing. Robin wasn't surprised. She had a delightful sense of humour: dry, subtle and ironic. Furthermore, her classical education enabled her to find something to talk about with almost anyone.

She must also have spent a fortune on a new wardrobe, he reflected. The dress she was wearing was stunning. She wore high-heeled, cream-satin shoes with crossed straps, and silk stockings. The skirt was long enough to cover the scabs on her knees, but Robin knew about them. She'd told him of her "brief encounter with a Messerschmitt," which had "literally brought her to her knees."

He'd responded by telling her she ought to have been in the shelter, but part of him was pleased that she had stayed to watch. No, of course, she should have been in a shelter, he admonished himself angrily. He didn't want to think about her getting hurt. Portsmouth was a bloody dangerous place to be these days!

"Here you are, Sir." The bar-orderly pushed a sherry and a scotch towards him.

Robin reached Kennel at the same moment that a flushed and overexcited Corporal did. "Sorry to disturb you, sir. But the Observer Corps just called in a sighting – a lone Me109. They claim it flew over Shrewsbury."

"They've lost their marbles," Priestman declared, handing Emily her sherry. "No 109 is going to fly that far north – it would never get home again."

"Quite right, sir! It didn't! It landed!"

"You mean crashed."

"Well," the Corporal scratched his head uncomfortably, "they *said* landed, sir. They said it eased down gently into a near perfect three-point landing at a civil airfield at Leaton."

"Are we missing a Hurricane somewhere?" Kennel asked.

"No, sir! That was my first reaction, but the Observer Corps gentleman was very indignant. He gave me quite a rocket for implying that his boys couldn't tell the difference between a Hurricane and an Me109. He went on at some length about it being so low as it floated over his head that he could see the crosses and the aircraft identification letters – I've got them written down, sir. He said, too, there was a red horse emblem on it as well. Presumably a personal or squadron marking."

"Where did you say this stray 109 went down?" Priestman wanted to know, and something in his voice made both Emily and Kennel look over at him sharply.

"Just north of Shrewsbury, sir. There's an old civil airfield – just a flying club really, and not in use any more – near Leaton." The Corporal answered readily. "There's a tower of sorts, and the pilot may have thought he was at an operable airfield."

"What are you thinking of, Priestman?" Kennel asked warily, his eye on the younger officer.

"A perfect wheels-down landing, sir. The kite must still be serviceable – maybe just out of fuel. If it really *is* a 109—"

"Intelligence will take care of it. It's not our affair."

"You can't mean that, sir! I'd sell my soul for the chance to fly a 109. Let me go down and take a look at it."

"It's probably just a Hurricane or some other less familiar aircraft."

"With swastikas all over it?"

"Be reasonable, Robin. What on earth would a lone 109 be doing over the Welsh Marches? It can only be some kind of mistake."

"Maybe the German pilot's. Or maybe he wanted to surrender? Maybe he was wounded and confused, dazed, lost, disoriented. It doesn't matter. If a perfectly serviceable 109 has fallen into our hands, then the only sensible thing to do with it is to test it. Put it through its paces."

"That's not your job."

"Please, sir, let me take a look!"

Kennel shook his head in resignation rather than denial. "Off you go, then. Take the Maggie."

Priestman had no trouble finding the stray Messerschmitt. There were police cars blocking all the roads in, and crowds of curious locals held back by a police cordon. There was already an RAF Anson on the field beside the little German fighter. Robin flew happily over the police cordon and set the Maggie down. He turned the little trainer about and taxied back to the Anson, which had evidently brought the half-dozen officers who were inspecting the Messerschmitt. Brass, he thought, as he recognized Air Vice Marshal Sir Quintin Brand, AOC 10 Group. That might not be such a bad thing, he decided. Brand had been knighted for flying from England to Cape Town some twenty years ago. Probably not a stickler for caution.

Priestman climbed out of the Maggie and walked over to the cluster of RAF officers beside the Messerschmitt. He saluted smartly and addressed himself immediately to Air Vice Marshal Brand. "Heard there was a serviceable Messerschmitt here, sir. May I fly it?"

Brand laughed outright – although the other senior officers looked considerably less amused. Then he cocked his head and considered Robin more critically. "You used to fly at shows, didn't you? Priestly, was it?"

"Priestman, sir. Yes, I flew in shows before the war. Flew Hurricanes in France. Currently, I'm training Spitfire pilots up at Hawarden. May I take her up?" He nodded towards the Messerschmitt.

"A test pilot is being flown in," one of the other officers answered definitively. "And ground crews. We can't be sure this machine is fully serviceable. The pilot died in the ambulance, so we had no opportunity to ask him about what state it was in – or what he was doing here. There is a rack under it that may have been for a bomb but was more likely for an extra fuel tank. We suspect he was on a long-range reconnaissance mission and somehow got tangled in a fight – though we've no report of a fight with a lone Messerschmitt. Possibly one of his own long-range bombers – not expecting a friend so far from home – shot him up when he came too close. In any case, he had a bullet in his neck and another had grazed his head. He was also very low on fuel."

"That shouldn't be a problem, sir. We can siphon some green stuff off the Maggie. I made sure she was fully topped up and used hardly anything to get here."

"There is absolutely no rush to fly this machine, Flight Lieutenant," a staff officer countered annoyed.

"We're losing the light, sir." Priestman pointed out with a nod towards the west.

"So, we can fly it tomorrow or the next day or next week," the man told Robin off with more sharpness. "It isn't the first one that has—" A look from one of the other officers cut the speaker off.

Priestman ignored them all and focused on Brand. "The sooner I know what it's like, the sooner I can tell our fledgling pilots what it's like and how best to fly against it."

"In due time, Flight Lieutenant!" The man, a Wing Commander, had clearly had enough impertinence, and he glanced to Brand for support. Brand, however, only raised his eyebrows and looked at Priestman.

"We're losing three to four pilots a day, sir. And I'm responsible for training the replacements. If I can tell them the strengths and weaknesses of an Me109, they might live longer. Sir."

Brand laughed, cutting off the staff officer's angry retort with a gesture, he turned to Priestman, admonishing, "Be honest; all you *really* care about is getting your hands on the controls of that little invader."

"No, sir," Priestman insisted. "Of course I want to fly it, sir, but anything I can find out about it will be extremely useful for my trainees."

"Do you speak German?"

"No, sir," Priestman admitted, not following Brand's logic.

"Then how do you think you're going to read the controls and dials?"

"I believe you can help me with that, sir." Priestman answered with a glance at the staff officers around Brand. He was betting that the AOC had brought at least one German-speaking intelligence officer with him.

Brand laughed again and answered, "We can't afford to risk a pilot of your experience, Priestman. It's dangerous flying any unfamiliar aircraft – let alone one that we don't have the specs for and which has been damaged in combat." Brand pointed to bullet holes that cut up diagonally from the wing root across the side of the cockpit.

"I thought I got paid for taking risks, sir."

"Only necessary ones," Brand answered, but then he snorted, shook his head, and clapped Priestman on the shoulder. "Go on, climb in. I don't have the heart to stop you."

"Sir—" one of the others started to protest, but Brand waved him silent. "Enough. At his age, I was exactly the same. Besides, where would this country be now if our pilots weren't keen? See about getting petrol siphoned off as Flight Lieutenant Priestman suggested."

Robin wasted no time scrambling up the wing of the waiting Messerschmitt. He could not have explained the excitement of it. It was exciting to get into any new machine, but this wasn't just another aeroplane: it was the type of aircraft that had shot him down twice. He had fought against seemingly countless numbers of these beasts. He had seen them from every angle – left and right, above and below, head-on, tail-on and yet never this close and never tangibly.

The metal was warm from the evening sun, the camouflage scratched from countless boots. Less appetising: the headrest was soaked with blood. Robin hesitated a second, then eased himself into the cockpit. It was notably narrower than either the Spitfire or Hurricane. It smelled both familiar and strange. One of the staff officers was beside him, squatting on the wing and holding on to the frame of the canopy. "What do you want me to read?" he asked.

They started going through the dials one at a time. Much needed no translation, but Priestman was careful to note that the altimeter was in metres rather than feet and the speedometer in km/hour rather than mph.

Meanwhile another RAF plane landed. This brought a Flight Sergeant and ground crew. One of the latter opened the cowling, and a rigger started an inspection of the rest of the aircraft. Canisters of fuel, siphoned off from the Maggie, were brought over to the Messerschmitt. The staff officer went down to help decipher the various cryptic designations along the wing and fuselage to facilitate refuelling.

A Flight Sergeant scrambled onto the wing. "You understand, sir, we can't be sure we're getting the right mix of things. For all we know the Huns use different oil or fuel mixtures. If you waited a couple of days, we could track down that information down."

Priestman looked up at him wordlessly.

The Flight Sergeant sighed. "As you wish, sir." He jumped back down.

Brand replaced the Flight Sergeant on the wing. "The Flight is right, Priestman. You're taking completely unnecessary risks."

"Are you telling me that everything else seems to be all right, sir?"

Brand laughed, "You're hopeless, Priestman. I hope I don't live to regret this." He slipped back on to the ground, just as a Hurricane put down in the now crowded civil field.

While the Flight Sergeant took over again, Brand walked over to where the Hurricane had come to a halt. AVM Park, in his distinctive white overalls and white flying helmet, climbed out. Brand shook his hand and they stood together by the Hurricane.

The sun was low. Shadows stretched across the field, and the air was turning cold. The Messerschmitt gave a sharp bark. Smoke belched from the Messerschmitt engine, but then it went dead. They tried again. And again. And again. Just when it seemed they would not be able to get it started, it roared furiously into life – rather like a lion whose tail had been trodden on.

Priestman leaned out of the cockpit and shouted to the erks. They shouted back. The engine settled down to a low growl. The Anson took off again, leaving only the Maggie and the Hurricane sharing the field with the Messerschmitt.

As they watched, Park remarked to Brand, "Isn't this the pilot who shot down a Heinkel in my Group just a couple weeks ago? I was told he was flying a Spitfire from Training Command down to the Supermarine works for a refit when a raid came in."

"That will be him. He also shot down a Dornier while on night readiness, but he's not a test pilot."

"I have the feeling I've heard his name from somewhere else. I wish could place it."

"He flew in air shows with our aerobatics team before the war."

"Maybe that was it..." Yet Park felt sure he'd heard something negative about this pilot. He asked Brand, "Where did you tell him to land?"

"I haven't told him anything yet, but I think it best for him to take it back to Hawarden. He'll have landing flares there, and we'll have better service and security until it can be flown over to the Royal Aircraft Establishment."

Park nodded and Brand crossed the distance to the Messerschmitt, which was now dancing about as the rudder, elevators and flaps were tested with the engine still idling. An erk had draped himself across the tail to keep it from lifting.

Brand climbed up the Messerschmitt wing again and ordered Robin to fly the Messerschmitt to Hawarden, adding "Fight checks only. Nothing silly. You're not competing in air shows now. This country can't afford to lose experienced Flight Lieutenants, so be damned sure you get it and yourself there and down in one piece."

"Yes, sir."

A fitter took Brand's place on the wing and closed the canopy. Robin noted that it was quite awkward as it opened to the right onto the wing, rather than sliding back along the fuselage. As a result, it couldn't be left open during take-off or landing as he liked.

At last the Messerschmitt was in motion. It danced about clumsily on the rough surface. Fortunately, while the erks had been working on the engine, some of the policemen had been preparing a kind of runway, removing rocks and filling in potholes. Tall poles with fluttering ribbons now marked a straight path into the wind. The Messerschmitt lumbered to the start of this improvised runway. Robin turned the alien aircraft into the wind and reved up the engine. Then he eased up on the brakes.

The Messerschmitt started to roll forward slowly. It started to bounce, hop, jump and leap across the field. The tail came up. Only after he was airborne did Robin realize he didn't know how to raise the undercarriage. It took several seconds of frantic looking over the instrument panel until he found something that looked promising. He lifted the flap and found two buttons. He chose the one labelled *Flug* on the assumption that meant "flight." He was rewarded with the sound of hydraulics. and the undercarriage clunked into position shortly afterwards. At last, he could concentrate on actually flying the beast.

He banked around to the north. With darkness descending rapidly, he didn't have a lot of time to play with. He took it up as high as he could and flew it through the most common maneuvers used in combat. Just as

Brand had ordered, he engaged in no showy aerobatics, flying just turns, climbs, dives, rolls and spins.

By the time he landed it was almost completely dark and the narrow undercarriage made the landing dangerous. As he bounced in, the fighter tipped dangerously and for a second he was sure it was going to put a wing in and cartwheel. He instinctively threw his weight in the opposite direction, and the second wheel came back onto the ground; accident avoided. He was relieved to come to a halt and happy to switch off the engine. Sweat was pouring down the side of his face.

No sooner did he come to a halt, however, than he was surrounded — the trainees, flying and ground staff, Kennel, Brand and Park closed around the fighter. The latter had evidently flown over directly, while he carried out the test manoeuvres. Emily hung at the back of the crowd looking a little forlorn and unsure of herself. Or had she just been worrying about him? He tossed her a smile as he pushed himself up out of the cockpit and jumped down from the wing.

"Well?" Brand asked pointedly.

"I can't give you an honest answer in present company, sir." Priestman replied.

Brand considered this answer, and then took Priestman's elbow and led him away into the darkness, away from the Messerschimtt and the exuberant crowd of trainees, and away from Emily. Park and Kennel followed them. The four officers walked behind the hangar. It was cool and damp and pitch dark.

"All right. Now." Brand ordered.

"It scares the hell out of me."

"What?"

"It's a bitch on the ground. You have to keep the canopy closed for take-off and landing, and I don't see how they open it fast in an emergency – although they do. It also has bars in all the wrong places, blocking your vision, making you vulnerable to attack. The throttle works backwards: you pull it *back* to open up. The damned thing can't be trimmed to fly straight and level – or this one couldn't. It required constant right rudder. Turning it at any significant speed requires considerable strength. The ailerons seem practically to freeze! After flying Spitfires, it was like having a bad-tempered donkey rather than a thoroughbred in my hands. It does dive nicely, I admit, but essentially, it's a machine designed for one manoeuvre only – the high-speed bounce from above. It's not a dogfighter, and landing it is a bitch. In a nutshell, I'd rather fly a Hurricane any day – much less a Spitfire."

"I'm not following you, Priestman. If you prefer our fighters and have found so many faults with the Messerschmitt, surely you must feel better about flying against them?"

"No, sir. Given all these faults with the kite, *their pilots* must be a hell of a lot better than that lot over there." With a jerk of his head, Priestman indicated his trainees on the far side of the hangar, who could clearly be heard laughing and chattering excitedly.

Park considered that a moment. "I take your point. Then again, *they're* losing their experienced pilots, too. Not just the killed and wounded, remember. Now that the bulk of the fighting has shifted over England, even if their pilots bail out, they become POWs. Ours get back into a new Hurricane within hours. One of these days, they are going to run out of experienced pilots – and start sending in lads like yours."

"If we last that long."

Park nodded thoughtfully, and then remarked simply and emphatically, "We bloody well have to!"

For a moment they all just stood there thinking about it, and then Kennel addressed himself to the two Air Vice Marshals. "You must both be very hungry. May I suggest you fortify yourselves with food and drink at our humble little Mess before you head back to your heavy responsibilities?"

"Thank you; that would be very welcome," Park agreed, and Brand added, "Excellent. That will give my staff time to send a car for me."

Together the four officers rejoined the crowd, and then the three senior officers led the way back to the Officers' Mess.

Robin hung back and slipped his arm around Emily. The gesture warmed her. As he guided her back to the Mess, his attention focused on the questions being flung at him from the trainees, his kept his arm possessively about her waist. It compensated Emily for feeling abandoned and forgotten two hours ago.

The three senior officers sat together at a little table. Brand was smoking a cigar. Kennel and Park had pipes. They had brandies as well, although Park was careful not to drink too much as he still had to fly back to London.

"Not one raid all day, although the weather was no worse than on other days when they've come over. I wish I could convince myself that *they* needed a rest – and not that they were just gathering their forces for the next wave of attacks."

"A bit of both, no doubt," Brand agreed. "Some of the German airmen we've captured seemed genuinely astonished that we still had squadrons in the West Country. I think Jerry underestimates our reserves."

"The problem is, we can't deploy them all where we need them,"

Park pointed out. "The control system can't handle more squadrons in 11 Group."

Brand nodded, and they fell silent. Park's eyes were on the pilots clustered around the bar. Priestman was the centre of attention, of course. "Tell me about F/Lt Priestman," Park requested of Kennel. He had remembered what he'd heard about him, and his instincts had been right; it wasn't good. He didn't know what to think of the young officer as a result.

Kennel felt no such ambiguity. "Priestman is one of the finest young officers I've met in a long time. I've put him in for the DFC." The two AVMs gazed at Kennel, evidently astonished. It was not normal to put a pilot from Training Command in for a DFC. "He's got 6 recognised kills," Kennel defended himself. "He's training pilots during the day, is on readiness every third night for 10 Group, and is the only one of my instructors with a night kill. Then on his only day off, he nipped down to Southampton in a bum Spitfire and bagged another Jerry. The trainees idolize him, and the ground crews eat out of his hand."

"The ground crews?" Park asked, surprised. "Why's that?"

"He has a wonderful way of making them feel appreciated and respected – and he gives them joy rides in the Maggie!"

Park looked decidedly more favourably on the young officer after hearing this and turned his attention back to the pilots crowded around the bar. He recognized the distinctive accent of a New Zealander and realized it came from a large man who stood like a bear with his arm over Priestman's shoulder. Around them the others were doubled up with laughter, while the girl with Priestman giggled behind her hand, as if she were a bit shocked but nevertheless enjoying herself very much.

"You know he has a bad blot on his record?" Park remarked.

Kennel frowned. "I saw his confidential report, but it wasn't very explicit. Something about misuse of His Majesty's Aircraft resulting in loss. Frankly, I know more than one damned fine officer who might have *that* in his record."

Park nodded, "True, but what Priestman did was dare an officer of the Imperial Japanese Navy to do what he did in his Vildebeeste. He then proceeded to fly a series of risky aerobatic manoeuvres at low altitude over running seas. In his attempt to imitate, the Japanese pilot crashed, killing himself and destroying the aircraft."

There was a moment of silence while the other two senior officers absorbed this information. Then Kennel said, "Right. Not exactly King's Regulations, but it proves he's a damn fine pilot."

"Hmm." Park answered ambiguously before asking, "Is he a good instructor?"

Kennel looked embarrassed. "No, not really. Flying comes so naturally to him that he just can't explain it to anyone else. And he's quick to let them know that he thinks they're pretty hopeless. The other day he told his flight that Jerry would eat them for breakfast the minute they went on ops."

"Well, that's good for morale," Brand observed dryly, and the three senior officers laughed.

Park got to his feet and went to the bar. Coming up behind Murray, he asked, "Is that another Kiwi I hear?"

Murray spun around, totally flabbergasted. "Sir? You're a New Zealander?"

The others were sputtering, "Kiwi? What's a Kiwi?"

"Some kind of stupid bird from Down Under, I think."

"Ugly little runt, as I remember."

"A bird that *can't* fly."

"Well, now you have met *two* that can," Park countered, his hand on Murray's shoulder. Turning to Murray again, he asked, "How are you getting on?"

"Food's bad. Beer's terrible. Weather's bloody awful. But the Spitfire's absolutely wizard, sir!"

"Except for the fact that it has a retractable undercarriage," Priestman noted dryly, causing the trainees to burst into a new round of whooping laughs.

"Yes, bloody nuisance that undercarriage, sir," Murray agreed soberly. "Couldn't they build the thing with a sensible fixed base?" he suggested.

Park smiled faintly. "I don't think we have time for major design changes at the moment. Now, I'm afraid I must be on my way, but maybe I'll see one or the other of you in 11 Group one of these days." He shook hands with each of the young pilots, one after another.

"I'm raring to go, sir," Murray assured him, "but the skipper here," he nodded to Priestman, "seems to think I still have a few things to learn."

"All I ask is that you land on the wheels rather than the belly."

Park laughed with them and then looked at each of them in the eye again. "Best of luck to all of you."

As he started for the door, Kennel caught up with him, and Park remarked as they left the Mess together, "Keep their spirits up, George. We need them like this." Another volley of laughter followed them out into the night, as if to underline what he meant.

Crépon, France

Christian's French girlfriend wasn't at all what Ernst had expected. And then again she was. On the one hand she wasn't the kind of stunning film-star beauty that he had anticipated: her hair was a non-descript brown and her eyes a pale grey. But on the other hand, every gesture she made and every movement of her lithe, supple body was not only elegant and sophisticated but, well, exquisitely *French*.

Ernst watched her in awe as she uncrossed her silk-clad legs and slid down from the high stool behind the counter. She was dressed very primly in a fitted but not tight dark skirt that came well below the knee, and a long-sleeved, high-necked blouse with a lace collar. Yet her nails were bright red and her lips not only red but moist. Furthermore, her eyebrows were perfect, curving lines and her lashes longer and thicker than those of any girl Ernst had ever seen in real life before.

She smiled at Christian languidly and called him "*Monsieur le Baron.*" Although they spoke French and Ernst couldn't understand what they were saying, from the way she tossed her head and looked at Christian through half-closed eyes, Ernst sensed that she was both inviting and mocking. She clearly had Christian eating out of her hand, and not the other way around. It was amazing, Ernst thought as he watched them together.

He'd seen the way the *Helferinnen* gazed after Christian with adoration or tried to attract his attention with tartness. No matter what they did, Christian was indifferently polite to them. Even to Klaudia. At first Ernst had been furious with Christian for asking her to his table. He thought it was very unsporting of Christian to seduce the girl he was in love with before his eyes. As the evening wore on, however, Ernst had recovered from his embarrassment and resentment enough to realise Christian had done it for him. That, however, had only embarrassed him more. Apparently the whole *Staffel* knew how he felt about Klaudia. Ernst sighed. It was hard to have secrets from the men you lived, flew, fought, and drank with.

Christian hadn't been able to keep Gabrielle a secret, either – despite it being against regulations. But ever since Hartmann became acting CO, Christian was not even pretending to keep her a secret. Still, Ernst knew he was privileged to be allowed to *meet* her. Up to now, the only other man in the *Gruppe* who had actually seen the mysterious woman in Christian's life was Dieter. Since Dieter had been tasked to fly something over to the *Jagdfliegerführer* at Deauville this afternoon, Christian asked Ernst if he wanted to come along. Ernst had not waited to be asked twice.

"If I showed up alone, Gabrielle would be suspicious and give me the cold shoulder," Christian explained.

Ernst found that hard to believe, but she certainly asked after Dieter and she kept her eye on Ernst, too – as if she were not sure whether she could trust him or not. Her colleague was downright hostile to Ernst, turning her back on him and disappearing behind the curtain at the back of the shop in an indignant huff. Gabrielle had smiled after her, and with a little shrug and gesture indicated to Ernst that her friend was "crazy" – but there was nothing she could do about it.

To avoid just staring at Christian and Gabrielle while they flirted with each other, Ernst started looking at the things in the shop. It was a typical little French luxury shop, full of the kind of things you couldn't buy in the Reich. Ernst had been in a lot of them by now, but he still found himself attracted by all the pretty, useless things they sold. It was precisely because everything they had was so frivolous and unnecessary that he liked them. At home everything was – well – practical.

The prices were quite fancy too, Ernst noted, but without particular indignation. There was nothing here that he could send home to anyone he knew. His mother would be outraged by such "flighty" things, and his sisters wouldn't know what to do with them. He sighed as his eyes caressed the silk scarves neatly laid out in squares, over-lapping so just a couple inches of the leading edge of each was visible. So many bright colours and different patterns: blue fleur-de-lis on white, or golden anchors on blue, silver gryphons on red, even brown horses on green.

Klaudia had said last night that she loved horses. She'd had a pony of her own when she was little, but her father had taken it away from her as punishment for some childish misdemeanour. Christian had said he knew a place where they could rent horses, but Klaudia had at once declined, saying she couldn't really ride. She said she loved horses, though....

Suddenly Ernst was certain she would love this scarf. It was a rich, shiny green and it had what looked like lots of horses in different poses on it. Of course, he couldn't see very much of it, because it was folded up and covered by the other scarves in the row. Ernst looked over at Gabrielle, but she was chattering away with Christian, waving the smoking cigarette he had given her in expressive, Gallic gestures.

Ernst redirected his attention to the scarves, trying to read the price. Were they all 180 F? His mother would have a fit if she learned he'd spent that kind of money on a silly scarf! But what was his money for? He was getting fed more than well enough, as his ungainly figure testified. His bed was free. He'd bought new uniforms and boots just before coming out to France. True, his Mess bills were not exactly modest, but it wasn't as if he couldn't *afford* the scarf. Besides, what was the value of a gift that was cheap? This scarf was so pretty it was *obviously* expensive.

Gabrielle called something over to him, and guiltily Ernst stepped backwards, clasping his hands behind his back.

"She just asked if you wanted to look at something from the counter," Christian explained.

"Well, yes, but there's no rush, really. I mean..."

Christian and Gabrielle sauntered over. "Which scarf did you want to see, Ernst?"

Ernst explained and Christian translated. Gabrielle pinched it by one corner and deftly opened it before him with a single, elegant flick of her wrist. It was exactly what Ernst wanted. A mare lovingly nuzzled her bright-eyed foal in the centre and various other horses frolicked around the edge. He purchased it at once and asked for it to be gift-wrapped. Gabrielle did this, with obviously flirtatious remarks to Christian in French that had him laughing. Ernst supposed they were laughing at his expense, but he didn't care. Holding his treasure proudly but carefully (as if it could break), he went back out to the open staff car to await Christian. They had to be back at the base in another hour, and there was no point in inhibiting Christian any longer.

But no sooner had Ernst settled down to wait for Christian, then he started thinking about how to deliver his present to Klaudia. He couldn't just stroll up to her in the CC and hand it to her. Everyone would see – and if she turned it down, everyone would laugh. If she didn't want his attentions, she would certainly turn it down. And, of course, she didn't want his attentions. Ernst knew he wasn't good enough for her. Never. He was just a plumber's son, and a fat one at that. A pretty, aristocratic girl like Klaudia didn't want him courting her!

He stared at the package in his hands with the pretty wrapping paper and a bright ribbon around the beautiful scarf, and he felt rising despair. He so wanted to give it to Klaudia. To see her delight when she discovered the mare and foal – but he couldn't. He couldn't possibly give it to her in any public place without risking the rebuff he deserved, and if he tried to give it to her in secret – No, it was impossible. Suddenly the scarf seemed to weigh a ton as he held it in his lap.

They were already turning into the base, past the saluting sentry, when Ernst finally found the courage to ask. "Christian? Would you give this scarf to *Fräulein* von Richthofen?"

"Why should I?" Christian asked back, adding firmly, "Give it to her yourself."

"But she doesn't want me courting her, Christian," Ernst explained miserably.

"*I* certainly don't want to court her!" Christian countered.

"I know, but you could say it was from someone else, from a friend, an admirer?"

Christian turned into the motor pool, stopped the car, switched off the engine and pulled on the hand brake. Then he turned in the seat and looked straight at Ernst. "She's not stupid, Ernst. She'd know exactly who it was from – and she'd think less of you for being too cowardly to give it to her yourself." This said, Christian flung open the door and climbed out of the staff car.

Ernst followed him towards the Mess, trying to find some argument that would bring him around. He found none. As they started up the steps, Ernst caught Christian's arm. Christian turned back expectantly.

"Please." Ernst looked up at him, begging him silently with his eyes. Christian frowned. "No!" He turned his back on Ernst definitively, and bounded up the steps to disappear into the Mess. He left Ernst standing in the dark with his precious – useless – gift.

Chapter 23

RAF Tangmere
18 August 1940

The morning was hazy and, after the quiet day before, Ginger almost let himself hope that they would have another day of rest. The sun burned down hotly by mid-day, when the first rumours spilled out of the Operations Room to the wooden squadron dispersal.

There was a massive raid building up over Calais. Bigger than anything the WAAFs in the control room had ever seen before. ("Woody" Ringwood had started dating ACW Hadley and so got "inside" information.)

"Just exactly what does that mean, old boy?" Jones asked irritably, shaking a crease out of his newspaper.

"200+ is the official designation, but apparently above a certain size they can't estimate any more. Liz tells me that this raid topped 200+ almost ten minutes ago and is still building."

"Well, I wouldn't believe a thing those girls tell you," Tommy grumbled; "letting girls onto RDF sets is as silly as letting them fly."

But Flight Lieutenant Hayworth wanted to know, "How many aircraft does the Luftwaffe have?"

"4,000 – I think," Debsen put in, trying to sound knowledgeable.

"Where did you hear *that*?" Jones demanded, scowling. "And when? Six months ago? I mean, really, old boy, we *have* shot down one or two of their crates, you know."

"Well, presumably they get replacements just like we do, don't they?" Hayworth pointed out.

The next rumour suggested the raid was moving towards London.

"Well, that should shake the Government up a bit," Jones observed, apparently satisfied; "maybe even give that madman Churchill something to think about."

But Ginger felt his stomach turn over. He'd only been to London once in his life, but it was so crowded. And all those houses right next to each other were crammed full of people. If the Luftwaffe hit London, there would be thousands and thousands of people killed – almost all of them civilians, including women and children.

"Kenley and Biggin Hill!" Ringwood shouted out to the dispersal hut, apparently after talking to the Ops room. That got more of a reaction. The pilots who had been dozing – or pretending to – sat up.

The act of sitting up made MacLeod's head hurt, and he scowled as he squinted up at Ringwood. There'd been a terrible scene last night. After all the fuss Lettice had made about being ruined and wanting to kill herself, she'd accepted an invitation to a dance in the Officer's Mess. MacLeod had confronted her as she started up the steps, and he couldn't remember exactly what he'd said, but it hadn't been nice. The next thing he knew, Debsen and Thompson were throwing fists at him, so he'd defended himself.

Rather well, too, he thought smugly, eyes closed. But, of course, Jones interceded and put MacLeod under arrest for the next three days – except for readiness and flying. Fortunately, he'd had a couple bottles of gin hidden away and had finished off the better part of both of them.

"Stand-by!" The shout from the dispersal reached them before the klaxon went off.

MacLeod somehow got his feet under him and managed a lame trot to his waiting Hurricane. He clambered up the scratched wing to drop heavily into the cockpit. With considerable effort, he directed his attention to the pre-flight check. Other machines were coughing into life.

An unfamiliar fitter helped Ginger into his Hurricane. The new fitter seemed almost as nervous as Ginger felt. He didn't have that same reassuring smile and calming manner that Sanders had had. Ginger supposed it wasn't fair to the earnest young man helping him with his straps, but he just didn't feel as safe without Sanders looking after his kite. He plugged in his R/T and heard: "Cotton Ball Leader, scramble. Steer 070. Angels 18."

It was odd to be flying northeast rather than west or south. Indeed, it felt *wrong* to Ginger. It meant they were no longer meeting the enemy at the border but fighting him inland – just short of London. Ginger felt even worse when he realised that the smoke rising up ahead of him was from RAF Kenley. It reminded him of what had happened to Tangmere two days ago. They were clearly going for the airfields, and there were hundreds of aircraft all over the sky. Ginger grabbed his paper bag and was sick into it. It didn't seem to help this time. He still felt sick.

"Cottonball Squadron, sections line astern! Line astern, go!" Jones ordered crisply, and Ginger dutifully took up his arse-end Charlie position. Today, for some reason, he was in Ft/Lt Hayworth's section. As he switched the guns to "fire," his stomach heaved again and he tasted vomit in his mouth. It was all he could do not to be sick again – in his mask. The effort not to was making him sweat hard. The sun was boiling and blinding.

"Look out! Break right! Break!"

They came straight out of the sun. He really couldn't see them at all. It was more as if the sun had blinked, and then the chatter of guns and tracer surrounded him. The Hurricane trembled and bucked as cannon shells riddled it.

Ginger grabbed the stick and flung the little plane into a left turn. He greyed out, and in that second it was almost as if he had died. Then his vision cleared, and he saw a Hurricane diving across his bows, flames pouring back from the engine. Ginger recognised the 606 "XT" squadron letters and "P." That was Hayworth. He'd better get out fast! But the Flight Lieutenant wasn't even trying. The canopy was shut, and he was making no effort to open it.

Ginger, searching the sky around him for the enemy, nevertheless tried to reach Hayworth on the R/T. "Cottonball Yellow One! Flight Lieutenant Hayworth! Sir! You're on fire! Get out!" Ginger swung onto a course beside the apparently injured Flight Lieutenant. Flying close beside him, Ginger could see that Hayworth was slumped against the side of the cockpit. Just when Ginger decided he must be dead already, he moved. Ginger distinctly saw him shift his position, saw him reach up one arm, and then saw it slump back down again – apparently too weak to struggle. The flames were licking around him.

"Hayworth!" Ginger called one last time – and the next instant he felt his own Hurricane shudder. He'd been bounced yet again! Oh, God, was he never going to learn? Why did God let this happen again and again? Why show him his incompetence, and then save him so he had to go through it all over again?

Not that he thought of just giving up. Not for an instant. They would have to kill him, because he wasn't going to stop trying to stop them until they *did* kill him. Already he was turning, the blood draining from his brain as he prayed incoherently and wondered at the same time: where did all the Messerschmitts come from? Why were there always so many more of them than there were Hurricanes?

It was hopeless. They were never going to stop the Luftwaffe. They were too few and the Luftwaffe too many. The RAF just *couldn't* stop all these planes! They could die trying, like Hayworth just had, but they couldn't *stop* the Luftwaffe. The Luftwaffe was too powerful. And the Nazis didn't give a damn about losses. They didn't care what it cost. They would just keep sending in more and more and more planes until the RAF was completely wiped out. Ginger gripped his teeth together and kept turning. He feared it wouldn't do any good, but what else could he do?

MacLeod evaded the first bounce by half rolling and diving, but the next thing he knew there were bombs falling around him. He glanced up and his heart stopped as he realised that there were German bombers *above* him! Not more than 1000 feet above him – and they had their bomb-bays open! He looked straight up into a rain of high explosives, and there was absolutely no way to take evasive action. He watched in stunned helplessness as one bomb tumbled down right towards him. He knew it was going to hit him just a split second before it smashed right through the fragile frame of the Hurricane wing and continued on its way to do more damage. But MacLeod had no chance to think about that. His right wing was gone and the Hurricane, usually so docile and co-operative, was tumbling out of the sky.

MacLeod didn't waste time trying to regain control of his aircraft. He had only one thought, and that was getting out. This was easier said than done under the circumstances. He was being hurled about inside the cockpit. He couldn't seem to get hold of the canopy release. He was seized with sheer, blinding panic, and then abruptly the canopy was open and he was flung out of the machine. He tumbled wildly, still disoriented, and it took seconds before he managed to find the ripcord. With a horrible yank and a wrenching pain to his groin, his fall was halted. The parachute opened majestically over his head, but MacLeod was doubled up, cursing inarticulately as he tried to ease the pain in his groin with his hands. The fucking parachute had probably just unmanned him, he thought in his agony.

Gradually the pain receded to a burning ache, and MacLeod became aware that he was caught by a brisk wind and was being blown sideways as he descended towards the earth. What was worse: he was fast descending towards a town. Being on the outskirts of London, the houses were close together, row after row with narrow back gardens all separated by walls. No place for a cushy landing! There was a railway line too. Bloody hell! He was going to crash right into the footbridge! He tried jerking the strings of his parachute to spill air and guide his descent, but only succeeded in making himself fall faster. He hit the ground and rolled as they'd been taught, but the roll or the drag of the parachute brought him up hard against something very solid and he staggered, fell down and blacked out.

He came to where he'd fallen, but now he was surrounded by people. They were all bending over him – not in sympathy but rather holding a shotgun in his face. "Hands up!" a gruff voice shouted.

"Fuck off!" MacLeod shot back, trying to get to his feet. This was truly the last straw, he thought. He'd very nearly killed himself defending these buggers and they greeted him with a shotgun!

The men crowding around him shoved him back to the ground, while from the back of the crowd helpful advice was shouted: "Knock him out!" "Tie him up!" "Kill the bastard, Babson!"

Story of my life, MacLeod thought: I survive the whole Jerry air force and get shot by a bunch of Sassenachs!

The squadron straggled back to Tangmere individually. Debsen was back first, of course; he'd had some engine trouble and had missed the whole show. Then Ringwood put down, followed by "Tommy" Thompson and Williams. Ginger limped in next, his engine spraying glycol and overheating, but he got the Hurri down safely. Dunsire came in with his tail shot up and Green had to crash-land just short of the airfield, but he walked away from the wreck. MacLeod called in from a pub, and the hospital at Croydon reported that they had Flying Officer Parker. He had been shot in the knee, thigh and hip and would be in hospital for "some time."

Appleby and Ripley stood before the remaining hangar and scanned the sky. Appleby raised a hand to shield his eyes from the bright sun. There wasn't an aircraft in sight. Ripley checked the time: only about 15 minutes of fuel left. Appleby had a horrible feeling. What if the canopy he'd installed had jammed? Jones had used the aircraft at least a dozen times since the repairs, but he'd never had to get out in a hurry. Appleby had noticed it still seemed to catch on opening. He'd filed it a couple of times, and yet....

Ginger reported how Hayworth had been killed before his eyes, and by late afternoon the wreck of his plane had been found and his identity bracelet removed from the charred lump in the cockpit. Pilot Officer Whittington was found next. He managed to crash-land his Hurricane in a field, but broke his neck doing so; he died on the way to hospital. There was no news from Jones, however, and no one could remember seeing what had happened to him. In the absence of a Squadron Leader and with one Flight Lieutenant dead – not to mention the complete loss of four aircraft and three further kites unserviceable – the squadron was stood down.

Allars watched the sun go down from the adjutant's office with phantom pains throbbing through his missing leg. He was numbed and horrified by his own sense of detachment. It seemed increasingly certain that the squadron had lost three pilots killed and one seriously injured – and was virtually leaderless – but all he felt was a weary sense of déja vu. Just like the last time around, his brain seemed to say. And like then, the best way to deal with it was not to let it get to you. Pilots come and pilots go. How did the Yeats poem go?

I balanced all, brought all to mind, the years to come seemed waste of breath, a waste of breath the years behind, in balance with this life – this death.

Allars sighed, and gripping his pipe between his teeth, searched his pockets for matches. Mickey sprang to his feet to offer him a light. Mickey was looking shaken by today's carnage. He wasn't a pilot, but he was very devoted to his squadron.

"Any news of Jones yet?" Allars asked.

Mickey shook his head, adding: "But you never know. In the last war, I heard one of the lads disappeared without a trace and everyone wrote him off. Then the next day he called in bright and cheery from some French brothel, where he'd spent a very jolly night indeed."

Allars smiled wanly. He'd heard that story, too. It was told a lot – and he supposed it might be true. Then again, it might not. It was the kind of story fighter pilots liked to imagine....

"Rowe just reported that he'll have all three damaged Hurricanes repaired by morning, and two replacement aircraft are already on their way."

Allars nodded. Rowe was nothing if not efficient – you had to give him that – but he drove the ground crews hard. Sometimes, Allars thought, too hard. That fitter with the broken back was a first-rate tradesman, and first-rate tradesmen don't make stupid missteps unless they're under too much pressure for too long. There could easily be other accidents, if he kept them at it like this. At some point, bad as the situation was, it would make more sense to have the squadron go on readiness with less than 12 aircraft.

The phone rang behind him. The WAAF clerk answered, "606 Squadron." The WAAF sprang to her feet. "Yes, sir! He's just here, sir. One moment, sir!" She covered the speaker and "whispered" in a loud voice to Allars, "Squadron Leader Allars, sir. It's Air Vice Marshal Park, sir! He wants to speak with you, sir!"

Allars stamped over to the phone and took it. "Allars here."

"Park. I've just had word that Squadron Leader Jones has been found dead. Apparently, his parachute failed – or was shot up. In any case, it didn't open." There was a pause.

Allars felt compelled to say dutifully, "I'm very sorry to hear that, sir." Was he? Not at all. He'd long thought Jones wasn't up to the mark.

"Doug, I'd like an honest answer from you."

"Of course, Keith," Allars answered, although he was alerted by the use of his first name that this was a special request.

"Wait until you hear the question, Doug."

"All right."

"First, is your remaining Flight Lieutenant up to the task of serving as acting squadron leader over an extended period? I mean until this show is over."

Allars didn't even have to think about that one. "Under no circumstances. If anyone had asked *me*, I wouldn't have made him a flight commander. He's an irresponsible, self-satisfied whelp, who thinks that just because his father inherited a coal fortune the whole world ought to dance to his tune. I'm not saying he can't fly, but he certainly can't lead – if you want my honest opinion, Keith."

"I asked for it. All right, then, is the rest of the squadron a write-off or not?"

Allars hadn't been prepared for that. "There are still fifteen other pilots, Keith, and as I said, Tommy can fly well enough. Also, I've been told we'll be back up to twelve aircraft by tomorrow."

"That's not what I asked, Doug. The question is: should I pull 606 out of the front line?"

"Pull them out?" The temptation was strong, but Allars also felt it was a disgrace. In the last war no squadrons had been rotated out to safety. He found himself saying, "Other squadrons have been in it longer. I think we can cope."

That did not sound terribly reassuring to Park. He didn't need squadrons that could 'cope;' he needed squadrons that could maul the Luftwaffe badly enough to stop it from coming back. Yet his options were limited. Taking a deep breath, he tried to explain. "The problem is this, Doug, almost every squadron we've rotated in from the north has been slaughtered within two to three days of arrival in 11 Group – often with hardly anything to show for it. The squadrons that have been here longer have much higher kill-to-loss ratios and have consistently lost fewer pilots. If I pull 606 out, the chances are that the replacement squadron will get badly mauled – maybe lose six or seven pilots – before the week is out. *Now* tell me if you think 606 needs to be pulled or not."

"In that case, definitely not. Most of the pilots are sound, one or two have leadership potential, if they survive long enough. Several are good hunters."

"You think a new CO could turn them around?" Park asked explicitly.

"The right CO could."

"I hope you're right, Doug."

"So, do I, Keith – if not, I'm going to have several young men's lives on my conscience, aren't I?"

"If you haven't already, Doug, you're a lucky man."

Not until that moment did Allars realise just how much Park's responsibility weighed on him. Suddenly, he wished he could take back his remark – wished he could say something to comfort his friend. But the moment was past. Park had already thanked him and hung up.

Allars stood for a moment listening to the dialing tone, and then hung up.

Mickey and the WAAF clerk were both staring at him expectantly. Mickey finally asked, "Is he going to throw us out of 11 Group?"

"No, not yet. I think he's going to try to find us a new CO – God knows where."

"Well, he could send us one of the experienced Polish officers..." It worked. Allars laughed, and together he and Mickey went over to the Mess to break the news about Jones.

JG 23

The sun sank below the horizon just as they made the French coast, and the sky was instantly darker, the water purple, the land black.

"*Herr Oberleutnant!* My fuel light is on!" an excited young voice called out over the R/T.

"Just now? You couldn't have done much dogfighting back there." Hartmann snapped back.

"But *Herr Oberleutnant—*"

"The rest of us have been flying on red at least since we left the English coast," another irritated voice told the newcomer off.

"Keep a look-out for a field to put down in," Hartmann advised wearily.

"Engine's just starved," Busso reported crisply, as if to underline the point, and already his 109 started to drop out of formation, gliding while the others pressed forward.

Ernst glanced nervously at the dark landscape below. He hated the thought of having to put down in a field at this time of day. It was the worst possible moment – well, not really, with every second it got worse. Better now with some lingering light left. His engine coughed and his heart stood still, but the plane kept going. Another aircraft was falling behind, its propeller slowly winding down, but Ernst couldn't make out the ID letters in the gloom. Christian was still ahead of him.

"There's the field." As so often at dusk, there appeared to be no wind at all. A small blessing.

"Go straight in," Hartmann ordered the Staffel. Ernst registered that he also called control, advising them that they were *all* making "emergency" landings, but he didn't hear the answer. Ernst touched down, bounced, clunked down again, and rolled forward, bouncing and bumping. Lousy landing, he thought wearily, too tired to be upset about it. He turned the Emil to the right, and it waddled across the dark field in its usual awkward fashion, until abruptly the engine died. The last of the fuel was gone, and the Emil rolled to a stop still 200 yards short of its dispersal point.

Ernst released his straps in preparation for getting out, then decided to wait for the ground crew to come over to him. He folded his arms above the instrument panel and dropped his head on them. He fell asleep instantly.

"*Herr Leutnant!*"

Ernst jerked upright in complete confusion, then blushed from embarrassment as he realised he'd fallen asleep in the cockpit. At once he started to get out, then remembered he'd run out of fuel. "We need—"

"Are you all right, Herr *Leutnant*?" the mechanic asked anxiously.

"Ja, ja. I just ran out of fuel, that's all," Ernst assured his ground crew, more embarrassed than ever.

"You and everyone else in the *Staffel*," the crew agreed. "You go on in, *Herr Leutnant*. We'll push the crate over to dispersal." His fitter was offering him a hand. Ernst took it gratefully. They'd flown four sorties today, the most ever, and all of them in the afternoon. Ernst was stiff and absolutely exhausted. He stumbled a bit as he hit the ground, and his flying boots seemed to weigh a ton. He wished he could fly in riding boots as Christian did, but his boots gave him blisters. (They'd been cheap and, according to Christian, not properly fitted.)

At the steps into the Mess inside, Ernst caught up with Dieter, and they went in together and straight down to the bar. They'd snatched a snack between their third and fourth sorties of the day, and they weren't so much hungry as desperate for the calming effects of alcohol. There were lots of pilots ahead of them, so it took several minutes to be served. They sat down at one of the tables and Christian flopped down into a vacant chair, still in his flight jacket. He stretched out his long legs and pulled the scarf off his neck. "All I can say is, I hope the RAF is as tired as we are." Then suddenly he stopped. "*Scheisse!* What day is it today?"

"Sunday," Dieter answered.

"*Scheisse!*" Christian sat upright. "What time is it?"

"20.25," Ernst answered for him even as Christian looked at his own watch.

"*Verdammt*! I promised Gabrielle I'd take her to a flick tonight."

"It's too late," Dieter pointed out.

"She'll be steaming!"

"Surely she'll understand," Ernst started, but Christian had already jumped to his feet.

"Gabrielle thinks flying is fun. *She* has to work all day standing on her pretty little feet, being polite to snotty customers, while I get to lark about sitting down. She says she has a *right* to a little entertainment in the evenings. The *least* I can do is take her out now and again. And she's been on about this film for *days*. Some French heart-throb in the leading role."

Christian was checking his wallet to be sure he had some francs. "Dieter, can you lend me ten francs or so?"

Dieter sighed, but he removed his wallet and handed a bank note over to Christian. Christian got as far as the steps up out of the bar, when a voice called out to him, "*Leutnant von Feldburg*?"

Christian looked back, clearly startled. The voice was unfamiliar to Ernst, and so was the face of the *Hauptmann* addressing him. No one had noticed him when they came in. He wasn't from the *Gruppe* at all.

"*Herr Hauptmann*?" Christian answered cautiously. Ernst could see his *Rotteführer* was tense and wary. He'd been on his way out to meet with a French girl, after all.

"Fischer," the senior officer introduced himself, as he got to his feet and went over to Christian. He took Christian by the arm and they went together up the stairs. Ernst looked at Dieter; Dieter looked back at him. The word Gestapo flashed through Ernst's mind, although the stranger had been in Luftwaffe uniform. But he'd always known Christian shouldn't say all those things about "the Leadership" and the Party. And maybe someone else had heard that mock speech making fun of the *Führer*? Dieter seemed to be having similar thoughts because, without a word, they both got to their feet and started out of the bar together. Halfway up the stairs, however, the strange *Hauptmann* met them coming down. He smiled at them. "May I join you gentlemen for a round? – on me, of course."

"*Herr Hauptmann*," Dieter answered ambiguously.

"Fischer," the *Hauptmann* insisted again, leading them back to the table as he raised his hand and called to the bartender, "A round for three, please."

Fischer took the chair Christian had just vacated. "So, who do I have the honour of drinking with?"

"Dieter Möller, *Herr Hauptmann*."

"Ernst Geuke, *Herr Hauptmann*."

He nodded, and then explained. "I've been sent in from I *Gruppe* to take over the Staffel. Hartmann is being given one in JG 53."

Ernst slipped up to his room as soon as he could. Fischer seemed nice and all, but Ernst was tired and wanted to be alone with his thoughts for a bit. He got out of his uncomfortable boots and tunic and settled himself at his writing desk, wearing just his shirt and trousers with the braces hanging down so they didn't cut into his shoulders. He took out his "diary" and entered the date neatly: Sunday, August 18, 1940.

Then he started, as he always did, "Dear Klaudia."

He'd bought the diary just before he came out to France, but it wasn't until he'd met Klaudia that he'd made the first entry. Somehow it had seemed silly to write to himself, but ever since he'd fallen hopelessly in love with Klaudia, he'd started writing to her. He put down in his diary all the things he wished he could say to Klaudia – but never would.

"Dear Klaudia, we flew four times today. That's a lot. Looking back on it, of course, it was OK. We lost no pilots today, even though we scrapped with the Tommies on three of the four sorties. The only aircraft we lost were due to lack of fuel. We finally seem to be getting the better of them now, and once today we were allowed to do a free-hunt rather than being tied to the bombers.

When we *are* with the bombers, they've upped the escort ratio to almost 5 to 1. That means the bombers are getting through almost every time. Today we hammered one of their airfields in waves – it was a total shambles, when we left it. There were bomb craters all over it and all but one of the hangars collapsed. They won't be able to use it again – not for weeks, anyway, and by then the army should have landed.

"But it's late now, and tomorrow will be here too soon. Then it starts all over again. Because we've knocked out the RAF's forward fields, the targets get farther and farther away. That means flying longer just to get to the targets, and that means less fuel for dogfighting. I suppose this doesn't sound heroic but knowing that we hardly have enough fuel to get home really nags at us during a flight. The more we mix it with the RAF, the more likely it is we'll have to ditch in the Channel. It's not just the extra time lost chasing after them, but the power-dives and power-climbs, that really eat up the fuel. Just five minutes scrapping can make the difference between landing safely here at Crépon or having to ditch. The water is bitterly cold, and the Tommies have been shooting down our rescue planes. The thought of ditching makes me—" Ernst broke off and crossed out this line. He started a new paragraph.

"Christian's French girlfriend doesn't understand how tiring flying is for us. She seems to think it is a sport. I know you know better. That means a lot to me. You and the other *Helferinnen* know just how tough it is out there, how good the Tommies are, and what the risks are. I know some of the officers think it's wrong for women to wear uniform and do men's jobs, but that's stupid, old-fashioned thinking. I know that you and the other *Helferinnen* love Germany just as much as we do and want to do your part. And you do a great job! Frankly, most of us wish there were more of you out here. Admittedly, not just for the work you do, but because we really like having German girls here."

Ernst stopped, decided that this might leave the wrong impression, and hastened to add: "Not that I would be interested in anyone else, even if there were a hundred Helferinnen here. I'm not like that. I don't fall in love easily. In fact, I've only done it once – with you." Ernst paused to reflect upon the importance of this sentence. He was so lost in thought and feelings that he nearly jumped out of his skin when there was a knock on his door.

"What? Who's there?" he called out in alarm. Surely Christian wasn't back already? He checked his watch. It was just ten pm.

"Fischer."

"*Scheisse!*" Ernst swore under his breath, jumped to his feet, and pulling up his braces looked about desperately for his tunic. "One minute, *Herr Hauptmann*, I'm not—"

The door opened and the *Staffelkapitän* entered. "Relax, Geuke. Sit down. May I?" He indicated the bed.

Ernst didn't know what to say – but he could hardly say "no." "*Herr Hauptmann.*"

The *Staffelkapitän* sank onto the end of Ernst's bed, and took out a packet of cigarettes. He shook them out towards Ernst. Ernst took one, more out of politeness than desire; he'd only started smoking because they all did. The *Staffelkapitän* lit up, exhaled towards the ceiling, and then considered Ernst earnestly. "I've been looking at the records, Geuke. You're senior to six pilots in the *Staffel*, now that Hartmann has been posted away. You could be – should be – leading a *Rotte*."

"*Leading, Herr Hauptmann*? But who'd fly wingman to Feldburg then?"

"One of the newer pilots, of course," Fischer retorted, with a whimsical smile at Ernst's apparent astonishment.

"But they can hardly fly, *Herr Hauptmann!*" Ernst answered indignantly. "They're as likely to lose Christian and land in an English prison as not."

"That's putting it a little strongly, I think. One or two of them have actually survived a half dozen combat sorties already."

"That only means they joined us two days ago, *Herr Hauptmann*," Ernst reminded him. "They still can't be trusted to keep Feldburg's tail clear. Now that he's started making kills at last, he needs a reliable wingman."

"One kill," Fischer pointed out with evident amusement. Fischer himself had eleven.

"It's a start!" Ernst insisted loyally. "He's got the hang of it now. He'll get better. It would be madness to give him a new wingman that he has to look after and train, rather than being free to concentrate on his shooting."

Fischer considered Ernst so intently that Ernst started to feel nervous. He looked about for his tunic again. The last thing Ernst wanted was to be given a *Rotte* with some inexperienced young pilot flying on his flank. They'd both end up getting killed, and all for nothing! He couldn't hit anything to save his life. In fact, he'd only fired his guns three or four times. Christian and he had become a *good* team. Ernst spotted his tunic at last and stood up to get it.

"Leave it," Fischer urged with a vague gesture. "I'm not going to force you to take over a *Rotte*, if you don't want it – but Feldburg assured me you were up to it."

"He did?" Ernst was non-plussed, and then again unsure how to feel about it. Did Christian want to get rid of him, or had he meant it as a compliment? "What did he say exactly?"

"I believe the phrase was, 'Geuke can have a *Rotte* any God-damned time he wants one. I don't have to bolster *my* image by turning a good man into a *Katschmarek*.'"

Ernst winced. "*Katschmarek*" was a derogatory term for wingman, equating them with slavishly loyal Polish servants from the large estates in East Prussia and Pomerania. It was also a clear slur on Bartels, who had never let his own wingman move up, despite being the second most experienced pilot in the *Staffel*. To Fischer, Ernst declared firmly, "He's right. He doesn't have to do that – and I'm no *Katschmarek*, either. But I don't want a *Rotte*, *Herr Hauptmann*. Not yet."

Fischer looked him straight in the face and their eyes met; then Fischer nodded, and took a deep drag on his cigarette. "All right. If that's the way you want it. I'm giving Feldburg a *Schwarm* and – if you insist on staying wingman to him – the other two pilots will be Ettner and Renz." Ettner had been with the *Staffel* nearly as long as Ernst, and he was a very serious, correct pilot. Ernst had never been able to warm to him, but he felt he was at least as qualified to lead a *Rotte* as he was himself, so he nodded. Renz had only arrived yesterday, and they'd taken him along on only two of the sorties today. They always did that: let the new pilots ease into the work-load while the "old hands" ensured adequate coverage for the bombers.

"OK. I won't disturb you any longer," Fischer declared, hauling himself back to his feet.

Ernst automatically stood as well, remarking sincerely, "Thank you for asking, *Herr Hauptmann*."

Chapter 24

Portsmouth
19 August 1940

The other girls were gossiping as usual. They always did first thing Monday morning while they made tea. They talked about films and film stars, about who had been seen with whom, about what ships were in and where they'd been dancing on Friday and Saturday nights. There might be a war on, but the sailors in Portsmouth still wanted to have a good time, and the city "defiantly" offered them a range of opportunities. Although Emily's colleagues had always gone dancing with sailors, they now made it sound like a patriotic duty. Emily found the attitude a bit hard to take.

Today, however, they were talking about the Luftwaffe with the supreme confidence of girls who had been out with a couple of erks.

"The Jerries fly in such large formations because they are herd animals. They only feel comfortable in groups. Just like sheep. They only have one leader and one navigator for the whole formation – not like in our bombers, which each have their own navigator. If we shoot down the lead plane, then the others don't know where they are or what to do."

"That's why they can't handle democracy," another girl joined in knowingly. "They all just follow orders without questioning them. Hitler gives the order and they all just do what he says."

"I wonder how he has time to give so many millions of orders," one of the girls remarked with just a hint of irony, but Emily didn't get a chance to hear the reaction. Her phone rang.

"Wyndham, Cassidy and Harper. How can I help you?"

"Resign. Meet me at the Queens at four – well, wait for me there. I'm just leaving Hawarden now and I don't know when I'll arrive exactly. I'm driving my poor old Austin, but I think I should be able to make the Queens by four. Is that all right?"

"Yes, of course." It was out automatically, but then she asked with alarm, "Has something happened, Robin?" He sounded so distant, detached, strange. And why hadn't he mentioned he was coming down to Portsmouth today when she'd been with him yesterday? She found herself asking into the telephone, "Do you have leave?"

"No, I've been posted to Tangmere and will pass through Portsmouth on my way. I need to pick up a scraper ring, in any case, and thought I could introduce you to my mum. If you want, that is. I know this is a bit unfair. I mean, *very* unfair. It's just, I'd really like you to be there for me, if you could bear it, that is." He paused a second, but Emily was still too bewildered to fully understand what he was saying. Pick up a "scraper ring"? What the devil was that? And what was unfair?

Robin started talking again, in a rush. His coins were probably about to run out — as usual. "Look, you don't have to give me an answer right away. You can think about it. But I'd rather like to know before I report at Tangmere. Then I could see about housing and such straightaway. I probably need someone's permission. Station Commander, I suppose. My coins are out. Will you be at the Queens?"

She barely had time to shout "yes" before the beepers started. Then she sat there trying to make sense of it.

Slowly she did, and she felt very, very cold. He wanted her to be there for him — at Tangmere. He'd been posted to Tangmere. That meant he was back on ops. Now? In the middle of a training course? That damn Messerschmitt. And Park. He'd seen him fly. The ring. What had he called it? A scrapper ring? "Oh, my God," Emily only whispered it, but the others were already staring at her.

"What is it, love? You look like you've seen a ghost."

"Oh, my God," Emily repeated, still not moving or seeing anything around her. She was chilled through.

"What's happened? That was your bloke, wasn't it? He can't be dead."

"No," she answered vigorously, adding in a lower voice, "not yet."

"What's he gone and done then? Has he broken off with you?"

"Has he got another girl?"

"He's not married, is he? I always thought he must be—"

Emily couldn't stand their mindless speculation any longer. "No! He just got himself promoted Squadron Leader." Only as she said it out loud did it really start to become real to her. Robin wasn't just going on ops, he'd been given a squadron at the forefront of the battle — and there was only one reason for such a pre-emptory promotion: his predecessor must have been killed, yesterday.

The other girls were being silly and congratulating her. Emily could have screamed at them. Didn't they realise what it meant? But why should they? They weren't important, anyway. Emily tried to remember everything Robin had just said.

Resign. He'd asked her to resign, and meet him at the Queens, so she could meet his mother. He wanted her to be with him at Tangmere, but he was being unfair to her. How? Of course: to expect that of her. He hadn't asked her to marry him, after all, just "be there" for him. That made her hot with shame for a moment, but then she wondered: would he really introduce his mistress to his mother? And what did he need the Station Commander's permission for? To have his mistress in residence on the station? Surely the RAF couldn't sanction that? And what did it matter? If Robin wanted her to be there, she would be. It was as simple as that. It didn't matter on what terms or for how long. Even if it were only for a single day....

RAF Hawarden

They were all clustered around. No new instructor had arrived yet and it was raining anyway, so his trainees were on the ground. Murray, now only referred to as "Kiwi," insisted on helping him pack his car, cramming more things into the boot than Priestman thought possible, and Goldman wanted him to accept a silver cigarette case as a thank-you present. "What for?" Priestman shot back. "I was just doing my job."

The adjutant was there too, giving him petrol stamps for the trip down, and Kennel was giving him advice on which route to take. Finally, he was able to climb in behind the steering wheel and start up. He gunned the engine to clear it out, and then backed out cautiously as the others reluctantly got out of his way.

"Send us a post card!" someone shouted. "Or the crosses from the next Jerry you get!"

Priestman waved out of the open window and set off. Clouds hung low and dark, scudding along the hilltops, driven by a brisk wind. Fine, misting rain blew in through the open window, so Robin rolled it up as soon as he was in fourth gear. The windscreen started to steam up on the inside almost immediately, so he turned the heater and fan on full, as well as the windscreen wipers. He sighed as he slowed down to turn out of the drive. It was going to be a miserable drive, but then again, he needed time to think.

Things had happened too fast. (Not a complaint a fighter pilot ought to make, he reminded himself.) But he really hadn't been prepared for Park's call at all. He wasn't entirely sure he was prepared for a squadron, either. The thought of all the paperwork was enough to make him want to take cover! That was dodging the issue. They'd given him a squadron, which had just lost it's the squadron leader and one flight commander. In his polite way, Park had been very explicit. The squadron was on the brink of collapse, and the remaining Flight Lieutenant "wasn't up to the mark."

Either Priestman turned the squadron around, or it would be pulled out of the front line. It was a compliment – almost.

Priestman didn't think Park had really selected him because he thought he was exceptional in some way. On the contrary, he'd mentioned Singapore, and made it very clear that he had his doubts, but Fighter Command was desperately short of experienced flight commanders and Robin supposed he was the first Flight Lieutenant to come to mind simply because Park had seen him fly that 109 two days ago. He'd seen him, thought of him, and decided to give him a chance *in spite* of what he'd done in Singapore. That was all.

But what an opportunity! Commanding a squadron was the best job in the RAF. Beyond squadron leader, a man got bogged down in even more paperwork and planning, tangled in bureaucracy and – worst of all – soon tied to a desk. Priestman *wanted* a squadron. He was excited by the idea of leading a squadron. He wanted the chance to do all the things right that he thought others had done wrong over the last five years of his life. He liked the idea of having his own personal aircraft. He liked the idea of making the decisions on tactics – and the first one would be to fly in a loose formation similar to the German one rather than in the RAF standard ones. Part of him even thrilled at the idea of "turning a squadron around" – and in the next moment he quailed at the thought.

He'd be flying with complete strangers, and at least four of them would be pilots straight out of flying school. If he'd found it nerve-racking worrying about incompetent pilots during training, how the hell was he supposed to look after them when the Luftwaffe bounced them out of the sun? He'd have to try to do some operational training, he promised himself. That was the way he'd learned: inside the squadron with the men he was going to be fighting with. But how the hell was he supposed to manage that with only one Flight Lieutenant or if he was on readiness from dawn to dusk?

Well, at least he could be sure the guns were harmonised at 250 feet or less rather than the standard 400 feet. That would improve the chances of shooting down Huns – at least for the more experienced pilots. And for the beginners he could institute gunnery practice – at least on fixed targets. In the training units, they weren't issued enough ammunition to give the pilots proper gunnery practice, but ammo was never an issue with an operational unit. Suddenly there seemed to be a great deal that he longed to do with a squadron to get it right. Yet with the airfields being blitzed, he couldn't assume that they'd have enough operable aircraft, get proper meals, or have a dry place to sleep.

Which reminded him, he'd made a hash of things with Emily. He'd intended to propose to her at the Queens. Assuming he could get down to Pompii soon enough, he'd planned to go to a tailor, put up his stripe, and then pop over to a jeweller to buy an engagement ring. But with his stupid remark about resigning he'd let the cat out of the bag, so he'd quasi come out and asked her on the phone.

Emily hadn't sounded exactly over-joyed. In fact, she'd pretended not to understand him at all. She'd acted as if she thought he was crazy. Maybe he was. They hardly knew each other. Then again, he felt he knew her better than any other girl he'd ever taken out. With the others, he'd done a lot of dancing and they'd gone to the flicks or concerts and shows together, but they hadn't *talked* much. Certainly, none of them had ever flown with him....

Still, he hadn't even thought about marriage until he got the squadron. Most squadron leaders were married. He couldn't remember a squadron leader who wasn't. The RAF even gave them a Marriage Allowance, which eliminated any financial concerns. Robin's memories were of Squadron Leaders with large, rambling country houses where the pilots were always welcome and often introduced to nice girls.

Memories of Singapore competed with the rain pelting on the windscreen. Squadron Leader Whiteley had had a wonderful house with a long veranda and a view down to the coast. The single officers had spent more time there than in the Mess because Mrs. Whiteley had put them all at ease. Robin knew that she had on more than one occasion very diplomatically intervened with her husband on behalf of one or the other of the pilots – including himself. She'd saved his career more than anyone, he supposed. If Whiteley hadn't been talked into defending him at the enquiry, he'd have been given a bowler hat and probably be in the infantry by now – or the Merchant Navy.

He could picture Emily in the role of intermediary. She was very different from Mrs. Whiteley, of course, but in her own way she would be a great asset to him and a good friend to his pilots.

Then he reminded himself that he'd known the Whiteley's in peacetime. He wasn't asking Emily to join him in the tropics with an army of Chinese servants to do her bidding or to dance with him at embassy balls and sail on the sparkling waters of the South China Sea. He was asking her to live in cramped married officers' housing that would be targeted by the Luftwaffe along with the rest of the Station. As to looking after the pilots, it might be better for her if she didn't get to know them too well. Emily was very sensitive. Maybe it was unfair to ask her to deal with so much death and injury at all? Not to mention that there wasn't time to plan a big wedding.

What did he mean, there wasn't time? Of course, there was time. It was pure selfishness that made him want to marry her now. Today.

Tomorrow at the latest. He'd made up his mind, and he knew he was going to have enough to worry about without dealing with wedding plans – or even just the bother of driving to pick her up, take her home again, etc., etc. He certainly didn't want an *RAF wedding* with the attendant stag night and the compulsory drinking and inevitable practical jokes. Or was that also just a peacetime phenomenon? What did he know about the morale of his new squadron – except that it was near to collapse?

He wasn't concentrating on his driving. Coming around the curve he saw the heavily laden milk cart a fraction too late. He slammed on the brakes, but the road surface was wet, his tyres no longer at their best. The Austin squealed, skidded and smashed into the back of the slower vehicle. Milk churns tipped over backwards onto the windscreen, shattering it, and then the engine cut out.

Milk was dripping through the shattered glass onto his sleeve and the suitcases on the seat beside him. Woodenly, Robin took his foot off the brake, opened the door and slipped out from under the steering wheel. The driver of the cart was coming towards him, cursing in very colourful language.

The constable, who arrived shortly afterwards, was more polite but more difficult. He fined Robin for speeding and added a long lecture on how motorcars were not fighter planes and shouldn't be driven with such careless disregard for the other people on the roads. Robin, who only wanted to get the whole thing over with, agreed to everything the constable said – which only seemed to encourage him to extend the lecture. "All you RAF boys think that you can do whatever you like these days, but that's not what this war is all about. What makes Britain strong is that everyone has the same rights and has to obey the same laws – even the King."

"Yes, God Save the King. May I go now?"

"It was being in such a hurry that got you into trouble in the first place, young man!"

"You made that point earlier, officer. I believe that I explained that I am under orders to report to my new squadron 'immediately.'"

"Well, you would have been there faster if you had been obeying the traffic laws and not speeding." And so it had gone until finally the tow-truck arrived and to haul the Austin to the next garage.

There the mechanic looked over the Austin, shaking his head and clucking his tongue. From the list of what was wrong with it, Robin thought he couldn't have done more damage if he'd crashed it at 500 mph from 5000 feet, but the bottom line was that the Austin wasn't worth more than two pounds scrap.

"Whole engine is worthless, sir. Piece of junk, really."

Robin didn't believe him. He was sure that this man could and would extract many valuable, working bits and pieces, which he would use for the repair of other vehicles. Robin knew he was being cheated, but he didn't have the time or inclination to argue. He let the man have his beloved – but now sadly shortened – Austin for two quid and started to unload his things. "Can I get a taxi to the next station?"

"Taxi? You must be joking, sir! You aren't in London you know!"

"Yes, I noticed that," Robin commented as dryly as possible, trying to imagine how he was going to get all his earthly goods and belongings down to Pompii and/or Tangmere without a vehicle of any kind.

Queens Hotel, Portsmouth

The longer Emily waited, the more her mother's words nagged at her. Her mother had taken a very dim view of the announcement that Emily had resigned from her job so she could be with Robin. Her mother had called her a "tart." Indeed, she'd insisted Emily was worse than a tart, because she was prepared to be at Robin's "beck-and-call" without the slightest compensation.

An hour or so after she arrived, a heavy rain had set in. Everyone who entered shook out their umbrellas and brushed rain off their over-coats. While bellboys hurried back and forth trying to relieve the guests of their wet things, the arriving guests glanced at Emily with mild curiosity, and every look made her more self-conscious. They all seemed to assess her: Oh, one of *those*, a girl with so little self-respect that she has to sit around waiting on her beau. She felt very, very silly. All dressed up and now where to go...

The rain became so heavy that before sunset the foyer of the hotel was dark. The staff closed the blackout blinds and turned on the lights. In the artificial light, Emily felt tawdrier than ever.

After more than two hours of waiting, the receptionist was starting to give her hostile looks. How much longer should she wait? What else did she have to do? Where else could she go? Not home like a stray cat dragging its tail between its legs!

There was a commotion at the door. The doorman rushed out with a hotel umbrella. People were saying, "Yes, my lord," and "right away, my lord." A gentleman in a bowler hat with a silver-headed cane entered the foyer, giving orders for a table and champagne. Then he stopped and scanned the foyer. It took her a second to realise that there was someone in Air Force blue in his wake.

When Emily saw Robin, her heart stopped for an instant. He had never looked so good to her. His hair was falling over his forehead as usual, and there was something vaguely rumpled about his uniform – as if it had become wet and dried on him. But he had both hands *out* of his pockets for once and was nervously playing with his cap as he scanned the foyer. His eyes, trained to look into the distance, swept right over her. He focused on the back of the room, anxiously scanning the entrance to the restaurant – as if he were looking for 109s in the sun.

"Robin!" she called out as she tried to get to her feet. The winged chair was so deep and low that she fell back into it. She struggled up again, and this time Robin caught her. He had her in his arms. "Thanks for waiting," he murmured with relief she could hear. "I crashed my motorcar and had to hitch a lift. I was very lucky that Lord Beaverbrook happened along and offered to bring me all the way; he even let me stop by my tailor and a jeweller he knew."

"That was Lord Beaverbrook?" Emily asked in awe and twisted around to get a better look at the gentleman who had just swept in. He had already disappeared into the dining room.

"His son's a fighter pilot, you know, and he said he couldn't drive by an RAF officer standing in the rain." As he spoke, Robin was fumbling in his pockets. He produced a box, a ring box, and held it out to her. "I hope you like it. The man said we could exchange it, if you didn't."

Emily didn't care in the least what the ring looked like. All that mattered was that it was from Robin and it expressed his honorable intentions. In a daze she snapped open the little box and caught her breath because it was beautiful: six little sapphires like leaves around a diamond. It was dainty, pretty and practical – and it was Robin's. She slipped it on her left ring finger, still staring at it in wonder.

"Does that mean you *will* marry me?" he asked, sounding uncharacteristically uncertain.

Emily broke into a beautiful smile. "Oh, yes, Robin. Very *definitely* 'yes.'"

RAF Tangmere

It was pitch dark and still raining lightly when Robin finally made it to Tangmere. It was a load off his mind that things had gone so well with Emily. His mother had been more charming than he could remember – a bit stiff but, given her disappointment about him not marrying one of those heiresses who would have transformed her life, he couldn't blame her entirely. Hattie had made up for it with her exuberance and warmth. She insisted on taking "some credit" for them getting to know one another, and she had happily offered to help Emily organise everything.

He'd been a little shocked to discover Emily was not only a professed atheist but had never been baptised. That would slow things down. She'd suggested a civil wedding, but Robin told her – maybe too sharply in retrospect – that he wasn't interested in "a stamp on paper from a low-paid civil servant." That was when Hattie intervened and assured Robin she would see that he didn't have a thing to think about – "except getting to the church on time."

The thought that Emily would be joining him as soon as possible was calming. He could now concentrate on the task in front of him with his tail covered. He was sure she'd make a comfortable home for him, a place he could retreat to and relax. That would give him added strength for the days ahead. For now, it was one thing less to worry about.

Priestman reported first to the Station Commander, who gave him a brief run-down on what Tangmere had been taking and the impact of the raid on the sixteenth. "We've got everything running again, but, of course, no replacement housing and the like. Many of the ground crews are sleeping in tents, and all the WAAFs are now billeted in a requisitioned house – just outside the main gate, fortunately. Luckily, the pilots' quarters were not seriously damaged, and we are still managing to do regular meals – at the moment, anyway, but we haven't got any replacements for the cooks and batmen killed in the raid, so services are not up to standard."

He also gave Robin a quick overview of the other squadrons assigned to Tangmere: 17 and 43, flying Hurricanes, and 602, flying Spitfires, from Westhampnett. 17 was still quite fresh. 43 was weary. 602 was top of the line. This said, the Station Commander sent for Allars and Michaels.

Both men had turned in more than an hour earlier but arrived within a few minutes to greet their new commander. Priestman then withdrew with them to the office assigned to the squadron commander of 606. This was nicely appointed with leather armchairs, a solid oak desk complete with wooden in-trays, a rattan wastepaper basket and a silver box for writing utensils. It presented a neat and tidy picture, and Priestman had the impression that either Jones had never spent much time in it – or they had done a very thorough job of cleaning his presence out of it. The only thing halfway personal about it were the many framed pictures of 606's planes and pilots.

In most of the photos, the pilots were lined up before an aircraft or an entire flight line. Here and there they sat or stood upon the aircraft itself. In one photo a small dog stood proudly on the tip of a Gladiator wing.

Robin paused to look at a photo, obviously taken here at Tangmere, with a Hurricane in it. It was a "casual" photo with some of the pilots in deck chairs and others lounging in the grass, most of them wearing their life-jackets.

"That's Squadron Leader Jones there," Mickey provided the commentary. "Flight Lieutenant Hayworth, Flying Officer Sutton, Pilot Officer Davis – he was killed just a couple days after this photo was taken. That's Flying Officer Ringwood and Flight Lieutenant 'Tommy' Thompson; they're still with the squadron. Tommy, as the only remaining Flight Lieutenant, is acting CO at the moment. 'Woody' is acting B-Flight Commander. That's our Canadian, Sergeant Pilot Green, and Sergeants Bowles and MacLeod. MacLeod's a bit of a troublemaker, I'm afraid. Got thrown out of his last squadron for brawling, and I'm very sorry to say, sir, he was just given three days arrest for doing it again. Saturday night."

"In a pub?"

"Worse, sir. Right here in front of the Officers' Mess with Flight Lieutenant Thompson and P/O Debsen."

"They're *all* under arrest?" Priestman asked in horror. This was worse than he'd imagined.

"Oh, no, sir. It was undoubtedly MacLeod's fault. The WAAF he's been seeing showed up for a dance at the Officers' Mess, and he tried to stop her going in. Indeed, he was very rude to her."

Priestman returned his attention to the picture. Mickey continued the commentary: "That's Pilot Officer Hughes; he's the one in hospital with several broken ribs. These are Pilot Officers Debsen and Williams, both of whom are still on the squadron."

"How long ago was that taken?"

"End of July, I believe. Wasn't it, Doug?"

"Yes, that's about right. Three, at most four, weeks ago."

Mickey used the pause which followed to start explaining himself in a bit of a rush. "S/L Jones wasn't one for paperwork, sir, and I'm afraid that he left quite a bit undone—"

"Let's sit down," Priestman suggested, and went behind the desk to sink into the chair with its rounded, wooden back. The air whistled as it went out of the leather seat. "Now, before you drown me in paperwork, could we cover a few of the essentials?" It was worded as a question, but Priestman's new subordinates could only agree.

Mickey nodded vigorously, regretting that he had brought up the detested subject of the neglected paperwork. Allars tried to make himself comfortable in a chair, his wooden leg thrust out in front of him, and kept his eyes fixed on Priestman.

"What is the operational strength of the squadron at this

moment?"

"In pilots?"

"In pilots. I'll talk to the Chief about the kites."

Allars and Mickey exchanged a glance at that. Mickey answered the question. "Fifteen – sixteen with you, sir, and counting Pilot Officers Hughes and Parker, both of whom are in hospital but should be fit in a few weeks or so. Also, I understand two replacement pilots are on their way. Whether they will be here tomorrow or the next day, I can't say for sure, sir."

Priestman couldn't count on pilots still in hospital, so he called that sixteen altogether. Full strength for a fighter squadron was officially 20 – and even that was down from the 24 Dowding had originally wanted. Two would be newcomers, whom he had only just resolved to keep out of the battle until he'd given them some gunnery practice and operational training. So very little extra for days off, injury, illness – or casualties.

"Can we go through the list one at a time?"

"Yes, sir, of course."

Mickey, with occasional comments from Allars, ran through the list of pilots from the most senior to the most junior, trying to provide a quick sketch of each. "Flight Lieutenant 'Tommy' Thompson is, ah, one of the originals, sir. In fact, his father, who's an MP, sir, was largely responsible for the Squadron being formed at all. I'm afraid Thompson thinks he's above things like 'King's Regulations.' He, ah, considered the 'amateur' aspect of the Auxiliary Air Force to be a point of pride, and he doesn't seem to have adjusted to the changed circumstances." Mickey coughed nervously into his hand and glanced at Allars, wondering if he'd said too much.

Instead, Allars reinforced him in a sharp tone. "The fact of the matter is, he looks on the squadron like his own preserve – the Lord of the Manor, one might say."

The two men waited for a reaction, but Park had warned Robin that his only Flight Lieutenant "wasn't up to the mark"; now he knew why. He nodded and asked about the next name on the list.

"Ah, Flying Officer Dunsire, is actually the most senior pilot after Tommy, but, ah, Tommy has reorganised the flights, so that he has all his friends collected together in 'A' Flight. He named Flying Officer Ringwood, who joined the squadron before the war but wasn't at Winchester with the rest of them, acting commander of B-Flight. All the recent arrivals – mostly Sergeants – are collected in 'B' Flight." Mickey clearly found it embarrassing to report this.

Priestman glanced at the Intelligence Officer. The older man seemed intent on lighting his pipe, remarking with it still in his mouth, "You're beginning to understand the situation, I believe."

As Mickey went through the next names, he clearly divided them into "old" – i.e., Auxiliary Air Force – and new, mostly Short Service, pilots. When he got to Debsen he faltered, and then decided to word it: "Ah, Debsen seems to have a lot of bad luck with aircraft, sir."

"In what way?"

"Well, he has a lot of engine trouble, or the oxygen runs out on him. His guns jam quite a bit, too."

Priestman looked sharply over towards Allars. Allars was still fussing with his pipe and said nothing. "Has he any claims?"

"Oh, yes, sir. Two probables. Quite browned off that no one could confirm either so although they were made they were not credited"

"I see. Go on."

Mickey did. He was notably enthusiastic about the one foreigner in the squadron, Sergeant Pilot Green. "Good mixer, Green," Mickey stressed. "Generous and full of good spirits. You know what I mean, sir. He took no end of teasing on account of his accent at first, but he never let it get to him. They call him 'Rabbit,' too – which wouldn't be anyone's choice of a nickname – but he doesn't seem to mind. He's got the right attitude."

Priestman nodded, satisfied. They had come to the last name on the list: George "Ginger" Bowles. Mickey was notably less enthusiastic than he had been about Green. There was – as with MacLeod and Debsen – a notable hesitancy in his voice. "Very nice, quiet sort of chap, but a bit of a loner."

Priestman was focused more on the flight commanders, however: "Tommy" Thompson and "Woody" Ringwood – he had noted the names carefully. Clearly, none of the senior officers – or Park – thought highly of Thompson, but there did not seem to be anything concrete against him – not like his own record. Nevertheless, Priestman sensed this would be his first challenge: getting firm control over a man who thought he held the squadron like a feudal fief. As for Ringwood, he'd have to see if he was really up to the job of leading a flight, or if Dunsire, the more senior pilot, was more suitable.

"All right, how many credited claims does the squadron have?" Priestman addressed this question to Allars as Intelligence Officer.

"Oh, let me see, Jones had nine all told – five destroyed, three probables and a damaged. Thompson claimed four destroyed and —"

Priestman cut him off. "Don't you know the *squadron* score?"

"Ah. The squadron. Well..." Allars didn't. He also registered that it was the kind of question Park might have asked him. Embarrassed, he admitted, "No, sir. I'd have to add it up for you."

"Do that – by tomorrow morning." (It was very nice indeed to be able to give orders, Robin reflected briefly, before continuing.) "Before I go and find the Chief to see about the kites, is there anything either of you think I ought to know about the squadron?"

The two administrators looked at one another. Mickey was tempted to make another attempt to explain about all the things Jones had left undone, but then decided against it.

Allars decided to risk a comment. "606 County of Gloucester Squadron had a very good reputation before the war, sir. They were a close-knit squadron, and that was good – until some big gaps got torn in those ranks over Dunkirk. You see, new pilots filled the *ranks* – but not the *gaps*. They couldn't – because they weren't allowed to. Jones – and Tommy even more so – felt that men like MacLeod or Bowles or Green didn't belong here. I won't go so far as to say they resented them for being where they felt their friends should still be, but they felt – and feel – strongly that they are a different 'calibre' – as Jones put it. What he meant, of course, was different accent, different background, different interests, different class. There's a lot of good material here, but it hasn't been cultivated."

Priestman digested that and glanced at Mickey. "Would you agree with that?"

"Oh, yes, very much, sir!" Allars continued, "And now, maybe you could tell us something about yourself, sir. What squadron have you been on up until now?"

"Actually, I'm coming direct from Training Command."

The faces of the other two men were priceless. Robin laughed. They continued to gaze at him as if they were about to lose their dinner. "Cranwell 1936. No. 36 Squadron in Singapore until '38. Did some aerobatics on the circuit and then joined No. 579 Squadron just before the balloon went up. Gained a bit of experience in France, if that makes you feel better." He removed his flying log book from his brief-case and tossed it on the table. "You'll find it all in there."

Allars didn't even glance at it. (He could do that later.) For the moment, he was still in shock. This squadron was a vital link in Britain's terribly thin line of defence against the Nazi hordes just across the Channel. The Squadron Leader was the linchpin of the squadron. And if this young man – and he was very young – was not good enough or if he got shot down on his first sortie, then the squadron would disintegrate. It was as simple as that – and it was a very sobering thought.

Chapter 25

RAF Tangmere
20 August 1940

It was still dark as the ground crews lined up for breakfast. Ever since the raid had destroyed a good part of the Airmen's Mess, 606's ground crews were both housed and fed in tents. Since the weather was warm and comparatively dry, it hadn't been too bad so far. Fowley, new to the squadron and still rather excited to be part of it all, thought it was rather like camping out. The only bad part was the food. Since most of the airmen's kitchen staff had been killed or injured in the raid and not yet replaced, they were being fed from the Sergeants' Mess. By the time their food got to them, it was already cold. Powdered eggs were bad enough warm; they were terrible cold. Besides, who wanted to eat at 4.00 in the morning?

Fowley pushed the yellow mush on his plate around a bit and then decided he'd throw it out. He stood up, then stopped himself; since the NAAFI had also been destroyed in the raid, there was nowhere to buy a chocolate or a sandwich if he got hungry mid-morning. Maybe he should force himself to eat the stuff after all?

He glanced around to see what the others were doing, and noticed that Tufnel was just sitting there with his head in his hands. "Are you all right, Al?"

Tufnel pulled his head out of his hands and gazed at Fowley. His eyes were sunk in his head and there were dark circles under them. "You know what that cow did?" he opened without preamble, as if everyone else automatically knew what he was thinking about. "She broke it off in a sodding letter! Didn't even have the decency to come and tell him to his face! Couldn't wait until he was out of hospital or whatever, either! Couldn't even send him a bleeding 'get well' card!"

Because Fowley had been working closely with Tufnel the past couple of days, he understood Tufnel's anger against Sanders' girl, but he couldn't *feel* it. He nodded and suggested sensibly, "You got to eat something, Al. It's going to be a long day."

Tufnel just frowned. "I'm gonna write to that cow and tell her what I think of her."

"We've got to be at the aircraft in 20 minutes," Fowley reminded him.

"Don't tell me my sodding job! I've been doing it a hell of a lot longer than you!" Tufnel snarled back, getting up and turning his back on Fowley.

Fowley sighed and left the table. He scraped the leftovers into the slops bucket and dropped the plate and cutlery into a basin of soapy water waiting for it. The water was already filthy, with grease more than suds floating on the surface. Most of the others were hanging around lighting up before starting the day.

Unnerved by the exchange with Tufnel and not having any other friends in the squadron yet, Fowley decided to walk over to the remaining hangar, where "H" was currently standing. (That was one good thing about the tents; they were closer to the hangar than Airmen's Quarters had been.)

The hangar was pitch dark inside. Fowley had to turn on the light switch. At once the whole interior lit up. It was very odd to be alone in the large, cavernous building. Fowley was fractious. He had a nagging feeling that he had forgotten something, failed to check something vital, left some lever in the wrong position. He'd barely scraped through training, passing his exams by the thinnest of margins. At the time, he hadn't given a damn about anything but passing out, since being a fitter with an operational RAF squadron had been his dream for as long as he could remember. But in training he hadn't had to look in the faces of the pilots whose lives depended on his skill.

Here at 606, by contrast, pilots weren't abstract nuisances who mucked up perfectly good machines. Suddenly they were people. They weren't all nice, of course, but that wasn't the point. Besides, the only pilot everyone really *dis*liked was Debsen because he always blamed his crew if something wrong. Debsen caused no end of trouble because he said this or that was wrong with the kite, and then his crew had to take the whole crate apart, and if they didn't find anything wrong, Chiefy said they hadn't looked hard enough, and if they still didn't find anything wrong....

But the others seemed nice enough. In fact, Sergeant Bowles, Fowley's pilot, was particularly nice. He'd offered to clean up his own mess, but Tufnel said that "wasn't done" and insisted that they do it for him. Fowley was glad of the extra money, and frankly a little in awe of Bowles. He couldn't imagine being that frightened – and then still doing it day after day. Unlike that braggart Appleby, Fowley knew he didn't want anything to do with flying, much less fighting the Luftwaffe in a fragile little crate made of wood and canvas that could burn up in seconds. He truly admired Bowles for being willing to do that even though, unlike some of the others, he was obviously acutely aware of the danger he was in. Which was precisely why Fowley felt so bad when he thought he might have forgotten something. If he had, he might be to blame for Sgt. Pilot Bowles' getting killed. He set his tea down on the wing of "H" and opened the cowling.

"Something wrong with her, Aircraftman?"

Fowley nearly jumped out of his skin at the unexpected question. He had thought he was alone in the hangar, and now there was a man in a Sidcot suit standing beside him – a man he had never seen before. The Sidcot covered all rank insignia, but he was obviously a pilot, because his hair was so long it was hanging in his forehead, and no Sergeant would have let him get away with that. He also had a silk scarf around his neck and tucked into the front of his overalls. Most important, he stood there with his hands in his pockets as if he owned the place – not to mention his upper-class accent.

"Not that I know of, sir," Fowley answered the question. "I was just checking. To be sure."

"What's your name, Aircraftman?"

"Fowley, sir."

"I'm new to the squadron," the officer explained. "Just come from Training Command. You don't mind answering a few of my questions, do you?"

"No, sir." Fowley thought the pilot looked old for coming straight out of Training, but maybe he'd been flying other aircraft, or had come from the Fleet Air Arm and had just converted to Hurricanes, or something like that.

"Any bum kites in the stable?" The pilot nodded vaguely to the other three machines in the hangar.

"Not really, sir. Those two there are brand new. They're in here to get their ID. 'B' is in for a fifty-hour check. 'Q' is here because Pilot Officer Debsen says the engine stutters, but we can't find the problem, sir."

"And this kite?" Robin nodded towards the aircraft they were standing next to.

"Well, it got shot up on the eighteenth. The glycol tank was hit and the engine over-heated, but I think it's OK now."

"Good. Then it needs a flight check. Would you mind getting it fuelled up and ready for me? I want to make a quick test flight – might as well make it doubly useful." The pilot was walking around the wing.

"Ah, sir, wait. May I suggest you take a different kite, sir?"

"Why?" The pilot stopped and gazed at Fowley in astonishment.

"This one – well – it stinks a bit, sir," Fowley admitted shamefully.

"Stinks?"

"Yes, sir. We try to clean it out, but, well, somehow it still stinks."

"All aircraft stink, Fowley," the pilot observed with a whimsical smile.

"No, sir, not like this. I mean, like someone's been sick in it."

"*Has* someone been sick in it?"

"Yes, sir. Sergeant Pilot Bowles is sick every flight."

The pilot was staring at Fowley so hard that it made him look down and kick at the cracked concrete under his feet with his thick-soled, scruffy boot. He felt bad to have betrayed Sergeant Pilot Bowles' secret, but this pilot would have smelt something anyway....

"What aircraft would you recommend then, Fowley?"

"Well, 'R' is brand new, sir – not just a pieced-together job. Straight from the factory—"

"Fowley! Oh! Sir!" Flight Sergeant Rowe had spotted them. He came up saluting smartly to the pilot – not his usual condescending salute to new pilots. Then he cast Fowley a look laden with threat. Even if he'd only been on the squadron five days, Fowley knew that look, and it made him cringe. Rowe was in a bad temper. "What can I do for you, sir?" Rowe asked the pilot, in a tone that was almost servile.

"The weather's lifting. I want to test-fly one of the aircraft. I've been on Spitfires for the last month or so."

"May I suggest 'R' or 'S', sir? Both were delivered by the ATA just yesterday."

"I'll take 'R.'"

"Yes, sir! Fowley!"

Fowley ran off, not giving Rowe a chance to even look at him twice.

"I want her armed as well."

"Of course, sir!"

Rowe was shouting again, and within minutes the Hurricane was rolled out of the hangar, her new squadron and aircraft ID letters still a bit sticky and shiny in places. A petrol bowser came up beside her and a team of armourers got her guns loaded. Fowley went for the starter trolley.

Priestman squinted up at the sky. The cloud cover was tattered. The first hints of light made the sky behind the clouds a lighter shade of grey. He scrambled up the wing and swung himself into the cockpit. It seemed roomy after the Spitfire – not to mention the 109. He took his time going over the dials. He found the whole cockpit reassuringly familiar. He'd flown Spitfires just over a month, but Hurricanes for more than a year. Besides, there was something endearing about the Hurricane that even his love affair with the Spitfire couldn't shake. This feeling was only reinforced during a smooth take-off; the Hurricane's broad undercarriage meant that she handled better on the ground and she had no inclination to overheat as the Spitfire did.

As soon as he was airborne, Priestman circled the field and called in to control. The eastern sky was getting steadily paler. "Beetle, this is Redcap Leader. Just getting re-acquainted with the Hurricane," he told them, and the controller acknowledged in a pleasant, relaxed voice.

Priestman sprinted away below the scattered clouds that hovered at roughly 5,000 feet. He flew towards the rising sun, enjoying the pale pink of the dawn. Just beyond Brighton, the controller suddenly broke in over the R/T. "Redcap Leader, we have a lone bandit not very far from you; can you handle it?"

"Why not?"

"It's your decision, sir. We can scramble your Duty Section in 15 minutes."

Priestman glanced at his watch. It was 5.10. "Do that, and I'll go look for trade anyway."

"Right, then. Vector 110. Angels 26."

"Vector 110. Angels 26. Roger." Priestman turned in the opposite direction to start piling on altitude before making his interception. As he passed 20,000 feet, on oxygen and grateful for his flight jacket, he asked again for a vector.

"Redcap Leader, fly 080, Angels 24. We think he's sniffing about, trying to get photos of the damage done to Kenley and Biggin Hill."

"Thanks." Priestman was impressed by the amount of information. In France the controllers had been notoriously taciturn and snotty, if asked for details. Priestman supposed the controllers in France hadn't had much information themselves, frequently moved from one provisional location to the next, and were poorly equipped in the first place. Nevertheless, he made a mental note to talk to this controller when he got down and thank him for being informative. It was always a good thing to cultivate a good relationship with your controllers.

"Redcap Leader, your bandit is weaving about. Vector 100."

"He's probably trying to find a break in the cloud," Priestman explained. "It's 6/10s to 7/10s overhere."

"Right oh."

There was a lull while Priestman searched the sky ahead of him, not forgetting to keep an eye on the sun, which was rapidly getting higher and more intense. He checked his watch. Nine minutes since he'd asked the controller to scramble his Duty Section. If 606 was good, they'd be in the air already. He thought he'd check. "Beetle, Redcap Leader here; what's the status of my Duty Section? Are they airborne yet?"

There was a pause, which was surprising. A controller usually knew the status of any scrambled section. Finally, the controller answered, "I'm sorry, Redcap Leader. They seem to be having a little delay. I'll let you know as soon as they're airborne."

Priestman wasn't listening any more. He'd just glimpsed movement to his left. He looked again. A Junkers 88 was flying a good 3,000 feet below him and weaving among the clouds to keep a good view of the ground below.

Priestman switched on the gunsight, switched the gun button on fire, and checked the sky around and above him again. "Beetle, I've got the bandit in sight. You're sure he's alone out here?"

"We've had no reports of snappers."

Good. Priestman climbed towards the sun, putting himself between it and the Junkers. One last look over both shoulders out of sheer habit, and then he tipped the wing down and dived for his prey. It was the perfect bounce. Robin felt it in every nerve, and the exhilaration of the dive was magnified as he came up below and behind the Junkers.

The German aircraft loomed in his sights, the black crosses outlined in white getting larger by the second. The hunting instinct was tremendously powerful, Robin registered in a detached part of his brain. He lined up his sights on the starboard engine, holding his fire, getting closer. He resisted the almost instinctive urge to check his tail, and opened fire.

He held the gun button down. The Hurricane staggered a little, but she was a wonderfully steady gun platform. The tracer went true, thick and fast. The cowling of the enemy's starboard engine shattered, exposing the mechanism. A blue-yellow flame leapt up; black smoke billowed backwards. Yet in the next instant the Junkers flick-quarter-rolled and dropped right out of his sights.

Priestman cursed himself soundly for being caught off guard. He'd just been out-flown by a bloody bomber pilot! He took off after his quarry, but it was gone in cloud. "Bugger!"

"What was that, Redcap?"

"I've lost him in cloud, Beetle."

"Bad luck."

Priestman tried to out-think the bomber pilot. He'd been hit in one engine and his primary concern would be getting home. He would also avoid flying straight and level. In his shoes, Priestman thought he'd turn south and – if the engine permitted – try to gain some altitude. He plunged into the cloud and started a shallow climb. When he re-emerged, he found himself utterly alone in the sky. Cursing, he searched the sky systematically. Abruptly, the Junkers lift out of a cloud on his left. He shoved the throttle through the wire and went after it.

The German gunner was alert. Although too far away to fire at the pursuing Hurricane, he was clearly giving instructions to his pilot.

The Junkers stood on a wingtip again and, although it briefly presented a magnificent target, it was out of range. Then the Junkers scuttled into the next cloud.

They kept it up for another ten minutes, and then abruptly Control cut in again. "Redcap, are you over water?"

"*Our* Channel, yes."

"Let him go, Redcap. Pancake."

Priestman considered that order for a moment. If he'd had the Junkers in sight, he probably would have ignored it, but it had just disappeared into cloud again.

"Do you read, Redcap? Pancake."

"Understood." As he turned to obey, Priestman remembered the Duty Section that should have reinforced him long ago. "What ever happened to my Duty Section, Beetle?"

"They are ready for take-off now, Redcap Leader, but there's no point in scrambling them any more."

Priestman checked his watch. It was 28 minutes since he'd asked to have the section scrambled. They had been on 15- minute availability. That was bad. Much worse than he'd expected. Priestman had never heard of an active squadron that couldn't scramble in *less* than 15 minutes. He turned west and sank gently down to 10,000 feet, where it was warmer and he could go off oxygen. He picked up Beachy Head below him on the right and followed the coastline home. It was nice to be at Tangmere, where he knew the land better than the back of his hand.

He was greeted by Flight Sergeant Rowe, who asked if everything was all right with the aircraft. Priestman assured him that all was fine and climbed down. Once his feet touched the ground, he shoved his helmet off and ran his fingers through his hair. Rowe at once pointed out two Leading Aircraftmen, who were also waiting for him. "LAC Ripley will be your fitter, sir, and LAC Appleby your rigger, whichever aircraft you choose to fly."

"Thank you, 'R' seems fine." Priestman replied to the Chief and then, despite being in a hurry to get over to dispersal, he took the moment to shake hands with his crew and asked them about themselves.

"I apprenticed with Rolls-Royce, sir," Ripley told him. "Joined up in April '39."

"Merlins?" Priestman asked hopefully.

Ripley nodded proudly. "Yes, sir." Priestman turned to Appleby.

"Ship's welder from the age of 14, sir – until I joined up in '38." Then, whether from frustration or impudence, Appleby added bluntly, "I joined the Air Force because I wanted to learn to fly, sir."

"Do you still want to fly?" Priestman answered, looking more amused than surprised.

"Yes, sir!" Appleby replied, his whole ugly face lighting up.

"Have you ever been airborne?"

"No, sir." Appleby at once looked rather dejected.

"Your enthusiasm may wane when you are," Priestman told him seriously, but then grinned and added "—or increase. We'll have to put it to the test. Now, I'd better get over to dispersal."

He took the time to step out of his Sidcot suit, however, and left the parachute and his flight jacket on the wing of the Hurricane. He was thus wearing his service uniform, the rank insignia clearly visible, as he started towards the dispersal on the far side of the field. It was a long walk, but it gave him time to prepare for what lay ahead.

He was much more keyed up than he would have liked to be or wanted to let on. In fact, he had not slept at all, because his mind was simply too stimulated by the impressions he'd gathered and the things he wanted – needed – to do. It was obvious last night that he was going to have to act fast to get a firm grip on this squadron, but the failure to scramble in 15 minutes focused things. He sensed that he was facing a confrontation, but there was nothing to do but meet it head-on.

A stiff wind drove the clouds briskly across the sky so that their shadows raced across the field, changing the patterns on its face rapidly. The windsock stood straight out, and the airmen's tents billowed and shook. Because of that wind and the morning chill, the pilots were gathered inside the dispersal hut. The deck chairs lay about unused outside. It had just gone 6.05 am. "A" Flight had been scheduled to go on fifteen-minute availability starting at 5.00 am. He'd asked Control to scramble the Duty Section at 5.10. Priestman checked the blackboard as he went inside. Red Section, led (as expected) by Fl/Lt Thompson, was Duty Section.

Priestman stepped into the dispersal and took in the scene spread out before him. The pilots were sprawled about on chairs or slouching against an iron stove. They wore bits and pieces of uniforms, supplemented by roll-neck jumpers, silk scarves, and a woollen vest in one case. Only three of them had their Mae Wests on. Those were the objective factors that Priestman could catalogue.

In addition, a thousand intangibles set off intuitive alarms. For a start, Priestman knew he'd been seen, yet all the pilots pretended not to notice him. They let him stand in the doorway surveying the scene without any apparent indication of curiosity, let alone greeting.

"It is customary," Priestman started slowly, "to get to your feet when your commanding officer enters the room."

A man with the two rings of a Flight Lieutenant was lying more than sitting in a chair and reading the sports pages of a newspaper. He glanced up with deliberate slowness, pretended to have only just seen Priestman, and with provocative non-chalance got to his feet. He saluted – after a fashion. The other pilots followed his lead, all warily watching for Priestman's response.

"Flight Lieutenant Thompson, I presume." Priestman opened.

"That's right, sir."

"You and the rest of A Flight were on fifteen-minute availability from five o'clock this morning, I believe."

"That's right, sir." Thompson answered, apparently unconcerned.

"What took you so long to get scrambled?"

"Sir?"

"Your Duty Section was scrambled at 5.10 this morning and not in the air 25 minutes later. Could you explain that to me?"

Thompson frowned but answered in a self-confident tone, as though he felt no shame, "The transport was late at the Mess, sir."

"Sorry. I'm not sure I understood you, just now. Are you saying you were not *already* here at dispersal at 5 am?"

"No. The WAAF from MT was late, and we didn't get away from the Mess until just after 5, isn't that so, Barry?" He explicitly sought support, only increasing Priestman's contempt for him.

The Flying Officer addressed came to his assistance. "Absolutely, sir. We waited and waited, but the lorry just didn't show up—"

"So why didn't you start walking?" Tangmere was an older airfield with decidedly more humane dimensions than many of the newer ones. There was no answer, so Priestman decided he had made his point, and continued. "If anyone in this squadron is late for readiness in future, they'll be posted. Furthermore, starting tomorrow, you will report for duty in proper uniform. The only exception allowed is to wear a scarf in place of a tie."

Thompson rolled his eyes provocatively, adding, "I'm sure things in Training Command are a bit more spit-and-polish, sir, but some of us have been fighting the war for the last three months."

Priestman could feel them all staring at him with bated breath, watching for his reaction. They reminded him of a pack of hounds waiting to see if a challenge to their leader was going to succeed or not. Priestman was so keyed up that he was absolutely calm. "I see. Are you suggesting, Flight Lieutenant, that you are getting fed up with this 'readiness' business and think it's someone else's turn to bear the brunt of the Battle?" Priestman sounded almost solicitous.

"Yes," Thompson replied in a tone of genuine grievance, "yes, I *am* getting rather tired of it all. You know, we were thrown into that total cock-up over Dunkirk and weren't given even a month's rest before we got chucked in again. There are other squadrons that haven't had a go at the Hun at all. All seems rather unfair, don't you think? Not to mention that none of us would have to be doing this at all if that madman Churchill would just accept Hitler's reasonable peace proposal. The PM's a bloody, irresponsible adventurer, and this is going to be another Gallipoli, if Halifax doesn't get him to see sense soon."

Priestman didn't answer. He was too furious, or was it frightened? Never in his life had he imagined things might be *this* bad. He turned to look at the others, still waiting with bated breath. It took considerable effort to keep his voice level as he asked them, "Do any of the rest of you feel like that?"

"Well, what would be so wrong with doing a deal with Hitler if it would stop this bloody war? And why *don't* they rotate squadrons in out of 13 and 10 Group, Sir?" the Flying Officer, who had supported Thompson earlier, asked.

"What is your name, Flying Officer?"

"Dunsire, sir. Barry Dunsire."

"You feel you're in need of a rest?"

"It wouldn't hurt. If you'd been here these last weeks, you'd understand better, sir."

"I think I understand well enough," Priestman countered. He turned and went into the cubicle at the back of the hut, in which an airman clerk guarded the telephone connected to the Ops Room. He asked for a connection to the Station Commander.

Within minutes the tannoy was squawking loudly: "606 Squadron, 'B' Flight: report to dispersal IMMEDIATELY. Repeat: 'B' Flight 606 Squadron: report to dispersal IMMEDIATELY."

Within a quarter of an hour, the pilots of "B" Flight came tumbling into the dispersal, looking disheveled and apprehensive. Flying Officer Ringwood pushed past the others, looked around, and identified his new commanding officer at once. He saluted, and then asked anxiously, "What's the flap, sir?"

"I'm posting two officers of 'A' Flight away from the squadron." Priestman indicated Thompson and Dunsire as if they were pieces of furniture.

"You're doing what?!" Thompson protested furiously. "You can't—"

"But I can. I've already spoken to the Station Commander. Besides, I am only responding to your own request. You said you needed a rest, Flight Lieutenant."

"I said the whole squadron needs a rest!"

"None of the others, except Flying Officer Dunsire, seemed to feel so strongly about it. Now, I want both of you out of here by noon. You have leave until new orders arrive."

"You can't do this!" Thompson protested once more, raising his voice this time, and now he got a supportive chorus of protests from several of the others in A Flight and Ringwood as well. They all were saying things like "if you'd been here" or "we were only trying to tell you what it was like." Priestman let them protest until they realised they were getting no response and fell silent on their own.

"You have your orders, Flight Lieutenant, Flying Officer. If you want to dispute them, see the Station Commander, but get out of this dispersal. I need to talk to my squadron."

This time Thompson and Dunsire left, but Priestman could hear their indignant protesting voices as they retreated towards the Mess. Thompson was saying he'd call his father and Dowding and the Air Minister.... Priestman closed his ears to it all and focused on the tense young men standing uneasily in front of him.

"Until replacements arrive, I'll lead A Flight myself. The flights will be reorganised as follows." Robin went to the blackboard and erased the Order of Battle as it stood. He divided the board into two columns headed by A and B. He put himself under A and Ringwood under B, and then listed the rest of the pilots randomly, trying to distribute ranks about equally.

"Furthermore, for those of you who didn't hear it, starting tomorrow, no one will come on duty out of uniform, with the exception of a scarf instead of a tie if they wish. Now, I'm going to take A Flight up for some unit training immediately, and while we're at it, B Flight is on Readiness. Is everything clear, F/O Ringwood?"

"Yes, sir."

By noon Priestman had flown with both Flights, and he headed for the Mess to get lunch. Before he reached the dining room, Mickey intercepted him. "Sir, could we have a quick chat?"

"Of course."

"It's about the officers you chopped. It doesn't have anything to do with what I said last night, does it?" Mickey was feeling terribly guilty for having been rather critical in his introductions.

"Of course not," Priestman assured him. Did it? Had he been influenced by the Adjutant's candid answers?

Mickey continued in a worried tone, "But, sir, can we really afford that just now, sir? Doing without two pilots, two *experienced* pilots."

"Two jaded pilots. This isn't about them being a bit cheeky, Mickey – although Thompson was certainly that. Thompson was on 15-minute availability and 25 minutes later he was still on the ground. By then, a bomber he might have intercepted was half-way across the Channel. Jerry got home with a belly full of valuable photos, and Thompson was here having a cup of tea. Worse: he tried to pin the blame on some innocent driver. I've already checked with the MT Officer, and he confirmed that his driver was sitting out in front of the Mess waiting for 'A' Flight for more than 20 minutes. There are few things I hate more than officers who try to blame subordinates for their own failings. That's unacceptable in my squadron, but it's not the reason I gave him the chop."

Robin paused to be sure Mickey was paying attention. Then he explained, "Thompson had the arrogance − or stupidity − to express a negative opinion about the PM in the presence of the entire flight. Worse: despite being a Flight Commander, he suggested in front of pilots on the front line of battle that we should do a deal with Hitler -- and Dunsire agreed with him." The words were acid with outrage. "I won't have either of them in this squadron. If Thompson's said things like that before, it's no wonder this squadron is in the state it's in! If that man stays a day longer, he will destroy what morale is left among the others!"

Mickey dabbed at his receding hairline with his handkerchief unhappily. He considered telling Priestman that the heretical views came from Jones' father in the Foreign Office, but then decided it didn't matter.

"I'm on my way to lunch. Why don't you join me?" Robin suggested in a warmer tone, anxious to make peace with his adjutant. "I believe you had a long list of 'unfinished business' that needed my attention," he added in a clear gesture of reconciliation.

"Oh, you can look at that later," Mickey replied, embarrassed. "You need a bite to eat before facing all the paperwork." But then he added hopefully, "But I could bring it over to dispersal later this afternoon, if you like?"

"Good. Then you'll join me for lunch?" Robin persisted.

"Yes, sir." Mickey looked pleased by his insistence, Robin noted, and he was glad he had.

He had barely started eating, when the klaxon went off, scrambling both 606 and 17. He left his dinner standing and dashed out. "B" Flight was already running to their Hurricanes. Ripley handed him his parachute as he scrambled up into the cockpit. "Where's your Mae West, sir?"

Priestman had left it in the Mess. "Nevermind. Is she re-armed?"

"Yes, sir, but the battery didn't recharge properly. I'd like...."

Priestman wasn't listening as he did his final cockpit check. He switched on the R/T while starting for the head of the runway. The other memebers of "A" flight were waddling behind him, while "B" flight was already on the circuit waiting for them. "Beetle, what have you got for us?"

"To be honest, Redcap, I don't know yet." Priestman resolved for the second time today to get to know this controller. He liked his honesty and tone. "What the RDF shows is two raids coming in quite low. Yours is at 40+, but we've no Observer Corps confirmation on type yet. Either it's a low-level bombing raid going for Portsmouth docks or the Supermarine works – or it's a fake."

"A fake?"

"Other sectors are reporting 109s doing fighter sweeps on their own – strafing and generally making a nuisance of themselves, but not doing any serious harm."

"Trying to lure us up."

"That's what it looks like."

"Thanks." Priestman took off, climbed rapidly and took over the lead of his squadron. He hadn't had time to explain, much less train them in, the tactics he'd developed in his mind over the last month. So all he could do was order a conventional RAF formation, namely Close Vics, Sections Close Echelon Starboard. S/P Green was flying Red Two on his right and P/O Debsen was Red Three on his left.

The controller meanwhile vectored them due west over Chichester, passing Portsmouth on their left. Ahead of them Southampton Water shimmered under broken cloud and, straining his eyes, Robin thought he could make out the Supermarine works at Woolston. If that was their intended target, they should have contact soon.

"Snappers, Redcap Leader!" It was Green's unmistakable Canadian voice – an octave higher than usual and very excited.

"Where?"

"Over the Solent! About 20,000 feet. They're coming for us!"

"Well done, Green. Turn left into them." There appeared to be about 40 enemy aircraft in a large swarm. That meant roughly four apiece. A bit daunting, but it didn't really worry Priestman. The Huns would pretty much get in each other's way.

In Training Command Robin had been required to read intelligence reports, and of course he followed the papers, particularly articles by American reporters still inside the Third Reich. They made a lot of the German fighter aces, who had run up incredible scores. Allegedly the three top Luftwaffe aces – Mölders, Galland and Wick – were all credited with more than fifty kills each.

It crossed Robin's mind, as the German formation swung into position with obvious and admirable ease, that he might be facing one of those aces. In which case, that lead aircraft, well protected by a wingman on his right and a pair of supporting fighters on his left, was very deadly. He was also focusing his attention on Robin, sending the rest of his large formation out to his left to take on 606's other sections.

Priestman could not afford to think only of his own approaching duel with the German, however. "Spread out, everyone! MacLeod, come up on my left. Give yourselves plenty of room to manoeuvre and aim for the leaders."

Priestman looked right to see that his order was obeyed and was satisfied. He then glanced left and registered with a shock that there didn't seem to be anyone there at all. "Debsen, MacLeod," Robin ordered, "cover me to port!"

The response was a very rude "You fooking bastard!" from the Scotsman.

There was no time for more orders, however. He was closing at a rate of nearly 700 mph with the lead Messerschmitt. The range of the Messerschmitt's cannon was greater than that of the Hurricane's machine guns. Priestman couldn't allow the German to get a good bead on him, and that meant abrupt and unpredictable movements. He therefore jerked up and then down and then opened fire on the 109 still coming straight towards him.

It was firing back, and the stream of tracer arched over the glass of his canopy. Priestman shoved the throttle through the wire and stalled out under the belly of the enemy.

The rest of the Germans were still falling out of the sky, and Priestman reefed the Hurricane around tightly in the glide and started taking pot shots at "targets of opportunity." He could see several Hurricanes dogfighting hard but did not catch their letters. In fact, most of the action had already moved east and north, leaving him behind in his stalled aircraft. Time to take care of that. He reached forward and tried to restart the engine. Nothing. He tried again. The engine didn't even sputter. It was as if the battery were completely dead. It took a moment for him to register and believe what was happening. After several more attempts, the realization penetrated his brain: his brand-new Hurricane had just failed him.

He was gliding down very gently. He had his parachute – but no Mae West. Well, he was over Spithead; there was a good chance the Navy would pick him up. But how fast? Could he really swim for several hours? The channel was cold and dirty. But his drifting Hurricane was bound to attract attention. If the 109s came back for him....

They were there already. A pair of them. Coming straight at him. The leader's cannons were flashing. He felt them punch into the side of the Hurricane – bang, bang, bang – then they were gone. No, not really, just swinging around for another pass. Time to get out and trust the Navy. He could swim after all. Stupid about the Mae West. What an inauspicious start to his command....

Priestman shoved the canopy back and started to get out, but the 109s were rushing at him again. He scrambled back into the cover of the armour-plated seat and the bullet-proof windscreen, crouching down as low as possible in the seat. He braced for the punches of the cannon, eyes closed. Pray God they don't make a direct hit. The cannon of a 109 would literally blow him apart.

The cannon fire didn't come. He opened his eyes. The 109s were wheeling around in front of him. He could see the lead pilot look over, wave, and then dive away towards the Isle of Wight.

That left him stunned for a moment. They must have seen him trying to get out and decided to treat him as "finished" without delivering the Coup de Grace. That was very chivalrous of them, given that he was over his own territory. Would he have done the same for one of them? He'd think about that later. Whatever else happened, today he owed his life to a chivalrous German pilot.

For a moment, Robin wondered whether it might have been one of the aces, but then dismissed the thought. The aircraft he had first engaged had continued forward, east and north with the milling dogfight. These two that had come for a lame duck were not the leaders, but more likely a couple of novices still full of romantic ideas about being "Knights of the Air." Better stop wasting thought on irrelevancies and focus again on his immediate situation.

The sky was utterly empty. He was still gliding down gently, horizontal and only very slowly losing altitude – the Hurricane was a true lady at times like this. There was cloud about, but Robin knew this coast. He'd sailed it all his life. Below him was Hayling Island, with Thorney Island beyond. Coastal Command had an airfield there. He'd make for that. Careful not to lose more momentum or altitude than absolutely necessary, Robin gently banked to starboard and adjusted his course to east-by-east-northeast.

As he got closer it became clear that to land at Thorney, he'd have to circle her down. That seemed a shame with Tangmere only a few miles further. "Beetle, Redcap Leader here."

The answer came back like a shot – as if the controller had been holding his breath, waiting for this call. "Good to hear you, Redcap Leader. Where are you?"

"Oh, gliding over Thorney Island at 7,000 feet. I'm going to try to glide her in."

"Engine's packed up?"

"Yes. What of the others?"

"All back safe."

"Good."

"Indeed. Right, then." After a short pause, the Controller was back, announcing, "Observer Corps have spotted you, Redcap Leader. Try to keep south of Chichester so you can make a soft landing if you have to."

A short while later, Robin reported: "I've got the *Old Ship* on my port beam."

"Well done. If you make it to Tangmere, I'll take you to dinner there."

"Well, in that case, I'll try harder."

"What's your altitude?"

"Four and half."

"Good."

They kept up the chatter right to the end. The only bad moment was as he turned into the circuit and realised that the wind was still gusting badly from the southwest – and while this had helped bring him home, it meant he had to do a half circuit to come in head-to-wind. He made it without incident. The Hurricane rolled to a stop almost directly before the hangar, like a horse heading for the barn.

Then, after the serenity of gliding home on a favourable breeze, all hell seemed to break loose. Rowe and the Appleby – one on either wing – were shoving back the canopy. An ambulance wailed up along with a fire truck. The bowser hovered just a short way off. Bit of a contradiction sending the bowser and the fire-truck at the same time, Robin registered, and then he accepted Appleby's hand to climb out of the cockpit. "Are you all right, sir?" Appleby asked anxiously.

"Why shouldn't I be?"

"Sergeant Green said two of the bastards were hammering you, while you tried to get out of the cockpit. There *are* cannon holes all along the fuselage!" The aircraftman pointed out the holes in the brand-new Hurricane.

Priestman gave them hardly a glance. "Remarkably bad shots, some of these Germans. Check the engine. It stalled on me at an awkward moment, and nothing I tried could restart it. Battery problem possibly. Be sure 'S' is fuelled and armed for me, would you, Appleby."

"Don't worry about 'S,' sir. She's already ready for you."

"Well done."

He dropped off the wing and stood a moment catching his breath. Funny. He hadn't felt any tension in the air at all, but now he felt he could use a drink. Bad idea. It was early afternoon, and although the Hun wasn't out in force yet, he was snooping about. Furthermore, for his first engagement as Squadron Leader things hadn't exactly gone as planned.

Of course, he hadn't reckoned with having his aircraft stall on him. It had never happened before. Factory-new Hurricane! But whatever his excuse, he'd failed to keep overall control of the squadron, and frankly hadn't the foggiest idea what had happened to the others.

A Flight Lieutenant with an eye patch and the spy, whose name he'd forgotten, were coming towards him. What a pair – one with a wooden leg and the other with a black patch over his eye. "Well, if you don't look like a couple of pirates," Priestman greeted them.

The man with a patch over his eye managed to smile, and it triggered a memory. "Don't I know you from somewhere?" Robin asked him.

The controller held out his hand. "Bainbridge, sir. I was at Cranwell –"

"Of course; a year behind me. What did you do to your eye?" Robin asked, very glad to have a familiar face around.

"Managed to knock it out on a telephone pole on an icy road."

"Silly thing to do."

"Very. I'm one of the controllers here–"

"Did you just talk me in?"

"Yes, that's right. I owe you dinner at the *Ship*–"

"Nonsense – though I'd be happy to have dinner with you there or anywhere. I've been meaning to drop by and meet you ever since this morning. Best controlling I've ever had – informative and candid."

The sincerity with which Priestman said it embarrassed Bridges, who found himself stammering. "Thank you. I try. Actually, I – or rather we," he indicated the stern-looking intelligence officer, "thought you ought to see the transcript of today's sortie."

"Transcript? You make transcripts?"

"Not all the time, sir, but I have a WAAF on the watch who's wizard at taking short-hand, and Squadron Leader Allars thought it would help him sort out the claims, so when she can manage, she takes down what is piped in. Not always very pleasant, I'm afraid."

"I can imagine! Poor girl! I hope she's not the sensitive kind!"

Bridges smiled. "Most WAAF are much more sensible than we give them credit for," he replied and held out a sheaf of papers, remarking as Priestman took them, "I'd better get over to the Mess or there won't be any lunch left. Pleasure having you here, sir." Bridges added.

"'Robin,' for God's sake!" Priestman countered.

"Thanks – and I go by Bridges, in case you've forgotten."

Robin had, but he just smiled and waved. Then he leaned back against the trailing edge of the wing and started glancing through the transcript. Within only a few seconds it riveted him; it appeared that Debsen had simply dropped out of the fight as soon as the enemy was sighted.

MacLeod – seeing this – had shouted at him – indeed, threatened to kill him – and then chased off *after him* rather than engaging the enemy. It seemed so incredible that he read the transcript twice. Then he looked at the Intelligence Officer, who was watching him very carefully, leaning heavily on his cane.

"Has this happened before?"

"Not quite so blatantly."

"What exactly does that mean?"

"Jones usually assigned Debsen Tail-End-Charlie in Sections Line Astern. Sometimes the Germans bounced him before he had a chance to get away. Sometimes he developed 'engine' or 'oxygen' or whatever trouble before an engagement. The Chiefy reported repeatedly that the crews sometimes worked all night trying to *find* something wrong, but there wasn't anything wrong. He's changed aircraft several times, and the aircraft only develop problems when he's flying them. If none of those things happened, then he simply came back with a report that didn't quite fit with the others. This is the first time someone saw him turn away."

"Have you debriefed them?"

"MacLeod is calling him a coward and saying that if he isn't hanged, he'll kill him with his own hands."

"Lovely. And what does Debsen say?"

"Why don't you talk to him yourself, sir? He's changed his story on me twice."

"Right." Priestman folded the transcript together, stuffed it in the inside pocket of his tunic and walked over to the dispersal hut. He called P/O Debsen outside into the windy sunshine. "Pilot Officer Debsen, would you mind telling me what happened just now?"

"I've already reported to the spy! You were there, sir—"

"Unfortunately, I was distracted by engine trouble. I want to hear what happened from you."

Debsen clamped his jaw shut and looked resentfully at his CO. Priestman stared him down. "Well, we got jumped and you ordered us to turn into them, and the next thing I knew there was a 109 on my tail. So, I dived for the deck, to try to shake him off. He was firing at me the whole time. I don't know how he missed. It's a miracle, actually. Maybe he was a beginner. Anyway, he ran out of ammo or gave up and turned away, so I returned to Tangmere." It was said in one unbroken flood of words. When he fell silent, the young pilot waited, his face still set in its indignant-defensive expression.

Priestman's eyes sought the distance, while inwardly cursing himself. Why had he been so bloody hasty this morning? Why had he posted both Thompson and Dunsire? Thompson had been necessary, but Dunsire's misdeeds now seemed insignificant: backing up a friend and leader. Debsen was a much greater threat to the squadron. Not only did his actions endanger the rest, his example could corrupt new pilots. At least two new pilots – very likely four – would be joining the squadron in the next few days. Priestman could not allow them to witness this kind of cowardice. He had been wrong about Dunsire, but that wouldn't make it right to keep Debsen. At last he turned back and looked straight at the nervously defiant young man: "Debsen, you have to go."

"Sir?"

Priestman pulled the transcript from his pocket and gave it to Debsen.

Debsen just stared at it without taking it into his hand. He swallowed.

"It's not ambiguous, Debsen. And it's not the first time. The ground crews are fed up with looking for problems that aren't there – and I can't afford to have them wasting time on imaginary problems when there are so many real ones. You put me at risk today. Tomorrow it might be one of our new, inexperienced pilots you leave in the lurch."

"My fitter's not up to the mark, sir. He—"

"Don't you dare try to put the blame for this on your ground crew! What happened today had nothing to do with any deficiency in your kite!"

Debsen realised that he'd just slipped up, and he held his tongue, his face fixed in a sullen expression.

Priestman said softly, "Go back to the Mess, pack your things and leave the station before we come off duty. Leave without any fuss or farewells. Just disappear as if you had never been here."

"But—"

"There isn't any 'but'."

Debsen still hesitated; then he turned and walked away very quickly.

Allars watched him go. "Three in eight hours. Must be some kind of a record."

"Jerry did it in one."

"True.... That's nearly 20%."

"Which one do you disagree with?"

"Not Debsen."

"And the others?"

Allars shrugged. "You're the CO."

"So I am," and with that Priestman entered the dispersal hut.

They waited all afternoon. The cloud cover gradually increased to about 9/10 and the Germans stayed away. At 18.00 they were stood down. The others went back to the Mess in a cluster of comrades. Priestman went alone to the same building.

Park arrived after dark. Priestman was in the Mess having a drink with Bridges when someone put his head in the door and called, "Heads up! It's the AOC!"

Priestman had the sinking feeling he was the cause of this unscheduled visit, and with trepidation got to his feet along with the others. The unmistakable, lean figure in his white overalls and helmet emerged. Park waved them to ease at once, and the Station Commander was quick to take him to the bar. Park kept glancing around, however, until he spotted Priestman. He signalled him over at once.

"So, Priestman, how was your first day with 606?" Park inquired pleasantly.

Although he didn't know the AOC had found out, Priestman had the feeling the AOC already knew about everything that had happened. He answered honestly, "Eventful, sir."

"So, I hear. Was your experience in the 109 any use to you in the scrap?"

"I didn't even think about it, sir," Robin admitted.

"I understand you have done a little weeding out." Park was watching Priestman intently, but it was hard to tell if he approved or disapproved. Then he added, "I had a phone call from a Conservative MP this afternoon. A Mr. Thompson." Priestman held his breath and waited for the blow to fall. "Of course, I told him that a squadron commander has the right to post *any* member of his squadron, but I must admit I've never heard of a Squadron Leader posting three pilots in one day before. Certainly not in the middle of an enemy offensive."

"Flight Lieutenant Thompson was commanding the duty section on 15-minute availability and not airborne after half an hour. I can't accept that, sir, and I told him so. I would have left it there, however, had he not — in front of the entire flight — called the PM a madman and suggested we should submit to Hitler."

Park flinched ever so slightly and considered Priestman searchingly for another moment in silence. Then he remarked dryly, "So, you're now seven pilots short of full complement."

"And I have no experienced flight commanders," Priestman admitted rather sheepishly. Might as well be hung for a sheep as a lamb....

"Um hum." Park looked at him as if to say: "Well, that is your fault and so your problem." But after a moment he asked simply, "Any suggestions?"

"For Flight Commanders, no, sir. But I'd like to have a couple of the pilots I trained myself, if that's not too much to ask."

Park nodded.

"And I think I can lower the casualty rate and increase effectiveness if you'd give me a free hand with regard to formation, sir." It was out, and from the reaction of the men around him Priestman feared he'd gone too far.

Park considered him hard and then, after a pause, he continued in a conversational tone, "I'm listening."

He wasn't the only one. The entire bar seemed deathly still, and Robin noticed that Bridges and Mickey and several of his pilots had drifted closer. He took a deep breath. "We need to fly in pairs, like the Germans do. One pilot concentrates on hunting, the other on protecting the hunter. Pairs can work together in sections of four, or flights of six, or squadrons of twelve – but the principle remains the same. A knight and squire." (The simile had come to him listening to Emily talk about her knights.) "One does the killing; the other ensures he isn't hit from behind. And the pairs fly in loose formation, so everyone can concentrate on watching the sky."

Park nodded. "It makes sense to me, and I've heard similar suggestions from other commanders – mostly men who, like you, flew in France. On the other hand, some squadron commanders swear by vics or line-astern. I'm reluctant to impose any particular tactic. I want every squadron leader to decide for himself what tactics he wants to use – provided, of course, his pilots can be taught to use them."

Park pointedly turned to Allars. "Doug, good to see you. What are you drinking?" Priestman and the others immediately understood that they had been dismissed and withdrew discreetly.

Park and Allars took their drinks to a corner table.

"And?" Allars asked.

"You were right. He had to do it. But it was still a huge risk." Park paused, drew a deep breath and admitted. "I sometimes wonder if we aren't asking too much of them. Priestman's only 24 years old...."

"And how old were you when you took command of 48 squadron in the last war?"

"Twenty-five, but that's not the point. Whether we like to admit it or not, our role in the last war was ancillary; the war was won by the army and navy. This time, the RAF is practically alone. Furthermore, the consequences of failure are infinitely worse. I don't know what terms the Kaiser would have dictated had he won the war, but it was unlikely to have included occupation of the British Isles." He took a sip of his gin and tonic. Then continued. "Make no mistake, Doug, the situation is extremely precarious. The margin of error is razor thin. The only reason the swastika isn't flying over Buckingham Palace is because of that lot of schoolboys over there," he gestured with his head towards the gaggle of pilots clustered around the bar and getting increasingly rowdy.

Again, he paused before adding thoughtfully, "and a handful of slightly more mature flight and squadron leaders. In short, the fate of this nation hinges on the ability of less than a hundred flight and squadron leaders to train, mold and lead a thousand youths too young to vote. That's why I have to take a chance on Priestman; at least he knows what's at stake."

Allars nodded soberly. From the radio at the bar came the unmistakable voice of the PM, and the airman behind the bar at once turned up the radio.

"The gratitude of every home on our island, in our Empire and indeed throughout the world, except in the abodes of the guilty, goes out to the British airmen who, undaunted by the odds, unwearied by their constant challenge and mortal danger, are turning the tide of world war by their prowess and their devotion."

Around the room conversation came to a halt, and men turned to look towards the radio in astonishment.

"Never in the field of human conflict was so much owed by so many to so few. All our hearts go out to the Fighter Pilots, whose brilliant actions we see with our own eyes each day.

Chapter 26

Crépon, France
21 August 1940

"Fatty's gone and given Galland and Mölders *Geschwader*," Christian announced, as Ernst arrived for breakfast. It was at a "civilised" time this morning, because the *Staffel* wasn't slated to fly escort until the afternoon. Morning fog clung to the Channel, delaying all flying.

Ernst whistled. He'd known that Goering had given the leading aces the Golden Flyer's Badge with diamonds at his hunting lodge, Karinhall, on this past Sunday. The papers had been full of pictures of them grinning beside the Reichsmarshall, shotguns over their arms, the slaughtered partridges inevitably likened to their mounting score of Spitfires and Hurricanes. Still, for all their legendary success as hunters, they were very junior – still majors – and to command a *Geschwader* was to command three *Gruppe* of three *Staffel* each, or roughly 100 aircraft and more than 1500 men. That was a lot of responsibility. Ernst considered Christian's expression and asked hesitantly, "Isn't that good?"

"Good? What's good about it? The Gallands and Mölders of this world only care about their personal glory. Haven't you heard? Their entire *Gruppe* had to hover about 'protecting' them while they attacked alone – bounce after bounce, running up their own score. Is that the most effective use of 40 fighters? Now, I suppose, they'll expect the whole damned *Geschwader* to 'protect' them! Glad we aren't in JG 26 or 51!"

"Ah, *Freiherr* von Feldburg, seeing the best in everything, as usual." Fischer thumped himself down in the chair opposite and shoved his cap back on his head.

Ernst sat up straighter and waited for what would happen next. Christian just remained as he was, side to the table, his long legs stretched out and crossed at the booted ankles.

"I do have some good news, you know. We aren't flying escort this afternoon. We've been given a free hunt again."

Christian sat up straighter. "That's more like it!"

"Apparently, Galland and Mölders talked Fatty into more of them."

"Of course! Gives them a better chance to run up their own scores." Christian's tone was instantly sneering again.

"Don't be jealous, Feldburg. It demeans you. Your own score *could* be higher, after all...."

Christian looked sharply at Ernst, but he knew Ernst hadn't betrayed him. Ernst had offered to lie for him outright. As Christian jumped down after returning from yesterday's sortie, Ernst had been waiting for him. He asked in a low voice, "Do you want me to say I saw it go in?"

"Of course not," Christian had retorted.

"But we can't claim it as it is," Ernst had protested in distress. "The engine was dead and the pilot was about to bail out, but we scared him back inside."

"So, we don't claim it," Christian told him simply. "We don't say anything about it at all."

Ernst had done just as Christian wanted. So how had the CO found out about it? Or was he referring to something else? Ernst noticed his hands were sweating, and he rubbed his palms on his trousers nervously.

But Fischer stood up again. "You need to decide what it is you want, Feldburg. Not knowing might be dangerous one day."

RAF Tangmere

An airman shook Ginger awake, calling urgently. "Sergeant! Wake up! You've got to get up!"

"But we're not on readiness until this afternoon," Ginger protested, still half asleep, his fine, red hair falling into his eyes, his pyjamas twisted as he turned over in answer to the disturbance.

"It's not readiness, sir. You have a telephone call. At reception, sir."

"A phone call? For me?" Ginger couldn't remember ever receiving a telephone call before. He threw the covers aside and staggered – still not fully awake – out of bed. Green turned over and pulled the blankets up over his ear, muttering something vaguely rude. Ginger grabbed his dressing gown from the back of the door and stuffed his bare feet into slippers, and then went out into the corridor. It was quiet. Most of the sergeants were already at their posts. Only the pilots had the morning off. It was a gloomy morning; fog clung to the ground, dimming the light from the windows.

It could only be his Dad. No one else would phone him. Or had something happened to his Dad? What if there had been some kind of accident? His father was doing that thatching job. What if he'd fallen off the roof and broken his back like Sanders? Ginger started moving faster.

He hurried down the stairs. In the reception was a switchboard manned by a WAAF. She motioned him to one of the wooden phone booths, and a moment later the telephone in it rang. Ginger grabbed the receiver. "Bowles. Sergeant Pilot Bowles," he improved.

"Ginger?"

It was his Dad's voice. Ginger let out a long sigh of relief. "Did you hear the PM's speech last night, lad?" The senior Bowles sounded excited, almost breathless.

The swing in emotions had been too rapid, and Ginger found his eyes watering. Annoyed with his weakness, acutely aware of his fragile nerves, Ginger answered with uncharacteristic cynicism. "I'm glad the PM thinks we're turning the tide of war, Dad, because, frankly, it doesn't feel like that from where I'm standing."

"That's not the point, Ginger! I mean, it was what he said about what we all *owe* you. After the BBC broadcast, everyone started congratulating *me* – people I hardly knew! Total strangers, even. They came up to me in the pub – I was down totown to shop and stopped in 'fore coming home for just a quick one. But the radio was on, and after the PM spoke, everyone started slapping me on the back and congratulating me – but it was all meant for you."

The thought of his despised and ridiculed father being the centre of approving attention was so poignant that Ginger had to fight back tears again. He was glad that his father was still talking excitedly. Mr. Bowles was saying breathlessly, "I had to tell you that, Ginger. The PM was speaking for all of us. We know you're all that stands between us and the Nazis. We know what the Nazis would do to us – if it weren't for you and your mates."

"They still might, Dad. No matter what the PM said, we haven't won yet." It came out rather harsh, because Ginger was so confused by his own emotions that he could only cope by being hard.

"I know, Ginger. But we're all behind you. And I've never been so proud in all my life."

"Thanks, Dad," Ginger's voice softened.

"Wish I could come and see you, lad. If I came to Chichester, could you get some time off? Just a couple of hours, I mean? Time for a quiet pint together?"

"It'd be an awful lot of trouble for you, Dad." Part of Ginger desperately wanted to see his Dad, but he was a little afraid of it, too. He couldn't introduce his Dad around to the others; they'd laugh at him for his country clothes, speech and manners.

"But you could get the time off, couldn't you?" His father pressed him.

"I don't know, Dad. I got a right to three days every fifteen, but we've got a new CO, and he's Cranwell. He chopped three pilots—"

His father wasn't listening. "Three days, you say! That's good then. I'll see about coming to visit. Is there somewhere cheap I could stay?"

"Don't worry about that, Dad. I can afford a hotel for you, but I don't really think I can get leave. Not three days, that's for sure—"

"One day's all I'm asking for, lad. Or an afternoon. Just to see you again."

"Well, I suppose I could ask, but don't you think—"

"I'll look into it tomorrow. Now, you take care of yourself, all right?"

"I do my best, Dad."

"I know you do. That's how you got where you are. Take care of yourself!" He shouted it into the receiver and then hung up before Ginger could hear how choked up he was – but Ginger heard anyway. They knew each other too well.

The Auxiliary Air Force pilots of 606 drove over in Sutton's Rolls Royce to the *The Kings Arms* in Chichester for a "proper breakfast." They were frequent guests and treated accordingly: taken to their usual table and brought both coffee and newspapers.

"Tommy called last night. His father talked to both Dowding and Park and they both stonewalled him." Sutton reported.

"What did you expect?" Donohue countered, taking out his silver cigarette case and offering it to the others. "Dowding is the most pig-headed man in the whole pig-headed Ministry! They've been trying to get rid of Dowding for years. He was due to retire, you know, and then the balloon went up and no one was willing to risk changing horses in the middle of the stream – though one wonders *why* one should stay on a *lame* horse. But his days are numbered, I can assure you of that. He'll be gone by Christmas."

"A lot of good that will do us! At this rate, so will we! I only hope the Butcher goes first!" Sutton replied vehemently.

"Who the hell does he think he is? That's what I want to know," Donohue reflected – lighting up his cigarette, inhaling deeply and blowing the smoke towards the panelled ceiling.

"Cranwell grad," Ware volunteered. "Aerobatics team, too. He was in the papers once or twice. Went out with some pretty grand corkers too, as I recall."

"Yes, quite. I thought I'd heard the name somewhere, so I rang my Mum – she's always one for remembering any gossip." Needham put in. "Just before the war he was dating – occasionally, anyway – Virginia

Cox-Gordon, and my Mum remembered that it caused quite a stir. It seems the family's a bit rum – not the Priestman side, his paternal grandfather's an Admiral, but apparently the Butcher's mother was a certain Miss Fitzsimmons and *her* father was this eminently respectable and highly successful industrialist who went completely bonkers and got involved with a French can-can girl. According to my Mum, he left his wife and family and fortune for this French floozy, and the child of that illicit affair is our fearless leader's mother."

"Charming. So, he not only *is* a bastard, but was born of one as well." Sutton concluded.

RAF Hawarden

David Goldman had bought a car, a used Jaguar, to be precise. He could afford it. He just couldn't drive it. He stripped the gears when he tried shifting with his left hand, and after they had nearly collided with oncoming traffic for the second time (because Goldman kept driving on the wrong side of the road), Kiwi couldn't take it any more. "Let me drive, would you?"

"You?" Goldman asked in a tone of utter disbelief, as he looked over at Kiwi in astonishment – and almost went into the ditch. The road was narrow and winding and Goldman was holding the steering wheel straight.

"Yes, me! For Christ's sake! We're supposed to take a Jerry or two with us before we die! Let me drive. I'm used to it." Goldman still looked sceptical, so Kiwi reminded him, "it's got a fixed undercarriage, for Christ's sake!"

"True. Right, then." Goldman stopped the car right where it was – in the middle of the road. The only other traffic at the moment was a herd of black-and-white Herefords slowly plodding towards them to the clang of their bells. Kiwi and Goldman swapped places.

After just a few minutes, David started to relax. Kiwi was much better at navigating the narrow, winding roads than he was. He found himself nodding off to sleep. Not too surprising, really. He hadn't slept at all during the night. The excitement of a posting to an operational squadron had been too much for him.

The news had arrived abruptly that all training was being cut to two weeks, and so all the pilots were being posted immediately – even Kiwi and himself, who had less than that. There had been a huge bash in the tiny Mess to celebrate, and almost everyone had drunk too much. Funny the way they all wanted to "get at the Hun." Or did they just talk like that? Had they all had sleepless nights once the carousing was over? Goldman hoped so. He lifted his head as if to look at the road, but really to glance at Kiwi. He looked contented and rested. He was even humming to himself and nodding his head as he did so. No, Kiwi wasn't having a fit of nerves.

Goldman laid his head back against the leather seat and closed his eyes again, but he was still far too tense to sleep. He had much to worry about. Hurricanes, for a start. Why send him to a Spitfire OTU, only to assign him to a Hurricane squadron? It didn't make sense. But the aircraft didn't really bother him. After his unpleasant taste of British anti-Semitism, he was far more worried about his fellow pilots than of the kite. He was glad that Kiwi was going with him. He'd have at least one friend. It was amazing how close he felt to Kiwi after just one week. Yes, that was the best aspect of this unexpected posting: that he and Kiwi would stay together.

But wasn't it dangerous to rest too heavily on the sturdy but soft Kiwi? After all, if you could believe the books from the last war, new fighter pilots only had a fifty-fifty chance of surviving their first combat. Who could say that Kiwi would still be there for him tomorrow? But, Goldman just couldn't imagine Kiwi going first.

His own death, by contrast, seemed near. Goldman knew only too well that he was a good pilot – for passengers. He could fly smoothly, meet schedules, navigate and fly on instruments. If he had a flight plan, he could follow it – almost regardless of weather. He could improvise when necessary too, deal with engine failure, head-winds, turbulence, ice – all that. But he wasn't a hot-shot flier like Kiwi, and he wasn't a hunter. That was what you had to be to survive in the air war. Look at Rickenbacker, Richthofen, Galland, Mölders.

Goldman knew that he should have gone to Bomber Command. He would have made a really good bomber pilot for all the qualities he had just listed. So why was he heading for an operational Hurricane Squadron on the front line?

Because he couldn't bomb Germany. Because – despite everything – he couldn't stand the thought of destroying his homeland. He hated the Nazis with all his heart, but they weren't Germany. David wanted to see the Nazis defeated, and Germany restored to what it had been before – a great, liberal and cultural nation. That was why shooting down German aircraft intent on bombing England was one thing, but bombing German cities – including all their great architectural monuments and the good people along with the bad – was something else.

But what if he wasn't any good at shooting down German aircraft? And why should he be? He'd never shot at anything in his life, and he hadn't fired a Spitfire's guns either. Maybe that came later in training, but the fact was, he had never fired even at a still – much less a moving – target.

The more David thought, the more certain he became that he would fail. Everyone knew the Luftwaffe was the finest air force in the world. Oh, the RAF was giving it a surprisingly good run for its money, but could anyone really doubt the Luftwaffe would win in the end? Of course, the Luftwaffe would get the upper hand sooner or later. What the hell was he doing throwing his life away in a lost battle? A kind of panic made David sit up sharply again and readjust himself in the seat.

"Shall we stop for lunch at that pub up ahead?" Kiwi asked innocently, unaware of Goldman's inner torment.

"Fine with me – but I don't think they do meals. All the pubs that do meals have signs out the front. It looks to me like they only serve drinks."

Kiwi ignored him and pulled in at the "Mortimer Arms," a nice fieldstone and half-timbered country inn. Kiwi had to duck to get through the door, and they found themselves in a low- ceilinged room with horse-brasses and oil-paintings of hunting scenes dimmed by layers of smoke. Kiwi went up to the bar. "G'day, Miss. Can m' mate and I get something to eat here?" he asked in his booming "down-under" voice.

The barmaid glanced up. Her eyes widened. "We don't actually do meals, sir, but I'll go and ask the landlady. Please sit down." She disappeared into the kitchen before Kiwi could stop her, and a minute later a grey-haired, pink-cheeked woman in a flowered apron appeared. "What would you boys like for lunch, then?" she asked happily.

"If you don't do meals, Ma'am, just tell us where to go, and—"

"But you're RAF pilots! Can't have *you* going hungry! You just tell me what you'd like, and I'll do my best. A cheese omelette, maybe? I've got my own chickens and have real eggs."

"*That* is absolutely irresistible, Ma'am," Kiwi answered with a wide grin, and the woman was gone in an instant, beaming happily.

"You're flying under false colours, Kiwi," David hissed at him admonishingly as soon as the landlady was out of hearing. "She thinks we're *real* pilots who have *done* something."

"Don't spoil her fun, mate. She's tickled pink to think she's helping pay her debt to some of 'the few.'"

RAF Tangmere

Mickey fussed with his pencils, straightened them for the umpteenth time, and then took off his glasses and wiped them clean. Even after all these years of service, he still found it difficult dealing with new pilots. It was hard being a commissioned officer in the RAF without having an inferiority complex about the absence of wings. Mickey's problem was compounded by the fact that he'd washed out of flight training some 14 years ago. He'd *wanted* to fly, but he just hadn't seemed able to get the hang of it. His short-sightedness had developed later – which in a way had made things better. Most people meeting him for the first time assumed that his eyesight had prevented him from flying from the start. Mickey, on the other hand, knew that every pilot was in some way better than he. Yet at nearly 40, he could not look up to a pair of over-grown school-boys like the two youngsters now standing in front of him.

Sergeant Pilot John Percy was a short, stub-nosed Northerner with a perfectly awful Geordie accent, while Pilot Officer Thomas Herriman was a puppy with a public-school-boy lisp. The latter clearly belonged in a school uniform rather than an RAF one – let alone one with wings. Mickey couldn't stop himself from asking, "Just how old are you, Herriman?"

"Almost 19, sir."

"'Almost' isn't an answer."

"18 years, 10 months, 3 weeks, 4 days and 6 hours, sir."

"Don't be cheeky, Herriman!"

"No, sir."

Cheeky little bastard! Mickey thought in exasperation.

"When are we going to meet the CO, sir?" The Sergeant Pilot entered the fray fearlessly.

"When he finds time for you!" Mickey told him off in no uncertain terms.

"But we arrived yesterday," the schoolboy pointed out.

"And he the day before. He has a lot more important things to worry about right now than the likes of you."

"Funny, I thought the country was short of fighter pilots," the schoolboy remarked in an aside to the Sergeant Pilot.

"Don't think that's what you are yet!" Mickey told them sharply. "The CO chopped three pilots yesterday – for insubordination – and they were veterans with more combat sorties than you have solo flying hours."

That took the wind out of the youngsters' sails. They were staring at him, rather agape. Taking advantage of their shock, Mickey continued, "The CO is a Cranwell graduate. He won't take cheek. And, incidentally, he also took trophies at a number of airshows before the war. He was appointed to 606 by AVM Park *personally*." Mickey was beginning to enjoy this, as the two new pilots were looking more and more intimidated. "And if that's not enough for you, he has six confirmed kills, was wounded in France, and came out of Dunkirk on foot – one foot, to be precise, because the other was broken."

"Don't over-do it, Mickey, or the poor chaps are going to think I can fly on one wing and see in the dark, too."

Mickey jumped to his feet. "I didn't see you, sir!"

Robin gave him a perplexed look and then held out his hand to the newcomers. "Priestman."

Mickey's speech had, however, had its intended effect. Both youths were rigidly saluting him, their eyes still fixed at some point over Priestman's shoulder.

"At ease," Priestman had to tell them, before they risked shaking his hand. When they relaxed a fraction, he considered them in bemusement. "So, tell me the bad news. Just how many hours have you had on Hurricanes?"

"Twenty-one, sir."

"Twenty-two and a half, sir."

Priestman dropped onto the front of Mickey's desk. "You are joking, of course."

The new pilots glanced at one another and then shook their heads.

"Right, then." Priestman stood up again. "Get out to dispersal, kit up, and let's get a couple more hours in before dinner. A couple after dinner. And then you can do some night circuits. Has either of you ever landed a Hurricane in the dark before?"

"Three times, sir," they said in a chorus.

"One night flight with three landings, right?"

"Yes, sir."

Priestman sighed, but he wasn't surprised. Just three days ago, he'd been training boys like this. Thank God the weather was so bad on the other side of the Channel that the Germans were laying low....

PART IV

Round Two

Chapter 27

RAF Tangmere
24 August 1940

"Good morning, sir. It's three-thirty. You asked for a wake-up call."

Priestman started. He had been in a deep sleep for the first time since he had taken command of 606, and for a moment he was completely disoriented – a fact exacerbated by the ugly face of the airman holding out a tray with a cup of tea on it. The face was familiar, but Robin's brain said "France," and that couldn't be. He dragged himself upright and peered at the airman more intently. He was sure it was the cook's assistant who had brought him a sandwich under the wing of his Hurricane in France. But he was definitely at Tangmere now. The solid brick walls and the tall windows with the heavy curtains and blackout blinds confirmed it. "Weren't you with No. 579 squadron in France?" he asked, reaching for the tea.

The airman broke into a wide grin. "There you are, sir. Just won me ten bob! I said you'd remember, but the others wouldn't believe me."

"What are you doing here?"

"They asked for cooks to volunteer to come south to 11 Group, sir, and I knew from France how important it is to look after you lot. When I got here, I heard you needed a batman and offered to re-muster."

Priestman was wide awake now. "That is the nicest compliment any one has ever paid me. I do hope you won't regret it. I'm not generally at my best at 3.30 in the morning."

The airman smiled. "None of us are, sir. Is the tea all right? I wasn't sure how you liked it."

Priestman took a sip. "Less milk and two sugars next time. What's your name again?"

"Thatcher, sir."

"What's the weather like this morning, Thatcher?"

"Clear as crystal, sir. Going to be a lovely, bright, sunny day."

What a perverse world we live in, Robin thought, when such good news is greeted by a sinking heart. Weather like that would bring the bombers out again. No doubt, all across Northern France the orders were going out at this very minute, and German airmen were being woken and told to ready themselves for a new onslaught. The short spell of comparative quiet had ended, and with it the respite for 606.

Bad weather had induced the Germans to fly only weak and sporadic fighter sweeps for the last three days, giving 606 three whole days to try to pull itself together. Priestman had concentrated on trying to get to know his pilots, flying with each of them. He'd also talked about his tactics and tried to practice them at flight strength, but bad weather and aircraft problems had got in the way.

The Germans, however, must be chafing to get on with the offensive as the summer slowly came to a close and autumn threatened. They were bound to send over practically everything they had. Priestman was certain that his four sprogs would be blooded today. Like a parent with teenage children, Priestman doubted if they were ready for the harsh realities of the world, but he knew he could not protect them any longer.

The dining room was still dark, but you could hear noise coming from the kitchen and the clatter of plates and utensils as the cooks started to prepare breakfast. The pilots would start trickling in about 4.30, but Robin had asked for the 3.30 wake-up call to get the weather report. If it had been bad again, he would have gone back to sleep, but there was no point in it now. Better check on the state of the kites and be sure everything was ready for the day ahead. Priestman asked Thatcher to bring some toast to him out in the dispersal hut and headed for the remaining hangar to talk to Rowe.

He didn't make it. Rowe intercepted him. "I was just going to send for you, sir. I'm afraid I have some bad news."

"How many kites are u/s?"

"Oh, it's not that. There are 13 serviceable aircraft. It's one of the riggers, sir. He was caught trying to go AWOL last night."

"What do you mean?" In Priestman's experience AWOL occurred most frequently when men did not return by the specified time at which their leave expired. Usually they arrived a few hours late, having missed train connections or whatever. Now and again, he'd known men to sneak off the Station for a night on the town that was not authorised, but they too always returned in due time. While these were offences, they hardly warranted the grave look on Rowe's face.

"He was caught trying to climb over the perimeter fence in the middle of the night, sir. Evidently, he was trying to desert."

"Are you certain?" Priestman asked, incredulous. Soldiers deserted. Sailors deserted. Airmen did not. At least, he'd never heard of it. Did the first recorded case have to be in his squadron?

"There can be no doubt, sir. He was wearing civilian clothes and carrying a bag with personal effects. Desertion in the face of the enemy is a capital offence, sir—"

"I know that!" Priestman retorted irritably. "But I don't think we should jump to wild conclusions. There are no enemy on this Station, anyway."

"The Germans have demonstrated that they can hammer us here, sir, and I was only trying to remind you, sir, that he must be held under arrest."

"Slow down. Have you talked to him? And who is it? Which aircraft?" Priestman was rapidly becoming aware that he had focused too intently on his pilots these last four days. He didn't know the names of any erks other than his own.

"Leading Aircraftman Tufnel, sir. He regularly serviced "H.""

"H" was the kite Sergeant Pilot Bowles usually flew, and Robin remembered that on his first morning here an airman had suggested he not take "H" because it stank. That was something else he had neglected: he hadn't talked to Bowles about being airsick. Suddenly, he realised that despite feeling as if he'd been working himself to death these past four days, in fact, he hadn't done half of what he *ought* to have done. For the moment, however, the issue was Tufnel. "What does Tufnel say he was doing?"

"He's refusing to talk, sir."

From somewhere out on the airfield, the first engine coughed into life. The pre-flight warm-ups were starting. The sound reminded Priestman that he still wanted to go over the Order of Battle and make a few adjustments based on the observations he'd made while flying yesterday. Herriman was over-confident and over-estimated his abilities. He needed to be well hemmed in. Kiwi was a natural leader, but it wouldn't do to put a sprog and a foreigner in command of a section yet, if he didn't want to alienate the old auxiliary pilots completely. So, he'd position him as Red Three, the most exposed position in Vics Echelon Starboard. He concluded that he didn't have time to deal with Tufnel just now. "Look, Rowe, I don't want any charges brought against LAC Tufnel until I've had a chance to speak to him personally."

"Sir, according to paragraph—"

"Pack it in, Flight! One day isn't going to make any difference. Who is servicing "H" in Tufnel's place?"

"I am, sir."

"Very good. And you said we have 13 serviceable aircraft?"

"Yes, sir."

"Thank you. I'll be at dispersal if you need me." Priestman turned and started for his own aircraft, which was rapidly becoming discernible in the pre-dawn twilight. His crew was working around it already – checking the tyres, polishing the windscreen, closing the gun-ports with canvas to prevent condensation at higher altitudes that could cause the guns to jam.

Ripley was just about to climb into the cockpit when Robin came up alongside. He stopped. "Morning, sir."

"Morning. Tell me, do you know LAC Tufnel well?"

Ripley and Appleby exchanged a glance before Ripley answered cautiously, "Well enough, sir."

"Any idea why he would want to desert?"

"No, sir. Tufnel's a first-class man. One of Trenchard's brats," Ripley said firmly, his expression one of earnestness.

"Problems at home, maybe?" Priestman pressed him.

"No, sir.... But he hasn't been himself since Sanders broke his back."

"Who?"

"Sanders, sir," Appleby took over from his taciturn colleague, coming nearer. "He and Tufnel were at Halton together and posted here together. Sanders had an accident just before the raid. He fell backwards off a Hurricane wing and broke his back. He's up in Southampton in hospital now. I heard he won't ever walk again. You might want to talk to Fowley, sir. He's Sanders' replacement." Appleby nodded towards one of the other Hurricanes.

Priestman thanked him and went straight over. Fowley's story was the same. It was getting light very rapidly because there wasn't a cloud in the sky. Priestman could see a lorry waiting out in front of the Officers' Mess to bring the pilots over to dispersal, so he started walking towards the dispersal himself. At dispersal Priestman made a note to himself to call Mickey after 8 am and ask him to bring over Tufnel's personnel files.

When the Sergeant Pilots arrived from their Mess, Priestman asked Bowles to step outside with him. "Sorry to get your day off to a bad start, but your rigger tried to go AWOL last night," he told the Sergeant Pilot. "Any idea what the problem might be?"

Ginger had expected some personal criticism from this terrifying new CO and was relieved by the question about his rigger. "Tufnel, sir?"

"Yes."

"He's been very upset about Sanders, sir."

"Sanders. The fitter who broke his back about a week ago."

"Yes, sir. They were good friends. The padre tried to get Tufnel a pass so he could go and visit Sanders, but the CO wouldn't approve it. And then the raid came and you came...."

That folder full of leave slips! Priestman thought guiltily. Mickey had mentioned that nothing had been approved in a long time and maybe he ought to look at it.... Better have him bring that along with

Tufnel's files. But the word "padre" was a good tip, too. He would ask the padre to have a talk with the erk. He nodded, "Thank you."

"Is that all, sir?" Ginger asked hopefully, anxious to end this uncomfortable one-on-one with a CO, who frightened even the commissioned officers.

"Now that you mention it, no." Ginger waited for the axe to fall. "I understand from your ground crew that you suffer from airsickness." Priestman levelled his eyes on Bowles as he said this.

Bowles looked down and his ears started to turn red. "If that's what you want to call it, sir."

"I'm surprised your instructors passed you out of training. Airsickness is no one's fault, obviously, but it is a serious impairment to effective flying."

Bowles' expression became very stubborn as he looked up and met his commanding officer's eye. "I didn't have it in training, sir. It has nothing to do with flying."

"But you have been sick when flying – repeatedly, I was told."

"I'm only sick when I see the enemy, sir," Bowles told him bluntly, adding provocatively, "Am I going to be posted, too?"

"Is that what you want?" Priestman retorted sharply. Mickey had told him that his nickname in the squadron was "the Butcher."

"No, sir." Bowles stood before him, his face flushed with shame, but his lips pressed together resentfully and his blue eyes flashing defiance.

"You want to keep fighting despite this condition?" Priestman probed.

"Yes, sir. I carry paper bags." Ginger pulled one out of his flight jacket pocket to show the squadron leader. "And I'll clean the aircraft myself if you want me to. I've offered to do that before, but Sanders and Tufnel wouldn't hear of it."

"That's not necessary, Bowles," Robin tried to ease the tension. "If you are prepared to keep flying despite this discomfort, then I for one am honoured to have you with me."

It took several minutes for Ginger to digest that, and he didn't quite believe it. "You're not going to post me, sir?"

"No, why should I? You're one of my more experienced pilots, and I understand you have a credited kill."

"That was just an accident, sir." Ginger hastened to explain, feeling embarrassed. "During the raid, everything was happening so fast that I didn't have time to be sick, and suddenly there was this Stuka right smack in front of me, so I shot at it and it blew up."

"That's the way it happens for all of us half the time," Robin told him with an amused smile. "Shall we go and get some tea?" He gestured towards the dispersal hut with his head.

"Thank you, sir," Ginger replied automatically, and then he realised that he really was thankful. The CO wasn't anywhere near as bad as the others made him out to be. At least he cared whether Ginger was sick or not. Jones must have known about it too, but he hadn't cared.

Crépon, France

Christian had started it, of course. Yesterday, after yet another inconclusive sweep in lousy weather, he had flung himself on the grass and said in a loud voice, "Leave. Also known in civilian life as Holiday, Vacation, or Time Off. It was under Bismarck, I believe, that the first laws governing mandatory time off – even for kitchen maids – were passed by the Reichstag. Certainly, the Socialists introduced laws about the maximum working week – which is the reverse side of minimum time off."

"Freiherr von Feldburg is *still* trying to find some way to become the Red Baron of this war," Fischer commented to the amusement of the others, not least Feldburg himself. (The "Red Baron" was the popular nickname for the highest-scoring ace of the last war, Baron von Richthofen; the "Red" in his nickname had referred to the colour of his tri-plane. But "Red" was also the designation for Socialists and Communists, while Christian was a baron in his own right.)

When they had stopped laughing, however, Christian persisted. "But it is true, Herr *Hauptmann*, we *are* entitled to days off, aren't we?"

"What do you want me to do, Feldburg?" Fischer answered tartly, "call the Herr *Reichsmarschall* and say: 'I know we're running out of time for the invasion, and I know you gave the Führer your word of honour that you'd defeat the RAF in four days, and I know the Me110 has proved almost worthless as an escort and that the bombers get slaughtered if they have no 109s protecting them, but my pilots want a day off'?"

"Yes, that would do nicely." Christian agreed smiling.

Fischer threw his cap at him, and everyone laughed.

Of course, nothing more was said about it at the time – or afterwards either – but Ernst suspected he wasn't the only one who thought about it now and again. After four days of exhausting and frustrating fighter sweeps, they were slated to support *three* raids: 1) to go in as the second wave of escorts to relieve the first wave on a raid on Manston, 2) to form the main escort on a raid against North Weald, and then 3) to escort bombers attacking Portsmouth in the late afternoon. All raids, no sweeps: a guarantee of opposition, dogfights, casualties. If only they were winning but that feeling, which Ernst had had just a week ago, was slipping away from him.

Every day they told themselves that the RAF *must* be as tired as they were. They listened to the intelligence officer, who carefully calculated British aircraft production, deducted their own claims, and proved that the British couldn't possibly have more than 50 Spitfires left and maybe a hundred Hurricanes. They wanted to believe it. It was simple mathematics. The game *had* to be nearly over. But there wasn't one German fighter group which was up to strength any more either, Ernst thought morosely, as he adjusted the straps of his parachute and pulled his helmet on in preparation for take-off. Beside him his Emil trembled, and the grass shivered in the slip-stream as his mechanic did the last-minute tests on the engine. The mechanic climbed out of the cockpit.

Ernst hauled himself up the wing and eased himself down into the still-warm seat. Was he imagining things, or had he really lost weight in the last couple of weeks? How ironic, if the British had succeeded where both the Hitler Youth and Luftwaffe had failed! Then he started the cockpit drill, with his mechanic still on the wing beside him.

"*Alles in Ordnung, Herr Leutnant?*"

"*Ja, alles in Ordnung.*" He waved his OK, and the mechanic pulled the canopy shut over Ernst's head before he jumped down off the wing.

Of course, a day off wouldn't really do that much good. What they needed was two weeks on the Baltic, or in the Alps or – why not? – on the Mediterranean. Two weeks away from everything: the RAF, the war, flying, Luftwaffe regulations and maybe even each other.

Ernst sighed and forced himself to concentrate. He plugged in R/T and oxygen, glanced right. Christian waved. Ernst nodded, pulled the throttle gently back and eased up on the brakes. For these supporting raids on targets further east, the *Staffel* flew first to the Pas de Calais, refuelled there, and then took off again. That was why they still had to get off at the crack of dawn, even though the raid itself was not being scheduled before 9.30.

RAF Tangmere

In the Operations Room the big clock on the wall clicked slowly forward. 7 am, 8 am, 8.30, 9.00, 9.25 – the first flurry of activity. The Germans were awake after all. There were plots building up at Calais. After a bit, they moved slowly forward on the big map of the control table. These raids were not going for Bainbridge's Sector. All appeared to be concentrated on the Hornchurch sector. And soon the confirmation came from Uxbridge. Bainbridge was told to hold his squadrons back for now. Then came the news: Manston had been hit hard; everything seemed to be burning, but at least the squadrons hadn't been caught on the ground.

By 10.45 the next raids were on the board. These too slowly edged their way across the Thames Estuary and then swung west, giving Manston a miss this time, but reaching North Weald. Park threw five squadrons at them from Kenley and Biggin Hill, but it was soon reported that at least 20 bombers got through. The Messes, married quarters and the stores were damaged.

Bainbridge could only stare at the table below him. It was all so clear from here. The Luftwaffe had finally worked out which airfields were used by Fighter Command and cottoned on to the English system of control. They were systematically going for Fighter Command, and particularly the Sector airfields. The concentration on the airfields to the southeast of London seemed a clear indication that the invasion was going to come at the narrowest point of the Channel. Tangmere might be spared – or rather ignored – if that was the case, but Bainbridge could not calmly watch the Germans pound England's air defences to bits. Besides, as the squadrons in the direct path of the bombers wearied, Park would have to ask the squadrons from peripheral sectors to assist.

JG 23

The supporting role they were flying now entailed going in on the same course as the bombers, but more than half an hour later. The escorting Messerschmitts of the first wave went in with the bomber but had only enough fuel for ten minutes of dogfighting. Once they'd engaged, they had to make a dash for France or risk ending up in captivity or the Channel. This, of course, left the slower bombers unprotected on the way home, unless a second wave of escorts could relieve the departing fighters. On this first raid, that was JG 23/II's job.

As they crossed the Channel at almost 10,000 metres, Ernst saw several Emils darting back to France far below them. Then more and more bombers passed by below, also heading the other way, often on one engine or trailing smoke. Meanwhile, the sky ahead of them became dirty with flak and smoke over the target. To the west, a field of barrage balloons swayed sedately over London.

Soon they saw the first evidence of a scrap as well. Vapour trails twisted about overhead, while now whole formations of bombers were streaming back in ragged swarms, mauled by the defenders.

Then Christian drew attention to the "last fifty Spitfires" while Fischer ordered them to attack the Hurricanes, which were feasting on the bombers. Ernst switched on his gun sight and took the safety off. He glanced further back to see if Ettner and Renz were with them as they dived, and then they were in the thick of it.

They had barely reached the bombers before the Spitfires Christian had spotted earlier were upon them. Ernst, who had been expecting them, saw them in time and called out the warning. Christian ordered Ettner to continue down while he and Ernst banked around to take on the Spitfires. These just kept diving past, either intent on Ettner and Renz or on the bombers still below. Christian was therefore in the advantageous position of being able to follow them down, Ernst still flanking him doggedly.

As they approached the bombers, however, Christian abandoned his quarry to come to the rescue of a bomber that was being shot up by a determined Hurricane. Christian was flying very well today, Ernst thought, as he watched his leader press in close behind the oblivious Hurricane. The English pilot was so intent on bringing down the bomber that he wasn't watching his tail. Christian had all the time in the world. He lined up neatly, slightly below and just a hair to the right of the Hurricane's tail, came in close and then opened fire. He registered hits almost immediately.

Textbook bounce, Ernst thought, and checked the sky above and behind them. When he looked forward again, the Hurricane's tail had been shot away completely, the aircraft was wobbling helplessly as the pilot tried to clamber out.

"Bravo, Christian!" Ernst called enthusiastically.

Christian answered by flicking his wings up and banking away exuberantly while calling over the RT. "Better rejoin the party." He was referring to an ongoing dogfight on the other side of the retreating bomber formation.

Ernst followed dutifully, automatically checking their tail. He got a shock. "Christian! More Spitfires!!"

A pair of Spitfires was so close one had already fastened onto Ernst's tail. Ernst broke out into a sweat of sheer terror as he heard the familiar chatter of guns. His Emil shuddered – clearly taking hits. A split second later, his knee and then his thigh jerked. His left arm was flung into the air. Blood splattered across his face, his chest. He was knocked to the right, against the right side of the cockpit, with such violence that his right shoulder felt broken. Then the pain hit him from his left leg upward.

"Dive!" Ernst heard the order shouted into his ears, while still in shock at what he had just seen happen before his eyes. He threw the little aircraft into the steepest dive of his life. They had been told the Spitfire couldn't follow them down. The English engines stalled out. Down, down, down. Flying with the right half of his body only, despite the excruciating pain in his right shoulder. How could it hurt more than where the bullets had hammered into him? It didn't make sense.

God almighty! He was blacking out. Going straight in. He was crashing at 1000 km/h. Pull out! Pull out! he ordered himself, and almost yanked with all his might on the stick – only to stop himself just in time. Don't tear the wings off her! Gentle. Oh, God, help me! I can't do this alone! I'm going to die!

His right leg was trembling so violently that his knee was knocking the side of the cockpit. His left leg was soaking the floor with blood. Oh, God. For a moment he didn't know if he was vertical or horizontal any more. He felt dizzy. His stomach was about to empty itself. He grabbed at the canopy release.

Idiot! Check the altitude first! He was at less than 200 metres. He had to get altitude to jump!

Christ! His right shoulder was killing him. No, it was from the bullet holes in his left side that his life's blood was draining away. He was drenched in blood. It has soaked the inside of his flying jacket and his trousers. His left hand was bright red with it. Soon there would be none left.

He had to get out of the aircraft and surrender to the Tommies. He had to get to a hospital before he bled to death! No, he had to gain altitude first. He had to concentrate!

Someone was shouting in his earphones. He paused in his despair to listen. "Geuke? Do you read me?" Christian was out there somewhere. "Ernst! Come in! Do you read me?"

"I've been hit," Ernst answered, just so Christian would know what had happened. He could write home, tell Klaudia.

"Where? Can you still fly? Where are you?"

"I don't know." And what did it matter? He'd never get home in this shape, and no one could help. In a single-seater, you were utterly on your own. He couldn't even bind his wounds to stop the bleeding.

"What's your altitude?" Christian persisted.

"I'm on the deck," Ernst told him, adding as he took note of it himself, "Near a town."

"Is there a square-towered church in sight?"

"Ja."

"Circle the town. Where are you damaged?"

"My whole left side."

"You or the Emil?"

"Mostly me."

"Can you still fly?"

"Sort of." He was, after all, managing to circle this quiet English village calmly. The trembling had at last stopped in his good leg.

Christian was still harassing him. "Is your Emil operable?"

"It seems to be."

"Do you think it can make it home?"

Home? He couldn't possibly get home. Then again, he couldn't just circle this town until he ran out of fuel and crashed. If he could fly in circles, why couldn't he fly a straight course? If he was going to crash land, then rather at Crépon than here. At Crépon they'd have an ambulance for him, and – if by some miracle he survived – he wouldn't be a prisoner. Yes, it was theoretically possible. "If I don't get bounced again."

"Don't worry. I'll be with you. Turn on a southeast course and I'll join you shortly."

Ernst dutifully pointed the Emil southeast and flew away from the village. Shortly afterwards, another Messerschmitt swooped down beside him and waggled its wings in greeting. Never had Ernst been so glad to see his *Rotteführer*. "We've got to get some altitude. Can you climb?"

Ernst nodded numbly. He supposed he could. The Emil seemed to be responding. Christian pulled a little ahead and led him up to 4,000 metres. It was immeasurably reassuring to be flying on Christian's flank again. Now all he had to do was follow him home. Ernst stopped thinking about everything else. He did not dare look at the fuel gauge. He did not care about altitude, speed, or course. Nothing mattered but Christian flying right there on his port bows, steady and confident and armed.

Sunlight flooded the cockpit, heating it like a greenhouse. Ernst was sure he was sweating now. Sweat was running off his face, down his neck, and drenching his sides from his armpits. His feet were horribly hot in his boots. But the pain had eased up in his right shoulder, and he didn't feel pain from the bullets any more. That is: if he didn't move or touch his left leg, then the pain was only dull and pervasive rather than acute. Even the bleeding seemed to have slowed down. Everything was slow. Ernst wanted to close his eyes and sleep.

This is madness! He woke himself up sharply. It was all very well to follow Christian in the air, but Christian couldn't land the Emil for him. It was hard enough to land the Emil on its narrow undercarriage when one was fit. How was he ever going to get it down in this state? He was bound to crash on landing. Maybe he should jump after all? But the thought of climbing out of his warm cockpit and trusting his awkward, bleeding bulk to a parachute was not appealing. No, he'd rather risk a crash landing.

As if his thoughts had communicated themselves to Christian, Christian was nagging him again. "Ernst? Can you hear me?"

"Ja."

"I'm going to lead you down. Just stick to me like glue. Do everything I do. Same altitude, same speed, same course. Got it?"

"Ja."

"All right. Here we go."

Ernst forced himself to concentrate. Don't even look down, he told himself. Just watch Christian. Trust him. He's brought you this far. He'll get you down. Believe it. Undercarriage down. Flaps. Throttle forward. Ooops. Not that much. Now a bit more. Ease her down. Gently. The nose is falling, pull it up! Up! No, ease down. Aaahhh! That was ground. Already he'd bounced up again, high, and then whacked down on the ground with such force that his punctured body was shaken horribly and the pain was intolerable. Instinctively he smashed his good leg on the brakes and the Emil pivoted hard and tipped up onto its nose. It tore along on its snout with a terrible crashing, screeching and whining. Ernst felt as if he was being shaken apart. The pain obliterated everything else. Ernst saw, heard and felt nothing but the blinding pain that seemed to come from everywhere at once.

"Ernst?" The voice was nearby, urgent, familiar. Christian. "Are you alive?"

Ernst nodded, but then realized that was not enough. He was only alive because of Christian. "Thanks, Christian," he mouthed it, but he wasn't really sure any sound came out. The pain was so loud....

RAF Tangmere

It was noon and the next raid was building up over Calais again. Bainbridge started to suspect that the Germans had concentrated their forces over the Pas de Calais. Otherwise, they couldn't mount so many raids in one place in such quick succession. Park would have to ask Tangmere Sector to support soon. Bainbridge's eyes wandered nervously between the boards below and the telephone connecting him directly to Park's HQ at Uxbridge. The raid moved inland. Manston again. This time communication to and from that airfield was knocked out.

Bainbridge stood and went to the railing of the gallery to stare at the map below. He tried to picture the coastline from Hastings to Ramsgate. That, apparently, was where the German Army intended to force its way ashore. Hastings would undoubtedly appeal to the superstitious dictator, Bainbridge thought flippantly – but without real levity. Someone had brought him a tray with lunch and he had not eaten a single bite. "Aren't you going to eat, sir?" ACW Roberts asked.

"No, you can take it away."

She seemed to do so reluctantly.

Hastings was too far west, Bainbridge decided on second thought. If they were going to land at Hastings, they would be concentrating more in the Kenley and Tangmere Sectors. They must be planning to land nearer Dover. Land below chalk cliffs? Were there cliffs all along the coast? Bainbridge was from Somerset and didn't know the south coast well. He was so lost in his reflections about the impending invasion that he was taken by surprise when a plot went on the board at Cherbourg.

That would be for them. He glanced at the clock; it was 3.40 pm. OK. Watch that carefully. Park wouldn't want them to scramble too soon. It was still building up. 100+ already, but the escorts were no doubt still joining up with the circling bomber squadrons.

Farther east, another raid was moving out of Calais again. Communication, meanwhile, had been restored to Manston. All accommodation had been levelled, and the airfield was so littered with unexploded bombs (aircrew error, an indication of declining German industrial efficiency, or an intentional new tactic?) that it was no longer usable. The order went out to the Manston squadrons to withdraw to Hornchurch.

Bainbridge noted: 15:45, August 24, 1940: the Germans achieve their second clear victory in the air war: they deny RAF Fighter Command one of its forward airfields.

The German raid from Cherbourg started to move north. Bainbridge licked his lips, and noticed they were raw already. He must have been licking them all day without noticing. The plot read 200+ now, and it was making straight for them. Park would wait a little. He had issued explicit instructions to avoid interceptions over the water. Too many pilots had been lost after successfully getting out of their damaged machines. For Stations like Kenley and Biggin Hill that presented little challenge, but for Tangmere it meant holding the squadrons back longer and that meant shorter interceptions, which meant that they had less time to gain altitude, which meant they were at a disadvantage. So, don't wait *too* long, Bridges begged Park mentally, gripping the rail of the gallery.

His assistant answered the phone that Bainbridge had heard and ignored. "Hornchurch is under attack, sir."

The airfields. They were definitely going for the airfields. But his raid seemed to be veering west. Ventor again? Or Portmouth? If the invasion was planned for the Pas de Calais, then perhaps Tangmere frightened Jerry less than the Royal Navy? Maybe Jerry even believed Tangmere was out of action already. It might look pretty useless from the air with all but one hangar collapsed. No, all recce photos would show the aircraft of four fighter squadrons still concentrated here. Perhaps the resources available in the Cherbourg area limited? This raid was clearly being thrown at Portsmouth.

At last the call from Uxbridge came. Seconds later, Bainbridge reached for the phone and rang 43 Squadron dispersal.

"Got something for us, sir?" the dispersal orderly asked.

"Yes, we've got a 200+ apparently making for Portsmouth. Take the whole squadron to stand-by, will you?"

"Will do, sir."

"Observer Corps on the Isle of Wight, sir," W/O Robinson called out, in a voice that betrayed that he too was getting the wind up a bit. "They're reporting close to 400 aircraft, sir. They say it's not more than 50 bombers, with about 100 110s and twice that number of 109s."

"Bloody hell!"

Park ordered Tangmere to scramble two squadrons. Bainbridge grabbed the phone to 43 Squadron again. "Scramble!" Then he called 17, putting them on readiness with a nervous glance at the clock. It was 3.55 and they couldn't be in the air for 15 more minutes. Still Bainbridge hesitated for a second, but he had no choice. He grabbed the telephone that connected him to 606 dispersal.

Priestman himself answered. "606 Squadron Dispersal." Cranwell to the end.

"Robin, we've got a 400+ over the Isle of Wight and apparently making for Portsmouth. That's 50 Junkers and 350 snappers of both varieties. Scramble at once."

"Roger."

Park asked him to scramble another squadron. That gave them 3 squadrons, something less than 36 aircraft (because 17 was not up to strength) against 350 German fighters. Not enough. Park told him to see if 602 could scramble. They had been released, of course, and it was hard to know how many pilots were even within reach, but he asked them to get ready to put whatever they had available in the air shortly.

"Right oh."

"How many aircraft will that be?"

"Twelve, what else?"

"Well done."

Bainbridge turned to his assistant, Warrant Officer Robinson. "I'll handle 43 and 606. You're responsible for 17 and 602."

"Right, sir."

43 Squadron came in over the R/T, demanding vector and altitude.

Bainbridge broke the bad news. The Germans were flying very high, estimated 25,000 feet, just 50 bombers and mostly fighter escort.

Next Priestman asked for vector and altitude. It was 16.02. 17 Squadron reported "at readiness." Jolly good. Just seven minutes of the fifteen allowed. They must have been expecting it. They would have seen the other squadrons scramble and gone on unofficial readiness. Bridges knew what the waiting around was like.

W/O Robinson took up the second microphone and ordered, "Scramble at once. 400+ approaching Portsmouth with more than 300 snappers at 25,000."

"The more the merrier, what?" The sarcasm was pretty thick.

That was everything Bainbridge had. Less than 50 fighters. He hesitated again, but then he called Uxbridge and asked for support from 10 Group. He was promised a Spitfire squadron from Middle Wallop. He glanced at the clock again. 16.10.

"Beetle, Lampshade leader, here. Tally ho! Right, chaps, ignore the snappers. Go for the bombers. Now!"

Half of Bainbridge's job was done. Now all he had to do was ensure the interception by 606. After that it was up to them. He looked down at the tables, but every nerve in his body was straining instead to hear the conversations coming in over the R/T. The WAAFs, too, stood with faces turned towards the speakers affixed to the wall. Some, Bainbridge noticed, had pushed one earphone off an ear to be able to hear the transmissions from the loud-speakers better. Behind him, Bainbridge's assistant controller, the liaison officers to the balloon and observer corps, and the WAAF clerks sat absolutely still.

"Come on, Red Two, don't be such a lame arse. Green One, take your finger out."

Bainbridge smiled at that. The pilots forgot – or maybe they didn't realise – that they were being listened to by the WAAFs.

"Bomb bays are opening! Stupid bastards! They can't aim at anything—"

"Break! Break! Break!"

"Chriiiiiiiiist!!!" It was a long, drawn-out scream that ended abruptly with an explosion that seemed to blow the entire Operations Room apart. Bainbridge was gripping the railing so hard his hands were cramping. The upturned faces of the WAAFs seemed whiter than ever. The air was suddenly oppressive.

"Jesus! Blue Three's just collided with an 88!"

"Dan! Break right NOW!"

"Redcap Leader to Beetle. Tally ho!"

Bainbridge jumped back to take up his microphone. "Good luck, Redcap."

"Redcap Squadron, turn left now! Blue Leader, take the left-hand flight. Red Section will take the right-hand flight. Try to skim over them and keep going for the bombers. Yellow Section, just keep making for the bombers."

Interminable seconds. Bainbridge's hands were wet. Sweat was trickling down his armpits. His eye patch was starting to itch and chafe.

"They're coming after us, Redcap Leader!" That was the unmistakable high-pitched accent of the youngster Herriman – already nicknamed "Eton" by the others because he had dropped out of this esteemed establishment to join the RAF.

"That's their job, Blue Four," his Squadron Leader reminded him. Adding to all of them, "Redcap Squadron buster."

17 Squadron gave the Tally-ho. Robinson wished them luck.

"I've been hit! Christ, I've been hit! There's blood all over the place."

"Got it! Look at that! It's going down in an inverted spin! Completely out of control!" The transmissions of the three engaged squadrons were mixing, impossible to keep apart.

"They must have hit a petrol tank down there. Look at the smoke!"

"Yellow Four, break right! Now, for Christ's sake!"

"Blue Leader, this is Blue Two; I'm being fired upon."

Bainbridge all but moaned out loud. The fool! If he took time to report it, it was too late. Who was flying Blue Two? And in which squadron?

The accent was odd. Might be the new pilot, Goldman.

A more experienced pilot was trying to sort him out. "Then turn until she stalls!"

"I've been hit. The rudder isn't responding!"

"Red Four, ye'rrre on firrre! Get ooot nu." That was MacLeod at his most Scottish – it always seemed to come out when he was under stress.

"They're bombing housing down there! Look at that. Just houses! Nothing but houses!" By the accent it was 606's new pilot from Newcastle, already known simply as "Georgie."

"Don't look down, Georgie! Look behind you! That's where the 109s are!"

"Gingerrr, yer bloody fool! Get ooot nu!"

"Bloody hell! There are more snappers! Where do they all come from!?"

"Tally ho!" That was 602 at last.

"Take that, you bastard! And that, and that!" Bainbridge started slightly as he recognised Priestman's voice.

"My leg! I've been hit in the leg! I can't move it!"

"Eton! Break off! That's a Spitfire, you bloody fool!!"

One of 602's, or had 10 Group's squadron engaged as well? Good work if they had. Must remember to thank them, Bainbridge thought.

"Christ, what was that?!" The astonished voice of the New Zealander.

"We're being fired on by the Navy!"

"Damn sailors! Afrrraid of any foocking thing that flies!" MacLeod again, and his remark brought a ripple of embarrassed laughter from the WAAFs.

"Skipper! We're getting too low. Pull up, for Christ's sake!"

"Not until I nail this bastard!"

"Blue Leader from Blue Four. Where are we?"

"Over the Isle of Wight!"

"Are you sure, sir?"

The answer was very rude.

Portsmouth

When the air-raid sirens had gone off, some of the sailors at the Salvation Army Mission proclaimed their intention to stay top-side since they didn't take cover at sea, but Miss Fitzsimmons would have none of it. She got everyone down into the cellar before the first cracks of ack-ack indicated that the bombers were in range. By then the sailors had noticed that the canteen was "below deck" and started clamouring for Cook to brew-up. Then the bombs started detonating all around them.

This was nothing like the last time, Emily noted with discomfort. This time they seemed to fall right on top of them, and she found herself cowering under the heavy kitchen table with a lot of strangers. The whole earth shook. Things crashed overhead. The ceiling plaster cracked and crumbled, falling like a rain of pebbles. The lights dimmed, surged, dimmed and then went out altogether. Someone started swearing in the darkness.

And still the shaking and the explosions continued around them. Someone was saying the Lord's Prayer. With a horrible crash and a shudder, a bomb exploded very nearby. The glass in the windows high up on the wall burst inwards with a horrible shattering sound, and with it came a flash of flame and billowing smoke. "Gas masks, everyone!" Miss Fitzsimmons ordered, but Emily had left hers hanging upstairs with her handbag. She held a handkerchief over her mouth instead.

The sound of sirens was coming through the window with the smoke. Fire engines, Emily registered. They pierced through her fear and calmed her. More, the sound of those sirens sent a surge of pride through her. Up there, although the bombs were still falling, firemen and rescue workers were doing their jobs. And not just the fire engines, she reminded herself. Up there, above the fire engines and ambulances, were young men in Hurricanes trying to claw the bombers out of the sky. They would have scrambled the squadrons at Tangmere. Robin was up there.

RAF Tangmere

The battle was starting to cool off, and Bainbridge started to relax a little. He glanced again at the table below. Were any more raids building up yet? Farther east one was moving north, but nothing at Cherbourg. It looked like Jerry had put everything into one massive raid here. Five-to-one fighter/bomber ratio. Bainbridge couldn't remember anything like it.

More and more aircraft started to call into Control for fixes home. This too was part of his job. Geordie called in, "Beetle, Redcap Yellow Four here. Can you read me?"

Something about the voice, small and tight, alerted Bainbridge. He grabbed the mike. "Reading you loud and clear, Redcap Yellow Four."

"I've been hit. My foot's all shot up."

"Do you want to jump or try to land?" Bainbridge asked him. "Land," came the very tense answer.

It was the pilot's decision. From here, in his bunker, Bridges could not possibly judge if it was the right one. He could only hope it was and do all he could to assist. He ordered Robinson to take the other calls and concentrated on talking this one pilot home. "Right, then. Do you know where you are?"

"No, sir."

"Not to worry. Just keep talking until we can get a fix on you." As he spoke he signalled to ACW Roberts, and she at once picked up the phone to the D/F room where their own fighters were plotted.

"Jerry must have dumped two hundred bombs on Portsmouth," Geordie was saying. "The whole city is lost in smoke. My foot is killing me. There's blood all over the floor now and the rudder pedals are getting slippery."

Roberts was back and pushed a note to him with the vector for Geordie. "Redcap Yellow Four, vector 065. What's your altitude?"

"Sixty-eight-hundred feet."

"Good. How's your Hurricane responding?"

"OK, Sir."

Bainbridge was sweating again. He knew what Geordie was going through, but he mustn't lose sight of the overall picture either. Nervously he glanced at the board showing the squadrons' status. 17 and 43 had already gone from green (in the air) to red (refuelling). If Jerry sent in a quick raid now, they'd be caught with their trousers down.

Bainbridge turned his attention back to Geordie. "You're doing just fine, Redcap Yellow Four. Coming in very nicely." Bainbridge reported the wounded pilot to the tower. "What have you got on the circuit?"

"Three aircraft at the moment. How far away is the lame duck?"

Bainbridge checked. "Five miles." Next, Bainbridge asked Roberts to find out how many planes were back and how many were still missing, and then went back to talking Geordie down.

"All of 17 are down, sir. 43 has lost 3 aircraft, and 606 has lost 2. 602 is still airborne."

"Find out which pilots are missing," he ordered. Meanwhile, the tower had sighted Geordie and took over talking him in. Bainbridge glanced at the board. All four Tangmere squadrons were refuelling – vulnerable. There were no plots on the board, but the Hun had sent in low-flying hit-and-run bombers below RDF in the past. If such a raid hit Tangmere now....

The WAAF handed him a piece of paper with the designations of the missing aircraft. Bainbridge turned to his assistant. "Robinson? Can you spell me for a bit? I need a smoke."

"Yes, sir."

Bainbridge went out into the bright glare of the afternoon sun. What a glorious day, and he spent it in a dark, windowless bunker! Yet the air smelt of petrol and wherever he looked, bowsers stood beside parked Hurricanes and ground crews clambered over them, rearming, checking oil and tyre pressure, cleaning windscreens.

At last he located it. The Hurricane flying low to the horizon and flying erratically: it sank down, then bounced up again, sank again, the wings wagged, the long snout swung from side to side. The engine roared as the throttle was shoved forward, then all but died only to roar again. The aircraft swooped up and down like a swallow. It banked dangerously as the undercarriage was cranked down. Then righted, but it was coming in too high. Much too high. It dropped down. Bashed onto the ground. Bounced up again. The wing tipped violently. It smashed down again. One of the undercarriage legs gave way. The wing tip went in and the aircraft started to cartwheel. Bainbridge stared in horror, oblivious to the sirens wailing around him. The tip of the wing broke off. The Hurricane flopped back onto its remaining undercarriage leg and screeched to a halt.

Bainbridge saw the pilot drop his head on the control panel and just wait. The ambulance stopped alongside. Two airmen from the ground crew were on the wings, sliding back the canopy. They pulled off the pilot's helmet and tossed it aside. They undid his straps, lifted him out of the cockpit, onto the broken wing. His right leg appeared to be soaked in blood, useless. He had blood on his right hand and the right side of his face too – possibly just from touching his wounded leg. The ground crew eased him down the slope of the wing to the waiting medics.

Another pilot came around the snout and went over to the stretcher. He talked briefly to Geordie. The stretcher was loaded into the ambulance and howled off. Priestman came towards Bainbridge. "Who's missing?" he asked without preliminaries.

"Sergeant Bowles and Pilot Officer Goldman."

Robin pressed the heels of his hands to his eyes for a moment. Then took a deep breath. "Right. Better get back to work. Anything on the boards?"

"Not yet. Did you get whatever you were chasing out there?"

"He was billowing black smoke from both engines and skimming the wave-tops so close his propellers were sending up spume. But I ran out of ammo and had to abandon him like that."

"A probable, then."

"Damaged. I've got to get back to dispersal," Priestman repeated woodenly and started walking towards the dispersal hut.

Mickey came up beside Bainbridge. "I've got a problem," he muttered miserably.

"What?"

"There's a Mr. George Bowles sitting in my office."

"Who's George Bowles?" Then something clicked. "Not any relation to Sergeant Bowles?"

"His father."

"Bowles isn't back yet."

"I know."

"Jesus Christ." Bainbridge was almost glad to be returning to his dingy, stuffy bunker after all. Anything but face the father of a pilot who had probably just been killed in action.

Mickey had no choice. He sighed and gazed at the airfield, where the activity was gradually slowing down as the refuelling and rearming was completed on one after another aircraft. He searched the sky one last time. But it was hopeless. Bowles and Goldman weren't going to fly in. The only hope for them now was that they'd bailed out or landed safely somewhere else.

Portsmouth

The explosions were receding, but the smoke billowing into the cellar was oily, smelly and seemed to be getting thicker all the time. "We've got to get out of here!" a man called in panic. A stampede started for the door. Miss Fitzsimmons tried to stop them, shouting for them to wait for the "All Clear," but they ignored her. They clattered up the stairs towards the back door and pushed out into the street.

Emily crawled out from under the table, but obeyed Miss Fitzsimmons. She noted the way smoke billowed in as the crowd of men opened the door and watched in horrified fascination the way it seethed along the ceiling.

Exclamations of amazement and horror from the men who had forced their way outside soon distracted her. The honk and wail of sirens was louder than ever. Someone said something about one of the Navy's oil tanks being hit. Against a background of more excited shouting, someone stuck his head back inside the Mission and shouted, "The cinema's burning!"

The sirens seemed to be converging on them. Miss Fitzsimmons stood uncertainly at the foot of the stairs for a moment, then she turned to the Cook and Emily and ordered, "Better get some tea made and prepare the mobile tea wagon. Fire-fighting is thirsty work." Wearing her tin helmet, Miss Fitzsimmons went up the stairs into the street as the "All Clear" wailed.

Emily and Cook got the tea wagon ready and together rolled it out onto the street. Emily wasn't prepared for what she found. The smoke from the burning oil tanks had obliterated the beautiful afternoon. Instead of sunshine and blue sky, heavy, stinking black clouds turned the sky orange. From nearer at hand, a greyish but foul-smelling smoke gushed into the alley from the main street. This was laden with ash and burning embers.

When they reached the corner of the street, they could see the cinema itself: the roof was completely gone already, only the steel girders remaining, while flame and smoke rose from the cauldron underneath. Several fire engines were pouring water into this fire without apparent effect. Bizarrely, the blue plush seats of the theatre had somehow been blown right out of the cinema and lay scattered about the street and even on the roofs of nearby houses, as if a giant had sprinkled them from the sky. Many people had converged on the cinema to search for the survivors among the rubble, accompanied by urgent shouts and agitated orders.

"Full of children," someone murmured. "An afternoon matinee for children."

The ambulances started arriving one after another. And then the first of the hysterical mothers appeared on the scene. The police started to cordon off the site. A sobbing mother was brought by a constable towards the tea wagon. Miss Fitzsimmons took her in her arms. "M' youngest!" the woman kept sobbing. "M' youngest!"

The rescue workers, dazed and black with soot, started to collect around the tea wagon. The sweat rolled down their blackened faces and when they tried to wipe it off on the back of the sleeves, they only smeared the filth around. They stank of sweat and smoke, and their hair stood on end from oil and ash. The whites of their eyes stood out.

"Were they all killed?"

"Wasn't there a shelter?"

"They were just filing out."

"Direct hit! Didn't have a chance!"

"Were there no survivors?"

"A handful at most."

In the rubble under the iron girders, the flames were gradually brought under control, and the fire engines started to withdraw one at a time. Their job done here, men climbed aboard their vehicles, and with a clang of bells hurried off to the next job. There were fires burning all over Portsmouth. But the ambulances were still shuttling back and forth between the cinema and the nearest hospital.

RAF Tangmere

Robin walked towards the dispersal very slowly. His feet were leaden. He felt as if he couldn't take another step. He was weighed down with exhaustion and emotion. Bowles was bad. He hardly knew him, but he couldn't get over his awe of a pilot who was so terrified he was physically ill before every combat – and still went in like he did today. Bowles had not lagged or hesitated or said a word. He just did his job. Robin hated to think that Bowles was dead – or badly wounded. Now he remembered someone shouting, "Red Four, you're on fire." Why did it have to be someone like Sergeant Bowles, who was so gentle? What was he thinking? Not even the bloody Huns deserved to be incinerated by aviation fuel!

Get hold of yourself, Robin.

He stopped where he was. Just stood in the middle of the field and let the wind blow through his hair. He concentrated on feeling the way it fretted with his silk scarf and slipped up his sleeves, making them tremble. He looked up at the sky, which was still clear except for some very high, thin cirrus.

Pull yourself together, Robin.

He couldn't walk into the dispersal hut like this. His nerves were taut as a drawn bow. If anyone said anything to him, he'd snap their head off.

Goldman. He'd killed Goldman. His selfish desire to have a couple of more mature and experienced pilots in the squadron had resulted in Goldman being shot down on his first combat sortie.

Robin had never been so conscious of killing someone before. All the German airmen in the planes he'd shot down just weren't the same. He hadn't known them personally. Besides, they were the enemy. They were bombing his country, his city, his fiancée's home, for Christ's sake!

Robin shifted uncomfortably. He didn't have to close his eyes to see

355

the way Portsmouth was burning just now. His mother was safe. The bombs had fallen predominantly near the dockyards – where Emily lived and where she and Aunt Hattie worked in the Seaman's Mission. That was what had made him lose his temper out there.

He'd looked down and realised that the bombs were falling on Emily's neighbourhood. For all he knew, she was dead, too. Just like Goldman. If Emily was dead, it was in part because they had failed to intercept in time. Failed to break up the bomber formation. Failed to shoot them down last time they were over. Failed to discourage this kind of bloody raid. Failed, failed, failed.

"Are you all right, sir?"

Robin jumped out of his skin. Then he looked over and saw Allars studying him very intently.

"No. No, I'm not all right. If you must know, I'm about to have a nervous breakdown. Any second now, I'm going to throw myself on the grass and start tearing it out with my teeth and throwing it at the heavens or – whatever. Something like that."

"Oh, well, if that's all, don't let me stop you. Before you start, however, I thought you might want to know that Pilot Officer Goldman has called in from some girl's school. It seems his parachute got entangled in a tree beside their hunt field. The sight of which sent quite a number of their silly, over-bred mounts bolting in all directions. The girls, it seems, are willing to forgive him, and the Head Mistress has promised to have him back here in time for dinner – but she insisted he stay at the school for tea."

Robin stared at Allars for a minute in disbelief before he finally smiled. "And Bowles?"

"Give me another half-hour on that, will you?"

"Half an hour? I'm a generous man. Take an hour. But get him back."

"I'll do my best. Now, would you like to tell me about the Junkers Kiwi says you 'nailed.'"

They were walking back to dispersal together. Both the weariness and the tension had eased. They weren't gone, exactly, but Robin could shove them into some corner and keep functioning.

Portsmouth

Marjory came up breathlessly. "Miss Pryce! Miss Pryce! Come quick. It's RAF Tangmere. They want to speak to you."

RAF Tangmere? Emily dropped everything and ran. She had been so proud to think Robin was up there defending her. What a fool! She hadn't given a thought to him being killed. How could she be so naïve?

She was out of breath by the time she got to the phone in the hall, where the receiver waited off the hook for her. "Hello? RAF Tangmere?"

"Miss Emily Pryce?" It was a strange voice, a female voice.

"Yes. Is—"

"Let me put you through to Squadron Leader Priestman."

Emily almost collapsed from relief, and then Robin was on the phone. "Emily? Are you all right?"

"Yes, I'm fine—"

"Next time, for God's sake, would you call in? I've been mad with worry, and I can't afford that."

"I didn't think I should bother you—" Emily protested.

"Just call the Adjutant, and he'll get the message to me. I need to have my mind clear for the job—"

"But I haven't got the number," Emily pointed out. "I haven't got *any* number where I can reach you. You've never given me one."

"All right. I'm sorry. It's just I could see where the bombs were dropping. It was so close to the Mission. You're sure you're all right?"

"The cinema was hit – full of children at a matinee. We've been trying to help a bit."

"Emily, I've got to go, but here's Mickey. He'll give you the number. And I'll take you to dinner tomorrow. Promise." He hung up.

RAF Tangmere

That settled, the next problem was Mr. Bowles. Mickey had put him in the waiting room. He'd offered him tea and then as the time crawled past, he'd offered him scotch. The man had looked at the Adjutant as if he'd pointed a pistol at him. His eyes widened. He put his hand to his chest and pressed it hard as if it were hurting him. "My boy's dead."

Mickey denied it. As he admitted to Robin, "I just couldn't bring myself to tell him. He's such a simple man. And he must love his son a great deal to come all that way."

"Well, we don't actually have confirmation yet, do we?" Robin found himself clinging to a straw of hope.

"No, but it's three hours since the squadron returned. Goldman reported in over two hours ago."

Priestman didn't need to be reminded of that. He glanced at the clock.

19.35. He picked up the receiver and called the control room. "Bridges?"

"Yes, Robin?"

"Anything on the boards?"

"No. All gone home for dinner."

"Not bloody all of them!" Priestman reminded him, with that same burst of anger he had felt while pursuing the Junkers this afternoon. His nerves really were raw.

"Sorry," Bainbridge soothed.

"Not to worry. Thanks." Priestman hung up. He took a deep breath and put his cap back on before he entered the anteroom. Ginger's father got to his feet at the sight of him. He couldn't read RAF rank insignia. He didn't know that Priestman was a Squadron Leader – but he sensed authority intuitively.

Priestman saw a farmer: short, stocky, no neck to speak of, with red skin and a flat face – rather like a bull. He was dressed in a worn suit that had apparently shrunk, leaving his ankles and his wrists exposed. His fingers were stubby, and his hands had so many years of ingrained dirt on them that, although scrubbed clean for this occasion, the torn fingernails were lined in black. He had big brown eyes, the eyes of a bullock facing the slaughter full of incomprehension.

"Mr. Bowles," Robin held out his hand, "my name is Robert Priestman. I'm the officer commanding 606 Squadron."

"My boy is dead, isn't he?"

"We don't know that for sure, sir. But he is overdue. More than two hours overdue."

Tears glistened in the man's eyes. His lips quivered slightly. He stood there clutching his hat in his filthy hands, and there was nothing either of them could say. Then the man croaked out in his broad West Country accent, "May I – Do you mind if – Could I just wait a little longer, sir? I won't be in anyone's way. I promise. If you want me to wait outside—"

"Of course not. You are welcome to wait here, sir. Or you can come to the Mess and have something to eat." Stupid thing to say, Robin noted even before he'd finished saying it. This man was obviously in no condition to eat anything. "Let me have tea or whatever you want brought in to you—"

The man shook his head. The tears spilled over and ran down his weathered skin. His hands started to shake. "He's all I've got. M' wife died years ago. He's the meaning of my whole life."

From outside the room came the crash of doors being flung open and loud, careless voices. Laughter, even. Priestman frowned. At that moment he could have killed whoever it was even though he objectively realised that they did not know what was transpiring in here.

"Mr. Bowles. I want you to know that your son is without doubt one of the bravest men I have ever had the honour—"

The door behind him crashed open and Priestman spun about furiously. Mickey was grinning in at him. A moment later a figure black from head to foot with dripping and stinking gunk walked into the room. Even his own father took a moment to recognise him. Then they were in each other's arms.

Priestman left them to it and retreated into the Adjutant's office. "What the devil—"

"He bailed out at 5.000 feet and landed in tidal flats – that's what that stinking black stuff is. Once he'd waded out of the guck, he *walked* back here. He says he couldn't have asked anyone to give him a lift with all that stinking mud clinging to him, and it never occurred to him to call in, since he knew he'd make it on his own."

"He'll get a bollocking for that!" Priestman promised, but he was grinning. The relief was almost too much to bear. Goldman, Emily and now Bowles all safe, and Geordie's wounds were not fatal. Given the intensity of the fight and the odds they'd faced today, he was satisfied with those results. Kiwi, Goldman and Herriman had all survived their first combat, two of them completely unscathed, and that improved their chances of surviving tomorrow by a large margin.

Now, he had to get on with the next order of business: seeing the padre, who had had a talk with LAC Tufnel, and then seeing Tufnel himself.

After that he planned a talk with the ground crews – as he should have done four days ago – and then there was the paperwork....

Chapter 28

RAF Tangmere,
25 August 1940

"Another lovely day today, sir," Thatcher announced cheerfully.

Robin opened one eye and gazed at him. Didn't he know what that meant? Another day of the Germans hammering Fighter Command's airfields. Another day waiting with nerves strained to the breaking point or scrambling wildly to face overwhelming odds. They'd lost Manston yesterday. For all they knew it might be Tangmere's turn today.

"Just a little milk and two sugars, just as you ordered, sir. And I've brought you some toast, too."

It was impossible to be angry with the man. Robin sat up and took the tea. "What's the mood among the erks this morning? You knew this job came with a mandate to spy and report, didn't you?"

"Yes, sir, and the mood has improved somewhat."

Robin had called the squadron's other ranks together in the hangar last night and given them a talk. He'd explained that Jones had sat on all leave requests for over a month and that there were so many requests in his file that he couldn't possibly grant them all without the squadron breaking down altogether.

He'd asked them to bear with him while a proper leave roster was worked out with the station Engineering Officer. Then everyone would get leave on a regular basis regardless of what was going on. Meanwhile, he promised that he would hear any requests for emergency leave – but begged them to keep these requests to "real" emergencies.

Next he'd addressed the subject of L A C Sanders. The RAF, he said, couldn't afford to lose first-rate tradesmen like Sanders to "avoidable" accidents. By "avoidable" he said he meant men working when they were exhausted or sick. He said he'd rather go to readiness with one less aircraft, than with one less aircraftsman.

"If you aren't doing your best, believe me, I'll know it." That had brought a ripple of laughter. After the savaging of the pilots five days earlier, his reputation for not tolerating any slack was well established. "But if you are doing your best, that's all I ask."

When he opened the floor to questions, the first one had been about Tufnel. The speaker, his own fitter Ripley, said that Tufnel was a good man and not a trouble-maker, and nobody believed he was trying to desert – certainly not out of cowardice.

Priestman replied that he agreed, and that Tufnel had been given three days leave to go and sort out certain problems. All charges were suspended. Only if he failed to return would they be pressed. He'd thought at the time that this news had been well received.

Thatcher confirmed that impression. "They approved of the way you handled Tufnel, sir, and although there was some grumbling that you could have granted leave in the order it had been requested, there was general satisfaction that something was going to be done about the situation. Now, if you'd just do something about the food, you'll have them eating out of your hand."

"The food?"

"Yes, the airmen's kitchen was hit and most of the cooks were killed, and so other ranks are being fed from the Sergeants' Mess, and it's always cold by the time we get it. The cooks in the Sergeants' Mess are overworked and fed up with the situation, too."

"That's really beyond my control," Priestman pointed out. "The Station Commander has to take care of it."

"I understand, sir. I brought you today's paper, sir. I know you come from Portsmouth."

The airman withdrew, leaving Robin staring at the paper. Filling almost the entire front page was a picture of a row of houses that ended in a heap of rubble, with broken lumber scattered upon the bricks and men in tin hats sifting through the mess.

The headlines read: "143 dead! Worst German raid in history!" Horrified, he read the details. The casualties had not been carelessly walking about. Several of the "Andersen" shelters, which people had been urged to build in their kitchen gardens, had been blown apart in direct hits. Also, a pair of slit trenches had collapsed.

A map showing where the bombs had fallen put him off breakfast altogether. It wasn't just the dockyards that had been hit, as he'd first thought. There were bombs all over the place — Orchard Road, Albert Grove, and worst of all, King's Road, just behind where his mother lived and close to where Emily had worked before. Thank God he'd told her to resign – but the sooner he got her out of Portsmouth, the better.

He was so absorbed in reading the paper, he forgot the time. When he put the paper aside and saw the clock, he had to rush. After the fuss he'd made that first day, he could *not* be late for readiness himself. He knew his pilots disliked him, but so far they respected him and obeyed him. If he did anything that gave them justification for not only disliking him but also viewing him as a hypocrite, he would lose control of them altogether. That meant not only being on time but also being sure he was washed and shaved and properly dressed when he showed up, too.

He tried to hurry, but he had just fifteen minutes left for breakfast when he made it downstairs. As he wolfed it down, the lorry pulled up outside and his pilots went out to it (rather conspicuously) in a group, leaving him drinking his tea standing alone. The driver of the lorry (probably at the inducement of one of the pilots) hooted the horn, threatening.

Priestman gave up trying to finish and stepped out of the Mess – only to be waylaid by the WAAF Officer Commanding.

"Squadron Leader Priestman. Just the man I was looking for."

"I'm on my way on readiness, ma'am. Could we have this discussion at another time?"

"Frankly, no. You're always busy, and I've been up all night trying to deal with a situation caused by one of your pilots. You might have the courtesy at least to hear me out."

Priestman took a deep breath and remained where he was. The WAAF driver – and all his pilots – could see that he was here and see that he'd been stopped by the WAAF Section Officer.

"Are you even aware that one of your pilots has seduced one of my WAAF?"

"I presume the WAAF involved was over the age of 18."

"Yes, 'though barely, and a very young 18, too—"

"In that case, Ma'am, anything that occurred between her and one of my pilots took place between two adults and really doesn't concern me."

"Are you saying that the morals and disgraceful behaviour of your subordinates do not interest you, Squadron Leader?" Newton asked indignantly.

"Half my pilots are probably still virgins, ma'am, and very likely to die that way. Do you want to have to say the same thing about your WAAF? Now, if you'll excuse me, I have to go on readiness. Any further discussion can wait."

Priestman left her standing – and sputtering – in his wake and made a dash to catch the lorry.

Bridges watched the board all morning with mounting unease, unconsciously fussing with the patch over his missing eye. Just one fighter sweep after another. It didn't make sense to him. They'd handed the RAF their first tangible defeat – the abandonment of Manston – two days ago. They'd pounded the sector airfields and the Navy with devastating effect yesterday. And now they didn't follow it up? They should have been back in double strength today. They should have been hounding the fox, now that they had him on the run – not giving him a chance to catch his breath. Hornchurch and North Weald were both reporting repairs complete.

Early in the afternoon, a raid finally built up over Cherbourg, and Bridges – ignoring his lunch again – sat rigidly at his desk and prepared for a new duel. He glanced at the board: 606 and 17 were at readiness and 602 available. No. 43 squadron had been released after the losses they'd taken yesterday; they needed the rest.

But this raid was veering very far west, clearly heading neither for Tangmere nor Portsmouth, nor even Southampton. It was 10 Group's business.

"Aren't you going to have your lunch, sir?" ACW Roberts asked with apparent concern.

He shook his head. "No thanks. Not really hungry."

"Is your eye bothering you, sir? Can I get you something for it?"

As he shook his head, he thought: Oh, dear. I hope she isn't getting personal or anything. That wouldn't do. It was bad enough that one of the plotters, Liz Hadley, was dating F/O Ringwood. Bainbridge couldn't bear to think what would happen if she was standing down there listening to the pilots on the R/T when Ringwood was hit – maybe wounded and calling for help, or screaming as he burnt to death. No, it didn't bear thinking about.

More plots came on the table. Now they were coming in after all. Both 606 and 17 went to stand-by. They could not risk them being caught on the ground. Tangmere had to be on the agenda sooner or later. But then the Isle of Wight Observer Corps reported, "Snappers only, repeat, snappers only. Not even the larger sort. A school of minnows on their own."

"Thank you." This information was given to Uxbridge too, of course, and Bridges took his squadrons from stand-by back to readiness, allowing them to leave their cockpits. Then he turned things over to Robinson for a bit and went down the wooden steps from the gallery and out into the bright, sunny afternoon. Windier than yesterday, he noted. He found his cigarettes and lit one with difficulty.

When he returned to the Ops Room, there was still nothing on the boards. After checking with Park, he called 606 dispersal and told them to go to 30-minute availability for one flight only.

Priestman turned to his pilots. "All right, one-flight readiness only. Ginger, Goldman and Eton, you can have the afternoon off."

"Why me?" Eton asked, evidently affronted. The others groaned.

"If Eton doesn't want to go, sir, I'll make the sacrifice," F/O Donohue offered with alacrity.

"You'll stay right where you are. Eton, just take the afternoon off, and don't argue with me."

"But, sir—"

"Ever hear the one about the Squadron Leader who chopped three pilots in one day for answering back?" Ringwood started casually to Ware.

Eton was out the door.

"It was only two for answering back," Priestman corrected.

"Hey, I haven't heard that one. Go on, Woody," Kiwi urged eagerly.

Priestman threw a magazine at him. Dodging to avoid it, Kiwi knocked over the chair Williams was sitting in. A general free-for-all followed, which only ended when they were all out of breath from laughing so hard. Gradually the laughter died out, and their breathing returned to normal. They resumed their normal poses, but Priestman knew that something good had just happened. He walked out of the dispersal hut and stood gulping the fresh air.

*****

Ginger's Dad had spent the night in a farmhouse bed-and-breakfast south of Midhurst. The vicar at home had a sister who knew the woman who ran it, and that was why he'd taken these particular lodgings. Ginger was grateful in one way: at least no one from the squadron was likely to find it. But it was rather hard to get to without transport. It had taken his Dad and him over an hour and a half to get there last night by bus. Not that it mattered. They were together. And once there, they had been able to talk by the fireside late into the night – almost as if they were at home. There had even been two dogs to keep them company.

Of course, it had taken Ginger half the night to get back to Tangmere again, and he'd been so tired he'd drifted off once or twice during readiness this morning, but he was feeling better. Seeing his Dad had done him good. That, and having a CO who really looked after them.

Priestman had given him an earful for not calling in yesterday, but only because he'd been worrying. Jones hadn't given a bugger what had happened to him last time. Priestman had also ticked him off about getting out of a burning aircraft faster. Next time, he said, he didn't want to hear Ginger being told twice by another pilot. That made him feel good, too – even if he knew he'd do anything not to land in the drink.

"Ginger?"

Bowles jumped and looked over at Pilot Officer Goldman, who was walking beside him. Goldman's face a wreck from the run-in with the tree yesterday; half was black and blue, and his nose was swollen up like a pig's. There was no question why the CO had let the two of them have the afternoon off. If anyone in the squadron needed it, they did.

"Do you need a lift anywhere? To get to your father, or whatever?" Goldman asked.

"Oh, my Dad's staying way up at Midhurst, sir. Miles away. I wouldn't want to impose."

"Please, don't call me 'sir,'" Goldman answered. "It makes me feel like I'm 60 years old or some stuffy banker." What he really meant was he wanted to make friends. The auxiliary pilots had started calling him "Banks" on account of his father owning one, and he was grateful that they hadn't chosen a less pleasant nickname such as "Judas" or "Jerry," but he still sensed their disdain for him. If he was going to have any friends here, then it was more likely someone like Ginger who was as much an outcast as he was himself, if for different reasons. To Ginger he noted with a tentative smile, "Nothing's that far away in this country."

"It is more than 10 miles, s— What do you want me to call you?"

"David or Banks like the others do. Ten miles is nothing. Besides, I've got nothing else to do with the afternoon. Couldn't I take you and your Dad somewhere? Chichester, for example? I hear the Cathedral is worth seeing."

Ginger was mortified. His Dad in this rich man's Jaguar? But how was he supposed to say "no"? "That's what I've been told too, but m' Dad – well, he's a very simple man. I don't think he's very keen on that kind of thing."

"In that case, I'll just drop you off and continue on my way."

"But it's out of your way. Midhurst is due north and Chichester is west."

"I've got nothing else to do."

Ginger sensed it would be rude to protest any more, so there was nothing for it but to set off together. In front of the Mess, however, they ran into the padre. He asked where they were going, and Banks told him.

"Oh, I was just on my way to Chichester myself," Colin answered. "I've got a list of things to pick up." He indicated a folded piece of paper, which he took out and then stuffed back into his breast pocket. "Would you mind if I tagged along with you?"

"Of course not," Banks agreed at once, glad of the company. "In fact, if you don't mind, you can drive my Jag. I strip the gears too much."

"May I?" Colin asked eagerly. A silver Jaguar was much more exciting than the hand-me-down old Bentley from his father.

With Colin driving and Banks beside him, they set off. Ginger was glad to be in the back. He didn't have to say anything that way, except what was necessary to direct them to the farmhouse bed-and-breakfast.

When they arrived, Ginger climbed out and hastily and thanked Banks and Colin. He was anxious to get inside before his father came out and the others saw him. Just as he straightened to wave the others off, his father came out of the house. He must have been sitting at the window watching – hoping – that Ginger would show up. He was dressed like the day before, in his Sunday best, and holding his hat in his hands.

Ginger cringed. Yesterday, he had been too overwhelmed by his father's unexpected presence to be ashamed, but now he saw all his flaws: the suit shrunk so that the sleeves revealed the frayed cuffs of his shirt and the trousers exposed his thick socks; the dirty fingernails; his terrible tie – and all that displayed for the rich banker's son and a future peer of the realm. It was horrible.

Worse. The officers were getting out of the car, coming over to offer their hands to his Dad. And his Dad – grinning like an idiot – was offering them his stained, stubby workman's hands. Ginger wanted to scream at him: That's the future Earl of Exmouth, Dad! You should knuckle your forehead, not shake hands. But already his Dad had worked out that Colin was the padre who had organised the telephone call on the night of Ginger's arrival. Rather than letting his hand go, he grasped it in both of his filthy paws and pumped it up and down vigorously as he thanked him earnestly.

When Colin finally managed to extricate his (nearly crushed) hand and introduce Banks, Mr. Bowles wanted to know right off what had happened to Banks' face. When he learned that Banks had bailed out, he started chattering about how Ginger had bailed out yesterday, too.

"They *know* that, Dad. Now, let them get on their way," Ginger intervened in a peeved voice.

"Oh, where are you off to, then?" Mr. Bowles senior asked.

"Chichester, sir," Banks answered readily. "Do you want to join us?"

"Chichester? Oh, yes! The vicar said I shouldn't miss the Cathedral. Are you going to the cathedral?"

"Yes, of course," Banks answered, with an amused smile to Ginger, as he opened the passenger door for the older man.

"Dad—" Ginger tried to stop him, but Mr. Bowles was already settling himself in the front seat of the Jaguar, looking pleased as punch.

"I always wanted to ride in a posh motorcar," he told Banks happily, his eyes taking in all the shine and the dials, his hands stroking the leather seats.

Ginger looked helplessly at Colin, who shrugged and got back in behind the steering wheel, while Banks climbed into the back seat. For a moment Ginger stood outside, trying to think of some way to make his father get out again, but he couldn't. He climbed into the car, feeling more embarrassed than ever.

First, Ginger's Dad wanted Colin to tell him what all the dials and knobs and "gadgets" were for. Then he enthused about what a pleasure it was to meet some of Ginger's friends. Ginger had been such a solitary boy, he told the others. "Lived too far from everyone, you see," his father explained. Finally, Mr. Bowles launched into his favourite subject: Ginger himself. He raved about how clever Ginger was and good with mechanical things. Good with animals too, but he "came by that naturally," his father insisted solemnly. "His gift with machines – that's something special." Next, he was telling Colin about how good Ginger had been at school – "like no one in the family ever before," and how he got a "scholarship."

All Colin could do was nod and make polite noises – he couldn't get a word in edgeways. Now and then Mr. Bowles would twist around to be sure Banks heard what he was saying, and Banks would nod and make the odd, encouraging comment as well, while Ginger tried to make himself smaller and smaller.

He wished his father had never come. He felt he couldn't bear it a minute longer, but it went on and on and on. It only stopped when they got to Chichester and Colin conducted a tour of the Cathedral. Here at last Mr. Bowles was awed into silence by the great Gothic cathedral and the presence of God. Abruptly, in the Lady Chapel, he dropped on his knees, folded his hands and prayed so earnestly that it made even the padre a little uncomfortable.

The three young men in uniform stood about awkwardly, waiting for the old farmer to finish. Finally, Mr. Bowles got up, dusted imaginary dirt off his knees with his hat, and announced in a loud whisper, "Just praying for you, Ginger. That you always get out safe. And I put in a word for you too, young man," he added to Banks solemnly.

"Thank you, sir," Banks said in surprise, unexpectedly moved. Ginger wanted to disappear through the flagstone flooring, Banks being a Jew and all.

They had tea together, Ginger's father asking Banks about Canada – all the stupid, ignorant questions that Ginger had been careful *not* to ask. And, of course, he slurped his tea noisily and soaked up the spilt liquid with his scone. Ginger thought he was going to die there and then.

After that, Colin had to do his shopping, and Ginger's Dad insisted on carrying everything. "Frail boy like you can't manage that!" he kept saying. "Give it here, boy!" The future Earl of Exmouth: "boy"! Ginger almost corrected him, but every time he opened his mouth to protest, Colin intervened graciously, thanking Mr. Bowles and saying what a big help he was.

At last the afternoon was over, and they returned to the Jaguar and drove back to Midhurst. Mr. Bowles sat in front again, humming tunelessly to himself, very happy. Colin asked him about where he'd come from, and his wife.

"Now that was the finest girl you ever laid eyes on," Mr. Bowles declared simply, with a smile that lit up his leathered face. "It took me almost a six-month to work up the courage just to ask her to walk out with me. I was *that* sure she'd say 'no.'" He shook his head at the memory, smiling faintly, and then he turned and looked over the seat at Ginger. "You take after her, Ginger. All your good qualities, you get from her."

Ginger knew that wasn't true, but at that moment he was so furious with his Dad for this whole, embarrassing afternoon, that he said nothing.

At last they reached the farmhouse. They all got out of the car, and Mr. Bowles asked generally and eagerly, "You want to stay to dinner, boys? I'm sure—"

"NO!" Ginger couldn't take it a moment longer. "We have to get back to the Station. I was much too late last night! I was a wreck all day. We have to get an early night."

For the first time this day, his father looked deflated. For a moment a look of bewildered hurt came into his eyes – as if he had only just noticed that Ginger had hardly said a word all afternoon. "But—"

"I'll try to ring tomorrow – but I won't be able to get time off," Ginger told him bluntly. Then, relenting a little, he gave his father a quick hug before climbing hurriedly into the back of the car again.

Banks and Colin exchanged a look, shook hands with Mr. Bowles, and then got back into the car. They waved good-bye, and Mr. Bowles stood at the end of the drive, waving as long as he could see the car. At the very last minute, Ginger remembered he might never see his Dad again, and turned sharply to wave back. But it was too late. The car had gone around a bend and a hedgerow got in the way. Sadly, Mr. Bowles wandered back up the drive to the house.

Ginger sat hunched in the back of the car, too ashamed even to apologise. His father had ruined everyone's afternoon – which wasn't that bad for the padre, maybe, but Banks could be dead tomorrow. Ginger thought he wasn't ever going to be able to look either of them in the eye again. Every time they saw him, they'd be reminded of his uneducated, selfish father rambling on all afternoon!

Banks and Colin glanced at one another, and then Banks turned around and said, "You're lucky, Ginger."

"You don't have to make fun of me, you know!" Ginger snarled back.

Banks glanced at Colin again, and then he said seriously, "I'm not. I'm absolutely serious. Your father thinks the world of you. He's truly proud of you." He paused and then admitted, "My father – even when I was a little boy, my father never had time for me. I was just an annoyance. My earliest memory is of him coming out of his office to reprimand my Nanny for letting me play too loudly near his study. He didn't honour me with so much as a glance or a word. He addressed himself to my Nanny alone. She curtsied and hastened to shoo me away.

"And when I went to boarding school, I was sent in a car with a chauffeur and servant and picked up the same way. When I played football at school, he never came to watch a match. My mother came once or twice, but my father never had time.

"I know what you're thinking, Ginger. You think your father is just a simple man while my father is an influential banker, but would you rather be a banker's disappointment or a workman's pride?"

Ginger gazed at Banks for a moment. It was hard to read Banks' face – misshapen and discoloured as it was at the moment – but Ginger couldn't believe he meant what he said. He started to protest, "I'm sure you aren't really a disappointment to your father. I mean, you're an officer—"

Banks' face twisted even more. "On a short-service commission. I failed to get a college education. Your father can't get over the fact that you can fly aeroplanes, while mine says I'm nothing but a 'glorified bus driver.' Flying is for him nothing more than a means of transport. The day I came home in my pilot's uniform for the first time – so proud of myself I was busting – my father greeted me with the words: 'You might as well drive a city bus. Change into proper clothes for dinner.'"

Even Colin gasped at that and exclaimed, "You can't be serious!" Banks turned to Colin deadly seriously. "The day I brought him the newspaper article about the RAF offering short-term commissions to trained pilots, he read the article and then looked up at me and remarked in all honesty, 'This is the first time that I've ever been proud of you.'"

Banks turned to address Ginger again. "*The first time, Ginger.* I'm 22 years old, and the only reason my father is proud of me is that I'm risking my life to fight the Nazis – not because of *me* at all. Not like your father, Ginger. Your father loves everything about you. If you were arrested for rape and murder tomorrow, he'd show up at the gaol with tears in his eyes asking what *he'd* done wrong – he'd never blame you."

Ginger swallowed awkwardly. He'd never thought about it. To him it was just natural. Fathers love their sons. That was all there was to it, nothing to be particularly proud of or happy about. But looking at David, some of the embarrassment and resentment he'd been feeling all afternoon started to ease. He realised that neither David nor Colin were looking down their noses at him. Neither of them was making fun of him or his Dad. They were calling him by his first name.

"What do you say we all go to dinner?" Colin suggested, suddenly elated, intuitively feeling what Ginger felt at the same moment. "Just the three of us," he added to be sure they understood.

"Good idea!" Banks agreed instantly, smiling so much his face hurt, and Ginger was grinning suddenly, too. They were friends.

Portsmouth

Robin was running very late. He'd said he'd be at Emily's at 7 pm, to give them an hour with her parents before going on to dinner. Dinner reservations were for eight. But by 7.45 he hadn't shown up, and Emily's parents, who had a Party meeting at which her father was giving a talk, had to leave.

They were not pleased. Mrs. Pryce remarked that she thought very little of a man who could not be punctual and wondered how much respect he had for a girl he left waiting for hours. Mr. Pryce shook his head sadly and sighed to his daughter, "You think this man wants to *marry* you when he hasn't even got the courtesy to be on time for his first meeting with your parents?"

They left her there in the dingy little house, waiting. Adding to the gloom was the smoke that still hung over Portsmouth from the fires started the day before. The big Navy oil tank was still burning, five houses had been lost in the next road, and an unexploded bomb was cordoned off in the middle of the rubble – something the sappers would have to get to when they had time.

Emily could hear the grandfather clocking ticking slowly in the living room, admonishingly marking the increasing length of Robin's tardiness. Every tick of the clock seemed like a disapproving reminder of her utter dependency. She had no life of her own any more. Everything turned around him.

Then she heard a car in the street and jumped up to go to the front window. A big, old Bentley drew to a stop right in front and at once attracted a hostile crowd from the men lounging around "The Queen's Head" at the corner. The driver's door opened, and Robin stepped out. Emily let the blackout curtain fall back in place and hurried to the hall to open the door, stopping only to check that her lipstick and hair looked all right in the hall mirror. But the doorbell didn't ring. She opened the door to look out.

Robin was still in the street, completely hemmed in b what looked like every schoolboy in the neighbourhood. They were hounding him with questions. He glanced up, caught sight of Emily and started towards her. The boys kept pace with him like a pack of hounds, still asking breathless questions. How fast could a Hurricane fly? How high? Had he killed many Germans?

"No, but I'm about to kill a very large number of English school boys if they don't get out of my way." That surprised them enough for Robin to bound up the steps and in the open door. Emily closed it behind him, and he turned, taking off his cap and bending to kiss her in one motion. The kiss was stronger, hungrier, than any that had passed between them before. Emily's pulse raced, but then Robin pulled abruptly away and glanced around nervously. "I'm sorry I'm late. Your parents must be very angry. I'd better go and make my apologies to them. I'll tell you what happened afterwards."

"They had to leave. My father was giving a talk tonight." In the harsh glare of the hall light, Robin looked utterly exhausted, as if he hadn't slept since the last time she'd seen him. He had dark circles under his eyes, and the skin around his mouth was red and dry from the chafing of his oxygen mask. His hair, falling over his forehead as usual, looked as if it hadn't been washed lately.

Without thinking Emily exclaimed, "Robin, you look absolutely knackered!" No sooner was it out than she bit her tongue. Why did she always have to blurt things out like that? She would have been hurt if he'd said the same about her.

Robin didn't seem to mind at all. "I *am* a bit tired. Things have been fairly hectic these last days. Then just as I was leaving to come here, the Station Commander sent for me. You won't believe it. I was given the worst ticking off of my life for some silly remark I made to the old bag commanding the Station WAAF. I planned to stop and get flowers for your Mum, but by the time the Station Commander was finished with me I didn't have time for anything but driving straight here. I couldn't even stop by a bank. Do you think the restaurant will take a cheque?" he asked, pulling out his wallet and peering inside. "I haven't got enough cash for dinner. I'm sure of that."

"Robin, we don't have to go to dinner. I can make you something here. Not that I'm a good cook or anything, but it's after eight. They may have given the table away already."

Robin looked at his watch and then back at Emily. "You wouldn't mind? Not going out, I mean?"

"I wouldn't mind at all. As long as we're together."

"I'll ring the restaurant then and tell them we can't make it." Emily nodded and went to the kitchen to start looking for something she could turn into a meal. She thought they had some rabbit left over from last Sunday, or should she "steal" the roast planned for tomorrow?

Robin joined her after a moment and stood in the door watching.

She wore a simple blue dress with white collar and sash, and the white, high heels with straps. Very elegant. Yet she had put on an apron to make dinner, and that gave her a domestic touch. Watching her efficiently set pans on the stove and collect a variety of ingredients, Robin congratulated himself. How many Cambridge graduates loved flying and could cook as well? "Shall I pour us something to drink?" he asked.

Emily hadn't realised he was back and turned around a little surprised. "Oh! I'm sorry. I hadn't thought of that. My parents are fanatical teetotallers. You'll find no alcohol in the house at all."

"Right. Then I'll just nip across to the local to buy a bottle. I'll be right back."

He was gone, and Emily was just as happy. She felt self-conscious cooking with someone watching. Realising the roast would take too long, she decided on a cabbage stew with spam and potatoes. She set to work, and hardly noticed that Robin was gone for a long time until she was nearly ready to serve and he still wasn't back. *Now* what was keeping him? Wasn't it bad enough that he was almost an hour late getting here?

Just then she heard the door open, and Robin swept into the kitchen with not one bottle but three – scotch, gin, and red wine. "Compliments of the Navy!" he announced. "I don't think they'd ever seen an RAF uniform in there before. I could have stayed until closing and never spent tuppence."

She could smell the scotch on his breath already, but he blew away her annoyance with a quick kiss. "Don't be angry, Em. Here, I'll mix you a gin and tonic. You'll love it."

Emily found it impossible to be angry with him. She brought two small tumblers (since there were no cocktail or wine glasses in the house), and Robin poured their drinks while she set dinner on the table. She had taken out her parents' best china and silver for the occasion – the things that waited unused in the dining room cabinet year-after-year. The tablecloth was the best Irish linen from her mother's "hope chest," creased permanently from decades of disuse.

When they sat down at last, it was almost 9.15 pm. "So, what did you say to get yourself into so much trouble?" Emily asked as she shook out her starched napkin.

"I can't remember exactly. I was on my way to dispersal at five am this morning, and suddenly this WAAF officer was in my way babbling on about how one of my pilots had seduced one of her WAAF – mind you, even *she* said 'seduced.' I suppose I was flippant and asked her if she really wanted her WAAF to die virgins—"

Emily burst out laughing. "You didn't really?"

Robin paused and glanced at Emily uncertainly. She was laughing delightedly – one hand over her mouth as she did when she felt guilty about laughing but couldn't help herself. "The Station Commander," he told her cautiously, "made it very clear to me that my remarks were most inappropriate. He said my remarks implied that there was something *wrong* with being a virgin and that this was an insulting attitude – I presume since I said it to a woman who is very obviously of that ilk!"

Emily doubled up with laughter, the gin and tonic on the empty stomach having gone to her head.

"Furthermore, the Station Commander intoned, one of our greatest monarchs, Queen Elizabeth, had been a virgin, which presumably—"

Emily went into another fit of giggling and shook her head so vigorously, Robin stopped, a little confused. "Actually," she managed to gasp between giggles, "she probably wasn't. There's considerable evidence that Queen Elizabeth had at least an affair – if not a long-standing relationship – with Robert Dudley, Earl of Leicester. One way or another, I'm sure *she* would have *agreed* with you about virginity being a deplorable state to die in."

Emily was still trying to get her giggles under control, but Robin's thoughts had moved on. "It certainly would be a terrible shame if *you* died in that state."

That sobered Emily by embarrassing her and making her suddenly self-conscious. She looked down at her stew, blushing and wondering if it had been such a wise move to suggest making dinner for him here. Did he think, maybe, that she was inviting greater intimacies? It wouldn't be unreasonable. They were engaged. Was she so sure she didn't want them?

Robin had the sense to change the subject. "We'd better eat before it gets cold. It smells delicious."

For a moment they concentrated on the stew, Robin complimenting Emily on it lavishly, making her to blush again. Emily changed the subject. "Tell me about the squadron."

Robin hesitated. "I don't know where to begin."

"Then start with the pilot who got you in so much trouble today." Robin looked at her, not comprehending. "By seducing a WAAF."

"Oh. Sergeant MacLeod. He's a rough and a troublemaker, and...." It poured out as if the floodgates had opened. He told her of the impudence of the auxiliary pilots. He told her about Debsen, who ran away at the sight of the enemy, and Ginger, who got sick at the same sight – but still did his best. He told about his Hurricane stalling in the midst of a dogfight and the German pilots who had let him live. He told of the ground crews driven to exhaustion and accidents by a Chief he dared not replace for sheer dependence on the man's efficiency. He told her of the aircrews living in damp tents with cold food, and Emily risked interrupting, "But why not let the Salvation Army organise something? We could probably bring a hot meal in – at least once a day. I'm sure we could – if you want. We have a mobile canteen."

Robin got up and kissed her for that. "Splendid idea! Do you think you could really manage a hot meal?"

Emily promised to look into it and let him know.

Robin sat down again and told her about Eton, who was just a school boy playing at being an adult. He explained about getting Kiwi and Goldman — now known as "Banks" — posted to 606. "Kiwi's brilliant. He's the calmest man I've ever encountered – almost phlegmatic but in a good way – and he has them all laughing in an instant. But Banks got shot down on his first combat sortie. Horrible black eye and bloody nose from crashing into a tree at some girl's school. Banks says it was a nightmare."

"I bet the girls loved it!" Emily told him with a laugh, "one of the PM's 'Few' dropping in like that!"

Robin laughed with her, and then asked for seconds. When they were married, he could do this every night, Robin reflected – talk to Emily about everything in the privacy of his own home rather than maintaining a pretence of cheerful imperturbability in a noisy Mess. "Have you done anything about our wedding yet?" he asked her.

Emily flinched guiltily. She had talked to Hattie about it, of course, but she was having problems with the idea of joining the Church. "I wanted to talk to you about that," she admitted, not daring to meet his eye. "I understand your feelings about some county clerk or whatever – but, well, I really don't believe in God, and isn't it terribly hypocritical to go through a lot of vows and rituals...." Her voice trailed off. She glanced up at him to see if he was angry.

He wasn't. He was, in fact, looking very contented as he sipped at the red wine. In a relaxed tone he asked, "Do you seriously think all Creation was an accident?"

"No, I'm quite willing to agree there might be some kind of a Creator, but I just can't believe in, well, a benign Being who takes an active interest in our *individual* lives. How could He? There are millions and millions of us. And if He's on our side, then He can't be on the side of the Germans, or the Italians, but they all pray to Him too, don't they? The Germans even have '*Gott mit Uns!*' on their belt buckles!"

"True but being 'with us' doesn't mean He's on our side."

"Well, what *does* it mean?" she asked, slightly annoyed, because he was acting so self-assured on a subject that she didn't think anyone had any right to feel confident about.

"Being with us is just that: being with and inside of each of us."

"You think God is with you?"

"Always."

"When you're killing?"

"And when I'm being shot at."

"I don't understand."

"God is always with us, but just as He doesn't always do what we want Him to, we often don't do what He wants us to do. For a start, we have to ask for His help, and then we have to listen to Him. We'll never get His help if we don't ask for it, but even if we do, he might just say 'no.'

"But I'm not a theologian or a padre, Emily. I'm not going to be able to make a Believer out of you – certainly not tonight. All I ask is that you indulge me in this. I am not particularly devout – not Church-going – but I take God very seriously. I do not believe that I would be alive today if it weren't for Him. He was with me when, as a stupid 15-year-old, I took an open 16- foot sailboat into a Force Six gale and capsized it. He was with me when I raced a Vildebeeste between breakers near Singapore. And He was with that German pilot who *didn't* give me the Coup de Grace the other day. So, I *try* to keep my faith with Him, and one thing I promised Him was that I would never sleep with an innocent girl unless I was married to her."

"Your pilots can, but you can't?"

"My pilots have a different God."

"What are you talking about? Surely they're all Christian!"

"Sorry. I told you I wasn't any good at explaining things. It's just that I believe God is so complex or far beyond mortal comprehension that any one of us sees only that tiny facet he or she is capable of comprehending. That means that inevitably the 'face' of God which each person sees is determined as much by who we are as by what He is. I don't presume to know the level of spiritual development of my pilots – or any WAAF, for that matter."

"That sounds as if you're saying that what is wrong for one person, might be right for someone else."

"In a religious sense, that *is* what I'm saying, but I wouldn't want to risk it as the basis of a civil society."

"You were wasted at Cranwell. You should have read theology at Oxford."

Robin shook his head. "No Spitfires."

They laughed and dropped the subject, but Emily had taken his meaning. He was not going to accept anything less than a Church wedding, and it was up to her to be more open-minded about the Church. "Where did you learn to argue like that?" Emily found herself asking.

"Thorton. It's a very good school, but it's young, poor and obscure. Being inter-denominational, our religion classes included lectures by rabbis, imams, Buddhist monks, and all and sundry. We even let the Seventh Day Adventists and the Mormons have a day. Not that you can make schoolboys equally respectful of all them, but they tried." They were laughing again.

Then suddenly a cold wind rushed in from the door behind Robin, and he turned around to find himself facing a haggard-looking grey-haired woman with her hair in a tight bun. "Just what is going on here!" she demanded furiously. Behind her stood a mousy, balding man, clutching his hat in his hands.

Robin got to his feet. Emily was saying, "Hello, Mum, we were just having something—"

"You said you were going to be taken to dinner, not that you were planning to tryst right here in my house! And what is that on the table? Emily! You know the rules of the house! How dare you let anyone bring *alcohol* in here!" Mrs. Pryce stormed into the little dining room, seized the bottle of scotch, and threw it into the fire-place. The bottle shattered with a loud crash and filled the room with the powerful smell of scotch.

While Robin and Emily were still stunned, Mrs. Pryce spun around on Robin and spat out at him, "I suppose you planned this all along – to arrive after we'd left so you could drink and seduce my daughter under my very roof." Her eyes narrowed down into slits and glinted with fury. Her lips were pressed together in a tight line.

"How dare you treat my guest like this?!" Emily demanded furiously. "It's not Robin's fault that he was late—"

"How would you know? You'd believe any stupid excuse your lover gave you. You've lost all your self-respect!"

"If you'll excuse me, Emily, I think I'd better leave." Robin walked out of the dining room, right past Mr. Pryce, who stepped out of his way but then followed him to the hall.

From the dining room came the sound of raised female voices. Emily protested her mother's actions and words, and Mrs. Pryce shouted her down with outrage over the alcohol – the gin and port following the scotch into the fire-place to the sound of splintering glass.

Robin took his cap and set it firmly on his head, the peak low. When he turned to leave, Mr. Pryce stood between him and the door. "Just what are you doing here? What sort of game are you playing?"

"I came to have dinner with my fiancée – and to meet her parents."

"Do you expect us to believe you really intend to marry Emily?"

"Why on earth shouldn't I?"

"She's not your class, for a start. She's just an ordinary girl—"

"I don't find her the least bit ordinary!" Robin retorted sharply.

"Well, for a girl you claim to want to marry, you don't show her much respect! Just what time did you get here tonight?"

"I'm very sorry I was late, and if you'd been here when I arrived, I would have explained myself. But, frankly, it's too late now. I don't think we are ever going to come to an understanding." Robin reached past Mr. Pryce to the door handle and let himself out into the night.

He had barely reached the car when the cottage door opened again, spilling light into the blackout. Emily came running down the path. He could hear her sobbing and he turned to meet her. She flung herself into his arms. "Don't leave me, Robin! Please. Take me away. Take me to the Salvation Army. I won't stay another minute in that house. My mother's mad! She's mad with class-hatred or jealousy or I don't know what. I don't understand it. Why can't she be happy that I've found someone like you? Why does she have to try to ruin everything?"

Robin didn't have an answer to her questions. He just took her around the car and helped her inside. "I'll take you to Aunt Hattie," he decided. "She has an extra bedroom."

Suddenly Mrs. Pryce was standing in the doorway of the cottage, lit up from the light streaming out of the house. The Air Raid warden would be here any minute, Robin thought clinically.

"If you leave now, Emily, don't think you'll be allowed back into this house! I won't have a child of mine acting like a tart!"

Robin glanced at Emily.

Tears streamed down her face, but she looked straight ahead. Her lips pressed together, she shook her head. "Take me away. I don't ever want to set foot in that house again. She just accused me of being pregnant! She says a man like you wouldn't even talk of marriage unless I'd shamed him into it!"

Robin turned the key in the ignition, gunned the engine and drove away.

Chapter 29

Boulogne
26 August 1940

A lot of the staff at the hospital were French – mostly the sisters that brought the meals and changed bedpans and that kind of thing. Only the doctors and senior nurses were German. When Ernst heard the sisters jabbering away in French, he was reminded of how close he'd come to ending up in an English hospital – if he'd survived jumping, that was. He certainly couldn't have landed on his own, and when he thought how much it had hurt just being jarred about in the cockpit, the thought of landing by parachute was intolerable.

He was lucky to be alive. They'd removed six bullets – two from his left leg, two from his buttocks and one each from his side and his left upper arm. They were now in a bowl next to his bed. Souvenirs. He twisted his head on the pillow and tried to see them. But he couldn't. He stopped trying. Every movement seemed to exhaust him, and there were the tubes with blood still connected to his arm. He'd lost a lot of blood, but the doctors assured him he'd survive. Everything was going to be fine, they said. None of the bullets had damaged anything vital. Ernst decided maybe all his "extra padding" was good for something after all.

The French nurses were nattering away out there very loudly, he noticed with a frown. German nurses would never have been so inconsiderate. *"Monsieur! Monsieur! Un ami—"*

"Christian!" Ernst tried to sit up and greyed out instantly, flopping back onto the bed but reaching out his hand.

"Lie still, you idiot!" Christian's hand gripped his good shoulder.

Ernst opened his eyes and gasped. "What happened to you?" Half of Christian's face was black and blue, and a big gash cut down from his forehead to the inside of his nose right across his right eye. Pools of blood were collected in the whites of his right eye under the thin membrane.

"Can't take care of myself without you. That's all."

"But what happened to your face?"

"I don't know exactly. It happened while bailing out."

"You had to bail out?"

"It seemed the sensible thing to do at the time. My fuel gauge failed, and I found myself over the Channel with a starved engine and two

Hurricanes coming in for the kill."

"Christian!" Ernst tried to sit up again, but Christian held him down.

"*Nix*. How are you doing? The nurses tell me you'll be back on your feet in no time."

"How do they know?"

"Good question." Christian grinned.

"What are you doing here?" Ernst asked next. "Aren't we flying today?" He tried to twist around to see out of the window, but although he couldn't, it was still obvious from the light in the room that it was a fine day.

"Got the day off," Christian told him with evident satisfaction.

"How did you do that?" Ernst asked in amazement.

"Do you really want to know? It's a bit of a story."

"Tell me!"

Christian looked around, found a chair, and pulled it up. "You aren't going to believe me."

"Does it matter?"

Christian laughed. "All right. For that, you get the *long* version! When I got back to Crépon after seeing you off in the ambulance, we were just about to take off for the second mission of the day, and Fischer fobbed off this brand-new *Fahnenjunker* on me – still wet behind the ears. I can't even remember his name. He couldn't keep up with me. I lost him on the first bounce, and we've never seen or heard from him again. Poor Fischer has to write home to his parents and probably doesn't even remember what the kid looks like – I certainly don't. Anyway, without you I couldn't concentrate on anything, so of course I couldn't get anything." Apparently unconsciously, Christian was holding his right eye closed with the fingers of his hand.

"You know how it is. Suddenly I was alone out there except for some Junkers on their way home. I thought I'd give them a little comfort – seeing as my fuel light wasn't on yet. Mind you, it seemed odd, but you know what they teach us at flight school: trust your instruments, not your instincts. So, I was happily weaving over them when I caught sight of two birds flying in formation and rapidly overtaking us. Peculiar behaviour for seagulls, I thought, and drew the correct conclusion: they were Hurricanes. Gentleman that I am, I turned back to face them, and that's when the engine cut out on me. It seems that the fuel gauge wasn't working, so the warning light hadn't come on. I was completely out of fuel."

"With two Hurricanes on top of you?"

"Precisely."

"I don't believe you."

"I knew you wouldn't. It gets better." Christian brought his hand down from his eye, but held the eye shut as he talked. "I managed to jump out and – to be fair – the Tommies were very decent and didn't try to shoot me in the 'chute. They circled as I floated down, but they held their fire. When I went into the water, they flew off and left me there alone. I was almost sorry to see them go." Christian's hand crept back to his eye as he talked.

"The Channel is huge from wave-top level – and bitterly cold."

"What about your rubber dinghy?"

"It had been shot up and didn't inflate, but I had my flare pistol and sent up flares. The Channel is *really* cold!" Christian repeated with emphasis. "By the time an E-boat picked me up, I couldn't feel my toes any more. I was ravenous, too, because I hadn't had anything to eat since breakfast, but the slops they offered me were inedible. Did you have any idea of how bad our sailors have it?" He took his hand away again, but as before, he kept his eye shut. "I don't even know what the stuff was – I think they called it *Eisbein*, but it bore no resemblance to any *Eisbein* I've ever eaten before. Fischer was quite decent about it when I got back to the base. He had the kitchen make me a steak extra and bought the champagne. We'd just started to have a pleasant evening when Fatty arrived."

"What?!" Ernst tried to sit up again, and Christian pushed him back down. "You're not serious?" Ernst asked breathlessly.

"Of course, I'm serious."

"The *Herr Reichsmarschall* himself?"

"Don't make it sound as if you would have *liked* to be there!"

"But I would have! What an honour!" Ernst spoke in all sincerity. The *Reichsmarshall* was the second most important man in the entire Reich. He wasn't just the C-in-C of the Air Force, but Prussian Minister of the Interior and many other things as well. "Of course, I would have liked to meet the *Herr Reichsmarschall*!" he told Christian earnestly. "My parents would be so proud! Did he shake your hand?"

"No. He was not in a particularly good mood. He seems to think we fighter pilots are shirking our duty – avoiding combat with the Tommies, abandoning the bombers, and all-in-all responsible for the fact that we still haven't obtained air superiority over England. In short, we alone are losing the war and disgracing him and the Luftwaffe."

"But, Christian, that's crazy...." Ernst couldn't grasp it. They were doing their best. What more could they do? "Doesn't he realise.... Didn't Rosskamp explain?"

"Rosskamp was miraculously absent. Must have had wind of what was coming. So, I felt it was my duty—"

"No! Christian! You didn't say something to *the Herr Reichsmarschall himself* – did you?" Ernst was horrified. He knew just how disrespectful

Christian could be. But surely....

"Under the circumstances, I decided to ask him for a day off."

"Christian! You couldn't have! Did you?"

"Well, all right, I didn't *exactly* ask for a day off. I said something about how if an officer's courage was questioned that he had no choice but to resign. Something like that. In any case, I threw my cap at his feet and stomped out."

Ernst hardly dared to breathe. He knew Christian wasn't teasing him. He was too uncomfortable. He wasn't looking at Ernst directly, and his hand had gone to his injured eye again, holding it shut.

Ernst was sure something terrible must have happened after this. Frankly, he was amazed that they hadn't already thrown Christian in a Concentration Camp. He certainly would have expected Christian to be put under arrest, but since he was here, that clearly hadn't happened – yet. "Have you been grounded, Christian?"

Christian tossed him a smile. "No. Fatty refused to accept my resignation. For some reason he decided my behaviour was 'spirited' – Fischer must have been very persuasive. After all the excitement on the day you were shot down, however, the bombers were too exhausted to fly again. Fatty ordered the 109s to 'restore their honour,' and so we flew one sweep after another all day. Only I suppose I wasn't flying very well. Fischer told me this morning that he didn't want me flying around endangering everybody else, and suggested I come and check on how you were doing instead. How *are* you doing?"

"I'll be fine. Is your eye bothering you?"

"Not really. It's just blurry. I can see better when I keep it closed."

"You should see a doctor – a specialist – while you're here."

"Sure. How many bullets did they take out of you?"

"Six. They're there." Ernst pointed. Christian peered at the bowl.

"Christian?"

"Yes?"

"Would you take one to Klaudia?"

Christian frowned. "Take it to her yourself."

"I don't know when I'm getting out of here. And the scarf I bought her, remember? Give it to her along with one of the bullets."

"You aren't dead yet! You aren't even dying. You're going to be fine and rejoin the *Staffel* soon."

"Maybe, but it could be a while. Please, Christian. I know you think I'm a coward—"

"Stop it! You know I don't think that!"

"Then you'll give Klaudia the scarf and one of the bullets?"

"This is blackmail."

Ernst just gazed at him. "Promise me, Christian."

"Scheisse!"

"—and in my desk, I have a diary. I want her to have it."

"What's got into you? The nurses said you're in no mortal danger."

"I want Klaudia to have my diary. Please, Christian. Promise me."

"Ernst, you are taking shameless advantage of the situation. Just because they've removed six bullets from your young body and you're lying in a hospital bed with tubes attached to your arms and all that, doesn't mean I should give in on this. It's a matter of principle. You should do your own courting."

"But I can't from here, can I? Please, Christian."

Christian pressed his hand to his bad eye and frowned as he considered Ernst with his remaining eye. Then he mumbled, "*Scheisse*" again, but took Ernst's hand. "If you insist, I'll do it."

Ernst grinned. "Thank you, Christian."

RAF Tangmere

Banks came to breakfast feeling comfortable, almost "at home," for the first time since he'd arrived in England. Tangmere, he had discovered the day before, was located in one of the loveliest corners of England. Furthermore, the night before he had enjoyed an excellent meal in a quaint pub and visited the village church of Bosham, dating back to Saxon times. Beyond the blackout curtains, you could hear the birds calling to one another, announcing another glorious day, defying the reputation of English weather. Most important, as he pulled out a chair and joined the others of No. 606 squadron sitting together at one of the long tables, they glanced up and greeted him. At 4.30 in the morning, they weren't wildly cheerful, but even their silence was a form of acceptance. Without a word, Ware passed him the tea-urn, and Woody gave him the sugar bowl. An airman emerged out of nowhere.

"Bacon or sausages, sir?"

"Bacon."

The airman disappeared. David registered that they were rather fewer than normal. Eton and Kiwi were missing – and so was the CO. That was unusual, but then he'd been a little late yesterday, too. Kiwi arrived humming "Waltzing Mathilda" happily to himself, causing Donohue to groan and ask if there wasn't some regulation against singing before dawn.

Eton stumbled in, looking very rumpled, at ten to five. "I'm sorry," he started to say, then noticed the CO wasn't even there, and so just plopped himself down at an empty seat and grabbed for the tea.

"Where's the Butcher this morning?" Ware asked, as if just noticing it himself.

"Got an earful from the Station Commander last night," Sutton answered gleefully.

"Whatever for? I thought they loved the bastard for bringing us to heel?" Needham observed.

"Rude to the WAAF OC," Woody told him smugly.

"Yes, something about it being a pity if the WAAFs died virgins," Sutton added.

"Well, he's got a point there," Ware declared.

"First sensible thing the Butcher's said, if you ask me." Donohue agreed.

The lorry waiting for them hooted its horn as a reminder. They dragged themselves to their feet to the scraping of chairs and clacking of cups on saucers, then spilled out of the Mess.

As the lorry lumbered around the perimeter to their dispersal, Banks looked out at the rapidly brightening day. There wasn't a cloud in the sky, and the sunrise had a canary-yellow tinge.

"Isn't that the skipper's aircraft over at the hangar?" Kiwi asked. They all looked towards the remaining maintenance hangar.

"Wonder what it's doing over there?" Ware spoke for all of them. Erks were clearly working on it, which seemed odd, since they had not scrambled yesterday afternoon.

The lorry came to a halt in front of the dispersal hut and stood vibrating and belching diesel smoke into the air as the pilots dropped down from the back rather wearily. Banks noted that, to the disappointment of the Auxiliary pilots, Priestman was already there, standing in the door of the dispersal, apparently checking the weather. Banks didn't like the way he looked; his hair was wet, apparently from a quick shower, and he was bleeding on his neck from a hasty shave. His eyes were sunken in his face.

"You're up early, sir," Woody managed.

"Didn't go to bed," Priestman retorted.

"Chasing night intruders, were you, sir?" Kiwi made the connection between the Squadron Leader's appearance and his aircraft being in maintenance.

Priestman nodded.

"Did you get something, sir?" Bnks asked.

"Didn't see a bloody thing. No search-lights."

"Something wrong with the kite?" Kiwi wondered.

"Not really, just overdue for a maintenance check. I'll be flying 'P' if 'R' isn't ready in time. But 'K' and 'D' are both undergoing checks as well."

A second lorry arrived with the Sergeant Pilots. Robin checked his watch; it was two minutes late. He watched as Green and Bowles dropped down from the lorry readily, but MacLeod moved like a man with a severe hangover. "MacLeod!"

The Scotsman frowned but came over and drew himself up into a semblance of attention. "Sir?" His eyes were badly bloodshot and his shave very rough. Worse: you could smell the gin on his breath.

Priestman stiffened as he inhaled it with a guilty conscience. Aunt Hattie had been wonderful about taking Emily in last night, but she had also made it clear to him that the whole thing was his fault. "You knew perfectly well no alcohol was allowed in the house – that's why there wasn't any there in the first place. Couldn't you go one single night without drinking? It sounds to me like you are becoming dangerously dependent on the stuff."

"Headache, MacLeod?"

"Now that you ask, sir, yes." He said it impudently, adding provocatively, "Nothing that a whiff won't cure."

There was dead silence from the other pilots, and Priestman could feel them watching with delight. No doubt, they already knew that MacLeod had been the reason for him getting a frightful ticking off the evening before. They were waiting for him to take it out on MacLeod. "Your usual aircraft is due for a 100-hour check. I've assigned you 'F' instead – it's just been flown in by the ATA."

Priestman turned his attention to Donohue, "Feel up to leading a section, Donohue?"

The Auxiliary pilot was clearly surprised. "Ah, if you say so, sir."

"Since Sergeant MacLeod appears to be less than top drawer at the moment, I think the section would be safer in your hands. You'll be flying Yellow One, with Pilot Officers Goldman and Sergeants Green and Bowles. MacLeod, you'll fly Blue Four."

He turned and addressed the others, "I want to go over our tactics again for this morning." He returned inside the dispersal, and as the others filed in, they found the blackboard had been "decorated" with a diagram of three sections of four aircraft. The four sections were in uneven vics: a leader with one aircraft on one flank and two on the other. The three vics were themselves in a rough vic, with the first section leading the other two.

Robin had had a difficult night. It was after midnight before he got back to Tangmere after settling Emily in with Aunt Hattie. It hardly seemed worth going to bed by then, so he'd gone over to the Ops room to see what was on the board. A number of intruders, particularly one that seemed to be making for Southampton, induced Robin to go up and see if he could intercept. The interception had been a failure, but it cleared his head and he'd been able to do some straight thinking on his return.

It was exactly one week since he had taken command of 606, and he didn't like the results. It was bad enough that he had made no kills since assuming command, but except for Woody and Donohue, none of the others had, either. In the same period, they had lost two aircraft and one pilot had been severely wounded. In short, they were 2 for 2, and that wasn't good enough. Jones' record had definitely been better. That meant either his tactics were wrong or they weren't implementing them correctly.

After mentally reviewing the combats since taking over the squadron, Priestman concluded that he'd failed to implement his tactics at all. Everything had just been a messy free-for-all. He decided to try to explain his ideas again. He'd had time for a quick bath and shave after his night sortie, so he was feeling quite good at the moment. He waited impatiently while the squadron collected in front of him.

They crowded around the blackboard in a ragged circle, in flying boots with their flight jackets hanging open or worn over one shoulder. Some – Needham, Sutton, Ware, MacLeod – looked openly resentful or bored. Williams, Donohue, Ringwood and Eton just looked tired. Bowles, Green, Banks and Kiwi were the only ones who looked interested.

"The idea," Priestman tried to drill into them, "is that we work in pairs. The odd numbers – Red, Blue and Yellow 1 and 3 – are the hunters, concentrating on getting a target in their sites. The even numbers – Red, Blue and Yellow 2 and 4 – protect their respective leader.

"The leaders, as you can see, are myself, Ware, Ringwood, Sutton, Donohue and Green. We have to rely on our respective wingmen to keep our tails clear and focus on shooting down bombers.

"The rest of you, the wingmen, are responsible for keeping a sharp look-out astern, above and – above all – in the sun. The slightest flicker of sunlight is probably an enemy aircraft crossing it, so watch for that – don't expect to see the aircraft itself. Remember, too, that a favourite German tactic is to dive below an intended target and then tip the nose up and rake the underbelly of the unsuspecting aircraft. So don't forget to look back and *down* now and again.

"When you see something approaching, don't just scream 'break' – unless it is a full-scale attack on the whole squadron. If the danger is just to your leader, then be sure to address him directly. For example, 'Red Three, break now!'

"Another thing. Don't shout 'Break!' unless the danger is acute. The minute we break up, we stop fighting as a unit and it becomes every man for himself. That's not the most effective way of fighting – particularly given the numerical superiority of the enemy."

As he spoke, it dawned on him that these pilots – with the exception of Kiwi and Banks – probably had not had any systematic instruction on the tactics of the current war. They had been flung into the battle with peacetime training and expected to learn while fighting.

"Can one of you – other than Kiwi or Banks – tell me the basic units of the Luftwaffe?"

The pilots looked rather blankly at one another. Finally, Eton raised his hand. "Don't they have squadrons and wings like we do?"

"Yes and no. The Luftwaffe's basic organizational unit is the *Geschwader*, not their equivalent of the squadron, the *Staffel*. A *Jagdgeschwader* or JG, the German fighter unit, consists of about 120 aircraft. A JG is composed of three *Gruppe*, and each *Gruppe* consists of three *Staffel*, or twelve aircraft. Although administratively organised around the *Geschwader*, in fact, they like to deploy in *Gruppe* strength – which is about 40 aircraft including the staff-flight, that is, three *Staffel* of twelve aircraft each and then a Section of four led by the *Gruppe* commander. They fly in sections of four, in the same formation I want you to fly. As you may have noticed, it is very effective!"

No laughter, but at least one or two of them nodded their head in acknowledgement.

Priestman continued. "The Me109 has a fuel injection engine, so it doesn't stall when it goes into a dive. This is a vital advantage. Never forget it. When you dive to avoid a 109, you are actually handing him an advantage. You are going to lose power for precious seconds while he gains on you. Don't do it! Climb, or better still, turn away from a 109. One very good evasive tactic is to climb to the brink of stalling out and then stall-turn away from him."

After a pause to let that sink in, he continued, "Better still, don't let him get on your tail in the first place. If there is enough warning – and that depends on the wingmen more than anyone – then the squadron as a whole can turn into the attacking 109s, robbing them of their advantage, and so avoid being caught from behind."

Priestman thought he had their attention as he continued, "If we are engaging bombers, then we can't all afford to turn into the attacking fighters, so only Red Section turns to face them and tries to disrupt them, while the rest of the squadron continues to press home attacks on the bombers – but with the wingmen watching out for the Me109s. Any questions?"

At first Priestman thought they were just going to stand there sullenly, but then Sutton roused himself. "Yes. I mean, what bloody good are four Hurricanes against forty 109s?"

"Four Hurricanes that engage the *Gruppekommandeur* will be distracting the top-scoring ace from pursuit and forcing him to engage in a dogfight he doesn't want. He wants to shoot us down when our backs are turned. Unless he's already wearing one, he wants a Knight's Cross, not a dip in the Channel."

By now, only MacLeod still looked resentful – or was his frown purely habitual? How could any girl be so stupid as to fall for the lout? Back to business. Priestman continued, "Another thing: the Me109 doesn't have the fuel capacity of the Hurricane. What this means—"

The telephone rang. They all froze. The clerk answered it. They were staring at him. He still jumped up and shouted as if they had been on the other side of the airfield. "Scramble! Squadron Scramble!"

They clattered out of the dispersal and scattered across the field towards their aircrafts as the tannoy blasted out the announcement. "Scramble 606 and 43 Squadrons. Repeat: scramble 606 and 43 squadrons."

The erks were starting up the engines and climbed out of the already vibrating Hurricanes as the pilots arrived at a run. The chocks were pulled away, and the Hurricanes nosed out of their sand-bag bays like eager hunters. Priestman had his eye on 43 Squadron. They were faster than 606, taking to the airfield first, and sweeping into the air. Why? It certainly wasn't the erks. Could only be his pilots. He throttled forward as the last of 43's aircraft waffled its way into the air clearly a bit mushy – probably one of their sprogs.

Then, as his own undercarriage tucked in under him, he called Control. "Beetle, this is Red Cap Leader; what have you got for us?"

"Large enemy formation has formed up over Le Havre and is heading north. We suspect another raid on Portsmouth. We want to you try to intercept over the Isle of Wight. Vector 210, Angels 20."

"Vector 210, Angels 20. Roger." He turned on course, noticing that there was quite a bit of cloud about, and it seemed to be coming in from the west. That was not ideal, and it would give the bombers somewhere to run and hide. If they were unlucky, they wouldn't even make the interception.

For now, however, he had to concentrate on getting his squadron into formation. He leaned forward in his cockpit and checked to his left and right. Kiwi was clinging to his left wing. "Spread out, Red Two – this is not an aerobatics exercise. I don't want you ramming me when you twist your neck to look for the Hun. Red Three, fall back more. Everyone *spread* out!"

On their right, Priestman could make out Spitfires climbing hard on a parallel course, clearly 602 Squadron making for the same interception.

They climbed through cloud at 10,000 feet, and Priestman called in to Control. "We've broken above cloud, Beetle. Are you sure the bombers are coming in high?"

Before Control could answer, Sutton, flying Blue Three on the port flank, made a sighting: "There they are, Redcap Leader! Looks like 100+ bombers."

"Some of them are 110s." Ringwood corrected.

"Watch for escorts. 109s are reported in loose escort, separated from the bomber formations." This extremely helpful advice came from Control.

"Thanks, Beetle. Redcap Squadron, turn port and follow me up to Angels 22." Although they had been steadily climbing, they had only just passed through 16,000 feet and were at roughly the same altitude as the bombers.

Priestman started the curve, leaning forward in his cockpit to check over both shoulders to be sure the rest of the squadron kept with him. "Wake up, Blue Four." Yellow Two was lagging a bit too, but Robin did not draw attention to it, guessing that Bowles was being sick. A moment later, Yellow Two surged forward and slotted himself into formation again doggedly. "Gunsights on, safeties off!" He ordered. "Now—"

"Snappers in the sun!"

"Coming down!"

"Blue and Yellow Sections, buster and maintain course. Go for the bombers! Red Section, hard a' port!" As he spoke, he up-ended the Hurricane onto the port wingtip and spun about, still climbing.

The Messerschmitts sliced through them without anyone having a chance to fire. As the 109s continued after the rest of the squadron, Priestman was in a position to turn Red Section around again. Within minutes, they were behind the Messerschmitts and chasing them.

Admittedly, the Messerschmitts were in hot pursuit of the other eight aircraft of 606, but these were closing fast with the approaching bomber formation. Both Ringwood and Donohue were among the bombers, blazing away. Smoke gushed up from the starboard engine of the bomber Ringwood hopped over. Priestman had no time to notice anything more, because he had to concentrate on lining up behind a Messerschmitt that was hounding Banks.

"Yellow Four, break right – now!" Priestman ordered. He was amazed and relieved when his order was instantly obeyed. As the Messerschmitt pivoted on a wingtip to follow Banks, Priestman racked him from spinner to tail. The canopy shattered, and the aircraft put the nose down and dived. It was streaming flame and smoke.

"That's one for you, skipper!" Kiwi announced.

Priestman had no time to answer. The other Messerschmitts had caused Blue and Yellow Sections to break off their attacks on the bombers, scattering in all directions, turning, diving, twisting and jinking frantically in a desperate effort to shake off their pursuers. The bombers were now unmolested as a result.

Control had suggested that the bombers were heading for Portsmouth, which was somewhere below the soft layer of cloud. The photo from the newspaper was vivid in Robin's mind – the row of flattened cottages only five minutes' walk from his mother's. There was no way he was going to let all these bastards drop their load on Portsmouth. He pressed in towards the lead bomber.

Robin wanted the lead bomber because, reputedly, they did the navigating for the entire group. If he could knock it out, the others might become disoriented – at least they might not be as accurate, particularly given the cloud cover that obscured the target. Robin was no longer sure himself where they were, but he felt fairly confident that they hadn't reached Portmouth yet. With luck they were over the Solent; if unlucky, still over the Isle of Wight.

To get at the lead bomber properly, however, he had to skim in under the two aircraft on its port flank. To be sure there wasn't a Messerschmitt behind him, he twisted around in his seat, squinting up towards the sun.

"Don't sweat it, Skipper. I've got you covered." Kiwi admonished.

"They're making for the clouds!" someone called out.

"Go on! I've got you covered!"

"Damn it! I can't see a thing!"

"Fucking English weather!"

Priestman could pay attention to none of it. He had drawn the fire of the bombers, could see the lead being pumped at him. He eased down. Bullets pinged and punched on the wings, causing him to wince involuntarily, and then the sky darkened and he lifted the nose and drew the orange lights of the gunsight onto the soft underbelly of the lead bomber and pressed the tit.

The Hurricane bucked violently and flipped over onto its back. The air around him was suddenly a cauldron of smoke and flame. Things were cracking against the airframe. Something soft and white smashed against the Plexiglas, leaving a huge red smear. The Hurricane fell out of the sky and went into a spin. It took Priestman several seconds to regain control of it again. His heart was pounding in his ears and his whole body was drenched in sweat. How bloody stupid could you get? Going in that close to a loaded bomber from underneath.

Breathing and pulse still racing, he tried to turn around and see what had happened. There was a burst of black smoke amidst the increasing white clouds – rather as though a gigantic firework had gone off. Another Heinkel was sliding down the sky sideways, apparently damaged. A third was tumbling down in a flat spin with a wing missing. A fourth was diving towards the cloud below, while another veered towards the columns of cumulus that were coming in from the west. There was not a Hurricane to be seen anywhere. Kiwi. Don't think about it.

The thudding of his heart was steadying, becoming less deafening. Priestman decided it was time to call in. "Red Two, where are you?"

Nothing. Don't think about it.

Try to raise Tangmere. "Redcap Leader here, can you read me, Beetle?"

Nothing.

He tried it again. Still nothing.

He tried raising the rest of the squadron. "Redcap Leader to Redcap Squadron. Come in."

Nothing.

There had to be some kind of damage to his R/T. Not important. He turned for Tangmere, but soon noticed his engine seemed to be over-heating. He had to throttle back almost to stalling speed to keep the temperature steady. It was worrying at first, but after he got used to it, it was almost soothing to fly so slowly — rather like being in a Vildebeeste again.

He was feeling quite calm by the time he put down onto the blowing grass. A quick count while on the circuit put the number of 606 aircraft at 10. One missing. Kiwi, he thought again guiltily.

His landing could have been better. He bounced a bit, but the Hurricane was wonderfully forgiving and settled down quickly. An ambulance started wailing and with irritating persistence continued to scream, even as he turned and cut off the engine. He shoved back the hood and pulled off his helmet with a deep sigh of relief.

Ripley was hanging over him. "Are you all right, sir?"

"The blood's not mine, if that's what you mean." Priestman gestured to the hideous smear which had now turned brown across the hood he had just shoved back.

The erk glanced at it and then looked at him hard again. "Flying Officer Ware and Pilot Officer Murray both said you'd bought it, sir."

"Kiwi made it?" Priestman asked anxiously.

"Had to take a walk, sir. Said his Hurricane was flung against a bomber, causing them both to crash. He said you blew up, sir."

"The bomber blew up. I was a bit too close and the Hurricane got knocked about a bit. Engine's overheating a little." This said, Priestman hauled himself up on the windscreen and stepped out onto the port wing. He was feeling very stiff and a little shaky at the moment. As he'd mentioned to Emily, there were some moments when one is more aware of God's presence than others. This was one of them.

Then, following Ripley's rather dismayed look, he realised his Hurricane looked rather ragged. In fact, the antenna was gone, and large pieces of fabric had been ripped completely off the tail frame, revealing the wooden construction. The sight made his knees weak. It flashed through his mind that a Spit probably wouldn't have survived.

Rowe arrived frowning, his hands on his hips as he surveyed the damage. "It'll take us all night to get her serviceable again, sir," he greeted his CO. "And Flying Officer Donohue's crate is also u/s. Pilot Officer Murray had to bail out. We haven't got any reserve aircraft left." He sounded rather irate about it.

"Are you finished with the inspections on 'R,' 'K' and 'J'?"

"Yes, sir. But 'D' and 'Y' are due at the end of the day."

"We'll put in for more aircraft, Flight."

Allars appeared around the tail of the Hurricane. "Good to see you back, sir. I gather you are putting in two claims?"

"Yes, that's right. An Me109 and a Heinkel 111. I believe I had witnesses. What state is Kiwi in?"

"Except for being understandably upset about you, sir, he sounded fine. Should be back any minute. He was getting a lift from the police. You'll be pleased to hear your sortie was an exceptional success. Although squadrons scrambled from Warmwell got lost in the cloud and failed to intercept, the three Tangmere squadrons together managed to divert the bombers from Portsmouth. They dropped their bombs harmlessly all over the countryside north of Cosham and Farlington."

Priestman liked the sound of that and nodded. Then thought to ask, "Anyone else get anything?"

"Woody's claimed a Heinkel, Donohue claimed a damaged 110, and Eton's claimed a Messerschmitt, but the latter doesn't sound credible."

"You think he's lying?"

"No, just over-excited. It would appear from the accounts of the others that the Messerschmitts were engaged at a higher altitude by Spitfires – presumably 602. Eton fired at a Messerschmitt that he says was diving and that he then saw go in. But the others claim several Messerschmitts fell out of the sky already in trouble. Eton admits he only got in a short burst, and his ground crews say he fired less than 50 rounds."

"All right, I'll try to sort him out. Anything else I ought to know?"

Allars hesitated, then remarked dryly, "Sounded a bit dodgy – not to say daft – what you just did."

"Stupidest thing I've ever done in my life. I won't do it again."

Allars nodded. "that covers it for the moment, then."

Priestman pushed himself upright from the trailing edge of the wing and started for the dispersal with great effort. His sleepless night was catching up with him now. All he wanted to do was lie down and sleep. Maybe he could catch a nap while waiting for the next scramble.....

As he approached the dispersal, something strange happened: The pilots were all lounging about in front of the dispersal in deck chairs or spread out on the grass. Donohue, Needham and Sutton were playing cards at a rickety table. MacLeod was sleeping off his hangover and the others were reading. Green glanced up, saw Priestman approaching, and called out in obvious amazement, "It's the CO!"

Ware glanced up from his newspaper and got to his feet. Suddenly they were all getting to their feet. By the time he reached the little group, they were all standing up to face him.

"We thought you'd bought it, sir." Woody admitted. He sounded more stunned than gratified.

"Not yet, so you'll have to postpone the party. Is there tea anywhere?"

"I'll get you some, sir," Ginger offered, ducking back into the dispersal.

The others were still staring. "I understand you got a Heinkel, Woody."

"Yes, sir."

"Well done. I saw you put one engine on fire on your first pass. Did you go back around for it?"

"Ah. No. Actually, I didn't even see that. It was afterwards. I broke left and chased after another one. It spun out of control and I saw two of the crew jump."

"Well done. Donohue?"

"I got in some good bursts at a 110 and saw the starboard engine catch fire, but I didn't see him go in. Got distracted by a Messerschmitt."

"Eton?"

"There was a bloody great free-for-all after you – I mean – we came out the other side of the bomber formation and got jumped on by a horde of Messerschmitts. It can't have been the ones that had been following us. They had to come from somewhere else. F/O Ware tried to climb into them like you said, but they were already coming down, and one cut in front of me. I got in a good squirt and when I looked back, there he was streaking down with a long tail of smoke. I know he went in."

"Very likely, but the 109s were coming down because they'd been engaged by Spitfires at higher altitude," Priestman pointed out. "You probably shot at an already dead pilot."

Eton frowned. "But, sir, he passed right through my sights."

"What speed do you think he was going?"

"400 mph at least, sir!"

"And how far away was he?"

"Maybe three hundred yards – four hundred at the most." The others just burst out laughing.

Priestman waited for them to quiet down. "Eton, do you want to step inside and let me give you a short lesson on the Browning machine gun." It was not a question, and the boy looked decidedly disheartened as he stepped into the comparatively dim light of the dispersal hut.

"Trigonometry wouldn't hurt either, sir," Sutton called after them.

"Oh, and, sir?" It was Donohue.

Priestman stepped back to the door and looked out expectantly. "I just wanted to let you know that I am *not* a virgin." There were guffaws of laughter from the others, and Priestman shook his head and turned away. "Eton—"

The telephone rang. Paralysis.

"606 Squadron Dispersal."

The clock ticked. The wind blew. The pilots of 606 hung in suspended animation. No one was breathing.

"One moment, sir." The clerk turned to Priestman. "It's the Adjutant, sir. He'd like to speak to you."

Priestman took the receiver. The others exhaled and resumed their activities. Eton fussed with his silk cravat. "Priestman."

"Congratulations, sir! You've just been awarded the DFC. The wire's just come in – and they didn't even know about the two you got today. I'm so pleased for you, sir! I've rarely known anyone who deserved it so much!" Mickey sounded so sincere, Robin was touched.

"Thank you, Mickey. Could you do me a favour?"

"Of course. What would you like me to do?"

"Organise something. A dance. With a real band. Something everyone can enjoy. The erks, too, and the WAAF, of course. Not in the Mess; the cooks and stewards are overworked as it is. Do you think you could do that?"

"For tonight, you mean?" Mickey sounded overwhelmed.

"No. There's no rush. What day is it today?"

"Monday."

"All right. Thursday or Friday."

"Don't worry, sir. I'll fix something up."

"Thanks."

There was a commotion going on outside. Robin put his head out the window to see what it was about.

Kiwi was towering amidst the others, still in his Mae West and parachute. The latter was dragging along behind him and occasionally billowed up as it caught the wind. "Down, boy, down!" Kiwi admonished the 'chute when it tugged at him. "Behave yourself!"

"Where the devil did you come from?" Priestman asked, very relieved to see him.

"Ahhhh!" Kiwi reacted as if he'd seen a ghost. "You were the one who blew up!" He crossed himself.

"I did nothing of the sort, but I hear you collided with a bomber and wrecked your Hurricane. That's what comes of not keeping your distance as ordered."

"I get your point, Skipper." Kiwi grinned at him, and then turned to admonish his parachute, "Behave! You're in company!"

"And Kiwi, get out of that useless 'chute and collect a packed one."

"See! You've got yourself posted!" Kiwi told the parachute. "I warned you not to muck about in front of the CO!"

Robin shook his head and withdrew back inside the dispersal hut to give Eton his lesson on the effectiveness of gunfire from different ranges. But the telephone was ringing again.

"Bloody thing!"

"606 Squadron Dispersal.... SCRAMBLE! SQUADRON SCRAMBLE!"

Chapter 30

Crépon, France
August 28, 1940

JG 23 wasn't slated to fly until mid-afternoon, and the ground and air-crews had the morning to themselves. Because of the fine summer weather, almost all off-duty personnel congregated around the periphery of the field where deck chairs and various pieces of portable furniture had been set up in the sun. A casual game of football was in progress on the actual field. Several of the men had stripped down to the waist to soak up the sun, and most had at least removed their tunics, rolled up their sleeves and undone their collars.

When they caught sight of Rosa in her dress uniform as she tried to slip past on the way to the motor pool, she was greeted by whistles and cheers – as if she were a beauty queen.

Axel frowned. He didn't like her attracting attention like this. "Hey, Rosa! What are you all dressed up for?" he called out to her, without getting up from his deck chair.

"I'm going to Paris," she told him with a toss of her head and continued on her way.

"Like hell you are," Axel retorted, thinking it was a poor joke. Rosa just continued towards the lorry that was already rumbling and trembling in the drive, preparing for the daily run into Cherbourg. Axel noticed she was carrying a little rattan suitcase. His frown darkened, and he dragged himself out of the deck chair to go after her.

"What's this all about?" he demanded as he caught up with her and grabbed her arm to make her face him.

Rosa set down her suitcase, and without a word pulled her leave papers out of her breast pocket.

Axel gazed at them in amazement, and then demanded angrily, "Why didn't you tell me you were putting in for leave?"

"Why should I?" Rosa shot back. "I don't need *your* permission!" The last thing she needed was Axel asking her why she wanted leave and trying to talk her out of it.

"What's eating you?" Axel asked back, baffled. They'd been friends now for almost two months. He considered her his girl. "I thought we'd take leave together."

"Really? When? If you've told me once, you've told me 100 times, the

Staffel can't get along without you even for a single day."

"Not now, but when things have calmed down a bit," Axel countered in annoyance, "then we could go away together."

"And just when will that be?!" Rosa countered.

"The Tommies are almost finished; they can't last more than a couple of weeks."

"*Ja, ja,* and then comes the invasion and the occupation, and we all know the war just can't go on without *Oberfeldwebel* Voigt!" Rosa sneered sarcastically, adding to rub it in, "The *Reichsmarshall* and the *Führer* can take a few days off, but never *Oberfeldwebel* Voigt!"

"What the hell has got into you, Rosa?" Axel snapped back. It would have been one thing if she'd asked him to take leave and he'd refused, but she hadn't even mentioned it.

"Nothing's '*got into me*'!" Rosa flung back. "I just need a little time off! Got a bloody right to it, you know!" Rosa's Communist pride boiled up in her unexpectedly. "Workers – even ones in uniform – have rights! They can't just work us to death like slaves!"

"What's that got to do with it?" Axel demanded, more baffled than ever and scowling furiously. "You've got the right to take leave, but why can't you wait until I can go with you?"

"Bugger off, will you. I'm going to take my three days when I can get them, whether you like it or not. You don't *own* me!" Rosa snatched up her suitcase and turned again for the waiting truck.

"If you're seeing someone else—" Axel started to call after her.

Rosa spun back, "Oh, that's just what you *would* think, isn't it?! Typical male! Just because *you'd* cheat on *me*, if you got the chance!"

"Well, why else do you want to go to Paris *without* me!?" Axel demanded, raising his voice still more.

From far away a frail female voice called out, "Wait, Rosa! Wait!" It was Klaudia, who had just learned from Ursula that Rosa had leave for three days and was trying to catch the 12.20 train to Paris. Klaudia was running across the field from the Mess. She waved and called out again, "Rosa! Wait!"

Axel, anxious to conclude his conversation with Rosa before Klaudia arrived, grabbed Rosa and tried to pull her off to the side. She yanked her arm free of his and shouted in his face, "Leave me alone! You've done enough already!"

Klaudia drew up and held her breath, hoping that Axel had found out about his baby at last – but no, he just barked stupidly at Rosa, "If that's the way you feel, then go to hell, for all I care!" He started to stride away, and then he turned back to shout at her – mostly for the male audience sprawled upon the deck chairs and watching the entertainment avidly:

"I hope who-ever-it-is bangs you up! But don't come crawling to me if he does! If you play the field, don't expect me to pay the bill!"

"Wouldn't think of it, love!" Rosa shouted back, her face bright red with fury and humiliation. Then she made a dash for the waiting lorry.

Klaudia just barely caught up with her as she scrambled up into the passenger side of the cab. "Rosa! Stop! Wait! Don't do it! Please—"

"Leave me alone!" Rosa screamed, and slammed the door shut.

The driver looked over at her with raised eyebrows, but she stared straight ahead. "Come on! We'll be late!"

"Hey! I've been waiting for *you*!" he reminded her, but he obligingly put the lorry into first and let in the clutch.

Klaudia stood in the drive, watching the Luftwaffe lorry lumber away with a horrible weight in her stomach. From one of the French women who helped out in the kitchens, Rosa had the address of a woman who did abortions in Paris.

When the truck was no longer in sight, Klaudia turned back towards the Mess. She wished she could sit out in the sun. Maybe it would calm her agitation about what Rosa was doing, but she was too shy to join the men – especially with some of them half naked. Besides, none of the other girls were here. No, she would have to find another spot, some place where she could think undisturbed about what to do. Rosa had threatened to tell everyone about Jako if Klaudia breathed a word about the baby, but Klaudia wondered if she should say something anyway. Not to the other *Hilferinnen*, but maybe to Papa Kahrs?

Lost in her thoughts she was surprised when a voice called, "*Fräulein* von Richthofen."

Christian von Feldburg was walking beside her. He smiled, but she gasped at the sight of him. Everyone was talking about how he'd stood up to Göring, but no one had mentioned that he'd bashed up his face bailing out. Half his face black and blue, and the white of his right eye filled with a puddle of blood.

As if in response to her expression, Christian put his right hand to his eye, covering and closing it at once. "I'd like to talk to you, if I may?"

"But of course, *Freiherr* von Feldburg," Klaudia answered. Christian had never been so attractive to her. He left his tunic somewhere and was wearing only his shirt, with a cravat twisted inside his collar instead of a tie. He was wearing the forage rather than the peaked uniform cap, albeit he was still in riding boots. The sleeves of his shirt were rolled up above the elbows, revealing well-muscled and tanned arms. Klaudia remembered being told once that it took strengthto fly an Emil in combat. When the officers were in their elegant uniforms, they didn't look particularly athletic, but now she could sense the latent strength in the arms of the man beside her. If only he would take an interest in her....

"I expected you to ask me about *Leutnant* Geuke," Christian remarked, in a tone of voice that was calm, soft and admonishing.

At once Klaudia felt guilty. "Oh, yes!" She looked over hastily, not wanting to disappoint this handsome baron by being callous towards his friend. "You went to visit him, didn't you? I heard he was all right."

"All right?" Christian'seyebrows shot up. "They removed six bullets. He lost litres of blood. He's very, very lucky to be alive."

"I understand he has you to thank—"

"No! He flew himself home!" Christian corrected sharply. "All I did was make sure the Tommies didn't bounce him a second time. You don't seem to appreciate what an excellent pilot Ernst is," Christian told her bluntly, and the look he gave her made her cringe. Christian was looking at her with only thinly disguised contempt.

"That's not – I mean—" How could she possibly restore herself in his eyes? Blushing, she tried to defend herself. "I don't know anything about what it takes to be a pilot. How should I?"

"That's fair enough," Christian conceded; but his expression remained hostile as he added, "But it can't have escaped your notice that Ernst is well liked and respected by the rest of us. That should have told you something."

Now that he said it, it seemed obvious, but she had never looked at it that way. After all, Lt. Geuke was just a wingman. "But he always flew wingman to you—"

"Don't tell me you're no better than some Roman matron eager for the sight of blood in the arena? Are kills all that interest you? Do you only like men who have blood on their hands?"

"No! I'm not like that at all! I even hate hunting innocent animals—"

"Then shouldn't you respect the pilot who *protects* more than the one who *kills*?" Helet the words sink in before adding in a different, less accusatory but more dismissive voice, "When I visited Ernst in hospital yesterday, he asked me to give you something. I admit I hesitated, and I'll tell you why."

He stopped walking, and Klaudia was forced to stop, too. They were in the middle of the airfield. Out of hearing in one direction were the off-duty ground crews lounging about in their deck chairs, and equally out of hearing in the opposite direction was the Mess.

Scattered about were the idle Emils in their sand-bag bays. A light breeze ruffled the long grass, and the shadows of the clouds loped silently across the lush, green landscape.

"*Fräulein* von Richthofen, I don't think you're good enough for Ernst Geuke. I think he deserves someone better than you. But God knows, love is blind. And I'm a prime fool when it comes to that, so hold your fire." He held up his hand as if he really expected her to lay into him.

In fact, Klaudia was too stunned to say anything at all. She should have been indignant. Perhaps she would have been if anyone else had dared to say this to her. But Christian was from her own class, and no one here at Crépon knew Ernst better than he did.

Christian handed her a package, which she had not noticed in his right hand until just now. It was something soft wrapped in pretty tissue paper, a leather-bound book and, dangling on the string that held the other two objects together, was a bullet. "That's one of the bullets they extracted from his flesh," Christian explained. "The wrapped present is something he bought for you weeks ago – but didn't dare give you for fear you'd humiliate him by rejecting it."

Klaudia gasped, horrified by the image. She would never have done that – even if she admitted to herself that she wasn't exactly *pleased* with Ernst's attentions....

"The diary is—" Christian shrugged. "All I know is he asked me to give it to you. I hope you treat it with the respect it deserves." Christian thrust the package at her and then turned and strode away, leaving her standing in the middle of the airfield with the unusual package in her hands.

After she recovered from her shock, Klaudia continued towards the Mess. She wanted to be utterly alone before she opened the curious present, away from all prying eyes. She hastened up to her room, closed the door and turned the key in the lock – technically against regulations, but this was no time to think of that. She sank onto her bed and started fumbling with the string holding the book and the soft package together. She couldn't bring herself to touch the bullet. It seemed a cruel, unrelenting reminder of how callous she had been, not taking *Leutnant* Geuke's wounds particularly seriously.

She started instead with the present wrapped in tissue. Although she opened the tissue carefully, it was so frail that it tore. Soon she had the silk scarf with the pictures of horses spread out on her lap. The mare and foal in the centre were touchingly sweet. It was exactly the scarf she would have wanted but would have been too ashamed to buy. Klaudia sat for a long time, her hands stroking the soft surface, touched beyond measure by the fact that Lt. Geuke understood her so well.

Then, with trepidation, she took the diary in her hands and opened it timidly. Geuke had a surprisingly legible hand. He wrote in modern rather than gothic script.

"Dear Klaudia," the diary began. "I know that I am not worthy of you, and that is why I can never say to you all the things I feel in my heart. But I can't just keep them bottled up inside, either. I have to let my feelings out before they burn me up. Please don't be angry with me...." Tears started to trickle down her face as she read, and before long she was sobbing desperately. Soon she was unable to read further. Instead, she clutched the little diary to her chest and stretched herself out on her bed, overcome with shame and regret and self-hatred.

Freiherr v. Feldburg was right. She didn't deserve the devotion of Ernst Geuke. She had slighted him and looked down on him just because he was fat and a plumber's son. How could she have been such a snob? Such a bigoted fool? She, who had let a bastard like Jako play with her, had kept the honest Ernst at a distance. She had allowed him feel her disdain. She had hurt him over and over again. It was all in the diary, and despite it all, he avowed his admiration and affection for her, blaming only himself. "I'm sorry that I embarrassed you today by stopping you on the way to the Mess. You were annoyed. I could tell even though you tried to be polite. I promise I won't do it again...."

Oh, God! She turned into her pillow and cried miserably into it.

RAF Tangmere

It was so warm and sunny that Mickey opened his office window, but this let in not only the fresh air but the noise from the airfield as well. The squawking of the tannoy and the sound of the squadrons taking off, returning and refuelling was louder than ever. After a while, Mickey couldn't stand it any longer, and decided to go over to the Ops Room to see what was going on. The Duty Controller was Gage, the WWI veteran. "Mind telling me what's going on?" Mickey asked.

"Not at all, old chap. The first raid appeared at eight am, and just like two days ago, it was composed of a moderate number of bombers escorted by four to five times that number of 'snappers'. Notably, there were no 110s on this raid – just the smaller, more effective 109s. Among others, our last squadron of Defiants was deployed against them, and got massacred, I'm afraid to say."

"Good lord."

"Furthermore, the bombers got through to both Rochford and Eastchurch, dropping more than 100 bombs on the latter. They just hit Rochford again, I'm afraid; that's twice in less than four hours. The damage reports aren't in yet, but first indications aren't good. What you can see down there are bombers from that raid on their way home. And what time is it?" He looked over at the clock. "11.46. They'll be back," Gage predicted stoically.

Mickey went back to his office. The phone was ringing wildly. It was the sailing club at Bosham, telling him the price they wanted for the use of their club. Mickey protested. "But you're closed! It's not as if anyone else could use the rooms."

"Yes, but that's the point. We'd have to open and clean up 'specially for you. Besides, we can't do meals since the cook went and enlisted."

"In short, you don't want our business."

"What's this all about anyway?"

"Oh, one of our Squadron Leaders just got the DFC – he's downed a total of eight Jerries now and wanted to celebrate with the whole squadron, that's all. Wanted to go off Station so it would be a bit more special. You're sure you couldn't let us have the club rooms for a more reasonable price?"

There was a pause. "Are you ringing from RAF Tangmere?"

"Yes, where did you think?"

"The message I got – never mind. If this is for the RAF, you can have the rooms free of charge, and I'll get back to you with a price for the catering."

"Oh, that's much better. Thank you."

The tannoy was squawking again. 606 and 43 were being scrambled. That was 606's second scramble of the day. The earlier scramble had not resulted in contact, so they had returned with their guns unfired, but Mickey knew that even such sorties were exhausting and hard on the nerves – as was the waiting. Mickey went outside to watch them take off.

They were down to 15 operational pilots and 12 aircraft at the moment. And still no Flight Lieutenants. Mickey had been nagging the Group Personnel people about Flight Lieutenants ever since Priestman chopped Thompson, but they weren't very sympathetic. The attitude was pretty much that no Squadron Leader in 11 Group was going to recommend promotion for a capable Flying Officer at a time like this, since they would thereby risk having him posted away. If they had anyone they could trust, they were guarding him jealously.

In short, Personnel implied, 606 would just have to make do with what it had. Ringwood seemed to be working out quite well, actually. As for new pilots, Personnel complained that they "couldn't produce pilots out of thin air" – always with an undertone of accusation, as if the front-line squadrons were careless with the pilots they did send. But there was no way they could keep up this pace with the pilots they had. Each engagement brought the risk of more casualties. Mickey thought they were bloody lucky not to have lost both Priestman and Kiwi two days ago. What the hell did Priestman think he was doing, firing from beneath a loaded bomber at less than a hundred yards? You could almost have thought he was suicidal – if you didn't know the bloke.

Mickey had warmed to Priestman. Yesterday he had come to the office with a bottle of champagne and insisted that they celebrate his DFC together. Mickey had been touched beyond words. Most men would have gone to a pub or celebrated in the Mess with the other pilots, without giving a thought to a paper-pushing ground-hog. Instead, Priestman dragged both Mickey and Allars out of their respective dens and made them join him for a bottle of bubbly.

Priestman led the squadron into the air this morning, with Kiwi on his left flank and MacLeod and Bowles on his right. The other two sections were led, as before, by Ringwood and Donohue respectively.

The sun was very bright and there was a heavy haze across the surface of the earth, obscuring the contours of the land and making it hard to recognise landmarks. The Channel gave off a sheen through the haze. Robin had to squint against the glare, and it seemed exceptionally hot in the cockpit. He shouldn't have put on his flight jacket.

"Bandits! One o'clock!" Williams' voice crackled through his earphones.

Priestman found them, too: from here they were only dark specks against the haze, but in fact it was a vast armada of enemy aircraft, the twin-engine bombers in neat formation and above them, a swarming beehive of 109s.

As they watched, a handful of planes flew in at right angles to the armada, evidently another squadron also vectored onto the formation and intent on attacking the bombers. Instantly, what seemed like a score of snappers fell out of the sky to start attacking them. One flamed almost immediately.

"Jesus Christ!" Donohue commented.

"Redcap Squadron, buster! Eton, don't fire unless it's got two engines on it. Do you read me?"

"But, sir—"

"I don't want you shooting at Spitfires again. If it doesn't have two engines, hold your fire."

"But what if it's shooting at me?"

"Then evade it."

"Redcap Leader! Those aren't bombers."

"Good God! There's nothing but snappers out there!"

The "bombers" were Me110s, and while these had proved ineffective escorts, they could still be deadly. For a start, they were faster than the Hurricane, and armed with four forward facing guns, one rearward firing gun and two forward canons. Furthermore, they were pure bait. The whole armada was nothing but an elaborate trick to lure the RAF fighters into the air where the 109s could get at them. Unfortunately, it was too late to disengage safely.

Priestman made a snap decision not to target the 110s, but to charge the 109s. He didn't have enough altitude to bounce them, of course, but he was determined not to let them do that to him, either. He ordered the squadron to bank hard right, away from the melee, and forced his Hurricane into a curving battle climb. His engine screamed and the little aircraft trembled with effort. He tried to keep his eye on the enemy, but his wing was in the way, blocking his view. Maybe this wasn't such a clever idea, after all. He couldn't risk this much longer. He flipped back to the horizontal, looked left, and his heart almost exploded from sheer terror. A swarm of 109s was coming straight at him, not more than 500 yards away. Another second or two and they would be in range.

The two formations clashed. Guns flashed. Tracer crisscrossed in the air. Someone screamed into the R/T. One 109 was so close that Robin could see the pilot's face. Robin thought, "we're going to crash," even as he instinctively flinched away. He found himself beyond, his heart battering his chest and his hands trembling. His breathing was ragged. But already, more 109s were coming towards him. They were hopelessly outnumbered.

"Could you try to give them a little more berth next time, skipper?" Kiwi was miraculously still with him, but there was no sign of the rest of the squadron.

Priestman didn't bother answering. There was no time. He sideslipped and then did a quarter-roll to take him between the leader and wingman of the next on-rushing pair of German fighters. Then he hauled the aircraft around to the right and tried to get in behind them. The Germans were turning, too. Again, Robin looked for the rest of his squadron. They had to be out here. But the chaos was too great.

A Spitfire chasing a 109 sliced across his bows. A lumbering 110 going full-out and hard on the tail of an unfortunate Hurricane swept by going the other way. It was from another squadron, but before Robin's eyes, the Hurricane seemed to disintegrate as the cannon and machine guns of the heavier German aircraft severed a wing off the fragile wooden British kite. Robin saw the pilot start to climb out of his cockpit. Saw the impact of the 110's cannon. Saw the body fall out, bang against the tail, tumble down lifelessly – and already he had the murderer in his sights, unconscious of anything he had done to position himself for a deflection shot.

His machine guns shattered the glass of the canopy. The Me110 jinked. Its engines started smoking as the pilot shoved them into full emergency power, trying to get away. The bigger plane was faster, and Robin had only another second or two. He held the trigger down furiously. But the 110 pulled away – straight across Kiwi's bows and into his stream of bullets. Abruptly, it started to dive.

"That's one for you, Kiwi."

But he'd hardly got the words out before he saw tracer flash past him on the right. Something hostile had him in its sights and had only just missed hitting him. Robin hauled the Hurricane around until he greyed out. He eased a fraction, but it was still there. Must be a 109. He turned tighter again. His vision faded. He couldn't take this much longer. He eased up on the turn, but his stomach cramped in anticipation of the bullets. Nothing. He eased a bit more. Looked in the rear-view mirror, over his shoulder. Left. Right. Nothing.

Disoriented, he looked around again. He was alone in the sky. Well, not entirely: a 109 was skimming over the surface of the earth maybe 2000 feet below him – making for home. Further away, there were other aircraft – scattered over the whole horizon. But the dogfight was over. The Germans had run out of playing time.

The telephone rang on Mickey's desk. "Adjutant 606 Squadron."

It was the front gate. Were they expecting the Salvation Army? Mickey had completely forgotten! Yes, yes, they were indeed. They'd had a phone call this morning from a Major Fitzsimmons, asking if she could come and bring a hot meal over to the airfield. The Station Commander had approved it, remarking that he should have thought of it himself much sooner. Mickey told the gate to let the lorry in and rushed off to welcome them.

By the time he arrived, the lorry had stopped between the ruins of two of the hangars. The sides of the lorry had been dropped down to reveal a mobile kitchen, and scores of erks had already lined up eagerly. They were drawn, Mickey decided, not just by the smell of a savoury stew, but by the two young women doing the serving as well. Both were quite young and pretty, the darker one particularly so – although the blonde was bantering with the erks with such ease and glib charm that waves of laughter met him as he approached. By her accent, she came from the same class as the men she was serving, and although she was still quite young, she was no timid maiden.

The other girl was much more reticent, almost shy. She just smiled and served, hardly saying a word.

"Hello," Mickey came alongside. "I'm the Adjutant of 606 Squadron. Just wanted to thank you in the name of the all the squadrons on this Station. Is one of you Miss Fitzsimmons?"

It was the dark-haired girl who answered in an educated accent, "I'm sorry, Miss Fitzsimmons can't leave the Mission. She sent us along instead. I'm Emily Pryce and this is Daisy Lewis. You must be 'Mickey.'"

"Yes, that's right." Mickey replied, flustered that she knew his nickname.

"I'm Squadron Leader Priestman's fiancée," she explained, holding out her hand.

"Good heavens! Is that how you heard about our problem with the catering?"

"Yes, exactly," Emily smiled.

When she smiled she was absolutely lovely, Mickey noted, even if he'd never pictured Priestman with a girl from the Salvation Army, of all places! Socialite would have been more like it.

The tannoy squawked into life and Mickey saw her eyes search the distance, clearly trying to make sense of her environment.

"606 is already in the air," he explained to her.

"Thank you." She smiled at him again. "Would you like something to eat? It's gammon steak with Brussels sprouts."

"Yes, please."

Emily was feeling exhilarated. The break with her parents had been like a thunderstorm ending a horrible drought. She'd woken up in Miss Fitzsimmons' sunny little attic guestroom in Eastney to the sound of the seagulls and the sight of Robin's model airplanes floating over her bed. It was like being at home for the first time in her life. Cambridge had enchanted her – but more like a dream or fairy tale with its elegance and history. In contrast, Hattie's house was so comfy and ordinary, she couldn't feel awkward.

She had gone downstairs to a breakfast of sizzling bacon and fresh eggs, which Hattie had been given by a "customer." "Black market, I'm sure, but it's just what you need." And they had talked.

Or rather, Emily had talked, and Hattie had listened. At the end of it, it had been so clear: she should never have gone home after University.

Whether she could get an academic job or not, she should have started her own life immediately after graduation – even if it meant working as a secretary in London or some other city – anywhere but Portsmouth!

"But I wouldn't have met Robin if I'd done that," she concluded a little whimsically.

"You might have met someone better," Hattie countered. She'd then put a hand on Emily's. "I adore my nephew, and I happen to think he is a very exceptional young man with wonderful qualities that might just make him a *great* man one day – if he lives long enough. But when it comes to women, Robin is a spoilt brat. Ever since he reached maturity, he's been taking what he could get from those fool enough to give it to him – and avoiding getting snared by those who wanted commitment. My opinion of him with regard to women went up by miles when I heard he'd asked *you* to marry him. He is *very* lucky that you said 'yes.' So, don't let him push you around! *He's* the lucky one."

"We're both lucky," Emily countered. "He's been absolutely wonderful to me."

"Telling you to resign your job and sit around waiting for him was *not* being wonderful! It was bloody silly and insufferably selfish! What does he think you're supposed to do? Sit gazing up at the sky for 16 hours a day and then run to him and smother him in love and kisses? Ridiculous! You're better educated than he is! You are full of energy and commitment. You need to be *doing* something – not sitting around like a silly spaniel!"

That was when Emily told Hattie about the ground crews needing a hot meal. Hattie had agreed at once. "Right. Start with that. You talk to Cook about doing a hot meal a day and see which of the girls want to help you with it – or rather, try not to start a riot over who gets to go with you! They'll all want to, but I think Daisy would be best suited.

"Next, you'll need to learn to drive, so you'd better see about taking driving lessons, too. But don't think this is enough. You need a job – a hard, demanding, challenging job that will keep your brain from calcifying. Don't, whatever you do, let Robin talk you into anything else. He fell in love with you because you were sharper than he was, and you had your own opinions. If you lose either, the *next* thing you'll lose is his affection."

Now, here at Tangmere, Emily was experiencing the same kind of excitement that she had during her first week up at Cambridge – despite the alarming sense of the acute proximity of the war. Portsmouth had been hit and hit hard, but in between times life went on as normal. At Tangmere, the war was all-pervasive. For one thing, the ruins of the hangars still exuded a smell that was a mixture of fire, smoke and petrol. And around the perimeter of the field were aircraft being serviced. One squadron was still on the ground and their aircraft waited purposefully in their bays. Their dispersal was surrounded by young men, and people moved in and out restlessly. A certain nervous energy exuded from it. The chattering crowd of airmen who came to collect a hot meal, although cheerful and grateful for the meal, were also a reminder of the war. They were dirty and unkempt in a way no one had ever looked at Hawarden. They also reminded Emily that Robin wasn't the only one at Tangmere who was approaching a state of exhaustion.

Emily's attention was also drawn towards the WAAF who joined the queue. They came in a little group, half a dozen of them. They were wearing oil-stained uniforms just like the men's – trousers and tunics, shirts and ties and rank badges. They wore neither make-up nor nail-polish, but they were powerfully attractive because they exuded self-confidence and contentment. Here was no pouting, no whining, no back-biting as Emily knew all too well from her colleagues at the insurance company. The girls were laughing among themselves – and with their male colleagues. Not *flirting* but chatting in a way Emily had not seen since leaving University.

They were getting low on food and starting to take the empties back at the other side of the lorry. Daisy offered to start the cleaning up. Emily noticed that the men were glancing up at the sky and checking their watches more and more frequently. "Are you expecting something?" Emily finally asked an airman as he checked his watch before taking the bowl of stew.

"Squadron's been airborne an hour and 18 minutes now, Miss. If they've engaged, they'll be running low on fuel soon and need to return. Need to eat up fast." He smiled and took the stew, spooning it into his mouth even as he walked away.

Emily leaned forward and scanned the sky, but it was clear and empty except for a few fluffy clouds. Then she saw something. Or maybe she only saw others see something. The atmosphere on the airfield changed. Men put aside their bowls and mugs, leaving them scattered about. Men started running, and the WAAF did, too. It took Emily several moments before she heard the buzzing and realised that it was aircraft. They came down in a ragged pack. One was lagging, dragging a wing and trailing smoke. They swung about to line up into the wind. She knew about that from Hawarden. They settled down just like a flock of gulls – not at exactly the same time, not in neat formation, just a flock of green-brown birds, trundling across the field and over to the far side of the airfield. Somebody said "43 Squadron" and she felt some of the tension leave her – until she realised that meant 606 was still airborne and presumably running out of fuel.

She noticed that a WAAF was driving the fire engine that rushed out to meet the Hurricane trailing smoke. WAAF were also driving the lorries hauling bowsers that rushed alongside the other Hurricanes. Airmen scrambled up the wings of the aircraft that had landed. They reached in to help the pilots out, or opened slots in the wings to feed petrol into the wing tanks from the bowser. Other slats opened to enable the empty munitions belts were pulled out. Meanwhile, airmen walked around the aircraft inspecting them for damage. The speed and efficiency of all these airmen and women impressed Emily. She didn't mind that they'd just tossed their bowls and mugs aside any more.

The arrival of more aircraft, distracted her. These were straggling in one and two at a time and one of the airmen, who had the courtesy to return his bowl before dashing off, was kind enough to say, "that's 606 now – you can tell by the letters XT before the roundel. The letter behind is the aircraft ID." Then he was gone.

Emily tried to count the aircraft with the XT on them. But some had already turned away or been rolled back into their pens. Indeed, one or the other of the earlier aircraft might have borne the XT. She thought she'd seen maybe seven or eight altogether. That hardly seemed enough. Then another one limped in, its engine sputtering and the aircraft rising and falling like a swallow. It came down rather hard, and the fire engine and ambulance rushed to meet it. Two more appeared. Then a last one.

Emily found herself watching this last one closest for some reason. The pilot shoved his hood back while still rolling out after landing and pulled his helmet off. Darkhair fluttered in the wind. Check the aircraft letter, she told herself. "R." That was him. "R" for "Robin."

The Hurricane moved purposefully across the field with Robin looking out of the cockpit on one side and then the other. Ground crew were signalling him over, signalling him to turn. Cut the engine. The chocks went before the wheels.

Oh, dear, Emily thought. It had to be dangerous to love anyone this much.

Almost at once she had a new crowd of customers – the pilots of both 43 and 606 had been given the word by their crews about the food, and they were crowding around. No queuing for the likes of them. They all wanted something at once. Daisy was up to the task, however, reprimanding them and chastening them to make them laugh.

Priestman cut the engine and was at once conscious of feeling clapped out. Ripley loomed over him, and without a word offered him a hand. Perceptive young man, Robin registered. He took the offered hand and let the young fitter help pull him out of the cockpit. He dropped to the earth with the weight of exhaustion almost overpowering him, while the fitter tidied up the cockpit, ready for the next scramble. Williams had called in saying he was going to have to jump. But from his quick count on landing, another aircraft was missing, too.

Allars appeared out of nowhere, and Robin got off the first question. "Who's missing?"

"Williams managed to break a foot landing. He'll be fine – but not on ops for a bit. Sutton is a hair overdue, but not seriously. He might still turn up at another field, or he may have taken to the silk."

"Anyone see what happened?"

"Not really, although Banks thought he saw a Hurricane get chewed up by a 110."

"So did I, but it wasn't one of ours. Not a Tangmere squadron."

"Right." Allars accepted his word for it. "Get anything?"

"Shot up a 110, but Kiwi got it. Is he back?"

"All the rest are back."

"Are they making any claims?"

"MacLeod says he got a 109, and Kiwi put in for half a 110 with you."

"Give him the whole thing. All I did was break some glass."

Allars nodded. "Green says he damaged a 109, but then got 'distracted.'"

Priestman snorted. "We were all a bit distracted. Mickey, what are you doing out here?" Robin had caught sight of the Adjutant.

"I wanted to bring you the news myself, sir. We've got Bosham Sailing Club booked for Friday night. I also got the Squadron stood down early on Friday – 5 pm, and the morning after you don't go on again until noon – so the lads can enjoy themselves Friday night."

"You mean to ensure the Defence of the Realm after they've been carousing all night. Good idea. Do we have transport laid on?"

"I'll see to that next, sir. Didn't want to make a lot of plans until the place and date were fixed. By the way, you'll also be pleased to hear that LAC Tufnel returned on schedule. Do you want to drop all charges?"

Priestman flinched inwardly when he realised he had completely forgotten about the rigger who had tried to go AWOL. "Yes, of course. Have you spoken to him?"

"No, Rowe just reported it to me."

Priestman looked around towards the hangar, wondering if he should go over and try to find the rigger himself, but he was distracted by the lorry with its sides open. "Is that the Salvation Army over there?"

"Your future bride, I believe. She's made a conquest of the entire Station. The food's jolly good, too."

"Think I'll go and get some."

Allars and Mickey let him go, but one of the erks who had been trying to repair the damage to "P" came chasing after him. "Sir! Squadron Leader Priestman! You've got to see what we found in the leading edge of 'P's wing!"

Robin paused frowning slightly, afraid for an instant they were going to give him fragments of bone or skull. He still shied away from thinking about that soft, white thing that had smashed against his canopy, coating it in blood. But the airman was not that morbid. He held out an Iron Cross. Robin gazed at it. It had a swastika in it, so it was from this war. Of course, old men don't usually fly combat sorties.

"Don't you want it, sir?" the airman asked, puzzled.

"No, you keep it."

"But, sir, it was your kill," the airman insisted. He seemed so disappointed that Robin felt he could not insist on refusing. He took the iron cross with a nod. "Thank you, Todd."

The airman grinned. Robin started to turn away. "Oh, and, sir?" the airman stopped him. Robin looked back. "You've got a wizard girl!" The airman scampered away after allowing himself that impertinence, but Robin was rather pleased by it; it indicated that the ground crews didn't think of him as a "butcher." He looked over towards the Salvation Army lorry. Thatcher had said he'd have them eating out of his hand if he did something about the food. If only the pilots could be bought so easily. Maybe the dance on Friday would help.

Chapter 31

**Boulogne
30 August 1940**

Klaudia talked Ursula into swapping afternoon watches with her. That gave her 12 hours between coming off at 9 am and going on again at 9 pm. She had already arranged with Oberleutnant Möller for a lift to Cherbourg Station, and he promised to meet her return train as well. In Boulogne she took a taxi to the hospital. By the time she arrived, she was inwardly agitated. She had rehearsed a thousand speeches in her mind, and none of them were worth anything because she didn't know how Ernst would react.

After reading his diary from start to finish more than once, she thought she knew him intimately. The problem was, that she felt she knew things she didn't have the right to know. When he'd been writing his diary, even if it was ostensibly addressed to her, he'd never expected her to read it.

The nurse at the desk of the hospital was unfriendly, telling her visiting hours weren't until four, but a doctor, overhearing the conversation, intervened. He understood she had to get back to her unit and told her where to find Ernst. As she made her way along the gloomy corridors, the smell of the place intimidated her. Now and then she caught a glimpse into the wards where men lay in rows of beds facing one another. They wore hospital pyjamas, and many were connected to blood or bed-pans. Klaudia, nervously clutching her handbag, became increasingly afraid of what she might find.

At last she reached Ernst's ward and timidly pushed open the door. It was a room for just four, but that was bad enough. One man had his leg in a cast from thigh to ankle and it was suspended on a sling. Opposite him was a man with both arms in casts. Then she saw Ernst and he saw her.

He struggled to sit up more, pulling the covers across his legs and waist without taking his eyes off hers. They were large and searching and worried. He was so apprehensive about what she was going to say to him, that he didn't even smile. "*Fräulein* von—"

"*Leutnant* Geuke," she began. Then, because all words seemed to clog in her throat, she felt the need to communicate without them. She timidly took his hand. It was surprisingly soft and warm, and it sent a surge of warmth through her whole body. She broke into a smile, because nothing she could remember had ever felt so right as his hand in hers. His eyes widened with surprise, while with his other hand he tried to comb his hair. "*Fräulein* von—"

"Please, I want you to call me Klaudia, and I think we should use the familiar form of address, don't you?"

"But—"

"*Freiherr* von Feldburg gave me your presents, Ernst. When I read the diary — I was so ashamed of myself—"

"But why? What did I say—" Ernst looked genuinely alarmed, and she had to wave him silent.

"I felt so stupid, so arrogant, so cold-hearted. I'm so ashamed that I didn't appreciate your feelings, Ernst. Didn't appreciate *you*."

"But that's not what I meant, not what I intended. I know I'm not good enough for you, *Fräu*—" He broke off and gazed at her, confused and frightened.

Klaudia saw Ernst through completely different eyes. She saw for the first time that he had a very well-proportioned face with expressive blue eyes. He had fine blond hair, and although he was very pale at the moment, his skin was unblemished and tanned and not marred by stubble. He was not even as fat as she remembered him. "*Freiherr* von Feldburg put it the other way around, Ernst. He told me bluntly that *I* was not good enough for *you*."

"He didn't!" Ernst gasped, sitting up in horror. "I'll kill him!" Ernst was outraged and felt betrayed.

"It's all right, Ernst. You know Feldburg. He even told the *Herr Reichsmarshall* what he thought of him."

"But that's different! That's political. Christian's going to end up in a Concentration Camp one of these days. But he's my friend — or I thought he was—"

"Ernst." She squeezed his hand until he was distracted enough to fall silent. "He *is* your friend. If he hadn't told me off and made me start thinking, I probably never would have woken up and seen you for what you are. Ernst? May I sit down?"

"Yes, of course, I'm sorry—" Ernst blushed at his rudeness and tried to reach out of bed to pull the chair closer. His whole left side, however, was stiff and painful. His efforts made him grimace and catch his breath.

Klaudia forestalled him with a smile. She set her handbag down on the floor, and settled herself in the chair. Then she took hold of his hand again, this time in both of hers. He closed his fingers around hers, looking at her as if he expected her to flinch away. Instead, she smiled steadily at him. At last a smile crept tentatively across Ernst's face.

She continued to smile at him. "Let me talk, Ernst. You see, from reading your diary I know much more about you than you know about me. It's only fair for me to tell you about myself, don't you think?"

Ernst could hardly breathe for the wonder of it. She was looking at him with the eyes of a woman in love. That made him aware that he was not exactly at his best in hospital pyjamas with his hair in disarray. He tried again to comb his hair with his left hand.

Klaudia had an innate maternal instinct, which she had never been able to indulge before. With a glance at the bedside table, she found Ernst's comb and combed his hair for him. "Better?"

"If you say so," Ernst answered in a state of shock.

"You look wonderful to me, Ernst. I can't wait to see you up and about again – though I hope the English will have surrendered before you have to return to operations." Klaudia was reminded – with a little inward start – of the *dis*advantages of being in love with a fighter pilot.

"The doctor says I'll be out of here in another two to three weeks," Ernst dismissed the topic almost irritably. He was not keen to go back on operations exactly, but he wanted to get back to the *Staffel* – and back to Klaudia as well. He was ashamed to be lying on his back in bed. He wished he were on his feet and in uniform because he could now risk picturing himself taking her dancing, to the flicks and fancy French restaurants. Not a few of the others would envy him. "Please. Tell me about yourself as you promised."

Klaudia took a deep breath and started explaining. She him told about the heavy debts that burdened her father's estate, about her father's injuries from the Great War and the uncles who never came home from it. She explained what a disappointment she was to her father because she was a girl, and she him told about her little brother, who had been killed in an accident when she was five. This latter incident was the greatest trauma of her young life, and Klaudia still found it difficult to talk about. So much so that Ernst suggested, "You don't have to tell me if you don't want."

"But I *want* to tell you, Ernst!" she countered earnestly. "I want to tell you everything. When I was five and my brother three, he fell into the duck pond and drowned. After that – I don't know how to explain it exactly – but my parents just seemed to lose interest in everything – especially me. They just didn't seem to care what I did. My mother became more and more withdrawn and reclusive. My father was always taciturn and stern. For as long as I can remember, I could never please them."

"That's terrible!" Ernst declared, unable to understand such an attitude. If Klaudia hadn't been in love already, his sympathy alone would have won her. No one had ever taken her side like this before. She squeezed his hand in thanks.

"Didn't you have any friends or relatives to help?" Ernst asked. He'd grown up in a large family and always had lots of friends.

"There was no money to go away to school, and although we were invited to the neighbouring estates for balls and parties, people seemed to keep their distance from us. My parents were not particularly pleasant company, bitter and grieving as they were, and I..." She shrugged and looked at Ernst's hands in evident embarrassment. "No one ever took an interest. I used to tell myself it was the debts. I suppose no one wanted to have to assume them, so young men were warned away."

Ernst was at once appalled that young men would let anything materialistic stand in the way of love for a wonderful young woman – but he was grateful, too. If Klaudia had lots of landed suitors, he was sure she would not be sitting here with him, the son of a plumber – no matter what Christian said to her.

Cautiously he asked, "And afterwards? I mean, in the RAD and training and with StG2?"

Klaudia flinched. There it was: the question she feared most. Now that she knew she *wanted* Ernst's affection and respect, she couldn't bear the thought of telling him about Jako. He mustn't find out. She shook her head sharply. "There was never anyone. You know what the RAD is like – just girls. And in training the instructors were older, married men." She hesitated, then said with a rush of nervousness, "And at StG 2 the pilots were all so stuck up and arrogant. Nothing like you and *Freiherr* v. Feldburg and *Oberleutnant* Möller. It was terrible there!"

She said it with so much conviction that Ernst didn't think to challenge her. Besides, her words echoed what Christian's fitter reported, and Rosa had obviously disliked it, too. Ernst accepted her explanation guilelessly, because it fitted with what he had seen of her behaviour since she'd joined JG 23. She'd been modest and shy from the very start. Why should he imagine she had behaved differently at StG 2?

Klaudia, aware that she was deceiving him, wanted to change the subject. She looked at her watch. "Ernst, I'm going to have to go soon, but I'll come again as soon as I can. You should know, however, that *Freiherr* von Feldburg is completely blind in his right eye. He's been hiding it for days, but somehow Fischer found out and – after giving him a rocket – sent him back to Berlin for treatment. It means he won't be able to visit you."

Ernst didn't care about that. He was glad Christian was getting proper treatment, but if he was blind in one eye, they'd ground him. That would be terrible....

Klaudia was saying, "Rosa has three days leave, but as soon as she's back, I can apply for some and come and visit you for longer."

"Not when I'm here in bed. Wait 'till I get released. We could go somewhere together." It was out before Ernst could think about whether he was being too forward. At once he regretted it.

Klaudia wouldn't look at him. She collected her handbag from the floor and fidgeted with it as she answered, "I don't know about that, Ernst." Why did men always want to have sex straightaway? Klaudia felt her first qualm about Ernst since she'd fallen in love with him while reading his diary. Was he going to turn out no better than Jako? And how could she keep Jako a secret, if he slept with her and realised she wasn't a virgin any more?

"I'm sorry. I didn't mean it that way. I mean, it's such a long trip to just sit here in a stupid hospital. I – I want to take you out to dinner and to the cinema – or for a day on the shore. Dieter says St. Malo is a wonderful town."

That mollified Klaudia at once. Ernst *was* different, she told herself. She smiled at him. "I've always wanted to see Rouen Cathedral—"

"Then we can do that. As soon as I'm back on my feet. I'm sure to get convalescent leave. At least a day or two."

"You'll get more than that if only the English would just see sense and surrender. Why do they drag it out? It only costs everyone more casualties! But when you get your leave, won't you want to go home to your family?"

"Only if you come with me," Ernst told her very earnestly, and the look he levelled at her was pregnant with a proposal he had not verbalised. Klaudia felt her heart beating faster. That was different from a weekend together. That was serious and respectable. Was she ready to face a plumber as her future father-in-law? But what did it matter? She was living in the Third Reich, not the *Kaiserreich*! And Ernst was an officer. "I'd be honoured to meet your parents, Ernst."

Ernst broke into a wonderful smile. "You mean that?"

"Yes, I do," Klaudia decided. With a smile, she bent and brushed her lips on his forehead. She drew back a foot, considered him up close, and then bent and kissed him again on the lips. It was a chaste kiss. Nothing like the way Jako had pressed her against the back of the chair and consumed her lips and then penetrated her mouth, but for some reason it was very exciting, nevertheless.

At the door she stopped and blew him a kiss, and then she was gone.

RAF Tangmere

Another hot and sunny day, and the operations room was oppressively stuffy. The girls started to wilt early, losing their usual smart, alert appearance and becoming increasingly frazzled and tense. Corporal Winters had allowed them to take off their tunics and roll up their sleeves, but ties were still required, and they were clearly sweating.

Bridges was sweating, too, and his eye-patch was chafing and irritating him. He kept fidgeting with it, which only made it worse. The Germans had changed tactics again. Instead of sending in large raids which built up over France and then moved majestically across the Channel several hours apart, giving squadrons a chance to refuel and regroup, the Luftwaffe was sending little raids across every 20-30 minutes. Some of them were just fighter sweeps, but some contained bombers. The RAF couldn't afford to ignore any of them but trying to meet them all was almost more than Fighter Command could handle.

By mid-day every single squadron of 11 Group was airborne, but the Hun still managed to knock out the Kent electricity grid, and RDF went dead all across the most critical stretch of coastline. The RAF was blind in the midst of its most crucial battle yet. From that point forward, squadrons were being thrown about fast and furiously, but interceptions were rare. Biggin Hill got bombed twice and Detling took over a hundred bombs, putting it out of action for the rest of the day.

Bridges starting glancing more and more frequently at the clock. He felt the way Wellington had at Waterloo: would that it were dark... No, on second thought, scratch that quote. The second half was "or the Prussians would come." He most certainly didn't need any more damned Prussians!

Mickey was only vaguely aware of the intense activity. Although he had his window open and the sounds of the tannoy squawking, the aircraft engines, and the sirens of ambulances and fire engines poured in, he was too distracted to notice. Mickey was determined that the dance tonight would be a success, but he hadn't had a chance even to look at the clubhouse. He wanted to get over there early. The padre had kindly offered take him over along with the band, which needed to get set up early, but that meant finishing his paperwork before leaving the Station.

There were two burning issues that could not wait. Flight Sergeant Rowe had come in with the requisition forms for new aircraft, and two new pilots were waiting out in the anteroom. Rowe had to be handled first.

Mickey called to the senior NCO, and the Flight Sergeant came into his office looking bleaker than normal. Never a man known for his smiles, his expression now was more than grim, it was as if he were biting down on something bitter. "I want this on the record, sir," He commenced, jabbing his finger on the desktop as he spoke. His nails were very thick, square and grimy. They made a distinct clicking noise above all the background sounds of bowsers pumping and lorries groaning back and forth. "I am officially reporting, sir, that if things continue the way they have been, this squadron will cease to exist within two weeks. The crews cannot – I repeat, cannot – be driven any harder. They're doing their best—"

"We know that, Flight. The CO himself has made it very clear that he doesn't expect more of the crews."

"Oh, it is all very well for him to make pretty speeches, and promise the men leave," Rowe sneered politely; "now, I'm down a whole crew every day while the men go off to see their popsies!"

"But we don't have 14 aircraft. We only have 11," Mickey tried to mollify him. Priestman had arranged with the Station Engineering Officer, Fl/Lt Kimbolton, that the ground crews be given a regular two days off on a rotating basis. Kimbolton, a very conscientious officer, had been receptive to the idea, and agreed that it made sense to send entire crews at the same time.

"That is exactly my point, sir," Rowe retorted sourly. "We *don't* have 11 aircraft. And I don't even want to talk about pilots who shoot at the bellies of loaded bombers from less than 100 yards. If they care so little for their own skins, then why should they worry about the Hurricanes? But Sutton's Hurricane is a complete write-off." Sutton had managed to crash-land his Hurricane in a ploughed field. The problem was that, in order to prevent the Hun from landing gliders in such fields, stakes had been set up. One of Sutton's wings had been torn off by such a stake. They had hoped to salvage it, but Rowe was reporting, "The engine's completely clogged with dirt and manure."

"Let Lord Beaverbrook's salvage teams have a go at it," Mickey suggested. The Minister of Aircraft Production had established repair installations that could rebuild, from apparent scrap, aircraft that flew like new. "I'll requisition a new one." He held out his hand for the form.

As Rowe handed it to him, he continued: "This squadron has lost four aircraft in as many days."

"My understanding is that aircraft production is keeping up with demand," Mickey assured him.

"For how long? We have eight aircraft in the air at the moment, and two undergoing repairs. When are the replacements due?"

Mickey opened one of the files on his desk. "I put in for them yesterday and got an acknowledgement this morning from No. 41 Group, stating that three Hurricanes assigned to us are ready for collection at the factory. The ATA will have Hurricanes on their way to Maintenance Units for final refit today, and we should see them tomorrow or the day after, depending on the workload at the MU."

Rowe didn't bother answering; his face said it all. After a moment, he drew himself up. "Very well, sir. I've said my piece. You know what I think. Two weeks. That'll be mid-September. If Jerry hasn't given up by then, we'll have nothing to stop him with."

Mickey was thinking to himself that at least the new aircraft were all equally perfect. The same could not be said of pilots. He'd seen the record of the two young men waiting in the anteroom, and they were both straight out of a training unit. He stood up and went to the door, asking both young men to come in.

Pilot Officer Reynolds was a tall young man with long blond hair and an easy, infectious smile. Pilot Officer Tolkien was solemn by comparison, with rather sharp, dark features and no smile.

"I'm afraid this is going to be very brief," Mickey told them. "We're having a dance this evening to celebrate the CO's DFC, and I need to get over to the club we've rented." As he spoke, he glanced at the clock. It was already 3.50. He'd promised to be out by the main gate at 4.00! He hurried through the formalities, checking their orders and having them sign the forms for their pay and Mess bills and the like. When that was done, he was out of time, so he simply said, "I'm sure you've been reading the papers and know the form. Why don't you tell me a little about yourselves. Tolkien?

"My father's an Oxford Don, sir. I was reading maths until the war started. I applied to the University Air Squadron, but they turned me down, so I did VR instead."

"Reynolds?"

"Actually, sir, I'm an actor."

"An actor? On the stage?"

"Yes."

"How extraordinary! Anything particular?"

"No – any job I can get." He tossed Mickey a grin. "Not a lot going, so I worked in a chippy shop to pay the rent."

Mickey liked that confession. "And how many hours have you had on Hurricanes?"

"Twenty-one, sir."

"Tolkien?"

"Twenty-one, forty."

"Mathematician," Reynolds muttered.

"Right then. There's transport on for the dance tonight if you want to join us. Good chance to meet the others. A lorry will be leaving from the main gate at 5.45 and again at 6.15."

Mickey left them and set off for the main gate himself. The padre was waiting in his Bentley with the three musicians crowded into the back. "Sorry to keep you waiting. Had to welcome a couple of sprogs," Mickey explained.

The Sailing Club at Bosham was right down at the foot of the town on the shore, with the tidal basin on the left and a long pier pointing out to sea. It had been closed all season because of the invasion threat and there were no keel boats in the water, only some sailing dinghies drawn up on the shore. The tide was out and the mudflats emitted a pungent smell. Yet bunting flew cheerfully from the mast out in front.

The club-room décor of half-hulls, yacht models and sailing paintings had charm of its own, but when the Club had called for volunteers to fix things up for the RAF, the response had been overwhelming. Members had brought strings of paper bunting and coloured lights to drape from the ceiling, and hung a large, mirrored ball over the dance hall. The band was greeted enthusiastically and one of the club members helped them set up. Mickey was ushered over to the bar and shown the kegs of beer and the bottles which had been purchased on their behalf and was then taken back to the kitchen to see the catered food. Everyone seemed very happy to be hosting the event.

Emily arrived at about 5 pm. She was dressed in a burgundy satin cocktail dress that had a crossed bodice and a skirt that hung in elegant folds to well below the knee. *Now* she looked like a match for Priestman, Mickey thought. He should have known there was more to her.

Next to arrive was a gaggle of four WAAF, who came in their own car. They too were in civilian clothes and looking very chic indeed. Mickey hardly recognised Corporal Winters, she looked so much more feminine in a black velvet bolero jacket over a grey, raw-silk dress. Jane Roberts and Liz Hadley looked like the ladies they were, and between them was little Lettice Fields.

The whole Station knew about her situation, which was the last thing she wanted, but one of those things you couldn't keep secret in such a close-knit community – certainly not if you wore your heart on your sleeve the way Lettice did. What surprised Mickey was the fact that she was looking radiant. She had her hair pinned up and was dressed in a pretty, pink off-the-shoulder gown with tight bodice and full skirt.

The girls went straight to the bar, manned by a club member, and ordered a bottle of champagne. "We're celebrating an engagement!" Liz Hadley announced in a voice to include everyone.

Mickey, Colin and Emily all went over to congratulate. "And whom do we have the pleasure to congratulate?" Mickey asked, assuming F/O Ringwood had proposed to Liz.

"Lettice is marrying Sergeant MacLeod," Liz announced, clearly enjoying the astonished looks from the two officers.

Emily leaned forward and kissed the younger girl on both cheeks. "Congratulations, Miss Fields! I'm so pleased for you!"

"Have you set a date?" Mickey stammered out, still dazed by this fortunate turn of events.

"Oh, there wasn't time for that! Malcolm just said to go ahead and arrange everything, and whatever date I set he'd live with." She was so happy, she seemed unaware of how indifferent her bridegroom sounded. Lettice giggled and added, "I think I'll make it *soon,* so he doesn't change his mind."

Mickey glanced at Colin, but the young clergyman looked as astonished as he felt.

"Here's the bubbly!" Liz announced, passing glasses out. "To Mrs. Malcolm MacLeod!" She raised her glass and the others echoed her, except for the now blushing Lettice.

"Do you want me to find a Presbyterian pastor for you?" Colin volunteered.

"Oh, yes, that would be lovely!" Lettice agreed at once. The exchange gave Emily the idea of asking the padre's help for her own predicament. He looked like a nice young man. This wasn't the moment to say anything, however. She didn't want to steal attention away from Lettice. The latter was telling them excitedly about how she'd already resigned from the WAAF. Winters confirmed, adding it was a shame because "Fields" was such a conscientious supply clerk.

"Oh, can't you be married and in the WAAF?" Emily asked, disappointed.

"You *can* be, but the RAF won't guarantee postings to the same Station!" Lettice told her. "I'm not taking the chance of being separated from Malcolm! Besides, I want to start a family as soon as possible. I want to have at least three children."

A handful of other WAAFs, these wearing dress uniform, arrived with Kimbolton. He'd driven them over in one of the Station cars. They came straight to the bar and joined in the congratulations. Kimbolton scorned the champagne and tossed back a double scotch.

"Rough day?" Emily asked him softly.

"Bloody awful! We've lost four kites so far already. Three from 17, one from 43 – and your future husband's squadron hasn't even landed yet." He seemed to catch himself. "Sorry."

Emily made a gesture of understanding, but it unsettled her a little. It was almost six pm. Surely, they should have been back if they were stood down at five pm as Mickey had promised....

Finally, the first lorry arrived from the Station. There wasn't a pilot aboard, but with relief Emily recognised Appleby – who had boldly introduced himself to her the other day. If he was here, then Robin must be safely on the ground. Yet doubt remained.

The band started to warm up while the men crowded around the bar. One of the WAAF who had arrived on the lorry in uniform slipped into the Ladies and re-emerged wearing a slinky gown with deep décolleté, bare back and studded with sequins. She joined the band and as soon as she started cooing into the microphone, she harvested a storm of whistles and applause. The erks cheered with hearty approval the transformation of a girl whom they usually saw in oil-stained overalls changing sparkplugs.

The band started with a light, rhythmic two-step, and several couples went onto the floor at once. "Woody" arrived with Sutton, Donohue and Ware. They had clearly spruced themselves up for the event and were wearing expensive silk cravats rather than ties. The linings of their tunics were black satin rather than regulation. Donohue smoked a cigarette from a holder – it looked ridiculous and very affected to Emily, but the other girls seemed to like it.

"If I only had wings...." the singer commented in melody, "All day I'd be in the sky.... You'd see my picture in the papers.... one little pair of those wings...."

The big New Zealander, the two Canadians and Sergeant Pilot Bowles arrived – windblown but in good spirits.

"...I adore that crazy guy who taught my happy heart to wear a pair of siiilver wiiiings." The singer was good, the applause sincere.

The second lorry arrived with Bridges and two new pilots. Mickey brought them over to meet Emily. The blond bowed low over Emily's hand as if she were a Continental countess. "Enchanté, Mademoiselle. Enchanté."

"Don't fall for it," the other pilot warned. "He's just an actor."

"Jawohl, mein Fraulein!" He clicked his heels and saluted.

Emily smiled, shook hands, welcomed them again, and then managed to squeeze her way through the crowds to Bridges. "Where's Robin? Isn't he down yet?"

"Robin?" Bridges seemed to jump out of his skin, then recover. "He's fine, Miss Pryce. I think he's got another claim in. Doug Allars will be bringing him over." But Bridges looked guilty as he said this, and he glanced over his shoulders, too. Then he dropped his voice. "It's Eton and MacLeod who're missing. Terrible mix-up with 109s again."

The band was playing "Blueberry Hill," and the dance floor was crowded. The efficient club members were going around and closing the blackout blinds in preparation for turning on the lights. Emily went to the door to look for Robin. It was still quite light, although the sun had technically set. Across the road to the left was the lovely old Saxon church. If she was going to have to get married in a church, she thought, that was the kind of place she wanted – something historical but not imposing.

From the car park of *The Blue Anchor*, two men in Air Force uniform were approaching. One had a cane. Emily waited for them. They both looked sombre. How do you celebrate when two young men have just been killed? Robin saw her and smiled sadly. She went towards him, went on tip-toe for the kiss. Then she stepped back. "Bridges told me. Is there no hope?"

Robin shook his head. "The Observer Corps saw him go in. He didn't flame out, and the Hurricane appeared to be in perfect order. Nor did he have a mark on his body, but his internal organs had all ruptured. Or several of them had. There will have to be an autopsy." Robin, the former aerobatics pilot, was clearly shaken.

"It's the G, of course. It's been known to happen once or twice before," Allars was saying. "I believe at least one test pilot died of similar injuries."

"And MacLeod, too?" Emily asked.

"That's who we're talking about," Robin responded, confused.

"But what about Eton? What happened to him?"

"Oh, Eton's all right. Nothing but a bit wet! Jumped when it wasn't at all necessary, the fool. But maybe he learned a lesson. He's been told to find his own way home."

Only then did Emily register that inside the clubhouse, where the band was now playing "*I wished on the moon*," there was a young woman in a pretty pink party dress who thought she was soon going to marry a man who was already dead.

They went in together; Robin had his arm around her waist, and she did not even let him go to the bar. She took him straight onto the dance floor, and he seemed to understand. Without a word, he held her to him and let her listen to the beat of his heart.

They had arrived in the middle. The song ended. The band took up "*I fell in love with an airman*," and neither of them wanted to dance at a fast pace.

"I need a drink," Robin admitted, and they started for the bar.

Lettice had caught sight of Allars.

"...I used to watch him doing crazy things in the sky..."

Emily caught her breath, relieved that the older man would have to break the news.

"Scotch, please," Robin remarked beside her. Emily was still watching Lettice. She saw her eyes widen.

"...what happened there, is my affair, and I'm not telling you..."

Even before the piercing scream shattered the club-room, Emily knew it was coming. She started running, pushing her way through the crowd.

"Nooooo! Noooo! Nooooooo!" the wounded girl was screaming as she crumpled up onto the floor, clutching herself as if she had acute pains in her abdomen. Allars was completely incapable of dealing with the situation. He just stood there staring at the girl in horror. One didn't *do* that! Not in England. Not in the RAF.

Emily reached Lettice and sank onto the floor to pull her into her arms. "Hush! Hush! Shhh!" She grasped the girl to her own bosom, trying as much to silence her as to calm her.

Around her everyone was staring in horror. The mood of the evening was wrecked, the band silenced, the music dead.

"It's all right, Lettice." Emily stroked her back, hugged her close as she burst into wet sobs. Lettice was still gasping, "No, no, no" and shaking her head.

Colin reached them. "Let's get her outside to the fresh air," the clergyman urged. Corporal Winters was there, too. Together they helped Emily get Lettice onto her feet, and Emily told her fiancé and guest of honour, "I'll just be a minute." He nodded and let her go.

Emily, Colin and Winters together got Lettice through the blackout curtains and into the balmy summer night beyond. There was a breeze off the sea and the tide was coming in. You could hear the waves lapping at the quay, and the air smelled of salt and France. (Or so Emily always thought.)

"Why does God hate me?" Lettice sobbed out. "Why? Just when everything seemed to be all right? Oh, God, why? Haven't other girls done the same thing? Why do I have to be punished? Why?"

"No one is punishing you, Lettice," Colin told her gently, releasing his grip a little out of propriety.

"Yes, He is!" she screamed furiously, and Emily glanced quickly back towards the clubhouse. Fortunately, the band had resumed playing, and she could hear laughter and voices again as if nothing had happened.

"No, he's not, Lettice," Emily chimed in, taking a firmer hold now that Colin had pulled back. "Our pilots are being killed by the Germans because the Nazis want to invade this country and turn us all into slaves.

Sergeant MacLeod gave his life for England."

"Why? Why him? Why not one of the others? Why not your bloody future husband, who drives them all to madness and shoots at bombers from only a few feet away! Why not *him*?"

"Tomorrow it very well *may* be him," Emily told the other girl calmly, but Corporal Winters admonished firmly, "Stop it, Fields! Wishing other people dead won't bring Sergeant MacLeod back."

Colin nodded with his head for Emily to return to the party. "We'll take care of her, Miss Pryce," he murmured. Then turning to Lettice herself he suggested, "Let's go across to the church."

Emily gave them a questioning look. Corporal Winters nodded and gestured for Emily to go back inside, while putting her arm firmly around Lettice's shoulders and guiding her towards the square-towered church, with Colin on the girl's other side, ready to help if needed.

Emily watched them for a moment, then glanced up at the moon rising high above the horizon and casting a bright light across the waters of the tidal basin. With a deep breath, she made herself start back into the clubhouse. The singer was finishing the song with great gusto, "... *but I'm nobody's baby, I'm nobody's baby now!*"

Chapter 32

Croydon
31 August 1940

Pilot Officer Alan Ainsworth didn't know what to think or feel any more. The last 24 hours had been the most confusing of his life, and he hadn't come to terms with them yet. First came his orders to join 606 (Hurricane) Squadron at Tangmere – not totally unexpected, since he'd just about completed the OTU course and several other pilots got their orders at the same time. Still, one is never entirely prepared for orders like that. After all, other pilots had been sent to 13, 10 or 12 Groups. They didn't all get thrown in at the deep end like this.

As he stared at the orders, he found himself wondering who and how the assignments were made. Was it all a great lottery? Someone in the Air Ministry put a piece of paper with each pilot's name in a hat, perhaps, and drew them out one at a time to be assigned to the vacancies starting at, say, No. 1 Squadron and so on?

Or did someone actually *think* about who was to be sent where? Did the instructors get together over a friendly pint in a cosy pub somewhere and say "Well, let's give Harper a bit more time to pull himself together, but Ainsworth's up to the mark, we can send him straight to the fray." Or was it the other way around? "Harper's got some potential, better keep him alive a bit longer, but Ainsworth's a useless sod, might as well send him straight to the slaughter."

Part of Alan would have liked to know – but then again, he didn't like the last scenario much. Better to think of it as some kind of compliment. He thought he was doing pretty well, actually. At least he hadn't bent any crates.

Why didn't the train get going? They'd been halted here in Croydon station for at least 10 minutes. Alan got up and shoved down the window. He leaned out and looked up and down the platform, trying to see the cause of the delay. Before he could figure out what was going on, the sirens went off. Over the loud-speaker someone barked. "Disembark from the train and proceed to the Air-Raid Shelter immediately! All passengers must disembark immediately!"

Ainsworth was the first out of the carriage. Along the length of the train, the doors opened, and people poured out. The wail of the sirens seemed magnified here in the station, and ARP Wardens in their tin hats officiously directed people towards the stairs, where large arrows pointed downwards. Ainsworth resisted. His instinct was to stay above ground to try to get a glimpse of the enemy. He'd be facing them soon enough, after all; but the press of the crowd and the shouting of the ARP wardens couldn't be ignored. The human herd moved down the steps into the bowels of the station. The smell of mildew and urine lingered over the stairs, and it got darker and cooler with each step. From behind them, the detonations exploded, and the whole station seemed to tremble.

"Blimey! It's real!" someone exclaimed.

"Get a move on! Get a move on!" one of the ARP wardens ordered. People started to move faster. The crump, crump, crump of explosions became more insistent and the building trembled continuously.

Ainsworth stared at the ceiling. That was silly. You couldn't see a bloody thing through the ceiling. Dust and plaster was falling off it and some got in Alan's eyes. Cursing to himself, he looked down and tried to blink the grit out.

Already the detonations were receding. In less than 15 minutes it was over. The All Clear sounded. The crowd shuffled up the stairs into the station, with many talking excitedly. When they reached ground level, Alan was amazed to find that although neither the station nor the train had been hit directly, dust hung in the air, and a couple of windows had been blown inwards, leaving shards of glass glittering about on the floor.

The passengers re-boarded the train. The engine started snorting and hissing (it was an old steam locomotive pressed back into service). Ainsworth stood at the open window and as soon as they had come out from under the roofing of the station, he searched the sky.

There they were! The tell-tale vapour trails entwined and went every which way. Tomorrow he'd be up there. What a thought!

The train gradually increased speed, and one of the civilians looked admonishingly at him over his reading glasses. "Could you close that window, young man! It's causing a terrible draft."

"Yes, sir." Ainsworth stepped back, closed the window and sat down, feeling like a chastened schoolboy. His cherished wings and the thin stripe on his sleeve apparently did not impress anyone but himself. He leaned his head back. The seat smelt dusty, as all old railway seats did. He closed his eyes.

At once he saw Mona as she had lain beside him in the hotel bed this morning. The mental image sent a jolt through his whole body and he stirred uneasily, his loins quickening. He couldn't get over it. It had been better than anything he had ever imagined. It was indescribable! A pity it had led to such complications.

Late into the night Mona had started crying, convinced that he now thought she was "a tart." He denied it, of course, and in the course of comforting her, he ended up promising to marry her. In fact, he promised to ask his new CO as soon as he got to the Station. This had transformed Mona into a happy, cuddly kitten, and after that things had gone very well.

Yet as the train hurtled him toward his new life on an active squadron, Alan started to feel uncomfortable about the proposal. Well, not so much the proposal itself – it would be bad form to back out of that now, but the promise to talk to his new CO straightaway. How could he possibly show up at his first operational squadron and start off with a request?

The train slowed to a halt, and Alan opened his eyes. They were in the middle of nowhere. He got up, opened the window and looked out. "Blimey! They're at it again!" Large columns of smoke were erupting into the air no more than five or six miles away, and the train shook slightly with each detonation. Alan searched the skies overhead. A thin layer of cloud at about five thousand feet had slipped in from the west. He couldn't see what was going on above that, but now that the train was still, the engine only hissing faintly, he could hear the drone of engines – the low rumble of lots of non-synchronized engines and the higher-pitched purring of smaller engines. Straining harder, Alan detected the rat-a-tat, rat-a-tat of guns.

By the time the train pulled into Chichester station, Ainsworth was over three hours late. He was collected by an airman/clerk and taken to Tangmere, where he found he'd missed lunch at the Mess, and even the Sally Ann mobile canteen was closing up and preparing to depart. He reported to the Squadron Adjutant, who seemed a nice chap but a bit distracted.

The Adj smiled, shook hands and said nice things like, "Nice to have you with us," and "You'll see, Tangmere is one of the best Stations – good local pubs, too." But he didn't really *look* at Ainsworth as he spoke, and he seemed to jump clean out of his skin when the telephone rang. He told Alan where to put his things and suggested he go over to the 606 dispersal hut.

Alan heard the klaxon go while he was unpacking his suitcase in the room assigned to him at the Officer's Mess. From the window he could see Hurricanes racing across the field and lifting off in a great thundering herd. He'd never seen anything like it before – in training they'd never taken off in more than sections of three. Here there were ten to twelve of the thoroughbreds racing across the broad field and then wheeling about in a wide arc. They were magnificent! His heart raced faster at the thought that he would soon be out there with them.

When he got to the dispersal, however, it was empty. Everything just lay about – half-finished mugs of tea, unfinished sandwiches, magazines, newspapers. A record was circling on the gramophone, making only a scratching sound. Ainsworth took the needle off the record and turned off the gramophone. Then he glanced around the room, his attention drawn to the Order of Battle. Beside that was a blackboard on which crude aircraft in strange, lopsided vics had been drawn. That wasn't a formation they'd been taught in training, he noted, and it looked sloppy. There was also a large 94 at the top of the board, underlined heavily. He wondered what that was all about. Was he in the wrong dispersal? Was this No 94 Squadron rather than 606? But the 606 shield was there, and from the markings on the blackboard the 94 clearly had been written over other numbers that had been erased. Must be some kind of score, Ainsworth decided. He stepped out of the hut to wait in the sunshine.

It seemed to take forever for the squadron to return. While he waited, a gaggle of aircraft landed but dispersed far away, and the pilots went into another dispersal hut. There were three squadrons operating from Tangmere, Ainsworth remembered. Finally, a second gaggle came into land, with one of the aircraft trailing smoke and flying unsteadily. Alan watched in fascination as the damaged aircraft was given precedence on the circuit and came in low, its engine spluttering, the hood shoved back and the pilot looking over the side as he put it down. Fire engine and ambulance rushed across the field towards it, but the pilot waved them away and rolled over to one of the blast bays. Erks rushed out and caught the wingtips. The prop slowed. The pilot jumped down.

The other planes were landing fast, one after the other, and Alan watched the way they spread out to their respective blast pens. Everywhere the ground crews swung them around and backed them in. The planes had hardly come to a standstill, before whole teams of erks were crawling all over them: opening the cowling, the ammo boxes, the fuel tank, checking and topping up oil, glycol, oxygen, petrol, re-sealing the muzzles of the guns, testing tyre pressure, etc.

Meanwhile, the pilots had gathered around the damaged machine. They seemed to be in animated conversation, pointing this way and that, gesturing with their hands as they inspected the damage to the crate. A man limping badly and walking with a cane went out to them. They converged on him like a school of ravenous fish attacking a victim. Eventually they calmed down, however, and started towards the dispersal hut in a large group.

One of them noticed Ainsworth. "What have we here?" he asked in astonishment, halting. He was a slender young man with a snobby accent. They all stopped, but then one of them came forward with an outstretched hand. "I gather you're a replacement pilot for 606?"

Ainsworth caught sight of the two-and-half stripes just in time and saluted. "Yes, sir. Ainsworth, sir. Alan Ainsworth."

"Straight from an OTU, I gather."

"Yes, sir."

"Don't tell me the bad news just yet; let's get in out of the sun first." The CO led them all into the dispersal hut, where the windows were open, allowing for a bit of a cross breeze. He tossed his flight jacket into a chair, while the others hung their jackets onto hooks.

"Ring for tea, would you, Woody?" the Squadron Leader suggested, while the others collapsed into the chairs.

The CO introduced them to Alan one at a time, but except for the big New Zealander they called Kiwi, Ainsworth was sure he wouldn't be able to put names to faces for a while.

"Could we have some more sandwiches, Skipper? These ones have got ants all over them."

"All right, who was the bright sod who left them on the floor?"

"Does it matter?"

"Why doesn't the Salvation Army bring us a hot meal like they do the erks?"

"It would just get cold."

"You're off your form today, Skipper, by about 50 yards. If you don't smarten up, it will take us forever to make 100."

"We're much nicer at the *The Ship*, believe me," one of the pilots told Ainsworth.

Two Mess stewards arrived with hot tea and sandwiches and were greeted enthusiastically. The pilots gathered around with their mugs. Ainsworth didn't have one, but a slight, fair-haired pilot noticed, and took a clean mug from a locker and handed it to him. A moment later silence had settled over them, as they were all eating with concentration and an almost tangible urgency.

The telephone went. The eruption of swearing was truly vile – not just rude but vehement. The clerk was absent for some reason, so the CO grabbed the receiver himself, still chewing. He managed a mere, "MMM."

The others waited absolutely still, staring at him. He gestured with his hand for them to relax and they audibly unwound, starting to eat and drink more calmly. The CO was nodding. "Um hum. Um hum. OK. Thanks, Bridges."

"Well?"

"Hornchurch was hit while 54 was still on the ground. They lost a whole section – though not the pilots – and Biggin Hill was struck again. Second time today. They also gave Debden, North Weald and Croyden a pasting. It seems Jerry is concentrating on the airfields around London. 12 Group was asked to patrol London and the 11 Group 'dromes while the squadrons refuelled, but they failed to show up in time."

"Typical 12 Group," a man with a posh accent commented.

"Leigh-Mallory thinks his squadrons are more effective if they are flown in wings of multiple squadrons," the CO explained.

"Well, I like *that* idea. It would be a nice change *not* to be out-numbered ten-to-one!"

"We never *are* out-numbered by that many, Woody," the CO countered in a low, serious voice. "And the odds are identical whether we deploy in big wings or individual squadrons. The difference is at best psychological, and frankly I much prefer things the way they are."

"Why?" the New Zealander asked bluntly, and by the reactions of the others Ainsworth had the impression they all wanted to know.

"Because large gaggles just get in each other's way. Look at the 109s. We generally have somewhere over thirty or even sixty of the buggers up there when we attack, but when it comes down to it, we only fight with about a score. The others never get a chance."

"Maybe, but frankly, once – just *once* – I'd like to face them on equal terms."

"You--"

The telephone and klaxon seemed to go off at the same time, and they were gone even before the returned clerk could shout "scramble" at them. Ainsworth was left standing. He went to the door of the dispersal and gazed after them, feeling more confused than ever. Shouldn't he be with them? But they hadn't given him an aircraft or a flight or anything. Maybe there weren't any extra aircraft? There had to be, because the damaged crate had been rolled into the one remaining hangar, but its pilot was clambering into the cockpit of another. From the scattered chaos of the scramble, the Hurricanes started to collect at the head of the field into a rough line. Their engines took on a more purposeful purring and the tails twitched nervously. Then they rolled forward, slowly gathering speed, until the tails came up. They bounced, leapt, floated.

Ainsworth watched them wheel around, their wheels folding up under them, wishing he was with them. He noted they flew in loose formation, not at all what he'd been taught. Why didn't they tighten up more? It looked sloppy. Were they that tired? They were climbing up through the thin layer of low cloud. He watched until the last speck was gone, and then he looked around the forlorn dispersal again.

In less than an hour they were back. All of them. This time they trickled into the dispersal separately, depending on how far away their blast pen happened to be. "Fucking little cowards!"

"I don't know. I sure as hell wouldn't want to have a bloody bomb clamped under the belly of my Hurri!"

"They used to send Stukas to do that kind of thing."

"Ah, those were the days! Stuka Parties, we called them. They were great fun. Got 15 of them the day they bombed us here, you know."

"Fifteen!? You alone?"

"Of course not, Idiot! The Tangmere Squadrons combined. A bit confused, actually, not at all clear who got what exactly, but there were wrecks littered all over the countryside. Those were the days...."

"And now they bugger up their best fighter with a ruddy great bomb."

"Bloody unfair, that. If they come in unmolested they bomb their targets, but if they see us, they just jettison the sodding bomb and take us on like equals."

"Did they put the RDF out or not?" The question was from the CO, who had just come in.

"Don't know, Skipper."

The CO reached for the phone and jangled it. "Bridges? Did they succeed?" A long pause. The CO hung up. "They got them. RDF is down again."

"Bugger! Now we're blind again!"

"The whole chain again?"

"Truleigh, Pevensy and Rye."

"Bloody hell!"

"Jerry's getting too bloody clever. Whatever happened to good old days when he attacked Convoys, Coastal Command and the Royal Navy?"

No one had an answer to that, and they fell silent. The CO noticed Ainsworth. "Sorry, Alan. Not very hospitable, I'm afraid. Tell us a little about yourself – start with the good news, *not* how many hours you've had on Hurricanes."

"Sir?"

"Sorry, bad joke. Tell us about yourself."

"I'm from London, sir. After leaving school I trained as an engineer and joined the Volunteer Reserve. I'd just finished basic training when the war started."

"What part of London are you from?" a Flying Officer asked with mild interest.

"Primrose Hill, sir."

"You don't have to call *me* 'sir.' Save that for the Skipper. Where—"

"What's that?" Woody interrupted in an alarmed tone.

They could hear a lot of small engines, but very low and directly overhead.

"Jerry wouldn't send his fucked-up fighters in a low-level attack against *us*, would he?"

They bolted for the door so fast that several of them collided in the doorway. Ainsworth just stood there, holding his breath, waiting for the first explosion or at least the crack of ack-ack. Instead he heard a burst of excited voices, and he went to the door. The others had stopped just a few strides beyond the dispersal watching Hurricanes, flying in neat vics, circle the field and come in to land one section at a time.

"Very nice," someone said.

"Bloody amateurs," someone answered.

"Where do you think they came from?"

"Oh, probably Scotland."

"What?! You mean they're *foreigners*?!"

"Not necessarily. That's where they send English squadrons to relax and recuperate from the rigours of life here in the South."

"Ah. You don't suppose they've come to relieve us, do you?"

"Fancy a trip to Scotland, Donny?"

"Yes, as a matter of fact. Never been there."

"Its charms diminish on closer contact. Rains 363 days of the year."

"43 is being sent North," the CO put an end to their speculation.

"Oh." They watched the newcomers taxi neatly to the periphery of the field. Now they noticed that there were a couple of strange Ansons and Dragon Rapides parked around the periphery as well.

A Flight Sergeant was approaching the dispersal. He saluted the CO. "I'm afraid we're not going to be able to repair 'D' ourselves, sir. It will have to go to a Maintenance Unit."

"Have you put in for a replacement?"

"If you'll sign here, sir." He handed a form attached to a clipboard to the Squadron Leader, who signed without further ado. The Flight Sergeant turned away, and the CO turned to Ainsworth. "Unfortunately, the news about the kite is bad. It means we have no aircraft for you at the moment. Just how many hours *do* you have on Hurricanes?"

"17, sir."

There was a long pause. The CO didn't say anything. He didn't even look particularly shocked; but the longer the silence, the worse Alan felt. Then at last the CO announced, "Well, I'm not taking you on ops until you have at least 22, so let's see how fast we can get a crate down here for you to do some flying on, while we go to work."

The Mess was very crowded, what with 607 Squadron down from

Usworth and 43 still at Tangmere and not leaving until the next day. The new pilots were quite excited too, and correspondingly loud. They'd seen a great dogfight going on to the east as they flew down but had been unable to join in due to dwindling fuel. It had got their wind up a bit, however, adding to the simple excitement of being here in the thick of it.

Robin watched them clustered around the bar for a moment, their voices exceptionally loud and so dominating the room. Then he scanned the rest of the Mess. He'd met Banks, Green, Tolkien, Bowles and the chaplain out in front of the Mess on their way to a pub. That way commissioned and non-commissioned officers could have a drink together He suspected these pilots avoided the more common watering holes such as the *Fox and Hounds* and the *Ship*. He was glad they were including the new bloke Tolkien.

The old clique from 606 (Woody, Ware, Sutton, Needham and Donohue) were in the Mess tonight, but they had "adopted" Kiwi, Eton and curiously Reynolds, too, so that the eight of them were at a table together and talking animatedly. That left just Ainsworth. As Robin had halfway suspected, Ainsworth was standing on his own, on the fringe of the crowd of 607 pilots.

"I think you need a scotch," Bridges diagnosed, coming up beside Robin at the bar.

"Yes, but first I need to have a word with Kiwi. I'll be right back." He went over to the table where his pilots were sitting together. "Kiwi?"

"Something up, Skipper?"

"Ainsworth is standing over there by himself."

"Understood, Skipper."

Robin turned and Bridges caught his eye, signalling him to a table with Allars and Mickey. He sank down into the vacant chair.

"Robin, I was wondering. Would you have any interest in buying MacLeod's MG?"

Robin looked over surprised.

"It seems neither of his parents can drive, and it's a nuisance to have it transported somewhere and run an advertisement and all. They asked if I couldn't sell it for them, which I said I thought I could."

Robin was interested. The MG would give him the mobility he lacked. With a car, he could indeed live off station – which was clearly what Emily wanted. "Did they name a price?"

"Heads up! The AOC."

The pilots of 607 didn't seem to understand and looked about somewhat bewildered when the others sprang to their feet. Park entered, still in flying overalls, with his leather helmet hanging halfway out of his trouser pocket. Even then the 607 pilots didn't recognise him, but finally caught on when the Station Commander went to shake hands and lead the AVM to the bar. Park went to the bar and had a drink there, but then he turned and searched the rest of the room. When he spotted Allars, he came right over.

Robin and the others at his table got to their feet again. "May I join you?" Park asked.

"Of course, sir." They sat down again.

A Mess steward was already there. "Brandy," Park ordered. The Mess steward retreated. "How's 606 treating you these days?" the AVM asked Robin.

"Haven't killed me yet."

"Are they trying?"

"Not very hard."

Park nodded. He looked very strained, skeletal, in fact. His eyes were sunk deep in their sockets and there were dark circles under them. His chin seemed more pointed than ever, and the creases down his cheeks were gouges. His eyes were scanning the Mess. At last he announced, "I don't see Squadron Leader Badger?" That was No. 43's Squadron Leader.

"He's already turned in, sir," Allars reported.

Park glanced at the wall clock; it was just ten past nine. "They want to get an early start tomorrow, before the fun starts."

Park nodded. The brandy was set before him. He sipped at it. Set it down. "They struck Biggin Hill twice, Hornchurch twice, Debden, North Weald and Croydon. They put three RDF stations off the air for hours, and we lost 37 pilots. 37 *killed*. That is the greatest loss on any one day since the start of the war. It is worse than our daily losses in France or over Dunkirk, and more than ten times the average daily losses in July."

The others were stunned. It was the equivalent of roughly two squadrons in a single day.

"Furthermore, our kill ratios have been declining steadily ever since Jerry pulled his Stukas out of the battle and increased his escort ratios."

"These fighter-bombers are bloody dangerous," Robin pointed out at once. "They come in below the RDF, hit and run. After they jettison, they're as agile as ever and fully armed forward."

Park nodded and sighed.

A loud voice called out, "Pilot Officer Ainsworth? Is there a Pilot Officer Ainsworth present? You have a phone call, sir."

Alan was embarrassed to be called in front of everyone – even the AVM. He excused himself, while the other pilots teased him on the assumption it was a woman – which only made things worse because, of course, it probably *was* Mona. He'd promised to call her this evening, and it was approaching 9.30. He slipped into the wooden telephone box the clerk indicated. "Ainsworth," he said into the receiver.

"Alan? I've been waiting all night for you to ring! I've been going mad! Have you talked to your CO yet?"

"Mona. I – no. I haven't had a chance yet—"

"How could you *not* have had a chance? You've been there all day! How long does it take to ask one simple little question? Not 30 seconds, really, does it?"

"Mona, it's not like that. Try to understand. There's a war on—"

"Spare me, Alan! I *know* there's a war on, for God's sake. I wouldn't be in this horrible ATS barracks with all these horrible, common girls working myself to a wreck, if there wasn't a bloody war on!"

Mona never swore, so Alan knew how upset she was. Furthermore, her tone of voice was becoming increasingly hysterical. "I was right last night about you losing all respect for me, wasn't I? You didn't mean a word you said about marrying me! You just used me, and now you're going to wash your hands of me! You know what you are, Alan Ainsworth? You're a cruel, horrid bastard! That's what you are!" She was sobbing furiously on the other end of the line.

"Mona! That's not true! Listen to me—"

"Why should I? All you tell me is lies! Lies! Lies!"

"I haven't lied to you. Listen to me. The train was late. And when I got here—"

"Oh, spare me your excuses! If you loved me, you wouldn't treat me like this!"

"Of course, I love you, Mona! Listen to me. I'll go and ask the CO right now. This minute. I'll ring you back in an hour!"

"You know that curfew is ten pm!"

"All right! I'll ring back *before* ten. I promise. I love you, Mona!"

"If you haven't rung me back by 10 pm, I'll know that's a lie, too!"

"It's not a lie. I'll ring you back before ten! I love you, Mona!" She'd hung up. Christ! What was he going to do now? He looked back across the reception towards the open door to the bar, and his heart was in his mouth. He hadn't seen a lot of the CO, but he wasn't exactly the kind of chummy officer that made you want to come to him with your problems. He'd heard someone say he was Cranwell.

Alan glanced at the wall clock. It was 9.40. He had to do it. He had to go in there and try to have a word with the CO. He rubbed his sweating hands on his trousers and walked back into the bar. He scanned the crowded room for the CO, and when he saw him his heart sank. He was sitting with the AVM! Why hadn't he said something earlier? When? In the dispersal in front of everyone? Or at the bar, when the CO was telling him he needed more practice flying before he could go on ops? The   CO seemed to think he was useless as it was. How could he ask for a favour? He couldn't go through with this. But if he didn't, Mona would never forgive him. She was really upset. Shouting and swearing like that wasn't like her at all. She was regretting last night. He glanced at the wall clock; it was creeping up towards 9.45. Oh, God!

He plunged into the crowd and squeezed his way past the bar to the table where the AVM, his CO and another Squadron Leader were sitting with the Intelligence Officer, the Adjutant and a Flight Lieutenant he didn't recognise. "Sir?" His throat was so dry that no sound came out.

Fortunately, the Adjutant saw him and glanced up. "What can we do for you, Ainsworth?" He asked the question in a friendly tone of voice, but his eyes were transmitting a warning.

"Ah— ah— may I have a word with the CO, sir?"

"This isn't a very good time, Ainsworth," Mickey warned him. "Air Vice Marshal Park is here." Mickey nodded in the direction of the AVM, evidently thinking that Alan hadn't recognised the senior officer.

"Yes, sir. But I only need to speak with the   CO for a minute."

"Can't it wait until the morning?" Mickey's tone had become pointed.

Alan glanced at the clock and licked his lips. "Not really, sir. Just a minute is all I need."

"This is not the time, Ainsworth—"

Bridges had been listening to the exchange, and he nudged Robin. Robin glanced up. "Is something the matter, Ainsworth?"

"May I have a word with you, sir?"

Robin glanced at Park and Park nodded. "All right. Shall we step outside where it's a bit quieter?" He led the way out of the bar but stopped in the anteroom expectantly.

"Sir, I realise that this is highly irregular and maybe—" Alan could hear the clock ticking; it was ten to ten. "Sir, I'd like your permission to marry at the first opportunity." There, it was out.

Absolute silence. Robin was thinking, I don't need this: a pilot with 17 hours on Hurricanes and entangled in a love affair that is clearly robbing him of his concentration, if not his senses. He said: "How old are you, Ainsworth?"

"Twenty, sir. I'll turn twenty-one in December."

Robin almost said, "At your age, I was doing everything I could to *avoid* getting trapped in a marriage," but he stopped himself in time.

What did that have to do with anything? He was a different person, and he'd lived in different times. There hadn't been a war on when he was 20, and any risk to his life had been entirely of his own making. Still, he felt constrained to at least point out, "You are not entitled to a marriage allowance, you know, until you are either 30 years old or hold the rank of Squadron Leader."

Ainsworth nervously licked his lips and glanced at the clock. All he said was: "I understand, sir."

For a second time Robin thought, I don't need this. This pilot is not going to be focused on the job. But he personally resented having to ask permission to marry, and he was not going to apply a double standard. If Ainsworth was old enough to die for his country, he was jolly well old enough to decide for himself if wanted to get married. "If you think you're ready for marriage, Ainsworth, then I'm not going to stand in your way."

"Then I have your permission, sir?"

"Yes."

"Thank you, sir!" Ainsworth looked very relieved.

Robin nodded and returned to the lounge with an uneasy feeling, while Alan rushed to the telephone booth to put a call through to Mona.

Chapter 33

Crépon
1 September 1940

Klaudia was sleeping so soundly that she was shocked to wake up. Disoriented, she looked about in the darkness. It was pitch dark, the middle of the night. What could have woken her?

Then she heard a croak from the bed opposite and realised it was Rosa. "Help!" Rosa gasped. Something about the voice – so cracked and dry, so weak and yet so penetrating – sent a chill down Klaudia's spine.

She sat up instantly. "Rosa? What is it?"

"Help," the other girl whimpered.

Klaudia flung her covers back and went over to the bed opposite, her eyes still adjusting to the dark. "What is it? Aren't you feeling well?"

"The doctor," Rosa whispered. "Get the doctor."

Klaudia peered at her friend, deciphering the dark blob of hair on the white pillow around Rosa's face. Rosa looked pale, and her eyes were closed. Then Rosa's hand moved, drawing Klaudia's attention. The hand was dark and glistening. There was blood everywhere, staining the sheets in a huge, spreading pool.

Klaudia screamed in horror, and then exclaimed "Oh my God!" as she grabbed her dressing gown from the back of the door and wrenched the door open. Her scream had awoken the girls next door, and one of them put her head out as Klaudia ran barefoot down the hall to the stairs.

"What's happened?" Ursula called out.

"It's Rosa," Klaudia answered without even stopping. She ran down the stairs to the floor below, where the officers were billeted.

Klaudia had no idea who slept where, and it didn't matter. She pounded with her fist on the very first door. A low growl answered her from inside, and she called out in a voice shrill with shock and terror. "We've got to wake the doctor! Rosa's bleeding to death."

Although the growl from behind the door was inarticulate, a door further down the hall and on the other side opened and a tousled dark head appeared. "What?"

Klaudia ran towards the man in pyjamas, who stood blinking in the doorway. With relief she recognised *Oberleutnant* Dieter Möller. "Rosa! She's covered with blood! We've got to wake the doctor!"

"I'll get the doctor and bring him up," Möller answered, already fully awake. "Go back up to her!" He was already striding down the hall in the other direction.

By the time Klaudia returned to her room, the other *Helferinnen* had gathered. They had stripped the upper sheets off Rosa and removed her blood-soaked nightdress. One of the girls was trying to wash the blood away from her lower body with a face cloth, but the others were standing around in helpless, wide-eyed horror. Rosa was clearly haemorrhaging profusely – a filthy, thick, black, foul-smelling blood.

A moment later, male voices made the girls spring back to make for the Medical Officer, followed by *Oberleutnant* Möller; both were still in their pyjamas. The MO took one look at the girl on the bed and ordered, "Wrap her in a blanket! We need to get her to the infirmary at once!"

Klaudia tore a blanket off her bed. As she wrapped it around Rosa, she felt how icy cold her friend's hands and feet were.

Möller shouldered her aside to lift Rosa into his arms. Rosa's head rolled against his chest; she appeared completely unconscious. Her arms hung limply as he turned sideways to get her through the door and was gone, the MO behind him.

"What happened?" Ursula asked Klaudia, her eyes wide with terror.

Klaudia dropped onto her bed and started sobbing. She was sure it had to do with the abortion.

By morning, Rosa was dead. Numb with shock and guilt, Klaudia withstood the tirade from first the Chief Communications Officer and then the Station Commander. They both told her that she should have reported Rosa's condition and her intention to "commit a crime" to her superiors. Her failure to do so would be noted "negatively" in her Service Record. Klaudia nodded. What did she care about her Service Record at a time like this?

Blind with tears and stumbling with exhaustion and misery, she left the CC and headed for the Mess. Suddenly Axel was standing in front of her. "You bitch!" he shouted. "You bitch! You knew! You knew all about it!"

Klaudia covered her face with her hands and started crying openly, but this only seemed to make Axel more furious. He shouted more loudly still: "Why didn't you tell me?! If you'd told me, I'd have stopped her!"

Klaudia shook her head, her hands still over her eyes. How could she explain? Rosa had threatened to tell about Jako, if she went to Axel....

Axel jerked her hands down away from her face and forced her to look him in the eye as he told her: "It's *your* fault she's dead! Rosa's blood is on your hands!"

All Klaudia could do was cry harder, because she knew it was true, and then she sank down on the grass in utter misery. Axel left her there and walked away in contempt.

RAF Tangmere

Ginger went out to dispersal to find Banks. The squadron was stood down until 1 pm today, and they had been planning to spend the morning together in Chichester. Banks had called over to the Sergeants' Mess, however, to say the CO had asked him to help train the sprogs instead. The sprogs and the CO were still at breakfast, and Ginger found Banks alone. Banks was kitting up, tucking his trousers into his flying boots. "What is this all about?" Ginger asked resentfully on account of his ruined half-day off.

"You heard the latest sprog. He's only clocked up 17 hours on Hurricanes and the other two barely have 25 — including the hours they got swanning around yesterday. The CO wants to spend the morning training them in his formation and tactics before we go on readiness at 1 pm."

"But why you? Why not Woody or one of the senior pilots?" Ginger wanted to know.

Banks looked uncomfortable. The bruises from his collision with the tree were at the yellow stage, but the cut on his lip wasn't healing because his oxygen mask kept re-opening it. "That's what I wanted to talk to you about. You haven't said anything to him, have you?" Banks was a little embarrassed even asking the question, but he had to know.

"Of course not!" Ginger protested hotly. Ginger had never had a friend like Banks before, one he could talk to. He valued the fact that they could talk about things they didn't want the others to know. In Ginger's eyes, to have told anyone else the things Banks had told him in private, off the Station, would have been a betrayal as serious as treason.

Just a couple days ago Banks had confided in him that he couldn't shoot. "I want to," he'd told Ginger. "Every morning I swear to myself that this time I'm going to do it. I hate the Nazis. I really do. But then I start to get a bead on one of them and I think: What if that's Andreas flying it?

Or Ulli?Or Joachim?" Banks had explained to Ginger that before Hitler came to power, he had belonged to a gliding club. There he had had three close friends, who shared his love of flying. They had built a glider together and had innumerable adventures, including a serious accident when the Hitler Youth sabotaged their kite. That shared love of flight made it almost certain the others had joined the Luftwaffe when they reached the age of conscription. The only question was, fighters or bombers and which one?

"I didn't think you had," Banks reassured Ginger with a strained smile, but his expression remained tense. "It's just the way the CO asked me to do this – it was as if he knew how hard the fighting is for me."

Ginger thought about that and then ventured. "He found out about my sickness from the ground crews. Maybe they told him."

"Told him what? I always fire my guns so no one can tell."

"You blow the canvas off with a one-second burst. That *looks* OK to the casual observer, but the armourers know that you only used up 20-30 rounds every flight – and you can't do any harm with that."

Banks stopped fussing with his second boot and gazed at Ginger. Then he pulled his flight jacket off its hook and said, "Let's go talk to the erks."

Ginger went with him out of dispersal and started across to the remaining hangar, where the erks of 606 were working hard to get all checks done on the serviceable aircraft. "What did he actually say?" Ginger pressed Banks.

"He took me aside last night in the Mess and asked if I'd be willing to help him train the sprogs. I could hardly say no. Besides, he made it sound like a compliment. 'You've got more flying hours than the rest of them put together,' he said."

"Well, that's true," Ginger agreed.

"But then he said he thought I'd be good at instructing. He made light of it – saying I'd certainly be better than he was – but he was deadly serious. He was looking at me with those eyes – you know what I mean? Like he could see right into my mind and read my thoughts. I felt absolutely naked."

Ginger thought about that, his hands stuffed in his trouser pockets, and nodded. "He does have an uncanny ability to see through all of us – like the way he cottoned on to Thompson, Dunsire and Debsen."

A lorry was coming towards them and they stepped aside to let it pass. Instead it stopped, and Priestman leaned out of the window. "Can I give you a lift to dispersal, Banks?" Not a question, really. "Want to join us, Bowles?"

"May I, sir?" Ginger thought that if he couldn't have the morning off in Chichester with Banks, than he might as well get in some more flying. Ginger still loved flying; like Banks, it was the fighting he hated.

"Of course. Climb aboard."

Banks and Ginger went around to the back and joined the three sprogs. Reynolds reached down to give them a helping hand up and then offered them each a cigarette. "Sorry to ruin your morning off," he apologised. Reynolds had managed to get completely separated from the squadron during their first sortie the day before, and so missed the second. Tolkien's showing had been similar; he had become completely disoriented during the first dogfight and landed at West Malling. By the time he was returned to the squadron, it was too late for the last sortie of the day.

"We don't mind, really," Ginger answered for both of them, with a glance at Banks. When they landed after the first sortie with both sprogs missing, the CO had made some colourful remarks about the quality of instructors at OTUs these days. When Kiwi remarked, "At least they didn't get eaten by the Hun," he had nodded with a look of smug satisfaction – as if he'd planned it all. Ginger was certain he'd also got AVM Park to approve the morning off somehow.

At dispersal, they climbed down and Priestman explained the formation to the newcomers, and then announced that what he planned to do was have them fly the formation with Banks as section leader, while he and Ginger tried to bounce them. "You'll have two-to-one superiority, so you should have no trouble getting the better of us," he assured the sceptical-looking sprogs. Then, taking Ginger aside, he taught him hand-signals so they didn't need to use their R/T when stalking and attacking.

An hour and a half later they were on the ground again, and Ginger was feeling good. It was fun flying wingman to the CO. Ginger was surprised to discover that his flying skills had improved dramatically in the last month. He'd been so busy worrying about the fighting, feeling ashamed of being sick and all, that he hadn't realised that he could handle his Hurricane without thinking. Listening to Banks talking the sprogs through the manoeuvres had been interesting, too. The last bounce had failed; Banks got them turned around in time. He really was a born instructor, Ginger thought, wishing he'd had more instructors like that than the ones who made you feel like a fool half of the time.

Bosham

Colin collected Emily at 11 am to drive her over to Bosham. She had told him about her desire to be married there and admitted that she wasn't baptised, so Colin had arranged for her to meet the vicar and discuss with him what could be worked out.

Emily had dressed in a neat suit with hat and gloves. She wanted to make a good impression. Colin smiled as he opened the door for her. "You look lovely, Miss Pryce."

"Please call me 'Emily,'" she urged as she settled into the car. He closed the door and walked around to the other side. As he manoeuvred out of the parking spot, Emily asked him, "How is Miss Fields doing?"

Colin took a deep breath. "Not very well, I'm afraid. She had to be sedated these last two nights, and she's not getting much sympathy from the other WAAF because of the way she behaved. Nor will she allow me to contact her family. It doesn't help that MacLeod will be buried this evening at Boxgrove Priory. We're all a little worried about how she'll manage that."

"Do you really think she behaved so badly?" Emily asked the serious young man behind the steering wheel. Colin looked over at her startled, his eyes wide behind the thick, round lenses of glasses. "I mean, what should she have done? Just slipped away? I know that's what was expected, but think about it: the man she loved, the man she wanted to spend the rest of her life with, had just been brutally killed. What sort of woman would sustain such a shock without showing emotion?" She paused very briefly, giving Colin no time to answer before noting, "I've thought about it a lot. I think it was horrible that we just carried on dancing and drinking and laughing. A man who has been part of a tight-knit group for months was killed, and the others didn't even stop drinking and dancing long enough to mutter a word of regret, sorrow or shock. I think it was almost perverse, don't you?" Emily pressed the young clergyman.

Colin recognized that Emily expected an answer. He evidently cared about his opinion. That was flattering, and he did not want to disappoint her. "No, I don't think it was perverse. Not at all. Because, you see, they're not as callous as you make them sound. I'm sure that most of them have thought often of MacLeod – and Lettice – ever since it happened. But there are two reasons why they can't show their feelings. First, it would be bad form to make a fuss about one of their own, because it would be a kind of self-praise."

"I don't understand," Emily admitted bluntly.

"Well, it's like the PM's speech the other day. Don't think they weren't bucked up by it, but mostly they make jokes about it. If they admitted they took it seriously, it would be like taking themselves seriously. In the same way, if they make a big fuss about one of their number buying it, it's as though they were making a fuss about themselves. What are they supposed to say? If the death was tragic, then their own lives are tragedy. If the death was 'unnecessary,' then their lives are 'pointless.' If the sacrifice was 'heroic,' then so are their lives. I think that is an uncomfortable burden for them."

There was something to that, Emily supposed, nodding to herself. "But to ignore his death altogether... I've been told that deer are like that. When a hunter shoots a deer, the others scatter startled by the noise, but within minutes they'll return to the same glen or pasture and graze across the bloodied grass without the slightest indication of discomfort. That's what it was like yesterday evening. I felt ashamed of myself when I went to bed. I felt I shouldn't have gone back in and just carried on dancing and drinking."

"Of course you should!" Colin insisted. "They all *needed* that evening! It was doing them good – and poor Lettice almost ruined it for everyone. She didn't have that right. No matter how great her pain, she didn't have the right to take away the precious few moments of relaxation and joy that the other chaps have. When you get down to it, it's probably for the best. MacLeod wasn't ever going to make her happy. The man was an alcoholic and a brawler and even if he'd married her, it would never have lasted."

"Don't you wonder," Emily started, and stopped herself. A Navy rating had stepped out in front of them and with his white glove signalled them to stop. From a walled-off area on their left, a convoy of RN lorries emerged and turned onto the road.

"Wonder what?" Colin prompted while they waited.

"Don't you wonder if there might not have been more to MacLeod than meets the eye? There must be some reason why Lettice fell in love with him. After all, Robin tells me his pilots hate him, and yet he isn't really a bad person. I certainly love him fiercely."

Colin considered her seriously and then told her in a soft earnest voice. "His pilots don't hate him, Emily. Not any more."

The Royal Navy convoy was on the road ahead of them. The rating stepped out of their way and signalled them onwards. Colin put the Bentley back in gear and they continued.

Emily remembered that he had spoken of two reasons for not showing any emotion at MacLeod's death. "And what was the second reason why they can't publicly grieve for their dead comrades?"

"Because it would remind them of how close they are to death themselves – and if you'll pardon my language — it scares the hell out of them."

RAF Tangmere

Three pm. The sun was at its hottest, and the pilots had abandoned the stuffy dispersal. The air was still and flies buzzed about lazily. Banks and Ginger were playing chess on a collapsible card table they had set up outside. Ringwood, Donohue, Sutton, Needham and Ware were trying to teach Green the rudiments of cricket. Kiwi was providing running commentary in the dry tone of a newscaster — albeit in a language that would not have been allowed on the air. Reynolds lay flat on his back in the grass with his eyes closed as if sleeping, while Tolkien was reading something that had come in a tattered manila envelope and kept fluttering and flapping in the wind, so that Banks cast frequent annoyed looks in his direction. Priestman was standing across the field in front of the one intact hangar, in conversation with Flight Sergeant Rowe. Two new Hurricanes had just been flown in by the ATA.

From the dispersal came the ringing of the phone, and two seconds later the klaxon started its tuneless blare. Robin glanced over, saw his pilots drop everything and start for their dispersed Hurricanes, then he started running. As he dropped into the cockpit, he pulled on his helmet and plugged in the R/T. "What have you got, Beetle?"

"Massive raid building up over Calais. Biggin is already burning. Kenley under attack." While listening to the controller, Robin checked fuel, oxygen, and oil pressure. He leaned out of the cockpit and Ripley gave him a thumbs up to his silent question.

He pressed the starter button and the airscrew started to turn slowly. Then the engine fired, and great puffs of smoke billowed back to engulf the cockpit until Robin throttled back. The engine settled down into its usual consistent purr, and the aircraft trembled steadily. Robin checked the controls again: temperature, rpms, oil. Then he glanced across the field to where the other Hurricanes of the squadron were nosing their way out of their respective pens, waddling across the grass to turn into the wind for take-off in a ragged line.

Priestman waved the chocks away and let the Hurricane have her head, while braking occasionally to keep her under control. He took up his position in the middle and slightly ahead of the others. Kiwi was on his left and the other two sections — led by Ringwood and Donohue, as usual — on his right. The sprogs Tolkien and Reynolds were in Blue and Yellow Sections respectively, but Ainsworth was still grounded. Even with the training flight this morning, he didn't have 20 hours on Hurricanes. Besides, they were still one aircraft short. Bowles was now flying with him as Red Four beside Ware.

Priestman took his feet off the brakes. The whole squadron rolled across the broad field, gathering speed. They bounced until as if randomly one after another they left their shadows on the ground behind them. Priestman was on the R/T to Control getting a vector and altitude.

"Bandits 10 o'clock high!" Eton's voice was an octave too high. Ginger looked over and his stomach turned itself inside out. He just got the bag in place in time. He spat once more, and then shoved the bag down beside the side of the seat. Luckythey weren't flying at an altitude to require oxygen, he noted with detachment, wiping his mouth with the back of his right sleeve before taking two-handed control of his Hurricane again with resignation bordering on despair. The Jerries were stronger than ever. They must have endless reserves of planes and pilots. It just didn't seem to matter how many of them got shot down, there were always more of them the next day.

"Where are the bloody bombers?" Ringwood wanted to know.

"Just what I was wondering," Priestman admitted.

"There are nothing but snappers out there – again!" Ware confirmed angrily.

"Look at those bastards with yellow noses."

"Beetle, this is Redcap Leader. We have visual contact with a large formation of enemy fighters. Repeat: Fighters. No bombers in sight."

"Have they seen you?"

"Not that we know of."

"Let them be, Redcap. I repeat. Leave them alone. Pancake."

"Roger. Redcap, you heard him. Pancake—"

"Look out, Skipper!"

"I've seen them. Blue and Green Sections, pancake. Red Section stay with me." Was he asking too much of them?

The squadron was already breaking apart. Blue and Green Sections broke left and right respectively, turning for home, but Priestman had to deal with the swarm of 109s which had peeled off from the formation ahead of them. The fighters he could see had only a moderate height advantage, but he had to assume that there were more of them flying high-cover that he couldn't see – yet. It occurred to him that they would report that they had "frightened" away two flights of RAF fighters. Well, as long as they didn't report wiping out the third one....

"Red Two, try to watch above and behind. Red Section, in and out. Don't stay to muck about. Get out as fast as you can."

Robin had already chosen a target, the leader of the approaching four

German fighters. They were closing fast. These Germans really did have bright yellow snouts. How odd. A distinction of some sort? Or a means of making them easily identifiable to the anti-aircraft defences of their army? Maybe it was to avoid friendly fire when providing close cover for the invasion?

The flashes of light and glowing beads floating through the air indicated that they were firing their guns, but Robin considered it a waste of ammunition at this range. He held his course and flinched slightly when the Messerschmitt farthest to his right bucked and started billowing black smoke. That could only have been fire from Red Four: Bowles.

The Me dipped a wing and dived down. "Well done, Bowles," he commented before opening fire on his own target. But he couldn't see if he made any hits before he had to yank the Hurricane up and over the enemy. Immediately afterwards, he flung the aircraft into a hard left turn, pirouetting on his wingtip. The last thing he wanted was to continue into the dense cloud of fighters still ahead.

"Ginger is in trouble!" Kiwi shouted in his ears, as a Hurricane flew so low over Robin's cockpit that he ducked instinctively.

He wrenched around, trying to see what Kiwi had seen, but he couldn't.

Kiwi was shouting, "Ginger! Behind you!" but they had dropped below Robin's plane of vision. Hundreds of enemy aircraft were streaming northwards, and below him was the smoke trail from the Messerschmitt Bowles had hit. A lone Hurricane was off to starboard, flying straight and level. That was not a wise thing to do in present circumstances. Robin checked the ID: "Q" – Tolkien. What the hell was he still doing here? He was supposed to have turned back with Yellow Section!

"Yellow Four, this is Redcap Leader. Close on me."

"Yes, sir." An awkward pause and then a shamefaced admission, "Where are you, sir?"

"On your left." That said, Robin checked above and behind him again. He couldn't understand why he wasn't being pounced on by dozens of enemy. They were out there. They must have seen him. Four had attacked, after all. What were the rest of them waiting for? Yellow Four fell in beside him.

But where were Kiwi and Bowles and Ware? He suspected they were below him, but it was too bloody dangerous to look down with a sky full of snappers. He could only risk quick glances, and he saw nothing. All right, time to get out as he had ordered the others. He swung due west and tried to put some distance between himself and the enemy behind. "Keep a look out behind, Tolkien – just as Banks had you practice this morning."

Although he gave the order, he didn't trust Tolkien and kept gyrating in the cockpit himself. As he drew away without any apparent pursuit, he tried to contact Kiwi. "Come in, Red Two. Come in, Red Four."

No answer. Not both of them. Surely not both of them. Bowles was an experienced pilot. Like MacLeod. Kiwi was.... As if his thoughts had conjured him up, the New Zealander's voice blasted out of his earphone. "Got him, Skpper! Got him clean and good! He gone in now."

"Are you all right?"

"Peaches and cream."

"And Bowles?"

"He's the one who got the yellow-nosed bastard!"

"I thought you said he was in trouble."

"He was."

"All right, explain it to me on the ground. Pancake."

Ware was already down and Kiwi and Bowles entered the circuit as Priestman and Tolkien landed. They were all back safely.

Robin taxied over to his waiting crew and shoved the hood back. The fresh air was welcome. He noted now that he was soaked in sweat. He hung the helmet on the stick and ran one hand through his hair. Ripley was on the wing. "All right, sir?"

He nodded, but took his time unhooking everything. He found increasingly that he needed a few minutes at the end of each flight, time when he was by himself without Control or the squadron making demands on him. Ripley, a perceptive young man, left him alone until he pulled himself out of the cockpit. Only then did Ripley give him a smile. "Any joy, sir?"

He shook his head this time, adding that Bowles had got a 109.

Ripley said "good show" and then climbed up the wing to start his checks and open the petrol tanks.

Kiwi came around the tail with an arm over Sergeant Bowles' shoulder, grinning. "That's 95, sir."

Ever since he'd posted the squadron score, they actually seemed to care about it. Which had been the point of it, of course, but at some level it surprised him. He held out his hand to Sergeant Bowles. "Congratulations, Ginger. That's two in one day, then."

"What do you mean, sir?" Ginger asked, genuinely bewildered.

"Well, at the first pass the Messerschmitt you were firing at started smoking and dived. That's certainly a damaged in my book."

"Yes, sir, but that was the same one I got later." Ginger swallowed and looked guilty. "I turned after it and got bounced by his wingman. Only

I didn't, well, notice, sir. Not until Kiwi started shouting at me. But by then Kiwi had scared him off, so I kept after the first one."

Not exactly recommended behaviour, and Ginger knew it. He couldn't even explain it exactly – except that he was so sick and tired of them always being out-numbered. He was tired of being sick at the sight of them all. When he'd surprised himself by hitting one of the bastards, he'd suddenly felt like he'd rather die than let it get away. That was a bloody awful thing to feel, and he was ashamed of himself – but it *was* the way he'd felt. He gave the skipper a sidelong glance, wondering what he'd get by way of a bollocking.

He knew Jones would have given him an indifferent bollocking for following the snapper down. Kiwi, on the other hand, wanted to make a fuss because he'd made a kill. But as the silence lengthened, Ginger realised that the CO understood. The Skipper smiled faintly and said only, "Well done, Ginger, but try to keep a better look out behind you next time. You can't rely on Kiwi to be free to chase off the next wingman."

"I know, sir," Ginger admitted with a faint smile, registering that the CO was calling him by his nickname – not his rank or surname. That felt good – like he really belonged to the squadron at last. Then he added, "That's why I thought I owed him a beer."

"I couldn't agree more, mate." Kiwi was quick to accept.

Robin noticing Tolkien swas tanding at the wing-tip, listening but hesitant to join the veterans. He signalled him closer. "All right?"

"Yes, sir. I'm sorry I lost the formation again. I – I greyed out in the turn."

Robin said nothing. They both knew that if he didn't improve his flying, he wasn't going to survive. No amount of shouting or bullying was going to frighten him more than that simple truth, so Robin saved his breath, suggesting instead, "Let'sgo and get some tea?" It had just gone four.

Together they crossed to the dispersal. The others were sprawled in front, their tea in their hands or already set aside empty. They glanced up, mildly interested, as the four pilots joined them. "Get anything, Skipper?" Ringwood asked for them collectively.

"No, but Ginger did."

"Well done!"

"Congratulations!"

"I say, good show!" They all seemed genuinely pleased, and Ginger was momentarily embarrassed. Green thumped him happily on the back, and he glanced at Banks. Their eyes met; Banks only nodded once, but Ginger felt warm all over with real pride. Meanwhile, Eton enthusiastically declared, "That's 95, then! Only five more to go!"

"What do you mean?" Robin countered. (Eton always managed to rub him up the wrong way.) "We don't stop at 100, you know?"

"No, but we can give ourselves a jolly big bash after the 100th, I should think," Needham drawled.

"True," Robin agreed, reminding himself that he must learn not to let Eton get on his nerves. Then, as things settled down again and the four returned pilots clustered around the table with the tea urn, Donohue called out from his deck chair, "So what's a hobbit, Tolkien?"

The sprog spun about as if he'd been shot, knocking over his mug in the process. "What did you say?"

"Hobbit. What the hell is a—"

"How dare you!" Tolkien flung himself at Donohue, ripping the loose pages he was holding out of his hand – or trying to. He only succeeded in tearing some while Donohue, in an effort to escape the violent assault, let the rest drop. The wind instantly caught these and started blowing them across the field. "You bastard! You bastard!" Tolkien screamed, and chased after the blowing pages.

Stunned, the others stared after him. Then Banks, Reynolds, and Kiwi sprang to help him, while Priestman turned on Donohue and demanded, "What the hell was that all about?"

"Sir?! He attacked *me,* not the other way around!" Donohue declared in a tone of outraged innocence.

"I don't know what the hell a hobbit is, but I gather you and Tolkien do."

"Honest, sir, I *don't*. I just found this manuscript lying about when we got back—"

"Since when does an Officer of the Crown read another officer's mail, Flying Officer Donohue?"

"But, sir! It was lying around—"

Priestman exploded, "And you bloody well know why! There's no time to pack up personal belongings when we're scrambled – which is all the more reason to *respect* other people's privacy. Am I commanding an active squadron of the RAF or running a kindergarten?"

Then, taking a deep breath, he said in a calmer tone to Donohue, "You'll apologise to Tolkien the minute he gets back here, and don't let me ever hear of anything like this again." He then glanced at the field, where most of the scattered pages appeared to have been retrieved, but Tolkien was still chasing a last sheet. Reynolds, Goldman and Kiwi were sorting the pages they had captured and stacking them into a single pile. At last Tolkien caught the last run-away sheet and joined the others.

When Priestman came up, Tolkien's face was a rigid mask, his jaw clamped. He took the sheets from the others with a choked "Thanks" that expressed no genuine gratitude. Kiwi raised his eyebrows, but Robin jerked his head in the direction of dispersal, and the others, with an exchanged glance, followed his hint. "Right, then," Priestman addressed the sullen pilot glaring at the ground. "What was that all about?"

"He was reading my stuff!"

"I've ticked him off for it, and he will apologise to you immediately. But, frankly, there are more mature ways of dealing with the situation."

"You don't understand, sir."

"You're damned right, I don't understand! I've got enough trouble on my hands fighting the bloody Hun, dealing with AWOL fitters, and priggish WAAF Officers, without my pilots attacking one another!"

"It's a manuscript my father sent me. Something he's writing for me – just for me! Its personal, sir. Completely personal."

"I understand, but you would have been far more effective if you had coldly pointed out to Donohue that by reading someone else's personal mail he had put himself on the level of spying chamber-maids."

"Yes, sir," Tolkien agreed, but his face was as rigid as ever and his tone resentful. Robin sighed; just when he thought the Auxiliary pilots were coming around, his sprogs started making trouble. Was he never going to get this squadron in shape?

Allars limped into the adjutant's office and let himself down into a chair. "What is it?" Mickey asked him, at once alarmed; he had never seen the one-legged veteran look so stunned before.

"Biggin Hill. They just hit it a second time today. That's the *sixth* time in three days! And this time it was a low-level raid – took it completely by surprise. Telephones, gas, water, electricity – everything's out. At least 30 dead and they haven't dug everyone out yet."

"What about the squadrons?"

"Airborne, but there's nothing to come home to by the sound of it. First all the Kent RDF stations, and now this." Fighter Command had been flying blind all afternoon – or rather, dependent entirely upon the Observer Corps, which could only report enemy formations as they passed overhead rather than seeing them coming in. For 11 Group, it was like fighting with one hand tied; many sorties had failed to find their targets at all, and the bulk of the bombers got in and out unmolested.

It had only been a matter of time before the Luftwaffe got an important target, but still the significance stunned Allars. When Jerry had taken Manston out last week, it had been bad enough, but Manston was a satellite field; Biggin Hill was a Sector Airfield. Without Biggin Hill Control, a huge gap was torn in Fighter Command defences.

Mickey's thoughts were rushing on. "Isn't MacLeod's funeral due to be held for this evening? Who'going, do you think? – after a day like this. Besides Priestman, I mean. He'll be there."

Allars grunted acknowledgement and dragged himself to his feet. "I'll remind them. Need to go and harass them about their reports anyway."

"But they didn't intercept this last time, did they?" 606 had been scrambled twice more since tea-time.

"All the more reason to harass them," Allars retorted. Pilots had to log their flying time whether there was combat or not, but the pilots were becoming increasingly negligent.

Allars went out into the late afternoon sun and limped towards the distant dispersal. The shadows were long and slanted. The air smelled of petrol as the last of the bowsers finished refuelling and pulled away from a Hurricane being backed into a blast-pen by two airmen. One of the erks nipped under the nose to put chocks around the wheels.

With this last bowser silenced, there was a curious stillness in the air. The wind had died away and you could clearly hear birds calling. The air was still warmed from the heat at noon to a balmy, summer temperature without the oppression of mid-day heat.

Funny that the pilots were all inside the dispersal hut in this pleasant weather, Allars thought vaguely; but nothing stirred outside the dispersal. He glanced at his watch: 7.20 pm. The squadron was due to stand down at 8.00 pm because MacLeod's funeral had been set for 8.30. The Station Commander would attend, of course, and there was a military trumpeter and a detail of airmen to fire a salute, and Mickey and he would go – but it would look bad if none of the pilots showed up. Still, it wasn't as if you could order them to a funeral.

He was close enough now to see the blackboard with the squadron score on it. They had 95 kills chalked up on the board with a large exclamation point behind it.

Allars almost tripped over the first body. Tolkien was lying flat on his stomach, his head pillowed on a tattered manila envelope – sound asleep. Startled, Allars drew up and looked around. Kiwi lay on his back, snoring softly through his open mouth. Green was curled up like a child with his head on his parachute. Even Priestman had drifted off, his hair falling in his face. They were *all* here, sprawled about on the ground around the dispersal, and all of them were out cold. That said more about their state of exhaustion than words could have done. Allars hesitated, but he didn't have the heart to wake them after all. He turned and limped back to the Mess.

Chapter 34

Boulogne
2 September 1940

"Do not believe everything you hear," the letter started. *"Wild rumours have been circulating that I am blind in one eye. This is a gross exaggeration. The only thing wrong with my right eye is that it cannot focus properly. I'm perfectly capable of seeing light and dark. Besides, the doctors are not certain that the condition is permanent, and even if it were, I would still be in an enviable position, since in the realm of the blind, the one-eyed man is king."*

Ernst sat bolt upright in bed in agitation. How could he write something like that?! Was he out of his mind? Ernst grabbed the envelope again to try to see if it had been tampered with. After all, the Gestapo might assume that the recipient, not just the sender, of such a statement was disloyal. Turning the envelope over, however, he noticed the stamp. It had been posted direct from OKH – the *Oberkommando des Heeres* – or the very highest Army command. Christian's elder brother was a General Staff officer currently serving at OKH, Ernst remembered. The Army was different from the Luftwaffe. They didn't allow any Gestapo interference with their officers – or their mail. But still, Christian was taking such a terrible chance. What if it had been opened at this end?

"Herr Meyer is very popular here at the moment – despite what happened the other night." Ernst frowned. Meyer? Who the hell was Herr Meyer? *"You see his picture everywhere, usually against a backdrop panorama of our bomber streams leaving the coast at Calais. That, or him with a shotgun over his arm in the company of Galland, Mölders and Wick."*

Now Ernst got the joke; Goering had reputedly said that if the RAF ever bombed Berlin "his name was Meyer." The RAF had hit Berlin on the night of Aug. 28/29. Fortunately, they had done very little damage – nothing compared to what the Luftwaffe was doing to English cities.

"They keep playing 'Bomben auf Engeland' on the radio, too," Christian's letter continued. *"It really gets on your nerves after a while. Especially when trying to have a relaxing evening on the Kurfuerstendamm with an attractive young lady.*

"No, I am not confined to hospital, and even if I <u>were</u>, I would still find a way to have dinner on the Ku'damm with an attractive young lady.

(*Gabrielle is, according to Dieter, dating three – please count: one, two, three – other men, so no lectures, if you please.*)

"The Ku'damm, for your information, looks better than ever. The shops are filled to the gills with products from Norway, Holland, the Netherlands, France, and Italy. Speaking of Italy, there's a new Italian restaurant, Don Giovanni, that is all the rage, with Italian waiters who make love to the women while taking their orders – well, verbally – and then serve such marvellous food that you actually <u>forgive</u> them their impudence.

"With the weather so fair, the Kneipe have put their tables outside on the pavements, and Berlin never seems to sleep. Blackout? Never heard of it. Are we at war? Not really. Apparently the Air Force is tossing bombs at England (please sing: Bom-ben auf Eng-eland!) and teaching the pig-headed English to show more respect for the Master Race, but this is considerably less important than the latest film released by UFA and starring our heroic national floating corpse, Christina Sönderbaum. (Same song, second verse, doesn't get better, it just gets worse.) This time she was seduced by a Czech rather than raped by a Jew, but it all ends the same way – with her (admittedly lovely) corpse floating on some body of water.

"If it weren't for the hope they'd show her naked somewhere in the prelude to the suicide (at least in the reflection of a glass or water or some such thing like they did that once), I wouldn't bother going to her films at all – especially not since now-a-days they have to start off with a Wochenschau full of steely-eyed Stuka crews and laughing fighter pilots. (We have been reduced to the role of Jesters!)

"At least our beloved leader has been defending our virility. The Army High Command (prudes that they are) wanted to ban a film because it depicts a Luftwaffe officer accepting the invitation of a famous and stunningly beautiful singer to share her bed before going off to throw bombs (presumably at En-ge-land), but Fatty went on record saying: 'The man would not be an officer if he did not take advantage of such an opportunity.' I hope he'll remember that line when I come up for court-martial because of Gabrielle – or her successor.

"Speaking of successors, there are really some very attractive young ladies here in Berlin. I was at the Esplanade the other night and ran into a friend who was escorting a couple of BDM leaders. Classic beauties, both of them. I'm sure you would have liked them. Just a reminder: there are other fish in the sea." Ernst frowned at that. What did Christian have against Klaudia? Why did he dislike her so much? Besides, Ernst didn't like ambitious women. He knew all about BDM leaders! They were more masculine than many men, disciplined as drill sergeants and fanatical on top of that. Who wanted a girl friend like that? Certainly not Christian himself, and nor did Ernst.

Christian's letter continued, "*Dieter says the Staffel is full of eager young boys now. He says they all look the same and they're all very 'correct.' No fun at all. The Bomber Boys are accusing us of breaking off the minute we see Spitfires (weren't they all shot down long ago? Must be the Supermarine Phoenix we are encountering now). Dieter says that can't be true, since the new boys never see the Spitfires until they are already being shot at – and even then they react in bewilderment. 'Herr Oberleutnant, my wing has just fallen off. How did that happen?' I kid you not! That is exactly what Dieter reported in his last letter!*"

Now Ernst squirmed unhappily in his hospital bed with a sense of intense guilt. He ought to be out there with them. He wasn't really injured. What were a few holes in his flesh? A few smashed muscles? Everything was healing well. Just stiff and painful. It wasn't right to send kids out there while he lay around on his back. He had to convince the doctor to pass him fit for flying. He had to get back to the *Staffel*. Fischer had already sent word that he would be leading a *Rotte* when he returned – if not a *Schwarm*. Now he regretted not leading the *Rotte* earlier. He should have learned to do that before taking a *Schwarm*. But there could be no question of hanging back any longer. He had to do his part.

After all they'd done and all the pilots they'd lost, they couldn't give up now. They had to defeat the RAF, and they had to do it soon! Time was running out for the invasion. Hadn't they been told at one of the early briefings that the Navy wanted the invasion launched no later than the end of September? After that the days were too short, or the winter storms started, or temperatures at sea dropped, or was it something about the tides and the moon? He was sure he remembered something like that. They had to get air superiority within the next few days, so that the invasion could be launched in the next week or two.

Ernst threw the covers off and pushed himself to his feet. He had to regain his strength and go back to the *Staffel*. He started hobbling around the room. He had to get fit again fast!

RAF Tangmere

The shortening days meant that dawn readiness had been pushed back half an hour to 5.30, and as the campaign continued at an unsustainable intensity, Group had realised that squadrons simply couldn't be kept on readiness 15 hours a day without a break. A rotation had been established that put them on no more than twelve hours a day and stood them down every fourth day. But while that all helped, the Germans had now taken to bombing at night. While the damage they did was marginal at best, it disturbed everyone's sleep.

Priestman was having a hard time staying awake as he forced himself to face the squadron's paperwork in his stuffy cubicle in the dispersal hut. There was too much red tape, and he just couldn't seem to catch up. Every accident and every lost or broken piece of equipment required a report. Every requisition and every leave request required his signature. And now Mickey had gently pointed out that the Confidential Reports on four of his officers were "over-due." He took off his tunic and hung it over the back of the desk-chair.

The voices of his pilots in desultory conversation drifted in the open window. It was a lovely day, and they'd all taken shameless advantage of the Salvation Army mobile canteen rather than going all the way back to the Mess for lunch. The good meal added to the general drowsiness of the early afternoon.

The sound of someone coming into the dispersal snapped Priestman upright. He'd drifted off to sleep. He looked out of the open office door into the waiting room and saw Ainsworth in flying kit putting things into one of the empty lockers.

"Ainsworth?"

"Yes, sir!" The youth came eagerly to the doorway.

"What are you doing in flying kit?"

"I heard my Hurricane had been delivered, sir."

"*Your* Hurricne?"

Ainsworth had the grace to look embarrassed. "I mean a replacement Hurricane, sir. That brings us back up to strength.

"No. It means we now have 13 aircraft and 14 pilots including myself; that is three aircraft and six pilots *below* strength," Priestman corrected. "Besides, you still haven't got 20 hours on Hurricanes in your logbook. We can go up again this afternoon when the squadron gets stood down at 5 pm. We'll still have a couple hours of daylight."

Ainsworth looked back at him with a mixture of disappointment and defiance. "Pilot Officer Goldman said I did very well yesterday, sir."

"Fine. Send Pilot Officer Goldman in here, but you are not flying ops until you have at least 20 hours on Hurricanes, and that's final!"

"Can I take the replacement Hurricane up for trials then, sir?"

"No. An experienced pilot will take it up for trials."

Ainsworth looked crestfallen, and Robin was tempted to relent, but the young man had turned away already.

A few moments later, Banks knocked at the door and looked in hesitantly. "You sent for me, sir?"

"Yes, come in and sit down." Priestman indicated the wooden chair squeezed between the door and the window.

Banks sat down warily. After a lifetime of being the son who always managed to provoke his father's wrath and the student with the poor marks, he associated interviews of this kind with unpleasant lectures on his deficiencies.

"Ainsworth says you told him he did well yesterday. Is that true?"

Banks was surprised. "Didn't you think we did well yesterday, sir?"

"The exercise went well enough, but I certainly didn't say anything to Ainsworth personally. Did you?"

Banks tried to think back and decided he might have done after they landed. He couldn't remember exactly. In his defence he said, "I was trying to be encouraging, sir."

"Meaning he *wasn't* any good?" The Skipper pressed him.

"I wouldn't go that far, sir. He was fine, really – when you think how little experience he has."

Priestman rolled his eyes. "That's just the point!" Then he paused and considered the frail young man in front of him. The bruises from Banks' collision with a tree had faded, and his face was nearly restored to its fine-featured, fair good looks – except for the dark streaks under his eyes. But Robin wasn't blind to the fact that Banks dreaded the klaxon in a way the others didn't. Yes, there were times when they all *hated* it. *Certainly,* there were times when they wanted nothing more than to be left alone. Yet for most of them there was also a sense of determination, too – a dogged refusal to let the bastards get the best of them. Most felt secretly proud to possess skills that made it *possible* for them to stop the bombers. There was a certain sense of satisfaction to be given the chance to strikes blows against the invaders. There was even, for most of them, an undying delight in flying that even exhaustion could not entirely extinguish. Banks seemed to lack all of that. "How are you getting on?"

Banks started and tensed. "What do you mean, sir?"

"I mean, you look .... very tired," Priestman hedged.

"Oh." Banks didn't know what to make of that. "Don't we all?" he asked innocently, inwardly dreading what was coming. Clearly the CO learned about his inability to shoot.

Priestman sighed. He did not want to insult Banks. That was the last thing he wanted. He just wanted to keep him alive. "You know how highly I think of your flying skills, Banks, but frankly, it seems to me you aren't the born fighter pilot."

Banks' stomach tied itself in knots, but he tried to play dumb – as he had so often with his father and his teachers. "What do you mean?"

"I mean, I think you're better suited to training other pilots than flying fighters." They stared at each other. Now that it was out, Robin felt better about it. There really wasn't anything insulting about that. It was true. Banks might not have the killer instinct or the drive to succeed so vital to a good fighter pilot, but he was patient and softly spoken. He didn't get flustered by the mistakes of others. He could remain calm and encouraging regardless – as he'd proved yesterday. Those were all fine qualities in an instructor. "I'd like to recommend a transfer to Training Command," Robin clarified.

Banks' emotions were instantly in turmoil. A rush of relief at the thought of getting away from the daily agony was replaced by shame at his own failure. He could hear his father's cold, contemptuous voice stating that he was "not surprised" that David had "failed yet again." He'd say it in German, the language they always used at home amongst themselves. (*"Nun, das überrascht mich überhaupt nicht: Du hast wieder versagt."*) "May I have a day or two to think about it, sir?"

"Of course. I'm not going to do it against your wishes. I'm *not* posting you, Banks. I'm *not* trying to get rid of you. But please think about it. Not everyone is cut out to be a fighter pilot."

Robin would have said more, but Sutton stuck his head through the open window and declared, "There's something out here with two rings on it, Skipper."

Robin, completely flustered to have someone putting his head through the window in the middle of what should have been a completely confidential conversation, snapped in annoyance, "What the hell are you talking about? Something with two rings on it?"

"Two rings as in Flight Lieutenant," Sutton explained.

"What's so – Flight Lieutenant?!" Priestman nearly broke his neck getting out of his chair and around his desk to the door. There was, indeed, a man with two rings on his sleeves standing in the middle of the others. "Are we glad to see you!" Robin declared, jumping down onto the grass without using the two steps.

The other man turned and saluted, then took Priestman's outstretched hand, evidently abashed by the enthusiasm of the welcome. Before he could say anything, Robin added a caveat, "That is, we're glad to see you, *provided* you've been posted to 606."

"Well, yes, didn't you—"

A cheer went up from the others that left the newcomer looking about himself, even more baffled and confused.

"That makes 15 operational pilots – if I can still count that high," Woody noted.

"Let's see, 15 pilots means that three can be off every day, right? So everyone gets at least one day off every five, doesn't it?" Sutton wanted to know.

"Let's get it sorted before that bloody klaxon goes," Priestman intervened, grabbing the newcomer by the elbow and pulling him towards the blackboard on which the "Order of Battle" – i.e., the sections, pilots and aircraft – were chalked in daily. Robin erased everything and with the chalk poised asked, "What did you say your name was?"

"Reed, Sir. Thomas Reed."

"Right. You've got 'B' Flight." As he spoke, Robin wrote the names on the board in order. "That'll be Ware, Sutton, Goldman, Bowles and Tolkien. The rest are in 'A' flight with Woody. Any questions?"

"Who gets today off?"

"Ainsworth."

"But he had yesterday off and the day before!" Sutton protested.

"He doesn't have 20 hours on Hurricanes yet, but I'll see that he gets them today. I'll tell you tonight who is in reserve tomorrow. Any other questions?" There were none. "Right, then, the rest of you can relax again, while I explain our formation to F/Lt Reed."

Banks slipped around the side of the hut and sank down into the grass, staring across the field. Ginger settled himself beside him without a word. They didn't speak until Banks volunteered. "The skipper wants to post me to Training Command."

Ginger felt his heart skip a beat. He hated the thought of Banks leaving. Better posted than dead, he reminded himself, but the very thought of not having Banks here in the squadron made him feel frightened – just like he had felt when he first joined the squadron.

Loneliness seemed to surround him already. Out loud he managed to say, "That's splendid." He just didn't sound as though he meant it.

"You think so?" Banks stopped and looked at him. He had heard the pause and noted that Ginger's expression was completely at odds with his words. "Would you be happy about a similar posting?"

Ginger swallowed. The CO had offered it to him that day he confronted him about his "air sickness." He had called it a serious problem and said if Ginger wanted, he'd have him posted somewhere where he didn't have to fly Hurricanes. But Ginger didn't want that. It would have been an admission of failure. He shook his head.

"Then why is it good for me?" Banks wanted to know.

"You'd be a good instructor, but with me. Ginger paused, sorting out his thoughts before explaining earnestly, "It's more about my Dad." Ginger faltered, but then continued, "My Dad was always looked down on. When I got it in my head I wanted to learn to fly, everybody laughed at us. No one believed I'd ever succeed. But, now, since the PM's speech, people are treating my Dad with respect for the first time in his life. I've become a local hero of sorts, but only because I'm one of the PM's 'Few'. If I stopped being that it would just make everyone think I was worthless like they thought all along. I can't do that to my Dad. It would break his heart."

Banks thought: it will break his heart more, if you get killed. But he didn't dare say that. There were some taboos even for close friends. He said instead, "I think your father would always want you to do what you wanted – no matter what other people say."

"But it would hurt him just the same, to hear other people say anything bad about me. It used to drive him round the bend when other kids were nasty to me, and it would be worse now. Besides, I wouldn't be a good instructor, and you would." Ginger grinned at Banks disarmingly.

"But that isn't the point, is it? Even if I'm not shooting Germans down, I can still keep a look-out. I can still fly wingman. I'm more use than the sprogs at that. I don't like the idea of going somewhere safe while the rest of you are here. I feel like I'm part of something here – something I haven't felt since I left Germany. It doesn't seem right leaving now."

"This can't go on much longer. If the invasion doesn't come soon, they'll rotate us out anyway."

"All the more reason to stay at least that long," Banks countered.

Ginger nodded, but part of him felt guilty about it. Something could happen at any time. As if to underscore the point, the klaxon went off, and they had to scramble to their feet and run for the waiting aircraft.

Priestman crossed both arms over his head and called out: "One at a time!" They fell silent and waited. He looked up. "Ware?"

"He can't fly, sir."

"What do you mean, 'he can't fly'? I saw him get into a Hurricane and take off without any difficulty."

"Straight into a cloud where he got disoriented, and that's how we got separated, and then he took us below the cloud and wandered about listlessly until we were all but out of fuel, while you and 'A' flight got clobbered by God-knows-what."

"We were not 'clobbered.' We were engaged by a somewhat larger force of enemy aircraft."

"Well, you were screaming into the R/T like the whole bloody Luftwaffe had jumped you."

"I was?"

"Not you *personally*, sir, but Kiwi was bellowing warnings to everyone under the sun, and Woody and Donny kept up a stream of rude remarks indicative of extreme discomfort."

The latter made a rude gesture in the direction of the speaker.

"By the look of your kites, it was a miracle you all survived.

"Miracles do happen. So where is our new Flight Lieutenant?"

"He said he had a tummy-ache and went straight to the MO!" Donohue provided this information with indignation bordering on outrage.

"Come on, chaps. Give him the benefit of the doubt. Maybe he does have a stomachache." Robin didn't want to face the possibility that his desperately needed Flight Lieutenant wasn't any good.

"Which one of us hasn't got a sodding stomachache?" Sutton snapped back, flushed with anger. Robin stared at him. He swallowed. "Sorry, sir."

"I'll go and check up on Reed," Robin said. "Woody, you're OC, if we get scrambled before I'm back."

Priestman was intercepted before he reached the sick bay. Flight Sergeant Rowe waylaid him to say that Donohue's kite was beyond repair here at the station. "Tell Pilot Officer Ainsworth to take up the reserve aircraft that arrived yesterday, would you? Better go over exactly what he needs to test."

Rowe looked indignant. "That's really not my job, sir. I—"

"Understood. Forget it." Priestman cut him off, and without another word changed course and went back to dispersal. "Ainsworth!"

The young man jumped eagerly to his feet. "Sir?"

"Get your kit! I need you to test-fly the reserve Hurricane immediately."

"Yes, sir!" Ainsworth was so eager he tripped going up the stairs into the dispersal hut to collect his jacket and helmet. The waiting around was killing him, making him feel useless while the Battle raged all around him. He was so ashamed of not really being on ops that he'd lied to Mona and his Mum about it, pretending he'd been on several sorties. In fact, he'd laid it on a bit thick, in retrospect, telling them everything was fine. No sweat. But he was sweating now.

The CO started for the hangar as soon as Ainsworth dropped onto the grass, and he had to run to catch up with him. As they walked towards the hangar, the CO ran through the drill with him, telling him exactly what he was to check and what to watch for. "The factories are under tremendous pressure to deliver, and sometimes they cut corners when doing the checks. The ATA has very strict orders to fly as carefully as possible, so they never put an aircraft through its paces. We need to be sure every kite is up to the mark before we trust it in combat." They reached the hangar and Robin called to his own fitter, who was sitting at a bench with a cup of tea in front of him. "Ripley?"

The young man clambered over the bench and came quickly enough, but he looked very tired. God, they were all knackered, and now they couldn't even get a good night's sleep on account of night raids!

"I want you to go over the drill for flight-testing a new Hurricane with P/O Ainsworth, please. He'll be testing 'U'."

Ripley nodded, and Priestman started again for the infirmary. This time Mickey intercepted him. "Robin, I've just been informed that there are two more Hurricanes on their way—"

"Good show! How did you manage that?"

"Oh, I'm sure it wasn't me," Mickey replied modestly, waving the compliment aside almost nervously; but Robin knew that Mickey had been nagging No. 41 Group. "And, ah, the other thing is that there are a couple of reporters here to talk to you. An American and—"

"Why?"

"Well, I gather it is about your DFC—"

"Couldn't they pick on someone else?"

"Well, I suppose they *could*, but the Station Commander has agreed to the interview, and they are waiting in your office."

"First I have to find out what happened to my new Flight Lieutenant."

"What happened to him?" Mickey gasped in alarm.

"I don't know. He reported sick – less than six hours after he arrived."

"Oh. Bad luck!" Mickey was devastated. He'd called in every chit he had, pulled every string, and harassed Personnel shamelessly to get a Flight Lieutenant posted here.

Robin gazed at Mickey exasperated, but the adjutant was so obviously doing his best that there was nothing more to say. Robin just sighed, and repeated, "I'm going to see what happened to him, and then

I'll come over to my office – and hope the gentlemen from the press have lost patience by then and moved on."

Mickey started to say something but thought better of it and let Robin go.

The MO pounced on him as soon as he entered the sick quarters. "Oh, there you are, Priestman. I was just about to send someone over with a message for you. I'm afraid I've got some bad news."

"What?"

"Well, your new Flight Commander appears to have hepatitis."

"What?!"

"Yes, he only just arrived from India last week, and, well, I'm afraid he has all the symptoms – yellow eye-whites, yellow skin, stomach cramps. I won't have the results of the blood-tests until tomorrow, but I don't think he'll be fit to fly for some time."

Robin nodded with resignation and turned to leave, but the doctor stopped him. "Squadron Leader?" Robin looked back. "I hate to mention this, but Flying Officer Sutton isn't well either. He's been pleading with me for medicine, but what he needs most is a long rest. I think he is getting a stomach ulcer."

Robin just stared at the doctor.

"And Donohue has developed a twitch," the doctor added, "just in case you hadn't noticed...."

Of course, he'd noticed, but this was just one remark too many. Robin snapped back, "Well, what do you recommend? Surrender?"

"No, of course not, but it is my job to keep an eye on the medical condition of all personnel at this Station—"

"And it's my job to stop the German Luftwaffe from gaining air superiority over the United Kingdom. How do you expect me to do that with a squadron that is *never* up to strength!"

The doctor seemed to consider that for a moment, letting the angry words hang in the air, so that Robin felt increasingly embarrassed about his outburst. Then he said gently, "You need a rest yourself, you know. You've flown every single sortie since you've taken command of 606, and I hear you're trying to train new pilots whenever you're stood down. You can't keep it up. If you don't let up, you're going to start making mistakes – fatal mistakes."

"I don't have a choice," Robin shot back, still furious. "I'm not going to let some sprog with less than 20 hours on Hurris fly combat!" Why didn't anyone understand this?

Still steaming, he walked into his office. A flash blinded him. Something smelling of perfume and dressed in velveteen and satin embraced him. The flash went off again twice in quick succession while

Virginia Cox-Gordon gushed, "Robin, Darling, I was so *thrilled*! Why didn't you ring? We simply have to celebrate. I've brought along some bubbly for you." She gestured towards his functional desk, on which no less than two sweating buckets of ice were cooling two bottles of champagne.

"I can't drink. I'm on duty," Robin told her, and tried to walk back out of the office.

She had him by the arm. "But, Robin, Darling! One glass never hurt. Don't you remember? I'm with the *Times* now. This is all *completely* official! When the DFCs were announced, I couldn't *help* telling how we'd dated all through 1939" (not the way Robin remembered it) "and then the Editor said I *had* to ring you and get an exclusive. He's promised to do a feature on you."

"I don't want a damned feature. I don't want any bloody article at all! I don't know why the hell the Station Commander approved an interview, but I don't intend to give one!"

"Robin, Darling, what *is* the matter with you?" Virginia sounded disoriented.

Robin supposed no one had ever talked to her like this before. He didn't regret being the first one to tell her off, but it was bad manners to use rude language to a lady. Besides, it demeaned him to lose his temper – especially in front of the Americans. The reporter and the photographer were watching avidly, soaking up every bad word he uttered with the eagerness of vultures. He really was getting ropey.

He gulped air to swallow his emotions and tried to regain a cool, calm exterior. He caught a glimpse of Mickey standing in the door between their offices with a horrified expression on his round, sweating face. Robin nodded to him to reassure him. Then he extricated himself from Virginia's grasp gently but firmly and went around behind his desk, putting it – and the champagne – between the intruders and himself.

"Bad start. You took me by surprise with your camera," he nodded towards the photographer and the American, who was grinning crookedly at him – apparently enjoying the whole scene, damn him! "Let's have another go. What can I do for you, sirs?"

"Briggs, Howard Briggs of the *Detroit Times*. Remember? We met once before, over near Liverpool, after you shot down a Dornier at night. That was what made me want to come along. I recognised your name, and Miss Cox-Gordon said she knew you and could arrange an interview. I must say, you looked a bit more relaxed back in Wales." He was smirking.

You and your whole damned nation of spoilt brats! Robin thought, glaring at him. Wasn't it bad enough that they weren't willing to help out despite all their riches? Did they have to come here and gloat, too?

Virginia glided forward and reached out a bejewelled hand to Robin's elbow. "Robin, Darling, I really did come by to celebrate your DFC and give you the attention you deserve. Howard told me about that bomber you got while in *Training* Command, and I told him about you getting out at Dunkirk on a broken ankle—"

"I know what happened to me, and I don't want it in the papers. Period."

"Fine!" the American agreed at once, raising both hands as if in surrender. "Then let's talk about the Battle of Britain. That's what my editor wants to hear about."

Once more Robin was tempted to refuse, but the Station Commander had approved the interview. "I'll try to answer your questions, but I trust you will respect my need to protect official secrets and understand that I may not be able to respond to all questions." Robin indicated the chairs before his desk and sat down himself, perching tensely on the edge of his chair.

"What about a little bubbly to loosen up with?" Virginia smiled at him, reaching for one of the bottles, but Robin shook his head.

"No. I don't drink while on duty, and I will not be stood down for another four hours. You, of course, are welcome to carry on without me."

Pouting slightly, Virginia settled herself into one of the leather visitors' chairs. She fussed to be sure her skirts were straight under her, and then crossed her legs. The men watched her automatically; she had great legs.

Briggs cleared his throat and asked eagerly, "Ah, Squadron Leader Priestman, could you tell us more about why you were awarded the Distinguished Flying Cross?"

The telephone on his desk rang, and Robin started so violently that he knocked over one of the buckets with champagne as he grabbed for the phone. Virginia screeched and jumped up to avoid the cascading ice and melted water, and the photographer dived to catch the bottle before it hit the floor. "Priestman!" Robin barked into the phone.

At the other end of the line, the Station Commander asked if he was aware that a *Times* reporter and an American newspaperman wanted to talk to him. Exasperated, Robin told the senior officer that he would otherwise be at dispersal, and, yes, he was giving a damned interview. "Calm down, old chap. Don't want to give the public the impression we're anything but confident and top-of-the-line, you know."

"Yes, I know."

"Do you want me to join you?"

"You're welcome to, sir."

There was a pause. "Yes, I think I'll drop by."

Robin hung up the receiver and looked expectantly at Briggs as if nothing had happened.

"You were about to explain why you were awarded the Distinguished Flying Cross.

"I haven't the foggiest. Ask the Air Ministry. They issued it."

Briggs laughed, but Virginia frowned and kicked her leg. "Oh, don't be difficult, Robin. Tell us about it." She was used to getting her way. She'd expected Robin to be flattered and delighted by her attentions. He ought to be eating out of her hand as he had in the past.

"It?" Robin asked coldly. "What, Miss Cox-Gordon, do you mean by 'it'?"

"Well, the Air War. Dogfighting. The Battle of Britain. After all, you're an 'ace' now, Darling, with six kills—"

"Ten," Robin corrected. Part of him hated boasting about it. Part of him knew that killing remained killing, no matter what the circumstances or the justification. He was not without conscience, but he knew, too, that Virginia loved his fame and success only. It gave him power over her that he had never had before – and he had just discovered he enjoyed that.

"Ten? But the official notification—"

"Was out of date at the time of issue, and in any case, a week old. The war hasn't stopped in the meantime."

The Station Commander emerged in the doorway, and Robin got to his feet. The civilians, surprised, followed his example, turning to look over their shoulders. As they had already met the Station Commander, introductions were unnecessary. The Station Commander, smiling graciously, remarked that he'd just dropped by to see if everything was "going smoothly," and looked about for a vacant chair. There wasn't one, but an attentive Mickey jumped up to get a chair from his own office. The Station Commander seated himself and Robin sat down again. "Do carry on," the Station Commander urged.

Briggs cleared his throat and gave Virginia a look to stop her interfering. "Squadron Leader, these claims for enemy aircraft shot down. Just how credible are they? The Germans are reporting very different numbers, you know. A lot of people in the U.S. think the RAF is fabricating the numbers just to try to keep up civilian morale – or to lure us into a lost war. It just doesn't seem possilbe that you could be shooting down so many Krauts with such minimal losses to yourselves – and still be losing the war."

"I hadn't noticed we were losing. As for minimal losses, I think Air Chief Marshal Dowding would disagree with you sharply. I certainly don't consider our losses 'minimal.' As for the claims," Robin shrugged, "they are made on the basis of combat reports recorded immediately following a sortie. The guidelines are very explicit, and no claim can be made for a destroyed aircraft unless the crew is seen to abandon it or it is seen to crash. Many pilots feel this is an unfair requirement, as we are usually fighting against superior numbers and generally have to take evasive action repeatedly – making it almost impossible to watch the results of our attacks. Furthermore, combat takes place at speeds exceeding 300 mph – in head-on attacks the closing speed exceeds 500 mph. Under such conditions, we must take aim and fire very rapidly, rarely getting in more than a 2-3 second burst before we have to take evasive action to avoid becoming a target or colliding with the enemy. I have personally returned from many sorties with the feeling of having achieved absolutely nothing – despite using all my ammunition. Sometimes it is completely impossible to get in any kind of shot at all – which is even more frustrating. I have never personally made a claim that I did not feel certain about."

"Could you tell us about your own claims, then?"

"I believe you saw with your own eyes the Dornier I shot down over Liverpool."

"But under normal circumstances, it must be more difficult to know just who got what?" Briggs persisted.

"Very, so it is all a matter of a good intelligence officer sorting through the reports and trying to make sense of them. Some intelligence officers are naturally better than others, and we can't exclude the possibility that some pilots exaggerate, whether intentionally or out of sheer excitement. Furthermore, in the course of any one combat, several pilots may shoot at the same target and each claim it. Last but not least, we have all returned to station with aircraft so badly shot up and spewing smoke or coolant that it seems a miracle. Doubtless the same thing happens to our enemy – albeit given the fact that they have the entire Channel to cross, they are far less likely to nurse a damaged kite home than we are. I would argue that many claims we *don't* make later ditch in the channel or crash on the French coast. That probably balances out the doubles and exaggerations we do make. Does that answer your question?"

"Yes, thanks, but," Briggs continued eagerly, "Churchill assured the nation recently that the RAF was turning the tide of war. It doesn't look that way to me. How do you feel about it?"

"I haven't the foggiest."

"But you're at the forefront of the fight here. Do you *feel* you are winning?"

The answer to this was "no" – but Robin knew he couldn't say that. He glanced at the Station Commander before insisting, "The Prime Minister is in a far better position to judge that than I am. I can only see one tiny piece of the picture. The squadron has good days – and it has bad days. We feel exultant now and depressed later. What we feel is quite irrelevant to the military situation."

"Would you say that your pilots are better than the Luftwaffe's?"

"Absolutely not. The Luftwaffe has excellent pilots."

"And your aircraft? Last time I talked to you, you seemed to think the German planes were pretty hot stuff."

"Our fighters are superior to both German fighters – particularly the 110." Robin insisted firmly.

"Even the Hurricane?" Briggs pressed him, obviously sceptical.

"The Hurricane is a first-class aircraft, and it is superior to the Me109 in a number of ways – particularly dogfighting. The 109 was designed to bounce an unsuspecting aircraft from behind using its superb diving capabilities, but if you can confront them, they can be out-fought by either British fighter," Robin insisted, earning a silent but definitive nod from the Wing Commander.

"But you used to fly Spitfires. Isn't the Spitfire better?"

"No. The Spitfire is a pleasure to fly – particularly for an experienced pilot. It is even more superior to the Me109 than the Hurricane – if handled correctly. But I prefer commanding a Hurricane squadron, because they are more forgiving of mistakes and so more likely to get a wounded pilot home."

Briggs took a minute to scribble this down, and then asked, "What are the decisive factors which will determine whether you win the Battle of Britain or not?"

"That is far beyond my competence. If the invasion is launched, it will be up to the Royal Navy, more than the RAF, to sink as many of the troop transports as possible and prevent or disrupt—"

"Sorry, I meant the air war. What is decisive in maintaining air superiority over the United Kingdom?"

"Every link in the chain – from our early warning system to our long-suffering and first-rate ground crews – is vital."

"What do *you* – as a fighter pilot – wish for most? What do you need to ensure you don't lose this struggle against the so-far invincible Luftwaffe?"

"Sleep."

"What?"

"More sleep."

The klaxon went off. Robin ran out of the office, ignoring the Station

Commander's gesture to relax and stay where he was.

By the time he was half-way to the 606 dispersal hut, it was clear that 607 had been scrambled, not 606, but he had no intention of returning to his stuffy office. He just slowed to a stroll and made his way to dispersal at a leisurely pace.

Sutton lifted his head. "Well? Does he have worse stomach cramps than I have?"

"As a matter of fact, he does. He has jaundice." Robin stretched himself down on the grass and put his arm over his eyes.

"Jaundice?!?" came from all sides.

"Well, I suppose it explains why he got a bit disoriented in the cloud," Ware conceded.

Robin had already dropped off to sleep.

Chapter 35

Eastney
3 September 1940

The phone was ringing incessantly, and Emily groggily looked at her clock. Good heavens! It was already 8 am. She threw back the covers, grabbed her dressing gown and ran down the stairs to the phone, wondering where Aunt Hattie was. Had she already left for the Mission? She normally didn't leave for another half hour.

"Fitzsimmons residence," she said into the receiver, but only the buzzing of the lines answered. Too late.

Who could it have been at this time? A chill went through her. Tangmere. Eight am. He would have been on readiness since 5.30. He could have flown at least one sortie by now. He could be dead by now.

With relief she heard Hattie's voice from the kitchen garden, apparently talking to a neighbour outside. Emily went into the kitchen but then the phone started ringing agian. She rushed back to the dining room to answer it. "Hello!"

"Well, Emily, have you seen the papers yet?" It was her mother's bitter, gloating voice.

"What papers? Why?"

"Your young man is making love to another woman all over them!"

"What?"

The kitchen door slammed shut and Hattie called, "Emily? Emily? Oh, there – sorry!" She stopped just inside the door to the dining room as she realised Emily was on the phone.

"What are you talking about, Mum?" Emily snapped, her back up already. She was convinced that her mother was making something up.

"Just go and buy any local newspaper you like," her mother retorted, "and don't come crying to me. Your father and I tried to warn you. All I can say is, thank God this happened *before* the wedding. You will have to call it off now. I suggest you return home at once. It is quite ridiculous living with his aunt after the engagement is over."

"In case you've forgotten, you threw me out, and frankly it was for the best. I have no intention of returning no matter what Robin has done. Furthermore, I can't think of anything he might have done that would be reason to break off my engagement." She looked to Hattie for support, but all she saw was distress on the older woman's face.

"Read the papers!" her mother sneered and hung up

"My mother—" Emily started, but Hattie just spread the localnewpaper on the table – open at the page with the picture of Robin and Virginia.

"I think I'd better go to Tangmere with the mobile canteen today. I don't want you exposed to any commentary from the erks."

RAF Tangmere

"I say, Skipper, you might at least have introduced her to the rest of us, you know," Donohue complained.

"Indeed," Sutton agreed. "After all, most of us *aren't* engaged to be married – even if we aren't virgins, if you see what I mean."

"Very streamlined crumpet, I must say," Ware commented, studying the picture with appreciation. "Better than I remember her as a Deb."

"That was just the dresses they were wearing that year," Sutton reminded him. "Too much fluff and duff frills."

"Is it true she's worth close to a million quid?" Needham wanted to know.

"A night?" Kiwi gasped.

Donohue threw his paperback at the New Zealander. "Her inheritance, you dolt!"

"What *does* she cost a night?" Eton asked in Robin's direction.

"Leave him alone!" Ginger ordered angrily, scowling furiously.

They looked over at the Sergeant Pilot in astonishment, and then shrugged and resumed the conversation among themselves, Donohue answering the question with: "Her brother will get the million-or-so, but she's got a nice sum settled on her, I should think."

"Somewhere near a hundred grand," Sutton confirmed knowledgeably, glancing over towards his Commanding Officer with new respect.

The telephone rang in the dispersal, and everyone tensed. The orderly emerged. "Sir," he addressed Robin respectfully, "it's the AOC."

Robin dropped his head in his hands, then shoved them through his hair and dragged himself out of the deck chair onto his feet. As he disappeared into the dispersal, all the others watched him go.

"They wouldn't really cashier him for something like this, would they?"

"Rather depends on what they think of him generally, I suppose. Stuffy strikes me as the type to take a very dim view of scandal. I'd say he's going to get a packet."

"On the other hand, experienced Squadron Leaders don't grow on trees."

Robin swallowed before picking up the receiver, which had been laid beside the phone on the orderly's desk. In a tone of complete resignation, he reported, "Priestman."

"Park. Would you like to give me your version of what happened?"

"I was told there were some reporters in my office who wanted to interview me, and that the Station Commander had already approved the interview. As I came through the door, Virginia threw herself at me and the photographer started snapping shots. I disengaged as soon as I could and got behind the desk. I did not drink a drop of the champagne, and I pushed off rather abruptly when the klaxon went."

There was a moment of silence, and then Park remarked, "You called her Virginia just now. Do you know her well?"

"We went out a few times before the war, when I was flying in air shows, and once or twice this past winter."

"I see. And what does your fiancée have to say about the whole thing?"

"I – haven't – talked – to – her – yet." Robin admitted feeling ill.

"Well, I hope for your sake – and the sake of your squadron – that she's sensible and doesn't make too much of this. Boret reported that you were sitting behind your desk and very correct for the part of the interview he witnessed. He praised your answers, and I quite agree that the *Times* article – without photo – is really quite good. I particularly liked what you said about Hurricanes, and you fielded the question about claims deftly. Your Adjutant, incidentally, gave the same version of events as you, but I have to tell you that the C-in-C is not amused. He feels it lends credence to those who portray all fighter pilots as frivolous and irresponsible. He also remarked that it wasn't the first time you've been impulsive and undisciplined."

Robin ruffled his hair with his free hand, but there was nothing he could say to that. He sighed. Park continued. "I think it will all blow over very quickly. There are more important things on our plates at the moment, to say the least. Nevertheless, I would appreciate it, if you would try to keep a low profile for a bit; would you?"

"I didn't ask for the interview, sir."

"I understand. Boret said you were clearly annoyed by it all. He was afraid you might be too blunt about just how difficult things are at the moment." There was a pause, and then Park added in a notably more friendly tone, "The PM was rather pleased, actually."

"The *Prime Minister* saw it?!" Robin couldn't grasp his misfortune. It had only appeared in the local Portsmouth papers, after all.

"He has a large staff that sifts through the papers, looking for anything that might be of interest to him. He rang me up about 30 minutes ago and growled at me that things couldn't be as bad as I was making them out to be if my front-line squadron leaders had time for champagne and socialites." Park paused and then added with obvious amusement, "He was tickled pink."

Robin could hear Park's amusement, but it didn't make him feel much better. Churchill might be amused, but Dowding and Emily held his future in their hands – and he was afraid that Emily was going to react more like "Stuffy" Dowding than the amiable Churchill. He *had* to find time to see her tonight. In fact, he ought to get her some roses or some jewellery – at any rate, a peace offering.

He went to the door of the dispersal hut and stood looking out at them. Reed was still in the infirmary, and Robin had written him off. But after the MO's words, he also felt he had to give Sutton the day off. Which meant, of course, he would be flying with all three sprogs. He'd been forced to re-organise the sections again, too. If everyone was going to have a day off, other officers had to get in practice as Section Leaders.

Reynolds was shaping up quite well, actually – or maybe he was just such a good actor that he could maintain an appearance of calm? Tolkien was more worrying, but the real concern was Ainsworth. Robin just had a rotten feeling about him. He was keen enough, and you couldn't even say he was a bad pilot. They'd been out for another hour last evening without incident. But Robin couldn't shake off his first impression from the evening of his arrival, when the boy had interrupted the AVM's visit to ask permission to get married.

At the moment, Ainsworth was all kitted up in his Mae West and flipping through a magazine at a rate too fast for reading. Oddly, Donohue was now reading the manuscript sent by Tolkien's father – evidently with Tolkien's consent. In fact, they were passing it around among themselves. Whatever kept them happy.

The sound of aircraft approaching drew his attention. None of Tangmere's squadrons had scrambled yet this morning, but by the sound of the engines, these were clearly Hurricanes. At last, he located the two Hurricanes flying nicely in tandem and watched them set down decorously on the grass. Precise ATA flying, not fighter-pilot bunk. They might be his two new replacement Hurricanes, he decided, and went over to take a look at them.

As he arrived beside the nearest Hurri, the pilot was climbing stiffly out of the cockpit while the chocks were put in place. He was evidently a rather elderly gentleman and seemed to be a trifle unsteady as he climbed out onto the wing. What is the country coming to, Robin thought to himself, when we have to enlist tottering old veterans to ferry our front-line Service aircraft about? "Do you need a hand, sir?" he asked politely.

The man turned around and Robin caught his breath. The ATA pilot was wearing an eye-patch, and one sleeve of his tunic was empty and pinned beneath his DFC, DSO and AFC. He smiled, but backed down off the wing saying, "Thank you, young man, but I can manage."

Robin was still trying to work out how a man flew a Hurricane with one arm, but the old man was all but laughing at him. "And you thought you were the cat's pyjamas, didn't you? Now you must live with the knowledge that even an old wreck like me can dodder about in your precious kites. Fly Spitfires, too. No trouble at all – provided I don't get bounced by the Hun."

"I'm sorry, sir. I didn't mean to be patronising."

"Don't let it bother you, young man. They don't call us Aged and Tattered Airmen because we're spry young things. Although, 'Always Terrified Airmen' might describe us better. I tried to deliver to Hornchurch yesterday and nearly went for six. It seems Jerry had just scrammed off and there were these UXB all over the place. Which was bad enough, but before my feet even touched the turf, the Chiefy tore a strip off for parking in the wrong place. It seems I was in everyone's way. I *do* hope you *want* these aircraft?"

"Yes, I do. Very much." Their eyes met, and Robin knew he had been understood. The older man dropped his remaining hand on his shoulder. "Don't worry about the crates. We'll see that you get them."

"You commanded a squadron in the last war." It wasn't a question.

He smiled sadly. "I did."

"Then you know."

He nodded. "I know. I know it's not the kites, it's the boys."

"They just sent me a lad with less than 20 hours on Hurricanes!" Robin gave vent to his exasperation.

"There's nothing magic about 20 hours," the Squadron Leader from the last war remarked. "Sometimes they came with less than 10 hours. I know, our crates were simpler, no retractable undercarriage and whatnot, but the air still froze our blood when it spilled out and the charred lumps of former aviators litter the Ardennes." He paused, looking hard at Robin. "You can't stop it. No matter how hard you try, you can't protect them. They are in God's hands. He will take to Him those He loves most. The rest of us are left to get old and stiff and useless."

"*You* certainly aren't useless," Robin hastened to assure the veteran."

He only sighed and shook his head again. "Not quite yet, perhaps, but soon."

The erks were waiting, reluctant to intrude. Robin caught sight of Fowley and Tufnel. He signalled them over. "You looking after this kite?"

"For the moment, sir."

"Good. I'll send someone over to do the test flights as soon as we're stood down."

He turned back to the ATA pilot. "Care to join us for lunch in the Mess?"

The older man shook his head. "Too early for that. Need to deliver some Tiger Moths up to Upavon for the fledglings there." Upavon was the RAF Central Flying School, where pilots got Basic Training.

"Be nice to them. They'll probably be reporting in here the day after tomorrow."

The ATA pilot laughed and laid his hand on Robin's shoulder one last time. "Keep up the good work. We're all depending on you, you know."

ACW Roberts set a tea beside him. "Here you are, sir."

Bridges glanced at it and thanked her, but his attention was riveted on the boards below. Yesterday they had plastered no less than five airfields, including Eastchurch twice, but it appeared to have taken a little out of them, because today had got off to a late start. Bridges glanced at the clock; it was almost noon now, and only two raids on the boards, both still in the assembly stage. Disturbingly, there was definitely something building up on the Cherbourg peninsula, and that would be for Tangmere.

As he watched, ACW Ross changed the disk on the raid, making it 200+. Another raid farther east was just crossing Dover. Could be heading for any of the London airfields – Hornchurch again, perhaps? Or poor old Biggin Hill.

Biggin had taken a terrible pasting this past week – hit altogether seven times in the last four days. The Operations Room had been knocked out for hours yesterday, and control of the squadrons had been turned over to the neighbouring sectors, while the Operations Room Staff moved into a preprepared "Emergency Ops Room."

At Kenley, the Station Commander had made the even more radical decision to move the Operations Room right off the Station into a disused butcher's shop. Bridges' counterpart, with whom he had trained, complained that it stank abominably, but admitted "It would take some wizard German intelligence to identify 'Spice and Wallis, Family Butchers since 1857' as a strategically significant target." The western raid was moving out into the Channel. "What do you think it will be, sir?" his assistant, Warrant Officer Robinson, asked, speculating:

"Portsmouth? I hear HMS *King George V* is at Spithead."

Bridges nodded, unconsciously wiping under his eye-patch with a handkerchief. "That could be it – or the Supermarine factory at Woolston."

Across the road from the Main Gate in the ivy-covered, red-brick cottage used as the "Waafery" since the raid of August 15, Lettice Fields was trying to pull herself together. It was two days since they'd buried Malcolm, and she'd stopped taking the sedatives, but somehow she still found it almost impossible to move. She'd re-enlisted, of course, or rather withdrawn her resignation. She wanted to keep working. Anything but go home to her parents! But she could tell that everyone's patience with her was wearing thin. Even Rosemary Winters and Liz Hadley were clearly fed up. Not that they said anything, but they no longer tried to help her. Oh, God, how had she got herself into this mess?

She washed herself cold to try to wake herself up, but they were hooting the horn on the lorry before she'd dried herself. They would leave without her if she didn't get down there in two minutes. They had to. Liz and Rosemary were part of the watch going on duty in the Ops Room at 13.00. They didn't dare be late. Nor did she.

She pulled her grey uniform knickers on her still-damp body, grey stockings, blue-grey shirt, blue-grey skirt. There was another loud, long hoot. She grabbed the tunic and shoved her arms in the sleeves but didn't take the time to do it up. She stuffed her tie into a pocket and ran down the stairs. She reached the door in time to see the lorry pull away. Coming towards her was the Sally Ann mobile canteen, so she'd missed lunch as well!

Bridges reached for his tea and glanced at the clock. He'd had the watch since 5 am and was to be relieved and have a spot of lunch. But the raid had now moved in straight over the Isle of Wight. They'd scrambled both 606 and 607 to try to catch it before it could reach Portsmouth or the Supermarine works. The squawking of the RT transmissions was coming in poorly, and they were reporting cloud rather than the enemy. Something had gone wrong with the interception.

A telephone was ringing, interfering with Bridges' ability to hear the R/T. "Where are the bastards supposed to be?" the CO of 607 was demanding in a clearly annoyed tone.

Bridges reached for his microphone to reply, "Black Cow Leader, they were last reported at Angels 27, bearing—"

"Sir! That was the Observer Corps!" Robinson interrupted – and it was unheard of for anyone to interrupt a controller when he was talking to an airborne squadron. The W/O didn't give his superior the chance to tick him off. "The Huns are flying due east!"

"East!?" Bridges repeated. Then he realised what it meant: they were coming for Tangmere.

"Can you repeat that, Beetle?" the R/T crackled. "What's the bearing?"

For once, something else was more important than the squadrons in the air. Bridges released the transmit button and called across the room to the airman clerk on the siren. "Sound the Air Raid Warning!" Then he grabbed the telephone to 17 Squadron. "Scramble!"

"But, sir—" the clerk on the other end started.

"Robinson! Get 602 in the air!" Bridges leaned over the railing and called down to the WAAF at the table. "Panic bowlers, everyone." Only then did he press the button on the R/T again. "Black Cow Leader, this is Beetle. Bandits have—" The transmission was disrupted by a large explosion that shook the earth and knocked the lights out.

Lettice had just managed to run through the Main Gate, still in the dust of the lorry, when the first stick threw her face-down onto the tarmac. A *Staffel* of Ju88s in tight formation hung directly over the airfield. Explosions erupted across the field in rapid succession, flinging dust and debris into the air. Lettice closed her eyes and clung to the earth for what seemed like ages. When there seemed to be a lull, she lifted her head to see where she might run.

What she saw was the lorry with the WAAF almost upside down, with the cab on fire. A white hand was sticking out between the tarp and the side of the lorry, struggling to release the tarp. The tarp was moving, too, as the girls inside tried to escape.

Lettice dragged herself up and ran towards the lorry.

"Get down, you stupid girl! They're still coming in!" a male voice shouted at her from the slit trench over to the right.

Lettice turned and screamed back. "There are girls trapped in that lorry! For God's sake, help me, you bastards!" Then she continued running towards the lorry. Gasping for breath and streaming tears, she barely reached the lorry before – as predicted – the second *Staffel* started their bomb run.

The earth shook, and detonations came from all sides. Lettice tried to tear the tarpaulin free, but she was too weak. All she did was rip her long fingernails. She could hear someone sobbing beyond the canvas and carefully kept her look averted from the cab, where Liz Hadley and the driver lay crushed. How much petrol was in that engine?

Suddenly four airman joined Lettice. Rather trying to open the tarpaulin, they sought to push the lorry off its roof and over onto one side. Shouting "Two-Six!" they heaved together and the lorry rolled enough to enable the WAAF inside to start crawling out the back.

Several girls, however, were groaning and sobbing in a heap. Corporal Winters tried to help them, but her left arm dangled uselessly at her side. Two of the airmen climbed into the lorry to help pull the injured out, and Lettice glanced once more toward the cab, but there was nothing anyone could do for Liz now.

The squadrons were demanding instructions. Bridges found a torch and used it to find the microphone. "Beetle here. We've just been hit. Electricity is down."

"There are craters all over the runway and probably UXB as well," came the reply – obviously from someone orbiting. "Our dispersal's gone for a burton, too!"

"Divert to Westhampnett, Black Cow Squadron."

The door opened below and a WAAF dressed in dirt, her stockings in shreds, and with a swelling eye came in. "I'm afraid there won't be relief for everyone," she announced simply, going to take the place of ACW Ross.

The other WAAF stared for a moment, and then ACW Ross told her, "Would you go to the infirmary? We can carry on perfectly well."

"Watch the yellow flags!" Priestman warned. "They mark unexploded bombs." Then he led the way down, choosing a bit of field off to the south that was almost untouched. They'd been properly outwitted this time. First the feint towards Portsmouth/Southampton at a fairly high altitude so the squadrons went in higher still, trying to avoid a bounce from the Messerschmitts. Then the very effective use of partial cloud cover, to disguise a sharp turn after passing over the RDF station at Ventor. After that, the bombers must have lost altitude very rapidly, so that they came in low enough for some pretty precise bombing.

Tangmere's equipment stores were ablaze and the Sergeants' Mess was smoking, too, although the fire engines appeared to be keeping that fire under control. No. 607 Squadron's dispersal had collapsed like a house of cards – bits of board and pieces of clothing all jumbled in an untidy heap. One Hurricane was burning out on the apron in front of the remaining hangar that miraculously still stood. Robin's Hurricane, usually so stable on the ground, was wallowing badly as he ran into bits of rubbish and clunks of earth thrown up out of the nearby craters.

At least their own dispersal was still standing. Ripley climbed on to his wing, pushing the Perspex back even before Priestman cut the engine. Appleby was dealing with the chocks. "What are the casualties?" Priestman got off the first question. "And what about the Sally Ann canteen?"

"Not to worry, sir. It had already left. As for our casualties, I'm not sure of the total, but ACW Hadley and Corporal Cawly bought it. A lot of other WAAF were in the same lorry, but ACW Fields and a couple of blokes managed to get them out just before the trailer caught fire."

"Fields? *Lettice* Fields? MacLeod's girl?"

"Yes, sir. You wouldn't have thought she had it in her, but she plunged right in – shamed the blokes into helping her, like." He grinned as he said that, and Robin had to laugh with him. Then he pushed himself up and out of the cockpit.

Almost as an after-thought, Ripley asked, "Any joy, sir?"

"Didn't even get a glimpse of the bastards!"

At the dispersal hut they were pretty browned off, too. Their lunch had been interrupted. They'd been out-witted by the bloody Hun and their Station hit behind their back. The squadron score still stood at 97. And there was no tea waiting for them. "How the hell are we supposed to win the war without a brew?"

"I dare say the cooks have more important things to do than feed us," Priestman pointed out.

"Like what?" Sutton wanted to know.

As if in answer to the summons, Thatcher appeared at the door with a heavily laden tray. The others converged on him like flies to honey, but Robin stood staring; the ugly little airman had swelling abrasions all over the right side of his face, and as he set the tray down on the clerk's desk, his hands shook.

"What happened to you?" Priestman asked.

"Nothing important, sir, just knocked about a bit."

"Weren't you in a slit trench?"

"There was some WAAF stuck in a lorry."

"You helped with that, did you?"

"I tried, sir. We was too late for—"

Priestman shook his head sharply with a glance at Ringwood. With a slow groan, the air-raid siren started to crank up. The pilots looked at one another. The telephone on the desk gave that click it always gave just before it rang, but Priestman didn't wait for it. "They're coming for us again! Get them airborne!"

"But, sir, they're still refuelling!" Eton protested.

"Get airborne NOW, you bloody fool!" Priestman shouted, already dropping out of the dispersal on the run. The others did the same. The erks had heard the sirens too and some were gazing up at the sky, while the more intelligent were scrambling down, pulling the fuel hoses out, backing the bowsers away.

The pulsing of the unsynchronized engines enveloped them. The ackack started to bark, and then with a bone-jarring crash the first stick of bombs went in. Robin pulled himself up onto the wing of his Hurricane, using the handle with a sense of déjà vu. It was France all over again.

There was no time for cockpit checks. He pressed the starter button and waved the chocks away, his mask hanging loose beside his jaw, nothing plugged in. He had only one thought: get airborne. Turning onto the airfield, he throttled forward, focusing on what looked like a clear run for take-off, but the flags marking craters and unexploded bombs were dangerously close, and towards the end there was a huge crater.

The Hurricane seemed completely lame – but that was only because nothing could be fast enough with the detonations going off all around. The crater was dead ahead. Priestman hit full flaps to bounce himself upwards and pulled the Hurricane into the air with brute force.

As he cleared the crater, a huge bang and whoof told him that whoever had been flying to his right hadn't made it. While still climbing, a more massive explosion shook the air, hurling his Hurricane sideways.

He recovered, pouring sweat, and glanced back to see smoke billowing up in a gigantic column from their ammo dump, located on the far side of the field from the hangars and other buildings. He dipped his wing the other way and looked back down to see that one Hurricane lay crumpled and burning in a crater, and another lay upside down – its undercarriage sticking up into the air like a dead bird's feet. All across the field, bursts of dust and smoke were still going up.

He switched the gun to "fire" and reefed the Hurricane around to hare after the still-neat formation of bombers, hooking his mask in place as he went. "Red Cap Squadron. How many of you are with me?"

They reported in one after another: Ware, Donohue, Kiwi, Woody, Green, Reynolds, Bowles, Banks and Tolkien, the latter sounding decidedly shaken. Eton and Ainsworth didn't report. "P/O Herriman? P/O Ainsworth?" Priestman tried it only once. There wasn't time for more. "Go for the bombers, but there are sure to be yellow-nosed bastards about somewhere!" he reminded them.

"Don't all talk at once!" Allars ordered above the pandemonium. They were crowded into the dispersal again, and Kiwi had already erased the 97 and put up 100 with three exclamation marks behind it. Donohue was insisting it was 101. Priestman was trying to get through to the infirmary to find out what had happened to Ainsworth and Eton. Through the open windows, the smell of cordite wafted along with the reek of aviation fuel and smoke. The clock was showing only 3.15. The second sortie had been very brief, as they had almost no fuel, but the interception had been short but sweet.

"Have they ever been known to hit a Station three times in one day?" Woody wanted to know.

"There's a first time for everything."

"The water mains have burst. There's no water for baths tonight."

"Who cares about that? Can they feed us? That's what I want to know."

"Aren't you claiming anything?" Allars asked Priestman.

"88. Flamer. Only two of the crew made it out."

"I told you it was 101," Donohue declared triumphantly.

"No, that makes 102!" Green started.

From the telephone came a distant-sounding voice. "Infirmary."

"Priestman here. You have two of my pilots."

A pause. "Pilot Officer Herriman has a broken collar-bone, sir, but otherwise he's quite all right."

"And Pilot Officer Ainsworth?"

A pause. "He's in the morgue, sir." Silence. "The aircraft caught fire inverted, sir, and he was burnt beyond recognition before anyone could even get near."

"Thank you." He hung up.

"You're counting Banks' and Bowles' Junkers twice!" Kiwi argued to Green.

Ginger glanced at the CO. "What is it, sir?"

He took a deep breath. "Ainsworth bought it on take-off."

The conversation ceased for a moment. "Pity. Rather nice chap, actually, Woodly remarked.

"Bugger!" Ware corrected. "He owed me five quid."

"Well, that will teach you to throw your money around," Donohue reflected. "Didn't your father ever tell you? 'Neither a borrower nor a lender be'?"

The phone was ringing in the reception of the Mess, and the clerk who should have been there to answer it was nowhere in sight. Probably helping clean up somewhere, Robin reflected. An unanswered phone is like a scrawling infant, however. It drives you batty. Besides, it might very well be Emily. Robin hadn't rung her yet, because he intended to drive over and speak to her personally. He'd had to change and bathe first, however, and had then dropped by the Mess to get something to eat before he faced her. Emily,however, might have heard about the raids and be trying to reach him. He'd told her to ring the adjutant, of course, but if Mickey wasn't in his office she might try here. Robin had just about made up his mind to answer it himself, when Needham reached over the counter and picked up the receiver. "RAF Tangmere, Officer's Mess... Oh... No, he's dead." He hung up.

"What was that all about?"

"Just some girl asking if she could speak to Ainsworth."

Robin opened his mouth twice before he managed, "How could you do that?

"What, sir?"

"That was probably his fiancée. And you just blurted it out like...."

Needham gazed at him, uncomprehending.

Robin turned and walked out of the Mess, heading for Eastney and Emily.

Eastney

Hattie answered the door. Robin was standing in it with a dozen red roses. "What a nice thought," she commented, backing up to let him in, adding, "Go and pour yourself a scotch. I'm sure you can use it. I'll fetch Emily."

"Is she very upset? About the papers, I mean?"

Hattie shrugged. "She's a sensible girl. It was pretty obvious, if you looked, that Miss Cox-Gordon was kissing you more than the other way around. Pour yourself a drink, and I'll fetch Emily."

"No need," Emily said, stepping off the last stair, feeling unsure of what to do or say. In the films, women were always hysterical and furious in a situation like this, but she couldn't conjure up those feelings. In part it was because she had known from the start that he must have had other girlfriends. Her parents had repeatedly warned her that since she wasn't "good enough" for him, he was sure to be unfaithful to her sooner or later.

Robin didn't give her a chance to say anything. "I'm sorry about that damned photo, Emily. I didn't mean it to happen. I didn't even know she was there, and the next thing I knew she'd flung herself at me and the photographer was snapping away. I was trapped. That's all. You will forgive me, won't you?"

"What is there to forgive, if you were just ensnared in a trap by a sly, predatory female?" Emily asked, with a solemn face but a little wicked amusement in her eye.

She was too clever by half sometimes, Robin registered, even as he retorted at the speed of gunfire, "For making you unhappy – even if only by mistake." He remembered the roses and offered them to her now.

"Time for me to go to the Mission," Hattie announced while Emily sniffed the roses. She took her hat down from the stand and her handbag from the table. "I won't be back until ten – not that you'll miss me." She laughed and went out of the door, closing it firmly behind her.

Emily excused herself to put the roses in water. Robin followed her to the kitchen and stood leaning against the door frame as she took a vase down, and then found a pair of scissors. "The problem isn't really this photo, you know," Emily told him from the sink, her back to him as she cut the flowers.

"What is it, then?" Robin asked, baffled.

"It's that I'm not your type."

"Who says that?"

"Well, look at the others. The Lady from the Paris Airshow and now this woman."

"There were lots. Do they matter?"

That put her on the spot. "No, of course not. Not if *you're* sure that you don't still want one of them – someone who can help your career, make life a luxury for you, open doors to unheard-of futures in politics or whatnot." Emily had learned at Cambridge just how very much the "right" connections could do for you in life.

"I went to a great deal of effort to avoid the snares of the lot of them and stay free," Robin retorted sharply. "I don't want to be married to a woman like Virginia Cox-Gordon or Caroline Merriweather."

The sharpness – almost bitterness – of his tone surprised Emily, and she noted with a rush of guilt how very gaunt Robin looked. He must have lost a lot of weight recently. As their eyes met, she had another shock: *he* was frightened – really frightened.

Emily left the roses standing and crossed the room to him. He pulled her tightly into his arms and clung to her. "Don't leave me, Emily."

"Forgive me, Robin. I had no right to give you a fright. I considered that I ought to give you up, and that I might be happier in the long run if I did, but I can't give you up now. If you want me—"

"I do. Emily, the others were playthings. The only person I can imagine spending the rest of my life with is you."

Emily lifted her head and they kissed. It was a long kiss, and at the end of it Robin drew back, only to hold her tightly to him again. "When are we getting married?"

"As soon as you can get some leave," Emily assured him.

Robin dropped her and stepped backwards. "You know perfectly well I can't get any leave!"

Emily was left bewildered by his abrupt change of mood. "Other people do—"

"Other people aren't commanding a fighter squadron – or if they are, they have at least one Flight Lieutenant! Woody's hardly up to leading a flight, let alone a squadron. Sutton and Donohue are cracking up on me. Ginger gets sick at the sight of the enemy, and Banks can't – or won't – shoot. At least Ainsworth bought it today, so that's one less worry. And Eton's broken his collar-bone."

"So how do you picture a wedding? I come out to the dispersal and the padre marries us between scrambles, or what?" Emily retorted, hurt to the quick by his tone and unable to follow his logic. It was as if he wanted to marry her only in the abstract.

"Of course not! We get stood down for one day every four now." He was scowling darkly. He thought she understood what things were like. He'd depended on it.

"One day," she sneered.

"Twenty-four hours; maybe I can stretch it to 36, if we have late readiness the next day, but frankly, if you're going to start making demands in the middle of all this, then maybe you're no better than the rest after all."

"Demands? You think expecting to spend one week with my husband is a demand?!" Emily shot back on the brink of tears.

"Who's talking about a week? I thought we were talking about a lifetime."

"That's what I *wish* we were talking about! But how the hell can you promise me a lifetime when you can't promise me an hour from the next time you go on bloody readiness!" Emily flung back at him, and then tried to run out of the kitchen because she was ashamed of herself. She knew she shouldn't have said it. It was against the rules.

Robin stopped her and pulled her into his arms. She broke down and started sobbing. "I'm sorry. I'm sorry. I know. All I'm asking for is a week." She sobbed into his tunic. "A week together without the war."

All his anger was gone. He felt only sympathy for her. And love. He held her without another word until she had calmed herself down. She sniffled, and muttered, "I need a handkerchief." She started to pull away from him to go and find one, but he held her fast with one arm and drew his own handkerchief out of his trouser pocket. He handed it to her, and she blew her nose, still enclosed in his arms. Then he pulled her tighter again, and she surrendered, laying her head on his chest, feeling the wet of her own tears and the scratch of his wings, and just waited.

When he was sure he had her attention, Robin said very softly, "We cannot build a future together on the assumption I am going to die tomorrow."

Emily took a deep breath. "I know."

"I'll put in for leave and see what they give me, but the reality is, I'm more likely to get a 48-er than a week. I'd rather do that, than live without you one day longer than necessary."

Emily only nodded, not trusting herself to say anything. After a bit she drew back and asked, "Have you had anything to eat?"

"I ate at the Mess."

"What?"

"I can't remember. I wasn't paying much attention."

"Let me make you something. You're too thin."

"You don't have to cook, Emily. That's not why I love you."

"Why do you love me?"

"Because you aren't in love with a trophy winner, or a fighter pilot, or a DFC. You're in love with me – a me I don't even know is there half of the time. You remind me that I'm more than just the brain of my Hurricane."

PART V

The Final Round

Chapter 36

Crépon / Paris
4/5 September 1940

The orders to report to *Luftflotte* 3 Headquarters in Paris were not only terrifying, they were inexplicable. Klaudia could not convince herself that her "failure" to report Rosa's condition was a crime serious enough to warrant the attention of the *Geschwader*, let alone the *Luftflotte*. To make things worse, her direct superiors acted as if they didn't have any idea of what the whole thing was about, either.

The situation was chaotic enough as it was. Frischmuth had failed to return on Sept. 2, and his replacement was due any minute. It was allegedly one of "Mölders' boys" – a man with 29 kills and Goering's ear. Rumour had it that he was being sent to "shake them up" and generally improve their "deplorable" performance. Everyone's nerves were on edge, and no one had time for the fears of a *Luftwaffehelferin*.

Just as she was leaving, Klaudia got a glimpse of the new *Gruppenkommandeur*, a lean, dark man with a sharp nose and a Knights Cross at his throat. He looked very young to Klaudia, young and predatory, like Jako. It made her shudder. She thought back to how nice it had been here when she and Rosa arrived, with Christian and Ernst and Dieter singing forbidden songs in the Casino. Now only Dieter, looking gaunter and more haunted than ever, was left, and no one played jazz on the piano in the bar any more....

She soon found herself on the train to Paris. The train was full of soldiers and sailors on leave. They were loud and rowdy, talking about all they were going to do in Paris. Some tried to pick her up, but she brushed them off and kept turned towards the window. The small towns of Northern France seemed bleak; the buildings were shuttered shut against prying eyes, the façades ill-kept, the gardens utilitarian. Even the outskirts of Paris disappointed. They looked just like industrial suburbs everywhere: monotonous blocks of housing and factories populated by drab, ugly people. As they got closer to the centre of the city, they went into a lot of tunnels and it was difficult to see anything, especially since the other passengers were dragging their things down and pulling on their tunics and caps. At last, with loud, squealing brakes, they pulled into a dingy but huge station, where the microphones squawked unintelligibly across a vast grey space in which the still steaming and hissing trains stood lined up on a score of tracks.

In the sea of people, Klaudia felt helplessly lost. Last time she had passed through Paris she had been no less intimidated, but she had been full of eager anticipation, too. And Rosa, competent, cheeky Rosa, had been with her. The thought brought tears to her eyes.

Abruptly, a young man in a very smart black uniform with gleaming boots and immaculate gloves was clicking his heels before her. "*Helferin* von Richthofen?"

"Yes," she admitted uncertainly, and then remembered to salute as she registered the rank of *Obersturmführer*, same as *Oberleutnant* in the Luftwaffe. But far more intimidating than the rank was the SD on his collar and the stiff, polished leather of his pistol holder. The *Reichssicherheitsdienst*! She was being arrested. Her mouth went dry with terror. She couldn't imagine what she had done. It had to be a mistake.

"If you would be so kind as to come with me?" He retained all the polished courtesies as he indicated the direction they should take. Klaudia was speechless with terror. He led them through the crowd like a hot knife through butter. Where he led, there was no resistance, no crowd at all; it parted before him without hesitation, whether French or German.

They emerged from the station into a drizzling rain, where a shiny black Mercedes waited with a driver in the smart, black uniform of the SS. The driver opened the door and saluted; the *Obersturmführer* stood back and gestured for Klaudia to get in first. She felt she could hardly breathe as she bent and entered the dark car. It smelled of leather polish, cigarette smoke and cologne of some sort.

Her companion went around to the other side of the car and got in beside her. The driver returned to his seat and set off. He obviously knew where they were going without being told. The seat was low and the windows tinted. Klaudia felt cut off from the outside world, as if she were already imprisoned, or at least on her way to that infamous "no-man's-land" of interrogation and concentration camps. No one would even learn where she had gone. She would just disappear.... She was too terrified even to look at this famed city as it sped past her.

The SD officer reached inside his tunic and removed a silver cigarette case. He opened it and offered it to Klaudia. "Smoke?"

"No," she shook her head rigorously.

He smiled, and remarked, "Good. I don't like women who smoke, and nor does the boss. Mind if I do?"

"Of course not."

"You seem nervous," he remarked with a faint smile.

"I don't know what this is all about!" Klaudia told him, a fraction desperately.

He smiled more broadly. "No, it is a big secret at the moment. I am not at liberty to tell you everything, but you have no need to be frightened. It is a great honour – provided my boss approves of you, that is."

They stopped in front of what, in peace-time, had been a grand hotel and now evidently served as some kind of headquarters. The doormen had been replaced by SS guards.

The door to the car was opened from the outside by one of them, who saluted as they climbed out. The grand foyer was still sumptuous, decorated in Louis XIV style, but all the visitors were men in SS uniform. Klaudia's escort indicated a lift. They went up to the second floor, along a carpeted corridor, and after a knock on a tall, gilded door, entered a spacious room, converted into an office.

Klaudia's escort saluted very smartly and she gave her best salute, acutely aware that much of the parade-ground smartness had gone out of it over the last months at Crépon. Nobody seemed to bother with saluting there.

A middle-aged man with the Golden Party Badge as well as the rank insignia of a *Sturmbahnführer* (Major) came out from behind his desk. He walked around Klaudia while she stood at attention and then nodded once. "Excellent. In fact, perfect! Absolutely perfect. Take a seat, *gnädiges Fräulein*. Would you like something to drink after your long trip? Tea, coffee, hot chocolate? The coffee is real."

"Coffee, then, if I may, *Herr Sturmbahnführer*."

The man went back to his desk, pressed a button and ordered coffee, while he gestured for both Klaudia and her escort to sit down. When he returned, he made himself comfortable in the Louis XIV chair opposite her. "You are here for a very important mission, *Fräulein* von Richthofen," he announced. "My office is responsible for contact with the Foreign Press. We have had a request from a certain American journalist who wishes to visit a front-line German fighter unit. He seems to think he can just go down and talk to anyone," he smiled as if over a silly child, "but that is not possible, of course. We have decided to take him on a visit to JG51, but fortunately my adjutant," he nodded towards the young man who had collected her at the station, "Gruber here, remembered seeing your name in some recent communication. We feel that having a Richthofen present would be a very good, subtle way of reminding the Americans of your legendary relative. We had planned on having one or two *Helferinnen* there anyway, but I confess, I was a little nervous as to whether you would meet the requirements of our Propaganda ministry. I am delighted to see you are really *exactly* what we want, isn't she, Busso?"

The young man grinned. "Perfect."

The older man nodded and looked more serious for a moment. The door opened, and a man in a white steward's jacket entered with a silver tray on which stood a silver coffee service. This was put on the coffee table between Klaudia and the two SD officers. The steward withdrew, and the adjutant poured the coffee for all of them into beautiful porcelain coffee cups. Only after she had her coffee in hand did the SD *Sturmbahnführer* remark, "Of course, we have to ask you a few questions."

Klaudia stiffened inwardly, although she tried to appear calm. "Of course."

"First, there was some incident with a colleague of yours who killed her own child."

"I tried to stop her! You don't know how many times I pleaded with her not to do it. I did everything I could think of to stop her!" Klaudia answered immediately. Her distress was genuine, and she had been expecting some sort of interrogation on this ever since she'd seen the SD on the uniform of her escort.

"Everything but report it to your superiors, it seems," the *Sturmbahnführer* remarked dryly – but not unkindly.

Klaudia looked down, tears pricking her eyes, "I know that was a mistake now, Herr *Sturmbahnführer*. But at the time, I – I didn't want to betray her. I was afraid she would get into trouble. I kept hoping I could talk her out of it. I know it was wrong. If I had only gone to someone, she would be alive today. I see that now."

The *Sturmbahnführer* nodded. "Well, you're very young, and I believe you have learned your lesson – the hard way, I might say. Tell us more about your relationship with Christian Freiherr von Feldburg?"

The question took Klaudia completely by surprise.

"Feldburg? I have no relationship with Freiherr von Feldburg whatsoever."

The *Sturmbahnführer* wasn't smiling. He looked at her very hard. "Don't think we don't know about him. A foolish and arrogant young man. He understands nothing about the New Order. He comes from a reactionary *Catholic* family." He said the word "Catholic" as if it were as much an anathema as "Jewish," and then continued, "His brother is no National Socialist either, but at least he is a very brave and loyal German. Earned his EKI with the Panzers in France. His brother we can trust to serve the State because of his love for his Fatherland. He is such an old-fashioned, die-hard aristocrat that he would shoot himself before he would break an oath – including the one he took to the Führer!"

"But Christian von Feldburg is made of different cloth." He continued. "An intellectual light-weight, and not even a particularly good pilot. On the one hand, too flighty and insubstantial to be a real threat to us, but on the other hand, subversive and dangerous, because he taints people's views by making light of things that are deadly serious. Don't you agree, *Fräulein von Richthofen?*"

"I – I hadn't thought about it," Klaudia stammered out.

"Well, what *do* you think of Christian von Feldburg?"

"He – he's – a very dashing and good-looking young man. Many of the *Helferinnen* have terrible crushes on him."

"But he prefers his French whore," the SD man told her bluntly.

"Yes. Exactly."

"Why do you think he would prefer a French whore to our gallant *Helferinnen?*"

"I – I suppose because she *is* willing to sleep with him, whereas he would have to marry one of us first."

The SD laughed. "Very good answer," the older man said, nodding approvingly, but Klaudia couldn't help wondering if he knew the truth about Jako. They seemed to know everything else. And now he pressed her, "You say the others have crushes on him. What about you?"

"He is not my type. I am engaged to Ernst Geuke."

"Geuke. Feldburg's wingman."

Guilt by association. "That's not his choice. He was just assigned."

"He was offered a Rotte and turned it down to stay with Feldburg," the SD countered knowingly.

"I didn't know," Klaudia whispered, frightened again. Surely Ernst and she couldn't be in trouble just because they *liked* Feldburg? Yes, they could. And Feldburg was such an arrogant fool! Telling Goering off to his face like that! "But Ernst's not like Feldburg at all. He's very loyal!" she protested. "He's devoted to the New Germany!"

The SD *Sturmbahnführer* considered her for a long moment, allowing her to sweat, but then he nodded and broke into a smile. "That was our conclusion, too. Good to hear you confirm it. Of course, for this exercise with the American press, you will say you are engaged to the young man we have selected for the interview, *Oberleutant* Lutze. He has 6 kills now, and I'm sure you will like him. But first we must make you look the part."

Before she fully grasped what was happening, Klaudia was turned over to a middle-aged woman, who was very obviously used to authority. It soon became evident she was in films, a close associate of Leni Riefenstahl, and she set about re-doing Klaudia. First, Klaudia was fitted for a new uniform in officer-grade cloth, and given silk stockings and new shoes. Then, while the adjustments were made to the uniform, the woman "made over" Klaudia's hair and face as well.

"Make-up mustn't be obvious. You represent a modest, decent

German girl, and there can be no hint that you might be even a little fast. No, not fast, but you mustn't look dowdy, either. The freckles are excellent – so wholesome! No cover make-up on them, but your lips are too pale, and we must do something with your hair."

There was no denying the success of the woman's efforts. Klaudia hardly recognised herself, and enjoyed being taken to the Paris opera by Gruber that evening, before being sent to bed in the hotel arranged for her. In the morning her new uniform was delivered to her, and a beautician came to do her face and hair again before she was picked up by a staff car at 9 am and rushed out of Paris to the airfield. On the way there *Obersturmführer* Gruber, who had been a journalist before the war, started to explain what would happen.

The American was scheduled to arrive at noon. He would first be taken to meet the CO of JG51, have lunch at the Mess, and would then offered a tour of the entire station. He would be given the impression that nothing was being hidden from him. When the car came abreast of Hangar Two, the ground crews would roll out one of the Me109s, and *Obersturmführer* Gruber would suggest to the American that perhaps he would like to talk to the pilot. They would stop the car and come over to talk to Lutze, who would be standing beside the Me109, putting on his parachute.

Klaudia was to keep herself inside the hangar until Gruber turned and looked over, as if casually. That would be the signal that she was to emerge. The gentlemen would then all pretend to be surprised to see her. Gruber warned her that he would look annoyed as well, and even try to send her away, but Lutze would introduce her as his fiancée. Gruber would ask the American if he knew anything about Luftwaffe Helferinnen, and Klaudia was given a short paragraph to memorise that, if asked, she was to recite, describing the selection process and training the girls had. She was also given extensive guidelines about how to respond to other questions.

Q: *Did she like her work? A: Of course; it was wonderful to be able to help "our young men."*

Q: *Didn't she think it was wrong for women to be on the front line? A: Of course not; women have always supported their men-folk in times of need.*

Q: *Was she frightened? A: What should she be frightened of? She was protected by the finest army in the world.*

Q: *Didn't she want to have a home and children? A: Of course, as soon as the war was over.*

Q: *Didn't she worry about her fiancé? A: Of course she worried. No natural woman did not worry about her loved ones; but she could not have fallen in love with a man who did not want to fight for his Fatherland, and she was proud of him.*

Klaudia started to get nervous again. She had always been bad at memorising things.

At the airfield, Klaudia was introduced briefly to Lutze, but the young man had also been given his script and Gruber was busy going over it with him. Very little was being left to chance. Even the ground crews had been carefully selected and controlled (they could wear dirty overalls, but they'd had their hair cut and were clean shaven.) They also were given strict instructions about how to act and how to answer any questions put to them. They were *not* to act as if they were forbidden to answer, only as if they didn't think they were *qualified* to answer.

Gruber took a good look at the selected Me109, too. It mustn't have any patched-over bullet-holes or evidence of combat damage, but it shouldn't look brand new either, he insisted. A few dents and scratches were just right – and, of course, the blackened smears around the guns from cordite. For this occasion, six RAF roundels were painted on the tail as well.

The American arrived with his cameraman. He wore ill-fitting civilian clothes, an old hat and worn shoes. His photographer was dressed even worse. Klaudia felt genuine contempt for both of them as she watched them climb out of the car to talk to Lutze beside the Me109. Gruber gave the signal, and Klaudia – feeling stage fright – left the safety of the hangar and joined the group.

Gruber frowned as he had warned, but Lutze played his part and signalled her nearer, saying, "Let me introduce my fiancée, Fräulein von Richthofen!"

"Any relation to the Red Baron of the last war?" the American asked at once – as if reading from the German script.

"My greatuncle," Klaudia replied, as she had been instructed. As predicted, the American showed an interest in her job and the role of the *Helferinnen*. Klaudia answered as best she could and was glad that Gruber interceded smoothly, explaining points more fluently. Although the American was speaking German after a fashion, it was clear that he preferred English, and Gruber spoke it fluently, "translating" (and improving) on Klaudia's answers.

Gruber stressed that the *Helferinnen* were all volunteers. "We have no female conscription in Germany, and never will! We respect our women too much for that – and, of course, their primary role is to be good mothers and wives. But young, single women who are not yet either wives or mothers can – if they choose – help their men-folk by providing support services as the *Helferinnen* do here. Miss von Richthofen is in communications. That's what that badge there indicates," he explained as

497

he pointed out her sleeve badge.

The questions came about how long she had been in her job and how she liked it. Klaudia smiled and said "very much" in her broken English, earning a big smile from Gruber and the Americans.

Then Gruber suggested that they mustn't keep *Oberleutnant* Lutze waiting. He was supposed to fly a reconnaissance flight, and there were several other officers waiting for the American. Gruber indicated the waiting staff car, and Lutze turned to climb onto the Messerschmitt.

The American interrupted. "Just one more questions, please. You've been fighting the English for four months now. Give me an honest answer: can you beat them?"

Lutze smiled broadly and answered in English (one of the reasons he had been selected for the interview). "But, of course, we already have! Their Army fled across the Channel leaving all their equipment behind. Their vaunted Navy cannot protect their merchant ships even in the so-called "English" Channel, let alone on the North Atlantic. Their Air Force is the finest we have yet had the pleasure to encounter. It has been great fun finally testing ourselves and our machines against worthy opponents! But look at them! Their airfields are in ruins. Their early warning system has broken down. They are vastly outnumbered in the air. It is to their credit that they come up at all! They are worthy opponents! But they are defeated."

"Then why don't you launch the invasion?"

Lutze laughed heartily. (Although to Klaudia's eye it looked a little forced.) "You will have to ask the High Command that! I am just a lowly pilot."

"OK, and as a lowly pilot, what do you think of the Spitfire?"

"Ha!" Lutze made a deprecating gesture. "Totally overrated. It is slower than the Me, has a lower ceiling and stalls in a dive."

Gruber was again indicating the staff car, but the American was not going to be lured away so easily. "Your bomber crews seem to fear it."

Lutze frowned. "Our bomber crews *fear* nothing! They respect it, perhaps, but not fear."

"Right. Respect," the American agreed, nodding. "But the English claim to be shooting down large numbers of your aircraft."

"The English are liars!" Lutze answered, apparently starting to get angry.

Gruber made a more determined attempt to pry the American away. "We really must let the *Oberleutnant* get off on his mission, or I shall get in terrible trouble for interrupting him at all."

Now, however, it was Lutze who had a point to make. "They are amateurs, these English. Always playing games and making jokes, and never taking anything seriously. They did not plan for war, and now they pay the price. They must cower in shelters and fear for their wives and daughters, while in Germany life goes on as before. In Germany no one is afraid. The people know they can trust us to finish off the English. But the English, they must live in terror, knowing the invasion will come any day and there is nothing – nothing at all – to stop it. Churchill is ridiculous with his 'we will fight them on the beaches!' With what? They have no army or weapons left."

The American nodded and stepped back. Lutze pulled himself hastily into the cockpit, and a moment later the Me109 coughed into life with a puff of smoke. The Americans went back to the waiting car, ready for the rest of their planned programme, which included dinner at the Officer's Mess by candle-light on the best Luftwaffe service, waited on by stewards in white jackets. But other *Helferinnen* had been selected for escorts there, and Klaudia's moment of "glory" was over. She was sent back to her unit by night train.

Portsmouth / Bosham
5 September 1940

Robin reached Emily at the Seaman's Mission. "We've just been stood down, so we thought we'd go over to *The Ship* in Bosham for a nice celebration. I'll pick you up at Aunt Hattie's in an hour. Is that all right?"

Emily was a bit flustered; it was only 4 pm. She hadn't expected to see him until much later – eight or so, as on the other nights. "Why have you been stood down so early?"

"Look out of a window; even the birds are walking." It was pouring rain.

"All right. Should I dress?"

"You'd be happier."

Ah ha. "Who else will be there, Robin?"

"I don't know exactly, but Reynolds rang one of his actress friends, and Donohue wheedled Virginia's number out of me. She's bound to bring some of her crowd along."

"Sounds as though all that's missing is the Duke of Windsor," Emily quipped.

"I didn't invite him," Robin retorted. "In an hour's time at Aunt Hattie's?"

"Yes, I'll do my best."

She left everything standing – but the others understood – just barely caught the bus and hastily bathed and washed her hair. She put on the only pair of silk stockings that she owned and chose the cocktail dress with crossed bodice and bare back that she knew Robin liked best. Her hair was still damp when he rang the bell.

Robin was looking freshly bathed and shaved, too, and driving MacLeod's old MG. He helped Emily into the passenger side, and then dashed around to the driver's seat. Pouring rain all but overwhelmed the windscreen-wipers, and the MG was so low to the ground that they seemed to submerge in some of the puddles. Robin drove the MG rather like he flew a Hurricane, aggressively and purposefully, which meant he concentrated on driving, which was just as well given the conditions.

Emily was left to her own thoughts. At first, she was uncomfortable, remembering that the car belonged to the dead Scotsman and thinking that they were going to celebrate a hundred "kills." What sort of a monster was she turning into? For a moment, her pacifist sentiments returned with intensity. War was madness! Why on earth should normal people, who really just wanted to follow peaceful pursuits, be turned into killers? She was reminded that the man beside her had blood on his hands. Rather a lot, even by the standards of his profession.

She looked over at the darkly handsome man on her right with his cap low over his eyes and thought to herself: this can't be real. He belongs to a different world. A world of glamour and danger. Abruptly, she realised that she *enjoyed* being part of it. It was as wonderful as flying itself – this fast-paced world of spontaneous decisions and unexpected encounters. It was – being alive. Maybe humans *needed* the proximity of death in order truly to appreciate and enjoy life itself?

The carpark at *The Ship* was already full, and a variety of vehicles lined the street and crowded the churchyard. "Have you set a date for the wedding yet?" Robin asked, with a glance at the church. They had agreed at their last parting that he would request leave as soon she had set a date with the vicar.

"How does the 21st sound?"

"Too far away. Why not sooner?"

"I have to be baptised and confirmed."

"Can't they do that the same day as the wedding?" As he spoke Robin held the pub door for her and they went inside and through the blackout curtains. They were greeted by shouts, cheers and whistles. Emily recognized Virginia Cox-Gordon from the newspaper article. The socialite swept up smelling of expensive perfume and feeling like satin.

"So, you're the reason Robin gave me the brush-off all summer," she exclaimed as she kissed Emily on both cheeks. "Congratulations." Donohue stood behind her looking very pleased with himself, and he winked at Robin.

They were drawn towards the bar. Champagne was poured for them. Virginia was reminding Robin of the names of the other girls leaning on the bar with Sutton, Ware, Needham and Ringwood. Many of the WAAFs were here as well, including Lettice Fields. She was looking remarkably perky considering what a wreck she had been at MacLeod's funeral six days ago. The Station Commander had put her in for a citation for her actions during the raids two days ago. Emily left Robin to go over and congratulate her.

She blushed. "I didn't do anything special," she insisted, but Rosemary Winters, her arm in a cast, contradicted her firmly. "You saved Elaine's life – and put the erks to shame! *They* would have just left us there!"

Bridges arrived with a drink for ACW Jane Roberts. Emily caught the look of adoration Jane gave him and decided it was time to withdraw, glad for both of them.

Ginger, Banks and Colin chose a table in a niche, to be a little apart from the antics of the others. An elderly gentleman in tweeds and ascot recognised Colin, however, and came over to clap him on the shoulder. "Good to see you, Colin. May I buy you and your friends a drink?"

"Thank you, m'lord. That would be very kind," Colin answered easily. "May I introduce David "Banks" Goldman, from Canada, and Ginger Bowles from Devon?"

The gentleman shook hands vigorously with the two pilots. "A pleasure to meet you! A pleasure to have you here! What are you drinking?"

They both assured him beer was fine, and as he withdrew to place their orders, Banks levelled a stern look at Colin and asked for both of them. "My lord?"

"Oh. Didn't you know? That's the Duke of Norfolk."

Banks and Ginger looked at each other. Banks shrugged. "What's a Duke or two?"

"Norfolk is one of the oldest peerages in the Realm," Ginger pointed out, awed.

"Lives just up the road at Arundel," Colin replied. "Owns several of the cottages across from the church. One often runs into him here at *The Ship*."

By the time Emily had had three glasses of champagne, she bluntly told Robin that if he didn't find her something to eat, she was "going to embarrass him."

"That would be interesting," he replied, but found her the menu, and she ordered the French Onion Soup followed by salmon.

The door opened and Vivien Leigh walked in with Rex Harrison and Lawrence Olivier. That electrified the entire room. Everyone crowded around while the celebrities graciously laughed, shook hands and signed autographs for their eager admirers.

Pilot Officer Reynolds followed in their wake, with a couple of lesser starlets as well as Green and Tolkien. Someone started playing dance music on the piano, and Kiwi was first off the mark to ask Vivien Leigh to dance. She laughed but put her drink aside to accept at once. Ringwood coaxed Lettice Fields onto the dance floor and soon there were a dozen couples on the floor. One of the starlets went over and spoke to Ginger, Banks and Colin. She was clearly trying to convince them to join in the fun. It didn't take her long before she had Banks on the dance floor with her. Ginger was soon dancing with Corporal Winters despite her cast, and Colin with one of Virginia's friends.

"Who's Colin with?" Emily asked Robin.

"Titled girl; Lady Margaret, I believe. She probably knows Colin's bloodlines. Aren't that many eligible heirs to earldoms around these days – and Colin's not about to go for six, either. Good bargain, if she can snag him."

Emily took a moment to absorb that, by which point the conversation had moved on. All that was left was a slight chill at the cold calculation of it all. The dark side of moving in these circles, she reflected: they were all predators.

Rex Harrison came to the bar beside Emily and ordered a drink. Then he turned and smiled at her. "Fine lot, aren't they?"

"Yes, but don't you think it odd that they were the same yesterday, last month and last year, yet no one seemed to take any notice then?"

"Ah, but my dear, they *weren't* the same last month or last year. Then they were just a bunch of spoilt youngsters letting the tax-payer foot the bill for their fun in the sky."

Before Emily could respond, Robin returned and remarked emphatically, "Quite right, and all this adulation hadn't gone to our wet heads yet."

Harrison laughed.

Robin took Emily onto the dance floor. "It *is* flattering," she insisted.

"The stars are here for their own publicity and image," he gestured towards a photographer eagerly snapping photos of the stars from the fringe of the crowd. "But I don't care. They've bucked up the lads no end. Look at Reynolds." He drew Emily's attention to the failed-actor-turned-pilot dancing with Vivien Leigh. "He said himself that he couldn't get even the third-rate actresses to return his calls a year ago, and look at him now!"

"It's only what you deserve," Emily insisted serenely.

Robin bent and kissed her for that. Then he dropped his mouth beside her ear and murmured, "What I *deserve* is for you to marry me sooner."

"All right. Fly me up to Gretna Green in the Maggie and we can get married tonight."

"Done." He started to lead her off the dance floor, then stopped himself. "Didn't I say even the birds are walking?"

They started dancing again.

Ginger took Rosemary Winters back to the table and offered to get her a drink. "I'd better not," she told him sensibly. "Not until I've had a bite to eat."

So Ginger offered to buy her a bite to eat as well. When he returned with a sandwich, he found that Lettice had joined their little round. She'd had too much to drink already, and felt she had to apologise for making such a scene at the last squadron do. Rosemary told her not to worry, and Banks offered to get her something to eat. Colin brought over the girl he'd been dancing with and introduced her around. She was very young and would have come out this year if there'd been such a thing as a "season" in the middle of a war. She was glowing and breathless with excitement, knowing already that this was a night she would remember for the rest of her life.

Some time later, when they were all very pickled, Kiwi started playing "Run, Rabbit, Run" on the piano, and Green obligingly climbed up on one of the tables to run – at least he took his shoes off first, Robin noted. Donohue and Virginia were inseparable by now. The celebrities had disappeared, but the lesser starlets had stayed. They clustered around the piano and encouraged Kiwi to keep playing, while they sang.

The sirens went off. The proprietor and the waiters looked rather alarmed, but Sutton told them sternly, "The bloody Luftwaffe ruins our *days*; they've got no damned right to wreck our nights as well." The civilians retreated to the shelters, leaving the RAF to their fate.

Robin staggered to his feet and went to the door to look out. The searchlights from Portsmouth probed the night, and the dull throb of unsynchronized engines came across the opaque sky above the gentle hissing of the waves on the shore. Emily joined him, and he held her to him. "Portsmouth."

"I hope Hattie's all right – and your mother."

"Mother practically sleeps in the cellar, and Hattie's no fool. You're the one I always worry about."

"Meaning I *am* a fool?" Emily teased.

He just held her tighter, and they started kissing vigorously until the ack-ack opened up rather close at hand. Flashes of light burst against the dark sky. One of the engines overhead took on a different note. Distant detonations and more flashes of light followed as the navy guns took up the fight.

From inside came the strains of Gilbert and Sullivan: *I am the very model of a modern major general....* accompanied by whistles, cheering and clapping as the pianist and singer increased the pace until they stumbled over the words and ordered another round.

"What time do you go on readiness tomorrow?"

"When we leave here."

"You're all smashed."

"I know.... There's a dance at the Sergeant's Mess Saturday night. Did I mention it? Wouldn't do not to show up. You'll be there, won't you?"

"Wasn't it only yesterday that you said we couldn't build a future on the assumption that you are going to die tomorrow?"

"Who's assuming I'm going to die tomorrow?"

"No one – you're just acting as though you thought it."

"No; but some of us are going to die tomorrow, so we can't stop living for a second, can we?"

Chapter 37

RAF Tangmere
7 September 1940

Allars clumped into the Adjutant's office, leaning heavily on his cane; his phantom pains seemed to be getting worse. He stopped at the sight of the Adjutant. The kindly man was looking down at something on his desk and frowning fiercely. "What's the matter?"

Mickey sat back in his chair, removing his thick glasses and cleaning them with his rumpled handkerchief as he spoke. "I'm afraid to show this log-book to Priestman."

"What log-book?"

He gestured with his head to the door. "There's another sprog here. This one has a total – *a grand total* – of 168 hours flying, and only 10 of that on Hurricanes!"

Allars sank heavily into the visitor's chair, his wooden leg thrust out straight in front of him. His face was marked with the sleepless nights. "Might as well send him back where he came from. Priestman won't let him fly ops with no more than that to his credit."

"I know." Mickey sighed again and used his handkerchief to wipe sweat from his head and neck, before replacing his glasses.

"I was just thinking that – that I shouldn't even tell him the boy is here. Just send him back."

"I'm a bit worried about Priestman," Allars admitted. "In fact, that's what I wanted to talk to you about."

"Oh? I think he's doing a damn fine job of it, actually."

"So he is – except that he doesn't have enough distance from it all. He takes everything too personally."

Mickey didn't have an answer to that; it was true.

Allars added after a bit, "Boret just turned down his request for 48 hours leave to get married. Gave him rather a nasty time of it, actually. Ticked him off for even thinking of it. Nothing going before mid-October, he said – unless the whole Squadron gets sent north, of course."

Mickey concentrated on folding up his handkerchief and putting it away. He thought that was a very poor decision on the part of the Station Commander. Priestman would benefit from having Emily on Station. For a start, it would get her out of Portsmouth, which regularly got a pasting from the Luftwaffe. And it would give him a refuge – somewhere to let down his guard and relax. Not to mention the sex, which was clearly important for a young man like Priestman.

"I quite agree," Allars remarked, as if Mickey had spoken out loud. "Bloody silly decision. I expected better from Boret. But he had a point about there being no suitable Flight Commanders who could take over the squadron for two days. That's actually what I came to talk to you about. I know you've been talking to Personnel about it."

"Daily. They groan the minute they hear my voice," Mickey admitted. "The thing is, to them it's only been three weeks since we lost Hayworth and Thompson, and just four days since they sent us the unfortunate F/ Lt what-ever-his-name-was with jaundice. They are still living in a world with regular hours and forms and regulations, after all. They assure me they are 'working' on it." Mickey sighed.

"Give it another try, would you?" Allars suggested, and then, with obvious pain, dragged himself back to his feet and clomped out down the hall.

Mickey picked up the telephone and dialled the number he knew by heart. "Ken? Mickey here."

At the other end of the line was the Group Personnel Officer. They had been in almost daily contact for weeks now, but this time Mickey was determined not to be brushed off.

"I say, Mickey, this really is being a bit pessimistic – to call up for a replacement even before one of your blokes has been shot down," the staff officer teased, trying to keep the tone light. "We haven't scrambled any squadrons yet today."

"I'm not calling about a replacement. I'm calling about an experienced Flight Commander – and I'm not going to hang up until you tell me one is on the way. Things just can't go on the way they are. The CO is killing himself."

"Now hold on, Mickey. It's not my fault the last Flight Lieutenant I sent you turned out to have jaundice."

"I'm not saying it was your fault, Ken; I'm just saying that the situation hasn't improved – in fact, it's worse than ever. And it's no good sending us sprogs with less than 20 hours on Hurricanes, either! All that does is add to the burden, because Priestman won't let them fly ops until they have at least 20 hours, and so he has to detail one of his experienced pilots to train them – if he doesn't insist on training them himself. He's led every sortie personally since he's been here, and I'm telling you now that he can't keep this up. If you don't send him an experienced Flight Commander soon, you're going to be looking for a Squadron Leader, too.

It's as simple as that."

"Slow down long enough for me to get a word in edgeways, would you, Mickey? It's all very well for you to demand a Flight Commander, but they don't just come off assembly lines."

"I know that as well as you do; but if you don't get someone down here soon, you're going to lose the whole squadron!"

"There's no need to exaggerate."

"I'm not exaggerating. They are nearly finished – *very* nearly finished – and he's the only thing keeping them going. If he breaks – or gets shot down and killed or seriously injured – there is no one here who can fill the gap. They'll go to pieces."

There was a long pause and then the Personnel Officer agreed grimly, "I'll see what I can do."

Warrant Officer Robinson met Bridges as he came on duty in the Operations Room just after lunch. Bridges had stopped by the Salvation Army canteen to say hello to Emily Pryce before coming to the Ops Room and was running just a little late. It was such a lovely day out there, and he hated burying himself in this bunker. Robinson greeted him with: "They've issued Invasion Alert Nr. 1, sir." That meant "Attack Imminent."

Bridges felt as if it had just become a little more difficult to breathe in the stuffy operations room, but he replied calmly. "What have we got on the table?"

"Nothing yet, sir. Group believes Jerry is holding back his planes to protect the invasion barges. There was unusual activity in the Channel all night, and reconnaissance reported troop movements as well."

"Right, then, we'll soon see if we're ready." Bridges went to his desk and sat down. Bridges wondered if he should tell his squadrons about the Invasion Alert. Would it increase their keenness – or only strain their nerves beyond the breaking point? In a way, it might almost be a relief when the "show" really did begin. And if Jerry thought that he'd succeeded in knocking out the Sector Airfields he'd been targeting for the last week, he'd have a rude awakening.

Despite Jerry bombing Biggin Hill ten times in the last seven days, it was still operational – although Bridges was jolly glad not to be a controller there! More than once, they had been knocked about so badly that the control of Biggin Hill squadrons had been temporarily passed over to neighbouring sector controllers. At Kenley, the Station Commander had blown up the last of his remaining hangars himself, to make it look as though the station was finished and so discourage further raids. The ruse appeared to have worked because it had been left alone since.

Briefly, Bridges wondered if they should do the same, but it wasn't his decision. He looked down at the WAAFs waiting patiently around the empty table. What a marvellous group of girls they were! They had all attended ACW Hadley's funeral, and Corporal Winters was back at her post despite the cast she was wearing.

Bridges risked a quick glance in the direction of Jane Roberts. He'd had a very pleasant evening with her the other night, but of course, if things were going to get personal, he'd have to ask to have her transferred to another job. It wouldn't do to work all too closely with her, if they started seeing one another socially. Think about that tomorrow, he told himself. There was an invasion alert, for God's sake! It was a warm, sunny day. The air was calm. The Channel would be as placid as a pond. Bridges sighed.

Ginger settled himself in the shade around the side of the dispersal, his back against the wooden side of the hut, and tried to collect his thoughts. For the moment, he didn't even want Banks near him – although he was very glad that the Canadian was still with the squadron rather than accepting the CO's offer of a posting to Training Command. That was selfish, of course, and Ginger supposed he ought to pray to God for forgiveness and more strength; but the fact was, he had another, more urgent problem at the moment. In the Order of Battle today, Ginger was down as Section Leader.

Ginger wasn't at all comfortable with that. Part of him resented that the CO had done it without even consulting him. He'd just chalked him in with a casual, "That's all right with you, isn't it, Ginger?" tossed over his shoulder.

Ginger could hardly say "no" in front of everyone, so of course he'd shrugged and said: "If you think I'm up to it, Skipper."

They were down to 12 pilots again, and although Ringwood had been given his second stripe and officially raised to "B" Flight Commander, it was pretty obvious that Sutton and Donohue were slowly losing their wool. Donohue had developed a twitch in his right eye, and Sutton's hands had spasms of violent shaking that seemed completely random – in the Mess at breakfast, lighting up a cigarette in the pub, reading a newspaper at dispersal.

Ginger wriggled uncomfortably in his Mae West, feeling hot and sticky. Then he leaned forward and pulled the life-jacket off entirely. Banks came around the side of the dispersal hut looking for Ginger, and at once sat down next to him. "Something the matter?"

Ginger discovered he wasn't so unhappy with company after all. Without hesitation he confided, "I don't understand why the CO just made me Section Leader. Needham and Ware are both better pilots."

"No, they're not," Banks countered loyally, leaning back against the dispersal hut and resting his hands on his bent knees. "But I heard him talking to Mickey about giving all the pilots a day off one after another as soon as some replacement pilots arrive, so he's got to have some back-up Section Leaders."

Ginger thought about that. It made sense.

The voices from in front of the dispersal suddenly got quite excited, and Ginger and Banks looked at each other. Several people seemed to be talking at once but they couldn't quite make out what was being said. Their eyes met, and by mutual, unspoken consent they pushed themselves on their feet and went around to the front of dispersal.

The other pilots were all on their feet around Allars, who was making calming gestures and scowling. "No one is reporting landings yet; it's just an alert."

"Invasion Alert!" Ringwood snapped back. "They haven't issued that before."

"Well, actually they have – but maybe the news didn't filter down to you because—"

"Why aren't we kept informed?" Ware interrupted irritably.

"Because it causes a flap, as we can see," Allars countered calmly.

"Well, it was pretty obvious *something* was up," Donohue retorted. "It's nearly 2 o'clock already, and it's been *ages* since Jerry let us have lunch in peace."

Ginger felt his stomach turn over – and he wasn't even in the air. If the invasion was to be launched, this was the last day he ought to be leading a section. Maybe he should talk to the CO about it? He glanced over at the Squadron Leader, who was off to one side talking to Tolkien. Tolkien had pranged a kite yesterday from sheer bad flying. The CO was furious – not because of the u/s kite, but because he said he couldn't trust Tolkien to fly with the squadron if he couldn't fly better than that.

The CO's face was thin, and his eyes were sunk in their sockets. His hair was hanging in his forehead as usual, but rather than giving him a boyish charm, it just looked unkempt. He'd shaved badly, too. It was obvious that the CO was none too happy about the state they were in. Nor was Ginger.

At 15.54 the first plot finally went on the board, but within minutes it was obvious that it was a massive raid. By 16.16 the Observer Corps had "hundreds of aircraft" in sight – and even these veterans of two wars and months of hard fighting were overwhelmed by what they saw. Post after post reported in evident agitation. By 16.30, every squadron within 70 miles of London was in the air or at readiness.

Park had recently issued orders for squadrons to be deployed in pairs – ideally, a Spitfire squadron to deal with the Messerschmitts and a Hurricane squadron to attack the bombers. Bridges therefore scrambled 17 (Hurricane) and 602 (Spitfire) squadrons first. When at 16.58 Bridges was asked to scramble his remaining two squadrons, 606 and 607, they were both Hurricane squadrons. Bridges sent 606 – which was more experienced and better led – in the covering role, and 607 for the bombers.

The pilots of these squadrons had heard and watched as 17 took off and seen the vapour trails of 602 as they swept upwards from Westhampnett. Anxiously asking if invasion barges had been sighted, they had already learned that the target appeared to be the airfields around London yet again – but in a single raid of unprecedented proportions. "Observer Corps is putting the bomber formations at 350 aircraft with an escort of double that."

The odd thing about this was that all previous raids on the airfields had been made by relatively small groups of bombers with much higher escort ratios. Why so many bombers this time? Did the Germans think their raids had been ineffective because of too little concentrated explosive? What if they were right?

606 Squadron had only been airborne a few minutes when Bridges broke in over the RT. "Redcap Squadron, the bandits appear to be targeting London."

Priestman acknowledged and strained his eyes as he searched the sky ahead of him; his gaze swept back and forth as he tried to penetrate the haze. At first, he couldn't believe what he gradually started to see. Dark specks that could only be aircraft were so plentiful that they dappled the entire sky – like a swarm of gnats or mosquitoes in the tropics. Mosquitoes in neat formation. Robin thought he'd seen a lot in the last few months, but this sight stunned him. Then his pilots saw them.

"Oh my God!"

"Would you look at that!"

"There are thousands of them!"

"Crikey – it's worse than Piccadilly Circus at rush hour!" Although they knew that 602 and 17 had to be out here somewhere – and dozens of other RAF squadrons as well – they couldn't see them anywhere. 607 was below and on the right because they'd been vectored simultaneously as a team, but visually no one in 606 could see any other RAF squadron. It made them feel far more out-numbered than they actually were.

Ginger couldn't help himself. After several days with only brief nausea, he found this sight so terrifying that it hit his stomach as the first sorties had. He just barely managed to unclip his oxygen mask and grab his paper bag before he lost his lunch into it. Oh, God, he prayed mutely. Oh, God, help me. Through his earphones came the unperturbed voice of the CO. "Redcap Blue Leader, can you deal with those 109s peeling off towards us?"

"Piece of cake, Skipper," came the sarcastic reply from Woody. There were at least 40 enemy fighters some 2000 feet above them, sliding into their attack. Ringwood had a total of four aircraft under his command.

The remaining two sections were flying straight for another swarm of 109s that was wheeling around to face them. "Redcap Yellow Leader, take your section down against the 110s."

Ginger flinched inwardly as he realised that meant *him* – and he hadn't even seen the aircraft the skipper was talking about. About 2000 feet below them was a formation of 110s flying low cover over the bombers another 2-3,000 feet below them. Ginger tasted vomit in his mouth again, and for a horrible second thought he was going to be sick right into the oxygen mask, but he managed to swallow it down and reply, "Roger, Redcap Leader."

He glanced over his shoulders, first right towards Green and Reynolds and then left towards Tolkien. Then he dipped his left wing and started sliding down towards the designated targets, blocking out all other thoughts and sounds.

The Me110 was faster than a Hurricane at these altitudes, but fortunately these particular aircraft were tied to the slower bombers below them. In a shallow dive, Ginger's section slowly overtook them. A sudden flurry of tracer fire from the aft-guns of the 110s indicated the RAF had been sighted by their quarry, and at once the 110s abandoned their flying formation to form a defensive circle.

Ginger concluded that they must have practised this manoeuvre often because they performed it to perfection, but it was purely defensive in nature and posed no threat. He pushed the stick forward, slipped under the "circus," and then came up again in the middle to start circling in the opposite direction, raking one enemy after another. Tolkien was still with him, while Green and Reynolds swooped about like a couple of happy swallows, taking pot-shots at targets of opportunity.

It was impossible to record individual hits, but in what seemed like a very short time, several of the enemy aircraft started smoking and lagging. The port engine of one burst into brilliant flame and a moment later the wing dropped off entirely, leaving the fuselage to keel over and then plunge downwards with a plume of smoke marking its rapid descent.

Instantly, Green plunged through the gap left by the downed fighter, firing at the plane that had been ahead of it at very close range before diving away. This surprised aircraft took violent evasive action by breaking hard to the right, causing the entire defensive circle to break apart. It was now "every man for himself."

Ginger tried to fasten on one of the diving 110s, but this was spewing smoke from both engines – not from damage, but from asking the maximum from them – and it soon pulled away from him. As it dived shallowly, turning gently, however, Ginger caught sight of the earth below. With horror he realised they were over London. Below him was a landscape of concrete and brick: row after row of housing crowded against the narrow streets, their back gardens pressed together.

Ginger had been raised in the country. He'd only passed through London once or twice, and he had never before been so conscious of how densely populated London was. There must be thousands of people living down there – *tens of thousands!* He couldn't calculate it, just sense it like one does the force of a gale that nearly knocks you off your feet. He was terrified by the sight of so much humanity crushed together.

Further away, the sun glistened silver on the lazy curves of the Thames, and Ginger could make out cranes, warehouses and ships lying alongside quays. There were huge oil tanks squatting beside the river and a gas works. Around the latter, little puffs of smoke marked the ack-ack. An instant later, huge black clouds erupted into the air.

Ginger shoved the throttle through the wire and kicked his rudder pedal hard, racing across the city to try to intercept the bombers, which were sedately dumping their loads of high explosive on the dockyards.

These bombers appeared to have come this far completely unmolested, because they still flew in neat formation. As Ginger closed, the lead section of three aircraft climbed up and away from their target. The next rows sank down towards the oil-tanks for their bomb run.

Ginger could see it all too well: the bombs tumbling out of the bellies of the bombers, the eruptions of smoke and dust running across the city in tight little patterns. He saw houses crumbling and collapsing before they were obscured by the debris flung into the air. Then a flash of light blinded him for a second followed by a pressure wave that yanked the Hurricane temporarily out of his control. The gas works had gone up in flames.

Ginger just managed to swing wide of the inferno shooting upwards. Deaf to the protesting howl of his Hurricane, he charged after the bombers. Still in formation, they banked contemptuously, turning away from the destruction they had caused and started for home.

"I'll get you!" Ginger screamed after them, as he flew straight through the smoke and debris that had been flung thousands of feet into the air by the explosion. "Bastards!" He sensed more than thought that such an explosion would have levelled blocks of housing, crushing people in their humble cellars, shattering even prepared shelters.

For all the fighting he had seen in the last months, for all the fear and strain, the injuries and deaths in the squadron, it wasn't until this moment that Ginger *hated* the enemy. He hated them with a searing, blinding fury that made him deaf to Tolkien's shouts. "Yellow One! Break! Break!" He did not hear the warning nor even feel the cannon shells hammering into his Hurricane. For him it was all part of the same madness.

"Ginger! Break! Break!" Tolkien screamed helplessly into the R/T. He pressed his own Hurricane to the limit, trying to get in range of the Me110 that was so close behind Ginger that it seemed to be nibbling at the delicate, wood-and-canvas tail of the little fighter. But he'd turned wider than Ginger and had lost ground. He was lagging almost 500 yards behind his leader when the Messerschmitt with its superior speed swooped down seemingly out of nowhere. He was still a couple of hundred yards out of range when the Me110 with its four forward machine guns and two cannons got Ginger's Hurricane in its sights.

If Ginger had reacted to Tolkien's shouts instantly, the greater manoeuvrability of his Hurricane might have saved him, but he was oblivious to the danger. Even as his own guns at last found their mark, Tolkien saw Ginger's tail disintegrate under the combined fire of the Me110's guns, and then the cannon were hammering into the back of Ginger's seat.

"Ginger!" Tolkien screamed one last time. But it was as much a howl of frustration and outrage – even horror – as a warning.

Tolkien would swear for the rest of his life that even then, as the bullet-proof glass of the Hurricane shattered and turned red under the 20mm cannon shells, Ginger continued firing. The bomber, Tolkien told Allars insistently, was hit *after* the canopy of the Hurricane had become opaque with blood. And then the gallant Hurricane's fuel tank erupted, and the remnants of the shattered aircraft crashed into the flaming chaos of the dock-yards below.

Robin's knees were shaking as he slipped off the wing onto the grass of the airfield. He paused there, leaning against the wing, to get hold of himself. Ripley and Appleby quickly assessed his state and with an exchanged glance, withdrew to the other side of the Hurricane. It wasn't that he was in anyway unpleasant to them when he was in this state, but they respected his need to be left alone for a bit before facing anyone after a difficult sortie.

Kiwi alone had managed to stay with him until they were both out of ammunition. His Hurricane had stopped a short distance away, but Robin had counted the squadron aircraft while on the circuit and knew that two were missing. He'd also heard Tolkien screaming at Ginger, and he feared the worst. The other missing aircraft was Reynolds'.

Robin thought he'd seen the worst, but the dimensions of this raid had shaken him. That the Luftwaffe could still put that many aircraft into the air at once was shattering. It was as if the RAF had had no impact on the Luftwaffe's strength at all. Likewise, although he knew that hundreds of RAF fighters had engaged – and had personally caught occasional glimpses of Hurricanes and Spitfires from other squadrons – it still seemed as if they were vastly out-numbered. Undaunted by the odds, my arse!

But it was Ginger that got to him. He found himself praying that the worst hadn't happened after all. Maybe he'd managed to get out in time, as he had twice before. Ginger was officer material. He'd been planning to recommend him for a commission – he just hadn't found the time to do the paperwork yet....

It was just after 6 pm, and the sun was settling down into the haze on the horizon. The air was distinctly cooler and a light breeze had sprung up. Robin tossed his helmet onto the wing and ran his hand through his hair, which was wet and sticky. He unclipped his parachute and left it on the wing, noticing as he did so that his "brand new" Hurricane of less than three weeks ago was looking rather run down.

Allars was coming towards him. With a sigh, Robin leaned back against the trailing edge of the wing, arms crossed over his Mae West, and waited.

Allars' face was marked by pain, and he grimaced a bit as he swung his wooden leg forward. He came to a halt three feet away. They gazed at each other. "Any good news?" Allars asked.

Robin felt the urge to shout at him: how the hell can there be any good news in circumstances like these!? Even if he'd shot down a dozen of the bastards, Robin felt it wouldn't qualify as good news. Killing was still killing, and what were a dozen enemy aircraft downed when there were still so many hundreds of them? He controlled himself and just shook his head stiffly before countering, "What happened to Bowles?"

"I'm sorry to say, he's dead."

"No hope?"

"Absolutely none. Tolkien saw his Hurricane shot to pieces by an Me110, and says the hood was covered with blood even before the fuel tank exploded and the Hurricane went in from 3000 feet. There was no parachute, and the Hurricane crashed in the midst of the flames of the burning dockyards."

No, there was no hope whatsoever. Sergeant Pilot George "Ginger"

Bowles was dead. Why did that seem so unreal? Robin had never had so much difficulty accepting a casualty before.

Kiwi emerged around the tail of Robin's Hurricane, but he must have heard what Allars had just said, because he looked stunned – and deflated. The big, imperturbable bear looked like a limp, defeated man. He even seemed smaller than usual – as if half the air had gone out of him.

"What about Reynolds?" Robin persisted.

"Green saw him bail out, but he hasn't called in yet. It is unclear if he was injured or not."

"Anyone else injured?"

"Ware has some shrapnel in his calf and foot, but the MO seems to think he'll be fit to fly."

Robin refrained from making a caustic remark about the MO deciding how much pain a man "ought" to be able to stand and still do his job well. Allars seemed to sense his thoughts, however, because he spoke soothingly, "It really isn't bad, Robin, and Ware himself insisted he'd be fine."

Robin was standing with his arms and ankles crossed, his seat resting on the trailing edge of the Hurricane. Allars could almost smell his hostility, and he hesitated to continue. "Anything on the table?"

Allars gratefully shook his head. "No. Nothing. They threw everything at us in that one massive raid, it seems. Ah, Robin...." He still hesitated.

"What?"

"You'd better talk to Tolkien."

Robin was about to ask why but decided against it. Instead he uncrossed his ankles, pushed himself off the wing and started back towards the dispersal. "Any claims, by the way?" he remembered to ask Allars as the older man lurched along beside him.

"Donohue says he got a 109, Green chalked up one 110 certainly and another possible, Ringwood says he damaged a 109 – and Tolkien claims the bomber Ginger targeted crashed with him into the gas works. That's all, I'm afraid – unless you have something, Kiwi?" He glanced at the New Zealander with this question, but Kiwi morosely shook his head.

There had been so many of the yellow-nosed bastards about that they were themselves attacked and had to break off every time they tried to latch onto something. At some point fairly early on in the scrap, Banks and Sutton had been lost in the ruckus, but Kiwi had followed his leader as he doggedly tried to claw something out of the sky. In the end, they were out of ammo with nothing to show for it – bad enough without Ginger being dead on top of it.

At dispersal all the pilots were sitting about in silence. Not one of them was talking – or even reading or eating. Several had cigarettes, others held mugs of tea, but no one had touched the sandwiches awaiting them.

Odd. Ginger had been a loner – a barely tolerated outsider – when Priestman had arrived at the squadron less than three weeks ago. The response now was a tribute to how much he'd come to be respected and liked in the end.

The pilots all looked up at Priestman as he entered. What the bloody hell did they expect of him? He couldn't bring back the dead! He looked for Tolkien, his eyes sweeping across their tired faces, and stopped briefly on Banks'. Their eyes met. Banks looked stunned, as though he couldn't grasp what had happened. Robin's eyes continued and realised that Tolkien wasn't here.

Allars muttered into his ear that Tolkien was in his office. Priestman turned and entered the little cubicle at the end of the dispersal. Tolkien was hunched over in the guest chair, holding his head in his hands. He caught his breath and jumped up at the sound of the door closing. Priestman waved him back down. He sank onto the chair, but his eyes were fixed on his CO as if afraid of something.

"Allars told me the details, Tolkien."

"Did he – did he say it was my fault, sir?"

"Of course not. Why should he?"

"If – if I hadn't lost station. If I'd been where I should have been—"

"No one can keep station in a mix-up like that. You couldn't have been doing so badly or you wouldn't have seen what happened—"

"But I was out of range!" the youngster protested, in an agony of guilt.

Priestman sank onto his desk exhausted. "Look, *I* heard you warning him. You ordered him to break several times. You did all that you could do. You've been at it long enough to know that we often get completely isolated from one another. It's the nature of the kind of fighting we do – always against superior odds and flying at over 300 mph. No one blames you for what happened to Ginger."

"His Dad will," Tolkien whispered, so softly that Robin barely heard him.

Robin remembered the stocky, ill-dressed man who had waited so piteously in his office the last time Ginger was shot down and believed killed. He could picture him vividly still – the too-short sleeves and trousers, the stubby fingers with ingrained dirt, the thick, red neck and the eyes of a bullock on the way to slaughter.

"Ginger and I may not have been close friends, sir, but he was as close to his Dad as I am to mine – not like the others."

Priestman nodded, and it dawned on him that he was going to have to write Ginger's father a letter of condolence. It was a horrible prospect, absolutely debilitating, actually.

The telephone on the desk rang and both pilots started violently. Then Tolkien went stock still, while Priestman grabbed the receiver. "Priestman."

Mickey was on the line. "Good news, Robin. Reynolds just rang in. He says he fractured his wrist hitting the tail fin as he abandoned his crashing Hurricane, but it's been put in a cast at St. Mary's Southwark and he'll be back with us by tomorrow."

"Well done. Thanks." Priestman hung up and passed the news on to Tolkien, who dutifully nodded and murmured something mildly positive. Priestman considered the young man in front of him with sympathy and then turned and picked up the telephone again. He put a call through to Bridges. "What's on the table?"

"Nothing. Absolutely nothing."

"What about standing us down then?"

There was a pause. Priestman gathered that there must be counter-orders. Bridges wasn't the kind of controller to keep them at readiness out of spite or misplaced zealousness. He'd almost resigned himself to a negative answer when Bridges said, "Yes, stand down."

"Thanks, I owe you one."

Priestman hung up and turned to Tolkien. "We've been stood down. Go and tell the others and take the rest of the day off. Maybe talking to your father would help," he suggested a little lamely.

Tolkien nodded and said, "Thank you, sir."

Priestman just stood leaning against his desk while the others filed out of the dispersal. A fly was buzzing about his in-box as if to draw attention to everything still in it. With a sigh, he went around behind his desk to get to work. There was a knock on the door. "Yes?"

Banks entered. "Sir?"

"Yes?"

"I'd like permission to drive down to Devon and deliver the news to Ginger's father personally."

Robin's first reaction was that the foreigner didn't have any idea of how far away Devon was. "It will take the rest of the day just to get there, and you'll have to turn around and drive all night to get back by tomorrow morning," he replied simply.

"If you give me tomorrow off, you'd still have ten pilots on readiness," Banks answered.

"That's assuming that both Ware and Reynolds fly injured," Robin pointed out sharply. Of course, they had both *said* they would, but it still seemed a bit unfair.

"Please, sir. We can't just send Mr. Bowles a telegram – it will kill him. And if I go, it will save you having to write a letter. We – Colin and I – can say all the things you would have said, sir, and it will be so much better coming from us face-to-face."

Priestman sighed, ran his hand through his hair, sighed again, and then nodded. What the hell difference did it make if they were 11 against 600 or just 10 to 600? "Tell him that his son was the bravest man I have ever had the honour to know."

"I will, sir. We'll be back as soon as possible, sir," Goldman assured him and went out, closing the door behind him.

Devon
8 September 1940

It was already starting to get light by the time Banks and Colin reached the Bowles cottage. They had made good progress at first, but then become thoroughly lost and confused on the dark, unmarked, country roads at the very end of the journey. At last they encountered a man on a bicycle, on his way to work in the pre-dawn light, who was able to direct them. Shortly afterwards they located the low and run-down cottage on the edge of the moors. They turned off the engine and sat for a moment in the gloom of pre-dawn, exhausted and dispirited.

"I suppose we ought to wait a bit," Banks suggested. "He'll be asleep now. We could sleep for an hour or so."

But from inside the cottage came the frantic barking of a dog. They exchanged a look of fathomless dread. "Bessie." Colin remembered the dog's name from Ginger's frequent accounts of her virtues.

"Might as well get it over with," Banks answered, swinging the door open and climbing out. He let the heavy door fall shut with a crunch. Colin slid out of the driver's side and his door fell shut, too.

From inside the house they could hear Mr. Bowles calling to the dog, "Hush, Bessie! What's got you all upset?"

Banks went around the car and stood beside Colin. They just waited. A moment later the cottage door opened and they could decipher a stocky, barefooted figure. The dog leapt out of the darkness and bounded towards them, barking loudly. She stopped abruptly but continued to bark while wagging her tail. She was confused and protective but not really hostile.

"Ginger?" Mr. Bowles had recognized the RAF uniform on the shadowy figures before his cottage in the waxing light, but Bessie's reception warned him that it couldn't be Ginger. "No, Mr. Bowles." Colin found his voice first and started forward, Banks in his wake.

As they approached, Mr. Bowles recognised them and started to smile. He held out his hand, but then realized why his son's friends had come in the middle of the night. He froze and then took a step backwards as if he could escape the message they carried. "Ginger." It wasn't a question any more.

"We're so sorry, Mr. Bowles," Colin murmured, stopping.

Mr. Bowles glanced at Banks as if hoping he would have a different message, but he saw only the shock on the young man's face and he closed his eyes, unable to bear it.

Colin stepped forward and took his arm. Gently he guided Mr. Bowles back into the cottage.

Neither Banks nor Colin had ever been in a home so humble. The old, half-timbered cottage had lacked a woman's hand for decades. While the surface of things had been cleaned, dirt and cobwebs had collected in all the "out of the way" places and then slowly started to creep forward, conquering more space from year to year. In confusing disarray, work-tools, newspapers, supplies, and unfinished projects littered the main room. There was a distinct smell of dog in the air, and a bone had been left in the middle of the very threadbare rug.

It took Colin only a second to shove aside his shock and focus again on Mr. Bowles. Although strong as an ox, he stumbled, and Colin had to hold him up as far as the sofa. Bowles collapsed onto it and with a loud gasp started to cry. Colin sat down beside him, and Banks put a hand on his shoulder from behind. They said nothing. There didn't seem to be any need for it. Bessie too tried to comfort her master; she laid her head on her master's knees and gazed up at him in silent sympathy.

Eventually, Mr. Bowles got hold of himself. He wiped his wet cheeks with the backs of his hands and, sobbing for breath, he started to talk. "He was my only joy, the only thing that made life meaningful. I mean, what am I? What good am I to any one? But Ginger—" He broke off, overcome again, his face crinkling up and the tears glittering in the darkness. He gasped for breath once, then held his breath until he had control of himself again. "How? When?"

"He was shot down over London trying to stop one of the bombers. You must have heard the news." Colin spoke softly, glancing up at Banks for reassurance. They had heard the news again and again on the car radio. London had been bombed again after darkness. The entire dockyards were reportedly ablaze, vast areas of the East End were in ruins, whole streets of housing had been destroyed, and 2000 civilian casualties were being reported.

Mr. Bowles nodded, holding his fist to his mouth to stop himself from gasping again.

"Tolkien warned Ginger he was being attacked from behind, but Ginger was so determined to get the bomber that he just ignored the warnings." Banks provided this information, and again Mr. Bowles nodded. He held his eyes pressed shut, but the tears escaped anyway.

"Can we make you a cup of tea, Mr. Bowles?" Colin asked. Mr. Bowles nodded, and Colin looked about until he spotted what he supposed was the kitchen. He stood and gestured for Banks to take his place before disappearing into it.

Banks started talking softly to Mr. Bowles as the latter fondled his dog absently. "Squadron Leader Priestman asked us to tell you that your son was the bravest man he had ever met."

That brought one short gasp from Mr. Bowles. Then he gasped out, "Thank him for me – but–" He cut himself off and fell silent.

Banks felt helpless and glanced in the direction of the kitchen, wishing for reinforcements.

Mr. Bowles started speaking again. "Ginger was so much more than brave. He was ...." He fell silent, unable to put into words the essence of his son.

The kettle started to whistle. It was turned off. From the kitchen came the clatter of cutlery and pottery. At last Colin emerged from the kitchen a chipped teapot, chipped mugs, milk in a bottle and sugar in a bag loaded on a tray. Banks had the presence of mind to jump up and clear a space for the tray on the table. Colin set the tray down. Banks sat down again beside Mr. Bowles. Colin – after putting a stack of old newspapers on the floor – sat down in a dilapidated armchair opposite. Banks looked towards him, pleading silently for him to say something.

It wasn't necessary; Mr. Bowles resumed speaking on his own. "Ginger was so pleased to have you as his friends. He never had friends before. Growing up here alone, he never had much chance. At school they looked down on him – even when he was better than them. You were the first friends he ever had – and such fine young men. You meant the world to him."

Colin and Banks exchanged a look, and Colin spoke for them both, "And he to us." His voice was shaky with emotion. After all, he'd been driving all night, and the reality of Ginger's death was sinking in.

Mr. Bowles at once reached out and grasped Colin's hand in his own great paw and clutched it hard. It almost hurt, but it calmed him a little, too. "That he had friends like you – it shows how much better he was than I could ever be. He never really belonged here – in this hovel," Mr. Bowles gestured vaguely to his run-down cottage. "He was made for better things."

Colin and Banks looked at one another helplessly again. Better things? Having his body ripped apart by 20mm explosive shells?

"He was everything I had in the world," Mr. Bowles repeated, "and without him—" He broke off. Bessie, whining miserably, pawed at his knee.

With his free hand, Mr. Bowles fondled her behind the ears. "I don't know how I'll go on without him, but I have no right – no right whatsoever – to complain. I have been so lucky."

Colin and Banks stared first at one another and then at Mr. Bowles again, baffled and speechless.

Mr. Bowles continued, "God in his mercy lent Ginger to me. He let me have that wonderful young man for 20 years. Me – a worthless, stupid, good-for-nothing! He sent me one of His own great treasures – a boy so good and so full of life and love that even He could not stand to be parted from him for long. He let me have him for 20 years. That is more than I ever deserved."

As Mr. Bowles spoke, tears streamed from his eyes and his nose, but although he was in pain, he was not angry or bitter or even bewildered.

Chapter 38

Boulogne
8 September 1940

What a change from her last visit, right after Rosa's death! Klaudia looked utterly transformed as she came through the door of his hospital room – and it almost frightened Ernst to see her looking *so* lovely. Looking as she did right now, every healthy male in the world would find her attractive – and she was surrounded by too many of those! She was wearing her hair differently, too (although Ernst would have been at a loss to explain just what was different about it). She was even wearing lipstick and perfume. It dizzied him a little as she bent over to kiss him on both cheeks.

"Dieter drove me over, Ernst. He's come to visit too," she said with a glance over her shoulder. Ernst realised that he had been so busy feasting his eyes on Klaudia that he hadn't even noticed that Dieter was with her.

Dieter smiled at him and held out his hand. "Sorry I didn't have the chance to come earlier, Ernst. How are you doing?"

"Fine; I'll be released next week. The wounds are healing fine. It's just a matter of being stiff and sore and all that."

Dieter nodded, and Ernst knew by his expression that he thought Ernst was lying.

"What do you hear from Christian?"

"Christian? He's threatening to 'escape' back to France. He's terribly afraid he'll miss the invasion." Dieter's tone was astonishingly lighthearted. Indeed, the usually sober and almost morose Dieter was actually grinning.

"Klaudia said things have been pretty tough," Ernst remarked with a quick glance at her.

"They *have* been, yes, but we've finally done it, Ernst. We've broken the back of Tommy Fighter Command." Ernst wouldn't have believed it if anyone else – even Klaudia – had told him that. But Dieter had shared Christian's scepticism from the start, and Ernst had never known him to be taken in by mere propaganda, much less engage in bravado.

Yet he still found himself asking sceptically, "You're sure?" He just couldn't believe that things could have changed so radically.

Dieter grinned. "Yesterday, when we struck at London, and there was almost no resistance. We put up every operational aircraft we had in both

Luftflotte Two and Three – over a thousand aircraft in one massive raid, and they had nothing – or practically nothing – left to stop us with!" Dieter was clearly delighted.

"What happened to their fighters, then?" Ernst wanted to know.

"You know, intelligence has been saying for weeks that their aircraft production couldn't keep up with the losses we inflicted, but apparently, they were able to pull aircraft in from other parts of the country – maybe even from the Colonies for a while. I don't know.

"But after weeks and weeks of fighting with no apparent progress, suddenly the Tommies were gone – and with so many bombers, it wasn't just that they didn't *want* to fight. We set half of London ablaze, Ernst. The light from the fires could be seen all the way to Calais at night! And they lit the way for the night bombers, too. JG 53 went in and out without encountering a *single* enemy fighter, Ernst! Not one! And the bombers reported only 4% casualties – can you imagine that? Less than 15 bombers lost for the sake of smashing London's entire dockyards! Ships were hit and warehouses, and a gas works. We haven't seen anything like it since Amsterdam."

Ernst was surprised by Dieter's enthusiasm. He wasn't usually bloodthirsty. Ernst could only suppose that the slow attrition of the past weeks had made even a gentle soul like Dieter anxious to get it over with.

"So you see, if you don't get better soon, you may be rejoining the *Geschwader* in London," Klaudia teased with a smile and reaching for his hand possessively. She was so relieved that the RAF was finally broken. Of course, there had been some casualties among the fighters – apparently the 110s had suffered again, but it looked like the risks to Ernst were going to be much, much lower in the future than in the past. With luck, it would all be over before he was released from hospital.

Klaudia wondered what it would be like being stationed in England. Even here in France she felt uncomfortable among the local population. She knew she was resented, and the Luftwaffe had frequently warned about radical elements among the French population who refused to accept their defeat. There had even been isolated incidents when French fanatics attacked the German occupation authorities when they thought they could get away with it. Klaudia suspected that things might be worse in England. After all, after so much bombing, the English were bound to hate the Germans more – or would they have the sense to blame their own government for stubbornly rejecting Hitler's generous offers of a compromise peace?

London

That was exactly the question that preoccupied Howard Briggs of the *Detroit Times* at this moment, too. In the last 24 hours, he and his photographer Joe Gonzales had experienced the most hectic and frantic hours of their lives.

First, they had taken refuge, like all other sensible people, in the shelters near their offices on Fleet Street. That's where Joe and he had run into that swank Brit reporter, Virginia Cox-Gordon. As soon as the "All Clear" sounded, they had tried – rather unsuccessfully at first – to get near the burning and damaged parts of the city farther east and south. Virginia had proved a terrific help, whoe really knew her way around London!

Unfortunately, their efforts had been thwarted not only by blocked-off streets where unexploded bombs threatened to go off and rubble, but by officious air-raid wardens, grim policemen and excited firemen, all insistent that they "keep away."

After harassing, pleading, and bullying their way closer and closer to the worst-hit area of the great city – Canning Town – the sirens had gone off again. The three reporters had soon discovered to their horror that there weren't enough official air-raid shelters here where they were most needed. Along with hundreds of other distressed and near-panicking civilians, they forced their way through the barriers of an Underground station and took refuge on the train platform.

The experience was sobering. No one had prepared the Underground for such an invasion, and the sanitary facilities were completely overwhelmed. In consequence, more and more of the refugees made use of the tracks, which was pretty disgusting. Nor was a well-brought-up young lady like Virginia used to being crushed together with "the unwashed masses." She naturally found the smells and the rude tone of the crowd very unnerving.

They were all very relieved to hear the All Clear and stampeded like the rest of the people towards the exits, only to find themselves in a new nightmare. The sky was lit up a lurid, smoky red, and the smell of burning rubber from a near-by warehouse made the heavy, smoke-laden air almost impossible to breathe. The sirens and bells of fire engines and ambulances seemed to surround them. Several fire engines sprayed the fronts of burning buildings. Ash and embers blew through the air, burning with sharp pin-pricks.

Howard shouted to Virginia that she had better try to get back to somewhere safe, while he and Joe went on alone. But the girl was spunky insisted on coming with them.

They soon discovered that fires were burning in every direction, and just getting back to the West End became an ordeal. Dawn was already greying the sky when they finally made it to Bayswater Road, and Virginia had been hobbling badly with blisters on both feet from her silly (if pretty) high-heeled shoes. Their faces were also black with soot and their clothes ruined by the ash, cinders and sweat. They reached the Americans' hotel, and Howard invited Virginia in to get rested and cleaned up. The concierge looked at them askance – and then rang for the hotel doctor.

The doctor didn't answer; it seemed he had already responded to a call from St. John's Ambulance Corps and gone into the East End to help out at one of the emergency first-aid stations. There were no taxis either, so Virginia had taken a room, while the two Americans dragged themselves up to their respective rooms, bathed and fell asleep.

But a reporter can't afford to sleep for long in a situation like this. First, Howard had to file a story on what he had seen the night before, and second, he had to get back out onto the streets and start getting the commentary and analysis. His first story, which he sent off just after noon London time, focused exclusively on the physical aspects of the German raid. Howard Briggs wrote:

Germans Launch Massive Air-Assault on London

In what appears to be the opening act of the final assault on the British Isles, the German Air Force demonstrated its superiority by launching a massive raid on London on Sunday. Reportedly more than a thousand German aircraft participated in the raid, dropping tens of thousands of tons of high explosive on the British capital.

The raid concentrated on the dockyards, with the apparent objective of choking England's vital life-line to its overseas Empire. Merchant vessels, which had successfully braved the U-Boat infested waters of the North Atlantic, found themselves trapped helplessly at the quay. As they attempted to off-load their precious cargoes in the heart of the Metropolis, they fell victim to the merciless rain of destruction from above.

Beside the burning hulks of the ships, warehouses full of vitally needed war supplies, from rubber to potatoes, were soon reduced to smoldering rubble. And all around the heart of the Docklands, the shabby, crowded houses of the dockyard workers were pulverized by the bombs, the flames and the shockwaves, which spread out from the center of the raid.

This raid claimed thousands of civilian casualties, and throughout the city fires continue to burn. This makes it impossible to currently calculate the full extent of the destruction to either life or property.

The inadequacies of the preparations for this inevitable contingency were rapidly apparent. The number of public air raid shelters proved woefully inadequate for the population near the dock-yards. Private air raid shelters are even less common here than elsewhere because the slum-dwellings have no gardens suitable for the popular Andersen shelters installed in more prosperous neighborhoods. Frantic civilians stormed the subways, breaking down the barriers to seek shelter on the platforms under appalling conditions. And still London burns.

Although it is far too early for an assessment of damage, two things are clear: first, that this is only the beginning; the Germans will return. And second: the claims of the RAF to have weakened the mighty Luftwaffe were – to say the least – greatly exaggerated. The German raiders reached London practically unopposed.

Since the Germans are going to return, and the RAF has no way of stopping them, the question quite simply becomes: how long will the British people stand by and watch their homes and workplaces, their monuments and places of worship, their future and their children's future being pulverised? How many casualties will it take before the populace demands peace?

RAF Tangmere
9 September 1940

Mickey was still a couple of hundred yards from the dispersal when the drizzle turned into a down-pour. He sprinted the last stretch, sprang up the steps two at a time, and flung his shoulder against the door. As he half-fell into the dispersal, he was struck by the smell of burning coal from the potbellied stove that had been pressed into service in a hurry. The sound of the rain on the roof drowned out the voices. He stood in the narrow hallway between the CO's and the orderly clerk's office, shaking the rain off his cap and brushing water from his tunic. What bloody foul weather all of a sudden!

He glanced into the main room to see if Priestman was there and was shocked by the chaos that confronted him. Good heavens, he thought, can't they ever pick up after themselves? Really! The room was a shambles. Life-jackets, magazines, dirty tea-mugs and discarded scarves lay all over the place. A military man to the core, Mickey was disgusted.

Not one of them was in regulation uniform, either, he noted, taking in the sudden blossoming of fisherman's sweaters and heavy socks pulled up *over* uniform trousers in a ridiculous fashion. They all – without exception – needed a haircut, and those old enough to grow beards were poorly shaved.

Just when Mickey was about to feel angry, he noticed Reynolds standing beside the stove and trying to pour himself tea with his left hand because his right wrist was in a cast. Someone – Mickey couldn't see who because his back was to him – reached out to help. Mickey's eyes wandered next to Ware, who was lying on a sofa with his bandaged leg propped up.

His anger dissolved instantly and turned to unease. What had the country come to, when this lot was all that stood between her and a Nazi invasion?

To his right the telephone rang, and the pilots spun about and gazed in the direction of the orderly office. A moment later the orderly put his head out of his cubicle and called, "Sir? Control wants to know if you can put a section up in this weather. RDF has picked up a mysterious lone bandit nosing around the Solent and Observer Corps is blind in this muck."

Mickey looked towards the ceiling where the rain was thundering down on the corrugated iron roof of the Nissen hut. Madness! They couldn't possibly fly in this. The field must be as wet as a rice paddy.

"Kiwi? You up to it?" Priestman asked.

"Have we got pontoons for the Hurri?"

That sounded like a "no" to Mickey, but Priestman interpreted it as a "yes." "Right, then, let's go."

Priestman and Kiwi started pulling on their flying jackets and Mae Wests, shoving their feet into flying boots. Mickey watched them for a second and then turned around and left the dispersal. He had completely forgotten why he had gone over in the first place, and as he plodded doggedly through the rain he hardly noticed it.

He threw his cap and tunic aside as he reached his office. Beyond the sound of the rain pelting on the glass and gurgling down the gutter came the distant, uneven roar of Hurricane engines straining across the soggy field for take-off. A man coughed into his fist to draw attention to himself, and Mickey looked over, startled.

A small man with a large moustache and bushy eyebrows was standing in front of his visitor's chair, apparently having just got to his feet. He was in a very smart uniform – knife-sharp creases on the trousers – and had two rings on his sleeves.

Mickey's face broke into a smile and he reached out his hand. "Flight Lieutenant! Am I glad to see you! Did you just arrive? Goodness, I had no warning, but then I never do! Sit down! I'll ring for tea."

The Flight Lieutenant shook hands, but his face remained solemn. "Before you get too excited, you might want to read this." He handed Mickey a sealed letter. Mickey at once became wary, took the official-looking letter from the Air Ministry and slit it open. The communication contained a copy of a medical report and a short letter addressed to the Commanding Officer of No. 606 (Hurricane) Squadron. It stated that F/Lt. Glazebrook, formerly of Nr.141 (Defiant) squadron, had developed severe problems with drink and been in rehabilitation for four weeks. Although he appeared "cured," there was no way of judging how he would behave once he returned to life on a squadron and the pressures of combat. It was left to the Officer Commanding whether he wished to have F/Lt Glazebrook in his squadron or not. If not, the F/Lt would be assigned to ground duties.

Mickey carefully folded the letter, put it back inside the envelope, and tucked it in his inside breast-pocket. "S/L Priestman just took off on a patrol. You'll have to talk to him when he gets back. For now, let's go and have tea."

Glazebrook agreed, and together they went to the Mess. It was rather crowded on a day like this, and Mickey guided Glazebrook as much as possible into a corner, afraid he would attract attention. After all, everyone knew they were short a flight commander and would assume that it was all settled. Glazebrook was clearly even less keen to attract attention in a Mess he might not be joining, and so they slipped quietly into a corner and settled down.

"Have you ever flown Hurricanes?" Mickey asked.

"No," Glazebrook admitted, not meeting Mickey's eyes.

"No matter. Defiants are much the same," Mickey replied, feeling ridiculous. Of course, it mattered! Defiants might fly like Hurricanes, but they were fought completely differently! The Defiants had gunners and rearward firing guns! "Wasn't 141 the squadron that—" Mickey broke off.

"—was slaughtered." Glazebrook finished his sentence for him. "Yes. They shot down four of us on the first bounce, and we lost a fifth aircraft before 111 Squadron arrived to help us. Three of the remaining four aircraft were badly shot up by then. My gunner was severely injured and in terrible pain. I had a bullet in my foot. I crashed on landing, and that killed my gunner."

No wonder he had taken to drink, Mickey reflected – but how would he take to facing the Luftwaffe again? Mickey hadn't been up there. He didn't know what it was like, but common sense said that someone who had gone through an experience like that wouldn't have the nerves for more – or would be dead set on revenge. Either way, it was likely to be bad for the men under his command. Mickey didn't think Glazebrook was a solution to their problems, but rather a new burden they didn't need. Mentally he started preparing the arguments he would make to Priestman, even while he tried to make small talk with the solemn officer opposite him.

Then with a gust of cold wind, Priestman and Kiwi blew into the lounge, laughing together. "Wet! Saturated! Drenched! Soaked!" Kiwi was declaiming loudly in his New Zealand accent.

They had discarded their outer garments, but the lower parts of their trousers were indeed soaked, particularly Kiwi's, and they were shaking water off their caps. There was no apparent reason for their high spirits. It had to be some kind of inside joke, but Mickey couldn't help smiling. "That's S/L Priestman now," he told Glazebrook, with a nod in the direction of the pair that had gone straight to the bar.

"Do all Kiwis swim as well as you?" Priestman was asking.

"Look, Mate, if you grow up on the bottom of the world—"

Priestman had caught sight of Mickey, and his eyes widened as he noticed the rings on Glazebrook's sleeve. He came straight over. "Welcome to 606! You have made my day! Whoever you are and regardless of where you've come from!" He held out his hand to Glazebrook, ignoring Mickey's warning gestures. Glazebrook stood up to shake hands, looking embarrassed. "What are you drinking?" Robin asked.

"Tea," Glazebrook answered, with a gesture towards his cup.

"We've been stood down. Have a scotch on me." Without waiting for an answer, Robin returned to the bar to get two scotches. He came back and set one in front of Glazebrook. The Flight Lieutenant drew back as if it was poison. Mickey hastened to explain. "F/Lt Glazebrook doesn't drink alcohol, Robin."

Robin looked at his adjutant sharply; he recognised the warning note in his voice. Mickey reached into his tunic and removed the letter from his breast pocket. Robin opened it, read it, and gave it back to Mickey. He turned and looked pointedly at Glazebrook. "Welcome aboard. What about a tonic *without* the gin?"

"Robin, F/LT Glazebrook hasn't actually flown Hurricanes—"

"I hadn't flown an Me109 either – until I flew a shot-up one from some unused hobby field up to Hawarden a month ago or so. Nothing to single-engine fighters. Know one, know them all." Robin signaled for the

WAAF steward and placed an order for a tonic without gin. Then plopped himself down in the vacant leather chair opposite Glazebrook. He raised his glass to the Flight Lieutenant. "Cranwell?"

"1938."

"Excellent. You aren't by any chance a sailor? I just discovered Kiwi – that's P/O Murray from New Zealand, who you just saw come in with me – is also a fanatical sailor. We've decided to buy a boat together next summer."

Glazebrook shook his head. "I'm afraid I'm more into motorcars. Did a bit of racing."

"Really? That's interesting. Oh – excuse me! I need to have a word with the Station Commander." Robin was gone before they could stop him.

Warily, Mickey watched him intercept Wing Commander Boret, who had just entered. He could see Robin gesture to Glazebrook, and he knew at once what was going on. The WingCo looked over, nodded, listened, frowned, but then seemed to reluctantly agree. Priestman beamed, thanked the WingCo, and returned to the table, but didn't actually sit down. "I've got to make a telephone call," he told Glazebrook, "so why don't you let me introduce you to the others. We can talk later."

Glazebrook dutifully stood up and followed Priestman, who took him first to Kiwi, who was still at the bar, then around to the others. Priestman left him in Kiwi's care and headed for the telephones.

It was getting dark when Priestman found Mickey in his office. Putting his head around the door, Robin opened without introduction. "You think I was over-hasty taking on Glazebrook."

"No, of course not, sir," Mickey lied in flustered distress.

Priestman came into Mickey's office, the door falling shut behind him, and stood looking down at the adjutant, his hands in his pockets, his hair falling in his eyes. Mickey felt instantly guilty. He was already half cadaver! "You think my growing desperation to get married got in the way of my better judgement."

"That is the farthest thing from my mind!" Mickey protested, adding more truthfully, "Although you *do* need a rest, Robin."

"The trouble is," Priestman concluded, dropping into Mickey's spare chair, where Glazebrook had sat only a few hours earlier, "you're absolutely right. I deserve to be posted – or at least have a strip or two torn off. Then again, doesn't everyone deserve a second chance? I've done quite a few stupid things in my career, as you well know." Mickey looked astonished. "Don't you? Well then, ask Allars one of these days."

"Have you been drinking, sir?"

"You mean you can tell?"

"Are you feeling quite all right, sir?"

"I've rarely felt better. Emily has reserved Bosham church for 3 pm Sunday, Sept. 29. You'll stand up with me, won't you?"

"Be your best man?" Mickey was astonished and sincerely flattered. He stammered out, "I'd be honoured."

"Good. Then that's settled. The invitations – such as they are – go out tomorrow. Emily gets herself baptized next Sunday and confirmed the Sunday after that, and I have a whole week's leave starting at midnight of the twenty-eighth. Meanwhile, the Met is more of the same. Kiwi – I don't know why he didn't think of this earlier? – knows some Maori ritual to the Rain God (or was it Gods?) which, if we perform correctly, will keep us drenched – or was it soaked? – until then."

Very abruptly, his tone changed, reverting to his normal, professional tone. "By the way, I want you to prepare commissioning recommendations for every Sergeant Pilot on the Squadron, and a request for transfer to Training Command for P/O Goldman's signature and my approval."

"Will he sign it?"

"He says he will. How long should something like that take?"

Mickey shook his head helplessly. "I have no idea."

"Not to worry. We will invoke the Rain God!" Robin stood and went to the door. He stopped, hanging on it, and looked back at a still confused Mickey. In a serious and sincere tone he said, "Thank you, Mickey."

"What for?"

"For keeping this squadron together." Embarrassed, Mickey started to deny it. "I'm serious, Mickey. We'd have fallen apart long ago without you. I can't ever repay you for what you've done, but I won't forget it, either."

And he was gone, leaving Mickey feeling moved beyond words.

Chapter 39

Ernst made it back just in time for the "final battle." On his arrival at JG23, he was briefed along with the others. After a week of bad weather that had inhibited daylight bombing, the Met was forecasting perfect bombing weather for Sunday, September 15, and Goering had ordered his Luftwaffe to deliver the "Coup de Grace" to the RAF and batter British resistance to its knees.

The plan called for two raids in quick succession. The first would have a preponderance of escorts (five to one), so that the RAF fighters would be lured into the air and then eliminated by the powerful escort. This would clear the way for the second wave, with a greater preponderance of bombers, which would deliver a message to London that the British would not be able to ignore.

Before the general briefing, Fischer informed Ernst that he would be leading a *Schwarm* as soon as he "was back in practice," but that for this first mission since his return from hospital, he would lead a *Rotte* in Dieter's *Schwarm* with a new pilot as his wingman.

Luftwaffe High Command wanted to deliver the double punch relatively close together and saw no need to burden the pilots with an early start. It was sufficient if they got up after sunrise, took a liesurely breakfast in their own Messes, and then gathered in the Pas de Calais where the fighters could refuel for the arduous leg to London.

Since JG 23 was slated to bring the bombers out rather than to take them in, they had a particularly relaxed morning and landed at Lille to refuel. It was a glorious, sunny autumn day after days of dreary rain, and it seemed warm after the damp and wind of the previous week. The leaves on the trees around the field were starting to turn, bright yellow against the deep blue sky. Everyone was in high spirits.

RAF Tangmere

"Redcap Leader, this is Beetle. Do you read me?"

"Loud and clear. What have you got for us?"

"I just wanted to warn you." It was clearly the conscientious Bridges, and Priestman always felt better when he was their controller. Bridges continued, "12 Group has put their 'Big Wing' up over London. At least that is what they promised to do. All Tangmere squadrons have been tasked with distracting the snappers on their way in."

"I could have done without that honour," Donohue remarked tartly in violation of radio silence.

"Right. Thanks." Priestman ignored Donohue and squinted upwards towards the sun. He couldn't see a damn thing up there. He had a very bad headache. Emily was right. He had to let up on the drinking somewhat. And get more sleep. Well, when they got married things would improve. Then he wouldn't have to drive to Portmouth to spend the evenings with her. She was looking for digs in Bosham

What the hell was he doing thinking about Emily when there were Me109s lurking up in the sun? He swivelled his head around and squinted again into the morning sun. They had to be there.

"Redcap Leader, Redcap Blue Leader here. Bandits at 10 o'clock, low." That was Glazebrook. He was always very correct.

"Bombers," Green identified the aircraft sighted by Glazebrook.

"Right. Let's go for them."

"I thought we were supposed to fight the Messerschmitts?" Woody protested.

"If we go for the bombers, the Messerscmitts will find us," Priestman told him.

"How reassuring," Sutton remarked sarcastically.

Priestman ignored him and led them in a curving dive to line up behind the German bombers.

"Yellow-nosed bastards above and behind us! Here they come!" Green saw them first, as he often did.

The Hun was already too close for 606 to be able to turn into them, and Priestman made a split-second decision: "Throttle back and they'll overshoot us!"

Unfortunately, half the squadron had already taken evasive action: Donohue and Sutton had both flicked to the vertical and peeled off to the left, while Glazebrook led Tolkien, Ware and Goldman sharply upwards which had the desired effect of leaving at least some of the Messerschmitts shooting past – but the last four saw what was happening and took up the pursuit with their superior climbing ability.

Priestman's ruse, in contrast, worked perfectly. His section of four aircraft suddenly had a Schwarm of Messerschmitts directly in front of them as the latter over-shot. The Messerschmitt pilots didn't have time to realise what had happened to them, and already the Hurricanes were opening fire from very close range.

Priestman had the leader in his sights, and the machine-gun fire crept along the starboard wing inwards, hit the back of the cockpit, then the gas tank, and the Messerschmitt exploded. Priestman flew through the debris, while to his right Kiwi sheared the delicate wing off his Messerschmitt with concentrated fire. Green and Reynolds didn't fare quite so well, but they scored hits and sent the Messerschmitts diving in fright, the Hurricanes in hot pursuit.

Priestman and Kiwi looked around for more quarry. They quickly discovered Glazebrook's section and it was in trouble. They shoved their throttles forward, asking their Hurricanes for all they had to give. It wasn't enough. One of the Messerschmitts was clearly scoring hits on "L." That was Banks.

Then more of the "yellow-nosed-bastards" fell out of the sky.

Boulogne

At exactly 11.40, II/JG23 took off to meet the bombers as they came out. Ernst was immeasurably glad to be flying again, and happy to be with Dieter. Leading a *Rotte* for the first time in his career, however, filled him with pride. He was meticulous about keeping station and all radio protocol, because he didn't want anyone to think he had forgotten anything while in hospital. In fact, he was so busy watching Dieter and not looking farther forward, that Dieter saw them first.

"Holy Mother of God, what's happened to them?" Dieter had caught sight of the bombers they were supposed to bring home; there didn't seem anywhere near enough of them. There should have been close to 30 bombers in the formation, but Ernst could only count 15. 50% shot down? It couldn't be. Still, he looked nervously over his shoulder and about the sky. Spitfires. There had to be Spitfires out there after all.

As they swung in over the bombers to assume their close escort role, they had another shock. Most of these bombers were shot up in some way. There were holes in the wings, fuselages or tails of seemingly all of them. Some of the cockpits had shattered glass. Admittedly, none were damaged enough to be lagging, but—

"Möller, take your *Schwarm* and go and look for lame ducks. There must be more than a dozen bombers back there who can't keep formation!" Fischer's voice sounded as tense as Ernst felt.

Dieter at once increased speed and veered off. Ernst was caught a little by surprise and lost station for a bit, but rapidly caught up. He searched the sky again, particularly up-sun.

"Two o'clock low – two friends in trouble!"

"*Achtung! Indianer!*" Dieter led them in a curving power dive to get behind the two Hurricanes, which were intent on attacking the crippled bombers. Dieter's bounce was perfect, but the Hurricanes sensed it just in time and broke away in opposite directions. "Ernst, see the bombers home!" Dieter ordered, as he pivoted on a wingtip to race after one of the Hurricanes with his wingman beside him.

Ernst settled his *Rotte* above and behind the two bombers, which were flying with nearly touching wingtips – like two school children holding hands for comfort, Ernst thought. He had to fly at full flaps not to over-take the bombers, but at least they had a stiff tailwind that was sweeping them out of England.

Ernst was drenched in sweat by the time they crossed over the French coast and he could relax a bit. To fly with the damaged bombers, he'd kept his *Rotte* at only 3,000 metres, and it was hot in the cockpit at that altitude – not to mention being a sitting duck for Spitfires. Why had everyone said it was so easy? Ernst didn't think it looked any better than when he'd been wounded. Maybe even worse.

Ernst let the wounded bombers land first, while he and Kreisel (that was his wingman) circuited around, then followed them down onto the concrete runway. What a luxury! On concrete, even the Emil acted like a lady on landing. Ernst was flagged over to the side of the field, next to one of the bombers he had just escorted, and gratefully flung the hood open. He unplugged and removed his helmet. Then he scrambled out of the cockpit and down the wing. As he came around his own tail, the ambulance went alongside the nearest bombr, and he held back to allow the aircrew of the bomber to lower one of their number into the waiting arms of the medics. Only after the ambulance had raced away with wailing siren did Ernst risk approaching. He was not alone. *Feldwebel* Kreisel followed him, and from around the field, ground crew and staff were pressing around the airmen who had just landed.

"There were Spitfires all over the sky!" an *Oberfeldwebel* with pilot's badge declared furiously. "All over the place! They came at us as soon as we crossed the coast — tore right into the escort, and in two minutes our fighters were cavorting around with them rather than covering us. The next lot hit us halfway to London!"

"We didn't have one God-damned Messerschmitt with us when we finally crossed the Thames!" his navigator put in.

"But there shouldn't have been any Spitfires left," a member of the ground staff protested.

"Like hell! There were hundreds of them! More than I've ever seen at one time before! All just sitting up there over London waiting for us! They were waiting there like a pack of wolves. Fucking, shitty Spitfires!"

"There were so many of them they had to line up to take turns shooting at us!"

"That can't be," a staff officer protested again, but the aircrew would have none of it.

"Take a good look at the carcass of our crate! What do you think made all those holes in it? Imagination? I'm telling you, the Tommies had at least 500 Spitfires up there today!"

Ernst had heard enough. They were slated to fly close escort on the second raid, which was due to take off in just 70 minutes. He felt the familiar urge to urinate.

RAF Tangmere

The engine was running very rough, and it was spewing glycol. Priestman had to nurse it all the way home, and as he turned into the wind to land, he could see the fire engine clanging and swaying as it rushed to meet him. Concentrating on flying, with the glycol spewing onto his windscreen and all but blinding him, he had no chance to count the number of squadron aircraft already down. A moment later, he winced at his own landing. He prided himself on his precise three-point landings — and he'd dumped the docile little Hurricane down like a bloody sprog! They'd all think he was wounded.

Sure enough, the blood wagon was in motion, too.

Appleby signalled him vigorously to a nearby sandbag bay. He turned into it and cut the engine. No sooner had he pulled his helmet off his soaking hair than Appleby shoved back the hood, letting in the cool air. "Are you all right, sir?" he asked anxiously.

"Fine," Priestman assured him, nodding. The rigger reached inside to release his straps for him and then, bracing his right foot against the side of the cockpit, he held out his left hand. Priestman was stiff, and gratefully grabbed the rigger's arm to help pull himself up and out of the cockpit. "Who's missing?"

"Only Pilot Officers Goldman and Murray, Sir."

"Only?"

The sound of a Hurricane drew their attention, but it was one from 17 Squadron. Banks and Kiwi. For an instant he saw them as they had stood before at him at Hawarden the first day he'd met them – roughly one month ago.

"Sutton says he got a Messerschmitt, sir, and Reynolds thinks he got one, too." Appleby informed him; he clearly wanted to be cheerful but wasn't sure of Priestman's mood.

"Green says the one he was shooting at isn't as pretty as when it set out this morning, and he says both you and Pilot Officer Murray had kills, too."

Robin nodded.

"Wouldn't that be some kind of a record, sir? Four in one sortie?"

"You're just looking for an excuse to celebrate," Priestman told the cheeky airman with a frown. Appleby grinned back happily.

"That's right, sir! If I'm going to be up all night getting this crate off the u/s list, I want something to look forward to!" Appleby agreed.

Another Hurricane came in to land and it was "K," Kiwi's aircraft. It had a rather tattered-looking fuselage, but Kiwi put it down neatly and didn't appear to be having any trouble with it. Priestman walked right over to where it was being signalled.

Kiwi shoved the hood back and heaved himself out of the cockpit, using the rear-view mirror as a hold before any of the ground crew could come to help. He jumped once on the wing and then down. "He's OK!" was the first thing out of his mouth. "I saw him get out, and I saw the 'chute open. No question about it! He might be a tad singed, but he's definitely alive. Went down in a sheep farm. Scared the sheep half to death! But he made it all right."

Boulogne

As JG 23 took over their close escort role, Ernst thought of how Christian always used to complain that the "aces" got the fun jobs – the flanking and forward sweeps. Because JG23 wasn't led by one of the leading aces, they got stuck with the more difficult and less rewarding job of close escort. It was a vicious circle, as far as Ernst could see. Since the fighters on sweeps could position themselves up-sun and manoeuvre to their advantage, they were able to bounce the Tommies and run up their scores further. The close escort was tied to the bombers and unable to use any of their advantages – not speed, height, position or tactical skill.

The only positive side of it was the gratitude of the bomber crews. Ernst and his wingman had been treated with more than courtesy during their short stay at Lille. The returned aircrews stressed more than once how glad they had been to see them. "We thought we were done for until you appeared," one of the crewmen had admitted. Another had thrown an arm around Ernst's shoulders and bought him a beer.

"The Tommies didn't waste time clearing out when they saw two Messerschmitts coming for them, either!" the gunner pointed out with satisfaction.

Although Ernst wasn't very happy about this second sortie, there could be no doubt the bomber crews were glad to see them. They waved to them as they took up their positions. It was a pity they had no radio communication with the bombers, Ernst thought as he settled into position.

As they droned across the sky, the now familiar landmarks swept slowly under his wings. Ernst reminded himself not to look down. He rotated his head around, searching the sky, squinting into the sun. Funny that he couldn't see any other escorts besides their own group – not even the top cover. Probably off hunting, Ernst told himself. They were now well inland, and still no sign—

"*Achtung! Indianer!*"

Ernst tensed and searched the sky with new concentration. "Report properly!" Rosskamp snapped, irritated.

"Coming up, 4 o'clock."

"A dozen miserable Hurricanes," someone commented contemptuously.

"III *Gruppe*, take care of those Hurricanes." Rosskamp ordered.

Ernst's *Gruppe* continued with the bombers, pressing deeper into English airspace.

"More Indians. One o'clock high."

Again, they were only Hurricanes, but Ernst didn't like the way they were clearly racing in for a head-on attack. The next thing he knew, they were coming straight at him. Everything was happening much too fast. The Hurricanes were getting larger and larger, and then their wings lit up as they opened fire. Ernst flinched and tried to make himself smaller in the cockpit, while pressing on his gun-button – more out of fright than conviction.

With a horrible roar, a Hurricane swept overhead so close that its slipstream rocked the Emil, and then Ernst heard a horrible explosion behind him. He was already reefing the Messerschmitt around, trying to get in position behind the Hurricanes, but by the time he had turned around, the bomber formation had been shattered by the Hurricanes. One bomber was falling away to the left, smoke pouring from a wing that dragged it downwards, and another bomber had lost its tail entirely, evidently in a collision. The crew was abandoning it as it went down.

Fischer called the Messerschmitts of his *Staffel* back into position over the bombers, but the Hurricanes were also coming back for a second pass. Fischer again ordered the Staffel to turn to meet them. But the Hurricanes plunged in among the bombers and the bomber gunners opened fire. Ernst didn't see what he could do without risking a collision. He was not alone. The entire Staffel hesitated on the fringe of the melee until they saw the Hurricanes dive away and took chase.

Fischer called them back. "Stick to the bombers! Watch your fuel!"

Scheisse! Ernst glanced at his fuel gauge and registered it was already nearly half empty, and they had only reached the outskirts of London. The bombers were only just starting their run in to the target.

"Spitfires!"

"Scheisse!"

There they were. Just as the bomber crews from this morning had said: swarms of Spitfires hovering over London. Well, not hovering any longer. They were launching their attacks. Fischer led them in a left curve to face the Spitfires, and then all hell broke loose.

Ernst could never remember exactly what happened. Things happened much too fast. There were too many aircraft, all twisting and turning. Tracer, vapour trails and burning aircraft left their stains upon the clear blue sky. The chatter of guns, the duller thud of bombs going off below, the shouts in the radio all blurred together in his memory.

Ernst was terrified. First, he had one Spitfire on his tail, then another. Then a Hurricane nearly killed him as it raced past just in front of his propeller, chasing another Messerschmitt. Ernst was sweating, breathless, and in pain. The effort of wrestling the Emil around at these speeds seemed to have opened up all his wounds. He heard himself sobbing from exertion and pain and fear. He felt a panicked need to just get away from it all. Just get away.

He flipped on his back and then shoved the nose of his Emil down and threw it into the steepest dive he dared. The speed mounted and mounted. The little aircraft trembled and the engine screamed. Ernst's vision blurred. He smelled hot oil. Glancing at the instrument panel, he had another shock. The engine temperature was far too high. *Scheisse! Scheisse! Scheisse!*

Pull up. Slow down. *Mein Gott!*

And then stillness. He was alone in the sky, flying over a wonderful autumn countryside with bright yellow woods and green meadows dotted with sheep and cattle. A castle sped by on his left. A river glistened in the sun. Fool! Don't look down! He searched the sky again.

Gradually, awareness of what he had just done penetrated his consciousness. He had run away. He had abandoned his charges and his comrades and run away like a coward. Had his wingman seen it? Did the entire *Staffel* know what he'd done?

Did it matter? He knew what he'd done. Ernst felt sick with shame. He wiped the sweat from his face on the back of his sleeve and looked about the sky again. With relief he spotted some bombers over on his left. He at once sped across the distance between them. He felt guilty for the friendly reception he received. If they knew how he'd abandoned them just a few minutes ago....

After a few minutes, two other Messerschmitts joined him. Dieter and his wingman!

"Where's Kreisel, Ernst?"

"I don't know. I lost him in the dogfight." Although ashamed to admit that, it was the truth, and he was a terrible liar.

They flew on in silence, pacing themselves to the slower speed of the bombers. Ernst started to nervously check his fuel every few seconds. The Channel could be seen ahead of them.

"Hurricane! Dead ahead." Didn't they ever stop?

Ernst unclasped the stick to dry his hand on his trousers. Both his hands were aching from being cramped around the controls so long. The lone Hurricane lifted one wing to line up perfectly and then deliberately smashed head-on into the lead bomber. Both aircraft exploded and fell to earth in a shower of tattered debris, while the following bombers broke apart in horror.

Dieter exclaimed "Holy mother of God!" There were no parachutes.

Suicide. Sheer suicide, Ernst kept whispering to himself. The Tommies must be out of their minds. They had never fought like this before....

A de-brief took place immediately after landing. Still in flying kit, their hair sticky with dried sweat, and their uniforms crumpled and smelling none too fresh, they collected in the staff dining room of the inn that served as their Mess. This dining room in the cellar had been converted for use as a briefing room, with a blackboard and map of southern England and northern France pinned to the wall.

Ernst noted that he wasn't the only one with unsteady hands as they lit up cigarettes and struck self-consciously casual poses. (Fischer wasn't one for protocol. He let them stand about leaning against the tables or slouching against the wall.) Only when he caught sight of Kreisel, however, did Ernst start to relax a bit. He pulled out a chair and sank down into it.

"You all right?" Dieter asked at once, giving him a piercing look.

"A bit sore, that's all," Ernst admitted, burying the shame of running away deeper in his own mind and heart.

Dieter nodded and sat down next him. Gradually most of the others sat down, too; only a few remained standing at the back, leaning against the wall. The new CO, Major Henning, came in with the Intelligence Officer. The pilots came to a sloppy approximation of attention – more a halfhearted hint that they remembered something about owing respect to their CO.

Henning frowned, but then waved them back "at ease" and, leaning on the podium at the front of the room, announced: "The casualties from this morning's raid are in: 18 aircraft, 12 of them fighters. For the afternoon raid, the numbers aren't complete, but it looks like we lost between 30 and 40 aircraft, 11 fighters. As you know, *Feldwebel* Schüster had to bail out over England, and the *Gruppe* lost two other aircraft and pilots."

"Where did they all come from, Herr *Gruppenkommandeur*?" one of the pilots asked in obvious amazement.

Henning shrugged, but before he could answer, one of the new pilots whom Ernst didn't know suggested, "Maybe the Americans are helping the Tommies secretly. Everyone knows they aren't *really* neutral!"

"Or they got reinforced from their colonies," someone else suggested.

Henning cut the discussion short. "After a week of focusing exclusively on London, the British guessed what our target was and concentrated their defences around their capital, denuding the rest of the country. The largest formations were directly over the capital itself – probably as much to calm the civilian population as to attack us. After all, the mood in London must be very explosive, and the RAF will have wanted to show that they still had some fight left. I'd say they threw everything they had at us today – and if Galland, Mölders and Wick are as good as they claim to be, we'll have eliminated a good deal more than just 23 fighters."

That brought a satisfied murmur from the collected pilots. "Keep in mind that we saw the worst of the fighting, because we were to the bombers. The two *Geschwader* on free sweeps will have been in a position to attack rather than be attacked. I feel confident we won today's engagement, and the desperation with which the Tommies pressed home their attacks suggests they are at the end of their strength – and know it. They are fighting with their backs to the wall and fighting very hard. You have to respect them for it. They are worthy opponents, but I'd say they are very nearly finished. Now, the bar is open."

The pilots responded to Henning's little speech – and the early opening of the bar – with a cheer.

RAF Tangmere

"The AOC is furious," Allars announced, dropping into one of the sofas around a low table in the lounge of the Officer's Mess. "We're claiming almost 200 aircraft shot down – 185 to be exact – and he says there is no way we shot down even half that amount."

"Well, there *was* plenty of opportunity," Bridges pointed out. This second big, set-piece battle had been very different from the party last week. Firstly, it had been divided into two raids, each only half the size of the one the previous week. Secondly, they knew in advance that the target was London, and so Park was able to deploy his entire fighter force along the line of attack, rather than holding some squadrons back to protect the airfields. Thirdly, knowing the target was London allowed Leigh-Mallory in 12 Group sufficient time to assemble his "Big Wing" and put it up at the limit of the 109s' fuel range. The meant the German fighters were unable to stick around for a real scrap. All in all, the massed attack on London played very well into the hands of Fighter Command, enabling them to deploy two Groups rather than just one.

"I hope the AOC isn't questioning our claims?" Mickey protested defensively. 606 squadron had reported five enemy aircraft destroyed.

"No, not at all. In fact, he sent his congratulations. He was very pleased with our score of kills for no losses."

Banks had been picked up by a farmer and taken directly to a nearby hospital. When Mickey called to see his condition, he'd been told "not to worry," he would "certainly" survive.

"It's Leigh-Mallory's boys in 12 Group the AOC thinks have gone bonkers, claiming everything they nicked as a kill," Allars explained. Park had been seriously teed-off about the 12 Group claims, which he suggested had not been vetted for credibility. He'd specifically noted that he had no doubts about Allars' reports and remarked he felt vindicated for taking such a risk with Priestman.

They were at *The Ship*, of course. They had pretty much taken it over. It was their pub, and not a few locals came *because* they wanted to rub shoulders with an active fighter squadron. The WAAF, who wanted to, knew where to find them, and Virginia and her friends had a habit of "dropping in," too – all the way from London. Tonight, Reynolds' starlet showed up, though none of the celebrities.

Robin and Emily sat in a window-table with Mickey and Glazebrook. In peacetime the bow window would have offered them a view of Bosham harbour, but the windows were covered with blackout paper, leaving them no view but the interior. This was not entirely uninteresting, offering the interaction of the pilots with each other and the girls.

It was noteworthy that they were all here, Priestman reflected, not without satisfaction: the Auxiliaries, the short-service commissioned officers, the "experienced" Sergeants, and his latest sprogs. This past week they had sent him another pair of Sergeant Pilots straight out of training, both with less than 20 hours on Hurricanes when they arrived. Banks and he had managed to fly with them over the past soggy week, but he had refused to take them up today when it was clear the enemy was out in force. They had therefore missed "the show" and appeared to be feeling a bit out of things as a result.

Robin felt an inner resistance towards even trying to get to know them. He felt an emotional weariness. He did not want to care about them particularly when they got shot down. He couldn't afford to be torn apart the way he had been by Ginger's death. Even the uncertainty about Banks had been bad for him. It would be better for his efficiency if he didn't bother to get to know these chaps at all.

But even as he thought it, he knew it was wrong. A squadron was nothing but a number and an administrative fiction unless the members felt strong personal bonds to it and each other. It was the relationships between the individual members that gave a squadron its character. Bad relationships made for bad squadrons, and since you couldn't choose your comrades any more than your relatives, the only way to make a squadron a happy place was to cultivate good relations among its members.

That was why they were here (again), for God's sake. It was why Glazebrook was here nursing a tonic without gin, and why Mickey was valiantly trying to engage the somber Flight Lieutenant in conversation. But the sprogs were looking left out and awkward, so Robin leaned over and murmured in Emily's ear. "I need to go and look after the sprogs. I'll be right back."

He slipped out from behind the table and went over to the bar. "Can I buy you a round?" he asked, coming up behind the two new Sergeant Pilots.

They jumped and straightened up at the sight of him. But then one of them, Wilkins, recovered and smiled, "Don't mind if you do, sir." He had long, straw-like blond hair that was unkempt, and crooked teeth in an engaging smile.

Robin signalled the bartender for another round for the two Sergeant Pilots.

The other youngster, Casey, a stocky redhead with freckles, ventured, "May I ask you a question, Sir?"

"Of course."

"Ah. What's an orc?"

"I haven't the foggiest."

"We heard the other pilots talking about how to kill them. Is it another word for Messerschmitt?" Wilkins took up the theme.

"Oh. No. Probably one of the creatures in the book Tolkien's father is writing. Tolkien's father sends him chapters as he writes them, and he's been passing them around. They're all quite mad about it. You'll have to ask Tolkien for a copy."

"What *is* the best way to kill Messerschmitts, sir?" Casey asked rather solemnly.

"Frankly, for the next few weeks I don't want you to worry about shooting anything down. Your job is to stay alive."

"Beware of the Hun in the Sun and all that?"

"Yes, but at the beginning, you'll find it very difficult to see the enemy. Green is our best pair of eyes. He generally sees them first and warns the rest of us. Depending on where they are, we then try to turn into them, break apart and fight in pairs, or we may try a repeat of what worked so well today – slow down abruptly and let them overshoot into our sights."

"Does that mean we'll be operational soon?" Casey pressed him.

Priestman sighed. He didn't have any choice. He only had twelve pilots with Banks in hospital. Fortunately, he'd been told that Hughes, a pilot who'd been injured before he joined the squadron, would be returning to them shortly. "Do you feel ready?" he asked the Sergeant Pilot back.

That gave the youngster pause, and he took a moment to answer. "Are we ever ready, sir? I mean, I've heard that even the most experienced pilots are surprised by combat."

There was truth to that, but Priestman couldn't help feeling that it was asking rather a lot of someone to fight in an aircraft he hardly knew how to control properly. He nodded more to himself than to the two young men in front of him. "Casey, you're in 'B' Flight with Flight Lieutenant Glazebrook. Wilkins, you'll fly in 'A' Flight with Flight Lieutenant Ringwood. Now, bring your drinks."

Dutifully the sergeants did as they were told, and Priestman led them over to the table where Tolkien, Kiwi and Green were sitting. "Tolkien, these two young men need to be told about orcs. I think that's your department."

Tolkien's face lit up. "You want to know about orcs?"

Robin left them to it and returned to Emily. She looked tired. He gave her a kiss on her forehead as he sat down again. "Something wrong?"

"Of course not," she smiled. "In two weeks' time I'll be a married woman – unless you leave me standing at the altar."

"I wouldn't worry about that," Robin told her. "After the fuss I made to get leave, I wouldn't dare not go through with it."

"Your Mum wants me to invite all sorts of people."

"I hope you've said no."

"Hattie has. What about the Squadron?" She nodded to the room generally.

"If we're stood down, of course; and Mickey's my best man, so he'll be there regardless. Which reminds me – Mickey?" he interrupted the Adjutant's now quite animated conversation with the Flight Lieutenant. "Did you manage to book that hotel I asked you to?"

"Hotel? For your wedding night?" Mickey remembered quickly. "Yes, of course. Don't worry about a thing." He smiled at Emily. "It's to be a surprise, my dear, but you needn't worry. You'll like it."

Emily wasn't worried – as long as she spent the night there with Robin and not alone.

Chapter 40

Crépon
21 September 1940

Ernst woke with a horrible hangover – the worst he'd ever had in his life. Yesterday, he had finally shot down his first enemy, a Spitfire, and there'd been quite a celebration. When he tried to sit up, his head was so heavy, it seemed to drag him right back down. It was impossible to focus his eyes. He groaned and flopped back onto his pillow.

What was that hissing sound? He opened one eye and tried to orient himself. Rain? Could it really be? Dear God, let it be rain! He staggered out of bed and fell against the windowsill, where he lost his balance and crashed down to the floor with a painful thud. He groaned again, as all his wounds seemed to start throbbing and stabbing at once, while his head was making a sound like a Junkers 88 at full power – brmm, brmm, brmm. He grabbed the curtains, used them to pull himself to his feet, and then shoved them aside.

What a glorious sight! The airfield was awash with rain – rain so thick it was blinding. Maximum visibility 10 metres! Merciful God! There would be no ops in this torrent. Ernst could have danced a jig – if his head hadn't been so heavy and his legs unsteady. He staggered back to his bed, flopped down and fell instantly asleep again.

His batman woke him gently. "Sir?"

Ernst opened his eyes with a frown. The headache was still fierce. He glowered sceptically at the airman, daring him to say they were flying in this weather.

"Message from the CO, sir. He's told me to tell you that you can have 72 hours leave."

"What?" Ernst sat up abruptly, causing his vision to fade as he swayed with dizziness. He grabbed his head to steady it. "72 hours leave? Starting when?"

"This morning, sir."

"What time is it?"

"11 am, sir."

"*Scheisse!*" Ernst threw off the covers and banged loudly down the hall to the bathroom. He finally had leave and he was wasting it here. 72

546

hours wasn't enough to go home on. He'd have to suggest Paris or St. Malo. What if Klaudia couldn't get leave on such short notice? But in this weather, there was little work for her to do, either. She'd taken no leave since she'd arrived at the Gruppe. Ernst was determined to spend the three days with her – if he had to go to Fischer or even Rosskamp himself to get Klaudia the time off.

In weather like this, it hardly made sense to go to a seaside resort, so Klaudia opted for Paris. Dieter drove them to the station to catch the afternoon train to Paris, which put them into the *Gare du Nord* just after 5 pm. Dieter recommended an affordable hotel near the Opera, too, and here they checked in – separate rooms. Then, together, they set out to find somewhere for dinner.

Ernst was feeling very much a "man of the world" because he'd been to Paris before. From his last trip, he also remembered and applied Dieter's golden rule of prefacing every attempt at communication with the French with, "*Je regrette, Madame/Monsieur, je ne parle pas Français.*" It still worked like a charm, transforming hostility into polite friendliness.

Indeed, Ernst had the distinct impression that the French were far more tolerant of him on this trip than on his last. It might be that they had adjusted more to being occupied, but from the glances directed at Klaudia, he suspected it had more to do with the fact that he was with a woman. Since he was already escorting a young lady, he was automatically less threatening to the French women, while the fact that *she* was German conciliated the men.

Being with Klaudia was wonderful in other ways, too. He noted approving looks from his own countrymen, regardless of rank or service. Waiters and taxi drivers and doormen were invariably gracious and attentive. Best of all, Klaudia clearly wasn't used to the admiration and blushed a bit, clinging more tightly to his elbow shyly.

The feel of her close beside him was intoxicating. She was wearing perfume again, and a dark, red lipstick like a film star. She had pencilled her eyebrows into perfect lines over her well-set eyes, and her lashes looked longer than normal. She wore her hair down and held out of her eyes only by two little tortoise-shell barrettes. Ernst was so proud to be seen with her, he was all but bursting his buttons – despite having lost more than five kilos in the last month.

Klaudia, too, felt as if she were walking on clouds. For the first time in her life she was dining alone with a young man – and in Paris! Last time she'd been here, she'd still been in a state of shock, and being taken to the Opera by an SD officer was akin to being halfway under arrest.

She was so happy with Ernst that the rain and mist only made the evening more romantic. After all, to take shelter under an umbrella or in a doorway waiting for a taxi meant she could press up against Ernst without seeming at all forward. And he was marvellously gallant: rushing out into the street to wave down the taxi and standing in the rain holding the umbrella while she climbed in.

Furthermore, Klaudia could not understand how she had ever thought of him as fat. Of course, he wasn't sleek like Christian, much less gaunt like Dieter, but he wasn't fat – just comfortably round. She loved the feel of his arm around her shoulders or waist – it was warm and reassuring without being at all imperative. She shuddered at the memory of Jako and shoved thoughts of him aside.

Best of all, Ernst was a real gentleman. He said good night to her in the hotel lobby, allowing her to go up to her room alone. She heard him arrive at the adjoining room a few minutes later. She listened to him moving about in the room next to hers. It filled her with a curious excitement to think he was beyond the thin wall, getting undressed, brushing his teeth, going to bed. When all was silent in the room next door, Klaudia tip-toed very carefully about her own room. She did not want him to hear and listen to her – that would have been embarrassing. But once she settled snugly into her bed in the tiny room, she could not sleep for excitement.

She thought back over the evening. They hadn't seen any of the sights of Paris in the dark and the rain, but the whole city was enchanting – the houses with their wrought-iron balconies and mansard roofs, the women in their daring hats and high-heeled shoes, the men with their approving glances. And then dinner! It was the best meal Klaudia had ever had in her life. Last time she'd been too frightened to notice any of it.

It made all the difference in the world to be with the man you loved. Even with Rosa it hadn't been like this, and if she had been alone, she would have been frightened and unsure of herself. She would have been too timid even to go out into the night to look for a restaurant; she would have eaten at the hotel. Alone, she would never have flagged down a cab. Being with Ernst made her feel like a sophisticated woman of the world. It made her feel like she was special.

Then she thought of him being in the next room. Maybe even lying awake like she was – and she became aware of a different excitement. Although she had spent months suppressing all thoughts of Jako, now she could not stop herself. He had taken advantage of her innocence. He had misused her trust. He was a horrible, callous, selfish man! – but in the secrecy of her own bed she had to admit that it hadn't all been brutality and pain. There had been excitement and an inexplicable thrill, too. With Ernst, who was so devoted to her, kind and gentlemanly, it would be like all the romances she had ever read. It would be magic.

But what would he do when he noticed she wasn't a virgin? Worrying about this, Klaudia tossed and turned in her bed until, only many hours later, she fell into an exhausted sleep.

It rained the next day, too, although now and again the sun tried to break through. Ernst was determined to show Klaudia the sights – the Eiffel Tower, the Arc de Triomphe, Notre Dame, Ste. Chapelle and the Louvre. Klaudia was tired and soon footsore as well, dressed as she was in civilian clothes with her new high-heeled shoes. Although she didn't want to spoil Ernst's fun and didn't know if she would ever come to Paris again, by mid-afternoon she had to admit that she was just too tired to "do" the Louvre. She asked to go back to the hotel so she could take a nap before dinner and the promised dancing. Ernst, anxious to please her in everything, readily agreed.

Klaudia had bought an evening gown in Cherbourg shortly after Ernst told her he wanted to take her home to meet his parents. It was very daring: close fitting with a lower neckline than she had ever risked before. It left a lot of neck, arm and back bare which she could not adequately dress with jewellery, but the look in Ernst's eyes as he helped her out of her coat at the restaurant made her feel like a film star.

Ernst too was in his best uniform, long trousers and shoes rather than breeches and boots. This uniform was practically brand new, and the creases of the trousers were razor sharp and the buttons dazzling.

Ernst waited until after the main course, after they had finished off a bottle of wine, before nervously handing over the little box with the ring. "You know how I feel about you, Klaudia. You read it in my diaries, and I've told you more than once since. I want you to meet my parents and my sisters and brothers, but – it just didn't seem right to wait. You will marry me, won't you?" At the very last moment, Ernst started to have self-doubts again.

"Yes," Klaudia said solemnly, looking him straight in the eye. She reached out and took his hand in hers for a moment. Then she opened the little box and gasped. "It's beautiful!" She took the ring out and put it on her finger at once. It was a bit too big, and the heavy stone fell over to one side.

"It's too big—" Ernst noted in distress.

"It doesn't matter. I can wind yarn around the back. It's truly beautiful, Ernst." She reached out, took his hand and led it to her cheek. "You've made me so happy, Ernst. I can't tell you how happy I am."

After that they danced. Klaudia's feet were hurting, and Ernst was a timid and inept dancer at best, so they ended up just standing on the dance floor in each other's arms, shifting their weight from one foot to the other and swaying to the music. Klaudia laid her head on Ernst's shoulder and closed her eyes. She didn't want tonight ever to end. She wanted to go on dancing in Ernst's arms in Paris forever.

Some part of her brain knew that her parents would be shocked and angry to hear she'd accepted a proposal from someone they'd never met — a plumber's son from Cottbus, no less. Another part of her brain was less than excited about the idea of going to meet her future in-laws. But Klaudia didn't want to think about any of that tonight. She wanted even less to think about the war, about the fact that tomorrow night they'd be back at Crépon and that the morning after, Ernst would be flying again.

Ernst couldn't think about anything except the way Klaudia felt in his arms. She leaned against him with her whole body, and the response of his own was embarrassing. His pulse was definitely faster than normal, and he was afraid she'd notice what was happening to his loins. She snuggled her head against him contentedly and innocently, and he was reacting like an animal! Then again, that was what marriage was all about. She had freely agreed to do with him exactly what he wanted to do with her. But not until they were married, of course, and that could be months and months away, and... what if he got shot down on Tuesday?

Uncomfortably, Ernst tried to adjust his hold on Klaudia so she wouldn't notice anything, but she only snuggled closer and smiled up at him languidly. In the films, a look like that was considered inviting. Could she maybe want it, too? Tonight? "Shall we sit down and order another drink?"

Klaudia smiled at him and murmured, "Whatever you want, Ernst." They went back to their table, and Ernst ordered water. He was thirsty — and after his hangover yesterday morning, he was reluctant to drink too much. Klaudia accepted the offer of wine, although she seemed to be getting very sleepy. To return to their hotel, however, would be the end of their enchanted interlude. Tomorrow they had to catch the afternoon train for Cherbourg. There wouldn't be another evening like this for a long, long time...

They danced some more. Drank more. Klaudia was definitely tipsy. Ernst was having trouble keeping his eyes open despite everything. Yet still they didn't want to admit the night was over. The restaurant emptied out. The little orchestra stopped playing and packed away their instruments. They had no choice. They collected their coats from the cloakroom and went back out into the drizzling rain.

At their hotel, Ernst didn't say good-bye in the foyer. They got in the cramped lift together, travelled up to the third floor. They stepped out into the dim and silent corridor. They walked to their rooms, side by side. They were both tense and silent. Ernst desperately wanted to take Klaudia in his arms, into his room, into his bed, but he didn't want to insult her. If she was insulted, she might throw his ring back at him. He didn't want to make a mistake.

He pulled her into his arms. She was very willing and pliable. She lifted her face for his kisses. They stood there in the hall, kissing and kissing, until another guest came along the hall. They pulled apart while the stranger passed by them with a short glance and a raised eyebrow.

"Come in where we won't be seen," Ernst suggested in a whisper, his throat dry with nervousness.

"All right," Klaudia whispered back.

Ernst fumbled with the key in a frantic effort to open the door before Klaudia changed her mind. They stepped into the dark room. The door fell shut, and Klaudia fell into his arms again. Now they were kissing more desperately. They had crossed the threshold to a new stage in their relationship, and they both knew it.

Klaudia was drunk, drunker even than she had been that night with Jako. She was so drunk she was half asleep already, and her thoughts were numbed with wine. She was aware only of now, tonight, the feel of Ernst's arms, the smell of his skin, the illusion of sophistication – being in a Paris hotel room with a fighter pilot. She was even play-acting a little, doing things she had seen in the cinema. But she felt very sure of herself – maybe it was the wine. She felt irresistible and beautiful, like a femme fatale. She knew intuitively that she could make Ernst do whatever she wanted him to. And unlike Jako, she could make him stop whenever she wanted him to.

Only, she didn't want to stop him.

She had been right, she thought as she drifted off to sleep in his arms. It hadn't hurt at all with Ernst, and if it had been a little less exciting and elating than in the novels, then that was probably because he was rather inexperienced. But that had its good side, she reflected as sleep closed over her: he hadn't even noticed that she wasn't a virgin.

Chapter 41

Queen Victoria Cottage Hospital, East Grinstead, 28 September 1940

The hospital was pleasant. It was small and sat amidst well-tended lawns – more like a country home than a hospital, really. There were flower beds in front, carefully planted with bright asters. The rain had let up a bit, and the sun started to break through. Colin parked the heavy Bentley in a space marked "Visitors" and the three RAF officers climbed out. "Not bad,"Kiwi commented for all of them.

They went up the steps and through the glass doors to the reception. A neatly dressed receptionist took their names and then lifted a phone and announced to the person at the other end, "There are three RAF officers here to see Mr. Goldman." A pause. She nodded, "Very good," and hung up. She looked at the three visitors and announced, "Matron will be right out to talk to you. Have a seat if you like." She indicated some vacant chairs around a coffee table with dog-eared magazines.

The three officers dutifully retreated to the seats indicated, but none of them felt like looking at the magazines – gardening, cooking, motorcars and golf. Finally, a short, plump woman in a blue uniform with a white cap and wearing a gold cross appeared. "You're here to see Mr. Goldman?" she asked cheerily, as the three men got to their feet.

"Yes, Ma'am," Priestman, as the senior officer, answered for them.

The Matron was indisputably "motherly." Her skin had aged into soft folds, and the creases around her eyes and lips were the fossils of countless smiles. Yet, despite her overall benevolence, the gaze she steadied on Robin was critical. She reminded him of a drill sergeant at Cranwell by the way she let her eyes run down him from cap to shoes as if looking for some fault. As with any self-respecting drill sergeant, the Matron found what she was looking for – at least her eyes clouded – but unlike a drill sergeant, she kept her opinion to herself. "Squadron Leader, is it?" she asked in a pleasant voice.

"Yes, Ma'am."

"Is it fair to assume you were Mr. Goldman's commanding officer?" she enquired.

"As far as I know, I still am," Priestman responded, annoyed with the use of the past tense.

"I'm sorry," she replied sincerely, adding, "I'm afraid I'm not familiar with the fine points of when an officer is removed from a unit. It's just that since it is unlikely that Mr. Goldman will ever fly an aircraft again, I don't think of him as being the member of an active squadron."

Kiwi choked, and the Matron's attention swung to him and then to Colin. She then turned back to Priestman and explained gently, "Mr. Goldman received severe burns to his face and hands. Unfortunately, he was first taken to a local hospital with little experience in burns. Only after Dr. McIndoe visited him there and realised how serious his burns were, could we get him transferred here. We almost lost him, I'm afraid. His condition has stabilised somewhat in the last 48 hours, but he is still receiving morphine regularly."

Priestman couldn't absorb all that. Kiwi had said he might be "a bit singed," but the initial reports had been so positive. He wasn't expecting this, and it left him speechless.

Kiwi, meanwhile, burst out angrily, "What are you saying!? There has to be some mistake! I saw him get out almost at once! He can't be that bad!"

At that moment a man with thick glasses in a white doctor's coat swept in. "Sounds like a fellow New Zealander," he remarked with a smile, and he held out his hand to Kiwi. "McIndoe."

The officers introduced themselves in turn and explained they had come to see David Goldman, who had been shot down almost two weeks earlier.

"We had no idea he was badly burnt," Priestman told the famous doctor. "The initial reports—"

"I'm sorry if you were misled. As Matron was explaining, I didn't get word until he had been in a local hospital for a few days."

"Is he too ill for visitors?" Priestman asked, and Colin added a touch urgently, "He's a Canadian, sir, and has no family here. I'm sure he'd like to know that we're thinking of him – even if you only let us stay a moment."

McIndoe smiled. "Of course, you can see him." Turning to the Matron, he suggested, "Please prepare Mr. Goldman for his guests." Turning back to the officers, he added, "He's not as abandoned as you think. Mr. Bowles has been sitting with him for the last three days."

"Mr. Bowles?!"

"Yes. Surely he's a relative of some sort? He arrived here in the pouring rain the other night, right after Mr. Goldman was transferred here, and begged to see him."

The three officers looked one another in amazement. "How did he find out?" Colin asked; the others shook their heads, as mystified as he was.

The doctor continued, "As Matron was telling you, after he was transferred here, he had a bit of a set-back. He was unconscious much of the time, but Mr. Bowles sat with him. It seemed to have a soothing effect, so we let him stay. We assumed he was a relative. Isn't he?"

"No. He's the father of another pilot who was shot down and killed a week before P/O Goldman." Colin knew the dates; for Kiwi and Priestman, the days just blurred into one another.

"I see. Well, he's here, and he has done Mr. Goldman a world of good. I'm sure you will, too. So, come along." He led them along the clean corridors. A man in a wheelchair passed them. His face was a sheet of tight, stretched, red skin – no eyelids, no lips, no nose. Farther up the corridor another man in a striped housecoat reclined in a chair, reading in the light of a large window; his hands were black claws.

McIndoe saw his companions stiffen and explained, "It's tannic acid – not his own skin." He paused and looked at them with the same intensity as Matron had done a few moments ago. "They *will* heal. We can rebuild noses, reconstruct lips and eyelids and ears. It takes a long time, strip by strip, and I'm not going to pretend it is comfortable or pleasant – but it is better than being dead."

The pilots nodded solemnly and continued. After a moment McIndoe asked, as if casually, "When was the last time you had any leave?"

Robin cocked his head, a frown of puzzlement on his face, and asked in an imitation of complete innocence, "Leave? What's that?"

McIndoe did him the courtesy of laughing, and they continued down the corridor until he stopped before a closed door. A pretty young nurse emerged from the room. She smiled and nodded to the officers before reporting to Dr. McIndoe. "He's awake, sir, and ready."

"Thank you, Alice." Turning to the officers, the doctor said: "Mr. Goldman can't see very well at the moment. He may not be able to recognise you, so be sure to tell him who you are." At last the surgeon pushed on the swinging door and let the pilots file in.

It was a single room with a large window over-looking the manicured lawns. In front of the window was a little table on which a vase stood with a large yellow rose in it. The petals were brown at the edges, and several had already fallen to the table. Beside the bed sat Mr. Bowles, leaning his elbows on his knees. He looked up as the door opened and, recognising Colin, he broke into a smile. "I knew you'd come. I told Banks you would. Come here! Sit beside him." Then, turning to the man lying in the bed, he said in a cheery voice, "I'll leave you with your friends, Banks, but I'll be back." Then he was gone. They gazed after him, but then could not delay any longer. They approached the bed.

Banks was no longer recognizable. Bandages covered his face like an Egyptian mummy, and his scalp was bald. His eyes glinted out of slits in the bandages, watery and colourless. His mouth was a dark slit. It was hard to look at him. Colin overcame himself first. "It's me, Colin. Kiwi and the Skipper have come, too."

The head shifted a bit on the pillow. "Thank you." Banks' voice emerged out of the apparition undamaged, clearly recognizable, and that helped a bit.

Colin smiled. "Surely you knew we would come?"

"I didn't know if you'd have time – or when."

"Glorious English weather – it's raining," Kiwi quipped back.

"They're still pounding London. I can hear it every night, but the daylight raids seemed to have eased off. Is that right?"

"They've gone for the aircraft factories recently," Priestman explained. "First, they hit the Supermarine Spitfire assembly at Itchen, killing 40-some workers and injuring 60 more. Then two days ago they struck Woolston, killing another 40 workers and closing down production." The news of the Woolston raid had shaken him. He'd been there. He remembered the men rising to give him a standing ovation despite having crashed on their runway. He remembered the little man with the fringe of greying hair and the oil-stained overalls and wondered if he were among the casualties. He would never know, because he didn't even know the man's name.

Fortunately, Kiwi was with them and he was up to being cheery. While Robin's thoughts were still with the workers of the Supermarine factory, Kiwi glibly chatted about the sorties they'd flown to intercept all these raids. Then he remembered, "Oh, Tolkien wanted me to ask you if you wanted to read his Dad's manuscript. He thought you might want something to read that would be distracting...."

Banks nodded. "Yes. I'd like that – as soon as my eyes get better." His head shifted a bit. "Is the new Flight working out, Skipper?"

"Very well, actually. So much so, I've got a week off. I'm getting married tomorrow."

Banks managed to sound happy. "Congratulations, sir! Say hello to Miss Pryce – Mrs. Priestman – for me."

"I will. I'm sure she'll want to come and visit you."

"How did Mr. Bowles find out about you, Banks?" Colin asked.

The head on the pillow turned towards the padre. "I don't know. What *he* says is that Ginger woke him up in the middle of the night and told him to come. He says Ginger *shook* him awake out of a deep sleep, and while he tried to find the light so he could see him in the dark, Ginger told him, 'You've got to go to the hospital in East Grinstead, Dad. Banks needs you. You've got to go first thing in the morning.' But when he finally got the light on, there was no one there, of course. I suppose it was a dream."

They stared at him.

Banks continued, "He says I can go stay with him when they let me out of here to recuperate. He says he'll fix up the cottage so it's as clean and pretty as when his wife kept it."

"That's good. It will give him something to do. What have you heard from your own father?"

Silence.

Embarrassed, Colin glanced to Kiwi to change the subject. The New Zealander gamely started, "Woody asked me—"

Banks lifted a bandaged hand and pointed to the bedside table. Colin glanced over and saw a letter in the distinctive, almost sheer paper used for international airmail communications. Colin reached for it with an inquiring glance. "Do you want this?"

Banks nodded. "Read it."

Colin removed the letter from the slit-open envelope and unfolded it. His eyes scanned the letter silently. His face was very stiff as he re-folded and replaced the message. He contained himself a little longer, but then he burst out, "The bastard! I'm going to take a picture of you and send it to him!"

Banks shook his head. "It wouldn't make any difference." The eyes disappeared – rolled back in his skull, leaving the whites showing because he had no eyelids to close over them.

"I'm afraid, it's time for us get going," Priestman suggested, unable to take any more. "It's a long drive."

Kiwi and Colin took the hint – Kiwi gratefully and Colin reluctantly. The latter promised, "I'll be back again, soon."

The head on the pillow nodded. Priestman and Kiwi said good-bye and wished Banks a rapid recovery. They started for the door. Banks' voice reached them. "You aren't hiding anything from me, are you? The others are OK?"

"OK? The others are a bloody wreck," Kiwi retorted quickly. "If we tell them you're just lying around all day letting *very pretty* nurses feed and clean you, they'll probably go out on strike for equal treatment!"

"All of them?"

"Oh, you may be right. Sutton would oppose a strike—"

Recognizing that Banks couldn't take any joking on this topic, Priestman cut Kiwi off and answered seriously "Yes, they are."

"You'll make them keep a slot in Training Command for me, won't you, Skipper? I don't want to be invalided out. I want to stay in the RAF, and I want to fly again."

"I'll see what I can do. First you have to get well."

"I'll do my best, sir."

"I'm sure you will."

They hardly spoke all the way back to Tangmere.

RAF Tangmere

Mickey was called out of the Mess and into the Station Commander's office. "Where the hell is Priestman?" the Wing Commander opened. "I can't find him anywhere! And don't tell me to try *The Ship*; Glazebrook just called me from there. F/Lt Ringwood has just been rushed to Chichester General Hospital with acute appendicitis, and no one knows where Priestman is! Furthermore, I can't have him going off on a week's leave with only one inexperienced and rather unstable Flight Commander to lead the Squadron."

"Sir! He's getting married tomorrow. Things have been planned for weeks—"

"Yes, well they shouldn't have been! I warned him not to plan anything until mid-October at the earliest! He wheedled this week out of me by taking me by surprise. It was very much against my better judgement!"

"But you can't make him call it off now! Think of the poor girl! She's been very patient, and this is the most important day of her life. You can't ruin it for her!" Mickey protested.

"No, damn it! I'm not totally heartless, but we can't risk having Priestman gone more than 48 hours."

"Sir, that's not reasonable." Mickey insisted. "He's flown every sortie with the squadron in the last five weeks. He hasn't given himself a single day off!"

"Well, if he hadn't posted his only Flight Lieutenant the day he took over the squadron, maybe he wouldn't have needed to! He's got a very dangerous, irrational streak in him – posting three pilots in a day, shooting at the belly of loaded bombers from less than a hundred yards not to mention throttling *back* when a Messerschmitt is on his tail! Bloody impulsive is what that is! It's his damn Quaker blood!"

"What, sir?" Mickey could not understand either why the Station Commander was so angry or what Priestman's Quaker heritage had to do with anything. He certainly couldn't be accused of pacifism!

"I knew a Quaker gentleman once and he explained it all to me — that they don't have priests let alone bishops, etc., because each and everyone of them talks directly to God — or thinks they do. Now, if that isn't bloody dangerous, nothing is!"

"I'm sure Squadron Leader Priestman has no such delusions, sir. He's C of E, after all. He's getting married at Bosham Church."

"Well, you ask him about it — when you find him. I'll bet you a bottle of the best scotch that's exactly what he thinks! Now find him and tell him his leave's been reduced to 72 hours from the minute he goes off duty."

Mickey retreated quickly, going straight up to Priestman's room on the fourth floor. There he found only a rather distressed Thatcher. "Have you seen Mr. Priestman, sir?" the batman asked before Mickey could get out the same question.

"No, I've come looking for him."

"He was acting very strange, sir. I was here packing up for him and getting his shoes shined for his wedding tomorrow, and he stormed in like I've never seen him before. He hardly acknowledged I was here — not the usual way he stops to chat with me. He's always so polite, you know, and suddenly he just barked at me, 'Where the hell's my cravat?' He's never been like that before. And when I showed him I had just ironed it, he snatched it right out of my hands and went out again, slamming the door behind him."

Mickey didn't like the sound of that at all. Priestman didn't even know about his shortened leave yet. What on earth could have made him so angry? Thatcher was looking at him as if expecting an explanation, his distress written all over his ugly face.

Helplessly, Mickey remarked, "I'm sure he didn't mean to be rude. Maybe pre-nuptial jitters." Even as he said it, he knew how ridiculous it was. Priestman was the last man to worry about his wedding night, but it certainly wasn't like him to be rude to the loyal Thatcher. Mickey admitted out loud, "He's not down at *The Ship* with the others, either. I expect, he feared they might try some trick or other on the eve of his wedding. It's been done before. Must go and find him."

Leaving the unhappy batman still trying to do his best for his abruptly and inexplicably unpleasant master, Mickey made his way back downstairs and across to the Admin Block. All the offices were dark. No one was working late tonight. He flipped the hall switch and went into Priestman's office looking for some clue as to where to look for him.

Something lay crumpled up next to the wastepaper basket, and, being an orderly man, Mickey bent to pick it up. It was the cable he'd left on Priestman's desk this afternoon while he was away. Apparently, Priestman had come to his office after he returned from his visit to East

Grinstead, and he'd found this cable transferring P/O Goldman to Training Command and posting him to Central Flying School at Upavon. Mickey crumpled it up again and dropped it in the wastepaper basket, starting to feel uneasy. That had been very stupid of him. He should have just filed it away, not reminded Priestman of the now meaningless transfer request.

Just then the sound of a Hurricane flying straight for the building sent a tremor of alarm through him. The Hurricane roared overhead, just a few feet above the roof – in clear violation of all regulations.

Mickey ran out of the office and looked up in time to see the Hurricane, silhouetted against the moonlit sky, tucking in its undercarriage decorously. He had not been able to read any identification letters, but no one below the rank of Squadron Leader could authorise his own flight.

Mickey started running towards the airfield itself. He could just make out three men in overalls walking towards the hangar. "Who was that?" he called out to them. "Who just took off and beat up the Mess?"

"Squadron Leader Priestman, sir."

"Damn him!" Now Mickey was truly frightened. What could he hope to do in the middle of the night?

The airmen were beside him. "Is something wrong, sir?" the cheeky Cockney asked.

"You tell me! What the hell is he doing flying around in the middle of the night?"

"He said he was going hunting, sir. They're having another go at London, after all." The airman indicated the northeast, where dull flashes of light and distant rumbles recorded another Luftwaffe attack on the city. It was like the artillery barrages of the last war, which had become so routine one hardly noticed them.

"Did he seem himself?"

The three airmen exchanged a look, and the more steady Ripley answered this time, "No, sir. He was curt and unfriendly – just barking orders at us like we wasn't – well, you know, like we wasn't his crew or anything. Like we was perfect strangers, or petrol station attendants."

"Damn it!" Mickey turned on his heel and hurried back to the Mess in search of Allars. He found him in the bar and in a low voice confided what he had learned.

Allars gazed up at him from his pain-ravaged face and said simply, "He's cracked."

"What's that supposed to mean?"

Allars dragged himself to his feet with his cane and a heavy sigh. "No doubt he remembers that Dornier he shot down while at Hawarden, andnow he thinks he can join the fight over London – forgetting that nothing is the same. This isn't a lone intruder, it's a whole armada! And London has barrage balloons, and the ack-ack is twice as hot as Liverpool. He's bonkers! The one I feel sorry for is that poor girl, who thinks she's getting married tomorrow. He's a bloody fool!" Allars stomped off on his wooden leg, leaving Mickey snapping helplessly for words.

Mickey had another thought and ran down to the Ops Room. They kept the lights dim during the night so that the watch could sleep when all was quiet. Several of the WAAF were stretched out under the Map Table, their shoes lined up against the wall. A voice called down from the balcony. "Hello? Someone there?"

With relief Mickey recognised Bridges' voice. "Bridges! It's me, Mickey." He grabbed the banister and went up the steps to speak to the duty controller personally. Bridges met him at the top of the stairs, and Mickey spoke in a low voice, hoping the others were asleep. "Robin just took off. Do you know what's going on?"

"No, not really," Bridges admitted. "I asked him his intentions and he answered simply: 'I'm going to kill someone.' It was horrid. It echoed around the room and I heard one of the girls gasp. Frankly, it frightened me, too. It was like a voice out of hell."

Mickey sank against the balcony railing, and Bridges solicitously pulled him away. "I don't think that's all that strong – not since the raid." He led Mickey to a chair instead, and Mickey sank into it. His eyes were adjusting to the dark and he gazed up at Bridges, who was looking every bit as distressed as he felt. "You don't think he was suicidal or anything, do you?" Bridges asked anxiously.

Mickey shook his head helplessly. "I don't know. I just don't know." They waited it out together. The wall clock loudly counting away the seconds of fuel remaining. Now and again one of the WAAF turned over under the table with a little rustle. W/O Robinson was reading a book under one of the shaded desk-lamps. Every so often he turned a page. Tea was brought to Bridges at midnight. Mickey couldn't stand it a moment longer. "He's got less than 10 minutes of fuel left!"

"I could try to raise him," Bridges offered, moving at once to his hand-held radio and clicking it on. It sounded very loud in the still room. "Redcap Leader, Beetle here. Can you read me?"

"Loud and clear."

Mickey and Bridges looked at one another in amazement. He sounded perfectly normal and in the same room with them.

"Where are you, Redcap Leader?"

"I just beat up *The Ship* to make sure the chaps started for home.

Shouldn't be drinking this late, you know. Tomorrow is another day, and all that. I wouldn't want them napping on the job when they are supposed to be defending me and my bride from the barbarian Hun."

Mickey grabbed the radio from Bridges. "Just where the hell have you been? The Station Commander has been looking for you for hours!"

"Well, I'll be on the ground in another 2 minutes, so he'll just have to wait."

Mickey and Bridges stared at one another. "I'm going to meet him," Mickey announced, and started down the stairs. Bridges called after him, "Please let me in on the secret when you find out what it is."

"Gladly."

Mickey reached the Hurricane after the engine had cut off, and Appleby was already on the wing to help Priestman dismount. He heard Priestman remark in a perfectly normal tone of voice, "Appleby! Have you been waiting up for me? I owe you joy ride for that. When I come back from leave, I'll take you up in the Maggie."

"Thank you, sir!" Appleby said with feeling, and Robin was out of the cockpit. As he jumped down, he called, "Ripley?"

"Sir?" The fitter had to duck under the wing. "I have the horrible feeling I was very rude to you earlier this evening. I hope you will forgive me."

"Of course, sir."

"No. There is nothing 'of course' about it what-so-ever. I was rude, and I am very sorry."

"I'm sure you had your reasons, sir."

"I was very, very angry, but not at you, and I had no right to take it out on you. I know I would have been dead a hundred times by now if you didn't keep patching up and repairing and servicing this machine." He patted the wing of the Hurricane affectionately. "I *will* find a way of making it up to you."

"That's not necessary, sir."

"It is to me. Shall we say I owe you a favour? You choose when you want to cash it in, all right?"

"As you say, sir."

At last Priestman moved away from the machine and towards Mickey, who had stopped some ten feet away. Priestman noticed Mickey with a start. "Mickey? Come to escort me to the Station Commander?"

"No, sir. He gave me the message for you, but first would you mind telling me what that was all about? And did you get it out of your system, for God's sake?"

"I think so. When I took off, I thought I'd strafe the Air Ministry

After all, with the Luftwaffe over London, who would ever have found out it was me? But then I realised that I might miss and hit innocent civilians instead, so I nipped across the Channel and strafed a Luftwaffe airfield instead."

Mickey let out a slow sigh of relief. He didn't know what he was expecting, but it certainly could have been worse. This could be put down to just a little "over-exuberance" or "excessive keenness." He couldn't resist asking, however, "Would you mind telling me why you suddenly took it into your head to go chasing off in the middle of the night?"

"Banks is never going to fly again. His face is gone, and his hands are useless, shrivelled claws – all because those bastards at the Air Ministry couldn't move their arses fast enough! A highly gifted instructor, who would have benefited the RAF immeasurably, is now a human wreck, who'll never again know the pleasure of flight nor help anyone else to discover it. It was one life too many!"

"So, you wanted to *kill*?" Mickey asked, his incredulity obvious.

Priestman stopped dead in his tracks, and the light-heartedness vanished. "That was wrong, wasn't it?"

Mickey cursed himself inwardly. "Not as far as I'm concerned. You can kill Germans whenever you want. It just surprised me – from you, that is. With your Quaker background and all."

"What's that got to do with anything all of a sudden?"

"The Station CO was going on about it. He seemed to think that all Quakers believe they can talk directly to God. That's surely not true?"

There was a pause. Then Priestman replied: "More the other way around. God, we hope, talks to us." Oh, dear, Mickey thought. "The problem is listening, isn't it? I go off my head and decide to kill someone, and I'm deaf to Him. Do you think He'll punish me?"

"You'd better ask the padre that, not me. All I know is that the Station Commander had cut your leave from one week to 72 hours because Ringwood got rushed to hospital with appendicitis."

Priestman was silent for a long minute and then he said softly – not lightly, but not bitterly either. "That was quick retribution, don't you think? When are we due on readiness tomorrow?"

"7 am."

"The wedding's not until three in the afternoon. I'll go on readiness until lunch so we can have until noon on Wednesday together."

Then he walked away in the darkness.

Chapter 42

Portsmouth
29 September 1940

It was a clear, crisp autumn day with bright blue sky and only a few scattered clouds. Even grimy Portsmouth seemed washed clean by yesterday's rain, and the little puddles left behind sparkled in the bright sunshine. There was a brisk breeze on the Solent churning up white-caps, and the sea looked murky, whitish green. A pair of Royal Navy destroyers charged purposefully through the chop, their engines throbbing and their white ensigns stiff against the blue sky.

Emily stood on the Promenade, clutching a cardigan about her because it was chilly in the wind. It was only six hours until her wedding. She had "loads" of things to do — the hairdressers, pick up her gown from the dressmakers, collect the bridal bouquet and the corsages for Aunt Hattie, Mrs. Priestman and her own mother. Then it would probably be time for lunch with Admiral Priestman at his club, before changing and driving to Bosham.

Emily glanced towards the sky. The wisps of cirrus cloud were harmless and very high. Jerry would be over. He couldn't let a day like this slip by. But it didn't matter. Robin had the day off.

Crépon

Ernst felt like a different man after his return from Paris. He couldn't say exactly why, but as he walked across the sunny airfield to his waiting fighter, he was acutely aware of it. He had come a long way from the awkward "mascot" of the *Staffel*. He was not only one of the most senior pilots still with the unit, he had a confirmed kill — a Spitfire — and he was leading a *Schwarm*. His wingman walked anxiously beside and behind him, awaiting his orders, just as he would in the air. And he had a woman.

Ernst glanced towards the Communications Centre and noted that the windsock was standing out stiff. Force Four, the Met people had said, gusting to Five. "It'll be freezing cold in the Channel," someone had commented from the back of the briefing room, and the CO had cast the speaker a scathing look with the retort, "Then don't land there!"

Well, no one *planned* to land there, Ernst reflected. He glanced back at *Oberfeldwebel* Kreisel. "Everything in Order?"

"*Jawohl, Herr Leutnant.*"

"Then let's mount up."

Ernst cast his wingman a reassuring smile and headed towards his own waiting Emil. They had given him a new one a couple of days ago. It still had a clean cockpit and no tears or patches on wings or fuselage. It even smelled differently, Ernst noted as he eased himself down into the narrow cockpit. It didn't seem at all tight any more, now that he'd lost five kilos. He turned his thoughts to the cockpit drill. Thumbs up to the ground crew. Flip the starter switch. The Emil roared into life with a short gush of smoke. A couple of backfires and then the engine settled down nicely. Ernst checked his watch. He was a minute ahead of schedule, but Kreisel started up with a roar on his other side. Beyond him, the other two fighters of his *Schwarm* were also vibrating, as the whirling propellers caught the morning sunlight and gleamed like golden disks.

They took off on schedule, joined up with the rest of the Group, and flew up to Boulogne for refuelling before the rendezvous with the bombers and the rest of the escort. Two weeks out of hospital, and it was all pure routine again, Ernst told himself – only lying a little. He'd be happier on the return leg, but he could tell himself there was nothing much to this, and the man he had become agreed with him firmly.

They had the high escort role today. That wasn't as prestigious as the flanking sweeps which the aces got to lead, but it wasn't as difficult as close escort, either. They could climb up to 10,000 metres where the Emil had a clear advantage over the Tommy fighters and look down on the whole battle from a position of sovereign detachment. Then if the English flung a couple of fighters at the bombers, they could dive down out of the sky and chase them away.

They crossed the English coastline just seven minutes behind schedule, and the first puffs of flak burst silently in the sky below. The flak was so far away that it seemed almost pretty – like little blossoms bursting open above the still green English countryside. Off to the right he saw Messerschmitts diving down purposefully. Ernst searched for the Tommies, but their camouflage appeared to be working well. No matter. The other *Gruppe* had seen them in time and was taking care of them.

They continued inland. Visibility was extremely good today. You could see the silly barrage balloons swaying over the city of London. Ernst couldn't see what good they did. They forced the bombers to fly higher, that was all, but from greater altitude the explosives were just as devastating, only a bit less accurate. Less accurate meant they would cause more civilian casualties than necessary.

Ernst had read newspaper reports about the chaotic situation in London. They said the people were without electricity and water for days on end. The corpses of the victims were left to rot in the ruins until they stank. Soon there would be widespread disease – typhoid and the like. The rich aristocrats had retired to their country homes, while the poor were left to take the brunt of the attacks alone. The population was getting angrier all the time. Maybe they would finally get angry enough to force their government to make peace?

Ernst sighed and admitted to himself that he wanted to go home. He was tired of this futile, senseless war against a country nobody really wanted to fight – much less humiliate and defeat. The *Führer* had made that perfectly clear. He said the English were Germany's natural allies. The English and the Germans ought to be fighting together against the Communists, not killing each other. If only the English would see reason, they could all go home, and he could marry Klaudia. They could have a place of their own and start a family. Ernst liked the idea of training and flying without being shot at.

"*Indianer*! To port. Going for the left-hand column of bombers."

"Understood," Henning acknowledged, adding the order, "5 Staffel, deal with them."

"*Jawohl*," Fischer responded and dipped his wing. He did not have to order the others to follow him; they had heard Henning and could see what Fischer himself was doing. As they dived, the three *Schwarm* spread out into battle formation. As they were two pilots short, Fischer was leading with his wingman only. Dieter led the right-hand *Schwarm*. Ernst led the left-hand *Schwarm* and was thus closest to the enemy.

They were facing an almost equal number of English fighters, Hurricanes fortunately. Ernst still preferred facing Hurricanes to Spitfires, even if his terror of Spitfires had declined noticeably since he'd managed to bring one down.

The Tommies spotted them in time, and the leading four aircraft turned to face the approaching Messerschmitts. Oddly, they were flying in an identical formation to the German *Schwarm* rather than the usual RAF vic of three.

Ernst tensed even more as he realised that the leader was coming towards him with apparent deliberateness. Nervously he swallowed and wished he could remove his gloves to wipe the sweat off his hands on his trousers, but there wasn't time. He had to switch on the gun sight and take the safety off the guns.

When had the Tommies become so fond of these head-on attacks? They made everything happen so fast, and the risk of collision was terrible. Ernst was sweating in streams as he tried to keep steady. In this head-on attack, height didn't give him any advantage. He was screaming down towards the enemy who was clearly aiming for him. The Englishman's wingman had even eased out a little to target Kreisel. "Oh, God!" Ernst prayed. "Don't let these be some of those suicidal Tommies that intentionally crash!"

The Hurricane confronting him started to flash at him, and in the next instant he felt the bullets shattering along his wing. The Emil shuddered. Holes appeared in the wings. Bullets were spurting through the side of the cockpit and then it darkened completely. The roar of the Merlin engine filled the whole cockpit, deafening and disorienting him. Ernst screamed.

Only after the sun reappeared did he realise they had not collided after all. At the same time he realised his left arm was useless – again. There was blood all over his sleeve. Although he didn't actually feel anything yet, he was seized with panic. He'd been hit again! The Emil must be damaged! And around him the dogfight whirled.

Kreisel had disappeared, but behind him and to his right there were aircraft going every which way. Tracer left dirty trails upon the sky in a crazy pattern. A turning Hurricane suddenly flipped over and started turning the other way – only in doing so, its wing brushed against the tail of a Messerschmitt. Ernst saw half the wing of the Hurricane break clean away. Another Hurricane dived past Ernst's nose with a Messerschmitt on its tail pumping lead into it. Another Hurricane was turning in a tight circle set upon by two Messerschmitts at once. Somehow there seemed to be more Tommies about than when they started – more Messerschmitts too, as if the whole *Gruppe* had come down to fight it out. The bombers were nowhere to be seen – not that Ernst looked very hard.

His thoughts returned inside the cockpit. He'd been hit. His left arm was useless. The sensible thing to do was to get away from here. Try to get home. The Channel will be awfully cold.... Ernst flipped the Emil on its back and pulled the stick back with just one thought: down, down, down and away.

Only after he'd dived to 1 thousand metres and levelled out, setting his course due south, did Ernst notice that the engine temperature was nearing the "danger" zone and the needle was still rising.

Alarm seized him instantly. He glanced forward towards the trusty engine, and saw the thin, telltale trail of white smoke rushing towards him on the slipstream. "Oh, God, no!"

Ernst glanced down. Where was he? How far from the Channel? He couldn't even see it – just a parachute floating down below him with a pilot swaying on the ends of the lines.

Oh, God, no, Ernst whispered again, but already he knew there was no hope. If he increased the power, the engine would burn faster; if he cut it back, he'd sink to the earth. He was not going to get home. He was not even going to make it to the Channel.

The smoke turned from white to grey and then black. The temperature was off the clock. Any minute now the engine was going to catch fire. He had to put the Emil down – now, here, anywhere he could. He looked desperately around for a place to land, rocking his wings to get a better view.

For the first time Ernst registered that the English countryside was cut up by stone walls and copses of trees and hundreds of other lethal barriers. The fields were divided into little patches – nothing big and comfortable to land on as in Normandy.

Oh, God, why now? When he'd been shot up last time, it hadn't mattered as much. He'd thought Klaudia didn't care about him. He'd had no one particular to live for. Now he wanted to live more than ever. Oh, God, don't let me die!

The smoke was getting thicker. It was billowing back at him, almost blinding him, and it made him nauseous as well.

Concentrate! There had to be somewhere he could land. An Emil didn't need a lot of room. Ahead the countryside got decidedly hilly and more forested, so Ernst gently banked and turned back to the flatter, more open countryside that he had just crossed. The parachute was still drifting down almost to the ground now, and it attracted his attention. It looked like it would land in an open meadow farther to the right. That looked like a good place to land.

Ernst banked around towards it gently. At least when turning the smoke blew off to the side, and he could see better. Yes. It would have to do. There were sheep in it. He hoped he wouldn't hit one. There was also a farmhouse at the end of the pasture. A big, stone farmhouse with a stone barn. It would kill him if he hit it. He had to put her down now! Ernst put on full flaps, lifted the nose and then throttled back, his eyes closed. The Emil smashed into the ground with a horrible jolt that flung him against his harness and drew an unconscious scream from him.

The Emil did not bounce. It just tore its way forward – grass, mud, stones and sheep crashing against it – until it came to a halt.

Ernst took a moment to get his breath, but then the smell of oily smoke brought him back to life. With his right hand, he released the straps, and reached for the canopy handle. It was gone. Shot away. How was that possible? The handle had to be here. But it wasn't. The hood was firmly latched closed, and he had no way of releasing it from the inside. He reached up and tried to push it open. It wouldn't budge.

This couldn't be happening. The cockpit was filling with smoke, and Ernst was dripping sweat as the temperature in the narrow space increased. The metal frame of the canopy burnt to touch. Then he caught a glimpse of orange flames licking out towards him from the engine. The engine was burning well and good now. In just a few seconds the flames would reach the fuel tanks and the unused ammunition in the wings. God knew he might even have ruptured the fuel tanks landing. There might be aviation fuel all over the ground around him.

With frantic desperation, Ernst struggled to push the canopy open. He couldn't get it to budge. In pain and bleeding, he started sobbing from frustration and effort. He was swimming in sweat. Flames were waving wildly at him from less than a metre away.

Abruptly loud thuds and bangs rained down on his head. His view was blocked by men hammering at the canopy. They were apparently trying to open it, but they were shoving and kicking, trying to slide it backwards. "No!" he shouted and gestured, trying to indicate the handle. He only succeeded in scaring them off entirely.

They were gone. Ernst felt the skin of his face start to blister. He was going to be burnt alive.

The hood suddenly sprang open. A rush of cold air enveloped him, whipping the flames to new heights. Yet Ernst felt someone grab him under the arms. He was being dragged out of the cockpit and clear of the Emil itself.

People were shouting furiously. There seemed to be lots of them. More hands grabbed him. They weren't exactly gentle. He was being dragged and hauled across the ground at a run. Were they going to lynch him? He caught glimpses of guns, bayonets – no, kitchen knives – glittering in the sun. They were going to kill him.

Ernst tried to protect his face with his good arm, and then he felt the earth lift under him and felt a wash of hot air as a tremendous explosion shook him. A piece of debris hit his leg so hard it numbed his foot; smaller bits and pieces rained down on him. The main fuel tank must have just exploded.

After that there was a curious silence – or what seemed like silence. The flames were still hissing.

Finally, someone stirred slightly. Ernst realised he was being held in a man's arms.

The people around him started speaking among themselves in urgent but not hysterical voices. Ernst tried to lift his head and orient himself. The man holding him released him a bit so he could sit up. The worst was over. He was going to live.

As he gradually took in his surroundings, Ernst noticed a crowd had gathered, including some young boys eagerly gaping from behind their mother's skirts, and several young women with scarves tied at the top of their heads, just like factory women at home, only these were leaning on pitchforks. Ernst was reminded of the RAD girls, helping out on farms. He wanted to smile at them, but they drew back when he looked at them.

That's right. He was the enemy. The enemy who had been bombing them. Maybe killing some of their friends or family in London. The thought made him sad, and he became aware of how weak he was. His vision seemed to be dimming too.

Suddenly a man in uniform – well, a silly tin hat and an armband, rather like the Block-Wardens – appeared. He started shouting orders. How familiar. The housewife, boys and the English RAD-girls retreated before this figure of authority. But the man holding him was not very impressed. He talked back. That produced a canteen of water, which Ernst gratefully gulped down. Then he was laid out on the grass by the man who had dragged him out of the airplane. Gradually, the realization that his face and hands were very badly burnt penetrated to Ernst's consciousness.

It felt good to just lie on the grass with the cool breeze blowing. If only the sun didn't burn so. Ernst raised his good arm and tried to shield his face from the sun. The man who had dragged him out of the Emil understood what he was trying to do and adjusted their position so his own body cast shade over Ernst's face. In the process, Emil thought he saw a yellow life-jacket on his rescuer, but he wasn't sure. Maybe he was just imagining things – wishing it was Christian.

The thought of the last time he had been wounded, of the way Christian had led him to safety and been there to help him out of the cockpit, made him moan, but then he tried to focus on his benefactor. His eyes, however, were starting to swell shut, and they were watering terribly. He couldn't see the man – just a blur of dark and light, blue and yellow, swimming in tears.

At last, he heard sirens. He could hardly see anything, but he detected new voices and felt people beside him. He was lifted off the grass and onto something clean and cool – a stretcher. They carried him out of the sun and into the shade. Ernst knew he was in an ambulance, and that was good. He heard the doors clang shut. The ambulance swayed a bit as the drivers climbed in front, and then the engine sprang into life. The ambulance trembled until it was put into gear and they drove off.

Only then did Ernst register that he was a prisoner. Poor Klaudia, he thought. He hoped someone would break the news to her gently. He hoped someone had seen him land. It would be horrible if she thought he was dead. He would be able to write eventually, but it could take months. Why did this have to happen to him now?

Bosham

The invasion barriers ran along the peninsula beyond the tidal basin, which was crowded with sailing dinghies. Families on outings were picnicking on the lawn of the boat club, watching. Many turned and watched – smiling – as a bride, attended by a small crowd of relatives, alighted in front of the ancient stone church. She was in a layered gown that fluttered in the stiff breeze, and her long veils were quite out of control.

"What a lovely day for a wedding," someone exclaimed.

"You must get in out of the wind, or your hair will be ruined," Mrs. Priestman insisted. Emily was reluctant to leave the glorious day outside for the relative darkness of the church.

Still, there was no arguing with Mrs. Priestman's logic, and Emily found it difficult to contradict Robin's mother in any case. She wanted to get on with her, since she was never going to get on with her own parents. At least they had deigned to come to the wedding, but her mother looked as sour as if she'd swallowed a lemon. She was also dressed more for a funeral than a wedding, in a grey, double-breasted suit with black cuffs and collar. She even wore black stockings and shoes. Emily's father just looked rather pathetic in his ancient, baggy suit, worn shiny over the years, and with his hair blown away from his bald crown whenever he removed his hat.

Robin's family, in contrast, looked very smart. The Admiral was a formidable figure: tall, straight, with a mass of pure white hair and a silver-headed cane. He wore dress naval uniform with a battery of ribbons on his breast and twisted braid on his cap. Robin's mother looked elegant in a raw-silk, three-quarter-length, green dress, while Aunt Hattie wore a tailored suit of teal blue. Emily registered that in this attire, Hattie looked younger and downright handsome.

That was the wedding party. The only friend Emily would have liked as her bridesmaid was now a WREN stationed in Liverpool. She hadn't been willing to take leave. ("We've lost over 50 ships this past month, Emily," she'd explained in a tone of utter devastation. The North Atlantic was her war. She had no energy for the Battle of Britain.) So, Emily had decided to do without a bridesmaid.

Inside the ancient church, the flowers were already in place. The vicar came over, smiling happily, to welcome them. He shook hands warmly with Emily's parents, prompting Mrs. Pryce to dispel his good-will by telling him pointedly that she and her husband were "free thinkers."

"So are we all, I hope," countered the vicar blithely, eliciting a short snort of amusement from the Admiral.

Mrs. Priestman started fussing with Emily's hair and veils to get everything back in place. Then she asked the vicar if they could take refuge in the sacristy so Robin wouldn't see his bride before her triumphal walk up the aisle. The organist arrived and started warming up.

RAF Tangmere

They stood in a tense circle inside the dispersal hut around Flight Lieutenant Glazebrook. Kiwi put their feelings into words. "We can't just let the poor girl stand there! Someone's got to go and tell her what happened."

"I understand the padre will go."

"You can't fob this off on poor Colin! He wasn't up there. He can't tell her a Goddamned thing!"

"We haven't been stood down."

"Well, stop waffling and get on the frigging phone to get us stood down!" Kiwi told the Flight Lieutenant in his best Down-Under accent.

"We don't all have to go," Green suggested sensibly; "it would be enough if Kiwi goes. He saw what happened best."

Glazebrook looked uncertainly from the pilots towards the orderly office, with its phone connecting them to the Operations Room. He licked his lips and ran his hand through his over-thin hair. First Ringwood was rushed to hospital with acute appendicitis, and then the CO was shot down during the morning. He was down to 10 pilots. How could he let any more of them go? His hands started to shake. To stop them, he shoved them into his pockets.

"OK!" Kiwi told him. "You can ground me, or Court Martial me, or – I don't give a bloody damn – hang me from the frigging yardarm! I'm going to Bosham whether you give me leave to go or not!" The big New Zealander plunged out of the dispersal, tearing his life-jacket off as he went.

Bosham

It was quarter past three, and even Emily was getting nervous. Her parents were giving her "we-told-you-so" looks and shaking their heads, lips pressed together. Mrs. Priestman kept rushing to look out of the door (there was no window in the sacristy) and exclaimed over and over, "Where on earth could he have got to! It's so unlike him to be late."

Admiral Priestman at first made sniping remarks about the "junior service" obviously knowing nothing about "punctuality," but then he became silent and broody.

It was after three-thirty before Hattie came in like a breath of fresh air – she'd been keeping watch outside. "Colin's car just pulled in at the *Anchor Bleu*," she announced with a wide smile.

"Finally!" Mrs. Priestman exclaimed. "Now we'll just let him get inside. I've already arranged with the organist to start playing the Bach Fugue you wanted as soon as he's in position. That's the signal for you and your father to nip around to the door while Hattie and I go inside with your mother."

Emily had heard this all before and found herself looking in her compact for the hundredth time. Why was she still so nervous?

There was a knock on the door. The vicar stood there. "Miss Pryce? I'm afraid—ah—"

Emily looked up and recoiled at the sight of Kiwi towering behind the clergyman. Kiwi was supposed to be on readiness with the rest of the squadron – and he wasn't in dress uniform, either.

No. No. No. No. Don't scream! She held her breath. Don't act like silly Lettice Fields. He wouldn't want it of you. But what was she supposed to do?

"Miss Pryce, I'm sorry we couldn't get here earlier," Kiwi floundered miserably, his eyes fixed on her with pity. "The new flight commander was being a" – he swallowed the expletive just in time – "bit difficult."

"Where's Robin?" she managed to get out in a flat voice.

"I don't know. I swear I saw him get out, but—" but he'd said that about Banks, too. Kiwi's distress was written all over his face. "He should have called in ages ago. It was just after 11 am when we scrambled. He took us into a scrap, going like a bomb just about three inches over the coop of the yellow-noses, but then got himself in the cart, pranged one of the bastards, and had to take a walk."

"He was on leave," Emily said in a steady voice. She was icy cold.

Kiwi drew three breaths before he could answer. "Right, but when Ringwood went to hospital last night, he put himself back on the board for the morning." Kiwi turned and looked over at Mickey.

Mickey was standing behind him looking devastated, and he tried to explain. "The Station Commander shortened his leave to 72 hours and in order to spend as much of that with you as possible, he thought he'd start his leave later...." Mickey's voice faded out helplessly. It sounded so stupid in face of what had happened.

Emily found herself thinking, "I could *kill* you, Robin! – if you weren't already dead. How could you do it? Why? Why? Why? Don't I mean anything to you?" She was furious with him, so furious she hated him. The arrogant bastard! He absolutely refused to admit that he was mortal! She was so close to tears of rage that she had to turn away.

Behind her, Admiral Priestman demanded to know what had happened "in *English*, not this RAF gibberish!"

Mrs. Priestman was saying to Hattie, "I don't understand. What's happened? Robin wasn't flying today. What's happened?"

Emily fled outside into the beautiful sunshine, which now seemed a cruel, malicious, divine joke. She started running, picking up her skirts in an unseemly fashion, but soon she was too out of breath to run any further. She was aware of all the picnickers staring at her. She supposed they thought she was running away from her wedding.

She slowed her pace and skirted around the boat club to go out onto the pier. Here she stood with the wind buffeting her, and her veils and hair whipping about in wild disorder, and just held onto the railing.

She didn't believe it. She couldn't. Every day since they had met she'd feared this, but this morning she'd thought she was safe – for one whole week. Was that really too much to ask? People like her parents who didn't love each other were married for years and years. It wasn't fair that she couldn't have even one short week with the man she loved. What did fairness have to do with it? No one was up there ordering things anyway. It was all just luck. Robin's – and hers – had apparently run out.

She stared at the sailing dinghies as they heeled over violently, their helmsmen leaning out of the little cockpits to keep them from going over. She watched the whitecaps form and break beyond the sea wall. She stared and didn't see. Or she saw and didn't think. She was out cold. After a while she became aware that Colin was standing a few feet away from her.

She looked over at him. Poor Colin. He looked miserable. He'd lost his best friend three weeks ago, and then Banks had been shot down and burned. Robin had told her he was going over with Colin to visit Banks yesterday.

"How's Banks doing?" Emily asked him.

Colin started, surprised that she had come to and by the question. He hesitated, but then admitted, "He's much more badly burnt than we'd been led to believe. But he is in excellent hands, and the doctor says he'll recover. Only he won't ever fly again. That upset us all a bit yesterday."

Emily nodded. Maybe that was the reason Robin hadn't rung yesterday; she'd assumed he'd just been out drinking. "What time is it?"

"It's almost five."

"That late? How long have I been standing here?"

"More than an hour."

Emily turned towards him and realised she was very stiff. "I suppose I can't stand here forever. I might as well go back and face them." The next wedding was scheduled for 5 pm. The vicar had told her that long ago, but she'd forgotten. Now the guests for the next wedding were arriving – lots of them. This being a more fashionable time or a more fashionable crowd, everyone seemed very dressed up. Hats and gloves were the rule; the men were in grey tails. A large, spacious Rolls Royce arrived with the bride and a silver-haired gentleman who looked very "gentry" to Emily.

She started back towards the church with Colin. Her own small wedding party had abandoned it to the newcomers and stood in a forlorn little group next to Hattie's battered old Morris. Mrs. Priestman was apparently crying, and Hattie was holding her up. God knew how, since Hattie had loved him as much as anyone. Emily's parents, Mickey and the Admiral, stood about stiffly. Kiwi had apparently returned to Tangmere. Emily didn't blame him.

A Royal Mail delivery truck came to an abrupt halt in front of the church, getting in the way of the arriving guests. Emily watched disinterestedly and realised dispassionately that her grief was robbing her of her senses. The man getting out of the passenger side looked for all the world as if he were in RAF uniform. Indeed, he was pushing his way through the offended crowds of smart guests in their fashionable frocks, wearing what looked like a flight jacket. Worse. He looked like Robin.

She started running, trying to get through the crowds of arriving guests who drew back aghast at the sight of her. "Good heavens!"

"Why the rush?!"

"Who is that??!"

"Emily!" He caught her and crushed her to him. "I'm so sorry. They wouldn't listen to me when I tried to explain I had to be released. They wouldn't even let me make a phone call. They locked me in. I had to leave by the window and hitchhike."

"I don't care. Tell me later. Kiss me."

He obeyed willingly – until he became aware of just how much attention they were attracting. Then he drew back, looking about without letting go of Emily – or she of him. "What is this? Another wedding?"

"For five o'clock." Emily hooked her hand through his elbow and started to lead him away, back towards their own little crowd, which had witnessed the dramatic meeting and was approaching them in an agitated gaggle. Robin looked at his watch, and she saw for the first time that his hands were bandaged.

"What happened?"

"Nothing serious. It wasn't my kite. I helped another pilot out of his cockpit just before it exploded. He was trapped inside."

"I could kill you! Why do you take such chances?"

Robin looked at her baffled. "I had to help. The civilians didn't know the 109 cockpit opens sideways." Before Emily could fully register the implications, he kissed her again, and then – having noticed Colin at last – turned and bade him, "Tell the vicar we're coming, would you?" Colin nodded and hurried away, still dazed.

Meanwhile, Robin's mother enfolded him in her arms, sobbing, "We thought you were dead."

"The rumors were slightly exaggerated." Robin deftly freed himself of her grasp and moved her to his left, so he could keep his right arm around Emily. To the others he explained, "I misjudged a flick roll and collided with a 109, broke the wing and had to jump. At least I managed to land very nicely this time – remembered all the rules about bending knees and rolling and what-not. As I was telling Emily, I got delayed by trying to help another pilot who was trapped in his cockpit with the engine on fire. By the time we got him out, he was in pretty bad shape, so I had to stay with him until the ambulance arrived. The orderlies insisted I come back with them to have my hands seen to – which seemed reasonable enough. It was only noon, and I thought I could still get back in time for the wedding. I told the ambulance to drive to East Grinstead because I knew that was the best place for burn cases, only Dr. McIndoe recognized me and thought I needed an immediate rest. He ordered his staff not to release me or let me make phone calls. As soon as they finished bandaging my hands, they locked me in one of the rooms. Fortunately, it was on the ground floor, so I got out the window without difficulty, but they'd kept my wallet, so I had to hitchhike. The gentlemen of the Royal Mail were very good to go so far out of their way. I seem to be talking rather a lot. Shouldn't we get on with the wedding?"

"I don't know if there's time, now." Mickey pointed out, with an anxious glance towards the crowd of guests gathered for the next wedding.

The vicar emerged with Colin, his robes fluttering wildly both from the wind and his hurried stride. He approached the evidently indignant gentleman in the Rolls Royce. With gestures in the direction of Robin, he appeared to be explaining the situation.

A moment later, the entire crowd turned to look in the direction of the little group at the side. The elderly gentleman lifted his top hat to Robin and bowed his head, smiling graciously, and Robin, lacking a cap, smiled and waved back. Robin at once started for the church with Emily still on his arm. His mother stopped him and reminded him that wasn't how it was done. At that point, the vicar also intercepted him. He held out his hand, "Squadron Leader Priestman, I presume. A pleasure to meet you at last."

Robin held out a bandaged hand, but pleaded, "Please don't squeeze too hard."

The priest took it very gently in both of his. "Bless you. For all you're doing and have been doing." He looked deep into Robin's eyes as he spoke, embarrassing the younger man.

Robin felt compelled to point out, "Before you get the wrong idea, I burnt them saving a German pilot."

Except for Emily, the others hadn't heard this. It provoked exclamations of surprise and outrage from his mother, the Admiral, Mickey and even the Pryces.

The priest's expression did not change. He simply smiled and explained. "The next wedding party has agreed to wait until you're finished, but with so much wind, it would be kind of you if you'd let the guests into the church."

"Of course," Robin agreed, and then thought to look to Emily. She nodded. She didn't care if the whole world was there – just as long as it happened NOW.

The vicar gave the signal and all the natty, well-heeled guests moved like a great herd towards the church door.

Mickey pried Robin away from Emily and took him around to the side. "What the hell were you trying to do?" Mickey asked as they got out of hearing. "Make up for being so aggressive last night?"

Robin stopped and looked at the adjutant in astonishment. "I hadn't thought of it that way, but I suppose you're right. If God was chivalrous enough to give me a chance to redeem myself, surely it would have been churlish to rebuff Him?"

Mickey shook his head in incomprehension, muttering more to himself than to Priestman, "You really do believe God arranges things for you, don't you?"

The Admiral started ushering Mrs. Priestman and Hattie into the church, leaving Emily alone with her parents and Colin. Colin took both her hands in his, smiling with inner bliss. "I almost doubted Him myself, for a moment."

The first chords of organ music wafted out of the open doors, and Colin offered his arm to Mrs. Pryce. They went together into the church, leaving Emily alone with her father.

For a moment they stood unspeaking, and then Mr. Pryce remarked, "I will never understand your young man. First, he does his best to kill Germans – very successfully, too – and then he turns around and risks his life saving one."

Emily thought for a moment and then, slipping her arm through her father's elbow, answered evenly, "It's really not that complicated. As long as the Germans are flying in their aircraft, they are attacking and threatening us. Once they have been shot down, they are vulnerable human beings deserving of mercy and respect."

"You've changed so much, Emily," her father said to her, as she rearranged her veil as best she could in the still gusting wind. "This man has turned you into a stranger."

"Not really. I was always different. You just didn't notice. All Robin has done is to give me the courage to start living the life I want. That's the fugue I asked for."

They went together into the church. The late afternoon sunlight streamed through the rose widow, scattering shards of translucent color across the entire church. As they progressed up the aisle, the roomful of strangers stood up row by row as if they were royalty.

For nearly a thousand years, Emily calculated, women had tread these worn flagstones towards the same ritual. Many must have been little more than frightened children, terrified of the stranger by the altar. Others must have been relieved or grateful to be wed at all. Yet she doubted if any had been as frightened as she had been today – or as amazed and grateful to see their bridegroom grinning at them as she did now. It didn't matter to her in the least that he was in flying boots and his dirty hair was hanging in his eyes.

He was going to turn her into a believer yet, she realised a little awestruck; for how could anyone in their right mind attribute his survival today to sheer luck?

Historical Note

For Hitler, the Luftwaffe's failure to defeat the Royal Air Force in the summer of 1940 was an annoyance rather than a major strategic set-back. He had long declared his preference to have Great Britain as an ally. He had hoped the British would not 'interfere' with his invasion of Poland. He had expected the British government to sue for peace after the fall of France. When the Luftwaffe proved incapable of creating the conditions for an invasion, Hitler turned his attention back to his long-held goal of invading the Soviet Union. The war against the Soviet Union was Hitler's passion; the war against the British Empire was an irritating complication about which he lost little sleep. To this day most Germans have never even heard of the Battle of Britain, and if they have, they attribute to it no major significance.

For Britain, the United States, Occupied Europe, and later even the Soviet Union, on the other hand, the significance of the Battle of Britain can hardly be over-stated. If the RAF had been defeated in 1940, the Luftwaffe would have been able to continue indiscriminate daylight bombing almost indefinitely, and the Wehrmacht would almost certainly have risked an invasion attempt.

Although many doubt this would have been successful, there is no certainty that it would have been repulsed either. The Royal Navy had been seriously weakened by the losses during the evacuation at Dunkirk and was over-stretched trying to protect the Atlantic lifeline. Furthermore, the British Expeditionary Force had abandoned all its heavy equipment in France, and in consequence, the British ground forces lacked tanks and artillery for fighting the heavily mechanised Wehrmacht. Churchill was not only being dramatic when he spoke about fighting a guerrilla war against the invaders.

But the Battle of Britain was more than a military victory. The Battle of Britain was a critical psychological and diplomatic victory as well. At the time, the psychological impact of defeating the apparently invincible Luftwaffe was enormous. The RAF had proved that the Luftwaffe could be beaten, and by inference that meant the Wehrmacht could be beaten. This fact alone encouraged resistance and kept hope alive all across occupied Europe.

Of even greater significance was the diplomatic impact. As a result of British tenacity and defiance in the Battle of Britain, the United States, which at the start of the Battle had written Britain off as a military and political power, revised its opinion of British strength. Because of the

Battle of Britain, the U.S.A. shifted its policy from 'neutrality' to 'non-belligerent' assistance. With American help, Britain was able to keep fighting until Hitler over-extended himself in the Soviet Union.

If the United Kingdom had lost the Battle of Britain, it is unlikely that it could have provided assistance to the Soviet Union, and even less likely that the United States would have been drawn into the European war. Without aid from the United States, it is improbable that Hitler would have been defeated. The Battle of Britain was the necessary pre-requisite for future victory in Europe.

Yet, interest in the Battle of Britain is not really a function of its military significance. There were many other critical battles in WWII from Stalingrad to Midway. Nor is the appeal of the Battle of Britain founded on its magnitude or cost. Compared to the slaughter fields of the First World War or the Eastern Front in the Second, the price of victory was affordable. During the Battle of Britain, the RAF lost 1,023 aircraft (compared to the Luftwaffe's loss of 1,887 aircraft). In fact, due to the dramatic increases in aircraft production introduced by Lord Beaverbrook, the RAF ended the Battle with more front-line fighter aircraft than it had at the start of the Battle. In contrast, the Luftwaffe's fighter strength declined by 30%. Furthermore, while the Luftwaffe lost 2,698 airmen during the battle (killed, wounded and captured), the RAF lost just 544 pilots killed.

Ironically, it is the very small numbers involved that account in part for our fascination with the Battle of Britain. As Sir Winston Churchill put it so eloquently, "never in the field of human conflict was so much owed by so many to so few." This image of a small "band of brothers" standing up to a massive and invincible foe was reminiscent of other heroic battles – Henry V at Agincourt, Edward the Black Prince at Poitiers, Leonidas and his 300 at Thermopylae. Such battles, pitting a few defenders against a hoard of enemy, have always appealed to students of history and readers of historical fiction.

Yet, while the numbers involved were small and the losses objectively smaller still, pilots were specialists who could not be readily or rapidly replaced. This is what made the Battle such a close run and dangerous confrontation. Pilot losses represented roughly 40% of Fighter Command's strength. In short, from the perspective of the *participants*, chances of survival were barely greater than 50%.

The situation was aggravated by the fact that the more experienced pilots had a 5-6 times greater chance of surviving than did novice pilots coming into the front line with very little flying and no combat experience. In consequence, there were pilots who fought throughout the Battle (four full months), but also pilots who did not survive even four hours. A core of experienced pilots watched waves of replacements arriving and being shot down in a short space of time. Meanwhile, sheer exhaustion gradually wore down the veterans. By the end of the Battle, it was the Squadron Leaders, Flight Lieutenants and Section Leaders who were falling victim to sheer exhaustion, which led to inattention and mistakes.

For an individual squadron engaged in the Battle of Britain, the pilots who were seriously injured and hospitalised also had to be replaced, so the effective casualty rate (killed *and* wounded) at squadron level was closer to 70% than 50%. This situation forced ACM Dowding and AVM Park to pull entire squadrons out of the front line (i.e. 11 Group) and replace them with fresh squadrons when a certain — albeit entirely subjective — level of exhaustion and depletion had been reached. Altogether 16 squadrons were withdrawn from 11 Group in the one month between August 8 and September 8, 1940.

The problem with this rotation was that the replacement squadrons — like replacement pilots — were far more likely to suffer casualties and far less likely to destroy enemy aircraft than the tired but experienced squadrons. This was because the replacement squadrons often had no pilots with experience of the combat conditions reigning in southeast England at the time. Without experienced leaders, these fresh squadrons were often mauled badly during their first encounters with the Luftwaffe. It was not uncommon for these squadrons to lose five to six aircraft and three to four pilots in a single engagement. Fighter Command literally could not afford such losses, if it hoped to win the Battle.

Furthermore, for Fighter Command the issue was not merely one of surviving — they could have done that by withdrawing beyond the range of the German fighters. The issue was causing enough damage to the Luftwaffe to make it either unable or unwilling to provide the necessary air cover for an invasion. In short, kills counted. If the Luftwaffe hadn't been losing aircraft and aircrew that Hitler wanted for his aggressive plans elsewhere, he might have very well opted for the invasion. Kills, however, came predominantly from a limited number (approximately 5%) of the pilots — on either side.

The German tactics, formations, promotion policy and public relations all encouraged individual leaders to run up large scores. German "aces" were not only admired by their peers and superiors, including Goering and Hitler himself, they were also lionized in the press and idolized by the public. More importantly, a German ace was given a first a wingman and then an entire "Schwarm" to protect him so he could concentrate on killing. Moelders, Galland and Wick all had more than fifty kills before the end of 1940; by the end of the war, many German pilots were credited with 100s of kills.

In the RAF, in contrast, the highest scoring English pilot in the entire war, "Pat" Pattle, was credited with just 51 victories including victories against Italy in the Mediterranean, while the highest scoring ace in the Western theater, "Johnny" Johnson had 38 victories in the course of the entire war. Certainly, the continuous rotation of squadrons and pilots in and out of combat areas resulted in far lower individual scores in the RAF. However, another factor was also at play: the RAF ethos. RAF pilots brought with them a notion of "team spirit" and viewed bragging as "bad form." The RAF did not really encourage the creation of "aces." Medals were awarded for exceptional bravery or outstanding flying, assistance to one's comrades and the like, rather than merely for "kills." Promotions went to men with leadership qualities not merely an aggressive spirit and good aim.

Despite not particularly rewarding victories, the RAF inflicted losses at a rate of almost 2 to 1 — and morale did not break. Given the losses and the sheer physical demands placed upon the RAF pilots at the time, it was their ability not only to keep flying but to keep drinking and laughing that awed their countrymen, their leaders and their enemies — when they found out. That morale was at least in part a function of the RAF's strong "team spirit."

Astonishingly, the RAF's culture of "team spirit" and high spirits (buoyed up by alcoholic spirits) held sway in an exceptionally heterogeneous body. In all, nearly 3,000 RAF pilots flew at least one sortie during the Battle of Britain. Only 80% of those pilots, however, were British citizens; 20% came from the Dominions and/or other Allied countries. The largest number of foreigners to participate in the Battle were Polish, accounting for 145 pilots, but the second largest foreign contingent flying for the RAF at this time came from New Zealand with 126 pilots. Pilots also came from Canada, Czechoslovakia, Australia, Belgium, South Africa, France, the United States, Ireland, Rhodesia and Jamaica.

Furthermore, fully one third of the pilots who flew in the Battle of Britain were Sergeants. Ever since its inception, the RAF had actively encouraged recruitment from all sectors of society, intentionally breaking with the class-conscious traditions of the Royal Navy and Army. The RAF had provided scholarships to the Royal Air Force College at Cranwell for exceptional young airmen and apprentices. It had launched a special program to encourage ground crews to receive pilot training. The RAF Volunteer Reserve was established to enable young men still in civilian life without the means to finance flying lessons to learn to fly at RAF expense.

These pilots almost invariably came from the very classes of society whose sons did not traditionally go to public schools, university or enter the officer corps. In the Battle of Britain they flew, drank and joked alongside the titled and privileged pilots of the University and Auxiliary Air Squadrons and the regulars. Literally, the sons of dukes and miners served in the same squadrons, fulfilling the same duties, taking the same risks, and reaping the same rewards. Most of the Sergeant Pilots of the Battle of Britain who survived were later commissioned, and many rose to senior command.

Yet — and this cannot be said often enough — it was not the pilots alone who won the Battle of Britain. The RAF had worked hard to ensure that its pilots were supported by some of the best trained ground crews in the world. With its "apprentice program," the RAF had attracted technically-minded young men early and provided them with extensive training throughout the inter-war years. In some ways, ground crews were better educated than many pilots. This and the fact that some pilots came up from the ranks, fostered excellent relations between pilots and crews.

Last but not least, at this stage of the war, individual crews looked after individual aircraft and so specific pilots. The ground crews identified strongly with their unit — and 'their' pilots. After the bombing of the airfields started in mid-August, the ground crews were themselves under attack, suffering casualties and working under difficult conditions. Yet precisely at this most trying time, aircraft were turned around — rearmed, refuelled, and checked over — in just minutes.

Equally notable was the RAF's early and exceptionally positive attitude towards women. The RAF actively encouraged the establishment of a Women's Auxiliary, which by the end of the war served alongside the RAF in virtually all non-combat functions. Even before the start of the war, however, the vital and highly technical jobs of radar operator and operations room plotter, as well as various jobs associated with these activities, were identified as trades especially suited to women. The C-in-C of Fighter Commander, ACM Dowding, personally insisted that the talented women who did these jobs move up into supervisory positions — and be commissioned accordingly. During Battle of Britain over 17,000 WAAF served with the RAF, nearly 4,500 of them in Fighter Command. A number of WAAF were killed and injured and six airwomen were awarded the Military Medal during the Battle.

Despite Nazi ideology about the place of women being exclusively in the home, the Wehrmacht was also forced to rely increasingly on women auxiliaries. The expansion began after the dramatic victories in the West in May/June 1940 and continued throughout the war, climbing from roughly 35,000 women in uniform in 1941 to over 150,000 when Germany surrendered. General conscription for women, industrial and military, was introduced in Germany after the loss of an entire Army at Stalingrad in early 1943, but the bulk of the women serving in Germany's women's auxiliary forces before 1945 were volunteers.

Please Note:

The squadron number 606 has never been assigned by the RAF. The same goes for No. 579. All characters in these two fictional squadrons are fictional. In contrast, the other squadrons, particularly those at RAF Tangmere, are real RAF squadrons who were stationed at RAF Tangmere at some time during the Battle of Britain. No. 36 Squadron was also a real squadron that flew Vildebeeste torpedo bombers from Singapore until the squadron lost its last aircraft on March 7, 1942 and ceased to exist.

On the others side of the channel, JG 23 is fictional, however, Stukageschwader 2 was the Stuka Group engaged in the Battle. With the exception of Generalmajor Wolfram Freiherr v. Richthofen, and, of course, Hermann Goering himself, all the German characters in the novel are fictional.

Although the main characters are fictional, nearly everything described is based on first hand accounts and memoirs. Readers familiar with the autobiographies of Battle of Britain pilots will recognize incidents and people described which have been woven into the fictional fabric.

Likewise, progress of the Battle in the novel follows the progress of the war, including the date, time and place of raids, the units involved and the level of casualties sustained on both sides. All the raids on Portsmouth depicted in the novel correspond with actual raids, including the number of casualties and targets hit. Only one major deviation was made from the historical record. In the last week of August and the first week of September when the Luftwaffe concentrated its attacks on Fighter Command's airfields, Tangmere was spared. Because othese raids arguably represented the greatest threat to the ability of Fighter Command to win the Battle of Britain, I felt it was important to show the reader what it was like for the bulk of RAF Fighter Stations. I therefore "re-located" two of the raids on Biggin Hill to Tangmere.

Photo Captions Interior Images

All interior images are used with the permission of the copyright holder
Chris Goss.

Call to Arms

Photo 1:   Sgt. Pilot Thomas Pyne of 73 Squadron in the cockpit of his
             Hurricane; Pyne would be killed in action May 14, 1940
Photo 2:   Unteroffizier Willi Ghesla, 1 Staffel/Jagdgeschwader 53,
             Rennes, August 1940

Warm-Up

Photo 1:   Pilot Officer Keith Ogilvie and Pilot Officer Eugene "Red"
             Tobin, 609 Squadron, Middle Wallop, September 1940
Photo 2:   Leutnant Alfred Zeis and Leutnant Ernst-Albrecht Schulz, 1
             Staffel/JG 53

Round One

Photo 1:   RAF Fighter Command Control Room, Bentley Priory
Photo 2:   German Maritime Reconnaissance planning their next
             mission.

Round Two

Photo 1:   Rearming Sgt. Thomas Pyne's Hurricane, May 1940
Photo 2:   Rearming an ME 109 of 1/JG 53 at Cherbourg, August 1940

Final Round

Photo 1:   A Spitfire of 609 Squadron destroyed by bombing, Middle
             Wallop, August 1940
Photo 2:   Civilian Bomb Damage, here Torquay, bombed in May 1943

Concluding Photo

Damaged Hurricane — here a symbol of the tattered yet still operable
RAF at the end of the Battle of Britain

Glossary

Anson A reliable, twin-engined aircraft ideal for transporting passengers and the mainstay of the ATA fleet of air taxis.

AOC Air Officer Commanding, Group Commander in the RAF

ATA Air Transport Auxiliary, a civilian organisation tasked with ferrying all RAF aircraft to and from factories and maintenance units

ATS Auxiliary Territorial Service, the womens' branch of the Royal Army

Available State of being on call, waiting for the order to take-off, ready to be in the air in 20 minutes or less: i.e not at dispersal but on the airfield

Bandits RAF slang for enemy aircraft

Barrage Balloon Large helium filled balloons tethered onto steel wires which floated over major cities or important targets such as aircraft factories. The wires made it extremely dangerous to fly below the balloons and so prevented low level bombing of the areas protected by these "barrages"

Bounce RAF slang for an attack from higher altitude on a enemy aircraft

Bowler hat The traditional headgear of London bankers, stockbrokers and other office workers at this time; in RAF slang it meant getting "washed out" of training or otherwise sent back to civilian life.

Bowser Mobile fuel tank from which aircraft were refuelled

Break Order to break formation and evade an attacking enemy aircraft

Buster Use emergency power

CFI Chief Flying Instructor

Crate RAF slang for aircraft

Deck In flyer's language the surface, ground or sea. Flying near the "deck" meant flying at low altitude.

DFC Distinguished Flying Cross. A 'bar' to the DFC indicated the wearer had been awarded a second DFC etc.

Dispersal/Dispersal hut To avoid having the aircraft concentrated in one place and thereby being an easy target, the RAF dispersed aircraft around an airfield; the pilots of a squadron on readiness waited for the call to action in more-or-less improvised small huts connected to the operations room and Mess by a telephone. These huts provided lockers to hang flying kit, chairs, tables, usually a gramophone, and pilots brought books, magazines, cards and board games to pass the time. They were heated by primitive stoves in winter.

DSO Distinguished Service Order

Emil The affectionate name used by the Luftwaffe pilots for their Messerschmitt 109E fighters. It was derived from the German military designation of the letter "e" and referred to the fact that this was the 109 series E. (Later the "G" series was known affectionately as the "Gustav.")

Erk RAF slang for airman/ground crews

Fighter Command HQ for RAF fighter operations

Flap RAF slang for panic

Gaggle Large number of aircraft, flock of aircraft

Geschwader Luftwaffe unit, consisting of three *Gruppen*

Gone for six Slang for being killed

Gone for a burton Slang for being killed

Gong RAF slang for medal

Green stuff RAF slang for aviation fuel

Gruppe Luftwaffe unit, consisting of three *Staffel*.

Hun British slang for Germans

Hurricane First monoplane fighter introduced into the RAF. Most Fighter Squadrons during the Battle of Britain had Hurricanes and they accounted for the most 'kills' in the Battle of Britain; they continued in service in secondary theatres throughout the war.

Indians Luftwaffe slang for enemy aircraft

Jerry British slang for Germans

JG Jägergeschwader, Fighter Group, the largest operational unit in the Luftwaffe's fighter arm.

Junkers German aircaft manufacturer. Two of the German aircraft most commonly used at this time were the Junkers 87, also known as the "Stuka", a dive bomber, and the more versatile Ju88, a twin-engine bomber with both high altitude and dive bomb capability. The Ju88 were popular with pilots and were often used on low-level raids.

Kette German flying formation of three aircraft, similar to the RAF's vic

Kite RAF slang for aircraft

LAC Leading Aircraftman, roughly the equivalent of a Pfc in the US Army Air Forces

Luftwaffehelferinnen German Air Force Female Auxiliaries, similar to the WAAF in the UK

Mae West Term used to describe the life vests in use at the time, allegedly because it gave the pilots the same profile as the actress

MAP Ministry of Aircraft Production

Me109 Messerschmitt 109—the principal German single-engined fighter

Me110 Messerschmitt 110—a twin-engined German fighter, which proved no match for the Hurricane and Spitfire and was later converted to tactical bombing and recce functions

MP Member of Parliament

MU Maintenance Unit—Repair and Maintenance units where RAF aircraft requiring greater repairs or servicing than could be handled by operational groundcrews were serviced.

NSDAP Nationalsozialistische Deutsche Arbeiter Party—National Socialist German Worker's Party—known as Nazis

O T U Operational Training Unit, a unit where pilots of the RAF were given operational and tactical training immediately prior to joining their operational Units

Pancake Order to return to base and land

Panic Bowlers Tin hats for protection in an air raid

PM Prime Minister

Pompii Colloquial name for Portsmouth, England, home of the Royal Navy

Popsies Slang for girls

Prang RAF slang for crash

R/T Radio/Telephone, the radio used in aircraft at this time

RDF British designation for radar at this time

Readiness State of being on call, waiting for the order to take-off, ready to be in the air in 5 minutes or less, i.e. waiting at dispersal.

Reichsarbeitsdienst Compulsory Labour Service for men and women

Reichsmarschall Imperial Marshal, title invented for Goering to place him above all the Army Field Marshals

Ring Another term for the stripes sewn on a pilot's sleeve indicating his rank: one thin ring = Pilot Officer, one thicker ring = Flying Officer, Two rings = Flight Lieutenant, Two thick rings flanking a thin ring = Squadron Leader, three rings = Wing Commander

Rocket To "get a rocket" was to be repromanded by a superior

Rotte The basic fighter formation of the Luftwaffe consisting of two aircraft, the "Rotteführer" (leader) and the "Rottehund" (wingman), who flew on the leader's flank

Sally Ann Slang for Salvation Army

Sapper Soldier/engineer

Schwarm German flying formation of four aircraft, in which two pairs flew together. It was very effective. The RAF and USAAF later adopted it

Scramble Order for a squadron to take off immediately

Sidcot Suit Flying Overalls in use by the RAF at this time

Snapper RAF term for fighters

Spit ire Single-engined, high-performance fighter, made legendary in the Battle of Britian

Sprogs RAF slang for newcomers/beginners

Squarebashing RAF/WAAF slang for marching and drill

Staffel Basic German airforce unit, similar to a squadron in the RAF

Stand-by Awaiting for the order to take-off by sitting in the cockpit with the engine ticking over, ready to be in the air in 2 minutes or less

Station RAF base

Stripe Another term for the rings sewn on a pilot's sleeve indicating his rank: one thin ring = Pilot Officer, one thicker ring = Flying Officer, Two rings = Flight Lieutenant, Two thick rings flanking a thin ring = Squadron Leader, three rings = Wing Commander

Stuka Generic German term for dive bomber, but interchangeably used to refer to the most common German dive-bomber of the war, the Ju-87

Tannoy Public Announcement system, magnifying a voice and blasting out over a large area

Ticking Off Repromand

Ticking Over Propellor just barely turning over, at minimum power

U/S Unserviceable

UXB Unexploded Bombs

WAAF Women's Auxiliary Air Force—The British women's auxiliary: WAAF were trained with RAF and filled jobs as qualified with little or no distinction due to sex. NCOs and commissioned WAAF commanded RAF of lower rank. By the end of the war, with the notable exception of flying, WAAF were allowed into all trades and branches.

Waafery British slang referring to the WAAF quarters on an RAF station

WVS Women's Volunteer Service, a British organisation which provided a variety of services to support the war effort including canteens for service personnel away from their bases.

Recommended Reading

Autobiographies and Biographies of RAF Battle of Britain Fighter Pilots

- Baker, E.C.R. *Ace of Aces: The Incredible Story of Pat Pattle.* Silvertail Books, 2020.

- Brickhill, Paul. *Reach for the Sky: The Story of Douglas Bader: Legless Ace of the Battle of Britain.* Naval Institute Press, 2001.

- Deer, Air Commodore Alan C. *Nine Lives.* Crécy Publishing, 1959.

- Doe, Wing Commander Bob. *Fighter Pilot.* CCB Aviation Books, 2004.

- Hillary, Richard. *The Last Enemy.* MacMillan, 1942.

- Johnson, Group Captain J.E. *Wing Leader: From the Battle of Britain to the Last Sortie by the Top Scoring Ace of the RAF.* Ballantine Books, 1957.

- Johnstone, Air Vice Marshal Sandy. *Enemy in the Sky.* Presidio Press, 1976.

- Kingcome, Brian. *A Willingness to Die.* Tempus, 1999.

- Page, Geoffrey. *Shot Down in Flames: A World War II Fighter Pilot's Remarkable Tale of Survival.* Grub Street, 1999.

- Richey, Paul. *Fighter Pilot.* Cassel, 2001.

- Stokes, Doug. *Wings Aflame.* Crécy Publishing Ltd., 1985.

- Townsend, Peter. *Duel of Eagles: The Struggle for the Skies from the First World War to the Battle of Britain.* Phoenix Press, 1970.

- Wellum, Geoffrey. *First Light: The True Story of the Boy Who Became a Man in the War-torn Skies above Britain.* Viking, 2002.

Secondary Sources

- Beauman, Katherine Bently. *Partners in Blue: The Story of Women's Service with the Royal Airforce.* Hutchison & Co., 1971.

- Bishop, Patrick. *Fighter Boys: Saving Britain 1940.* HarperCollins, 2003.

- Bungay, Stephen. *The Most Dangerous Enemy: A History of the Battle of Britain.* Aurem Press, 2000.

- Clayton, Tim and Phil Craig. *Finest Hour.* Coronet Books, 1999.

- Collier, Richard. *Eagle Day: The Battle of Britain.* Cassell Military, 2000.

- Davidson, Martin & James Taylor. *Spitfire Ace: Flying the Battle of Britain.* Channel 4 Books, 2003.

- Deighton, Len. Fighter: The True Story of the Battle of Britain. Alfred A. Knopf, 1977.
- Goss, Chris. *Brothers in Arms: The Story of a British and a German Fighter Unit, August to December 1940*. Crécy Books, 1994.
- Kaplan, Philip & Richard Collier. *Fighter Aces of the RAF in the Battle of Britain*. Pen & Sword Aviation, 2007.
- —. *The Few: Summer 1940, The Battle of Britain*. Blandford, 1989.
- Levine, Joshua. *Forgotten Voices of the Blitz and the Battle of Britain: A New History in the Word of Men and Women from Both Sides*. Ebury Press, 2006.
- Oliver, David. *Fighter Command 1939-1945*. Harper Collins, 2000.
- Orange, Vincent. *Sir Keith Park*. Methuen, 1984.
- Price, Alfred. *Der Deutsche Luftwaffe 1939-1945: Fuehrung, Organisation, Aussstattung*. Motorbuch Verlag, 1979.
- Saunders, Andy. *RAF Tangmere in Old Photographs*. Alan Sutton Publishing, 1992.
- Seidler, Franz W. *Blitzmaedchen: Die Geschichte der Helferinnen der deutschen Wehrmacht im Zweiten Weltkrieg*. Wehr & Wissen, 1979.
- Wright, Robert. *Dowding and the Battle of Britain*. MacDonald, 1969.

Find out more about Helena P. Schrader's other novels and non-fiction books at: http://helenapschrader.com